THE NIGHTBLADE EPIC VOLUME TWO

GARRETT ROBINSON

THE NIGHTBLADE EPIC
VOLUME TWO
Garrett Robinson

The author greatly appreciates you taking the time to read his work. Please leave a review wherever you bought the book or on Goodreads.com.

Interior Design: Legacy Books, Inc.
Publisher: Legacy Books, Inc.
Editors: Karen Conlin, Cassie Dean
Cover Artist: Sutthiwat Dekachamphu

1. Fantasy - Epic 2. Fantasy - Dark 3. Fantasy - General

First Edition

Published by Legacy Books

To my parents
who enabled me to do this

To my wife
who got me to where I am

To my children
who keep this and everything else fun

To the Vloganovel crew
who keep me going

And to my Rebels
who are the best gift I could have asked for

GET MORE

Legacy Books is home to the very best that fantasy has to offer.

Join our email alerts list, and we'll send word whenever we release a new book. You'll receive exclusive updates and see behind the scenes as we create them.

(You'll also learn the secret that makes great fantasy books, *great*.)

Interested? Visit this link:

Underrealm.net/Join

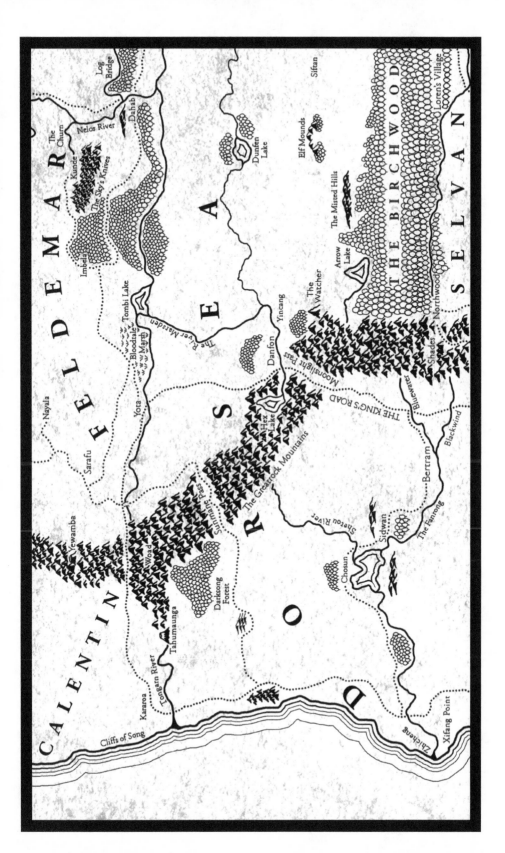

THE NIGHTBLADE EPIC VOLUME TWO

GARRETT ROBINSON

SHADEBORN

BEING BOOK ONE
OF THE SECOND VOLUME

OF THE
NIGHTBLADE EPIC

ONE

LOREN SLOUCHED IN HER SEAT, SEARCHING AND FAILING TO FIND ANY reason why this day should be better than the one before.

Her companions still lay upstairs in slumber. Even Albern had not yet risen, though the bowyer always woke before the coming of the sun. But Loren had been awake through the night, unable to close her eyes for fear of what she would see in her dreams. So a cup of wine had turned into two, and then a bottle, and some food just as the moons set, and now the sky outside crept towards the grey of dawn.

The innkeeper, Mag, stood behind the counter, polishing it with a damp rag, though to Loren's mind it shone bright already. Every so often the woman would gaze around the room, observing those within: the early wakers who had joined Loren for breakfast, or the night-time arrivals who had come to the city of Northwood for purposes unknown—and, mayhap, best not asked after. Mag's gaze never sought Loren in particular, but neither did it shy away.

In the days since Loren and her friends had first arrived at the inn, that was what Loren appreciated the most. Whatever thoughts Mag kept to herself, outwardly she never treated Loren differently from any other customer. Loren could not say the same for the others, who mostly sought to avoid her gaze. Either that, or they tried to draw her into conversation, speaking soft words she was not yet ready to hear.

All of them except Chet, of course.

Mag noticed Loren's empty goblet, hers the keen eyes of a barkeep with experience. She sidled out from behind the thick oak counter and made her way across the room. Without a word she scooped up the goblet, as well as an empty bowl.

"Will you be wanting anything else, love?" The words held neither judgement nor too much concern. It was as though Loren were any other girl who happened to be visiting the inn. Yet in that plain tone, Loren thought she heard another kind of care.

"Another glass of wine would suit me well, except that I feel my debt to you grows large," said Loren. "When will you let me cease to be a burden, and pay for my custom like the rest of your patrons?"

"Another time, mayhap. But not yet." Mag swept up the cup and dropped it in the bowl before returning to the bar. From the shelves she pulled a clean cup for Loren's wine, and then another, which she filled with ale. She brought them both to the table, and to Loren's surprise took the seat opposite.

Now at last she means to speak her mind, thought Loren. She should have expected it. Mag had seemed more understanding, less intrusive, than any of the others. But she must have felt the way they did all along, and chosen now to finally say something. Loren wondered idly why she had waited so long.

"I have heard what the others say to you, trying to urge you towards better spirits," said Mag. "You must know that they are wrong, and that this is not something you should try to hasten."

Loren blinked. "Those are not the words I thought to hear."

"I imagine not," said Mag, smiling gently and sipping her ale. "You thought I would lend my voice to theirs."

"They seem to think they know what is best for me, no matter whether I wish to hear it or not." Loren took a pull from her own cup, a deeper and longer drink than Mag's.

"Yet you will note that Albern has not joined them in their insistence. Nor would I. He and I have seen many dark times together. Both of us have felt loss. Both of us have done deeds we wish we could undo, deeds that have haunted us every day since."

Loren saw a flash of a broken body draped in a red cloak. She saw

4

an arrow protruding from a thigh, and a hateful man crawling through the dirt. She shivered and blinked hard, drinking again in desperation.

Mag's hand came gently to rest upon Loren's. "Only time can rid us of these wounds. You are fortunate to have that time. Take it—as much as you need. Let the pictures in your mind's eye fade away, one by one, until they trouble you no longer, neither while you sleep nor in your waking hours. It is not something you should try to hurry along, unless the healing stops on its own."

Loren picked at the cuff of her sleeve. Though it had been only a few days since they came to Northwood, she had seen no improvement in her mood, nor in the dark thoughts that plagued her day and night. "And what if it does? What did you and Albern do, when the darkness in your minds refused to leave you?"

"Only then are you close to the end. Embracing our grief plants the seed of healing, and once it is well-laid we must take it upon ourselves to foster the growth. If that crop lies untended, it twists within the earth. That is a sorry harvest, and one you have likely seen before: the drunkard who cannot think to spend his time anywhere but the tavern, his coin spent only on oblivion."

The wine soured in Loren's mouth. "You might as well say what you mean: *her* coin. Yet you will not take mine."

Mag's mouth twisted in a stern frown. "If I meant to rebuke you, I would do it without bandying words. I only mean to tell you that when the time comes for your next step, you must take it, or you shall lose yourself. Action can help you along the road—any action, though deeds filled with purpose are best. Or sometimes, the comfort of another can be our medicine. That boy Chet, for example."

"He is trying. Often have we gone walking in the Birchwood, and under its eaves with him I find something closer to peace than I do with the others, with their soft words and careful glances."

Mag gave her a look that lasted a moment too long, and Loren blushed. Quickly she took another swallow of wine to hide it.

"You should eagerly embrace anything that helps," said Mag stoically, and Loren thought she heard the hint of a smile behind the words. "Remember: do not let the others push you sooner than you are ready. There will be time enough for their cares later. First you must tend to yourself."

Boots clumped heavily down the stairs at the back. Loren looked up to see Albern descending into the common room. He gave her a quick glance and a half-hearted smile. Mag rose quickly and went to the bar with him, there to take his order and fetch his breakfast. Loren sat in the quiet and thought upon the innkeeper's words.

She did not have long to enjoy her solitude. Soon Albern joined her at the table with his eggs and a rasher of bacon. He spoke no word to her, but he did not have Mag's skill at hiding his curious eyes. And soon Loren heard boots upon the stairs again, and looked up to see Xain glowering there.

The wizard's limbs had gone thin and bony, his cheeks so gaunt that from the outside she could see his teeth pressing against the flesh. His hair was thinning now. Loren knew that if she tugged on it, it would come out in clumps. He was like a specter of death, and the effect was not lost on the room's other inhabitants. Some had drunk too much to care, but others averted their eyes or stood to leave with quick, muttered excuses, though there was no one close enough to hear them.

Xain seemed not to notice, or mayhap he did not care. He stalked towards Loren and drew out the chair beside hers, slumping in his seat as his eyebrows drew still closer together. He leaned close, his voice a harsh whisper, though Loren was sure it carried to every corner of the quiet room.

"Tell me you have had enough at last of sulking, and are ready to take the road again."

"Xain," said Albern in a warning tone. His fingers tightened on the handle of his mug.

"And a good morrow to you, fair sir," said Loren. She tried to make the words light, but could not entirely keep an edge from them. "Break fast with us, I pray, and help yourself to some fine wine." She held her cup before him, wiggling it back and forth.

Xain failed to appreciate the humor. He snatched the cup from her to drain it in a single gulp. "I take it you do not mean to move on, then. Do you think we have an eternity to waste?"

"Have we spent an eternity here already, Albern?" said Loren, looking towards the bowyer with feigned wonder. "Sky above, I thought it had been a few days only."

"Your jests are stale, and grow more so each time the sun passes us," said Xain. "When will we speak, away from this room and its prying ears? Day after day passes, yet still you will not tell me that which you once thought so urgent."

She knew full well what the wizard meant. They had not yet decided where they must go next, and Loren had grave counsel for him, which might shed light upon their path. But that counsel had come from Jordel the Mystic, and he had died moments after uttering the words. Recalling them now was akin to recalling the man, and Loren could not think of him without her heart wanting to stop in grief. Nor had the past week made it any easier, for in Northwood she had learned a dark truth. A truth about herself, and about the cruel man she had shot in the thigh. The man she had once called Father, but whom—by her own hand—no one would speak to ever again.

"Soon," said Loren, her voice quieter than she meant it to be. "I promise you. Only give me a little more time. My grief still presses itself too close upon me."

Xain growled. His gaze darted about as though searching for another argument. Without thinking, he picked at his coat sleeve. A deep hunger gnawed at him, Loren knew, and his mind was not entirely his own. She was only grateful it was not like last time, when his thoughts had grown so dark that she had feared to be in the same room as him.

"Good morn," said a familiar voice, a warm and welcome sound. Chet appeared by Loren's side.

"Good morn," said Loren quickly. She rose from her chair before Xain could choose his next bitter words. But she had moved too fast, forgetting the many cups of wine that had passed her lips. She lurched and nearly fell, and would have, had she not seized the edge of the table. She steadied herself quickly, cheeks flushing with embarrassment. "I thought to greet the sun from under the branches of the Birchwood. Would you join me?"

Chet looked worried. "Are you sure you need no rest? Did you find any sleep last night?"

"Who needs sleep when the world is waking? Come." Loren seized his arm and nearly dragged him from the table, taking each step carefully to see that she did not stumble. As they walked away together, she thought she saw Albern trying to hide a smile.

TWO

THE CRISP AIR OF MORNING DID MUCH TO CLEAR HER HEAD, AND SHE drank it in with a long breath. If she was honest with herself, it felt better to walk with Chet than to sit at her table and drink, but sometimes facing the wine was easier.

Dawn's thin grey light was just creeping into the sky from the east, and Northwood had begun to stir into wakefulness. She heard the sharp hiss of a smith's forge firing up, and the first tentative squalls of cocks greeting the day. But they met few faces upon the streets, and for that Loren was grateful. It let them walk to the northern gate with few curious eyes to see them. She no longer held much fear that her many enemies had followed her here, and yet the fewer people who saw them within Northwood, the better.

A single guard sat at a table by the open gate. She was well accustomed to seeing Chet and Loren take their walks, and gave them only a cursory glance before turning back to the game of moons that lay before her. Soon Loren and Chet found themselves among the trees of the forest they had once called home. A few steps farther still, and Northwood had vanished behind them, blocked from view by the trunks.

Now Loren felt herself truly relax, as though the last cobwebs had been swept from the edges of her mind. Here within the wood, her eyes saw things differently. Bent blades of grass told her of the passing of a deer, and when she heard a skittering within a bush, she knew it at once for the rustling of a vole. The forest was altogether different from the world of men, and she had greatly missed it since she left. It was all the more enjoyable because she knew Chet saw it just as she did. Sometimes they would speak as they walked. Other times, as now, they walked in silence and let their feet carry them where they would.

They found a narrow brook, making its eager way to join the Melnar to the south. In silent agreement, they turned to find a crossing upstream. Soon they came upon one: a place where the banks rose high above the surface of the water and drew together, close enough for a long jump to carry them across. Just as they reached the other side, the sun peeked its face above the branches of the eastern trees, and all the birds of the Birchwood burst into song together. Some hours later they came upon a clearing some thirty paces across, with a great boulder in the middle like a tombstone. There they sat, their backs against the rock, its cool surface chilling them after the eager pace of their walk.

Chief among the reasons Loren enjoyed their walks was that Chet seemed content with silence, or with speech, as Loren wished. He would converse with her eagerly, answering questions about what had happened in their village since she left. From him she had learned of her mother, who had vanished without a trace the same day Loren had. Loren had some half-remembered notion of family in one of the northern outland kingdoms, and assumed her mother had gone to find them. Too, Chet had told her that some time after his mother passed away, his father had begun to court Miss Aisley. Loren thought that a fine pairing, though Chet himself seemed unsure just what to think of it.

But when Loren wished for silence, silence was what Chet gave her. Now he simply looked with her into the trees, his hands toying with a stick he had snatched from the ground. Together they reveled in a quiet comfort. And without any pressure to speak, Loren found her tongue moved more freely of its own accord.

"In the city of Wellmont, I was caught trying to steal a man's purse," she began.

Chet glanced at her and smirked. "I thought you were a great thief. Is that a lie, for you to be so easily caught?"

"I was not *easily* caught," said Loren, shoving his shoulder. "I was betrayed by my own kindness. I saw the man beating his son and thought to relieve him of his coin—but then at the last moment, I thought the child might relish a life free from his father. That was a mistake. The moment I made the offer, he told his father of my words, and the father called the constables."

"A foolish boy," said Chet lightly. "He could have gone with you, and been pitched headlong into mortal danger. But at least you would not have beaten him."

"Mayhap," said Loren quietly. She had not meant to turn the conversation towards a father and his child, for that subject reminded her too closely of things she would rather not think of. "But in any case, the constables brought us to their quarters within the city. And there, to his shock as well as mine, I found Jordel inside. I will remember the surprise on his face —and the anger—forever."

Chet grew quiet, as he always did when her words turned to Jordel. Chet had never met the Mystic—something Loren desperately regretted. It seemed a crime that anyone should not have known the man, as great as he was, as quiet and heartfelt his praise, and as cold and terrible his wrath. She doubted she would meet his like ever again.

"What surprised me then, though it should not have, was how quickly Jordel guessed at what was going on. As soon as he heard that I had been caught stealing from the woodsman, his eyes grew sharp with suspicion. With barely a glance, he seemed to know the whole tale, and he was as merciless with the father as the father was with the son. And though his anger with me remained, it softened, and turned more to annoyance, as though he thought I was right to do as I did, though his duty meant he could not say so."

Her voice drew dangerously close to a tremble. One tear leaked from her eye, so she leaned her cheek on her fine black cloak where it draped over her arm, to soak up the drop and hide it.

Once more the clearing was silent, save for the morning birdsong.

She spoke again into the stillness, forcing her voice to remain steady. "Where did they find my father?"

Chet glanced at her from the corner of his eye, and then looked away again. "It is no tale for a day so beautiful."

"Likely it is too ugly for any day that may come to pass. Tell me, then, and let its darkness fade away once and for all."

"You have seen too much evil of late. I would not bring more upon you, not at least until you are ready. When I tell you this tale, I wish to tell it only once, and in full, so that we need never speak of it again."

"Then tell it now," said Loren.

Chet sighed. Then he pushed himself from the rock and sidled over to sit in front of her, his eyes fixed on hers, though she turned her gaze away.

"His corpse was a league south of the village when we found it. He lay on his belly, his head turned to the side, eyes open and staring. There was no blood in his spittle, but it had frothed greatly and gathered around his lips."

Loren swallowed hard. She knew what would come next: the tale of his wound, the one that had slowly bled him out beneath the trees of the same forest in which they now sat. Chet watched her, gauging her reaction. She kept her face as still as she could.

"We could see at once that he had bled to death. Though the fletching had broken from the arrow, the shaft still stuck from his thigh. It had struck a vein, or nicked it as he crawled, and all his lifeblood had drained out. The trail of it stretched far away south, mayhap half a league more. When we followed it, we found at the end the signs of a struggle. Between him and, I guessed, you, but also a third person who we did not know. I hazarded another guess that it was the wizard the constables sought."

"You were right in that," said Loren, glad her voice had remained steady. "That was Xain. My father nearly strangled the life from him."

"He would have, if you had not stopped him," said Chet quietly. "And he might have killed you, too."

Loren remembered the fight as though it were happening again. She saw the spite that filled her father's eyes, the spittle that flew from his lips with each hateful word. And now she imagined him crawling north after the fight, the shaft protruding from his flesh, his life pouring into the dirt beneath him. She saw him shuddering and convulsing as he died at last, and wondered if he had spent his final words cursing her—his own flesh and blood, whom he had never given anything so wasteful as love.

"Likely my words cannot help you," said Chet. "But you should not blame yourself. You restrained your hand beyond all reason. You might have planted your arrow in his eye, or his heart. You did not. You tried to show mercy. And mayhap, if he had stayed where he was, he would not have died in the end."

But Loren knew better. She remembered when she would chop her father's logs for him, how he would come and threaten her so that she would work faster. And she remembered how he would take her into the woods and beat her, his thick and meaty fists leaving bruises beneath her clothing that would last for weeks. And she remembered going back to chopping his logs, and gripping the axe tightly in her hands, and picturing it lodged in his skull, or in his back.

Her breath came faster as her thoughts raced on. Images flashed through her mind's eye, the corpse, and the arrow, and the axe and the corpse and the spittle and the blood and the corpse and the corpse again. And then the corpse became Jordel's and she saw his twisted body upon the floor of the valley that lay between the arms of the Greatrocks.

She fought the urge to vomit and rolled to her hands and knees.

"Loren!" cried Chet.

He knelt by her side and placed a hand on her shoulder. Loren pushed him off, breathing faster until stars danced in her vision and her head spun. She tried lifting her gaze to look upon the sky, but she could see only blackness where there should have been blue. *Black and blue, like my bruises.*

She screamed and slammed a fist into the earth, and then struck again, and again. Her fist flew into the boulder, and she felt the skin of her knuckles break.

The pain gave her focus, and she clutched her hand to her chest. At last she could sit back without her gorge rising. Rage turned to hot, bitter tears that left their trails of grief upon her cheeks. Chet sat beside her with one arm around her shoulder, and his other hand cradling her mangled one.

"It was not your fault," he kept murmuring. "It was not your fault."

Soon she felt in control again. And as she had so often, she took her rage and her grief and hid them away, deep inside herself where no one else could see. At last she looked up at Chet and tried to smile. But she feared she only looked sick, for his look of concern deepened.

"I am all right," she said softly. "I am all right. Come. The children will have risen, and they are likely driving the others mad."

She rose shakily to her feet, shrugging off Chet's helping hand. Together they set off into the trees, walking slowly now. But Loren no longer saw the green of the leaves, nor the crystal clarity of the brook as they crossed it. She saw only black and blue, and the red of blood.

THREE

GEM HAD BEEN AN URCHIN CHILD WHEN LOREN FOUND HIM ON THE streets of Cabrus, hungry and picking pockets in the service of a guild of young thieves. Annis had been a daughter of wealth and plenty, her every whim tended to by the comforts her mother's coin had afforded.

Their circumstances could scarce have been more different, yet they had surprised Loren equally since their arrival in Northwood—for both of them had spent every spare moment helping Mag around the inn. From tending to the stables to running drinks and meals to visitors when the common room grew busy, they took eagerly to even the meanest task. Neither had been raised in a life of honest work, and yet they took their roles as Mag's helpers very seriously.

They seemed to enjoy Northwood greatly. Loren told herself that one reason she had lingered so long was to give them a rest, which they greatly deserved. Even to her own ears, though, that excuse sounded thin and flimsy.

"With the cook's compliments," said Gem, arriving at the table with a tray, upon which he had balanced five bowls of stew.

"And the lady's," said Annis, swooping in with another tray that held five mugs of ale and two loaves of bread.

"Our blessings upon the cook and the lady," said Albern, scooping up his bowl and his mug. He tucked in with great abandon, tearing the heel from one of the loaves and dipping it into the stew.

The sun was nearing the horizon, and many within the town had joined the inn's tenants for supper and a drink. The common room buzzed heavily with talk and occasional bursts of laughter. Loren could hear the plucking of strings from somewhere in the back of the room as some minstrel readied to earn his dinner. But still her mind lingered on dark thoughts, and though her stomach growled at the smell of the stew, it tasted bland as paper upon her tongue. Chet tried valiantly not to show his concern, but Loren could feel it emanating from him like the glow of a torch.

"None of you will be surprised, I am sure, to learn that I have spent another day proving my worth," said Gem brightly as he ate. The first spoonful of stew did nothing to slow his words, and the food mashed noisily between his teeth as he talked around it. "Today I cleaned the hooves of all the horses in the stable, and laid fresh hay for each steed. Then I found that the dishes had stacked into a mighty mountain, and so I cleaned them all, every one, without even having to be asked. I hardly know how this place managed before I arrived."

"Oh, they must have pined for a dishwasher like yourself, master urchin," said Albern with a smirk. "Poor Mag must have spent her nights crying herself to sleep for want of such noble, scrubbing hands as yours."

"Just so," said Gem, missing the humor in the bowyer's tone.

Annis sniffed primly and dipped just the end of her loaf into the stew, nibbling on it with perfect manners. "Well, while you have been getting yourself filthy down here, I have been striving for cleanliness. I cannot guess when the rooms upstairs were cleaned last, and some of them stank of something which I am sure I would not like to know about. But they are clean now, and I have only knees and hands worn to the bone to show for it. Give me a few more days here, and I am sure I shall make the place fit for the custom of the High King herself, though why she should find herself in such a town as this I am sure I do not know."

Gem blinked and looked uneasily at Loren. "But . . . surely we will not be here that long," he said slowly. "I thought we would be leaving any day now."

Loren could see—or rather, feel—Xain's irritation from the other side of the table. She held her peace, excusing her silence with a mouth full of food, which she chewed slowly so as not to be obligated to answer.

Albern caught her unease, and likely Xain's dark look as well, for he shrugged and said lightly, "You shall all set forth when you are ready. There is no great rush. Certainly Mag enjoys your company."

"But she cannot enjoy the food we eat, nor the wine we drink, nor the rooms we sleep in, without so much as a copper penny taken in exchange," said Chet. Despite his words, he took a deep pull on his mug of ale before continuing. "I do not understand why she will not take our coin."

"It gives her pleasure to give you comfort," said Albern. "Do not ask about it again, or she might bring her spear from its retirement, and then you would be doomed."

"I can handle myself," Chet muttered.

"Not against Mag, I promise you," said Albern. "Years might have passed since she wielded a blade, yet I would wager all my coin upon her if she were to fight anyone in all the nine lands. You would too, if you were wise. When we were young she was called the Uncut Lady, and renowned as the greatest fighter in our company, and when she hung up her shield—"

"Every mercenary captain across the land poured a cup of wine into the dirt," Chet finished. "You have said that before."

"And do you doubt the truth of it?" said Mag. She had emerged from the common room's crowd to stand over the table. At the sound of her voice, Gem and Annis both turned to her with delighted smiles. But she fixed them with a stern look and gestured at the table. "Where is my plate? Where are my mug and my chair? Surely the two of you know better courtesy than this."

The children's faces fell. Gem scuttled off towards the kitchen, while Annis ran to fetch an empty chair. They were few and far between in the crowded room. Finally she found a drunkard slumped unconscious on a table and tipped him unceremoniously from his seat.

"Our apologies, Mag," said Annis as she pushed the chair up to the table. "We thought you were busy in the kitchen, and did not guess you would sup with us tonight."

"Sten finally rustled his useless hide out from the stables and came to relieve me," said Mag. "Tonight my company is yours, if you will have it."

"We will, and gladly," said Gem, who had returned with a bowl and a mug for her. These he set down with great reverence, as though he were serving a king. "And mayhap you can settle a matter over which I have spent much thought. None of us doubt Albern's words when he calls you the greatest fighter he has ever known. But how can that be, when you look no mightier than most of the people in this room? Why, your arms are not even so thick as his."

"If you think me a weakling, mayhap you will wrestle me, and see how long it takes me to pitch you into the dirt," said Mag, arching an eyebrow.

Gem stammered and stuttered and finally fell silent, looking down into his lap.

Albern laughed out loud. "Come, Mag, leave the boy alone. He has never seen you dance. You can't blame him for wondering, when he has only seen the sort of fighting you get from common street thugs and city guards." He leaned over to speak conspiratorially to Gem, as though he were confiding a great secret. "Not in the strength of the arm, little master, but more often in skill will you find the greater warrior. What use a soldier's brawny bulk when their blade cannot come within a foot of our Mag? The most dangerous fighters are the ones who dance with their foe like a lover, and who can stay on their feet and swinging long after the other man is ready to vomit his guts into the dirt."

"Surely you have seen the truth of that, Gem," said Loren with a half-hearted smile. "If all things in life depended on strength alone, you and I would have died in a ditch long ago."

Albern shook a finger at her and nodded "Just so. Why, once Mag and I and the company were fighting in the kingdom of Calentin, putting down the insurrection of some upstart who thought he could seize the throne because he had a flock of pretty knights at his back. One of these dullards came riding down on Mag with lance lowered, but she—"

The crash of a fist on the table threw them all into silence. Xain had slammed his hand down, and held it there now, his gaze roving across their faces. Loren's heart went to her throat as she remembered his madness in the mountains, when he had cast thunder and flame upon them with abandon, stricken with the magestone hunger just as he was now. Without thinking of it, she moved her hand to the hilt of the dagger beneath her cloak. From the corner of her eye she saw Albern's hand steal beneath the table, likely to his own weapon. Around them, the common room had grown quiet.

"If I must listen to one more of your tales, I will fling myself into the Melnar and drown," growled Xain. He shot to his feet and, seeing Albern tense, held up a hand. "Stay yourself, bowyer. I need only the girl. Loren, you have avoided this for too long. Come with me now, or do not expect to see me darken this inn's doorway again. If you are determined to sit here and pity yourself until the nine lands fall, then I will carry on with our task alone."

With that he stalked between the tables and out of the inn. A few of the patrons he passed by gave Mag a doubtful look, but she shook her head gently, and they let him pass.

"Something gnaws at that man," she muttered when Xain had gone.

"You speak more truly than you know," said Loren quietly.

Chet leaned over to murmur in her ear. "You need not go if you do not wish it."

Inside, Loren was fuming. Xain spoke to her as though she were some child, whimpering in the corner because she wanted second help-ings at supper. He had been there in the mountains when Jordel had fallen. Then, he had wept as openly as the rest of them. If his mood had darkened since, and if his cravings for magestone scratched at the edges of his mind, he had no one to blame but himself. How dare he mock Loren's pain, speaking as if she had forgotten her duty?

But she only shrugged. "He speaks at least some truth. I should have had words with him days ago. If it will stay this foul temper that has seized him, I will have them now."

"I can go with you," said Albern.

"No," said Loren quickly. "Stay. Tell the children your story. Surely they will enjoy it." And she rose to follow the wizard into the city.

FOUR

Xain stood across the narrow street. A lamp on the building beside him bathed him in its sickly yellow glow. His nails scratched furiously at his sleeve, and his head darted back and forth in the darkness. When he saw her emerge, she thought she saw him sigh with relief. But she approached him slowly. If he was going to be so difficult, she was in no hurry to give him what he desired.

"I . . . I may have spoken harshly," he muttered once Loren was in earshot. "Forgive me."

"Mayhap," said Loren easily. "Still, you have me here now, wizard. What shall we speak of? You make it sound most urgent, though you yourself have had days to speak to me. A conversation takes not one, but two at least."

"What we have to say—what I have to tell you, at least—I would not utter in anything above a whisper, and not at all here in the city," said Xain. Suddenly his voice was no longer bitter, or even exasperated. Instead he sounded afraid, and his words carried a darkness that made Loren shiver. She tried to disguise it as a sudden chill in the night air, and drew her cloak closer about herself.

"What, then? Do you mean to fly us into the air with your magic? For we are within the city still."

"At my best I could not do so, and I am far from my best. If it pleases you, Nightblade, let us take a stroll beyond the walls of Northwood."

Loren did not relish the idea of walking unknowing into the darkness with him, but his calling her "Nightblade" mollified her somewhat. It was a foolish daydream of her childhood, and only a few knew of it, though Gem kept trying to spread the tale of her—an effort she found more irritating than endearing, but she rarely had the heart to tell him to stop.

Xain pushed off from the wall and strode down the street, and Loren felt she had little choice but to follow. Rather than north, as she often went with Chet, Xain now took her east. There the gate lay open still, despite the late hour. Northwood had been removed from the wars of the nine lands for so long that it felt no need to lock its doors against them. The guard at the gate gave them a close look, peering at them in the weak light of his torch, but let them pass without question or comment. Soon they were in the empty darkness of the farmlands beyond the city, with only the tiny glow of candlelight through the windows of farmhouses to break the inky black.

From behind him, Loren saw the faint glow of Xain's eyes and heard him muttering words of power. A small spark of flame sprang to life in his hand, but almost immediately it guttered and died. Xain muttered a curse and tried again. This time the fire remained, hovering above his palm, though it was thin and wispy compared to the flames she had seen him cast in times gone.

"Your gift has not entirely left you, I see," she said.

"It weakens by the day," said Xain. "Soon even this small magelight will require all of my power and concentration. Then it will be a long time before my powers return to me."

"How long?"

"I do not know. I have never witnessed the recovery of one plagued by magestone sickness. They are, as you may know, strictly outlawed by the High King."

He barked a harsh laugh, and Loren found herself joining him. But she also thought, with some trepidation, of the small packet of magestones she carried in her pocket even now. Xain knew nothing of them; she had made very certain of that. She did not like to imagine what he would do if he ever found out.

Soon even the lights of the farmhouses had vanished behind them, and Xain's was the only flame in sight. But the moons had risen already, and they gave Loren enough light to keep from stumbling—most of the time.

Finally Xain stopped and turned to her. Without a word he sat cross-legged upon the ground beside the road. With a furtive toss of his hand, he indicated for her to do the same.

"A moment," said Loren. She stepped off into the darkness, searching around in the grass. Though it was still green, it was dry, and from the hedge that ran beside the road she pulled a few dead branches. These she made into a little pile before Xain, and waved her hand at it. "Light this. It will save your strength, for if we must finally speak of dark matters, I would have all your concentration."

"My concentration? I find it difficult to think of anything else," said Xain. But he lit the tinder, and soon the branches caught above it. In no time they had a little fire going, and Xain let the flame die in his hands.

"First I should tell you what Jordel said just before he died," said Loren. "Though I know little of its meaning. He said the Shades' dark master had returned, and that Trisken was some captain of special significance. He said—as you and I saw—that magic is no proof against them."

The Shades were a secret order that Loren had only learned of a few weeks ago, when she and her friends had become lost in the Greatrocks and stumbled upon their stronghold there. Jordel had said precious little about them, only that they were an order somewhat like the Mystics—except the Mystics, who wore red cloaks, preserved order and upheld the King's law in the nine lands. Loren had never learned the Shades' true purpose, though she had an uncomfortable feeling that would soon change.

"All of this I had guessed already," said Xain, waving a hand in dismissal. "Any fool could have pieced it together."

"Then it was no great crime for me to wait so long to speak to you," said Loren, her irritation growing. "Tell me, then, what *you* know, and why it is of such great importance that we must meet out here where only the grubs in the dirt can hear us. Who is this dark master of the Shades?"

Xain looked at her a long moment. His eyes looked black in the darkness, black as they were when he cast his spells under the power of magestones. It made Loren shiver, though she refused to look away. Then Xain averted his gaze and picked at his sleeve again, and when he spoke it was not with an answer.

"What do you know of magic?"

Loren blinked. "Only a little. I heard tales as a child, and Jordel taught me some little more when we were searching for you. I know of its four arms, which you call . . . oh, I cannot remember their scholarly names just now. But they are firemagic, mindmagic, weremagic, and alchemy."

"Elementalism, mentalism, therianthropy, and transmutation," said Xain stiffly. Loren ground her teeth, but he went on quickly as though sensing her impatience. "Yes, every child in the nine lands knows this. Wizards are few and far between, but rare is the man, woman, or child who goes a lifetime without seeing at least one. Yet we are all of us ignorant. For there are two other branches, hidden, never taught to children. For in them lies the fate of us all, and a dark and terrible fate it is."

Loren felt as if the world around them had gone still. She had to struggle to hear even the crickets, for it seemed that everything had gone completely silent.

"What—" her voice cracked, and she stopped. She swallowed hard and tried again. "What are the hidden branches?"

"Ceremancy and necromancy," said Xain. "Life. And death."

Loren frowned. "Those . . . those are not magic. They are . . . they are . . . they simply *are.*"

"So I, too, thought," said Xain. "Yet in Wellmont I spoke with Jordel for nearly a day, and he taught me the truth of things. Life magic and death magic are the source of all the other branches. They are the essence of power itself. My power, the power of all wizards, the power of magestones. All are interlinked, forever entwined with the two hidden branches."

"But there are no life wizards and death wizards," said Loren, irritated. "Surely we would know of them if there were. You were the first wizard I had met, Xain, but I had heard tales aplenty before then. Four branches I was told of. Not six. And nothing of two hidden branches."

"That was by careful design," said Xain. "And you are wrong: there are life wizards and death wizards. Or rather, there is one of each. The Necromancer, master of death. And the Ceremancer, though that one is more often called the Lifemage."

"Only one?" said Loren, more confused than ever. "Why, when there are a great many of the other kinds of wizards?"

"Because they are the source," said Xain. "They were the first, and from them sprang all the other, lesser powers. And though the first Necromancer and the first Lifemage died long, long ago, they were reborn. Again and again they returned, in later times and places, in new bodies, but always together, and always with the same powers. Life and Death, returning to wage their great and endless war for the fate of all men."

"I have heard tales of great warriors, wizards, and kings," said Loren. "And thieves as well. Yet never have I heard of either a Lifemage or a Necromancer."

"Many centuries has it been since they last lived in the nine lands," said Xain softly. "And in such times, the in-between times, the Mystics hide all knowledge of them. Every record is expunged, every tale snuffed out. They wish for no one to know of the Necromancer, for then followers might take root, and gather in strength in preparation of his coming."

Loren felt she understood at last. "The Shades. They serve the Necromancer. Do the Mystics, then, serve the Lifemage?"

"That is their true purpose. But they have forgotten. All but the highest and greatest among them, who guard the secret as carefully as the existence of the Necromancer. To know of one is to know of the other."

They fell to silence, and for a while the only sound was a light wind rustling the grass about them. Xain shivered and pulled his dirty grey cloak tighter. The weather struck him harder, as thin as he was.

As she began to digest his words, a thought came to Loren that made her heart skip a beat. "Then if the Shades are gathering in strength, does that mean the Necromancer is reborn?"

"That is what Jordel guessed," said Xain. He picked at the cuff of his sleeve.

"And while they grow in power, the Mystics do nothing to stop them," said Loren, stomach sinking. "Because they know nothing. Only Jordel discovered the truth, and he died in the Greatrocks. And now I have made us sit here and wait in a faraway city, when we should have been warning all the kingdoms."

Xain looked away. "You can hardly be blamed," he said, though his voice was gruff. "We all keenly felt his loss."

"I should not have let that stop me. Jordel would not have." She brushed the fingers of one hand across the battered knuckles of the other. Almost she struck at the ground again, but she did not wish to open the wound. "I am sorry, Xain. I should have listened to you from the start."

Xain grunted and moved to rise. "I will not argue there. Only see that you remember this in the days to come."

Loren shot to her feet easily and lowered a hand to pull him up. "I will. Clearly you are too weak to do much of anything useful, and have chosen to be wise instead to make up for it."

He glared sharply up at her, but then the moonslight showed him her smile. A wry twist came to his lips, and he took her hand to rise. Together they strode back for Northwood, and Xain flicked a finger to douse the embers of the fire behind them.

FIVE

THE NEXT MORNING, THE TRAVELERS READIED THEMSELVES TO DEPART. Though they had all seemed happy enough to remain in Northwood, once spurred to action Loren thought they seemed relieved to be on the move again. All of them except Chet had spent many weeks riding from one place to another. A rest had been welcome, yet now their feet itched for the road.

While Albern went into town to fetch supplies, Loren went to the inn's stable to prepare their horses for travel. Chet, for lack of anything better to do, came with her. Midnight gave a great cry the moment Loren approached, and she smiled to hear it. The horse was wise beyond the custom of beasts, and Loren thought she must know they were preparing to leave.

"Still your braying, you nag," said Loren, but she patted Midnight's nose with affection. "I have kept you waiting only a few days."

"Look at the way she nuzzles you," said Chet, looking Midnight over with appreciation. Loren had told him the tale already of how she had come to steal the horse. "She has taken you for her own, and no mistake."

"I took *her,* you mean," said Loren. She fetched a brush from the wall and took it to Midnight's coat, though she could see almost at once that the mare needed no grooming. "Though I suspect she thinks differently, I am her master and not the other way around."

She grew quiet for a moment and looked at Chet from the corner of her eyes. She had been meaning to ask him a question for some time. Now it had grown in urgency, but with the moment finally here, she found the words hard to say.

"Chet," she said slowly, carefully. "What will you do? Once we leave, I mean."

His eyes flew wide. He pushed himself from the wall where he had been leaning, and rested a hand on Midnight's flank. "Why . . . I mean to come with you, of course. Unless my company is not welcome, though I had hoped it would be."

Loren felt a rush of happiness, though she tried to still it. Chet had heard much of their journeys, but not all. Though he no doubt thought he understood his decision, he could not possibly imagine its implications.

"Of course you are welcome, always," she said. "And nothing would make me happier than for you to join us. But I would not have you come out of obligation."

"It was not obligation that made me leave the Birchwood," said Chet quickly. "I wanted to follow you. How often did we wish to leave the forest behind, when we were younger? How many lands did we see in our dreams, day after day, longing only to walk their roads with our own feet?"

"Yet in all my daydreams, I never foresaw the peril that has plagued me since I left," said Loren. "And though I would like nothing more than your company, I am loath to bring that peril upon you, and you unaware of it. Dark things hound our steps, Chet, darker even than I have known."

He paused, his hand scratching Midnight's side idly. "Things the wizard told you of? Is that why you make ready to go with such haste? Are you sure you can even trust his words? Mayhap your fear is misplaced."

"It is not," said Loren. "If what lies ahead is half so terrible as what I have left behind me, it will be a road far more perilous than any you have traveled to get here. I will walk that road with you—but only if both your eyes are open."

"They are," he said, shrugging. "I can handle myself in a fight, and have learned to ride a horse. What else would I do except take the road beside you, traveling as we always meant to?"

"This is not some fanciful journey. You must not come with me if you think so."

Chet smiled. "You have told me of the danger, Loren. That is enough. I still mean to come, unless you wish to lock me in these stables, or tie me to the trunk of some tree."

She gave a lingering sigh. "Very well. We will take you into our company, and happily on my part. But know that if you ever wish to turn aside and go your own way, no one will think less of you. And we shall have to find you a horse, unless you wish to be tied across the back of Midnight's saddle."

After readying Midnight and the other steeds to ride, they went back to the inn to see about a horse for Chet. There they found Mag already busy in the common room, her well-muscled arms glistening with sweat as she bussed trays back and forth from tables to kitchen. But she stopped at once when she saw they sought her attention, and came to speak with them at the bar.

"We need a horse for Chet," said Loren. "Do you know where we might find one from an honest seller, who will not give us some beast with a cracked hoof?"

"Why, beneath this very roof," said Mag. *"Sten!"*

Her roar was sudden and sharp, as could often be her way. It always made Loren jump a little. Her husband came hastily out from the kitchen, wiping flour from his great arms with a greased rag, his bushy eyebrows drawn together and his wide mouth muttering darkly.

"Sky above, Mag, how many times have I told you not to bray after me like some donkey?"

"And how many times have I told you how I love my little ass?" said Mag, though she stood a full hand shorter than he did. "See to the common room, will you? These two need a horse."

"The chestnut from that southern man?" said Sten.

"The same. And one last thing." She seized the front of his collar and pulled him down for a quick kiss. But when she tried to pull away, Sten wrapped his arms around her and lifted her from her feet, burrowing his thick beard into her neck. Loren and Chet looked away, shifting their feet. Mag squealed like a little girl, but gave him a sharp chop in the ribs at the same time. Sten groaned and dropped her like a heavy sack.

"The customers!" she snapped, though she could not hide her smile. "I will be only a moment."

Mag led them back to the stables. It held more than a dozen stalls, and most were full, four of them with the beasts Loren and her friends had brought. Near the back was a huge chestnut with a flowing golden mane. Loren had seen it as she came in and out.

"Two southern men came through here some weeks ago, from Idris or some such," said Mag. "They each rode a horse when they arrived, but had to sell one to pay for the rest of their way north. It is a good enough beast—no warhorse, but no swaybacked farm animal, either."

"Why did you buy it?" said Chet. "Do you often go riding?"

"Any innkeeper buys a horse for sale," said Mag. "A good bit of business, horseflesh. Often the folk who come through my doors need a steed to carry on their journey."

"And we will pay you handsomely for it," said Loren firmly.

Mag pursed her lips. "Not handsomely, though I cannot give him away for free. You know I will take no coin for your room and board, but a horse is another matter. Ten gold weights I paid. That is what I will take from you, and not one more. Just passing him on, so to speak."

"And if we were any other travelers, how much would we pay then?" said Loren, folding her arms.

"That I shall keep to myself, if it is all the same to you."

"It is not," said Loren. "But so be it. Ten gold weights, as you say."

After grasping wrists to seal the pact, Mag returned to Sten in the common room while Loren went to their room upstairs. She took from her coin purse ten gold weights and dropped them in a spare purse. After a moment's thought, she added five more. She did not know if it was a fair price—if anything, it seemed somewhat high. But the extra could pay for their food and rooms, for Mag had been far too generous. It left her purse somewhat lighter than she liked, but she would have to worry about that later. As long as they had enough to reach Jordel's brethren in Feldemar, that was all that mattered.

With Chet still by her side, she went back to the common room where Mag stood speaking with a customer. She threw the spare coin purse to Mag, who scarcely looked up as she caught it with a deft hand and carried on speaking. She did not open it to look inside. Satisfied, Loren went to her usual table in the corner, where Albern, Xain, and the children were already tucking in for lunch.

"I have fetched as many provisions as I thought the horses could carry," said Albern as they sat down. "It should see you at least halfway through Dorsea, though you shall need to stop for more supplies at some point."

"We will stop as rarely as we can afford," said Xain. "The fewer people who mark our passing, the better."

"Once you are deep into Dorsea, I think the danger shall lessen," said Albern. "In the south their kingdom is preoccupied with the war, and in the north they remain as untroubled as ever at the goings-on of the nine lands."

"Who is that man there?" asked Gem.

Something about the boy's tone raised the hairs on the back of Loren's neck. She looked over her shoulder to see Mag talking to someone new: a thin man with a hooked nose and spindly fingers, whose head darted about constantly as he spoke. He was altogether different from the simple folk she had grown accustomed to in Northwood, and it set her nerves on edge.

They all watched him for a moment, until Mag looked up from the conversation and caught Albern's eye. She tossed her head at him, and wordlessly Albern rose to approach her. Loren quickly found her feet and went with him, but when Chet, too, started to rise, she waved him back into his seat.

Mag wore a dark look as they reached her. "Len, tell them."

The thin man pinched his nose and sniffed. "There is a man. He is wandering about the city, searching for a girl in a black cloak."

Loren felt the blood drain from her face. Albern's mouth set in a grim line. The thin man nodded, pinching his nose and sniffing again.

"Aye, that is what I thought when I heard," he said, though Loren had said nothing. "Black cloak and remarkable green eyes, he asked for. Used that word, remarkable. Calls himself Rogan, which sounds foreign to me. He is dark of skin, like the girl with you, though from their looks I would not call them kin. Big. He carried no weapons, but he felt like one, if you follow me. When I heard him asking around, I thought to myself that I seen eyes just like that, and a black cloak as well, here in your place, Mag."

"Our thanks, Len. Drink up, and tell Sten it is my gift." He sidled off, and Mag fixed them with a hard look. "Is this Rogan some friend of yours?"

"I do not know that name," said Loren. "We should have left long ago."

"Stay your concern, at least for the moment," said Albern. "We know nothing for certain. Mayhap there is cause for fear, but mayhap this Rogan is some friend to Jordel."

"He said nothing of a red cloak."

"Hist!" Albern glanced over his shoulder. "Speak not so openly of our fallen friend's order where others may hear. And if this Rogan is one of them, and he sought us in secret, do you think he would show himself so openly?"

"We should go and see after him, and mayhap find our answers," said Loren.

"I think the same."

"I shall come," said Mag. "Len is a good sort, but his nerves can get the better of him. I may recognize the man's face where Len could not."

Loren ran quickly to put her black cloak away upstairs and fetch her dirty brown spare. When she returned, Chet again rose to go with her.

"Stay," she said. "Albern and I have something to look into. It will not take long, and too many at once may draw attention."

"Is it some trouble?" said Xain sharply.

"It may be, or it may be nothing," said Loren. "Rest assured, we will return in safety. Wait—but mayhap ready the horses, just in case."

She returned to the bar, where Albern still waited for her. Sten, too, was there, and through his beard Loren could see his frown of concern.

"Not long at all," Mag was saying. "Do not trouble your ugly little head over it."

"When have you ever given me cause for concern? I fear only for anyone who may think to tussle with you," said Sten. But the creases in his forehead deepened.

Mag placed a hand on his arm and stood on tiptoe to kiss his cheek. "See to the customers. Get those layabout children to help, if you need them." He let her leave him then, with no more than a long squeeze of her hand to see her off.

SIX

THEY SET OUT INTO THE STREETS, AND THOUGH IT WAS WARM LOREN quickly raised her hood to mask her face. Its shadow would hide her eyes—or at least, so she hoped.

Mag took them into the heart of the city. Northwood was no burg so great as Wellmont, or even Cabrus, the first city Loren had seen after leaving her forest home. Here there were hardly any buildings more than a single storey. The city was wide rather than tall, sprawled across the land with its streets twisting haphazardly in upon each other. Yet with unerring certainty Mag wove her way through them, until it was all Loren could do to keep up.

"Len said he was near here," said Mag, looking around in the lazy afternoon sun. "Stay close to the walls, and find shadows to stand in if you can."

Loren needed no second urging, already doing all she could to avoid being seen. Yet it seemed she need not have worried, for though the streets were well-peopled, not a single eye turned to her.

Search as she might, she could see no sign of the man Len had described. They searched every street and alley they could find, but had no luck for a long while, until Loren began to wonder if there was anything to worry about after all.

"There," hissed Albern at last. He seized Loren's arm and drew her against the wall of a smithy. Loren peeked out from under the very edge of her hood.

She saw him at last. Len had spoken truly: this man Rogan felt dangerous, and though he wore no armor his size protected him like a suit of plate. His arms were covered, yet under the sleeves she could still see his strength. Dark was his face, and he had scars across both eyes, though he had lost neither of them.

Something about him seemed familiar. Loren could not place the reason, and the more she searched for it the more she grew afraid. She knew she had seen something like him before. Not in Jordel, nor any of the other Mystics she had met upon her road.

Albern put words to her thoughts. "Do you see it? He moves like Trisken."

Loren thought her heart might stop. "We must leave. We should have fled the city last night. Why did I delay? We must leave."

"Albern, what is it?" said Mag.

"Nothing, or at least no great matter if we leave at once," said Albern.

His grip on Loren's arm tightened, and he very nearly hauled her down the street. Mag quickened her pace to match them. Loren glanced back over her shoulder once as they fled—and in a frozen, terrible moment, her eyes locked with Rogan's. Then he was gone, buried in the crowds that filled the streets.

"He saw me," she said, trying not to wail.

"We were too far away," said Albern. "He could not have remarked upon you, not dressed like this. You are not the only girl in the nine lands with green eyes." Yet he redoubled his pace. Now they were half running.

"Is it them?" said Mag. "The ones you fought in the mountains?"

"Mayhap."

"We have no time," said Loren. "I only hope the others have readied the horses."

Albern looked quickly back over his shoulder. "Mayhap I should come with you."

Loren wanted to refuse. Albern had sought to part ways with them and return to his home in Strapa, far to the south. But now she welcomed the thought of his company, for Albern was as skilled at using a bow as he was at making one. Indecision kept her silent, and she could not sort through her thoughts for the fear that filled her heart.

She saw Jordel's broken body on the valley floor.

She saw Trisken's bloodied grin.

The brute Trisken had commanded the fortress they found in the Greatrocks, the one filled with Shades that had inspired such fear in Jordel. Jordel, who had always been a solid rock for Loren to lean on. Trisken had fought them in the mountain's caves, and there they had cut him down with arrows and with swords. And Trisken had risen again, mortal wounds stitching together before their terrified eyes, and they could do nothing but run.

They had slain him at last. But in the slaying they lost Jordel, the greatest among them.

Mag's inn loomed above. Loren ignored the back door and burst in through the front, running at once to the table where the others sat. Gem and Annis looked at her in surprise, but in Xain's eyes she saw a dark recognition—he knew something was amiss.

"We are leaving," Loren said. "Now. Where is Chet?"

"With the horses," said Annis. "What did you see in the—"

"*Now,* Annis," snapped Loren. "Go with Gem and fetch our things, as quickly as your feet can carry you. Meet at the stables."

Annis and Gem caught Loren's panic like a fever and ran away upstairs. Xain tried quickly to rise, but stumbled and had to catch himself on the table. On thin and shaking legs he ran after Loren as she made for the inn's back door.

"A man in town searches for us," said Loren, before he could ask. "He is one of them, certainly. He holds himself as Trisken did."

Already pale, Xain's skin turned Elf-white. "We are too long delayed."

"We can be miles away before they learn we were ever here," said Loren.

"That is true enough," said Albern. "And unless they are mightier woodsmen than I guess, I shall see to it that they have trouble following us once we are beneath the eaves of the Birchwood."

"You will find Chet and me no slouches in that regard," said Loren. "We are children of that forest."

They struck the doors of the stable so hard the hinges nearly broke. Chet's gaze shot up from where he was inspecting his chestnut's bridle.

"Loren? What is it?"

"We are leaving," said Loren. "I hope you are ready to sit that saddle."

"I am," said Chet, eyeing Albern and Xain. "But I do not understand what—"

The sharp blast of a horn cut the air outside. Chet went quiet. Screams tore at the silence that followed, and somewhere far away, a bell began to toll.

SEVEN

LOREN WAS ON THE VERGE OF RUNNING BACK TO THE INN WHEN GEM and Annis appeared at last, bags tucked under their arms and eyes wide with fright. Chet and Albern took the supplies and began throwing them upon the backs of the mounts, while Xain slowly gained his horse's saddle.

"What are these horns?" said Gem, his voice quaking. "I heard shouting."

"An attack," said Loren. "I knew he saw me."

The stable door flew open again. The party whirled to the sound as one. Loren drew her dagger without thinking, and Albern his sword. When she saw Mag and Sten, Loren relaxed for a moment—until she saw the blades they held in their hands, and the shields upon their arms.

"The city is under siege," said Mag. "We shall see you safely beyond the walls."

"You should go back inside," said Loren. "Wait until we have gone. They will pursue us beyond the city and leave Northwood in peace."

"That I doubt," said Mag. "There is already killing in the streets.

And you have no time to convince me otherwise. Mount your horses. Quickly."

Loren began to reply, but Albern seized her and nearly threw her into the saddle. "You are nearly a match for Mag in stubbornness, girl, but not quite. Heed her."

Loren ground her teeth, but she stuck her boots through the stirrups. The others were quick to follow. With Mag and Sten on either side, she led the way through the streets, away north where the gate to the Birchwood waited. From the west rang the screams of the dying, and Loren heard the clash of steel.

"They would kill all these people just to find us?" cried Annis. "How can they hope to keep themselves a secret after this?"

"If none live to tell the tale, it will remain hidden," said Albern with grim finality. "Even if some spare few escape to spread word of the attack, most will assume it is an army of Dorsea."

"You mean to say it is not?" said Sten. Mag had heard the tale of their journey, but her husband had not, and knew nothing of the Shades.

"Time for that explanation later," said Mag. "We should hasten. If I were them, I would move to cut off escape to the north and east. With luck, we should gain the gate before then."

But just as she said the words, they came into an open square to find their foes before them. Shades in blue and grey stormed into view, mail shining and blades flashing with the sun. Folk fled before them, but the Shades cut most down as they ran. They were so intent in their slaughter that they paid no mind to Loren and the others.

"This way!" cried Mag.

She led them aside and down another street, away from the killing. Loren caught sight of Chet's face as they rode on. It was white as a sheet, his teeth bared in a grimace of horror. She gripped his arm as they rode, and squeezed until he met her gaze.

"Try not to look," she said. "Keep your eyes front, and your mind on where you are going."

He gave her a shaky nod. Beyond him, Loren saw Gem and Annis. Their mouths were grim lines, and their shoulders were set. The rest of them had seen so much death that even this wanton slaughter did not make them despair. She was unsure whether that was a good thing or not.

Mag took them through many twisting alleys, but the next time they came into the open they happened upon more Shades. Here some citizens of Northwood had taken up arms, shovels and pitchforks turned to makeshift weapons. But the Shades were disciplined, and fought in coordination. One or two had fallen in the fighting, but scores of their victims littered the ground.

"No use. It will be a fight," said Mag. Her voice was a chilling monotone. It had turned flat and lifeless—a terrible sound from the woman who had been so warm to them, so motherly to the children. Loren found herself shivering despite the afternoon's heat.

Albern drew an arrow from the quiver at his hip and turned to the rest of them. "Stay behind Mag and Sten. Stay your blades unless you have no other choice, for they will try to seize them and pull you down. Now, charge!"

Then, for the first time, Loren saw death made beautiful.

Mag struck, filled with battle-lust at the sight of her fellows killed in their own homes. She fought, blade lent the speed of her rage, her shield like a castle wall in motion as it warded their blows. Not once did her blade strike without drawing blood, faster than a serpent's strike, elegant and fluid as a flowing waterfall. Beside her Sten used his size and strength to batter his foes, knocking them back until he could find an opening for his sword. And behind her Albern let forth a flurry of arrows, each finding its mark, his archery like wizardry to Loren's eyes. But Mag's blade was coated in death, her fighting cry the wail of a banshee, and no foe came under her gaze and survived. In twos and threes they fought her, but they could not pierce her guard, nor could they stay her blade once it swung towards them.

The fight was over almost before Loren knew it had begun. The Shades who did not fall to their assault turned and fled through the streets, vanishing behind the buildings and into the alleys of the city. Mag turned to them, her face spattered with a mist of red. Loren saw flecks of it on her bared teeth.

"On!" growled Mag. "Do not stop moving, not even for a moment."

Wordlessly they followed. From the side Loren could see Albern's dark expression, and Sten looked sadly at his wife as they pressed through the streets. But Mag had no eyes for them, only for the road ahead.

Twice more they came upon Shades in the streets, and twice more Mag drove them back with a furious charge. Sten could barely keep up—indeed, even Albern's arrows seemed to strike a moment after Mag's lightning blows. Loren and the others tried only to stay out of the way, quaking in their saddles as they watched Mag slice through the heart of her foes like a scythe.

At last they came within sight of the city's north wall. But there they paused. More Shades came marching in through the gate, in rank and file. It was an army of them, a far greater strength than they had seen even in the Greatrocks.

"There are so many," breathed Loren.

"Surely not even Mag can defeat them all," said Gem. "Albern . . . what do we do?"

Albern hesitated. Sten had stopped in his tracks, and even Mag paused, as though the sight of so many foes had at last broken through her killing rage.

The moment's silence grew long. Loren tugged on Midnight's reins and began to wheel around. "Come. Mayhap they have not reached the eastern gate yet. We can try to—"

"They will have reached it," said Mag. She spoke in a battle commander's bark, but still it held no fire, no anger. Only emptiness. She turned to them, and Loren saw none of the warmth she had grown used to in the woman's eyes. "Come now, little children. Do you fear so few of them? Come with me, and you shall reach the Birchwood. I swear it."

"Mag!" But Albern was too late. She ran straight into the heart of the Shades, blade held aloft, glittering except where it was caked in gore. Sten came two steps behind, trying and failing to match her furious pace.

Albern drew another arrow. His quiver was half-empty. He turned to Loren and Chet with a snarl. "Make use of those bows on your backs, or give me your arrows, but do not stand here idle while she risks her life for yours." Then he kicked his mount's flanks and he, too, charged the Shades.

Gem, sitting behind Annis in their saddle, drew his short sword from the belt at his waist. Loren saw it shaking in his hand, but his eyes were hard. "Well, then," he said. "I had always thought to perish old in bed, but slain in battle seems a fair enough choice."

"Can you help them?" said Loren, turning to Xain.

He was shaking in his saddle, his hands looking almost too frail even to hold the reins. She knew his answer before he spoke. "My flames are nearly guttered out. I might conjure enough to stop one of them, or two. But even that little effort would exhaust me."

"Loren?" said Annis, eyes wide with fright. "What do we—"

"Between my horse and Chet's," said Loren. She drew forth her bow and nocked an arrow. "Gem, do not dare to strike at them except to save yourself and Annis. Stay close to the others, but above all, stay alive."

They rode after Albern. Loren drew the fletching all the way back to her ear, and sighted along the shaft. Mag stood against a squadron of foes now, and more were trying to circle around behind her.

Loren aimed for one of them, lowering her bow to strike him in the leg.

Blood dripping from his thigh, a trail of it for miles through the woods.

She tensed as the picture flashed into her mind, and the arrow went wide to rebound from cobblestones. Cursing, she drew another. Beside her, Chet loosed a shaft of his own. It flew true, skewering a soldier's calf. Beside them, Albern's bow was singing. Gem sat shaking in his saddle, holding his blade forth as if to ward any of the soldiers from coming too close. But they had no eyes for Loren and the others, only for Mag in their center.

Still she fought on, and her strikes had not slowed. The Shades could not get inside her reach, nor could they approach her from the side unawares, for Sten was with her. At her back he stood, guarding her rear as she guarded his, and if he could not kill as many as she could, still he could keep her from being outflanked. Any who threatened to break his guard soon found themselves with one of Albern's shafts in their throats.

So intent were the Shades on bringing the warriors down that they had drifted to one side of the street, leaving the other side open. And beyond them, Loren saw that at last they had stopped pouring through the entrance. The way to the Birchwood was clear, at least for her and Xain and the children. But despite their best efforts, Mag was hemmed in now, and the Shades were close to surrounding Albern besides.

"Albern!" cried Loren.

He risked a glance at her, and she pointed at the city's gate. Quickly his gaze followed, and she saw a light in his eyes. But then he turned back to Mag, and the light went dark.

Sten slipped.

A powerful blow to his shield sent his feet sliding in the blood that slicked the ground. His knee struck the dirt of the street, and a sword flashed around in a wide arc.

He jerked his head back, and for a moment Loren thought he had avoided the blow. Then she saw a red torrent gush from his throat.

Mag was behind him and could not see it, only that he knelt. She gripped his arm and tried to pull him up. Rather than rising, he fell onto his back, his lifeblood bubbling forth.

Mag screamed.

The sound of it was nothing human. Loren had never heard its like before. She knew at once that she would remember it for the rest of her life. For a moment the whole world held its breath. Chet froze with an arrow drawn. Even Gem stopped quaking. Xain had leaned forwards in his saddle, one hand outstretched as though to send forth flame or thunder.

But nothing came. Nothing but the scream, piercing and terrible and filled with rage.

Before it finished, she was already on her feet again, already killing. She pressed into their mass, hacking at them like a woodsman at a cluster of logs. Even with her back unguarded, they could not bring her down, but now at last their strikes found flesh. Loren saw deep red rents appear on her arms. *The Uncut Lady,* Albern had called her, but no longer. Yet she fought on.

Albern looked back at Loren, and then to the open city gate that now seemed leagues away.

Loren grit her teeth and spurred Midnight forwards to help.

"No!" cried Albern, and she reined up. "Fly, while you still can!"

She wanted to ride into them, and damn her vow not to kill. She would draw Mag from their midst, and the darkness protect any of them that tried to stop her.

A hand gripped her arm. She turned, expecting Chet—but it was Xain instead, and his eyes were grim. "Fly," he said. "Remember Jordel."

She ripped off her quiver and raised it, then tossed it to Albern. He caught it with a solemn nod. Then he drew his sword and threw himself into the fight, trying to cut his way through to Mag. But Loren would not watch. Midnight wheeled at her touch, and they spurred to a gallop. In seconds they had passed beyond the city and reached the Birchwood, and Northwood vanished behind the trunks of the trees—this time, mercifully.

EIGHT

THEY DID NOT STOP THEIR MAD RIDE WHEN THEY REACHED THE TREES, but they had to when the sun went down. Loren scarcely noticed, and it was Xain who finally called them to a halt.

She did not understand for a moment, and she looked at him in confusion. It was Chet who spoke first.

"The moons will not rise for hours, Loren." His voice trembled. "We can ride by their light if we must, but pressing on now is folly."

Loren stared a moment longer before she heard the words. Then she nodded and slid from the saddle, letting Midnight wander.

She set off through the trees, away from the others, eyes wide to catch every mote of starlight and avoid a stumble. But she did not see the forest around her. Rather, she saw only a ghostly and wispy aspect of it, just enough for her feet to avoid upturned roots and stones. Instead of the trees and the silvery starlight, she saw Albern's charge, and Mag's skin covered in wounds, and Sten's slashed throat.

It was some time before she could muster her thoughts. When she did, she realized she had wandered far from where the others had stopped. She turned to retrace her steps, and when she found their camp again they had started a small fire beneath the trees. Part of her wanted to douse it, to keep them hidden in case they were pursued. But she could not muster the strength to care for so small a thing.

Chet sat alone, outside the fire's light. His knees were pulled up against his chest, and his arms lay across them. He seemed to be looking at the firelight, but his gaze was far away, as though he saw nothing at all.

A sharp pang in her gut reminded her she had not eaten for hours. She went to Midnight's saddlebag to fetch some meat and bread.

Something went *clink* as she opened the saddlebag. Her brow furrowed. When she lifted the flap, she saw a small coin purse. It was her spare, the one she had given to Mag. Slowly she untied the strings and poured the contents into her hand. Ten gold weights sat there, gleaming in the firelight. She stared at them for a while. Then she put them back in the purse and put the purse in the saddlebag.

Her appetite had vanished, so she closed the bag again and went to sit by the fire. But by the time she reached it, she did not want to rest, so she kept walking past it and over to Chet. She had nearly reached him before he noticed her and looked up.

"You should eat," he said. "I suppose I should, too."

"I tried. Will you walk with me?"

He shrugged and stood to go with her. Together they went back into the darkness—only to her surprise, Loren found it easier to see, and she realized with a start that the moons had risen. She had spent more time alone than she thought.

Chet stopped and heaved a shuddering breath. When she looked to him, she saw his shoulders shaking gently. She laid her hand on his back and turned him around. Once he faced her again, she saw his cheeks wet with tears.

"They did not even seem to care who they killed," he said. "I saw children fall beneath their blades."

"So it often is when armies sack cities," said Loren. "Or so I have heard. I was there for the battle of Wellmont, but the city held. There was no killing in the streets."

He looked away and cleared his throat. When he spoke again, she could hear him trying to sound carefree, as though his tears were not there. "You all hardly blinked as you rode through it," he said. "I thought I would die of fright."

"We have seen killing before," said Loren. "Some of us more than others."

"I am sorry about Albern. I knew him only a few days, but he seemed to have a good heart. Mag and Sten, as well."

"They did," said Loren.

He swiped a hand across his eyes, but tried to make it seem like he was only wiping sweat from his brow. "Loren, we must get away from here. We should ride into Dorsea and vanish where no one will find us. If that army came to Northwood looking for you, and was willing to sack the city just to find you, they will not stop pursuing you now."

"That is why we must ride east, to warn the Mystics of their coming."

"Will they not expect that?" said Chet. "Will they not hunt us all along the road?"

"That does not matter," said Loren. "It is the duty I have taken upon myself. I have been hunted before."

"Duty?" said Chet. His voice had gone high and hysterical. "Why would you wish this upon yourself? I thought to travel with you, not die beside you. Oh, I know that all the nine lands may be dangerous, but this is another thing altogether. Did you not spend enough time, unhappy and trapped by your parents, out of some misplaced sense of duty?"

"That was nothing I chose," said Loren. "But this is my life now. It has been almost since the moment I left the Birchwood. Doom follows in my footsteps. That is why I urged you not to come with us. Even now I urge you to turn away, to let your tracks lead you home."

He stood there, looking at her in fear, and with a sinking heart she realized he was considering it. But at last he looked away and shook his head. "No. I said I would come with you. Who could call me anything but faithless, if I turned away because the road grew dark?"

"Who cares what anyone would call you?" said Loren. "I would happily have you by my side, but I would rather see you safe."

"And I you," he said. "That is why we should go, and now. Let others tend to duty. You and I have spent all our lives as its victims."

"I cannot," she said, in a small voice. "I owe it to him—to Jordel."

Chet looked as if he might say more, but then her stomach gave a gurgle. He stopped, collected himself, and shook his head. "We should eat. The road will grow darker still if we find ourselves starving upon it."

"I said I am not hungry."

"Hungry or not, I think you can swallow. Come."

They made their way back to the firelight. By the time they reached it, Chet seemed to have shaken off the darkness in his mind. Loren wondered if it had been so easy for her, the first time.

When she had first seen men killed in anger, it had been with the merchant caravan where she met Annis. Annis' mother, the merchant Damaris, had ordered a company of constables to be killed to preserve the secrecy of the goods she was smuggling. Loren remembered her horror at the senseless slaughter, at how the merchant had forced her to help dig graves for all the bodies. But looking back on it now, she hardly blinked at the thought of the constables dying. She had seen so much since then, so much worse, so much more frightening.

And yet she could not banish from her mind what had happened during the battle. She had chosen her target, and then had hesitated. The thought of her father's corpse had flashed into her mind, and the shot had gone wide. Mayhap, if she had been able to fire the arrow . . .

But such thoughts were ridiculous. There had been scores of Shades. Her arrow would not have made a difference. All the arrows in her quiver would not have made a difference.

Yet mayhap she *could* have done something. For one brief, thrilling moment, she had meant to charge in and rescue Mag by whatever means she could. She knew, looking back on it, she would not have hesitated to spill blood. That prospect terrified her—and yet it made her wonder again: why did she still hold so tightly to that ideal, when she had already taken a life?

That was different, she told herself.

Gem and Annis had eaten already, and lounged at the fire's edge while staring into its heart. Loren had not seen Xain touch his food, but then the wizard's appetite did not seem very great these days. He, too, watched the flames, but every few seconds he would look over his shoulder into the darkness beyond their camp. When he saw Loren and Chet return, his eyes flashed with interest.

"Good," he said. "We must discuss what we plan to do next."

"I myself am most curious about that," said Gem. "We have made our escape, and a narrow one. But what now?"

"We must warn the Mystics," said Loren.

"We know *that*," said Annis, "but where do we mean to go? South to Cabrus? The High King's Seat? I do not relish either of those choices, for my family would be thick about us. And you will remember that even Jordel did not trust all those of his order. How will we know the right redcloaks to speak to, and which ones will ignore our warnings to hang us as criminals instead?"

"If *you* will remember, Jordel told us where he meant to go," said Xain. "His stronghold of Ammon, in Feldemar. He told me where it lies, and that is where I think we must lay our course. His master lives there—a man named Kal, of the family Endil."

"And you think this man can be trusted?" said Loren. "Have you met him?"

"I trust few, Mystics least of all," said Xain. "But this, at least, we owe Jordel: to deliver his message to his master, and let the Mystics do what they may with the tale."

"But how shall we get there?" said Loren. "I have scarcely any idea how to make our way to Feldemar. I know only that it is north and east of Selvan."

"A far ways north and east, yes," said Xain. "Ammon is in Feldemar, and somewhat near the northern shore of the Great Bay. I visited that kingdom once in my youth. Ships travel to that area from all ports on the Bay."

"The King's road, then?" said Gem. "We could take it to the Seat, or Garsec, Selvan's capital."

"That would be like walking into the lion's den," cried Annis. "We would certainly be spotted, and then I would be taken by my family. The rest of you would not be so lucky. You would likely take long in the killing."

"No, Garsec and the Seat seem poor choices both," said Xain. "But there are other ports in Selvan, ports farther south along the Bay, from where we might sail. But traveling there would take a long while, and the voyage would be longer besides. No, I think we must sail from Dorsea."

Loren blinked, gawking at him in the firelight. "Dorsea? Have magestones addled your mind so much, wizard? They are at war with Selvan, and no safe place for us to wander. Especially since, as you have all pointed out so carefully, I speak like a child of Selvan birth. Chet is from my village, and most likely has the same accent."

"Yes," said Gem and Annis at once.

"Accent?" said Chet.

"That was true enough when we set out from Wellmont," said Xain. "But now the war is far away, in the southwest corner of the kingdom. Likely those in the northeast of Selvan have hardly heard of the fighting. Citizens of Dorsea will be even less concerned, so far away from the conflict. And so close to the border between the two kingdoms, we will find many families with both Selvan and Dorsean kin. Your quaint voices will scarcely bear mention."

"So that is our plan, then?" said Annis. "We will strike north into Dorsea, then travel east until we reach the coast? I daresay I like it better than the thought of riding to the Seat, where, if I have my way, I will never set foot again in this life."

"It seems a prudent course," said Gem.

Chet's eyes lit up, and he turned to Loren. "Mayhap—or mayhap there is another way. Traveling across the open country of Dorsea poses its own dangers, and we do not know the land. But there is another road to the coast of the Great Bay. And it is a road for which we already have two guides."

Loren caught his meaning at once. "The Birchwood."

"What of it?" said Gem.

"It runs all the way to the Bay. And Chet and I know it well. Mayhap we are not woodsmen so great as—" She stopped short just before she said *Albern*. "—as some others. But this is our home. I do not think the Shades can follow us beneath these trees."

"If there is one thing we should have learned by now, it is not to underestimate our foes," said Xain darkly. "Think of this. The Shades attacked Northwood from the west, but also from the north. They have been gathering in strength, much greater strength than we knew. Where did they all come from? They did not conjure so many soldiers from thin air. They are men and women of these lands, of Selvan and Dorsea and likely other kingdoms besides. And if they know we have fled into the forest, they will send trackers after us who know it as well as the two of you."

"You think any Selvans fight on their side?" said Loren angrily. "You think they would march into one of their own cities and murder their fellows in the streets? I think you know little of our kingdom."

"And you think too highly of your fellows," snapped Xain. "Mayhap they were starving, and the Shades gave them coin. Mayhap their homes were ravaged by war, and the Shades offered them safety. Mayhap they were dying from plague, and the Shades provided refuge. And mayhap their suffering was not at the hands of some whimsical fate, but their fellow citizens of Selvan. Do you think, then, that they would stay their blades?"

Loren fumed, though in the back of her mind she knew she had little reason for it. She had met evil men and women before. Few acted as they did for the joy of it. She turned away from Xain, refusing to answer him.

Chet frowned, but spoke to appease the wizard rather than to argue. "Still, we have a lead. I think we can evade them. And in any case, it would let Loren and me return home. If the Shades do indeed wander these lands, we owe it to our families to warn them." He stopped short, glancing at Loren from the corner of his eye. "And to our other friends, of course."

Loren turned to see Xain's dark eyes fixed on her again. Though she had never told him the full tale, he knew something of why she had left the forest. When he had found her there, a young girl who wished to flee her home, she had shown him the bruises her father used to leave upon her body. That was what had prompted him to bring her in the first place. He had to know she had little reason to return—not like Chet, whose father loved him, and who had had many friends in the village besides.

But still, Loren remembered some folk from her childhood with fondness, though it seemed many years since she had seem them last. Mayhap Chet was right. Mayhap they could warn the village and let them escape . . . but to where? She did not know, but anywhere had to be better than a kingdom overrun by Shades.

She met Xain's gaze defiantly. "Yes. We will make for the coast by way of the Birchwood. Rest, all of you. We ride again at first light."

Xain glowered at her. "I will stand the first watch." She held his gaze a moment longer before she turned to fetch her bedroll from Midnight's saddle.

NINE

Dawn broke grey and cold, with the sun struggling to pierce the clouds and find them beneath the trees. Loren felt a sore spot under her shoulder. After days spent in Mag's inn, which was comfortable, if plain, the forest floor was an unpleasant reminder of life on the road.

"Do you think it will rain?" said Annis, who had already awoken. She was looking up at the clouds.

"No," said Chet. "The air is not right, and this part of autumn rarely gives rain."

"It gave us plenty in the Greatrocks," said Gem.

"Mountains are different," said Loren. "This is the Birchwood."

Xain still sat where Loren had seen him last night. She realized suddenly that he had not woken any of them to stand watch. The skin on the back of his hands was raw where he had been picking at it, and she saw him shivering as he rocked back and forth. He seemed unaware of the rest of them.

The magestone sickness must be terrible for him now. It had been weeks since last he had eaten the precious black stones, and the darkness took time to leave his body. Last time it had taken more than a

47

month before his mind had righted itself, and his body had still been recovering its strength when she fed him stones again.

Now his countenance worried her. They could ill afford such weakness—the weakness of his body, or his judgement. For Loren knew his thoughts must be as frail as his skeletal frame. And she worried what the magestone sickness might spur him to do, especially if he imagined he was being betrayed. For Loren had shared much with him the night before, but she had not told him everything.

Could she now? Or would that only bring about the very crisis she hoped to avoid?

What would Jordel have done?

Her jaw clenched with resolve. No. Jordel had seen too much value in secrecy. He had valued Loren, and trusted her—but not enough. If he had told her more about her dagger early on, she would have had less trouble on the road from Cabrus. If he had told her about the magestones, she never would have given them to Xain. And if he had warned her about the Necromancer and the Lifemage, mayhap she could have found some way to save him from Trisken.

No. She would follow in Jordel's footsteps, but not too closely. Xain must trust her with his whole heart, and that could never happen while she hid secrets from him.

And what of your magestones?

That thought stopped her short. Could she tell him that she still had some of the stones? Did her desire for trust extend so far?

She glanced at him again. He had wrapped his arms about himself, and one hand picked at the other elbow.

No. He would go mad with hunger, she knew. She could not tell him—at least not now. That was not dishonesty, but mercy. And in the meantime, she would share all that she could.

Loren walked over to the wizard and motioned to him. "Come with me a moment. I wish to discuss the road."

His eyes snapped up to her, and for a moment she saw the fog of confusion in his eyes, as if he did not recognize her. Then they cleared, and he levered himself to his feet with some difficulty. Loren took his elbow as he stood, and then led him off east into the woods. Once they were out of sight of the others, she stopped.

"The road, eh?" said Xain. "The others are no fools—that boy of yours, least of all."

Loren gritted her teeth and chose not to correct him. "Last night you told me of the Necromancer and the Lifemage. But there was something else I did not tell you, something I was unsure I should speak of. But you deserve to know it, especially now. I am done keeping secrets between us."

His brow arched, and she saw interest spark in his eye. "Say on, then. It can hardly be darker news than I have heard already."

"It might be, in its own way," she said. "It concerns this."

She reached to her hip and drew forth her dagger. Xain fixed it with a wary eye. The black designs along its length were spiked and twisted—unmoving now, though Loren had seen them writhe like the tendrils of a living thing.

"Your dagger," he said. "From whence you took the name Night-blade."

"This blade was my parents'. I found it when I was a young child."

Xain arched an eyebrow. "And you stole it from them when you left?"

"It, and other things besides," she said. "Only I did not know what I carried with me. Nor do most who see it—except some very few, and to them it is an object of great terror."

Xain's brow furrowed, and he reached out for the dagger. Loren hesitated, but then she handed it to him by the hilt.

"It is a fine weapon, elegantly made, to be certain," said Xain. "I do not recognize the craftsmanship. But I do not see what makes it more fearsome than, say, a sword. Especially when you will not even use it to defend yourself."

"To kill, you mean," said Loren sharply. "The dagger's power lies not in its steel, but in its magic. It was crafted and imbued with spells centuries ago, in the time of the Wizard Kings."

His eyes darkened. "That is an ancient weapon, to be found in the hut of a woodsman."

"Ancient, yes. And mightier than can be seen with the eye. Jordel recognized it from the moment he saw it, and eventually he told me its tale. It is a weapon of the mage hunters. A blade for hunting wizards. And killing them."

Xain sucked in a sharp breath through his teeth, and suddenly he held the dagger gingerly between thumb and forefinger. He handed it back to her, and Loren took it gratefully. Now the wizard looked at the blade with distrust.

"I have heard tales of such weapons," he said. "There were dark whispers of them—and of the mage hunters—that passed among the students at the Academy. If our instructors heard us whispering these tales, we were sharply reprimanded and beaten. Of course that only made the tales spread farther. I had heard that one such blade was found recently, some time within living memory."

"The High King Enalyn discovered it, or it was revealed to her," said Loren. "And she grew wrathful, and reinforced the Fearless Decree because of it. To carry such a weapon means death—not only for the wielder, but mayhap for the Mystics themselves."

"As it should," growled Xain. "They used these weapons to slaughter my kind in droves. No wizard could rest easily at night, knowing such blades were carried in the nine lands. Who knew but that some Mystic might not appear upon your doorstep the next morning, immune to your magic and intent on taking your life? They say it was a time of great fear for us, and the very reason for the dark wars of the Wizard Kings. After I heard of how they hunted us, I could find no fault with my forebears for beginning those wars."

He had begun to pace as he talked, and his voice rose louder and louder in its wrath. Loren stood back from him, and found her hand gripping the handle of the dagger more tightly. But almost as soon as the anger had come upon him, it fled. He sagged like a sack of grain with the bottom sliced open and placed a hand over his eyes.

"No," he muttered. "No, those are wrathful words from days I have left behind. I have eaten of the magestones and come back—twice now. I have seen what plagued the Wizard Kings, what madness took hold of their minds and led to the dark times."

"The Wizard Kings ate of magestones?" said Loren. "I had not heard that."

"You had not heard of magestones at all until you left the Birchwood behind you. Yes, many of the Wizard Kings consumed the stones with reckless hunger. Their power was all the greater, but so were their madness and their wrath. Those who abstained were no villains—at least no more so than any other kings—but as the kingdoms vied for power, wizards ate the stones in greater numbers."

He looked at her, and she saw in his eyes the same man she had first met under the trees of this very forest: bitter, yes, and quick with biting wit. But mostly sad, and frightened, and a little lost.

"Now I have learned of their madness. And it makes me wish there were more such weapons in the nine lands."

Loren gulped. "What, then, do you think I should do with it?"

"Keep it," he said. "I have lived my whole life a wizard, and until recently I gave little thought to what it must be like for the rest of you—those without the gift, and the curse, of our power. I can only imagine the fear you must feel, living in these kingdoms where magic runs rampant. Unless I miss my guess, you will cross paths with many more wizards in the course of your life. Keep it, and use it to your advantage."

He pushed past her and made for the camp, leaving Loren standing on her own. Just before he vanished between the trees, he turned and called back over his shoulder.

"I only hope I never make an enemy of you again, Nightblade."

TEN

THEY SET OFF SOON AFTERWARDS, MOUNTING THEIR HORSES AND HEADING east through the trees. Despite the cast of the sky, the day soon warmed to a nearly unbearable heat. Loren cast her cloak back over her shoulders. Chet removed his own, stowing it in his saddlebags, and the children did the same. Only Xain still felt chilled, and clutched his cloak tighter as they went, trembling.

Loren set a good pace for them, but nothing too drastic. Though she thought they were most likely safe, she had not entirely discounted the possibility that they were still being followed. They could need their horses' strength for a sudden burst of speed. But they saw no sign of pursuit, and at midday she felt confident enough to let them stop for a meal.

It was a strange feeling, she reflected, sliding down from atop Midnight. For so long they had had Jordel to set their pace, and he had pushed them hard or let them wander, according to the urgency of their mission. Now they were without his guidance, and Xain, though older than Loren, was in no condition to set their course. Loren realized with a start that the others now looked to her for leadership. It was not an entirely comfortable feeling.

"So, do you know any songs?" said Gem, lounging in the grass and looking towards Chet.

"Gem," said Loren in a warning tone.

"What?" said Gem. "Albern knew songs, and was happy enough to sing them. He had a fine voice, too." His eyes grew solemn, and he looked down at his nails.

"I heard him sing," said Chet. "But I do not have his gift for it. There were only a few in our village who knew many songs, let alone had the voices to carry them. They guarded the secret jealously. I think they enjoyed the attention it earned them when we would have a dance."

Loren suddenly laughed out loud, and the others looked at her, startled. "I am sorry," she said. "But do you remember when Miss Aisley grew drunk on wine, and forgot the words of the song she was singing?"

Chet's crooked teeth flashed in a grin. "And she had set her cap for Rickard, but she was so befuddled she seized Bracken instead and gave him a kiss so deep the old man nearly fainted."

Loren doubled over, and by now the children had caught their humor and chuckled along. She even saw Xain smirk. "Rickard would not speak to her for months, and Bracken kept hanging about her house day after day, and stayed a week longer than normal."

Their deep belly laughs rang out through the forest, echoing from the trees. Loren had almost forgotten what it was to laugh, and certainly at a memory of home.

Chet fixed her with a look, and it was as though he could read her thoughts. "You see? Not all our past is dark. I am happy we will see our village again. Mayhap, now that those who made it so terrible for you no longer dwell there, you will change your mind about it."

Loren thought she heard the words he did not say: *and change your mind about our journey.* She frowned; she did not wish to keep arguing about this with him, least of all in front of the others.

"I wish I could see Bracken again," she said, as a way of changing the subject. "When last he came, I was still just a little girl. I wonder what he would think of me now, chasing after the tales of Mennet he used to spin for me."

"Mennet!" cried Gem. "I heard many stories of him. He was my favorite. The other boys in Cabrus always said I looked just like him."

"We heard of him as well upon the Seat, but never as a hero," said Annis, sniffing. "He was a scoundrel, a lawbreaker whom the king could never bring to justice. I heard he slew maidens in their beds and took toys from children."

"Mennet? Never!" said Loren. "He took from evil kings who taxed their subjects too highly, and kinslayers and murderers. Always he made right what others had done wrong."

Annis looked at Gem, but the boy only shrugged. She looked to Xain, but he shook his head. "I care little for children's tales of a thief who likely never lived in the first place," said the wizard. "Everyone has heard of Mennet, but the wise know he is nothing but a legend."

Loren glared daggers at him, but Chet spoke first. "Still such tales may have worth. But I never loved them like Loren did. I loved the stories of kings and warriors, brave knights and cunning constables who brought down those who broke the King's law."

"Mayhap one day you will hunt me, then," said Loren with a smile. "For I am no friend to constables."

"Why do you think I left the village in the first place?" said Chet, feigning an evil smile and forming his hands into claws. She shoved him into the grass as the children laughed anew. It felt as though a dark storm that had followed them from Northwood was now blowing away.

They went to their bedrolls that night in far better spirits than the day before, and Loren insisted on standing the first watch to let Xain sleep. She did not know if he ever actually found slumber, and more than once in the night she saw his eyes glittering in the light of the fire. But she woke Chet as the moons were descending, and then fell into a deep sleep that lasted until just after dawn's first light.

But they were not long on the road that second day before something happened to darken their mood. The land rose sharply up across their path, forming a range of hills that were just shy of being proper mountains. But there was a clear path up, so they found its base and then Loren and Chet led them in the ascent.

They were halfway up the rise when Loren chanced to look out at the land they had crossed. And there, some leagues away, she caught a flash of movement that did not look like a bird or a bear. She called them to a halt and stood stock still, searching.

"What is it?" Gem said from his saddle. Loren hushed him with a sharp wave of her hand and kept staring.

Chet came to her side and spoke softly. "Did you see someone?"

"Mayhap," she mumbled. "Somewhat south of our course, and—there!"

She saw it again. There were several shapes moving beneath the trees. Even from this distance she recognized riders on horseback.

"I see them," said Chet. "They are many. Mayhap a dozen."

"A dozen what?" growled Xain.

"Riders," said Loren. "Mayhap a league behind us, but traveling in the same direction."

All were silent for a long moment. Then Annis said, half-heartedly, "We do not know they are Shades. They could be simple travelers, like us. Surely some people must travel through the Birchwood on their journeys, or because they do not like the roads, or simply because it is more pleasant than the lands beyond."

"We are hardly simple travelers," said Loren. "But mayhap you are right. We do not know that we are pursued."

"After the luck we have seen upon our road, do any of you truly doubt it?" said Xain darkly. "They are riding east. That means they come from the direction of Northwood."

They did not answer him, but carried on up the path. And their steps came a bit quicker.

ELEVEN

THEY SOON CRESTED THE RISE. THERE AT THE TOP THEY STOPPED AND looked away west again, peering through the tops of the trees. But they could see no sign of their pursuers, if indeed they were being pursued. Quickly they rode down the other side of the ridge, and with many a backwards glance towards the top.

The Birchwood rose about them as they reached the bottom, and soon there was nothing but the sound of hoofbeats. No one talked as they rode, nor sang. When Loren's gaze did meet one of the others, she saw a hunted look that surely matched her own.

Often they glanced behind them, and after two hours of riding Chet reined his horse to a halt. Loren turned to follow his gaze. At the top of the rise they had crossed, they saw figures on horseback against the sky. At this distance, they were too small to be anything more than silhouettes. She could catch no colors in their clothing.

"They are making better time than we are," said Chet. "We should ride harder."

So they did, spurring their horses to a trot that they kept up the rest of the day. Deep in the heart of the forest, it was impossible to see very far in any direction, particularly behind. Turning from the path could lead the horse into a root or a tree. But now Loren thought she could feel eyes behind them, watching their progress, and it was all she could do to keep from staring backwards as they rode.

As the sun neared the top of the ridge far behind them, she searched for a stream. Fortunately, such were plenty in the Birchwood, and she soon found one to suit her purpose—shallow enough for the horses to walk in, yet deep enough that hoof prints on the bed could not be seen from above. Chet saw her aim at once and led them north in the middle of the stream, the water foaming white around their mounts' hocks.

"Ugh!" said Gem as a splash of water soaked his feet. The shoes they had bought for him in Wellmont were now worn and had holes. "This water is cold."

"Mayhap, but it will keep us safe," said Loren. "They cannot track us in the water."

"How long must we ride it?" said Xain. "I agree with Gem—I do not wish to sleep in a soaking bedroll, my wet clothes clinging to my skin."

"And I do not wish to sleep with Shades lurking in the forest all about us," said Annis. "We will ride as long as Loren and Chet tell us to."

Loren looked at her gratefully, and Annis gave her a smile. It was plain the girl was frightened, but her hands were steady as they gripped the reins, and her mouth was set in a grim line. Loren had not forgotten Annis' face in the Greatrocks when she confronted her mother. A spoiled merchant's daughter she might be, but there was pluck in her.

Soon the soft loam of the forest floor turned to hard and rocky dirt. The light was fading fast from the sky. "A cave," said Loren. "For the horses."

Chet nodded and led them out of the water. They searched about for a place they might conceal their mounts. Soon they found one: a cleft in the earth, wide and tall enough to ride inside, and with a corner behind which they could hide. There they hobbled the horses and left them with some oats, and then dragged branches to block them in and discourage them from wandering.

"Now back to the river," said Loren. "Quickly, all of you. Chet and I will follow."

"Why are you not walking with us?" said Gem.

"Enough questions, boy," said Xain. He gripped Gem's shoulder and pulled the boy along. "Do as she says."

Chet had a hatchet, and with it he cut two wide branches from nearby trees. With the limbs in hand, he and Loren retraced their steps to the river. Wherever the sparse grass had been disturbed, they used the branches to brush it back straight. With their boots they smoothed any soft spot in the forest floor where hooves had left a mark. Soon they found themselves back at the river, all signs of their trail removed.

"Now cross it, and strike out in the other direction," said Loren. "Hurry! Soon it will be dark."

"It is dark enough for me now," said Gem. But he had had enough rebukes for one day, it seemed, and he followed Xain obediently.

Into the forest they plunged, Loren letting Chet lead the way while she brought up the rear. Chet knew her mind without having to hear it, and led them to a rise in the earth that could be seen not far away. They came to its base, and Loren took the rest of them up the rise while Chet remained at the bottom and built a fire.

"Why are we climbing if we mean to camp at the bottom?" said Annis curiously.

"We do not mean to camp at the bottom," said Loren. "We mean only to build a camp at the bottom."

Xain's eyes flashed with recognition. "We have left a trail to it," he said. "If we are being followed, they will come to the fire. But from atop the rise, we can see them without being seen ourselves."

"Very clever," said Gem. "I only wish it did not mean we must sleep without a fire tonight."

"If we are right in our suspicions, it will be many days yet before we can light a fire at night again," said Loren. "Now quickly, let us find trees where we may sleep."

"Trees?" said Gem. "What are we, owls?"

"Leave *off*, Gem," said Annis.

Chet soon had a small campfire going, and he abandoned it to join them atop the rise. Together he and Loren found trees with wide branches that were hidden from the ground, and in them they built small platforms from branches they cut with the hatchet. Soon they had places for the children and Xain to lay their heads. For themselves they found two thick branches side by side, and lay lengthwise upon them.

Together they lay, arms hanging down just a few feet apart, and peered out into the darkness towards the campfire. Though a fair distance away, it glowed like the sun in the pitch-black night. All was quiet, save for the sounds of Gem and Xain rustling about, uncomfortable in their makeshift beds.

"Do you still think this course is wise?" said Chet quietly. "If they have caught up to us so early, what makes you think we can evade them until we reach our village, or the Great Bay beyond?"

"If they have tracked us this far, why do you think we would evade them if we were to change our course now?" countered Loren.

He sighed. "Mayhap. But then again, if they see we have turned aside, they might guess that we no longer mean to warn the Mystics, and leave us be."

Loren thought of Trisken and the cruelty in his smile—the same cruelty she had seen in Rogan's eyes, in that brief moment on the streets of Northwood. "You do not know them," she said. "They are not the sort to leave matters be, nor to show mercy."

He did not answer that at first. After a moment he said, "Mayhap this is all needless worry, and the riders we saw behind us are not even following our course. But if you are right, and we are pursued, what do you mean to do?"

"Find some way to evade them, I suppose. I have not had time to think that far ahead."

"Well, mayhap it will be needless. I hope so."

Loren snorted, and thought she saw him smile at the sound. Then suddenly he thrust a finger ahead and whispered, "Look."

She tensed, expecting to see figures approach the fire. But he was pointing instead at the moons, which had just crested the horizon to shine their silver light across the tops of the trees. Below them, the familiar leaves of home had turned into something else, a thousand thousands of fingers of pewter rather than lively green, swaying in the gentle breezes of the night. Far away they heard the songs of whippoorwills and owls, prey and predator joined in a nighttime chorus. Loren let out a long breath, and for just a moment felt the tension of the day's flight leave her. She looked back to the moons. Merida, the smaller, was especially bright, while Enalyn was partly hidden behind her sister.

"Merida leads the way tonight, her lantern searching the Birchwood for her mother and father," Chet said quietly.

"Enalyn follows cautiously, urging her sister back home to await their return," said Loren.

"Always I have wondered if I would live to see it, the day when the sisters at last find their way to those who search for them. I wonder what it would look like, a sky with no moons."

"It would be a sadder thing, I think," said Loren.

"I think you are right."

They were quiet for a while after that. Even Gem had stopped rustling above them, though Loren still thought she heard the occasional noise from Xain.

Finally Chet spoke again. "This part of the journey is not so bad."

"You are right. It is the times before, and after, that make up for it."

He snorted a brief laugh, and then grew dour. "I . . . I cannot stop seeing the streets of Northwood," he said in a voice scarcely above a whisper.

Loren looked at him. He was easier to see now in the moonslight, and she saw a faraway look in his eyes that she felt far too familiar with. "It may be some time until you can."

"Was it the same for you?"

"That I cannot tell you, for I cannot see inside your mind," she said. "But I can tell you that, when I first saw soldiers killed by other soldiers, I dreamt of their lifeless faces for days afterwards."

"What made it stop?"

Loren thought of the long road since. "Seeing many things worse."

He did not look comforted, and turned his face back to the moons. Seized by impulse, Loren reached out and took his hand in hers. Almost at once she felt unsure of herself and began to draw back. But his fingers tightened, not in restraint but in comfort. So she left her hand where it was. He did not look at her, nor she at him. Together, they only watched the moons.

Then a shadow passed in front of the fire below.

They pushed forwards to peer into the night. There—she saw it again. A dark figure crossed the light, and then another. Now she could see them illuminated in the orange glow. Six figures she counted, and she caught glimpses of their horses in the trees beyond. She saw at least one cloak of grey, but none of the blue-and-grey uniforms the Shades normally wore. Still her heart sank, for she knew the truth: whoever the figures were, they were hunting her and her friends, and had at last found signs of their prey. A moment later, they stomped out the fire and cast dirt over it, and vanished into the darkness beneath the trees.

Loren let out her breath in a sharp *whoosh*. "You left no trail that might lead them up this rise?"

"None," said Chet. "With any luck, they shall think we doubled back and made for the river again. They will follow it farther north, and by the time they realize their mistake, we shall be leagues gone."

"With any luck," said Loren. "But my travels have not given me reason to rely overmuch on fortune."

"Let us wait an hour, and then wake the others," said Chet. "If we wish to make use of our lead, we cannot spend the night here."

"You are right. Close your eyes now—I shall wake you when the moons change places."

Her gaze followed Chet as he curled up closer to the tree's trunk, propped between the branch on which he lay and the one just next to it. Soon his eyes were shut in slumber, his lips slightly parted and deep breaths wheezing between them. She turned her eyes outwards again, but she rubbed her thumb across the palm of her hand, and kept doing so until she woke them all an hour later.

TWELVE

They roused the children first, who woke with many grumbles. When Loren swung herself up to rouse Xain, she found him already awake and staring at her in the moonslight. She suppressed a shiver.

"They followed us to our camp," she said. "When they found it empty, they left. Now we mean to ride on, while darkness still hides us."

He nodded and rose. Together the party climbed down from the tree to land softly upon the grass. Loren and Chet led them off into the trees, with Xain bringing up the rear. Her gaze roved the woods before them, searching for any sign of movement. Most likely Chet was right, and the Shades would follow their trail all the way back to the river. But she was keenly aware that they could be walking into a trap.

They saw nothing all the long way back to the river, nor after reaching the other side. Swiftly Loren led them to the cave where they had hidden the horses. She heard Midnight's gentle nicker and breathed a sigh of relief. They fetched their mounts and gained their saddles before making for the river again. Once they had crossed, Loren spurred them on as quickly as she dared in the dim moonslight.

All night they rode, until the sky before them grew grey and finally broke with dawn. They rode a little farther still, until they found a stream where they might water the horses. Finally Loren called them to a halt.

"Well?" said Chet. "We have seen no sign of them, and have gained many leagues. Do you think they will abandon the chase?"

"I doubt it," said Loren. "We should guess that they will be at least as tireless as we are, and mayhap more so. Then we cannot be surprised, except pleasantly."

"What do you mean to do, then?" said Gem, yawning wide. "Ride on until we collapse? I do not think that will help our cause. I am blessed with great stamina, but even I tire eventually."

"Yes, we are all well aware of your great endurance," said Annis, rolling her eyes. "Never have I called you the Prince of Snores under my breath."

He narrowed his eyes at her. "Good."

"Children," said Loren in a warning tone. "I am not ready to let us rest. Not yet, at any rate. If indeed we mean to lose them, we must ride at least a little longer. Eat now, and stretch your legs upon the grass. But then we must continue, and quicker than before."

Annis and Gem began to grumble again, but she ignored them and went to fetch her breakfast from Midnight's saddle. Then, because the mare had run hard all night, she fetched an apple from the bag and fed it to her. But Chet seized his hatchet and walked off into the woods. Curious, Loren went after him.

She found him a ways off, looking at the lower branches of a young oak. He chose one and gripped it firmly, then began to hack at it near where it joined the trunk.

"What are you up to?" she said.

"I hope we have left our pursuers behind," he told her. "But then again they might find us, and next time it may come to a fight. If it does, I would see us armed. But we have no blades to hand, nor would I wish to use one if we did, any more than you. I thought I could make us some staves. Indeed, it would be nice to have a walking stick in any case, for when the ground grows rough."

Loren smiled. "A wise thought. I am glad to find you so helpful, for I had thought you saw this road as folly."

"Oh, I do," he said quickly. The branch came off the oak at last. He stood it up, measured the right height, and began to cut away at the other end. "I still think we should abandon our course and ride north, or south, or anywhere other than where we mean to go. But as long as I am trailing in your footsteps, I might as well try to make that road less perilous. Who knows? If indeed they are still following us, mayhap we might find help in the village. A score of woodsmen could help us fend them off in short order."

Her spirits dampened, and she looked away. "Chet, that is a poor idea."

He shrugged. "Why? They know the Birchwood better than anyone. Do you think they could not drive away a dozen fighters, even these Shades?"

She turned away. "I do not wish to argue. Just let us hope we have lost them."

Leaving him to his work, she went back to the others. The children sat in the grass and ate. The horses had taken their fill of the stream and now grazed along the ground.

"Where has Chet gone?" said Annis.

"He is fashioning staves for us," said Loren. "In case we should come upon any more trouble."

"I shall keep my blade, if it is all the same to you," said Gem. "I am still practicing the stances Jordel taught me, but I think I could take one of these Shades in a fight."

"Of that we are all very certain," said Xain, rolling his eyes. Loren smiled. Though the wizard still looked thin and haggard, it was encouraging to hear him jest, even so feebly.

They sat and enjoyed the morning sunlight for a time, until Loren began to think she would have to go and fetch Chet to ride on. But just then he returned, and in his arms he carried five staves of different sizes. One he threw to Loren, and she caught it easily in her hands. Three others he dumped on the ground before Gem, Annis, and Xain, and kept one in hand.

"Here you are. Some fine walking sticks if we must dismount—or weapons, if we are forced to fight."

"I told Loren already, but I prefer my sword," said Gem. He nudged his staff away with a toe, though Annis had taken hers and was hefting the weight of it curiously. Meanwhile Xain had scarcely glanced at his.

"But a sword can rarely prevail against a staff," said Chet. "A blade is a fine weapon for a battle, I will give you that. But if you are not standing in rank and file, you should take the weapon with the longer reach."

"Fah!" said Gem. "Do you think you could have stood against Mag, if she carried her sword and you a staff?"

Chet pursed his lips and cocked his head. "Mayhap not against her. Yet the point stands. Here, I will show you. Take up your blade, and come for me."

Gem looked suddenly doubtful. "I—I do not wish to hurt you."

"I doubt very much that you shall. But move slowly, if it comforts you to do so."

The boy stood and adopted his first stance. Loren still remembered the day Jordel had given him the blade and shown him the forms, back when they rode together through the Greatrocks. Gem had taken to the training with gusto, but even to Loren's eye he still seemed very much a novice. She leaned back, her hands planted in the grass, watching with amusement.

Gem stepped forwards and swung, a wide and slow arc that Chet could easily have sidestepped. But instead he lashed out with his staff, so hard it knocked the blade from Gem's hand. The other end of the staff came around to rest on Gem's shoulder.

"And you are bested," said Chet.

Gem greeted the words with a glare. "I was moving slowly."

"Then try it faster."

He did. This time he struck with much greater vigor, though Loren could tell he still withheld himself. Chet struck back faster than before. He did not even aim for the sword; he merely swung the staff at Gem's head. The boy yelped and leaned back, away from the blow, his own stroke turning weak and ineffectual. Chet flipped the staff at the boy's ankle, and Gem tumbled into the grass. Annis cried out and flung herself back as his short sword flew through the air, landing where she had just been sitting.

"I am sorry!" said Chet, face filling with remorse as he dropped his staff and ran to her. "Did it strike you?"

"I am fine," said Annis, though she looked at the sword with distrust.

But Gem had grown angry, and he leaped up from the ground to jump at Chet from behind. Before Loren could move to intervene, he had wrapped his arms around the older boy's neck, his legs wrapping around Chet's waist to try and restrain him. Quick as blinking, Chet seized the boy's spindly arms and lunged forwards, flipping Gem over his shoulder to land hard on his back. All his breath left him in a *whoosh,* and he lay there, gasping.

"A fair attempt at an ambush," said Chet without a hint of anger. "Mayhap later I can teach you wrestling to go along with your sword training."

"It would please me greatly if you would fling yourself into the river," said Gem through wheezing gasps.

"Enough," said Loren. "Gem, take your staff or not, as you will. But the rest of us should carry ours, for we have no other ways to defend ourselves. Xain, can you carry yours on your own?"

"I am not so feeble as you seem to think," snapped the wizard, glaring at her. But the weakness in his voice betrayed his words. Still, he snatched up the staff where it lay at his feet, then used it to lever himself up. He stood there, leaning heavily on the stick, looking for all the world like some wise old sorcerer from tales.

"Now he looks a proper wizard," said Gem, grinning. Xain's frown deepened, and he twisted his fingers. A globe of flame sprang to life and crashed into the ground by Gem's head. The boy shrieked and rolled away.

THIRTEEN

THEY MOUNTED AND RODE ON. THE BREVITY OF THEIR REST AND THE long ride since had left them all weary, but the beauty of the Birchwood in summer did much to raise their spirits and keep their wits sharp.

Fifteen autumns Loren had spent beneath these trees already, but until recently she had thought her sixteenth would pass elsewhere. When she fled south, she thought the forest had revealed all its secrets to her. Now it was as though she looked upon it with new eyes. The green leaves, the gentle brown of the branches and trunks, seemed more beautiful to her than they ever had when she dwelled there. The birdsong came more pleasant, and the rolling slopes of land seemed more gentle and inviting. Many dark months she had spent elsewhere in the nine lands, in dirty and crowded cities, along the soggy banks of the Dragon's Tail, and in the unforgiving crags of the Greatrocks. Now, returned to her childhood home, she could see in it the beauty she had never noticed before.

Her unexpected attachment for the forest grew throughout their ride, and it remained with her when she called a stop for the night. As the next day passed much the same, she felt homesickness growing in her heart, and she remembered Chet's pleading words. A desire grew in her to lengthen the visit to their village, as Chet wished.

She shook that thought off. That sort of thinking had kept them in Northwood for far too long, and might have brought about that town's death. It had almost seen them all killed, and would have, if not for the sacrifice of Mag, Sten, and Albern. She owed it to their memories, and to Jordel, to press on. Once they warned the Mystics, and Jordel's order knew of the coming danger, mayhap then she could return to the Birchwood and live in peace—or visit for a time, and then resume her journey as she had often dreamed, this time with Chet at her side.

Three days she wrestled with these musings while they passed ever farther east in the wood. Sometimes they would find rivers or streams, and then Loren would guide them along through the water for some miles in case anyone was still on their trail. But eventually that wary practice seemed less important, and they would simply cross. Soon the land sloped down again, and when the trees grew thin they could see a wide bend in the Melnar many leagues ahead.

"That loop is only a few days' journey west of the village," said Chet, and Loren could hear the eagerness in his voice. And now, she felt that eagerness echoing in her own heart.

Faster they spurred their horses on, for it seemed that even the children caught the mood. Only Xain remained reluctant, scowling and shivering atop Jordel's charger. Soon they found a narrow road. It was little more than a dirt path worn by hooves and boots, but Loren thought she recognized it as the one that ran all the way to their village. At midday they stopped again to eat. Loren wanted to keep going, to ride on until she saw the familiar houses of home ahead, but that was a foolish thought. Even on the road, it would take them some days yet to reach the village.

As they sat in the underbrush beside the path, Loren felt a prickling on the back of her neck. She faltered as she ate, looking about and wondering at the feeling. Then she noticed that Chet, too, had stopped eating, and was looking off into the shadows beneath the trees.

"What is it?" said Loren, quietly.

He shook his head. Then she heard it: silence. The birds and beasts around them had fallen quiet. The only noise was the wind and the creaking of trees. Gem and Annis watched with wide eyes; Gem looked as if he would burst, but still he managed to keep his mouth shut. Xain was watching Loren, his eyes narrow.

"On the horses," whispered Loren.

They mounted as quickly and silently as they could. Loren led them north into the trees, for she had no wish to follow the road now. She scanned all around for another river or stream. Inwardly, she cursed herself for losing her caution. If they had kept hiding their trail, mayhap they would be home free now.

They found a stream and began to ride south along it. After a time it passed under the road they had been on, where a slender wooden bridge crossed it. They did not slow, but rode beneath the bridge, ducking their heads to pass under its bottom rafters.

Still the forest around them remained silent. The babbling whisper of the stream was now a grating sound against the quiet, and she was painfully aware of how loud their horses' hooves were. Even her pulse thundered so loud that she wondered if their pursuers could hear it.

Soon she grew frustrated. The water slowed their steps, and if the Shades were close behind, a stream would do little to deter them. She leaned over to whisper in Chet's ear.

"We should cross the river and make for the road again. I think speed will save us now, more surely than silence will."

He looked back over his shoulder. "That would mean turning around, mayhap into the waiting arms of those behind us."

"Then let us cut east, and turn north if we feel it is safe."

He shrugged and pulled on the reins. The party passed between the trees again. Still all remained too quiet. Now it was maddening.

Loren was half-ready to turn and scream into the woods, when suddenly the Shades struck.

Arrows whistled out from the trees, but none struck true. Annis screamed, and her horse reared. Gem barely stayed atop the beast.

"Ride north, and quickly!" said Loren.

They spurred their horses and fled. Loren whispered thanks for Midnight's sure steps and quick reflexes, but she watched the children's horse with worry. Annis was sure in the saddle, but her mount was easily frightened. Often it tried to break from the others, and Annis had to wrestle it back into line.

But it was Chet's steed that nearly doomed them. An arrow came flying from their left and passed within a handbreadth of the beast's nose. The horse screamed and lurched left. Chet pitched from the saddle at the sudden change in direction. He landed hard on the forest floor, and Loren's heart stopped. But he scrambled to his feet quickly, lifting his staff. His bow lay in the dirt a few feet away—thankfully unstrung, or surely it would have snapped.

"Chet!" cried Loren. She wheeled and went to him, reaching down a hand to pull him up. But it was too late, and figures in blue and grey appeared beneath the trees.

Another volley they loosed, but all arrows went wide. Then they leaped from their saddles and attacked with swords held high.

Loren dropped from Midnight's saddle and landed catlike beside Chet. Her hands shook, but she managed to string her bow. From the quiver at her hip she drew an arrow. With shaking hands she fitted and drew it as Albern had taught her. But still she could not aim for the heart. The shaft went wide, though it did make the Shade she aimed at dive to the side.

Then the Shades were on them with swords, and Loren snatched up her staff from the ground. Together she and Chet managed to ward off the warriors' blows. They used the trunks to their advantage, ducking behind them and letting the Shades' swords bounce harmlessly off the wood.

One of the blades stuck in the bark. Chet lunged forwards and slammed the butt of his staff into the man's head. The Shade fell to the ground in a heap. But another came just behind, forcing Chet still farther back.

A high, thin scream ripped the air. Gem came running into the fray with his sword held high. Behind him came Annis, blanched with fright but still gripping her staff firmly. Gem's wild swings proved little danger, but at least distracted one of the Shades long enough for Loren to take him unawares. She struck him first in the gut, and then on the back of the head with a sharp overhead swing. But then his companion pressed forwards, and Loren had to give ground before her.

The woman knew her way about a blade, and though Loren could keep her at bay, she could not knock the sword from her grasp. Whenever Loren lunged to strike, the sword would be there to block it.

Gem leaped to the attack. The Shade blocked his first stroke, and then delivered a powerful backhand blow. He crashed into the trunk of a tree.

"Gem!" said Loren.

Her hands loosened on the staff. With a cry the Shade kicked out, knocking it from Loren's grip, and then she swung her sword hard. It missed Loren, barely, and she danced back out of reach. But then the

Shade swung again, and this time let go the sword, which flew spinning towards Loren's face.

She dropped on instinct and heard the blade whistle by overhead. By the time she rose to her knees, the Shade was already on top of her. Loren was borne to the ground, one arm across her throat. The Shade whipped a knife from the back of her belt. Loren barely caught the woman's wrist in time, choking for breath as she fought to push the knife away.

Annis screamed and swung. In her panic she struck the Shade in the back, not the head. But it made the woman grunt and loosen the pressure on Loren's throat for a moment.

Then the air rang out with a sharp *crack,* and a bolt of lightning from Xain struck her in the chest. Loren felt the bolt through her body, rocking her with a sharp and sudden pain.

The Shade lurched back with a cry. She reached for Loren again, but Chet had defeated his foe, and he struck Loren's in the chest with his staff. The Shade fell to the ground. Loren flipped up and on top of her, one hand gripping the woman's throat.

"Killing children in the woods? Is that the manner of person you are?" she screamed.

The dagger was in her hand before Loren knew what she was doing. She raised it high. Only at the last moment did she stop herself.

The woman's eyes had rolled nearly all the way back, and her hands feebly tried to pull Loren's fingers from her neck. Loren could see where her nails had dug into the skin, turning it an angry red under her grip.

She screamed again and turned the dagger. The pommel came crashing down on the woman's head. The Shade's skull slammed against the ground, and she lay still. Only then did Loren's fingers loosen.

When she looked up, she found Chet staring at her in silence. The look on his face nearly made her weep. It held no anger, nor shock, nor even fear. It was sorrow—the same sorrow she had seen in his eyes when he sat beside her in Northwood, and held her as she trembled and cried, murmuring that it was not her fault.

Quickly she turned away. "Annis, fetch rope from my saddle. Now!"

She started to drag the Shades to the base of a beech tree. After a moment's hesitation, Chet moved to help her. Soon Annis came running with the rope, and then ran to revive Gem with a splash from her water skin. Loren bound all the Shades' wrists behind their backs before tying the bindings to each other in a circle around the tree. When they woke, they would be able to rise if they all stood together, but they could not move away.

"It will not hold them forever, but long enough for us to make our escape," she said. "Now get the horses back, and quickly. With luck they will not have run far."

Chet's mount had fled after throwing him, but they soon found it a little ways to the northwest. The other horses were nearby, and the travelers swung themselves into their saddles.

Loren feared to look at Chet as they made ready, but finally forced herself to do it. He was studying her from the corner of his eye, and he looked away quickly when he saw her turn towards him.

"We cannot return to our village," said Loren. "If they followed us this far, it is folly to believe they will not stay on our trail. We will only bring their wrath down upon our home."

Chet said nothing. Xain watched him for a moment before looking to Loren. "Where, then, do we ride?"

"North. North to Dorsea, and then east to the coast." She spoke again to Chet. "But that does not have to be your course. You could go on alone, for you can hide your tracks better than the five of us could. They would not follow you, and you could return home in peace. No one will speak ill of you for doing so. Indeed, I would call you wise."

Still Chet said nothing, and now all the others noted his silence. Gem watched him, mute, an angry bruise growing on his cheekbone.

"That is a fine dagger you have," Chet said at last. He kicked his horse and rode north, and was soon out of sight among the trees.

"Do not get used to seeing it," Gem called after him.

After a long and doubtful look, Annis spurred on after Chet. Xain still sat, waiting and watching Loren.

"Turn your eyes, wizard," said Loren. "They should be on the road ahead."

He shrugged and pulled on the reins, and together they went after the others.

FOURTEEN

Now their steps felt hounded, and traveling through the woods no longer gave Loren any sense of peace. All that day, she could not banish thoughts of their fight with the Shades. Over and over she saw in her mind's eye the dagger held aloft, ready to plunge into the soft flesh of the woman's throat.

For she *had* been ready to strike, that she knew. Fueled partly by her worry for Gem, whom the Shade had attacked, and partly by the thrill of the fight, she had very nearly taken the woman's life.

But you did not, she tried to tell herself.

Yet it had been a near thing. So near, in fact, that she could almost imagine the feeling of the dagger sliding through skin.

And why stop yourself? came a voice in her mind.

She had been a killer before she first left the Birchwood, though she had only recently learned that fact. Along all the road south, and then west and north and east again, she had counseled peace to her companions. She had called Jordel bloodthirsty, and admonished Gem and Annis when they wished violence on others. Now those words became a bitter ash in her memory, and she half wished she could take them back.

More than the dagger, though, she saw Chet's sorrowful eyes. He had not moved to stop her. He had not even cried out. He had only watched, and if Loren had struck, he would have let her. What would she have seen in his eyes, she wondered, if indeed she had killed the Shade?

They stopped as the sun set and evening came over the Birchwood. Still Loren could not meet Chet's eyes, so she made a show of adjusting Midnight's saddle.

"We will rest here for a time, but we should ride again once the moons rise."

"Another midnight ride," said Gem. "They seemed romantic at first, but repetition has dampened their appeal."

"You may stay and sleep the night here, if you wish," said Loren, much more harshly than she had intended. Gem balked and looked away without an answer.

"Loren, he meant nothing," said Annis quietly.

"I grow weary of his complaining. I will return in a moment."

She hobbled Midnight and walked away, hoping they would think she was going to make water. In truth, she only wanted to be alone. Soon she came upon a clearing, the other end of it invisible in the dimming twilight, and sat with her back against a tree. Sightless she stared into the darkness, her hands fiddling in her lap, trying to banish the anger and the melancholy that plagued her.

"You cannot lie to me, you know."

Chet's words came from nowhere, and frightened her half to death. She jerked to her feet. He stood by the tree she had rested against, leaning there with arms folded. Loren shoved his shoulder hard.

"Do not sneak up on me like that!"

He gave a smile, but it was tinged with sadness. "You would prefer I tramped around the forest like an ox? I thought we sought to go with stealth."

"You know what I mean. Go back to the others. Leave me be."

"Why? What ails you?"

She glared. "Why, nothing at all. It is only that murderers chase us through the forest, and twice they have nearly killed us. No matter what we try, we cannot evade them for long. Indeed, it is only by the greatest miracles of luck that we are alive at all. So as you can see, it is nothing. What could I possibly be worried about? Clearly our fortune is such a blessing that we need not concern ourselves with any worldly troubles."

He did not answer, but only looked back at her, and now the stars shone bright enough for her to see him. He had the same look he had worn earlier, when she nearly killed the Shade.

"Stop that," she snapped.

"What?"

"You look at me with pity. I do not ask for it, I do not need it, and most importantly, I do not *want* it. Save it for Xain, who suffers greater than any of the rest of us."

"I do not pity you, though I will admit it pains me to see you suffer the way you do."

"I do not suffer!"

It came out as a shout. She drew a deep breath and spoke in a more measured tone.

"I do not suffer. Yes, I am worried, and if you do not understand why, you are a fool."

"You cannot lie to me, as I have said already."

Her teeth ground together, and her words came with great effort. "You think I am lying? Very well. Tell me the truth."

"I saw in your face the moment when you almost killed that woman."

"I did not almost kill her."

"You cannot—"

"I am *not* lying!" She no longer cared how loud she was. "I am not a murderer!"

"I know it. You stayed your hand, and for that I am proud of you. I know few others—in fact, I know no one—who would have shown such restraint in the heat of a fight."

Her anger fled like a gust of southern wind, and like the wind it left her cold. She slumped, shoulders sagging, and sat down again. Slowly Chet came and sat before her. She thought for a moment that he might take her hands, but he did not.

"Ever since I left the forest, I have told myself I was better than those who would kill without thinking," she said quietly. "There are so many times when it would have been easier, but I refused. And I chastised those who I thought took lives too easily."

"You were not wrong," said Chet. "Not even now. You have been sorely tested, and you faltered. But you did not fail. I only wish you did not have to take the test at all. Do you understand now? I wish you could abandon this quest, and not only because I fear for your life. I do not want to see your mind broken by whatever madness runs rampant in the nine lands."

Loren shook her head. "To turn aside now would make me a coward. If we do not act, the madness you speak of would gather in strength until all things were swept away before it. Mayhap, if Jordel were still alive, I could leave it in his hands. But he died, and now I feel as though right and wrong slip through my fingers, pooling together upon the ground until I can no longer tell one from the other."

"All the more reason to go," said Chet. "I do not believe in a darkness so great that we cannot outrun it."

"You do not know what I have seen. These Shades are not the worst of it. They are but servants of a dark power, a wizard they call the Necromancer."

"Who is he? I have heard nothing of it. And besides, what is one wizard in all the nine lands?"

"He—if he is a man, for we do not know—is not just a wizard. He is the master of death itself. The nine lands will fall before him if he is not stopped, and only the Mystics can resist him."

Chet looked away, thinking. Then he said, "Very well. You say you must tell them, for the memory of your friend. I pledge my help in that. Let us give this warning, and then they may fight their war. We need take no part in it. We can return home, or go to any other land you wish."

Loren met his gaze. "I do not know that for certain. But if no more is required of me once I have brought these tidings, then I will go with you."

"Promise me that—"

"No," she said quickly. "I will not promise anything. I will promise only to try. That must be enough."

The moons shone in his eyes as he studied her. Finally, he nodded. "It is."

She sighed. "Good. Then let us return to the others and ride on."

"In all haste," he said. "For the sooner we reach Feldemar, the sooner I mean to ride with you away from all this, if I must tie you to my saddle to do it."

She kicked his shin, leaving him to hop painfully back through the trees to the horses.

Loren let them stop again when the moons set, and in the three hours of darkness before dawn, they slept in restless fits. Xain stayed on watch once again, but when Loren rose, she thought she might as well have stayed with him. She had found it hard to get any sleep at all.

Dawn came with no sign of pursuit, but still they rode north as quickly as they could. Now they had resumed their earlier caution, so whenever they reached a river they would ride in it for a mile or more before getting back on course.

Just after they stopped for a midday meal, Chet called them to a halt and pointed. Far above the trees ahead, they could see thin wisps of white smoke rising.

"Signs of a village," said Loren.

"I thought we turned away from your home," said Gem.

"Not *their* village, you dolt," said Annis. "Do you think there is only one in all this great expanse of forest? My tutors used to tell me there were hundreds, all within a day's ride of each other, but who never saw each other at all, more often than not. They say that living so far from any other people, the tongues they speak can change throughout the generations, so that sometimes when they meet each other they must talk with their hands."

"That is ridiculous," said Loren. "We knew of other villages within the Birchwood, and would meet with them on occasion. We never had to speak with our hands."

Annis shrugged. "Mayhap you did not go deep enough into the woods."

Xain had been grinding his teeth, but now he spoke. "Will you all be silent? Do we make for the village, or avoid it?"

"I say we go there," said Chet. "They will be friendly, and mayhap we could pay to spend the night under a roof, rather than the stars. It would be wise to replenish our supplies in any case. We lack for nothing now, but that may not always be so."

"The wise man keeps his larder full, even in times of plenty," said Xain. "Very well. Lead on, huntsman."

"Hold," said Loren. "What if the Shades come to the village after we have gone? They will learn of our course, and can guess where we mean to go."

"What if they have reached the village already?" said Gem quietly.

That gave them all pause for a chilling moment. Annis looked into the trees distrustfully.

"I doubt very much that they reached it already," said Chet. "Or if they did, they at least did not attack it, for then I think we would see darker, thicker smoke, from the burning of the homes."

"Mayhap," said Loren.

"And mayhap your other concern may be turned to advantage," said Xain. "If we meet villagers, we may tell them we are heading west. The Shades, if they come after, will think we are doubling back, or making for some other destination. It may throw them off our trail."

"It might," said Loren. "Or it could endanger the village terribly. If the Shades believe they know something of our whereabouts, they may strike the village down in wrath."

"If the Shades believe the villagers are hiding something, they will strike regardless," said Chet quietly. "Therefore let us give information willingly, and with no sign of deception, so that they may pass it on freely. That may be their greatest chance of avoiding slaughter."

She could not deny that, though it was a chilling thought. "Very well. Only let us approach the village from the east, so that we lend credence to the lie."

"A fine plan," said Gem, licking his lips. "I enjoy all that talk of wise men, but I like a full larder best."

FIFTEEN

IT TOOK THEM SEVERAL HOURS MORE TO FINALLY REACH THE PLACE, A group of homes built in a part of the wood that had been cleared for the settlement. As they came closer, approaching from the east as they had planned, Loren saw signs of the inhabitants all around—a small shed built out in the trees, a woodsman's saw and axe lying near a tree, and even some food that had been abandoned.

But when at last they came within sight of the village, they saw that all their caution had been in vain.

At first Loren saw nothing amiss, for the place was quiet. There was no one in sight, and the only movement was the same thin white wisps of smoke they had seen from afar, rising lazily from the chimneys.

They saw the first body only moments later.

It was a woman, or had been. A wound gaped in her back, her guts spread out on the forest floor around her. She lay face-down, and had clearly been crawling.

Annis screamed before Gem's hand shot up to cover her mouth. Loren's stomach twisted, and her teeth clenched. She turned her eyes quickly away. Beside her, Chet had gone the same shade of Elf-white as he had been when they fled Northwood.

"Xain, stay here with the children," said Loren. "Chet, come with me."

"It could be dangerous," he said, still pale as a sheet.

"Someone could be alive. Mayhap they need help. Stay if you want, but I will not."

So saying, she leaped from Midnight's saddle and pulled her bow from her back. After a moment she heard the heavy *thud* of Chet's boots landing in the grass, and then his soft footsteps as he came after her. That was a relief, but still the hairs on the back of her neck rose ever higher the farther she advanced.

The village had become a charnel house, with bodies strewn about everywhere. As in Northwood, no one had been spared. Their blood had pooled together, and the bodies lay prone in it, like weary travelers cooling their brows in a river of red. Some had been maimed, their limbs lying close by, while others had been skewered or flayed open. But of the attackers there was no sign, nor were any of the homes cast down or burnt.

"Why did they leave the village standing?" whispered Chet. He walked a half-pace behind her and to the side, his staff held in his hands before him like a spear.

"Why should they not?" said Loren. "The Shades have no interest in this place. Likely they were searching for us."

"But we left them vanquished in the woods days ago."

"Only four. You and I saw more than that when they came by our campfire, and I would guess that there are many, many more in the woods. Likely they have divided themselves into several parties, roving through the Birchwood in search of us."

A sharp cry made them both jump. But they saw no threat, nor indeed any source for the voice. It sounded again.

Loren saw where it came from, and she felt the need to retch.

One of the corpses was not a corpse at all, but still alive. He was a young man, probably no older than Chet. At first she thought he was standing against the wall of one of the homes. Then she saw the metal spikes, and the angry red wounds in his hands. He was not standing. He had been nailed there.

"Get him down," she cried, running forwards. She grasped the head of one of the spikes and pulled as hard as she could. It barely budged. Chet tugged the other spike, and it came out easily. The young man sagged, screaming as all his weight was put on the other hand. The spike ripped out before they could remove it, passing all the way through the flesh. Another scream tore the air.

His eyes had been gouged out. The wounds were burned, as though with a red-hot poker. Blood gushed from his hands, but there were no more cuts on his body, only deep burns and many, many bruises. He lay there whimpering like an animal, and Loren nearly retched again as she saw both his legs were bent at odd angles.

"No more," he said. "No more, I beg of you."

"It is all right," said Loren, though the words came from nowhere, and she knew them for a lie. "They have gone. We are here to help you."

"Who are you?" He reached for her arm. "Who is that? Is that Dinna?"

"No, it . . ." Loren struggled for the words. "I am only a passerby. No one else is here. They are all . . . they are all gone."

He broke into sobs at that, though no tears came from his ruined sockets. Loren whipped off her cloak and rolled it up, gingerly lifting his head to place the cloak beneath it. The boy only kept weeping.

"Loren . . ." said Chet gravely. She knew his mind without needing to hear the words. They had no healing for these wounds. Nor would any healer in the nine kingdoms.

With a look to Chet to silence him, she gently put her hand over the boy's. His fingers tried to close over hers, but the pain of his mangled hand was too much, and he gave up.

"Who did this?" she asked him, her voice soft and gentle.

"Loren!" repeated Chet, this time in astonishment. But he fell silent as she gave him another hard look.

"They were soldiers," said the boy. His voice gurgled a little in his throat. "I do not know. They had weapons, and armor. Their captain was a beast."

Loren felt a chill of premonition creep over her. "What did he look like? Was he dark of skin?"

"Yes, dark as the night," said the boy. "He called himself Rogan. He asked us for a girl, a girl in a black cloak, and . . . and something else."

Loren's throat had gone bone-dry. She swiped the back of her sleeves across her eyes and went on in a shaking voice. "What then? How did the fight begin?"

"There was no fighting," said the boy, his sobs deepening. "He gathered all of us together here. We told him we knew nothing of the girl, and he started killing us. We tried to run, but they chased us down. All but the children."

She and Chet looked at each other. "What did he do with the children?" said Chet.

"He took them," said the boy. "He said he was their father now. Then some tried to fight him, those whose children he tried to take, but he and his men killed them, too. He killed them, and when I tried to help, they . . ."

The boy bit his lip and sucked in his breath, but then he broke down and began to cry again. Loren put her hand on his shoulder, one of the few places on his body the Shades had not mangled, the only comfort she could think to give him.

"I told him I did not know where she was, that none of us knew where she was," he said as he wept. "Finally he told me he believed me. But he did not stop. He never stopped."

Eventually his cries subsided. Loren leaned forwards, fearing he had died. But his lips moved again, barely able to whisper now.

"Who are you?"

Loren could not answer past the tightness of her throat.

"Are you the girl?"

She would have given anything not to have to answer him. But she could not stop herself.

"Yes."

"The one he sought?"

"Yes. I am sorry. I am sorry."

He turned his head away from her. A short while later, his chest shuddered in a breath, and then he lay still.

Chet came to Loren's side and put a hand on her shoulder. She threw it off and walked away. He let her go, slowly turning and going back to the others. Loren walked out of the village on the west side, to the edge of the forest, shaking as silent tears ran down her face.

In fury she stared off between the trees. She wished they were there, Rogan and the Shades and all of them. Let them fight her here and now, and be done with it. Who knew but that villages just like this one were being ransacked all throughout the forest? What death had she rained upon her homeland by her reckless flight into this wood?

A small voice, a voice of reason that sounded very like Jordel, told her that she could not hold herself responsible for this. But the white-hot anger in her gut refused to listen.

She stayed there, alone, until the tears passed and the sun had nearly set. Then she went back to the others, circling wide around the village so she would not have to pass through the death and blood once more. They had retreated into the trees, and were sitting silently in a circle. The children were staring at the ground, while Chet watched nothing at all. Even Xain had a grim look, his mouth twisted with more than its usual bitterness.

"We will rest here for the night," she said. "The Shades have come already. They will not be back, at least not for a time. We will ride on before first light."

"Should we . . . I mean to say, the corpses . . ." said Gem.

"We cannot bury them all, not without spending many days here."

"The Shades will have done this in other places," said Chet.

"I imagine they will have."

"Can we not warn them? Or can we not, at least, give the Shades reason to pursue us instead of killing innocents who have never even heard our names?"

"How do you mean to stop them, Chet?" said Loren, growing angry. "We could march into their midst and offer ourselves up for sacrifice. But as long as we are outside their grasp, they will hunt for us wherever they think we might be found."

"So you mean to let them?"

"We do not let them do anything," said Xain. "Did we invite them into the Birchwood? Did we tell them where to find this village? Did we tell them to put these people to the sword?"

Chet shook his head. "There must be something we can do."

"There is not," said Loren. "As is too often the case, we can only flee, and survive, to someday deliver a greater stroke that might secure victory."

Loren thought of when she and Jordel had left the city of Wellmont under siege. Others had begged the Mystic to stay, to aid in the defense of the city. He had refused, and when pressed, he had grown angry. At the time, Loren had thought him somewhat heartless. Now, at last, she understood. The wrath was a mask, a bandage meant to cover the gaping wound of his guilt. Doubtless Jordel would have fought upon the very walls of Wellmont, and given his life in defense of the city without a second thought. But he had known, or suspected, that a greater battle lay just over the horizon, and so he needed Xain to survive. How long must he have traveled the nine lands with that burden, letting ill deeds go unchecked in the service of stopping a far greater evil?

Loren looked at them all, at Chet and Xain and the children, their faces turned to her, angry and hurt and expectant.

"I will take the first watch. Rest, all of you. Even you, Xain. Tomorrow is another long ride to an uncertain end."

SIXTEEN

THE DAYS AFTERWARDS PASSED LIKE BITTER MONTHS OF WINTER: COLD, reluctant, and lingering in the mind long after passing. No one spoke often, nor laughed, nor told any jokes, for the memories of the village in the forest plagued them. They slept only a few hours at a time, when neither the sun nor the moons were there to guide their way. Often as they pressed on, their heads would sag against their chests for a moment, only to snap upwards at a jostle in the road.

Xain's condition was growing slowly worse, and though Loren tried not to pay it too much mind, she could not ignore it entirely. Fortunately, it was not as bad as it had been in the Greatrocks. Then he had been driven to madness, half the time forgetting who and where he was, and the other half filled with a murderous rage that he sought to unleash upon Loren and the others. This was more of a quiet wasting away, a slow breaking down of his body. Loren often saw him wincing as he dismounted, and his skin had begun to bruise easily at even a light touch. But he spoke no word of complaint, and always matched the pace Loren set, and so she kept her thoughts on the road ahead.

Five days after they found the village slaughtered in the Birchwood, they came at last out the northern side of the forest and down into the kingdom of Dorsea. Early on that day, Loren noticed that the trees were sparser and shorter, and seemed less hearty than those in the south. The ground turned from soft loam and grass to a brown and brittle dirt, which kicked up much dust that took long to settle.

Dorsea itself, when they reached it, was much the same. The land was not quite mountainous, but rolling and hilly as far as the eye could see, browner than it was green. What vegetation there was came in small, scrubby bushes and spindly trees that sucked what water they could from the earth.

"To the west and to the south, Dorsea is much like Selvan," said Xain. "But here, it is half a desert. The land may be tilled, but not easily, and so the people are as hard and stubborn as the land upon which they feed themselves. Still, adversity has made them somewhat kinder than their western and southern brethren who, like all fat and happy people, begin to turn their eyes outwards to what more they can claim for their own."

"I know much of Dorsean greed," said Loren. "It is what brings them to war with Selvan, over and over again." Chet nodded firmly.

"You speak with many dramatics, and little truth," said Annis, rolling her eyes. "Why, I have met many merchants from Dorsea, and members of the Dorsean royal family, and they were no more or less crafty than any other inhabitants of the High King's Seat. Those from Selvan included. You are a gem among women, Loren, and you seem a decent enough fellow, Chet, but you must know that not all people of your kingdom are so good and kind-hearted as you."

"It is no less foolish to claim great knowledge of all people, when you have spent all your life upon the Seat," said Xain. "It could be said, rather, that the wealthy and the powerful are much the same from one kingdom to the next, though the people they rule may vary wildly. But this is idle philosophy, and we have little time for it. Let us press on."

Now they were in open territory, and a land about which Loren knew little. Xain took to guiding them, for as he told them, he had traveled Dorsea well as a young man.

"Do not tell me you hail from this kingdom?" said Annis in surprise.

"It is hard to say where I hail from," said Xain, "especially since my first answer would have been the Seat until recently, and they will no longer claim me as their own. But as for where I was born, that is

Wadeland to the east, though I left it as a young boy when my parents found I had the gift of elementalism."

"And how did they find that out?" said Gem, leaning forwards with interest. "Were you bandying about the horses one day, when you accidentally set the stable boy on fire?"

Xain chuckled—an odd sound from him these days, and one Loren welcomed. "Nothing so crude as that, though I can hardly blame you for thinking so, since you are a commoner and know little of the practices of the wealthy. When a child of royalty nears his sixth year, he is required by law to see a representative of the Academy. Wealthy families, even those who are only distantly related to the nobility, such as my parents, pay in coin for such a representative to visit them. These men know how to test for the gift, and they put the child through a series of trials, meant to discover if any of the four branches have presented themselves in any strength."

"I took the trials," said Annis, sounding as if she were trying very hard not to boast. "They found nothing. What do they do, I wonder, if a child shows the gift of more than one type of magic?"

"That is impossible," said Xain. "Wizards are gifted with only one—even the most powerful among us."

With those words he fixed Loren with a look. She thought, as he must be thinking, of the Lifemage and the Necromancer, and the two branches of magic that had lay hidden for centuries. How did the wizards of the Academy detect them, if they even could? She doubted if they would ever know.

SEVENTEEN

THEY MADE CAMP ON THE WIDE PLAINS OF DORSEA THAT NIGHT. They
found a crag of a hill in the midst of the flatlands, and settled down to
the north of it, so that it might block the light of their campfire from
anyone who would follow them out of the Birchwood. Loren knew
there might be Shades in Dorsea already, and they might be seen from
the west or north. But as they had seen no sign of their pursuers for
days, the warmth of the fire seemed worth the risk.

Chet took the first watch. Loren had half expected Xain to volunteer, as he so often did now, but the wizard looked weary and worn.
Almost as soon as they had built a fire he curled up in his bedroll and
slept. Loren hoped that was a hopeful sign. When he had suffered from
the magestone sickness in the Greatrocks, he had gone through a time
of great anguish and pain, followed by a bone-deep exhaustion. If he
had come to that point already, it meant his recovery from now on
would be less taxing.

Loren's thoughts were still much occupied with their fight against
the Shades in the Birchwood, and the village full of corpses, and she
feared that sleep might well elude her. But it was a warm night for

autumn, and the soft glow of the fire quickly lulled her off to a deep slumber, one without dreams or dark thoughts. She woke feeling refreshed, more so than she had in all the many miles of their journey since Northwood, and as relaxed as if she had spent the night on one of Mag's softest mattresses.

Then she saw the moons in the sky above her, and realized with a start that it was still the middle of the night.

She looked about in confusion. Had a noise woken her? If so, it was gone now. Only dying embers remained of their fire, and the others were all curled in their blankets. The world was silent, save a faint whisper on the air and far-off birdsong.

When she lifted her head, she saw Chet sitting by a rock near the edge of their camp. His head was bent down into his chest in slumber, and her mouth twisted in annoyance. It was foolish, and she would have words with him—but in the morning. For now, she would simply take the watch and let him sleep. They were all of them weary.

But when she rose, she saw the Elves.

There were six of them, standing glowing in the starlight, only a few paces away from her sleeping friends. She knew them at once from the tales she had heard all her life. Those tales were told in quiet whispers in the night, for it was said that to speak of the creatures too often was to invite their wrath. The stories always came from survivors, of which there were precious few. When humans came upon Elves in the nine lands, more often than not they did not survive to speak of it.

They were all of different hues, but shared white clothing and the same raven-black hair, which hung long, down to the smalls of their backs, wafting gently with every movement. They wore no armor and carried no weapons, clad only in the white robes, the edges of which frilled and floated as though underwater. Their eyes were as pale as their clothing, a thin and ghostly gossamer with no pupils or irises, so that it was hard to tell where they were looking.

Except that they were looking at Loren, and somehow, in the deepest part of her soul, she *knew* it.

She was frozen, unable to move so much as a muscle. What should she do? What *could* she do? Her first thought was to rouse the others, to get to the horses as quickly as they could and ride for their lives. They were powerless if the Elves should choose to harm them—even Xain, were he at the height of his power, and he was far from that now. Elves could not be reasoned with; they could not be talked out of slaughter if that was their intent. Indeed, so far as Loren knew, no one had ever spoken to Elves, nor knew the words that they used.

But she and her friends could not run, not now. They could never move fast enough. Even if Loren left the others to save herself, the Elves could be upon her in an instant. They would kill her, and all the rest of them, if that was their whim. And she could do nothing to stop it.

A thought came into her mind. *The dagger.*

It was on her belt—she never removed it, even when she slept. But she immediately dismissed that furtive instinct, for it was ridiculous. Mighty knights and kings had tried to battle Elves, but none ever survived. What could such a tiny knife do against them?

The dagger.

This time the thought came more insistent, like a shout in her mind. And with a start, Loren realized that the idea was not her own. The Elves had given it to her.

She studied them. They had not shifted so much as a muscle. Only their clothing and their hair moved, wafting gently as though in a breeze, though the night held no wind. They had not spoken. The words had come directly from their minds to her own.

Loren reached for her waist, desperately hoping that this was not a terrible mistake. If they thought she meant to fight them, they would kill her for certain. As quickly as she could, she drew the dagger and then flipped it about, holding it by the blade, hilt forwards. One tentative step she took towards them, then another. When she was a few paces away, she knelt and placed the dagger on the ground.

Then they moved at last—or at least, one of them did. It stepped away from the others and came forwards, and watching the movement of its limbs was like watching a courtly dancer. The Elf was pure grace, and ease, and at the same time it imparted a terrifying power. It held out a hand, its fingers curled as though around the dagger's hilt. Loren pictured that hand circling her throat, and she quailed with fear. Then the dagger appeared, as if from nowhere, in the Elf's hand. If it had reached for the blade, or moved it with some magic, Loren had not seen it. One moment the dagger was not there, and then . . . it *was.*

The Elf turned to the others and lifted the dagger. It flashed in the light of both moons, which were directly overhead, and Loren thought she saw the silver glow of the Elves reflected in its steel as well. And then the Elves began to sing.

Loren burst into tears. Her knees failed her, and she fell to the ground in a heap. She buried her face in her hands, wailing, giving no heed to the sound of her voice or whether it might wake the others. The sound of the song was too beautiful: incomprehensible, for it was sung in no tongue she had ever heard; soul-shattering, for Loren felt that when it ended its grace would break her mind and leave her wishing always to hear it again. She felt as though it were transforming her from the inside out, changing something deep within her, something beyond explanation or hope of memory.

The song stopped. Loren lay there, still a wreck, aching to hear just one more note. And then, though they had sung to the dagger in chorus, as if in reverence, the Elf took the blade by the tip and dropped it in the dirt.

The dagger. The thought came to her again, and this time Loren knew it for the Elf's. She struggled to hands and knees; the thought of standing seemed more than her body could bear. Slowly she crawled forwards, searching the ground for the blade. But she was too far beyond the fire, and her eyes were filled with tears besides, and she could not find it.

A hand gripped her shoulder, and where it touched her she felt an incredible warmth. It was not a warmth of the body, but of the soul, and where it ran through her it filled her with hope and courage. But the hand was uncaring, uncompromising, and it lifted her to her feet without waiting for her to act. She found herself standing before the Elf, looking into its gossamer-white eyes, and then she realized that the glow in those eyes was the same glow she saw in Xain whenever he reached for his magic.

This is the end, she thought. The Elf would kill her now, for she had moved too slowly. She only hoped it would leave the others be.

The dagger, came the thought, impatient. The Elf was holding it now, its hilt towards her.

She found her hand wrapped around the hilt, though she had not meant to move it. The Elf released the blade, and then her shoulder, and the world seemed darker and more horrible than it had before she felt its touch.

The stones. And now in her mind's eyes she saw the magestones, the small packet wrapped in brown cloth that rested in one of the pockets of her cloak.

"What?" she said out loud.

She caught a movement—just the barest twitch of a muscle in the

Elf's jaw. Then it seized her again. Loren wanted to burst out in hysterical laughter at the feeling of it, the power and the joy. But the Elf, uncaring, reached into her cloak and seized the packet. From the brown cloth it drew one of the stones, and then broke it in half to hold before her eyes.

The stones.

Loren took the stone between thumb and forefinger, gingerly. And in her mind's eye, she saw herself putting the stone in her mouth, crunching down upon it, and swallowing the dust. Her eyes widened with fear, and she thought of Xain.

"No," she stammered. "I cannot—"

The Elf seized her throat. She felt its skin upon her own, no longer dampened by the cloth that had protected her when it took her shoulder. Her mind threatened to collapse upon itself. She saw herself, *all* of herself, the bone and sinew and flesh beneath the skin, and a bright white light at the center of it all. But it was all of it distorted and misshapen, turned about so that she could see every angle of it at once. And from each part Loren saw what looked like a thin thread, a silvery wisp of *something* that ran off back and forth in all directions, in *every* direction at once and none of them, and through time as quickly as through the many leagues they had traveled, and would travel still. With the sight came *knowing*, and she knew that she beheld the skeins of time, laid out before and behind her, and all of the many twists and turns that had led her to where she stood now. And farther, beyond the place where the camp lay, she saw those threads touching others, one at a time and then great clusters all in a group, and twisting endlessly around each other in a pattern that covered all the nine lands.

The twisted, broken thing that was Loren's body twitched, and from its mouth croaked the words, "I cannot . . . I cannot . . ."

Then the Elf placed the magestone in her mouth and released her, and the world was as it had always been.

Loren swallowed hard on instinct, and she felt the half-magestone slide down her throat unbroken. She gasped, for she *felt* it creeping through her. She thought it might be like a black corruption, or some great sickness sliding through her veins. But it was nothing so terrible. It was . . . a sharpening. Her mind had been a dull blade all her life, and the magestone slid through her like a whetstone, honing its edge.

With a start she realized she could see all the world around her, clearly as if it were day—except that she could see *better* now. She saw the pores on blades of grass, and the threads that made up Gem's bedroll, and the hairs that clung stubbornly to Xain's thinning scalp. Although it was a poor kind of sight next to the vision of the Elves, this was something her mind could comprehend, and she found it beautiful.

She looked at the Elves in wonder, and the glow that poured from them seemed thrice as lovely as before. But now their eyes were black, black like Xain's when he had cast darkfire, and she quailed under their gaze.

The Nightblade, came the thought in her mind. *The one who walks with death.*

Then their eyes turned from her. All of them looked skywards, to where the moons continued their long path across the sky, west towards the horizon where they would finally set. As one the Elves turned, though Loren did not see their feet move, and they began to wander off into the west. Back and forth they strayed, but always westerly, and though they did not seem to hurry, they were out of sight beyond the horizon in what seemed like no time at all.

When the last glow of their presence faded from sight, Loren went suddenly weak and fell to the grass again. She still felt the glamour of their presence in her mind, but without it there to sustain her, she was exhausted. What was more, the night vision of the magestones had faded. The world was black around her again, black save for the silver moonslight—a light she already knew would remind her, for the rest of her days, of the Elves.

At the sound of her dropping to the ground, Chet started awake where he sat against the rock. His head jerked, his eyes blinking furiously, and then he beheld her.

"Loren!" he said. He tried to rise, but he was still groggy and nearly toppled over. "I fell asleep. Sky above curse me, I am sorry. I hardly thought myself tired, but then a deep weariness overcame me, as though . . . what is the matter?"

She looked at him, and only then realized that tears still trickled down her face, leaking from the corners of her eyes to leave their tracks upon her cheeks. Hastily she wiped at them with her sleeve.

"Nothing," she said. "Nothing. Go, sleep in earnest. I will take the watch."

"I have slept enough—too much, it seems." He still looked worried, and he peered at her in the night as though trying to read her expression. "I can keep the watch, for a while longer at any rate."

"No. I cannot sleep now. Rest yourself. I . . . I wish to be alone for a while."

She could tell he was still worried, for he did not look away from her for quite a while. But he did not argue, only turned and went to his bedroll. Soon he was asleep like the rest, and Loren marked that Gem's snores had resumed, loud as ever.

Loren took the other half of the magestone the Elf had fed her. She put it between her lips and bit down, and then swallowed, though her stomach clenched with fear to do so. But the magestone went down the same as last time. Only now, she saw nothing, and the night was dark as ever.

Brow furrowing, she reached into her cloak for the magestone packet again. But in reaching for it, her hand brushed against the dagger's hilt once more. The night sprang into stark daylight, a vision beyond vision where even the horizon seemed near.

Her hand jerked back in surprise, and the vision vanished. She stared at the dagger a moment. Then she took it again, and could see as bright as day.

Jordel had told her that her dagger held many magicks, and one day he would teach them to her. He had died before he could teach her this one. But had he meant to teach it to her in the first place? Did he know the dagger held this power, or was it some secret of the Elves? Or had Jordel known, but withheld it, because of the magestones?

Would they act on Loren the same way they had acted on Xain?

That thought came with its own terrors, and she shoved the magestones as deep in her pocket as she could. Then she pulled them out and stood, intending to throw them into the darkness. But at the last second she stopped. Mayhap she was wrong. Mayhap the magestones would have no ill effects, if she was not a mage. Mayhap the dagger itself protected her.

She could not know, not at least for a while yet. And until she knew, it seemed foolish to throw away such a great amount of wealth— and a great amount of power.

Loren put the magestones back in her cloak and leaned against the rock once more. She put her hand on the dagger, then removed it, over and over again, watching the world turn from night to day each time. After a time the vision faded, and she saw nothing more with the dagger in hand than she did without. But her thoughts went on wild journeys long afterwards, recalling all she had seen when the Elf touched her, and the words it had put into her mind.

Nightblade. The one who walks with death.
Those words stayed with her the longest.

EIGHTEEN

Loren woke Chet an hour before dawn, when the sky was just beginning to grey. He roused slowly, but when he moved to wake the others, she stopped him.

"Come with me," she said. "I have something to tell you, and I would not tell the others. Not yet, at any rate. Come."

He did as she asked, though she could see the questions in his eyes. Loren led him up the side of the hill, until they sat on a flat shelf in its northwest side. From there they could see the camp down below, and the open plains for many leagues to the north and west. All the land was empty, as far as they could see, though Loren wondered if she would see anything different if she was to eat another magestone. But that was something she was not yet ready to test.

Loren told Chet everything that had happened, as best she could remember it—for already the memory had begun to fade, a grey and hazy thing, like a dream half-remembered. But all she had to do was recall the Elves' black eyes when she had eaten the magestones, and she knew with certainty that they had been real.

When she first mentioned them, Chet went white as the Elves' robes had been, and made the sign of the plow over his heart. Loren doubted that would have helped, for she guessed that the Elves cared little for such superstitions.

She did not tell him of the magestones, for she had never told him that she still had a packet of them with her. But she told him all the rest of it, and how it had felt when the Elf touched her, which she said was because she had not fetched the dagger quickly enough. By the time she finished her tale, Chet was looking down at the ground between his feet in thought. Loren waited a while, but when he still said nothing, she began to feel uncomfortable.

"You must promise not to tell the others," she said.

He looked up in surprise. "Why not?"

She paused, for in truth she had not thought overmuch about it—she only knew she did not want to tell them. "I am not certain. Only it feels like something that was for me, and me alone."

He chuckled. "Why tell me, then?"

"I had to tell *someone*," she said, sighing. "The memory fades even now, against my wishes. I was terrified for every moment of it, and feared that we might all of us be killed where we lay. Yet at the same time it was beautiful, like something from one of Bracken's tales, and I would not be the only one to know it happened. And somehow . . . I feel that if I were to tell them, they might not believe me."

"I believe you," he said quietly.

"I hoped you would. Come. We have rested long enough, and should put as many leagues behind us as we can."

They went down the hill again and woke the others. But when Loren shook Xain awake, his gaze locked with hers.

"What happened to you?" he said, eyes wide with wonder.

"What?" she said, feeling a chill run down her spine. "Nothing."

"Your eyes . . . something is different about them," he said slowly. He sat up straighter and peered at her more intently. "Something I feel I should recognize, but I cannot."

Loren swallowed, and thought she could feel Chet's eyes on her back. "Nothing," she said. "Mayhap it is a symptom of the magestone sickness."

Xain stared a moment longer without answering. Then he sighed and turned away. "Mayhap. I am weary, and feel as if I have hardly slept a wink."

When she turned, Loren saw that Chet was indeed looking at her with worry. But she smiled at him, and he looked away, and they readied for the day's travel.

The ride went swiftly. They turned their horses due east around midday, for the land seemed flat and easy, while to the north and south it was rocky and harsh. Three more days they rode this way, and each night Loren went to sleep thinking of the Elves, and woke to memories of their faces in the moonlight. The party gave a wide berth to any villages or farms they spied from afar; doubtless someone would mark their passing, but they wanted to leave as little information in their wake as they could.

On the fourth day, Loren found Xain studying their saddlebags with worry. Her earlier optimism about his recovery seemed to have been justified, for he was slowly regaining his strength. But now he was looking at their supplies, and seemed displeased.

"We do not have enough to reach the coast," said Xain.

"We thought we might not."

"That worry was far off when we were still in the Birchwood. Now it presses close. I would counsel that we should stop at the next village we see, only I fear that if the Shades still follow us, it could freshen the trail."

"We have seen neither hide nor hair of them for days now," said Gem, piping up from behind Annis on their horse. "And I would welcome a change from the endless, unbroken brown of this kingdom, and the wilting scrub brush that covers its landscape." He had taken to complaining day and night about Dorsea, never tiring of pointing out its flaws when compared to the lush green of Selvan, until Loren had to grit her teeth to keep from cuffing him.

"He is right, Loren," said Annis. "And I try not to complain, but I too would welcome a stop. This road is lonely and dirty and boring."

"Very well," said Loren. "We shall rest in the next town we see. Mayhap we will even spend the night in an inn."

"It will seem poor compared to Mag's," said Chet quietly.

They all rode in silence for some time after that.

They did not have to wait long, for later that afternoon they saw a small cluster of brown houses near the horizon. Loren stowed her black cloak in the saddlebag, for it was far too distinctive. But despite misgivings about the wisdom of such a stop, Loren found herself nudging a bit more speed out of Midnight. The mare seemed to catch her mood. The town sat on a small stream that headed to the northeast, and likely ran all the way to the ocean many, many leagues away.

The sun was nearing the horizon as they reached the place. From a ways off they saw some folk at the town's western end, waiting, or so it seemed. But once they got close enough to be seen more clearly, the villagers turned and shuffled off back to their homes. As they left, Loren saw weapons in their hands: staves and simple cudgels, no blades or spears. It gave her an unquiet feeling.

"Did anyone else find that odd?" Chet said, and she knew he had seen the same thing.

"Again you forget that we are in Dorsea now," said Xain. "Villages and towns cannot afford to be so friendly as in Selvan. And we would not do well to mention it, either, for that and your voices would mark us as foreigners."

The village was a small place, but a road ran through it parallel to the river, and there was an inn at the southwestern end. They caught a few glances as they rode past the homes, but the villagers seemed filled with curiosity rather than suspicion. The inn was low and squat, only a single storey high, with the rooms around the outside of the building and all their doors leading straight to the common room at the center. A fat and bearded innkeeper greeted them cordially at the door.

"Evening, good folk," he said. "You will need rooms for the night, I imagine?"

"We will," said Loren. "And stalls for the horses, if you have the room."

"That we do, though you have a couple of fine steeds there. Likely they are used to finer quarters than ours."

Annis smiled down at him. "We value hospitality more than feather pillows, and yours seems in plentiful supply, good sir."

The man grinned wide at that, and he gave Loren a low bow. "Always a kindness to have guests of such fair words under our roof. My boy Ham will take your steeds. Get yourselves inside for a pint."

They dismounted, and Loren raised a questioning eyebrow. Annis smiled, suddenly shy. "Dorseans hold hospitality as a high virtue, and disdain finery, which they see as unnecessary luxury," she said. "Or so I was taught upon the Seat."

"Mayhap you should do all our talking while we are here," said Chet. "He grinned wide enough to split his head open."

Annis ducked her head, cheeks darkening with embarrassment. They found a table inside, and soon the innkeeper came personally to bring them supper. After they had eaten for a while, and had drunk of his ale, which was fine enough (though nowhere near so good as Mag's) he asked if he might sit with them for a time, and they happily obliged. He introduced himself as Crastus, and did not ask for their names in turn, though they had prepared false ones.

"Where might you be headed? If my asking is no discourtesy, I mean," he said once he had settled down and taken a swig from his mug.

"Southeast, for the Seat," said Loren, for they had discussed this story before they entered the town. "Bridget here has a cousin in a courtly position who means to take her for a handmaiden. We are friends of her father's, and promised to see her safely to her destination."

"I have family north and west of here," said Crastus. "From where do you hail? Mayhap I know the place."

"It is only a tiny village, many leagues north of the King's road and deep within Feldemar," said Loren smoothly. "Too small a place to warrant a name."

"Like our own village," said Crastus. "Do you know the family Mennet? They are my kin, and are from around about those parts."

"Mennet?" said Loren, Gem, and Chet all at once.

Annis' eyes widened, and she pursed her lips. With a quiet look to Loren, she urged them all to silence. "I have met many Mennets through my father, though it pains me to say I cannot remember their names," she said. "You must forgive my friends their surprise. They are travelers, as you can plainly hear by their tone, and not from Dorsea by birth."

At that, Crastus gave them all sharp looks. "I should say not. Were I a wagering man, I would lay a gold weight that you three come from Selvan. The dark fellow there has hardly said a word, so I would make no guess as to him."

"From Selvan stock, but born in Feldemar," said Annis, cutting off Gem, who had begun to open his mouth. Loren kicked the boy under the table. "And certainly they hold no truck with that kingdom now, what with the goings-on in Wellmont."

Crastus eyed them a moment more. But then he shrugged and went to his mug again. "Ah, it is no worry of mine. As long as the fighting stays far, far away, I care nothing for it. Though you might wish to keep your words to yourselves, for some hold more tightly to their kingly bonds—more tightly, I would say, than seems reasonable."

"Thank you for the warning," said Loren. "Is that why we saw some men waiting for us when we rode in, bearing weapons?"

"No, that is something else entire," said Crastus, leaning in to speak in a hushed voice. "Some say there have been Elves sighted west of here."

The others' eyes all widened—all but Loren, who tried to keep her face calm. From the corner of her eye she saw Chet looking at her.

"Elves!" said Gem, giddy. "Truly?"

"I would rid myself of that smile if I were you, boy," said Crastus. "Elves are no playthings for children such as yourself."

"I have heard they are beautiful—though, to be certain, few enough have seem them and lived to describe it," said Gem. He had done nothing to follow the innkeeper's advice, for his smile remained.

"Aye, and that is because they will kill you without a second thought," said Crastus. "I pray they stay far, far away from here, that I do."

Loren cleared her throat and took another bite of her dinner. She had become aware that Xain, too, was looking at her now, and his brow had furrowed in thought.

The conversation turned to other things, and soon Loren rustled them all from their tables to go into town and get the supplies they had come for. Food they bought, and oats for the horses, and from the river they filled their waterskins to bursting. All these they put in their room, ready to be packed and loaded in the morning.

Night had fallen by then, and they met back in the common room for a drink before bed. Crastus joined them once more, and began to tell them a story of a time the king of Dorsea himself had come through the town, and tried Crastus' ale and proclaimed it the best he had had in years. The innkeeper was a fair tale-spinner, better at it at any rate than his ale was to drink, and Loren was leaning back in her chair enjoying the story when a man poked his head in the front door and gave a sharp whistle. Some rose from their seats and moved to the door outside.

"What is that?" said Xain, eyes suddenly sharp.

"Another party spotted coming in," said Crastus. "Probably just more travelers like yourselves, but half these boys will go and fetch their weapons expecting Elves. As though swords would help if indeed those demons decided to put our town to the torch."

He went on with his story, but Loren gave Chet a worried look. It might be more travelers, or it might indeed be the Elves. What if Loren had done something wrong since they saw her last, something she could not understand? From the look in his eyes, Chet seemed to understand something of her worry.

"You will forgive me, Crastus, but I think I shall take a stroll for the night air," she said, standing from her chair. "I have had more of your fine ale than is good for my head, and I wish tomorrow's ride to be a pleasant one."

Crastus looked somewhat miffed that she would miss the end of his story, but he waved them off, and she and Chet walked into the darkness. Quickly they made their way through the city streets to the west, and soon came to the edge of the town. There stood many of the villagers, more than had waited for them when they came riding in, and all of them held their weapons at the ready. Loren felt her pulse quicken, but she could not see beyond them yet. Grabbing Chet's sleeve, she pulled him to the side, moving around the men so she could see into the west.

She did not see Elves, or at least not the silvery glow she had seen from them before. At first she saw only torches, like a dozen orange eyes coming at them through the darkness. When the torches neared, she finally saw the figures carrying them—and then blanched, for they were soldiers on horseback, wearing armor and clothing of blue and grey.

NINETEEN

"Shades," she whispered.

"We have to go," said Chet, and she could hear the panic in his voice.

"This village . . . the people . . ." said Loren. But she did not know what to do. Certainly they could not do anything from here, without their horses and the others. "We must tell Xain and the children. Come."

Now they ran as fast as they could, feet pounding along the dirt streets, their cloaks flying behind them in the night. They nearly ran over one or two passersby, who shouted after them, but they never slowed to listen. The front door of the inn slammed into the wall as they threw it open, and everyone in the common room fell silent and turned to look at them.

"Riders," said Loren. "Dozens of them, with arms and armor, coming from the west."

She found Xain's gaze and held it, and he understood at once. He rose from the table, while Crastus stood and began shouting orders at the townsfolk in the room. Loren and the others ran to their room for their supplies, while outside the Dorsean villagers mustered themselves in case there was a fight.

"They found us," said Gem, voice quivering.

Annis took his hand. "That is unlikely. If they were so close behind us, we should have seen them days ago. Likely these riders came from the south, or some other direction entirely. They do not know we are here, and will remain ignorant if we leave at once."

"That is our course," said Loren. "Bring your things to the horses as quickly as you can. Gem and Annis, see to mine, and help Xain with his as well. Mount up as quickly as you can, and ride east."

Chet gave her a look. "You speak as if you will not be with us."

"I will be just behind you," said Loren. "I must find out what the Shades know—if indeed they are aware we are here already. Once I find that out, I will come running out the eastern end of the town, and you had best have Midnight ready for me."

"That is far too dangerous," said Annis. "And it is a worthless piece of information next to your life. Whether they know we are here or not, our path seems the same: ride for the east until our horses drop."

"It makes all the difference," said Loren. "If they know where we are, we must learn how, or we will never evade them. And there is no time to argue this. To the horses, *now.*"

She went running from the room, but Chet was on her heels. When she turned to him, he shook his head. "There is no time to argue with me, either. I will come with you. I am as sneaky as you ever were, and two are safer than one."

Loren nodded, and they went off. First Loren went to Midnight and took her bow from the saddle, strung it, and slung it on her back. Then she led Chet back the way they had come through the village. By the time they reached the west end again, the Shades had come to a halt just beyond the buildings. There were more than she had seen before, scores and scores of them.

She shook in her boots as she recognized Rogan at their head.

Chet joined her in cover behind the edge of a house, Loren thanking her stars that they had not been seen. Rogan sat high in his saddle, his horse covered with thick plates of armor the same as he was. His helm left his face exposed, but chain mail hung from the back of it to cover his neck. She remembered the tattoo on the back of Trisken's neck—the tattoo that had kept him alive, and which Jordel had destroyed in order to kill him, though at terrible cost.

They had missed some words between the Shades and the villagers already, but now Rogan was speaking. "We will not turn back. All my life I have heard fine tales of Dorsean hospitality, and I will not be greeted with anything less. Or would you have me spread tales of your dishonor to the neighboring towns?"

"We have no room for so many," said a man from the village. He was somewhat older than Loren, though still young and hale, and he stood forwards from the rest of them as though he were their leader. "If you must rest for the night, we shall not begrudge you that—only do it beyond the town's borders, in the fields outside."

Rogan studied him. Tall and strong the man might have been, but before Rogan he looked like a child. The Shade captain rolled his shoulders, and when he spoke it was as though he had not heard.

"We are looking for someone," he said. "A girl. She is young, and clad in a black cloak. If you came close enough, you might remark upon her eyes, for they are a bright shade of green. Has anyone seen such a girl?"

There was quiet for a moment, and some of the villagers shifted on their feet. Loren saw Crastus among them, and his boy Ham standing next to him, look at each other. But no one spoke any word.

"Come now," said Rogan. "She would have passed through recently, no more than a few days ago, if she came here at all. Certainly someone would have remarked upon her passing?"

"As I said, take your horses back out into the plains and stay the night there," said the man who had spoken before. "If you wish, some of your men can come and buy supplies in the town."

Rogan pursed his lips. Then, with more speed than Loren would have guessed from his massive frame, he slid from the saddle. The townsfolk took half a step back at that. He came forwards, and Loren saw the axe slung across his back. It was huge—the head of it was at least half again as wide as Loren's torso, and she doubted she could wrap her hands around the haft.

The villagers were backing up slowly now, but the man at their head did not falter. Instead, he took a step forwards and hefted the club in his hand. Even he must have realized how frail he looked before Rogan, but he did not turn away.

"Leave here, now!" he said, and his voice was strong. "You are not welcome!"

Rogan's hand flew to the haft of his axe, and it sprang from his back in a flourish. He did not strike the man with it, but swung it into both hands and sent the butt into his chest with a *thunk*. The man fell to the ground, gasping, and Rogan seized the back of his collar. He dragged him up to his knees, and then brought the axe around again until the blade was pressed to his throat.

"I will ask again, since hospitality has failed us all," said Rogan. "I look for a girl in a black cloak, with green eyes. Who has seen her?"

The rest looked at each other, and for a moment Loren thought they might answer. But Rogan did not wait. The axe jerked, and the man's throat spilled blood out into the dirt. Some in the crowd screamed, and they all drew back as though from a burning flame.

"Take the town," said Rogan. "Collect the children."

Chet was tugging at her arm, but Loren stood unmoving. She felt the urge to run with him, to flee to the others and leap atop Midnight's saddle and ride off into the night. But these people would die under the swords of the Shades, and all to find her.

She remembered the boy they had found in the Birchwood. *Are you her?* he had asked her, for he could not see Loren through the sockets where his eyes had been.

Loren threw off Chet's arm and stepped out into the open, drawing her bow from her back. "Rogan!" she cried. "I am here!"

Everything stopped at once. The villagers looked at her in fear, their faces orange in the light of their torches. But Rogan looked at her like a wolf looking at a meal, eyes glittering.

"Loren, of the family Nelda," he said, almost sweetly. "We meet at last. I have eagerly awaited this moment."

"Let them be," said Loren. "Whatever your quarrel with me, they are no part of it."

"Whatever our quarrel?" said Rogan, and then he threw back his head with a laugh. "Loren, do not feign ignorance with me. It says you think ill of my wisdom, and that is the height of bad manners. Do you think we would let you live to reveal what you know to the Mystics who hold your leash?"

"No one controls me. No one commands me," said Loren. "And you cannot win, whatever you might do here. Word of your coming will already have spread through Selvan at least, and has likely already reached the Mystics' ears. They will find you, and crush you in your infancy, before your plans ever bear fruit."

All of Rogan's false courtesy vanished in an instant. He had the look of a brute then, his thick layers of muscle enshrouded in the plates of his armor, and the gore that kissed his axe was full of dark promise. But his eyes were bright, and filled with a wisdom that frightened Loren all the more.

"Our infancy? You think we are new to this kingdom? I drew blood before you first drew breath. I serve death itself. I am shadeborn. My master is my father, and in his name I will lay all the nine lands low."

"I think you boast overmuch."

"I think we are alike in that. You say you have spread word of us, but I think you lie. You have no friends in the nine lands, Loren. The Mystics themselves hunt you to put you to death, and the constables would throw you in a dark cell if ever they laid their hands upon you. No one else will help you. We killed your companions in Northwood, and your woodland kin in the Birchwood. We even found the village where you were whelped and raised, and put it to the torch."

"No!" cried Chet. He rushed forwards as though he would charge Rogan, alone and unaided. But Loren seized him and held him, and when still he struggled, she twisted his arm back until he winced.

"He baits you," she hissed. "Leave it be. He is probably lying."

"You saw what he did to that village," said Chet. His voice sounded as though it might break. She knew he was thinking of his father, who had remained behind when Chet had left.

"Your companion shows more spirit than you do," said Rogan. "A promising protégé. Sadly, he is too old for my purposes. But there are many others here who will serve the master well. Take them. I will deal with the girl."

The Shades at his back moved at last, jumping from their horses and charging at the villagers. The townsfolk raised their weapons, but as in Northwood, they were a rabble facing trained soldiers, and they were cut down. Loren saw them hack apart men and women both, until the ones left standing turned to flee.

But they did not kill the children. Her heart stopped as she saw them pause, lower their blades, and seize any child they saw by the arm. Then they threw them over their shoulders and began to carry them back to the horses.

One of them took Ham, the innkeeper Crastus' son. The boy screamed with tears pouring down his cheeks as the Shade carried him away.

"Loren!" cried Chet. She saw that she had stood frozen too long.

Rogan was almost upon them. Instinct took over, and she snatched an arrow from the quiver at her hip the way that Albern had taught her. She drew and fired, aiming low, and by good fortune the shaft buried itself in the joint between his thigh and his hip. Rogan sank to one knee with a grunt, but soon fought his way back up, snapping the arrow off where the fletching stuck out.

"Run!" she cried, and then turned to follow her own command. They vanished between the buildings in the village, Rogan limping after them.

"Fly, little girl!" came his booming voice through the night. "Fly, and leave these innocents to die in your place. The bodies at your feet will stack higher and higher until they wall you in and there is no place left to flee from us."

She had hoped the Shades would come after them, but she should have known it was a futile wish. They stayed and cut down everyone before them, even those who did not fight. Panicked glances behind her showed her more children being carried off, slung over the Shades' shoulders, or simply dragged screaming by their scrawny limbs.

Just beyond the village's eastern edge, they found the others waiting for them, eyes wide with fright and horses ready to run. Together Loren and Chet climbed into their saddles. For one brief moment they stopped to look back. Some of the buildings were burning, burning in a bright red blaze that spread from roof to roof. The air was filled with the screams of men and women, silenced with sharp violence, and the screams of children, which lingered on and on until they faded into the dark.

"What happened?" said Gem. He sounded as though he might start crying at any moment.

"I cannot say it," said Loren. "If you value our friendship, never ask me again. Turn now, and ride."

They did, while the nameless village died at their backs.

TWENTY

THEY PUSHED THEIR HORSES NEAR TO BREAKING, THOUGH THEY SAW NO sign of the Shades' pursuit. The burning town was a memory behind them before long, but Loren thought she could feel the heat of the flames all the rest of that night.

Dawn came bleak and hopeless, and after a brief pause to survey the horizon behind them, she let them dismount to eat.

"I do not understand," she said, pacing while the others sat. "I do not understand. He barely even chased us. Why stay to kill those villagers?"

"He is a cruel man," said Gem. "Cruelty does not always need a reason."

"He is *not* some simpleton," said Loren. "I have seen savagery so strong it is almost madness. We all have. Rogan is different. He is cunning, and wise. He does not kill just for the joy of it, but for some greater purpose."

"Trisken loved his cruelty well enough," said Xain. He rubbed at his throat as though at a phantom pain. The brute Trisken had given him many dark memories when they fought in the Greatrocks.

"Rogan is *not* Trisken," said Loren. "He is something worse."

"If that is true, then all the more reason he would stay to kill those who cannot defend themselves," said Annis. She was looking up at Loren with concern, and with empathy, neither one of which Loren was glad to see. She was not some child who needed consoling.

"I think you look for reason in madness," said Xain. "Those touched by a berserker's fury do not act the way reasonable folk do. You cannot hope to control them as you normally would."

Chet's head jerked up. "What would you do then, wizard? Put them down? We are not killers." He spoke harshly, surprising even Loren. Xain glowered at him without answer. Chet stared a moment longer, and then returned to his meal.

They downed their hasty breakfast and rode on. That day was no hotter than the last, yet the sunlight seemed harsher, and the wind of their riding seemed to bite at Loren's skin. She was likely imagining it; the village, and Crastus, and Ham, were only the latest fuel thrown on the fire of her guilt that had been building since Wellmont. It made her irritable, and that made her cross with the others. When they stopped to relieve themselves, or water the horses, she did her best to avoid them. Soon they took her hint, and rarely spoke unless it was absolutely necessary.

By evening the children were nearly dead in their saddle, and Xain was slumped across his horse's neck. Though she felt she could ride for days if she must, Loren realized she could not force them on forever. She found a high rise in the ground and led them there, where they could rest while keeping a watch on the land all around them. The others threw themselves into sleep at once, and Loren stood watch all night. As the moons made their way across the sky, she kept her eyes upon the plains, for when she looked at the campfire she saw the burning of the village.

Three more days passed without incident. Whenever they saw signs of other people, Loren went to great pains to avoid them. The others followed without question or comment, though Loren sometimes took them many miles out of their way and slowed their progress considerably. But she would not endanger any other lives, not if there was a way she could possibly avoid it.

And then, in the middle of the fourth day, they crested a rise and came at last to view the sea.

In truth it was only the Great Bay, and not the wide ocean itself.

But the Bay stretched for leagues and leagues beyond counting, wider than some of the nine kingdoms were long, and so it seemed as vast as the ocean to Loren. Indeed, it took her breath away when she first saw it, the sun cascading off its breadth and glowing like a thousand precious jewels. For just a moment, she forgot the dark thoughts that had plagued her for the last many days.

"The Great Bay," said Xain. He straightened in his saddle, and his voice took on a new strength. "Where the first High King, Roth, first came to the Underrealm from the northern lands, which are forgotten. Many long months has it been since I last glimpsed its blue expanse, and I never thought the day would come when I would miss it. Yet while my heart sings to see it, my mind is less convinced. We may be in more danger now than before."

"I think I feel the same," said Annis in a small voice. "The world has been emptier without the sound of the sea, but now I can only think of how close we are to my family."

"And to the Academy," said Xain. "My face would be most unwelcome there."

"Where do we go now?" said Gem.

"We must find a port," said Xain. "There are many along the coast, although we will not be able to see them until we are much closer. There we will find passage on a ship to Dulmun, and then ride to Feldemar."

"Should we turn north, or south?" said Loren.

"Neither," said Xain. "Our best choice is to make straight for the coast. It will be faster to ride the road that snakes all along the Great Bay, than it would be to turn our path now."

So they rode on, their horses' hooves devouring the miles. But the Bay was farther away than it looked, thanks to its great size, and by the time the sun set they had not even closed half the distance. The next day they rode as quickly as they could, eager to reach the water now, but the coast hardly seemed to draw nearer. Instead the massive blue stretch of water only took up more and more of the horizon.

"How large is it?" said Gem.

"Larger than you can imagine," said Xain. "Large enough that you cannot see either side, standing on a boat in its center. From the middle, it would take two days of hard sailing to find a coast. And it is only a fraction of the size of the great sea beyond."

But at long last they could see the coastline approaching, and by that evening they had reached it. Then Loren saw the black and rocky sand of its beaches, where waves came crashing with thunderous roars. She sat there in her saddle for a moment, watching, wondering that there could be so much water in the world.

"Come, let us water the horses," said Chet.

"No!" said Xain sharply. "Do not let them drink from it, nor should you do so. The waters of the ocean are filled with salt, and though they hold no poison, they can have much the same effect. If you tried to drink your fill, your thirst would only grow, and you would retch and spill anything in your stomach. It is all too easy to die of thirst upon the sea, though you are surrounded by all the water you could imagine."

Chet drew back, giving the waves a distrustful look. But Gem sat up in his saddle and said, "Is it safe for swimming?"

Xain looked at him, perplexed. "Yes, if you remember not to swallow the water."

With a whoop, Gem leaped to the ground and ran off, throwing off his belt, breeches, and tunic, his lack of smallclothes thus rendering him stark naked. He flung himself into the water with a scream, thrashing about in the waves. Annis looked away and lifted her chin demurely.

"At least he will come out cleaner than he normally is," she said.

Loren bid them to rest and eat. She drank from her water skin. It was strange, having to resist the urge to fill it, but she had no wish to taste the water and test Xain's claim. Before long Gem came running back out of the waters, hugging his arms about himself, and scooped up his clothes.

"It is cold!" he cried. "Colder than I thought it would be, anyway. Does the ocean think it is winter?"

"It cares little for our seasons," said Xain. "A great current sweeps through the Bay, up from the south and around and then back out to the north, and it brings the ice with it."

"Gem, for pity's sake, clothe yourself!" said Annis. Loren found herself smiling, and shook her head. The merchant's daughter had always had such strict ideas about decency, ever since Loren had first met her. It seemed that was one thing, at least, that had not changed in the long months since.

Gem shrugged and began to pull on his clothes again. "You are right about the salt. I got a little in my mouth by accident, and it nearly made me retch. I had never heard this of the ocean."

"Urchins of the city streets would have little cause to know it," said Xain.

Loren looked to Chet to see him smiling at her, and she gave him a little smile back. But then his face froze, his eyes focused over her shoulder, and he hunched forwards. She looked behind her.

"Chet, what is it?"

"I saw something. Something moving—a man, I think."

At once she reached for her bow, and Chet for his staff. Xain got to his feet, though it was a slow and painful process.

"That dune," said Chet, pointing. "Towards the southern side."

"Remain here," said Loren to the children. "Chet and I will look to see what it was. Do as Xain tells you."

She tossed her head, and together they ran west. Loren took them in a wide circle so that they came to the dune from the northern side. In a few minutes they had reached it, and they slowed as one. Forwards they crept, an inch at a time, silencing their footsteps with long practice. Loren found the going difficult, for the sand shifted beneath her feet and left her stance uncertain. But the sound of the waves helped to mask the noise.

They crept around the edge of the dune with deliberate slow steps, until Loren saw it: a figure in grey and blue. She froze, ducking back, but she had not been seen. It was a man, similar to Xain in age and appearance, with long dark hair that went to his shoulders. The beginnings of a beard dusted his chin, but it looked to be there from neglect, rather than by design.

Loren met Chet's gaze and made two quick motions with her hands. Then she went left, staying behind the thin scrubby bushes that clung to the coastline, until the man was between her and the dune. Meanwhile Chet climbed up the sandy slope until he stood above the Shade.

The man was looking out, away south and west where Xain and the children were, though they had hidden themselves. He leaned forwards, straining to find them again, when Loren sprang forwards with a cry. The Shade wheeled, grasping for the sword at his belt. But then Chet attacked, his staff cracking down on the man's shoulder. The Shade fell in a heap, and when he saw Loren standing above him with an arrow drawn, he did not try to rise again.

"Mercy!" he cried. "Mercy, I surrender!"

"Fetch the others," said Loren, her voice like steel. She had heard cries of mercy from the Dorsean villagers as the Shades slaughtered them, and found her heart unmoved by the man's pleas.

Soon Chet returned with Xain and the children. The wizard came at once to stand over the Shade. Loren kept her arrow trained on him, though she relaxed the draw to half.

"Where are your companions?" said Xain.

"I have no companions."

At once Xain knelt, wrapping his hand around the man's arm. Flames sprang to white-hot life, and Loren heard the sizzling of skin. The man screamed. In Xain's other hand appeared a knife, and this he pressed to the man's throat.

"Where are they?"

"Xain," said Chet, a warning sound in his voice. But Loren met his eyes and shook her head.

"I lost them," said the Shade, gritting his teeth as he spoke. "A storm struck the coast, and its thunder made my horse bolt. By the time I got control, I could not find them."

"Where are you bound, and for what purpose?"

"North, to find them again."

"And us?"

The man did not answer. Flames sprang forth again. Loren saw the sweat that beaded on Xain's face, and knew it did not come from the heat of the fire. This must be taking a terrible toll on his strength. But the Shade screamed again, and this time he had an answer.

"We were searching for you!" he cried. "We sought a girl with green eyes, and a wizard, as well as two children. When I spotted you from afar, I saw that you matched the description."

"What were you to do when you found us?" said Xain. The flames in his hand died, but Loren could still smell the cooked flesh and burnt cloth beneath.

"Stop that," said Chet.

"Chet, take the children away from here," said Loren.

"What?" he said, looking at her in disbelief.

"Take them away," she said. "Quickly."

He looked a second longer, and for a moment Loren thought he would refuse. But then he ushered the children away. He returned a moment later while the Shade was still answering Xain's question.

"We were not to engage you in battle. If we saw you, we were to send two messengers at once—one west, to find our captain, and another south, to the Seat."

"The Seat?" said Xain. "Who is your master there?"

"I do not know," said the Shade at once. When he saw the baleful look in Xain's eye, his arm flinched and he screamed. "I do not know! I swear it! Our sergeant knew, but she never told me. Only if the messengers were to be sent would she give them the name."

Loren thought it sounded like the truth, and just the sort of wise cunning she would have expected from Rogan. Xain studied the man for a moment, and it seemed he thought the same.

"I believe you," he said.

Then he plunged his dagger into the man's neck.

"No!" cried Chet, rushing forwards. Loren stepped into his path and stopped him with her hands on his chest.

"It is done," she murmured. "You can do nothing."

"He surrendered. That was murder!"

Xain looked up at them, eyes dark. "Mayhap. Or mayhap it was justice. Have you forgotten the screams of the village we left behind? I have not."

Even now, the man's fingers grasped at his own throat, trying to close the gaping hole there. Dark red seeped between his fingers, staining the already-dark sand beneath him. Loren wanted to look away, but could not move her eyes. She wanted to join Chet in admonishing Xain, but felt she had no place. What words had the Elves placed in her mind?

The Nightblade. The one who walks with death.

She thought they had meant she carried a doom with her, but mayhap they had meant Xain.

"I have forgotten nothing, wizard," said Chet. "But your sort of justice is the kind that brings war and death to all the nine lands in the end." He looked at Loren, eyes filled with fury, urging her to join him.

"He had no choice," said Loren. "We could not have let the Shade go south, to tell his compatriots where we were."

She hated the look on his face then: the shock, the disappointment. Most of all, she hated the sadness, and the sorrow. Loren was almost as surprised as Chet was to hear the words coming from her lips. Had she not once spoken just as Chet had? Did she not believe as Chet did? She knew she had, once. But she was no longer so certain.

"We had best move on," she said, turning away from them. "Let us go back to the horses. Quickly, for the night will not be long in coming."

TWENTY-ONE

BY THE TIME THEY STOPPED FOR THE NIGHT, THEY COULD SEE THE GLOW OF
fires from a town far ahead. It was on the horizon, and Loren guessed
they could reach it in just a few more hours' ride.

"We should reach the town tomorrow," she said.

"Why not ride after the moons rise, and get there tonight?" said
Xain.

"And then what? We could not find a ship at night. And if the
Shades have come this way they might have gone to the town, and then
they might hear of our presence before we could leave."

He nodded, saying nothing more, and they found a spot near the
shore to camp. Loren would not let them start a fire, for finding the
Shade that day had made their pursuers seem altogether too near.

She took the first watch, and sat it atop a dune overlooking the bay.
From above, she could just see the sleeping forms of her friends in the
silver moonslight that reflected off the water. One of the shapes moved,
and then rose to climb the dune towards her. Her heart sank as she recognized Chet. She did not wish to face him just now. But as he neared,
she scooted over to let him sit on the sand beside her.

He was silent at first, and she avoided looking at him. She focused on the cool breeze coming in off the water, for autumn was much warmer here in the north. But she held no illusions: he had come to speak to her, and she knew it. It was plain in the nervous twitching of his hands, the way he turned his head to her often, and then turned away when he saw she was not looking.

At last she found herself growing impatient. "Out with it, Chet," she said.

He folded his hands over each other. "That man today. The one that Xain killed."

"Yes. I was there."

"I do not blame you for it. You could not have stopped it, nor could I. But I did not expect you to speak against me."

"Did I speak against you? Once the deed was done, there was nothing more to be said. We needed to carry on."

"You did not only urge haste. You said Xain had no choice. Those were never words I thought to hear from you. What he did was wrong. The man was our prisoner, and was half-dead from lack of food and water besides. He was no threat."

Loren stayed silent. In truth, she did not know what answer to give. Chet turned towards her, edging closer.

"I know you agree with me. Yet you spoke in Xain's defense. You cannot tell me you have grown as bloodthirsty as the rest of them."

"It is no thirst for violence. It is wisdom. We cannot leave enemies all about us, aware of our plans and intent on our harm. I have done that ever since I left the forest, and it has brought nothing but tragedy to my friends, and myself."

"You would never have said that in the Birchwood."

She looked at her hands as they lay in her lap. They were fidgeting, fingers twisting themselves about her thumbs. "Mayhap not. I used to think as you do. Always I would chastise the others when I saw them as violent, when they would kill or urge me to take a life. Still I will not do it with my own hands."

"That is not enough, and you know it. I think you were right before."

"But I am responsible now—for them, for the fate of the Mystics and the Shades both." She looked at him, his light brown hair glistening in the moonslight. "And for you as well. Those who hunt us will kill without a second thought. You saw that yourself. I may not approve, but neither can I stop to slap the wrists of those who would embrace violence to answer violence."

He looked back out across the bay, and she could see from the twitching in his jaw that he was holding back harsh words. She did not like to see such frustration in his eyes, any more than she liked to see him look at her with pity or sadness. She knew that, if she were to see herself six months ago, she would have looked at Jordel in much the same way when she thought he killed too freely.

"I have known you all my life, and most of yours. I was there when your father . . . when he treated you the way he did." His fists clenched together. "Often I was on the very brink of raising my own hands to stop him, however I could. Always you warded me off, either with words or with the look in your eyes—eyes that have always been able to say so much, even when I felt like the only one who could hear you. And it enraged me. You never lifted a hand to him yourself. If you had, no one in all the nine lands would have said a word against you. You had every right to do it. Yet you did not. I thought it foolish for a time. I felt the way you say you feel now.

"And then I grew older, and somewhat wiser, or so I thought. I felt I finally understood why you acted thus. Because to raise your hands to him, or to lift your axe and end him, forever, would be to lower your-self to his level. If you killed him, though anyone would have called it justified, you would only have beaten him by becoming him. And that was far, far worse than suffering. That was how I was able to still my fists all those long years. Because I knew that you were winning your own victory by proving yourself the better person, though it might take all your life to do so. Or so I thought. Was I wrong?"

Loren wanted to say he was. Since she left the woods, she had seen so much—Damaris' slaughter of the constables, and all of Auntie's hor-rors in Cabrus, and the terrible battle in Wellmont, and Jordel's death in the Greatrocks. The world seemed filled with evil, evil far more po-tent than her father's simple, stupid hatred that rotted the core of his soul. That evil she could have borne forever. But she could not stomach the thought of letting a much greater evil envelop the kingdom she called home.

And yet, she wondered, what good would it do to defeat those dark forces, if doing so meant she must accept the darkness into herself? She still believed that those who killed for a just cause could turn to killing when it suited them. That was mayhap the source of all wrongs that plagued them; for even Rogan had had a curious light of righteousness in his eye, when he slit the villager's throat and let his lifeblood pool in the dirt.

"I do not know the answer you want," said Loren. "Or rather, I know what you wish I would say, but I do not know if I can say it with any ring of truth. I have seen so much and traveled so far, Chet. And I am tired."

"Forget the road. Forget what you have seen. Try to remember how you felt when you lived with me in our village. And try to remember why."

She cast her mind back, all the long way to when she was a child, when her father had first pressed her into doing his labor, when she had first felt the crushing blows of his fists. And she remembered fleeing from the work, and his beatings, and escaping into the woods with Chet to sit in a clearing and listen . . .

"Mennet," she said. "It was Bracken's tales of Mennet. I was just a young whelp, and I wished great harm upon my father. And Bracken listened to me, and he heard me, and then he told me of Mennet, the thief who could bring down a king without spilling a drop of his blood. Yet now they tell me Mennet was nothing more than a legend."

"I do not believe that, and I do not think you do, either," said Chet. "And even if it is true, why should we care? I have heard it said that even false tales may have great value."

"But how can we know which have value, and which are simply stories for scared little children hiding from their parents in the woods?"

"Is there no value in that?" said Chet, his voice soft. He reached out and took her hand, as he had never done before, for it was always Loren who reached for his. "The value of a tale is what we take from it. The choice is our own. That is one lesson I learned from none of Bracken's tales—or mayhap all of them at once. And that belief kept me from falling into despair as I grew older, and thought you might be something more than only my friend. When I wished to wed you, though your parents would never have let me."

She held his hand, and felt his thumb dragging across her palm. And then she did not know what she was doing, but she leaned across the space between them and touched his cheek, and met his lips with her own.

The shores rustled down below them, and the wind whispered, and the moonslight sang its own song that seemed sweeter than all the rest.

Loren leaned away again, relishing the smile she had put upon his face. She matched it with one of her own, though smaller, and stood.

"I suppose I have much to think upon," she said. "But we will be no good to the others if neither of us sleeps. And I find myself weary, so I will leave you to the watch. Wake me when the moons are straight overhead."

She went down the dune and away from him, but not too quickly, and it was a while yet before she could close her eyes in sleep.

TWENTY-TWO

As they drew closer, Xain recognized the town, and told them its name was Brekkur. They could smell it long before they could make out the guards who stood above the gate. It was a fishing village, and the pungent odor wafted far upon the coastal winds.

The walls were wooden, not stone, and looked newly built. "That is likely because the town is growing," said Xain. "Many such towns wax and wane with the seasons, and in summer they fill to brimming with fishermen. Then they take down their walls and erect them again farther out, only to bring them in close once winter sets in and people flee for warmer climes."

They found little resistance at the gates. Loren guessed that the towns must have received no word of the Shades who marauded across the kingdom. It seemed an ill omen that so wanton a slaughter could be carried out with not so much as a whisper of warning reaching the coastline. But then again, they had seen only the killing of a rather small village, and likely that was of no great consequence to the kingdom at large.

In any case they were soon making a careful way through many shacks and stalls, put up against the ramshackle huts that were the town's permanent structures. Behind each one stood old vendors, leaning forwards to hawk their wares to Loren and the others. Many had fish, but others offered hooks, nets, and lines.

"Do they think we are fishermen?" said Gem, sniffing as one particularly malodorous old woman came too close.

"Most are, who come here," said Xain. "In summer these places are like farms for seafolk, who spring up out of nowhere to ply the water and return filled with bounty, which is then brought all across the nine kingdoms in preparation for winter."

"But fish will not keep that long," said Annis. "Even in the kitchens upon the Seat, which were often stocked with ice, they did not last long."

"They do not need to," said Xain. "When food is suddenly plentiful, and may be traded for, the citizens of towns and cities in all directions may turn their attention to other things. And so for a while, Dorseans near the coast eat mostly fish while they turn to crafts like smithing and clothes and such. Thus summer is a happy time for the common folk, for they may turn their hands to things of beauty rather than the meager business of survival. Though you would likely have never noticed, in your fine halls where food was always plentiful and you never had aught to do but your embroidery."

The words came surprisingly harsh, and Loren looked at Xain with worry. He ducked his head almost as soon as he had spoken, and looked away from Annis as though with shame. His shoulders were shaking in the stiff breeze that blew in from the sea, and Loren guessed the sickness was wracking his body harder than normal.

"I am sorry," said Xain quietly. "The sickness . . . it plagues me, though I weary of giving you that excuse."

"I know," said Annis.

"I will still my tongue."

"You need not," said Annis. Xain paused and turned to look at her. She shook her head. "I know how it hurts you. It is a cruel punishment."

"For cruel crimes," said Xain, frowning.

"You were not in your right mind," said Annis. "And I know that, though I have often tried to pretend otherwise."

The wizard's jaw clenched, and he turned away, bowing his head. His shoulders shook harder for a moment, and Gem looked away uncomfortably. Loren reached across the gap between them and took Annis' hand. The girl tried to give her a smile, but in her eyes Loren saw barely-restrained tears.

The conversation, however, had made Loren realize something else: she had suffered no ill effects from eating the magestone on the night the Elves had visited her. The day afterwards, she had mayhap been a bit weary, but that she attributed to the fright of seeing those other-worldly creatures. Now, though, she had had no cravings to try the stones again, nor had she felt any madness creeping into her mind the way it had crept into Xain's from the very moment he had eaten them. It seemed, then, that the illness struck only mages who ate the stones—or mayhap her other guess had been correct, and the dagger somehow protected her. Either way, it was a great relief.

They came to the docks soon enough, and Xain began to inspect the ships with a practiced eye. Loren had not forgotten when they sailed together on a riverboat down the Dragon's Tail, or how practiced Xain had seemed with boatcraft. She had wondered at it then, but she was grateful for it now. Several smaller boats he passed by at once. He spent a few minutes longer studying a large ship with its sail unfurled for cleaning, but then inspected the waterline and turned away, shaking his head.

They were riding slowly down the docks, in no particular hurry, when they came to a great ship with two masts. Loren found it breath-taking, though she knew little of sailing. It towered above them, and a long wooden ramp ran down from its deck to where they stood on the dock. Upon its prow was fixed a carving of an eagle, wings behind it as though it was diving. Its beak was split in a scream.

"You have an eye for ships, I see," came a voice.

Loren looked down to see a solid-looking man on the dock before them. He had spoken to Xain. Close-cropped black hair covered his head, from the top of it down to the thin beard that barely left his chin. His shirt seemed altogether too small, sleeves buttoned tightly around thick muscles that were well browned by the sun. His breeches and tunic were all faded, clearly from long wear in the sun and ocean wind.

"This is your vessel?" said Xain.

"He is," said the man with a nod. "The *Long Claw*, we call him, and I have commanded him across the Bay, and beyond, for nigh on a dozen years now."

"You are a man of Dulmun, judging from your speech and the

make of him." Xain spoke with curious interest, his voice more alive than it had seemed in many weeks.

"You have an eye for many kingdoms, I would guess," said the man. He stood forwards and thrust a hand up towards Xain on his horse. "I am called Torik."

"A pleasure, Captain," said Xain. He took the larger man's wrist, but said quickly, "Gentle, if you will. I have taken a spell of something on my journey here, though it is nothing catching, I assure you."

"A man must be bold to admit when he is ailing," said Torik with a grin. "Though I cannot say as I would let such a man on my crew."

"Fortunate for us both, then, that I am not searching for such a position," said Xain with a smile.

They both laughed, which surprised Loren—Xain's dour mood seemed to have vanished in an instant. She remembered the last time he had surprised her like that, when they met the riverboat captain Brimlad in the town of Redbrook. Something about sailing seemed to put him in good spirits.

Torik threw an arm towards the gangplank. "I would guess you seek passage, and that is something we have plenty of room for. If you wish, I can take you aboard and show you his quality."

"I can see it for myself from here, but gladly will we take your offer," said Xain. He turned to the others. "Come aboard. I think this ship will do nicely."

"You have not even asked him where he is sailing!" said Gem.

"He makes for the High King's Seat, and then to Dulmun," said Xain. "It is the usual route for Dulmun ships that sail from the coast of the Great Bay. Is that not the truth, Captain?"

"Certainly enough," said Torik. "Give your horses to the boy. He will take good care of them, on my word."

A young deckhand came running up, reaching for their reins. Another stood nearby, expectantly, and Torik caught his eye.

"Run up and tell the boys guests are coming aboard. Make sure they keep the sheep guts out of sight."

The boy's eyes widened, and he scampered up the gangplank. Annis looked uncertainly at Loren. But Xain spoke first to reassure her.

"In Dulmun, a ship is considered blessed if its decks are regularly polished with the insides of a sheep. But worry not, for you have already heard the captain means to keep such gruesome sights from you."

"I am not afraid of sheep guts," Annis snapped.

If Loren had thought the ship impressive from the dock, it was doubly so once they stood upon the deck. The mast seemed to stretch out of sight into the sky, and the vessel was longer from one end to the other than some of the largest buildings she had been inside. A large crew ran about, pulling lines and doing other things she could scarcely guess at. Torik led them all about, pointing things out here and there. She was soon lost in the many strange words he used, though Xain nodded his head appreciatively and seemed to listen with rapt attention.

"Now let me take you into his hold," said the captain. "We have many fine cabins down below—and some not so fine, if you are short on coin. I can show you where you would stay, if indeed you wish to secure passage."

An open hatch awaited, with a staircase leading down. Loren did not find the darkness below very inviting, but she swallowed her misgivings and followed the captain. The passage hooked around immediately, leading into a long hallway with doors on either side. It looked for all the world like the upper floor of an inn, like many she had stayed at in her travels. Metal grates in the ceiling let the light in, and the place seemed far cozier and more inviting than she had expected.

"If you will all step in here," said Torik, throwing open a door.

Still looking about in wonder, Loren led the way inside, with the others close behind.

The door slammed shut behind them with a *snap*. The air filled with the hiss of steel, and Loren saw half a dozen swords pointed in their direction. Behind them stood broad men and women in red cloaks.

She gave a shout and reached for her dagger. Beside her, Xain muttered words of power, and his eyes glowed white. But the magic sputtered almost as soon as he reached for it, and his shoulders sagged. At the other end of the cabin, which was spacious enough, Loren saw a Mystic woman with her hands twisted to claws. Her eyes glowed white, and Loren felt herself unable to move, held in the mindmage's grasp.

"Stay your hands," said the woman. "You will find you have no choice in the matter, after all."

"Stand down," said a deep and booming voice. "We will not harm you as long as you keep your hands away from your blades."

From behind the Mystics came another, and with one glance Loren knew him for their leader. His shoulders were broad, and his beard long. Many lines of care and worry criss-crossed his face, deep as the scars she saw there also. The other Mystics parted way before him, as if on instinct, or as if some invisible force surrounded him and pushed him aside. He marched forth to stand before Loren, glowering down at her. She felt her resolve crumbling despite herself, and slowly moved her hand away from her belt. It moved easily now, for the glow in the Mystic wizard's eye had dimmed.

"You will forgive us our surprise," said the Mystic. "Or mayhap you will not. It is no matter either way. I am Kal, of the family Endil, chancellor of the Mystic Order, and I have been searching for you for some time. Word has it, you were last seen traveling with Jordel."

Loren was so surprised that for a moment she could not speak. From the corners of her eyes she saw the others looking towards her, wondering. Her mind raced, trying to guess the right words to speak to save them all. In the end she did not know which lie to tell, and settled for the truth instead.

"I am Loren, of the family Nelda," she said. "And yes, it was our honor to travel at Jordel's side, for a time. We have come to Dorsea at his bidding."

"I am not one to take a woman at her word," said Kal. "If you rode with Jordel, where is he? And why would he send you, rather than come himself?"

"If I may show you proof?" said Loren. She reached slowly for a pocket within her cloak. The Mystics by Kal's side tensed, but he stilled them with a look. Loren retrieved Jordel's Mystic symbol, the badge of office she had seen on his chest the first time they met. She had retrieved it from his body when he died, thinking she might one day have use for it. That day seemed to have arrived at last.

Kal's eyes widened as he beheld the badge, and then narrowed to slits. "Jordel would not have given this into your hands, not even if you were his messengers."

He said it flatly, and yet Loren heard the question behind the words. "I am the bearer of ill news, I fear. Jordel fell in the Greatrocks, passing from this world to the next. We have carried on in his memory."

It was not that Kal moved, or made a face at her words. In fact no muscle in his great body so much as twitched. Yet she saw the words strike him like a hammer blow, turmoil raging in his eyes, though he made no sound. Indeed, he gave no sign that he had heard her at all. Then finally, at last, he reached out and took the badge from her hand, gently, as though lifting a babe from her arms.

"Sheathe your blades," he said. The air whispered with steel again, and in a blink the Mystics were standing at attention, any hint of threat vanished. Even the woman in the back had loosed her hold on her magic.

For a long while Kal looked at the badge in his hand, turning it over and over in the firelight. Then he thrust it back out towards Loren, where it lay in the palm of his hand. She reached out to take it, and put it in the same pocket where she had carried it all this way.

"Very well, Loren of the family Nelda," said Kal in a gruff voice—gruff, but soft at the same time. "Come and sit. It seems we must have words, and not a few of them, I wager."

TWENTY-THREE

KAL BROUGHT THEM TO A SMALL TABLE IN THE CABIN, WHICH LOREN quickly guessed was his own. There were only two seats besides his, so she took one and gave the other to Xain. The children and Chet sat around the edges of the room, on the floor. Two of the Mystic swordsmen remained, as well as the wizard, but all the fight seemed to have gone out of them.

"I was Jordel's master," said Kal. "Taught him from a young pup, I did. And when he took his knighthood and went on his journeys, I would often command his stronghold of Ammon in his stead."

"Ammon!" said Loren in surprise. "But that is where we are bound."

"So I guessed," said Kal. "I thought nothing of it when I had not heard from Jordel for some time, for often his duties would take him far, and word takes time to travel. Then I heard he was exiled by our order. Still I feared to leave Ammon, for I thought he would make his way there, and I wanted to be there when he returned. But when more weeks passed, and still I got nothing so much as a letter, I decided at last to act. Too late, it seems. We left Ammon two weeks ago, and just arrived here. I had put word out through the ship's captain that we sought you, and he recognized you the moment you showed your faces on the dock."

"It was good fortune, then, that we came when we did," said Xain.

"I will call nothing good fortune that begins or ends with the death of Jordel, nor has it somewhere in the middle," Kal snapped. "And I will hear the tale of that now, as quick as you can, girl."

At Kal's urging, and with Xain's help, Loren told him the whole tale of their journey: how she had first met Jordel in Cabrus, and how he had urged her to confide in him from the first. Then she told him of how Jordel had smuggled her out of the city and into the south of Selvan. When she told of how they rejoined Jordel in Wellmont, she stopped and looked warily at Xain.

"I know he is Xain Forredar, and called by some an abomination for eating magestones," said Kal in a brusque tone. "I see also that he suffers from magestone sickness. You may as well carry on with the story, for I suspect that has some part in what took place after."

Still Loren looked to Xain. But he only shrugged, so she went on, keeping nothing back. When she spoke of the magestones, she made the whole thing sound like her idea, hoping to divert some of the blame from Xain. But she could think of no way to gloss over the wizard's madness on the King's road, when he had coated Vivien and the other Mystics in darkfire. Kal's face grew stony at that, and she heard the other Mystics in the room shift. But she barreled on, telling them how Jordel had insisted they spare Xain's life, and then the road they had taken into the Greatrocks.

When she came to the Shade fortress in the mountains, her voice faltered and she bowed her head. But the cabin only sat silent for a moment or two before Kal slapped his hand on top of the table.

"Say on, girl. Do not stop talking for favor of weeping, for you are not so young as all that. There is no shame in grief, only do not get it on my rugs."

So she told him all that they had seen in the mountains, helped here and there by Xain, who had some knowledge of the Shades from what Jordel had told him in Wellmont. They came at last to the battle on the bridge, where Jordel had given his life to stop Trisken. Then she did weep, though she kept telling the tale. Behind her she heard Annis and Gem quietly sobbing together. Even Xain cast his head down in sorrow.

The journey from there she told much more quickly, for she had no great wish to dwell on the death of Wellmont, nor of the villages in the Birchwood and the plains of Dorsea. When she had finished, Kal studied her a long while, obviously displeased.

"These are dark tidings," he muttered under his breath. "Far, far darker than I had imagined."

"Would that they were anything but," said Loren. "They have been a heavy burden, and are delivered at great cost."

"Aye, and too slowly," said Kal. "What madness made you wait in Northwood for so long before you set foot upon the road again?"

Those words were like a punch to Loren's gut, and behind her she heard Chet shifting where he sat. But Kal raised a hand to wave off their hurt looks.

"Spare me your doe's eyes. What is done is done, and no use in anyone harping on about it—even me. Only you cannot blame me for wishing I had known of this sooner."

"Jordel always urged us to haste," Loren said quietly. "I should have heeded those words, even after he was no longer there to say them."

Kal's fist clenched on the table, and he rapped his knuckles twice in quick succession against the wood. It was a moment before his muscles relaxed, and looked as though he did it with great effort.

"Jordel was a bright and eager young knight, and it was my job to teach him to hunt mages."

Xain stiffened beside her at that. Loren saw the Mystic wizard sit up a bit straighter, eyeing Xain suspiciously. But Kal went on with the story as though he had not noticed, and only a glitter in his eye told her that in fact he had.

"I have never been called aught but a hard man. That is what is best for the soldiers in a commander's care, and anyone who says different will have corpses on their conscience. Jordel took it as well as any mage hunter I have trained before or since, and never once a hint of insubordination. And more, when I would tear apart one of his fellows for being a blamed idiot, Jordel would take them aside afterwards. He would piece them back when I had shattered their fragile pride into splinters. He had a way of making the soldiers feel they could succeed, that they could become mage hunters even when I knew they never could. But once in a while—a long, long while, mind you—he was right, and I was wrong."

He shifted to lean forwards in his chair, planting his elbows on the table and glowering at all of them. "And now I am saddled with his latest flock of novices. What is more, we have a task that is likely too great for me, and certainly too great for the likes of you. Yet we have little choice but to use what strength we have. And the appearance of the Shades may prove a boon. Mayhap now, at least, my useless compatriots will get off their arses long enough to do what they have been meant to do for centuries."

Loren balked at that, and looked uncertainly at Xain. But he seemed just as confused as she was. "Who do you mean?" she said.

"Why, the other Mystics, of course," growled Kal. "Useless layabouts though they are, now that we have some proof, mayhap they can trouble themselves to lift a finger where they never could before."

"I have met many Mystics," said Loren. "Never one I would call a layabout."

"Oh, they get riled up enough when they think a wizard has taken magestones," said Kal. He was fairly spitting now in his disdain. "But they have all but forgotten our purpose—the very purpose that drove Jordel, and which brings you here now. Even the so-called greatest among them, the ones who imagine themselves my superiors, would sooner bury their heads in palace intrigue than seek to find the dark master."

Loren shuddered at the word. "You mean the Necromancer."

"Aye, that one," said Kal. "The dark master, the lord of death, and a thousand other prettier names that they have worn through the ages. For more than a score of years I have warned of their return, and never will anyone listen. Mayhap now that will change."

He sat up straighter, and reached for a flask that hung on a strap from the wall. The stopper came out in his hand, and he took a long pull. "Right. You lot have got more road ahead of you, though less than you have left behind. You will be the ones to bring warning of the Shades to the lord chancellor—fop that he is—and the High King."

"What?" said Loren, incredulous. Beside her, Xain looked ready to fall from his chair. "What makes you think they will listen to us above you?"

Kal's frown, which Loren was already learning was perpetual, deepened. "For one thing, I have no time to sail for the Seat. Now that I have learned of Jordel's fate, I must return to Ammon with all possible speed. Our actions in the northern kingdoms must be coordinated, in Dulmun most of all. It is the oldest kingdom, and likely our greatest point of strength if indeed the Shades should make open war. Moreover, every redcloak at my command must be dispatched, at once, to find where the Shades may be gathering in strength. Worst in all this news is that they have been able to accomplish that, and all of us unaware of it. That speaks to traitors within our ranks, and rooting them out will be a dark business."

"The lord chancellor will never give us an audience," said Loren.

"He will if I tell him to," said Kal. "But such audience would be useless. He would still never raise the Mystics to war. Not unless the High King herself commanded it."

"And there you speak madness," said Xain with a harsh laugh. "If an audience with the lord chancellor will be hard to come by, one with the High King will be impossible. Not unless you wish to see my head on a spike on her palace wall, and our tale still untold."

Kal's mouth twisted in a grim smile—an expression that looked utterly alien there, and made Loren squirm in her seat. "Yet that is the great beauty of it. Who better than you, Xain Forredar, to get the High King's attention? Doubtless you will be brought straight to her throne room if you show your face upon the Seat. It is a much faster route than any other courtier, who would have to wait weeks or months for a meeting."

"They will kill him," said Loren angrily. "And then what help will he be to your cause?"

But to her surprise, she saw a grim resolution settle on Xain's face. He sat straighter in his seat, and his hands were steady on the table.

"He sees it. Here, boy, drink up," said Kal, and he slid his flask into Xain's hand. The wizard took a long drink. "I think you have little reason to fear, girl. Those who hate Xain upon the Seat are many—the dean and the lord chancellor among them—but rumor has it the High King is not among their number. She may have issued the decree for his arrest, but she has put no word in writing calling for his death. That was done by the Academy when that young whelp Vivien told them about the magestones."

"You guess that the High King will pardon him?" said Loren with a snort. "That is quite a risk to take—and with someone else's life, I might add."

Xain dropped the flask on the table with a sharp *clack*. "Yet it is a risk I will take."

Loren stared at him, incredulous. "Xain, you cannot be serious."

"I am, Loren. Kal is right—it is the fastest way to see the High

King. There, I will be able to tell her my tale. Whatever may happen afterwards is not important."

"It is important!" Loren cried. "I did not drag your wasted hide across all of Selvan and half of Dorsea only to see you throw your life away now. And what of your son, Xain? Have you lost all hope of recovering him?"

He stared at her, his eyes cold and dark. "Do not dangle my son before me in hopes of changing my will," he said, voice harsh. "There are duties higher than even the bonds of family, and the promise made to a dying friend is one such. Especially when that promise was made in payment of sins forgiven."

His anger left him as suddenly as it had come, like a thunderstorm vanishing from the summer sky. "By my hands many have burned," he said, quiet now. "Jordel forgave me that, though the ones I slew were his brothers and sisters. Now I must earn that forgiveness. And if fortune smiles, mayhap Enalyn will at least let me see my son. One last time, at least, before the end."

TWENTY-FOUR

As Kal told them often and loudly, they had little time to waste. Still, he allowed them one day on the ship to recover from the road. Besides, the *Long Claw* needed to be restocked for the voyage, while Kal had his own plans to make for the return to Ammon.

"I shall be taking another ship," he told them. "No use delaying my own passage home just to go to the Seat, when there is much work to be done back at the stronghold."

With them he was sending four Mystics—good soldiers, he said, ones he trusted. From what she had seen of him so far, Loren thought that his trust did not come lightly, and was grateful for his offer. He brought the Mystics by later on the same day they had arrived, while they were preparing themselves to sleep in the cabins belowdecks.

Three of them Loren recognized from Kal's cabin, though when she had seen them first, they had been behind swords. Their leader was a man named Erik. He was a hale warrior, with red hair and a beard almost as great as Kal's own. With him were a huge young man named Jormund and a woman named Gwenyth. Though Erik spoke easily enough, and in fact was far more polite than Kal, the other two hardly said a word when they were introduced.

The fourth Mystic was another mage, a woman named Weath, who Kal told them was an alchemist. Almost from the start, she and Xain fell into animated conversation. Among a blur of words Loren hardly understood, she gathered that they had attended the Academy at around the same time, though Weath had completed her training with the Mystics. But they soon excused themselves to continue their conversation elsewhere—or rather, they were forced to leave when Erik nearly threw them out of the room.

Erik then sat with Loren and shared with her a bottle of wine, for he had many questions. In particular, he wanted to know of the Shades: their strength and the composition of their troops, their strategies and any weaknesses he might exploit. Loren felt that she was little help, for she had no mind for warfare or strategy. But when she told him of Trisken, and the man's ability to cheat even mortal blows, Erik took a great interest.

"It was the tattoo on his neck," Loren explained. "It held some dark enchantment. I would wager the Necromancer put it there, for it had the power to stay death itself. But when Jordel destroyed the tattoo, Trisken could at last be killed."

"And you say it was on the back of the neck?" said Erik. "Do they always place it there?"

"I do not know for certain," said Loren. "But Rogan, another man like Trisken, goes to battle with mail hanging from his helmet, which protects the same area. It seems a safe wager."

"You are certain Rogan has the same power?"

"I shot him in the hip with an arrow. He snapped the shaft off as it if were a fly's bite, and came for me again." Loren shuddered at the memory, and at the baleful look she remembered in his eye.

"I have seen men do much the same in battle when their blood is up," said Erik.

"Not like this, I promise you," Loren assured him.

Whenever he paused to think of more questions, Loren asked him about himself and the others with him. She learned he bore the title of knight. But when she asked if that was true of the other Mystic warriors she had met, he shook his head.

"The greater part of Mystics are simply that—Mystics. They follow orders and fight at the command of others. In time they may be promoted to a knight, like myself, and then to the rank of captain. Captains answer to chancellors, who answer to one grand chancellor in each kingdom, who answer only to the lord chancellor himself. The lord chancellor answers to no one, save the High King."

The others bore no rank—not even Weath. That confused Loren, for it seemed a wizard such as she would be more than a match for Erik in battle, even if he was a mighty warrior.

"It is not only strength in battle that determines worthiness of rank," said Erik. "If that were so, the lord chancellor should never have risen to his position. That one is no warrior."

"How did he rise, then?" said Loren.

Erik looked around, though no one else had come into the room since they began speaking. "There are many rumors, and little known for certain. But he hails from the family Drayden, and their influence is powerful in the nine lands. The dean of the Academy hails from that black clan as well."

Loren shuddered, for she had heard that before. Annis, whose family of Yerrin was fearsome enough, had feared to do more than whisper at the dark machinations of the Draydens.

When at last Erik had exhausted his questions, and Loren had no more for him in return, he took his leave. Loren found herself alone in her cabin, for Gem and Chet had gone to the deck, while Xain and Annis had left her some time ago. She rose from her seat, pacing back and forth. There were two hard decisions to be made, and they had weighed heavily on her ever since Kal had first told her of his plan.

Just as she had made up her mind to go and put her thoughts to action, there was a sharp rap at her door. Before she could answer, it swung open to reveal Chet. His face was troubled, and he shut the door silently behind him as he came in. Then he came to stand before her, and though he looked as if he wanted to reach out and take her hands, he did not.

"You mean to go through with this mad plan, then?" he said.

Loren met his gaze and nodded. "I have no choice, Chet."

"We all have a choice. You told me you had a message for the Mystics, a message that might let them save all the nine lands from peril. That message is delivered now, it seems. Yet still you march by their orders."

She found herself annoyed at that, but she let it pass. "The message has not yet reached as far as it must. You heard Kal, and I know you saw the wisdom in his plan. Without the High King's order, the nine lands may wait forever for the Mystics to act."

"Xain is already determined to go and tell her of this, whatever the consequence he himself may face. Yet you, too, are a criminal under the King's law. You might face the same penalty."

"That is unlikely. I would be surprised if word of my doings have even reached the Seat."

Still he did not look satisfied. But Loren had only just mustered the courage to go and do what must be done, and she had no time to console him now.

"I hope you will come with me still," she said. "But I will understand if you wish to wait here. Stay on the coast, and I promise I will return to you the moment the High King has been told of the Shades' threat. I mean to visit Ammon after, if only to see Jordel's home. Beyond that, I have no aims—mayhap we can return to the Birchwood, where I am certain your father awaits your homecoming."

"Would that I could believe that," he murmured, looking past her as his eyes grew far away.

"I believe it. But now I must go and speak to Annis. You need decide nothing until tomorrow."

She moved past him. At the last second his hand jerked out to brush against hers, and she let her fingers trail against his for a moment longer than she needed to.

Upon the ship's main deck she found Annis. The girl sat on a large coiled rope, which formed a perfectly sized seat. She was watching Gem, who had somehow persuaded one of the Mystics to practice his swordplay with him. The boy had stripped down to the waist, and his bare feet danced upon the planks of the boat while he swung back and forth with his blade.

Though her mind had been made up, she quailed the moment she saw Annis sitting there. The girl looked up and saw her, and in her smile Loren saw the same quiet panic she herself felt. So rather than speak, she only sat next to Annis on the deck, and together they watched.

Gem's weeks of practice seemed to have paid off, for he matched the Mystic blow for blow. The man was one Loren had not yet been introduced to, but he was thin and wispy, and seemed a perfect match for Gem's small frame. Only now that she watched him, Loren saw that his frame was not so small as it had once been. In the months since she had met him, he had shot up like a beanstalk. And from all their many adventures, as well as the sword practice that he had thrown himself into after Jordel died, thin and sinewy muscle had developed where once there had been only skin clinging faithfully to bones.

She looked to Annis by her side, and saw that the merchant's daughter, too, was no longer the child she had been when first she had met Loren. She was neither so plump nor so short as she had once been. And her eyes as they watched Gem showed something Loren recognized, something that might not yet be womanly, but was not entirely childish, either. It was a disconcerting feeling, to recognize that two people she held to be her closest friends in all the world should have grown so much in such a short space of time, and she herself hardly recognizing it.

Annis caught her looking and blushed, turning her eyes away from Gem as he practiced. "Am I staring so boldly?" she said. "I do not mean to—you probably think me a fool."

"Sometimes you can be," said Loren, nudging the girl's knee. "But not just now."

Annis slapped her hand, but the girl's smile could not banish all anxiety from her eyes. She opened her mouth as if to speak but then closed it again. When she finally found her voice, Loren could tell the words were not the ones she most wanted—and needed—to say.

"What do you think I should do? About Gem, I mean."

Loren shrugged. "Whatever you wish. Your feelings are your own."

"You could give me *some* advice. After all, you and Chet . . ."

Loren felt her cheeks burn just a bit. "That is not the same. We have known each other all our lives, and Chet wished to marry me for years. You and Gem only met a little while ago, though indeed it seems much longer." Her smile dampened, and she spoke more softly. "But I do not think that is what chiefly troubles you, Annis."

For a few moments the girl attempted to feign ignorance, but the mask soon fell. She hung her head, her thick black hair cast down about her face. "No, it is not."

"We are going to the Seat," Loren prodded. "From all that you have told me, many of your family are there as well, and even more of their agents. For all we know, Damaris herself might have returned by now."

"I doubt that," Annis said quickly. "I do not think the Seat is much safer for her than it is for me just now, if indeed the Shades' influence reaches so far as it seems."

"And yet . . ."

"And yet."

"If you wish to come with us, you may, of course. But I cannot see that as a wise choice, though it breaks my heart to say it."

Tears sprang into Annis' eyes, which she tried to keep fixed on Gem. "I do not wish to be parted from you all. I told you as much in the Greatrocks. I tell you again now."

"And it is the last thing in the world I would wish for. But this is not forever, or even for very long—only until we have done our duty there, and can return to you."

Annis barely held back a sob, and turned it to a sniff instead. "But you will take Gem."

"Gem will not be hunted high and low by his family, for he has none."

"What do you mean to do with me, then?"

"Nothing without your agreement," said Loren. "I tried before to make such arrangements without asking you. I will never do that again."

"You know my meaning," said Annis. "Where would I go?"

"With Kal, I think. I will ask him to take you to Ammon. I can scarcely imagine a safer place for you in all the nine lands. And I mean to make my way there in any case, once we leave the Seat. There I will find you again, and together we will set forth upon the road once more."

"Do you promise me this, Loren? You will not abandon me there and go your own way?"

Loren snatched her hands and pulled her down to sit on the deck so that they were facing each other. "I swear it by the sky above and the darkness below. When I sent you on ahead of me in Cabrus, I did not stop searching until I had found you again. When Xain was seized by madness and took you from me, I found you and plucked you from his lair. Hear me now: I will come for you in Ammon as soon as I may. You are my dearest friend, Annis of the family Yerrin."

"You are more than a friend," said Annis, who could no longer keep her tears within. "You are my sister—nearer to me than blood, and twice as dear." And she fell forwards to throw herself into Loren's arms, letting her tears spill silently down. Loren kept her own from falling—but only just.

TWENTY-FIVE

THEY ALL SPENT A RESTLESS AND FITFUL NIGHT ON THE BOAT. LOREN had not slept well when they sailed on the riverboat along the Dragon's Tail, and she found it no easier on a ship so large. Almost she thought to go into the town and find herself an inn for the night. But she feared discovery by the Shades, and Annis would have been distraught besides. The girl spent the night in Loren's bed, curled up to her like a pup to its mother, and seemed to have no trouble with her slumber. So Loren stayed, waking in fits and starts, and when morning dawned she was miserable.

She had spoken with Kal the night before, and to her surprise he had agreed easily to the idea of taking Annis with him. "It is a sensible choice, and one I am surprised to hear the two of you make," he said curtly. "Mayhap Jordel saw something of worth in you after all. I cannot promise you the girl will enjoy Ammon, but neither will she starve there. I shall put her to work."

So, on the deck of the *Long Claw*, they bid each other farewell just after dawn. Annis would scarcely let go of her, although she no longer wept. Then she said her good-bye to Chet, which was somewhat awkward for the both of them, and then to Xain, which was somewhat cool, for Annis could not entirely forget the way he had acted in the battle of Wellmont, or after. Gem she saved for last, and Loren half expected some grand confession to spring from the girl's mouth. But she only held him close, and made him promise to come for her when he could. Gem, for his part, seemed mostly confused, and said of course he would be with Loren when they all came to fetch her.

Annis watched them go from the dock, and stood waving until she was out of sight. Probably, Loren guessed, she stayed there long afterwards, until she could no longer see her friends, but only the thick black dot of the ship growing smaller and smaller upon the sea. Some time after, she would no doubt shuffle halfheartedly onto Kal's vessel, there to take passage with him to Dulmun and complete their journey to Ammon.

"Do you think she behaved at all oddly?" said Gem. "It was as though she feared we would never come for her. And twice I thought she meant to say something to me, but both times she closed her mouth again."

Loren rolled her eyes and turned away from him. That was not a conversation she was at all prepared to begin.

She returned to her cabin once they were upon the water, and there rested upon the pallet that Captain Torik had provided for her, trying to recapture some of the sleep she had missed in the night. But if sleep had been hard when the ship was docked at night, it was much harder under sail when the waves tossed them back and forth. After an hour of fruitless trying, there came a knock at her door, and Xain let himself inside.

"There is something we must discuss before we reach the Seat," he said. "I have only just thought of it. It concerns your dagger."

Loren blanched, reaching for its hilt. "Sky above. I did not think of it."

"I thought not. You cannot march into the High King's palace with it. It could spell the very end of the Mystics."

"What must I do, then?" said Loren, fear rising thick in her throat. "There is little between here and there save the open water. Must I cast it into the waves?"

He smirked. "Not quite. I have a friend upon the Seat, someone in whom I have the utmost trust. He will take care of your dagger for you, holding it out of sight and out of mind until you come to reclaim it."

She let loose a great sigh of relief. "That is well. But what if I never do return? You cannot have forgotten that that is a distinct possibility."

"Indeed I have not. In that case, he will sail out into the Bay and cast the dagger into the water. I do not think you will miss it, if it comes to that."

Her smile was weaker than she meant it to be. But just then, she heard pounding steps in the hallway outside, and Chet burst into her room.

"Loren!" he cried. "Come quickly! It is the Seat!"

She stood from the edge of the bed and went up to the deck with him, Xain hobbling along more slowly. Seizing her hand, which no longer felt so strange to her as it once had, Chet took her to the railing near the prow.

There sat the High King's Seat, like the prize jewel in a great crown made all of sapphire. It shone in the midday sun, golden and bright and glistening like a dewdrop. Even from so far, at the edge of vision, it took Loren's breath away. Beside her she saw Chet and Gem's mouths hanging open in awe, and realized with a start that her own mouth gaped wide as well.

The closer they drew to it, the more it dazzled her. Soon she saw golden spires shooting up from the white stone walls that bordered the whole island. A tower that looked to be made of silver stuck up like an arrow from the back of a practice target. Perfectly cylindrical, it caught the sun's rays from every direction and flung them into their eyes, so that they could scarcely bear to look at its splendor. And from every battlement, rampart and tower flew the many banners of the high kingdom, blue and green and red and gold all together, fluttering in the wind like the feathers of some great bird.

Loren looked over at last to find Xain standing there, observing them all with clear enjoyment of their dumbfounded excitement. "Welcome to the High King's Seat, Loren of the family Nelda," he said. "I hardly thought I would ever come here with you. Yet it pleases my heart to see the look it puts upon your face, nonetheless."

"You lived here?" said Loren. "How did you ever go about your life? If I lived upon the Seat, I could do nothing but walk around and look at it all. I have heard tales and stories aplenty, but it is ten times better than any of them."

"It wears on the senses soon enough," he said, his tone a bit darker than before. "I am certain you will soon find yourself as weary of it as I was when I left."

He drew up his hood as they sailed closer. The dock itself was a masterpiece. Loren had seen docks before, but only of wood and never of stone. The ships she saw moored there were more grand even than the *Long Claw*, their masts reaching for the sun.

Torik skillfully guided his ship into the port, and in no time his crew had lashed it to the moorings. Then they all followed Xain and threw up their hoods, setting off down the pier and into the streets of the Seat.

The city was not paved in gold, as Loren had heard, but with fine white cobblestones that were perfectly fitted and sealed together, and then worn flat by some craft she did not know. Few people were on foot. Many constables rode horses, and royalty or wealthy merchants rode in fine carriages. Some craftsmen drove wagons, but even those were of far finer make than anything she had seen on the streets of Selvan's cities. Every building was of stone, none of wood, and each was an exquisite display of craftsmanship. Even a butcher's shop was no lowly venue; burning braziers hung outside above the door, and their pungent, sweet aroma banished the normal charnel stink.

Erik marched before them with Weath, and the other two Mystics behind, so that most passersby gave them a wide berth. Their steps took them towards the High King's palace at first, but Xain tugged at Erik's sleeve for a quick word.

"We have one burden we must deliver first. Do you know the way to Aurel's smithy?"

"I do not," said Erik.

"Then follow me, and closely."

He turned them to the left, so that they began to move around the palace in a wide circle. The streets were well-ordered, and in no time they stood before a fine-looking shop with a low, red door made of wood. Above it hung a sign with the mark of a silversmith burned into it. The door stood open, but Xain took them around to the back of the building, where a more modest service entrance awaited.

He rapped sharply on the door, and they had to wait only a moment before it swung open. Behind the door stood a thin little man, his grey hair sticking out in all directions, spindly hands clutching each other in curiosity. When he saw the four redcloaks waiting outside, Loren saw him square his shoulders.

"What is this about?" he said. "What service can I be to the Mystics this day?"

"Not to them, old friend," said Xain, and he threw back his hood. "But to me."

The man looked as though sheer surprise might strike him dead on the spot. He rushed forwards, eyes watering up, and clutched the front of Xain's cloak. "Xain! Xain, is it truly you? I never thought to look upon you with my own two eyes again." Then he recoiled, not in fear, but to look around in sudden suspicion. "But my boy . . . you must know the island is not a safe place for you. Come, come inside, and quickly."

"No time for that, Aurel. I have a burden I must ask you to bear, for a little while at least. It is for the girl here."

"A . . . a burden?" said Aurel, blinking at Loren as though he could not quite see her.

"You must keep it hidden from all eyes, even your own," said Xain. "If all goes well, she shall be back to fetch it presently. If not—if you hear that anything has happened to us, or if you hear nothing at all for a month—you must take it into the middle of the bay and drop it into the waters."

"Of course, my boy, of course." And though the old man's eyes burned with curiosity, he ushered Loren inside. Xain waited on the street for her, raising his hood once more.

"Do you have a box I can put it in?" said Loren, reaching for her belt.

"Yes, my dear, of course. Take your pick," said Aurel, gesturing around. Loren found herself in his workshop, with many tools lying about on benches and tables, as well as many crafts in progress—everything from serving platters to buckles to fine pins with exquisite designs. And against one whole wall was stacked a massive mountain of boxes. Loren chose one and pulled dagger and sheath from her belt to drop them inside. Then, struck by a thought, she reached into her cloak and drew out the packet of magestones. They joined the dagger at the bottom of the box. She would no sooner be discovered with them than with the dagger, after all, and both could spell her death within the High King's halls.

She closed the box again, twisting the little silver latch on the front, and then placed it in Aurel's hands. He blinked at her again, then stared down at the box, hefting the weight.

"I can keep it in my floor easily enough," he said. "And rest assured, girl, no harm will come to it. I shall not even look inside myself, that I vow."

"Thank you," said Loren, bowing low to him. That seemed to surprise him, and in his haste to return the bow, he nearly dropped the box.

Soon she had rejoined Xain on the street. But before they set off, the wizard drew close to Aurel and spoke quiet words in his ear. But not quiet enough, for Loren overheard much of them.

"I do not think I go to my doom, Aurel. Yet I cannot see all ends. If things should go poorly, I would have you send a message."

"I think I know it, my boy."

"Still, I will tell you. Send word of my love—and my death—to Trill, whatever you must do to find her."

"Of course, Xain. Of course. Only, do not place such a burden on an old man. Return here, and send the message yourself."

"If fate be kind."

Then Xain pushed past her in a rush, face hidden within his cowl again. Loren followed, cautiously, not wishing to upset him any further. Trill was the name of Jordel's sister, and the Mystic had told Loren how she and Xain had fallen in love. Trill was the mother of his son, but she had been married off to another man after their child was born, and Xain had not seen her since.

Now Xain marched like a man possessed, and even the Mystics struggled to keep up with him. Through the streets he passed like a returning prince, and indeed mayhap he was such in his own mind. He stepped in front of carriages and horses without heeding them, and more than one reared at his coming. Everywhere he went, heads turned to watch, though they could not see his face beneath his hood.

Soon the walls of the High King's palace loomed before them, though its splendor was somewhat lost on Loren. They were near the end of their road now, or might be, and the fear of what they might find dimmed the sight of the place. Still, she could not help but notice the high walls trimmed with gold, and the fine white stone that made the black battlements stand out all the more.

A guard stood before the gate, clad in the white and gold armor of the High King herself. She took one look at Xain, and Loren and Chet and Gem beside him in their plain clothes, and raised her spear to cross it over her chest. "Begone, beggars," she said. "There are kitchens aplenty for you, by the High King's charity. That is where you will find your next meal, not here."

Xain's bitter laugh poured out from beneath his brown hood. "Ah,

Sera, you old fool. Do not tell me you have forgotten the sight of a friend so quickly." And he threw back his hood to show the guard his face.

Many things happened then, and all of them quickly. The guard nearly froze in her shock, but kept just enough composure to call the alarm. Then many more guards rushed out of the gates, surrounding Loren and the rest of them with sharp spears. They were grabbed firmly, their hands tied behind their backs—even the Mystics—and then they were marched through the gates and into the palace, prisoners at the High King's mercy.

TWENTY-SIX

LOREN WAS DRAGGED THROUGH THE HIGH KING'S PALACE SO QUICKLY that her feet scarcely touched the floor. She could not see the beauty of the high, vaulted ceilings or the mural-covered walls, for her mind was filled with dread of what might lay ahead. The elegance that surrounded them barely registered in her mind, something noticed only by instinct, stowed away to be examined later—if she would have any time later to think of it, and was not put to death at once.

Beside her, Xain seemed frighteningly calm. Indeed, a grim smile played across his lips beneath his gag—for the guards knew he was a firemage, and had taken steps to remove him from his power. Loren thought she might be able to guess at the reason for his high mood; since before they first met, he had been a fugitive from the King's justice, fleeing from city to city and kingdom to kingdom to evade punishment for his crimes. Now at last that flight had come to an end. One way or another, Xain's days of running were over.

They came soon to the doors of the throne room, which lay open. Guards raised their polearms to let the procession through. These wore more splendid armor than the guards at the front gate, their plate gleaming with white enamel and trim bedecked in gold leaf. Their eyes were harder, and Loren could see the strength in their frames. They looked upon her with contempt as she passed.

The throne room was so wondrous that it dragged her mind to the present, as if the place itself were impatient for her to notice its finery. Pillars rose high to form arches along the walls, and the arches rose up until they joined in points that ran all along the center of the roof. From each point sprang golden spikes that ran across the white marble ceiling, like starbursts all in a row. They shrank in size from the entrance to the rear of the room, descending to the far wall so that they formed a sort of arrow, commanding the eye to look at the throne upon its dais.

Upon that throne sat the High King Enalyn. Loren had never had cause to see the High King, but she had heard many descriptions—and in any case, there was no mistaking her now, for no one else would dare to sit in that high chair. It was made of silver, with gold for the armrests and surrounding the head, and cushioned in plush white cloth. Enalyn sat in a pose of rest, one arm draped over the throne's right side, while her other elbow was propped up so that her chin might rest on her fist. She was a slight woman of no impressive height, but her gaze was keen and piercing. A thin golden circlet rested upon her hair, which had once been as raven-black as Loren's own, but now showed many strands of grey. Rather than any appearance of old age, it only gave her a mighty dignity that radiated through the room.

It was quite a long moment before Loren could tear her eyes away from the High King to see the others in the room. Many guards there were, in the same fine white and gold of the royal guard that she had seen at the throne room door. Then there were the courtiers, clustered in their splendid suits and gowns all along the sides of the hall. She also saw quite a number of Mystics in attendance, their red cloaks marking them as certainly as the badges upon their chests. But where all the Mystics she had seen before wore armor, and tended to look somewhat threadbare, like breeches worn from many months of hard travel, these ones were as clean and well-kept as the courtiers themselves. It was somewhat of a shock to Loren to see them wearing patterned breeches and tunics, and draped in cloaks of fine cloth and fur that she would have laughed to see upon Jordel.

They came to a stop at the foot of the dais. Loren raised her gaze to the High King—and then she noticed the two men standing to either side of her. One wore a red cloak over a suit of armor that looked more ceremonial than functional, and Loren took him at once for the lord chancellor of the Mystics. The other man wore grand, ornate robes of black with silver-threaded trim, and curious designs embroidered with gold and purple. That, and the hateful way he glared at Xain, led her to guess he must be the dean of the Academy.

A sharp kick from a plated boot made Loren's legs give out, and she fell to her knees before the throne. The guard who had met them outside the palace stepped forth, helm under her elbow, and spoke sharply to announce them.

"Your Majesty. I bring before you Xain, of the family Forredar, criminal beyond the King's law, sentenced to death by order of the Mystics."

"I see him, Sera," said the High King. Her tone was neither condescending nor sharp, but Loren thought she heard the hint of a joke inside it. "And who are these others you drag in his wake?"

"We do not know them, Your Majesty, but they came in his company."

Loren looked up to see the High King wave a hand, and Sera stepped back. "You may speak for yourselves then, travelers. Who are you, and why do you walk in the company of this wizard? Come, you Mystics. Speak up."

Erik looked up doubtfully from where he knelt. When no one seemed likely to shove him back down, he lifted one foot to plant it flat on the floor and then laid his arm across the knee, in the position of a soldier reporting to a battlefield commander. "Your Majesty. I am Erik, knight of the Mystics. You do me great honor—but this girl, in the black cloak, is the one who should speak for us."

Loren's stomach did a somersault at that, and stars danced before her eyes as the High King turned to look at her with one eyebrow arched. Titters and excited murmurs burst from all the courtiers in the room, who whispered to each other behind their hands.

"Indeed?" said the High King, and now her voice betrayed real interest. "I find myself curious why a Mystic would cede the floor to one so young. Unless she is from some noble family, and I do not know it?"

Loren looked sideways, panicked. Xain only raised his eyebrows at her. She shot to her feet and raised her head—then, mortified, she realized where she was and fell back to one knee. The courtiers burst into subdued laughter.

"No noble girl, then, I take it," said High King Enalyn, but her voice was not unkind.

"No, Your Gra—Your Majesty," said Loren quickly. "I am Loren, of the family Nelda, hailing from the Birchwood."

"A forest girl," said Enalyn. "Tell me, Loren. Why do your words hold more weight in this room than a knight of the Mystics?"

Loren reached into her cloak and withdrew the letter from Kal. "Your Majesty, I . . . I bring a letter."

Enalyn looked to Sera, who took the letter from Loren's hand and gave it to one of the royal guard. The man climbed the dais to place it in the lord chancellor's hand. The lord chancellor was a spidery man, with spidery fingers, and Loren did not like the grimace on his face as he pried loose Kal's wax seal. Though he hardly paused before speaking aloud, Loren saw his eyes flit quickly back and forth across the paper, taking in the message before he spoke.

"She bears a letter from Chancellor Kal, of the family Endil. It declares that these travelers bear grave news of utmost importance to all the nine kingdoms, for the ears of the High King and her closest advisors only."

"This is a gesture so haughty as to be almost offensive," said the dean from Enalyn's other side. "Lord Chancellor, can you not keep your own Mystics in better order than this?"

"This was done without my knowledge or consent, of course, Your Majesty," said the lord chancellor, who looked as though he very much wanted to burn the letter in his hands, and mayhap the Mystics at the foot of the dais as well. "Please, allow me to remove this matter to my own chambers, and deal with it there where it need not trouble you."

"The Mystics may be your concern, but Xain is not," said High King Enalyn, her voice just sharp enough to bring the throne room to complete silence. "It was I who issued the order for his arrest—an arrest that your men have failed to carry out all these long months. Now he comes to the throne room of his own accord, bearing a letter from one of your chancellors. I think I shall pay it heed."

She nodded to one of the royal guard, and he moved quickly to clear the throne room. In no time it was done; the only ones who remained were Loren's party, the lord chancellor, the dean, and the royal guard.

"Now, Loren," said Enalyn, and once again Loren's heart skipped a beat at hearing her own name. "Tell me this grave news that threatens all my domain. And for goodness' sake, stand as you tell me, for the top of your head is not nearly so comely as those remarkable green eyes."

Loren swallowed hard, and found for a moment that her legs had failed her utterly. But at last they heard her command, and she forced herself to stand.

"Your Majesty. I have come . . . that is to say, we have learned . . ." She faltered, for the words would not come, no matter how hard she tried to muster them.

Enalyn leaned forwards, clasping her hands in her lap. "You need not worry at your choice of words," she said gently. "Nor for how they will sound. If it helps, simply say it as plainly as possible. And worry not, for you are not the first to find your tongue tied in this room. Indeed, that was mayhap the greatest purpose of its design."

Loren smiled at that, if weakly, and cleared her throat. "Your Majesty. The Shades have returned, and the Necromancer with them, after many centuries. Even now they muster to make war upon all the nine lands. We found them in the Greatrock Mountains, and they have pursued my friends, and myself, ever since."

The High King's eyes flashed. But at her side, the lord chancellor only scoffed. "She comes here barking the words Kal has taught to her. He has said much the same thing to me, and many times over the years, as has his pet, Jordel. If he wished to trouble us with this nonsense, he could simply have sent a letter and saved us all much trouble."

Against her good judgement, Loren found wrath rising hot in her breast, and not the least at the lord chancellor's use of the word *pet* to describe Jordel, who had been one of the greatest men she had ever known. She spoke almost without thinking, and did nothing to hide her anger. "They *are* real, and they *have* returned. We know, my friends and I, for we have seen them. And Jordel would be here to tell you himself, but he cannot, for he died fighting the Shades, alone save for us, far away in the highest peaks of the Greatrocks. You should consider yourself honored if you ever so much as stood in the same room as such a man."

The room fell silent as death, save for the echo of Loren's own voice rebounding from the walls. The lord chancellor fixed her with a glare, while the dean's mouth sat open in a small *o* of disbelief. But the High King stood from her throne, one hand falling to hold on to it, as if for support. Immediately the lord chancellor and the dean fell to their knees, and Loren dipped her head again.

"Say again, girl. Jordel, of the family Adair, is dead?"

Loren's rage had fled her, and now she found it hard to speak around the lump in her throat. "Yes. He fell in battle, saving our lives at the cost of his own. Our road has been darker ever since. Your Majesty."

Enalyn bowed her head, silent. No one moved, or dared even to breathe too loudly. When the moment passed, she sat again. The lord chancellor rose, as did the dean, although somewhat stiffly.

"Remove Xain's gag," said Enalyn.

"Your Majesty," said the dean quickly. "I urge against that. He is a criminal, and sentenced to death for his crimes. Furthermore, he is an abomination, an eater of magestones. We cannot know that his mind is his own."

Enalyn turned to him, mouth twisted in displeasure. "Look at his gaunt cheeks, his wasted limbs. He is half-dead. Can you, as the dean of the Academy, not protect me and my court from so weak a wizard as this? For if that is the case, I know I would feel more comfortable with a much more powerful wizard holding your position."

The dean glared down at Xain, and there was more than a hint of anxiousness in his look. But he shook his head quickly. "Of course I will, Your Majesty, and it will be my great honor."

"Good," said Enalyn. "Remove it."

A royal guard hastened to obey, and once the cloth was removed, Xain flexed his jaw once or twice until it popped. Loren saw the dean holding his fingers in a claw by his side, lips parted as if ready to strike with magic. But Xain only rose to one knee and looked up at Enalyn—neither with anger, nor with shame. He looked only expectant.

"Did you speak over his grave?" Enalyn asked him.

Loren had not expected that, and by his look neither had Xain. He bowed his head. "No, Your Majesty. None of us could, for the grief of his loss was heavy upon us. But he fell from a bridge that spanned a great chasm, and into the stones of that bridge I inscribed my words."

"Tell me."

Here fell a great man
A clarion trumpet against danger
In darkness where none could see
His name was Jordel

Xain spoke the words as if they were a prayer, and suddenly Loren was back on the bridge by his side. She saw Jordel's mangled body once more, and the cairn they had built him of rocks, and his red cloak, which they had buried him in. She bowed her head, and tears sprang unbidden into her eyes.

Enalyn nodded at Xain when he was finished, a quiet smile on her lips. "That was very like him."

Then she clapped her hands, and it was as if a spell had broken. "Very well," she said. "If you speak the truth, and the Shades are indeed gathering power once more, we must put a stop to it immediately."

"Your Majesty, it would be a mistake to act too quickly upon this," said the lord chancellor. "You would be taking action based on the words of a known traitor and criminal, witnessed only by street urchins and children of whom we have never heard."

"They came escorted by four of your soldiers," said Enalyn.

"Soldiers who will receive appropriate discipline," said the lord chancellor, staring daggers at the Mystics, who studiously avoided his gaze.

"I fear I must confess myself still in mystery," said the dean, eyes narrowed as he looked from Xain to Loren and back again. "Who are these people the girl speaks of?"

"Time enough for a history lesson later," said the lord chancellor. "For now, I recommend that we rid ourselves of these . . . visitors. Your Majesty, with your leave, let us dismiss them and hold an emergency council to determine the best course of action."

"But you cannot mean to simply let Xain go free," said the dean quickly. "He has committed many crimes against the King's law, and must face his punishment."

Enalyn cut him off with a look. "No. At least not yet. If he has returned here of his own free will, then I can at least entertain the possibility that he has atoned for his crimes—or begun to." She turned to Loren and the others. "You will remain here, in the palace. Under guard, I am afraid, for I cannot let Xain roam free any more than I will consign him to a swift and brutal punishment. But you will not face justice until I know what is just, if you take my meaning."

"Your Majesty," said Xain, raising his head. "My son. If I could be permitted—"

But she fixed him with a hard glare, and he subsided. "I have not yet decided what to do with you, Xain. I will not reunite you with your son only to force him to part from you again. That is a cruelty I would visit upon no child, least of all my own kin, however distant."

Xain bowed to her once more, but Loren could see him fuming. The palace guards came forwards, lifted them to their feet, and escorted them towards the throne room door. But just as they turned, Enalyn called out sharply for them to halt.

"Forest girl," she said. "I had heard that a young girl of the family Yerrin was traveling by your side. Was I misinformed?"

Loren found her head spinning at that, for it seemed impossible that the High King should know anything at all about her. But she forced herself to think hard, choosing her words very carefully. "The girl was with us upon our road, but no longer."

Enalyn's head came up slightly, like a dog catching whiff of a scent. "And do you know where she is now?"

"I have some idea where she might be, but not exactly, Your Majesty." That was true enough, she reasoned. She knew Annis was on her way to Ammon, but she knew not where she was on the voyage, and in truth she did not even know where Ammon lay.

The High King nodded, and Loren felt that nod held understanding beyond words. "We will speak more of this. Farewell."

Then the guards' hands were upon her again, and the throne room was soon behind them.

TWENTY-SEVEN

THEY WERE WHISKED THROUGH A SERIES OF SERPENTINE HALLS IN which Loren was soon lost. Erik and the other Mystics were separated and led in another direction before Loren could say farewell. Soon she found herself before a chamber with a great wooden door. Inside were quarters more lavish than any she had seen in her life: in the middle was a large chamber with plush chairs around the walls, as well as an ornate table surrounded by many smaller chairs for eating. Many doors led off from the main room into bedchambers, each one of which was as large as the common rooms of any inn Loren had ever visited. Gem's eyes nearly popped from his skull at the sight of it all, and Chet was struck dumb. But Xain shrugged as he surveyed it.

"They are modest chambers by the palace's standards," he said. "Still, it is better than the prison cell I thought to find myself in."

Outside their door were posted several guards. There were two palace guards, as well as two Mystics—neither of whom had been among the Mystics they arrived with. One of them carried no weapons, and Loren guessed she was a wizard. Then there was a wizard from the Academy, wearing the same type of robes as the dean had worn, though nowhere near as lavish. Each type of guard looked at the other with as much distrust as they gave to Loren and her friends.

They spent all the rest of that day in the chamber. Gem ran about, ruffling the plush pillows and jumping on the beds until he had chosen one for himself. But Loren, Chet and Xain sat in the main room, silent save for the occasional answer to one of Gem's questions. Loren could not forget that, as fine as the quarters were, they were still prisoners, and they had no guarantee of any future safety. It put a damper on any conversation, and that night they went to sleep in their separate rooms with heavy hearts (though Loren still liked the soft feather mattress a great deal more than the hard ground of the road).

The next morning, servants brought them breakfast in the main chamber. There were eggs and sliced ham, and fine juices that Loren did not recognize the taste of. Gem wolfed his meal down, but she and the others ate more slowly. After all, they had nothing to do after they ate, and so there seemed no reason to hurry.

But in the midst of their meal, they heard an animated discussion just outside the door, and one voice in particular speaking very loudly. Then the door was thrown open, and a young man in fine clothing came barreling through. He took one look at them, and then fixed his eyes upon Xain.

"Xain!" he cried. "You mad, mad, *mad* fool. What in all the nine lands ever possessed you to come back to this forsaken island?"

Then he leaped forwards, dragging Xain from his chair and into a tight bear hug. Xain's eyes widened as though the very life were being squeezed from him. Loren and Chet stared at the man in shock. His clothing was nearly as fine as the High King's own, and was gold and white like hers with the same kind of breeches and a fine shirt. But he also wore a coat, and it was silver, and its threads shone in the early morning light that poured through the windows of the east wall.

"Loren, and Chet," said Xain, when the man had finally released him. "May I introduce, with some reservation, the Lord Prince Eamin."

Then Loren felt her throat seize up, and she shot to her feet just as Chet did the same. She wondered briefly if she should kneel, but before she could act upon it, the Lord Prince had her wrist in his hand and was shaking it as though she were a bag filled with coins that he hoped to loosen.

"The girl and the boy from the Birchwood, or so I have heard," said Eamin, and the smile upon his face was brighter than sunlight. "And

156

you will be Gem, of the family . . . was it Noctis? I have never had a gift for names."

Loren thought Gem's smile might split his cheeks and keep running all the way to his ears. "You have mine perfectly, Lord Prince, and so I would call you a liar."

"Gem!" said Loren, gripping his ear tight. The boy squealed, but the Lord Prince laughed and patted his shoulder. But as he looked at Loren properly for the first time, his smile vanished, to be replaced by a look of wonder.

"You . . . Loren, is it? Come here a moment."

Loren looked at Xain uncertainly, but he seemed just as confused as she was. Slowly she stepped towards the Lord Prince. Without warning he took her shoulder with one hand, and with the other he tilted her chin up to look him full in the face. She smelled a faint whiff of perfume on him, pleasant and not at all overpowering, and on his breath was the scent of mint.

"You are touched with Elf-glamour," he said, voice scarcely above a whisper.

She swallowed hard and looked over to Chet. He had looked somewhat annoyed as the Lord Prince drew her so close, but now he seemed concerned.

"Your . . . Your Highness?" said Loren, unsure of what else to say.

"I can see it in your eyes," said Eamin in wonder. "You have had concourse with the Elves. Only once before have I seen such a thing, and the tale behind it is well worth the telling. Speak, child. How came you to meet them? What did they say?"

Loren swallowed hard and looked nervously at Xain. She saw in his eyes the same wonder that was in Eamin's—and also a sort of understanding. He had seen it too, she realized. The day after she met the Elves, he had noticed something different in her eyes, though he knew not what he beheld.

Eamin seemed to think he had frightened her, for he released her shoulder and stepped back quickly. "My apologies. Only I have always been intensely curious about the Elves. It made me forget my manners. Forgive me."

Loren shook her head quickly. "There is nothing to forgive, Your Highness."

"You need not tell me the tale of this if you do not wish it," he said, insistent now. "I pressed too hard, and we have only just met."

"Though I, for one, would like to hear such a story," said Xain.

"Leave it be, Xain," said Eamin in a warning tone, though it was couched in a smile. "Tales of the Elves are things magical and precious, and belong to those who have lived them. If the girl does not wish to speak of it, you must not press her."

"As you say, Your Highness," said Xain. But Loren saw the look in his eyes and wondered how long he would keep that promise.

"Others have often told me I may have some relation to the Elves," Gem piped up, apparently tired of having lost the Lord Prince's attention for so long. "I doubt there is much truth to it, but they must be fooled by my exceptional appearance and cunning wit."

Eamin laughed out loud at that. "City children are such a welcome change from the stuffy sort we always get around here. And foresters, too," he said, beaming a quick smile to Loren and Chet. "Really, anyone who has not spent the last few years upon the Seat is preferable to anyone who has."

"Have I been away long enough to fit in that narrow category?" said Xain with a wry grin.

"Xain, my dear, dear friend, you have never been better company than *anyone* in this thrice-damned place." Eamin gave lie to the words by wrapping him in another embrace. Loren half expected to hear a rib crack. "Now, take your seats again. I am livid that I missed your arrival, and so to make up for it, now you must tell me the tale of all your journeys since you left the Seat."

Loren suddenly found her food bland in her mouth, and her appetite gone. It seemed that all she had done for the past few days was recount the stories of their travels, and she had no wish to do so again. Standing and pushing her chair back, she nodded to Eamin. "Forgive me, Your Highness, but I will take my leave."

He looked up at her with concern. "I hope I have done nothing to offend you."

"Not at all," she said quickly. "Only I lived the tale, and have told it too many times, and have no wish to live through it again."

He nodded, and in his eyes she saw compassion. "Of course. And you need not call me Your Highness—in this room, you need call me nothing more than Eamin."

She bowed again, but could not stop herself from saying, "Thank you, Your Highness."

He smiled, and she left. Chet stood silently to go with her. Gem, however, stayed behind, for his eyes had lit up with glee from the moment he had beheld the Lord Prince.

Loren and Chet went to her room. It had a door set in the back wall, which led out to a wide stone balcony that overlooked a peaceful courtyard. There were chairs in which to sit, but she felt the need to stay on her feet. She went to the railing instead, leaning her elbows upon it and looking at the grounds below. Chet joined her there in silence. A beautiful garden was laid out before them both, and they saw gardeners going about their business among the flowers and the hedges.

"I know we are confined to these quarters," said Chet. "Yet it is hard to feel as though we are being cooped up. Scarcely in my life have I imagined such luxury as this."

But Loren had stopped looking at the garden, and instead she stared away north and east. Beyond the grounds below was the palace's outer wall, and then the city, and then the Great Bay stretching for miles. Somewhere on those waters was Annis. Or mayhap she had landed already in Dulmun, and was on her way to Ammon.

"I wonder how far away she is," Loren said softly. "And in what direction. I hardly spared a thought for her yesterday, but now I find myself missing her far more than I expected."

"She will be safe. I know it."

"You cannot know that for certain."

Chet turned so that he was leaning back against the railing. "But I can. You devised the plan for her safety, and if I have faith in anything in all the nine lands, it is your cleverness."

She gave a wan smile at that, but said no more. They spent a while looking out at the Bay, and then at the courtyard, and when Loren tired at last of standing they went to sit in two of the balcony's chairs. There they rested in the sun and the silence, until the door swung open and Gem came running out to find them. He looked thrilled enough to burst.

"The Lord Prince just left," he said. "Never have I met such a man as he. Always quick with a joke, yet courteous to the border of fault. And Loren, you will not believe this—when I told him of the swordplay Jordel taught me, he promised to join me in practice. I will practice with the Lord Prince! I could never have dreamed of this when I was a starving little boy scuttling along the rooftops and gutters of Cabrus."

Loren smiled at him, and he fawned like a puppy whose ears had been scratched. He ran to the railing and drank deeply of the scent of flowers wafting up from below. But then Loren saw his gaze drift up-wards, just as hers had, until he too was looking out across the Great Bay. He turned to them, seeming somewhat deflated.

"I wish I could tell Annis of this. I miss her."

She felt a pang of sorrow at the look upon his face, and rose from her chair to stand beside him. With one arm around his shoulder, she tried to mask her own worry with an encouraging tone. "I miss her as well. But mayhap we could write her a letter. Not to Annis herself, you understand. But we could write to Kal to tell him of the success of our mission, and include a secret message for her."

Gem perked up at once. "That is a fine idea. I can write it, since I know you have not learned your letters. But where will we find a quill and parchment?"

"Ask the guards at our door," she said. "I think they are under or-ders to provide us with anything we may require."

"Be quick about it, and remain cheerful," said Chet with a smile. "We will soon see her again, for with the Lord Prince at our backs I am certain this will be sorted out in no time."

TWENTY-EIGHT

THEY SOON DISCOVERED THAT CHET'S OPTIMISM WAS, IF NOT FOOLISH, AT least misplaced. Day after day passed, and they received neither word nor summons from the High King. Nor could they leave their quarters, and spacious as those rooms were, Loren felt chafed by them before a week had passed. There were only so many chairs to sit in, so many soft cushions upon which to rest, before she felt she would rather fling herself from the balcony than spend one more day idle within her room. Their pleas to the guards outside their door fell on deaf ears, and even the Lord Prince Eamin grew frustrated. He visited often, and told them that he spoke to the High King every day on their behalf, but to no avail.

"I am on her council," he said, "yet she pays me no more heed than one of the guards standing in the corner. Everyone seems intent on doing nothing more than dragging their feet. Though the dean only learned of the Shades' existence less than a week ago, he acts as if he were the greatest authority in all of Underrealm when it comes to their motives and intentions. When he is not pontificating as to their next probable course of action, he claims that this is all a ruse on Xain's part to distract my mother while he destroys all the nine lands. Meanwhile, the lord chancellor counsels only caution—except that my version of caution would entail investigating the Shades' whereabouts, whereas his version means that we should do nothing."

If the rest of them were anxious for action, Xain was nearly beside himself with impatience. "What of the High King?" he asked, for what seemed to Loren to be the thousandth time. "In which direction does she seem inclined?"

"She withholds her judgement," said Eamin with a sigh. "She is not so shy as the lord chancellor, but neither does she wish to rush into a rash decision."

"There is wise prudence, and then there is indecisiveness," said Chet. "I would call this the latter."

"When your decisions can change the lives of many thousands, you yourself may find much reason for being indecisive," said Eamin. But though he spoke in defense of his mother, Loren could hear the frustration beneath his words. Xain only snorted and stared out the window with a dark expression.

After nine days had passed, the Lord Prince brought them different news altogether. This time he spoke to them in a low voice, leaning across the table with a sidelong glance at the door. "I thought I should tell you that the family Yerrin has been trying desperately to see you—or, I should say, to see Loren in particular."

Loren's throat went dry. Sweat sprang out upon her palms. "What do they want?"

"What do you think?" said Eamin, arching an eyebrow. "They seek the girl Annis. But the High King has forbidden them from obtaining an audience with you. Their representatives grew so insistent that finally she banished them from the palace grounds while you remain here."

"Well, at least that is one worry sorted," said Gem hopefully.

"I would not be so optimistic as to call that the end of it," said Xain.

"Nor I," said Eamin.

"Was it Damaris who was asking after us? Or servants of hers?"

Eamin blinked at her. "I am sorry, I thought you would know—no one has heard from Damaris or her caravan in weeks. Not since the time that you saw her last in the Greatrocks. When you arrived here and told the High King that part of your tale, all the palace chatter about her ceased at once. Either she has fled, knowing the High King would seek justice against her for siding with the Shades, or something else has happened to her that we do not know."

That gave Loren some relief. And at the same time, she found herself wondering after the caravan's fate. She doubted she was so fortunate that she would never hear from Damaris again. But then, she had assumed the merchant was alive. Now that she thought further, it seemed entirely possible that the Shades, or mayhap the Necromancer himself, had taken revenge on Damaris for the disaster in the Greatrocks.

It was a chilling thing to think that Damaris might be dead, and to her surprise she was not entirely certain how she felt about it. Moreover, she did not look forward to telling Annis the news. That would be no matter for a letter; it would have to be done in person, once they left the Seat.

If indeed we ever do leave the Seat, she thought to herself.

It was twelve days since they had arrived at the palace, and evening was working its way towards night. The dying red of sunset filled the sky through the window, and servants had already come to light lanterns throughout the room. The Lord Prince sat with them at their table for supper, and he and Xain were deep in their wine. Loren and Chet had poured themselves each a cup, but Loren found the palace wines too strong for her, and had only sipped gingerly.

Nightfall was the worst time for their mood, for it meant another day had passed without anything happening. Gem was slumped so far down in his chair that he looked like he might fall out of it at any moment. Though the Lord Prince tried to engage Xain in conversation, the wizard stared silently at his plate and hardly moved. Chet tried to smile each time Loren looked at him, but she could see it was forced. She felt, as she had for so many days now, the deep lethargy of their confinement.

There was a sharp sound outside their door. In her distraction, Loren almost did not recognize it, but deep instinct prickled the hairs on the back of her neck. Half a moment later, she placed it: the hiss of drawn steel.

They heard a great crash, and then the screams of people being killed. The door crashed open, and in rushed many figures holding daggers.

Loren shouted and leaped to her feet, and together the rest of them rose from the table. At once she dove for their weapons; the High King had ordered they be returned, but they had sat useless in a corner for the last twelve days. Now Loren snatched up her staff and turned to face their attackers. Chet was only a heartbeat behind her.

The figures struck, two of them coming for Loren with their knives bared. She backed up, forced away from Chet in the fight, and swung her staff wide to keep them at bay. They wore hoods and black masks that kept her from seeing their faces. She could only see their eyes, glittering in the light of the lanterns, and the flash of their daggers as they swung.

Though they had caught her off balance, she swiftly recovered. One of them fell to a heavy blow from her staff. As the other backed off a step, Loren struck the one who had fallen once more across the temple.

Behind her foe, she was scarcely aware of Chet facing another of the attackers. Farther off, the Lord Prince used his chair to fend two of them away from a weakened Xain. Gem battled another with swings of his sword. The boy showed far more grace than Loren had come to expect from him. It seemed his training had paid off at last.

All this she took in at a glance, and then the masked figure came for her. Her staff batted his dagger away, but he kept his grip. A smaller knife appeared in his other hand. This thrust towards Loren's stomach, but she sidestepped—almost too slow. The blade grazed her side, and she winced with the pain. But her attacker had stepped in close and was off balance. Loren brought her fist crashing into his nose. In surprise he dropped his blades, and Loren drove her fist into his gut. As he doubled over, she brought her staff down upon the back of his head with all her might. He fell to the floor and lay still.

Chet and Gem were still fighting. The Lord Prince had managed to down one of his opponents, and had found a sword to deal with the other, who was being forced slowly backwards. Chet was holding his own, but Gem had his back to the wall. Loren could see the terror in his eyes.

She ran for him. He saw her coming and with a scream swung wildly at his opponent. The man leaped back, arms wide—and Loren drove the butt of her staff into his lower back. He clutched at where she had struck him, until she brought her staff about to knock him senseless.

Wincing at the pain in her side, she turned to Chet.

She was just in time to see his opponent drive a dagger into his chest.

The world seemed to freeze. All she could see was the shocked look in Chet's eye, and the silver hilt of the dagger that protruded from near his heart. The blood that poured from her side, and the glowing pain that came with it, vanished. There was only Chet's face, which even now grew pale before her sight.

Someone was screaming, and with some surprise Loren realized it was her. She tackled Chet's foe from behind, bearing him to the ground. With both hands she gripped his head, then slammed it into the floor twice in quick succession, until the man lay unmoving beneath her.

But above her, Chet was still on his feet, and his eyes had moved past her. She looked back to see the last attacker had disarmed the Lord Prince, and sat atop him trying to press the blade into his throat. Chet rushed past her and threw himself at the attacker, knocking him to the ground. The Lord Prince rose up and took the knife, using it to slit the man's throat.

Chet rolled off and away, falling to his back on the stone floor. He shivered, clutching with both hands at the hilt that stuck straight up from his breast. His teeth were gritted, lips peeled back in a grimace of pain. Loren was kneeling by his side, holding his hands, trying to stop him from pulling the knife out, for surely that would send his lifeblood streaming out of the open wound.

She was shouting, Gem was shouting, both of them screaming for help. Finally, far, far too late, guards came running through the door. They tried to pull Loren away from Chet, but she fought them off. Dimly she was aware of Eamin ordering one of the men away, away to find a healer, but she did not look up to see him go. She was looking at Chet, holding his gaze, willing him to keep his eyes open.

But she failed, and his eyes slid shut, while she screamed at him to open them again.

TWENTY-NINE

THE HEALERS WORKED THEIR CRAFTS UPON CHET THROUGH THE REST of that night, and through the following day, and still they were there the morning after. All the while, Loren sat by his bedside and held his hand. Again and again Xain told her to try and rest, until at last Gem shouted at him to leave. Someone, probably Eamin, told her that the healers were the High King's own, and the best in all the nine lands. She did not listen. It did not matter. All that mattered was seeing Chet's eyes open again, yet hours turned to days and still they remained shut. Only the rise and fall of his chest, and the ragged breaths that scraped their way from his throat, told her he had not left her forever.

Gem stayed with her, sitting on the other side of the bed, and Xain was there during all the daylight hours. The Lord Prince was there nearly as often, now always escorted by members of the royal guard, and when he came Gem would give up his chair to sit at the foot of the bed, like a dog hovering near an ailing child. Eamin only left for the most vital duties from which he could not excuse himself, and always with deep and regretful apologies. The words fell empty on Loren's ears, but Gem would thank him, and greet him warmly whenever he returned.

On the second day, with Chet's eyes still closed, Eamin told them in muted tones of all that had transpired in the palace since the attack. "I owe you all a life debt now, and that is not the sort of thing I take lightly. We know the attackers were Shades, of course, and so I have been speaking strongly to the High King on your behalf. It is clear now that their threat is altogether too real. If they are confident enough to strike even here, then they must be wiped out before their power grows any greater."

"And is Her Majesty heeding your advice at last?" said Xain.

"Oh, indeed," said the Lord Prince. "She may not show it often in courtly settings, but as it turns out, my mother is actually quite fond of me. I can tell she is leaning towards our way of thinking, and now the dean and the lord chancellor fear to speak against me. When the dean tried, the High King nearly tore his head off."

It all passed like water over Loren, and when the words did register in the back of her mind, they came with a great wave of guilt. Chet had urged her often to turn from this course. He had come here only out of loyalty to her, and mayhap out of love, but not because he believed in their cause. And now he was the one with the gaping wound in his chest, clinging to life with his chances stacked against him.

Finally, on the fourth day, he opened his eyes—but only to shoot up in bed with a cry, fingers grasping at the bandages that covered his chest. Thankfully one of the healers was present. She commanded Gem and Loren to hold Chet's arms down while she gave him dreamwine. This soon calmed Chet, and he drifted back into slumber nestled in the thick pillows of the bed.

Thus came the second stage of his healing, and it was far, far more terrible for Loren than the first. Now Chet would awaken, but only to groan in great pain, and mayhap to weep into his pillows. Always she was ready with the dreamwine, and after a few swallows he would drift back to sleep, senseless. His eyes never seemed to fix upon her, nor did he recognize her voice. He existed in two states: the numb oblivion of sleep, and the unthinking agony of wakefulness. It tore at her very soul, and whenever she was alone she whispered her fervent prayers to the sky that it would end—but then, too, she was aware it might yet end in his death.

And then, on the eighth day, he opened his eyes and looked at her, and he smiled.

"Chet?" she said, taking his hand gently. "Can you hear me?"

"Scarcely," he said, the word coming slurred. "I feel as if my head is stuffed with wool."

"That is the wine," she said, voice cracking as tears came to her eyes. "You are likely as drunk as anyone I have ever seen."

"So I am," he murmured, lips barely moving. "Only I wish I were drunker still, for my chest hurts terribly."

"Do you remember what happened?" she said.

"Yes," he said, his voice grim for a moment. But it soon lightened again. "I am some sort of hero, I suppose."

"Some sort, mayhap," she said, laughing.

The healer came in just then, and when she saw Chet was awake she rushed to his side. She asked him many questions, of his pain and his breath and if there was any feeling in his hands, and so many other things that Loren lost track. In the midst of the questions Chet drifted back off to slumber.

"That is very good," said the healer, and Loren could hear the stark relief in her voice. "It means the worst is over. It will get easier from now on."

"When will he awaken in earnest?" said Loren.

"It will be several days yet. Such things take time. But he will gain more and more strength, and by tomorrow he should be able to talk for a while."

She left then, and Xain entered a moment later, accompanied by Gem, who had been off to relieve himself.

"He awoke?" said Gem. "What did he say?"

"Drunken ramblings," said Loren. "He has had more wine these last few days than I have in my entire life."

Gem clutched Chet's other hand, giddy, and even Xain gripped the foot of the bed, as though relief had made him suddenly weak.

Chet's eyes opened once more that night, and then again the next morning. Loren gave him more of the dreamwine, and fed him some breakfast when he asked for it, at the healer's instructions. But as she was spooning eggs into his mouth, the door of the chamber swung open, and High King Enalyn strode in, surrounded by members of the royal guard.

Gem fell to his knee before her, and Xain lowered himself more slowly. Loren did not move, though she did put the plate down upon the bedside table. The royal guards fixed her with an ugly look, but she stared right back at them in defiance, for nothing in the nine lands would make her move even that far from the bedside.

For her part, Enalyn did not seem bothered. All of her attention was for Chet. She went to his side at once, and lifted the bandages on his chest. He winced slightly, and she quickly replaced them.

"I am sorry," she said. "I only wished to see for myself that you were being well tended to."

"It is no trouble, Your Majesty. Only a mild stinging," he said weakly.

Enalyn sat in Gem's chair, which he had left empty, and scooted it closer to the bed. She graced Loren with a brief but warm smile, and then turned back to Chet.

"I have instructed my healers to give you the very best of care. Do you want for anything? Anything at all?"

"No, Your Majesty. They have been most satisfactory. The wine they provide, in particular, is very pleasing."

Enalyn smiled at that. "I imagine it would be. The wound will heal, but you will bear the scar of it forever. I wish that were not so, and yet you should wear it with pride, and with my gratitude. It is the price you paid to save the life of my son, and such a debt is not easily repaid."

"I will, Your Majesty," said Chet. "And it was my honor."

She laid her hand over his. Loren saw his face grow a little paler, and his jaw twitched as he gritted his teeth. The pain was coming back. Quickly she stood and reached for the wine, leaning over to help him drink it.

Enalyn stood from her chair with one more gentle pat of his hand. "Rest now. I will come visit you again when you are healed, to ensure that you have been well tended to."

When Loren had finished giving him his drink, the High King fixed her with a look. "Now, Loren of the family Nelda, I must ask something of you. I know you do not wish to leave him, and no one could blame you. But my advisors and I require your counsel—and yours as well, Xain."

Loren set her jaw. "Your Majesty . . . I hardly think my words could be any more useful than theirs. I am a simple forest girl."

"I am beginning to think, as the Lord Prince has told me often in the last few days, that there is nothing simple about you," said Enalyn. "And in this case, I am afraid I must insist, for the fate of the nine lands may well rest upon it. We are all of us on the brink of a great and terrible time, and the bravery you have shown thus far might be the only thing that saves us in the end. But I must ask you to be brave again, and lend your wisdom to our plans, for they will need every bit of help to succeed."

She hardly knew how she could refuse such a request, though she still did not wish to go. But she felt Chet's hand close around hers where it rested on the bed, and he spoke gently to her. "Go. I shall be fine, and will eagerly await your return. But for a short time, I think Gem can get me drunk enough on his own."

"And happily will I apply myself to the task," said Gem brightly.

Loren looked to Xain, the only one who had not spoken. He gave her a solemn nod.

"Very well," said Loren. "I serve at your pleasure. Your Majesty."

"Thank you," said Enalyn. "And you may be assured of his safety—I will leave two of my royal guard here to watch him, and they will remain on post for as long as his healing requires."

"Thank you, Your Majesty," said Loren, this time with earnest gratitude. In the fitful snatches of sleep she had managed, her dreams were filled with visions of more Shades breaking into their quarters to finish them all off. With a final squeeze of Chet's hand, she set off and into the halls of the palace, trailing in the High King's footsteps with Xain at her side.

Enalyn led her back to the throne room, and this time Loren was able to take more time to appreciate the palace's finery as she passed it by. But the trip seemed to take no time at all, for the High King's pace was quick with urgency. They passed through the throne room in a rush, though it still seemed to take an age to cross the massive space. Behind the dais was a door, and Enalyn led them through it into a small chamber beyond.

It looked to be some sort of war room. Upon the great table in the center was laid a map of the nine lands, which Loren marveled to behold. She had seen only one map before in her lifetime, and it was a small, crude thing that Bracken had carried with him. This was drawn in exacting detail, with the names of all the great cities inscribed with beautiful penmanship. But her attention soon went from the map to the men who stood above it, for waiting in the room for them were the dean of the Academy and the lord chancellor of the Mystics.

The dean looked angrily at Xain the instant he stepped in through the door, while the lord chancellor cast a dark look upon Loren. Clearly neither man thought they should be there, and yet she could see that they were not eager to speak up about their displeasure. Instead, as Enalyn bade them to stand at the table over the map, the dean and lord chancellor endeavored to stand as far away as they could without actually fleeing the room.

First Enalyn made them tell their tale once more, in brief, and point out where each event had occurred on the map. Though Loren loathed to recount her journey yet again, she found it more bearable this time, for the High King was understanding and let her skip briefly over the darker memories. She seemed peculiarly interested in the battle of Wellmont, and had both Loren and Xain tell their sides of it, though Loren did not know how her account could be helpful.

"I was within the city, Your Majesty," she said, after she had told the tale. "I saw very little."

"And my mind was greatly preoccupied during the battle," said Xain.

"Yet every detail helps," said Enalyn. "Something happened at Wellmont. Something we do not yet understand, and may not for a while yet. But say on."

Loren wondered what that meant. But she did as she was bidden, until they had spoken of the fall of Northwood, as well as the location of the Shade stronghold in the Greatrock Mountains. But the map clearly showed where the battles had taken place, and so they spent the greater part of their time trying to pinpoint the spot on the map where they thought the Shade stronghold had been, for of course it was not marked.

"It is as I suspected," she murmured. "All their activities are concentrated in the west, and have likely been strengthened by Dorsean troops."

"It seems that way, Your Majesty," said the lord chancellor.

"Your Majesty does not think the battle of Wellmont was the beginning of some petty border war," said Xain. It was not a question.

"No, I do not," said Enalyn. "I think it is a conflict motivated by the Shades, who seek to sow discord among the kings in preparation for an assault on Underrealm. If we are correct, then you have saved the nine lands by bringing me this information."

"What do you mean to do with it, then?" said Xain.

"The High King will put forth her strength, and the Mystics shall do the same," said the lord chancellor. "Together we will quell this uprising, unifying the kingdoms in preparation for the coming war."

"The Academy will send some of its strength as well," added the dean, sounding like a child who did not wish to be left out of a game.

"I am grateful we discovered it this early," said Enalyn. "As well as for the fact that you survived your journey to the Seat, Loren. Good fortune has blessed your travel, though I am certain it does not seem that way looking back on it."

She thought of Jordel, of Albern and Mag and Sten. "Thank you, Your Majesty, but it does not."

"Then there is only the matter of what to do with all of you," said Enalyn. "Certainly I cannot continue to treat you as prisoners, if for no other reason than your actions to save the Lord Prince. But neither can I allow Xain to leave."

Loren balked, but when she looked to Xain he only looked at Enalyn with grim understanding. "Your Majesty? I do not understand. Has he not proven himself?"

"Mayhap," said Enalyn. "Yet you are still a criminal by law, Xain, and I cannot discount the possibility—however remote—that this is all a deception for the purpose of clearing your name. If indeed we uncover a plot by the Shades behind the war in Wellmont, then I will consider your crimes paid for in full, and grant you pardon. You will be returned to full honor, and I will find you a place in my court, or in any court you wish across the nine lands."

"Your Majesty," said the dean. "You cannot mean to pardon his blatant—"

"That is enough," snapped Enalyn, and she stared at him until he subsided before turning back to Xain. "In the meantime, however, you may go wherever you wish inside the palace itself, though if you leave your chambers you will have to be escorted. And while you remain here under my care, you may see your son."

Xain tensed, his spindly knuckles going white where they held the edge of the table. Loren saw tears welling in his eyes, though he blinked furiously to hide them.

"Your Majesty . . . I . . ." His voice broke, and he shook his head as if to clear it.

"No gratitude is necessary, Xain," said Enalyn. "Go now and see him. You have both waited long enough."

He tried once more to speak, but it only came out as a sob. Hastily he turned, swiping at his eyes, and ran from the room as fast as his legs could carry him.

THIRTY

THE PALACE FELL TO BUSY PREPARATIONS AS THE HIGH KING'S ARMY prepared to march off to war. Eamin could not come and visit Chet so often now, though he still came by at least once a day. Xain spent most of his time with his son, and was reticent to bring him to their quarters where the guards at the door plainly marked him as a prisoner. Loren saw him but once, a small, wide-eyed boy not half Gem's age, who looked at her green eyes in wonder and blushed as he hid his face in his father's pant leg.

Loren stayed with Chet always, even when Gem finally grew bored and went to practice swordplay with Eamin as promised. When he was finally able to sit up in bed, she would help him rise each morning, and aid him in lying down again each night. When at last the healers would let him try to walk, she would take his arm as he hobbled out to the balcony, there to sit with him and watch the sun make its slow way through the sky. Always Gem would come and visit them with news of the palace's goings-on, but the boy had clearly determined that Chet was no longer in any danger, and meant to experience every minute of the excitement.

For Loren, it was enough to simply remain with him.

Then at last, the day before the armies marched forth from the Seat, the healers came to remove his bandages once and for all. When they arrived, the High King came with them. Chet hastened to sit up, and Loren took his arm to help him. He left the bed and tried to kneel, but Enalyn took his shoulder and bade him to remain on his feet. Xain stood to the side, watching alongside Gem.

Slowly, layer by layer, the healers unwound the bandages from his wound. Soon he stood there bare-chested, clad only in his breeches, and Loren could see his embarrassment by the color in his cheeks. On the right side of his chest was the scar, an ugly and twisted mass of flesh, treated as best the healers could, but not quite enough to leave the skin smooth.

"Now you must still treat yourself with care," said the healer, tilting her greying head as if Chet were a wayward child. "Engage in nothing too strenuous, and you will remain healthy enough."

"Thank you," he said quietly. The healer bowed and backed away.

"It is you who are owed thanks, Chet of the family Lindel," said Enalyn. "You stand before me healed, and yet scarred by a blade that was meant for my son. Only two men in this room can claim that."

She looked at Xain as she said this, and he bowed his head.

"For that I owe you a great deal. Any service I may give, so long as it does not break my vows to serve the nine lands, I will grant you. Ask for land or a lordship, and it shall be yours."

Chet swallowed hard, and his hand gripped Loren's shoulder more tightly. But he shook his head at last, and ducked his head.

"Thank you, Your Majesty," he said quietly. "I have never longed for anything like that. I only wish to go forth and see a bit of the nine lands, and see if I can find a better place to live than my home. And if I fail, then there I mean to return, for the woods are good enough for me."

Enalyn smiled, and she reached forwards to tilt his eyes up to hers. "That is well. But the young heart may seek to wander, while old bones wish to sit at rest. So long as you roam the nine lands, you shall do so with my blessing. And if the day should come when you wish for yourself a home, only say where, and so long as I sit my throne, I shall grant it to you."

Chet bowed to her, with Loren's help and many words of earnest thanks. Enalyn smiled once again, and then left them alone. All the excitement had rendered his knees somewhat weak, so after she helped him don a tunic, Loren helped him hobble out to the balcony where they spent the rest of their day.

As they sat there in the afternoon sunlight, she found herself studying him from the corner of her eyes, and her heart thundered loud in her ears. To see him there, so happy and carefree, overawed by the grace bestowed upon him by the High King, was a far greater thing than she had hoped for just a week ago. And she knew at last, and for certain, what she had long suspected.

They ate an early supper, alone, for Gem was somewhere wandering and Xain was with his son. Then she walked him to his bed, there in case he needed her support. But he did not reach for her, except to grip her fingers with his own.

He sat at the edge of the bed, and she helped him remove his tunic. But when he lay back and reached for his covers, Loren stopped him. With trembling fingers she undid the strings that held her own tunic closed at the top, and then lifted it from her body. When the cloth came away, she saw him looking at her with wide eyes.

"Loren . . ." he murmured.

She shushed him and undid her belt before climbing onto the bed, and then reached to undo the strings of his breeches.

From the palace walls the next day, they watched the armies march forth. All in a row they stood at the ramparts, Loren and Chet and Xain and Gem. Below them in the streets, the Mystics were gathered in rank and file. They wore shirts of mail and carried shields on their backs, and at their hips hung blades of castle-forged steel. Then came the High King's army, not so great as any of the standing armies of the nine kingdoms, but better trained and equipped with the finest of arms and armor. The tramp of their boots shook the ground so that those upon the wall could feel it, a deep shudder that still struck them long after the soldiers had vanished around the first bend in the road.

"The army will grow bigger as it proceeds south and west," said the Lord Prince, who stood with them to watch the march. He had already told them, with some disappointment, that he and the High King herself would be staying upon the Seat, with a token force to guard the island. "More Mystics shall join them from every city, and all of the Selvan army—that portion of it which was not already committed to the war in Wellmont, that is."

When they decided at last to leave the walls and return to the palace, it seemed incredibly empty. Many of the castle's servants were soldiers in times of war, and they had left, so that only enough remained to serve the royalty who stayed behind. Fewer guards patrolled the wall. The very air seemed subdued, waiting expectantly like a sailor's wife at the door.

Later that afternoon, Loren was sitting with Xain in the main room of their chambers. Chet was napping in his bedchamber, for watching the armies march had tired him out. Xain had a cup of wine in one hand, but he drank from it sparingly. Loren had discreetly asked one of the kitchen maids for silphium, and concocted a tea from it. It did not taste quite so bad as she had heard, for which she was grateful, but still she had lessened its bitterness with some honey.

"I think I know the smell of that tea," said Xain, keeping his eyes on the contents of his own cup.

"Mayhap you do," said Loren, and though she felt her cheeks glowing she refused to look at him. Still she could feel him smiling secretly to himself, and the silence that followed stretched just long enough to grow uncomfortable. "What do you plan to do with yourself now, wizard?"

He looked up in surprise. "Now? Why, wait for the armies to return, of course, and for my fate to be decided."

She rolled her eyes. "You know what I mean. The armies will return, and the High King will grant you your pardon. What then?"

Xain pursed his lips and shrugged. "I will tell you the truth: I had not thought upon it overmuch. Until only recently, the notion of earning my pardon seemed too far-fetched to plan for. But it seems, to me at least, that you and I have done our jobs. And a wizard is of little value without a court to serve, they say. Who knows but that the High King will wish to keep me around for herself. If not, I am certain the Lord Prince would take me. What of yourself, forest girl? Where will Loren of the family Nelda, the Nightblade, journey from here?"

"First to Ammon, of course, to join with Annis again. After that . . . I suppose I am like you, and had not thought that far ahead. The road here occupied quite enough attention while we traveled it."

"But you still mean to continue your journeys?" said Xain.

"Why not? The nine lands are wide, and I have seen precious little of them. I thought for a time to visit Hedgemond, where Jordel hailed from, and see his family if I could. I may still do that. In any case, the world will always have a place for a thief."

"You are no longer a simple thief, if ever you were," he said. "And though your heart seeks to wander now, it may not always feel the same."

His eyes wandered to the door of Chet's bedchamber as he said it. Loren blushed again, and drank of her tea.

THIRTY-ONE

ONE NIGHT, AS LOREN LAY IN CHET'S BED, HER HEAD RESTING UPON HIS arm, she heard a crash from outside the window. She shot up straight, eyes peering into the darkness. Nothing followed at first, but then she heard voices shouting, and the sound of many running feet.

Quickly she threw on her clothes and ran out upon the balcony, leaving her boots for the moment. Below her in the courtyard she saw guards running, all of them towards the front of the palace. But soon their footsteps faded from hearing, and the night was still again.

She went back inside, her nerves on edge. Too easily, her mind turned to memories of the night the Shades had attacked. She wished she had her dagger, but settled for fetching her staff and placing it on the floor near the bed. But she could not find sleep again that night, and looked up suspiciously at every wayward sound.

The next morning the Lord Prince came to visit them for breakfast. He seemed cheerful as ever, but she thought she saw worry lurking deep in his eyes. After they had eaten, she leaned back in her chair to look at him.

"Did something happen last night? I heard shouting, and guards running in the courtyard."

His smile dampened, though he fought to maintain it. "A small disturbance, and not cause for much concern. A Shade was discovered within the palace grounds. The guards found him, but in the pursuit they killed him before he could be questioned."

A shiver ran down Loren's back. Chet's brow furrowed as he looked back and forth between them.

"Another Shade?" he said. "That seems cause for a little concern, at least."

"Constables tracked down his dwelling within the city," said Eamin. "He stayed alone at an inn near the western gate, and arrived two weeks ago. It seems likely he was a lone informant, sent to spy on our doings and report to his masters. But they will receive no information from him."

He quickly turned the conversation to other matters, and soon had Chet and Gem talking animatedly. But Loren thought only of the Shade for the rest of their meal, and for the rest of the day besides.

"I think I will go into the city today to retrieve my dagger," she told Chet, as they sat together in his room later.

"Why?" he said. "The guard around our room has been doubled, and the palace is on high alert. The Shades would not try to attack us again."

"It will give me some peace," she said. "I have thought of it often, and though I trust Xain's friend Aurel, still as long as the dagger is gone from me I feel as though something is missing."

He slid closer, and slipped a hand about her waist. "Are you sure? Is there any way I can persuade you to stay?"

She slapped his hand and kissed him, and when at last she pulled back he was smiling. "No, there is not, brigand. I will return presently. If you remain awake, then you may do all the persuading you want."

Her black cloak had hung unused on a hook by the door since almost the first day they arrived. Now she went to fetch it, wrapping it around herself before slipping out the door. She and the others had been given free rein to explore the Seat—all but Xain—and so the guards hardly glanced at her as she slipped past them and out into the night.

Guards challenged her at the gate, but she told them she only wanted to go for a stroll. They let her into the streets, which were now lit by torches against the darkness. Though the sun had set many hours ago, still there were plenty of wanderers, and she soon lost herself in the crowd.

She remembered the route they had taken to reach the silversmith's shop, and soon found herself standing before his large red door. As they had done last time, she slipped around the back to knock on the service entrance. Aurel opened it after just a few knocks, peering out at her from the warm glow of his home.

"You . . . you are Xain's friend," he stammered. "Forgive me, my memory . . ."

"Loren," she said, with an easy smile. "I have come for my things."

He blinked twice, and then whirled and scampered into the workshop. "Of course, of course! Come in, come in. They have been kept safe, of course, for I heard about all those goings-on at the palace. So glad to hear you and Xain were not beheaded after all." He gave a little cackle, and Loren forced a smile.

There was a crack in the floor she had not noticed, and into it the smith drove a metal spike. This he levered up until one of the stones came loose. Beneath was a shallow hole, and in the hole was her box. Aurel fetched it for her and placed it gingerly in her hands.

"There you are, girl. No one knew it was here, and no one knew what was inside—not even me!" He gave another odd little giggle.

"Thank you," said Loren in earnest, for just to hold it was a relief. He turned away discreetly while she fetched her dagger and the packet of magestones from the box. When she was done, she closed it and handed it back to him.

"I am in your debt. If ever I can be of service to you—"

"Do not make me laugh," said Aurel, waving his hand. "Anything for a friend of Xain. Come and visit whenever you wish, or if you ever need goods of silver."

"I shall. And if anyone asks me who is the best silversmith in all the nine lands, I will tell them it is Aurel of the High King's Seat."

He kissed her cheek at that, and she vanished back into the night. Ducking into a back alley, she pulled forth one of the magestones and bit into it. She drew her dagger and held it reversed in her hand.

The dark streets lit like day, and the torches became like tiny pinpricks of light, weak and ineffectual compared to the illumination provided by her own sight. Now she moved with greater confidence, running through the darkest streets as she made her way west.

Once she reached the gate, she looked about for an inn. She soon discovered a problem: there were too many. The Seat was grander and more populated than any place she had seen before, and offered plentiful places for travelers to stay.

She found an old man leaning in the doorway of a shop, tugging at his beard as he watched her pass by. Loren stopped short, went to him, and gave him her friendliest smile.

"A good evening, friend. I heard tell the constables came through here, searching the room of some dead man. Can you tell me what inn they went to?"

"I heard something that sounded like that," said the old man. "But age is the great poison of memory, they say, and has only one antidote."

Her smile lost some of its warmth, but she dug into the purse at her belt and drew forth a gold weight. "Is this the antidote?"

The old man snatched the coin with a flourish. "It may well be. The very inn behind you, called the Shining Door, is the one you seek." And he walked away, clicking his heels on the stones of the street.

Loren threw back her hood and stepped into the common room of the Shining Door. It was bustling with occupants, and in the commotion no one gave her a second glance. She studied the room, wondering if she would have to pay another gold piece to find out which room the Shade had paid for. But when she took a look upstairs, she found that unnecessary. One door hung loose, slanted on its hinges, and the jamb was splintered where it had been kicked in by the constables.

Looking over her shoulder to ensure she had not been followed, she ducked into the room. No lamps were lit—a welcome advantage, for while the darkness would keep anyone in the hallway from seeing her black cloak, it was no proof against her sight.

She went to the bed, hoping the sheets had not yet been changed. A quick sniff told her that was unlikely. Running her hand along the pillow, she found what she was looking for: a few pale hairs clinging to the fabric. These she picked up before leaving the room and making her way outside.

A moment's search revealed the nearest torch, which she pulled from the wall and carried into an alley far from sight of any major street. She held the blade of her dagger over the flames as Jordel had taught her, until the air above the blade wavered in the warmth. Then she dropped the hairs onto the metal, where they fizzled and vanished in a puff of smoke.

The black designs on her dagger began to twist and shift, coiling around each other as though they were grasping for something. Then they snapped together, all pointing in one direction: east.

Loren grimaced. This was the magic Jordel had taught her, and now it told her several things. First, that there had been more than one Shade, for the one they found in the palace had been killed. The dagger would not reveal a corpse. Second, the other Shade—or mayhap there had been more than two?—was a wizard of some description, for the magic only worked upon them. And third, the other Shade had left the inn. Mayhap they had even left the Seat.

She owed it to herself at least to search, and so with the dagger acting as her compass, she ran through the city. She never faltered or stumbled, for in her eyes the streets were as bright as day. So she made her way tirelessly eastward, running at the loping, easy pace she had learned after years of running between the trees of the Birchwood.

But at last she reached the city's eastern end, and before her loomed the gate that led to the docks thrusting out into the Great Bay. Still the designs on the dagger pointed east.

Mayhap it meant the Shade was on the other side of the gates, on a ship but still on the Seat. Loren doubted it. More likely the Shade had fled when their companion was killed, and was even now far away on the sea—mayhap in Dulmun, mayhap even farther. Wherever they were, they were beyond Loren's reach, for the guards would not open the gate for her now, at night.

Shoulders slumped in defeat, Loren turned and made her way back through the city to the High King's palace, and spent a fitful night thinking of the Shades.

THIRTY-TWO

SOME DAYS AFTER THAT, THE LORD PRINCE EAMIN VISITED THEM ONCE more. He had taken to wandering listless about the palace, slouching in his stance and dragging his feet. When he and Xain would sit together and drink wine, Loren overheard him confide to the wizard that he was bored out of his skull, and would much rather be on the road with his mother's army than cooped up here like some prize hog. But today when he came to them, there was a bounce in his step and a rare light in his eyes.

"We received the first messenger back from the army," he told them. "They reached Redbrook some days ago, and now march west for Wellmont."

"They have made good time," said Xain.

"They are fighters, and have sat here on this island for years and years, with no wars to fight," said Eamin. "They were eager. The letter says the Dorsean army has already retreated from Selvan lands, and its generals have sent messages to the High King's army begging for mercy."

"Have they guessed that we know of their scheming with the Shades?" said Xain.

"That is what it sounds like," said Eamin with a shrug. "And more is the pity! The first time we have marched to war, true war, in my lifetime, and it is over before a single battle can be fought."

Loren found herself looking askance at him. She did not see it as any great loss to have avoided a battle between such mighty armies. But then, the Lord Prince was just the sort of man to long for the glory of battle. As he himself said, he had never truly fought in one. It was a curious thought, that she had seen the horror of war when such a great man had not.

"In any case, my mother—Her Majesty—thinks it might be a ruse. So we will accept their surrender, but proceed with caution just the same. The Dorseans will present all their military leaders, who will be put to the question by the constables' most able practitioners for any connection to the Shades. Those who are found guilty will be executed."

"A neat affair," said Xain. "Though there will likely be more work to do afterwards. The Shades undoubtedly have pockets all over the nine kingdoms. None may be a threat in and of itself, but if united by the Necromancer their power could be disastrous. I do not think you need lament our current absence of war, for the fighting will surely—"

His words died on his lips as horns blared across the walls of the palace.

They all sat there frozen for an eyeblink. Then everyone tried to rise at once, making for the door. It flew open and they nearly fell out of it in their haste, but then the guards were there, blocking the way with their weapons.

"The wizard must remain," said one of them. "By the orders of the High King."

"He is allowed to leave with an escort, you twit," said Eamin.

"While there are horns upon the wall, he shall stay," said the guard. "Forgive me, Lord Prince, but I obey Her Majesty."

Eamin looked as though he might argue it, but Xain pushed his shoulder. "Go. I will remain here. Only do not leave me waiting forever!"

Then they were all running down the hall, and soon they reached the courtyard and took the steps up to the wall. Chet was leaning heavily on Loren as they moved, and his breathing came hard, but still he kept pace with the rest of them.

"The horns come from the east!" said Eamin. "Quick!"

He ran along the wall until he reached the eastern battlements, and there slid to a stop with his hands on the stone. He leaned out, looking with squinted eyes across the sea. Loren and Chet joined him a moment later, searching in silence. The bay was shrouded in mist, for it was still early morning, and at first they saw nothing.

Then at last, they burst forth from the mist. Thousands of sails, lining the horizon from north to south. It was a fleet of Dulmun ships, each of them mightier than the *Long Claw* that had brought Loren and her friends to the Seat, and all ready for war. Though the distance was great, Loren could see the soldiers and sailors running back and forth across the decks as they prepared for a landing.

"Give me a moment," she said quietly, and then ducked away from Chet to run for a torch that sat, unlit, in the wall. She pulled it out, then used her flint and tinder to light it before thrusting her dagger into the flames. It had been days since last she used it, and she had no idea if it would still work. But it did, for the designs twisted upon themselves almost immediately, and just as they had before, they all pointed towards the east.

Loren cursed and stomped out the torch before running back to the others. "The Shade the guards found in the night," she said breathlessly. "He was not alone. His companion fled the Seat and went east to Dulmun, there to raise this fleet."

Eamin stared at her in wonder. "How could you know that?"

"Trust only that I know it," said Loren. "This is not some insurrection by Dulmun, but a planned stroke by the Shades."

The air erupted with horns again, making Gem jump. He stomped his foot and shouted at the spires atop the palace. "Yes, we have heard you! You may stop blowing now!"

"Those are not the same horns," said Eamin, looking fearful. "They came from the west."

Wondering what could possibly be going on now, Loren took Chet's arm again and helped him along as they followed the others in a mad run to the west wall. When they reached it they stopped, and Loren felt hope flee her. Before them lay the narrow strait between the High King's Seat and the shores of Selvan. And upon those shores, still pouring out of the Birchwood forest, came a great army of Shades in grey and blue, mounting their boats and making ready for an assault upon the island.

THIRTY-THREE

They ran back to Xain as quickly as they could. Loren had already started putting the pieces together in her mind, and when they reached the wizard, Eamin said what she had already begun to suspect.

"It was all a ruse," he said, gasping from their run. "The Shades meant for us to think that Wellmont was their doing. They meant for you all to warn the High King, so that she would send out the Mystics and the greater strength of her own army to put a stop to the fighting. They never meant to start a war between Dorsea and Selvan. They always meant to take the Seat."

Xain's eyes were wide, and for the first time since she had known him, Loren thought he looked truly terrified. "They will sack the city. They will kill anyone they can get their hands on."

But Loren herself felt sick, as though she could barely keep down her gorge. "It is our fault. We thought we were warning them, but we were only delivering the very message the Shades wanted us to bring."

Eamin shook his head quickly. "You cannot blame yourselves for that. You could have done no differently than you did. We have been outfoxed, as simple as that."

"Nothing is simple. I have doomed the Seat, and mayhap all the nine kingdoms. All because I thought to assume Jordel's place, and take charge of a war I was never prepared to fight."

"You did just what he would have done, and so you cannot insult yourself without insulting his memory," said Eamin. "So ask yourself now: if Jordel were here, what would he do?"

Loren swallowed, eyes darting around, trying to think. She could only picture the sails coming in upon the horizon, and the shapes of grey and blue pouring from the Birchwood. "He would . . . he would save the High King. That is the only thing we can do. She must survive."

"Just my thought," said Eamin. "Let us see to it."

They went to the door, but once again the guards stopped them. There were three of them, two swordsmen and a wizard, and their faces were hard.

"I am sorry, Lord Prince Eamin," said the one who had spoken before. "I cannot disobey the High King."

Eamin looked over his shoulder as though exasperated. But he fixed Loren with a knowing look. She nodded.

Quick as a blink, Eamin seized the guard's tunic. His forehead came crashing down on the bridge of the man's nose, and the guard crumpled to the floor. Loren leaped past the other for the wizard, whose eyes glowed white as she reached for her magic. But Loren knew she was a firemage, and Jordel had taught her something of how to deal with them. She clapped her hand over the woman's mouth to keep her from speaking, then drove a fist into her gut. The light died in her eyes, and as Loren punched her in the jaw, those eyes rolled backwards. The woman collapsed.

Behind her, Eamin had already knocked the other guard unconscious. "A poor reward for doing their duty," he said. "I shall have to remember to make things right with them, if any of us survive this."

Then they were flying through the halls of the palace, which had erupted into a torrent of confusion. Soldiers, guards, and servants ran every which way, none of them seeming to know which way to go. But everywhere they went Eamin cried, "Warriors, to me! To your Lord Prince and the High King! The rest of you, flee the Seat! To me! To me!"

They heard him, and armed soldiers in plate stopped their scrambling to follow. Soon they had a fair little procession making its way through the palace, until they came to the throne room and found it guarded by men with spears. They leaped forwards to attack, but stopped when the saw the Lord Prince, and raised their weapons.

Eamin kicked open the door and ran in, Loren and the rest at his heels. The High King stood by her throne, and to Loren's amazement a squire was helping her into a suit of plate armor. But she looked at Eamin and the rest of them as though this were any ordinary afternoon upon the island, and raised an eyebrow as if in mild interest.

"Lord Prince Eamin," she said. "Have you any more news about what is happening, or must I continue listening to counselors who have no counsel?"

"Erin!" Xain saw his son standing among the courtiers clustered near the throne and went running for him.

"Papa!" The boy leaped into his father's arms and held him tight.

"I ordered him to be retrieved the moment the horns sounded," said the High King.

"Thank you, Your Majesty," said Xain, his voice shaking.

"Your Majesty, the Shades attack from the shores of Selvan," said Eamin. "They are pouring from the Birchwood in great strength. Even now they board boats to cross the channel, and may already have arrived at the island's western gate."

"Do you think we can hold them?"

"Mayhap we could, but at the same time a fleet comes from the east. They are ships of Dulmun. We thought the Shades had enlisted the help of Dorsea, but that was a deception. They have mustered Dulmun to their banner, and mean to take the Seat to stake their claim to power."

"A clever ruse," said Enalyn. "I might have known the warning came to us too easily."

"Your Majesty," said Loren, throwing herself forwards and dropping to one knee. "No words can express my—"

"Oh, *stand*, girl. You cannot think to blame yourself for this, for you did nothing wrong. Indeed, had you acted any other way, it would have been treason." The last plate was strapped to her arm, and her squire helped her don gloves of interlocking metal scales. "Now it seems we must have a fight, if we wish to leave this island alive."

"Your Majesty," said Loren, rising to her feet. "I do not see how you can fight your way through so many. There might be another way, a means of escape besides—"

"Be silent, girl," said the lord chancellor, staring at her with venom.

"Beside the High King stand the greatest warriors Underrealm has ever known, and each of them would give their life for hers if need be. We will fight our way through, you may count on it."

"Where is the dean?" said Enalyn, as though she had not heard either of them. "I should have thought he would be here by now."

One of the royal guard standing nearby looked about uneasily, and then stepped forwards to speak. "Your Majesty . . . when we went to find him, we found his chamber empty. A student at the Academy said they saw him fleeing west, probably trying to escape the city before the battle."

"Craven to the very end," said Enalyn, shaking her head with a steely glare. "Let that be a lesson to you, girl: never appoint a wizard based upon his political convenience. Are we ready?"

"Your Highness—" said Loren, looking to Eamin, who was donning his own armor with the help of a page.

"Thank you for your counsel, Loren, but these are warriors all," he said. "They will break through, if it can be done at all."

With that, the High King raised her sword. Around her assembled the members of the royal guard, and outside them a sizable force of castle soldiers. Together they pressed forwards to the door of the throne room.

"Stay close to them," said Xain, holding his son tight in his arms. "Look for a chance to help, but do not join the fighting if you have any choice. Wars fought in cities are often the bloodiest."

Loren did not need the warning, for she still remembered Wellmont. But she nodded.

Quickly the procession made its way into the palace's main hall. Still there was no resistance; Loren hoped they might reach the city before they encountered the Shades. Out in the streets, she thought she might be able to find a path to escape if the High King should become surrounded. Here in the palace, with only a single door to march through, it felt as if they were walking into the jaws of death itself.

The palace's front door crashed open, and soldiers in blue and grey charged in with a roar. Over their heads flew black arrows, some landing among the High King's guard while others narrowly missed Loren and her friends. She fell to the ground with a cry, dragging Chet with her. He landed with a grunt, and together they huddled until the rain of arrows ceased.

When they could stand again, they saw Enalyn's force heavily engaged with the Shades who still poured in through the door. At once Loren saw the truth of what the Lord Prince had said: these were fine warriors. Their armor was thick and true, and the blows of their enemies could not pierce it. Their swords were sharp and gleaming, but soon streaked with the red of blood. Enalyn and Eamin were in the press, and every time an enemy drew near they struck quickly to cut them down. But for every Shade they killed, another stepped into place, and still more came through the door. Loren could see no end to their number. And each man of the palace guard who fell was irreplaceable.

"Retreat!" she cried in panic. "There are too many!"

Mayhap someone heard her, or mayhap they saw the truth for themselves. In any case, someone with a battlefield voice called the withdrawal, and they backed away slowly, making the Shades pay in blood for every foot of their advance. Armored hands seized the High King and the Lord Prince and dragged them backwards, out of the fighting and into the open space behind. The royal guard came with them, while the rest of the soldiers formed a rearguard to slow pursuit.

"Quickly!" said Eamin. Blood ran down his face, but Loren could not tell if it was his own. "They will cover our escape. Into the palace!"

They fled, and quickly, but still the clash of steel on steel followed them through the halls.

THIRTY-FOUR

THEY STOPPED IN THE MAIN COURTYARD, THE ROYAL GUARD STILL IN A protective ring around Enalyn. Loren and the others came to a halt nearby, and with a sharp gesture Enalyn beckoned them forwards.

"There is another entrance we mean to try," she said. "The rear gate is smaller and more easily defended. The Shades might have ignored it, focusing their strength instead on the wider front gate."

"But then again, they might not," said Loren. "Your Majesty, let us find some way to get you to safety other than force of arms, for I do not think that will serve us."

"She is informing you, not asking for your counsel," said the lord chancellor. "It is a courtesy you should be grateful for."

"If we escape to the east, that only means it will be even harder to make for the western docks and escape," Chet said angrily. "Your duty is to save the High King, not die gloriously in battle beside her."

The lord chancellor's face turned ugly, his voice to a low snarl. "I know my duty, boy. I wager I have had it longer than you have been alive."

Enalyn silenced him with a stern look and turned to Loren. "There is a hidden entrance. But it runs from the palace to the eastern docks. Those docks are currently occupied by the Dulmun fleet. Our foes have planned their attack well, and likely they were long in concocting their strategy. These men know their way about a battle. Put your faith in them."

The sound of tramping boots filled the air, and a fresh group of palace soldiers marched into the courtyard to join them. "There are the reinforcements," said the lord chancellor. "Your Majesty, we should be moving."

He led them on, back into another wing of the palace that Loren had never explored. She soon became turned around and lost, and resigned herself to following the armored backs of the soldiers before her. Before long they pushed through another, smaller door, and found themselves in a narrow open space between the back of the palace and the eastern wall. There was the gate, smaller than the one to the west. Above, guards on the wall loosed arrows at unseen foes on the other side. But they could scarcely peek out from the battlements without having to duck a hail of enemy fire.

"It looks as though there are many of them beyond the gate," Loren called out.

"Let us hope not enough," said the Lord Prince. "Open the gate!"

The shout went up the wall, and guardsmen in the gatehouse leaned to the wheel. With the groaning of chains, the gate swung slowly inwards. Almost at once, Loren saw swords and spear tips pushed through the gap.

Eamin held his sword aloft and gave a battle cry. The palace guards charged into the fray, and the Shades were thrown back from the wall. They turned in a rout, many fleeing into the streets and vanishing into the alleys of the city. But some of their captains managed to rally, and slowly the grey and blue uniforms came together once more. The Lord Prince's charge stalled, and the palace guards were pushed into a circle against the wall. Loren and her friends could not get through the gates, for it was blocked by armored bodies.

"They cannot get through," said Gem. "They will be cut down."

Loren did not answer him, but looked at Chet, and in his eyes she saw the same fear. Dread seized her heart. She had brought the enemy here and doomed the High King, and now she was powerless to save them.

Shadeborn. Shadeborn. Shadeborn.

A chant had begun to build beyond the wall. Loren quailed, for she recognized the word. That was what Rogan had called himself when they met in Dorsea. She craned her neck, and above the fighting she saw him. He had pressed through his troops to stand at their head, blocking the High King's escape into the city.

Shadeborn, shadeborn, shadeborn.

Bolstered by their captain, the Shades were pressing forwards in earnest, and the palace guard were forced back through the gate. She saw the lord chancellor hacking desperately, trying to cut a path through the enemy. With a cry of rage he threw himself forwards, attacking Rogan himself.

His blade caught in the hook of Rogan's axe and was turned aside. Then they danced, the lord chancellor striking with sword and shield both, while Rogan held his axe in both hands, his shield slung across his back. With the haft of it he blocked strike after strike, the lord chancellor pressing forwards. But Loren could see Rogan's smile beneath his helmet; he was toying with the Mystic, drawing him out and into the midst of his army.

A sword came swinging from the left, and the lord chancellor caught it on his shield. But in that moment's distraction, Rogan struck. His axe came down in a punishing blow that the lord chancellor barely avoided. But he was off his balance now, and Rogan pressed him back. Where before they had been matched blow for blow, now Rogan's axe was a blur of speed, striking so quickly that it took all the Mystic's skill to hold him back.

The axe bit deep into the joint at the shoulder, and the lord chancellor dropped his sword as he sank to his knees.

Twice more the axe rose and fell, first severing an arm, and then taking the head at the neck. The lord chancellor's body fell beneath the boots of his enemy, and the Shades roared their approval.

With renewed vigor they pressed forwards now, and Rogan led them in another charge. The palace guards had to retreat through the inner gate. But the guards atop the wall had been slain, and the portcullis remained raised. Loren, Chet, and Gem threw themselves at one of the doors, struggling to push it closed against the mass of bodies. Loren stood at the edge of the door, just a few paces away from the fighting. Her heart thundered as steel flashed and blood soaked the pavement at her feet.

"Loren!" cried Rogan, drawing her gaze. He wore a rictus grin, blood covering his armor. She saw the hilt of a sword sticking from the side of his breastplate where someone had landed a blow, but the Necromancer's dark magic kept him on his feet. "Daughter of the forest. You have done your duty well. Thank you for laying the path of our conquest."

She gritted her teeth and stepped away from the doorway to snatch her bow. In the blink of an eye she drew, and whether it was by Albern's training or some stroke of luck, her shaft sank into Rogan's left eye and out the back of his head. His body went limp as a rag doll, and he fell beneath the press.

The palace guards gave a great cheer, and the Shades wavered. The Lord Prince led a counterattack, and they pushed their foes back through the gates. But the press of bodies was too thick beyond the walls, and it was all they could do to push the gates closed. The royal guards seized the Lord Prince and the High King and dragged them back into the castle, with Loren and her friends hastening to follow.

THIRTY-FIVE

"That was a well-placed shot," said the Lord Prince. His helmet had been knocked loose in the fighting, and Loren saw a bruise blooming to life on his cheek. "I had heard from Xain that you had no taste for killing."

"He will not die," said Loren grimly. "A dark enchantment protects him, binding him to life."

"Still, it secured our escape, and I thank you," said the High King, who had knelt to wrap a bandage about the knee of one of her royal guards. The woman had taken an arrow.

"You are welcome, Your Majesty," said Loren. But the words were scarcely out before she turned on her heel and ran down the hallway towards the staircase.

"Loren!" said Chet. "Where are you going?"

"Finding us an escape," she said. She took the stairs two at a time. Chet hastened to follow her, but he soon slowed, wincing at the injury in his chest. Though she wanted to scream with impatience, Loren stopped and went down, taking his arm to help him.

"Why go up?" said Chet. "We cannot fly away from here."

"Mayhap, but one never knows. Certainly it seems that the ground floor has no escape."

She threw open a door leading to one of the wide open balconies that ran all around the palace exterior. Below them she could see the fighting at the eastern wall. As she had expected, Rogan stood at the head of his soldiers again. The gaping wound where his eye had been was already stitching itself shut.

Loren looked around in desperation, searching for some other way, some hidden door she had not noticed before. It seemed impossible. She had been a guest here less than a month. How could she find a new route of escape more easily than those who had lived in the palace their whole lives? But she had to try. She ran down the balcony, around a corner of the building, and the sun blinked as it vanished behind the arches for a moment.

Chet nearly ran into her as she stopped in her tracks. When he saw her looking up, his gaze followed. "What is it?"

She did not answer him. She was looking at the arches. The palace stretched out in five great wings. Along the top was a balcony, just like the one they stood on now, but thirty feet higher. And from the end of each wing sprang an arch, rising gently before dipping back down to meet the towers that stood at each of the five corners in the castle's outer wall.

"Come with me," she said, and ran back into the palace.

When she reached the High King, the royal guard were engaged in a furious argument with the Lord Prince about what to do next. Xain and Gem stood apart. Gem saw them and came running, eyes wide.

"Where were you?" he said. "I thought you had run off and abandoned us."

"You are not so lucky as all that," said Loren. "You must suffer our company a bit longer—quite a while longer, if I have my way."

"What do you—" he began, but she pushed past him to speak with the High King.

"Your Majesty," she said, cutting through the argument between the Lord Prince and the royal guard. "There may be a chance to get you to safety."

They all stopped at that and stared at her. But where Loren had quailed under their gaze in the throne room, now she had no time. She pressed on before they could answer.

"We have no chance of victory by warfare, as any of us can plainly see. All the castle entrances are blocked. This is not a time for blades and armor, but for stealth and secrecy. Shed your plate and follow me, and I can get you beyond the palace walls."

"How?" said the Lord Prince, incredulous.

"The arches. They stretch from the top of each wing to the towers. They are high, but they are wide enough to walk on, and not too steep. But we have to go quickly, for it will be a dangerous crossing, and if they see us they will try to shoot us down."

"That is madness," said one of the royal guard. "It is fifty feet in the air."

Enalyn studied Loren's face for a moment before turning to Eamin. "What is your counsel, Lord Prince?"

He looked at Loren in wonder, and she could see the thought working its way through his mind. "I . . ." he began.

THOOM

They heard a great crash outside, and the roaring of an army.

"They have broken the eastern gate!" said one of the palace guard. "They are within the walls!"

"Enough," said Enalyn. "If they are in the walls already, we have no choice. Up the stairs, and quickly!"

Loren led the way, jumping up the steps like a satyr on a mountainside, with Chet and Gem just behind. The High King followed, while the Lord Prince helped Xain and his son make the climb. Four of the royal guard came with them, the rest staying behind to guard the ground floor against the invaders.

Up and up the stairs wound in a spiral, and Loren ran past every floor. Only when she reached the top at last did she take the door leading out of the staircase, and quickly turned about to get her bearings. In a moment she found the door leading outside, and took it to another balcony. She went to the railing and looked down at the courtyard far below, where she saw the Shades doing battle with the palace soldiers on the pavement. The sight of it drew her gaze for a moment, but she forced herself to break away.

A few paces farther along the balcony, she found the spot where the arch joined the castle wall, some two paces below the balcony railing. It was not such a far drop, but it made Loren dizzy now; the arch was mayhap two paces wide, and if they stumbled upon landing, it was another fifteen-pace fall to the courtyard below.

"That is not an easy jump," said Chet beside her.

"It is the only way. Would that we had a rope! There is one in my pack, but I left that in our quarters."

The door opened behind them, and the rest of the procession came out onto the balcony. Xain took one look at the height and reeled heavily away from the railing. But Gem stood brightly on tiptoe, leaning far over the edge. "I made far more difficult leaps than this on the rooftops of Cabrus," he remarked.

"Your Majesty, you cannot think to go through with this," said the royal guard. "It is certain death."

"Certain death is the battle that rages in the palace even now," said Loren. "This is a hope, however slim."

"Two paces, is about how slim I would call it," said the Lord Prince.

"Unless someone is willing to suggest an alternative, my decision has been made," said Enalyn. "Now help me out of this armor."

She and Eamin and the royal guard shed their plate as quickly as they could. Loren tried to help, though she knew little of how the pieces strapped together. Before long they stood only in their regular clothing and light shirts of chain, which would not hinder their movement.

"Now, we must go down one at a time," said Loren. "We should send one or two ahead of the High King, to help catch her and steady her landing."

"I will go first," said Chet, and before she could argue, he seized the railing and vaulted over the edge of the balcony.

"*Chet!*" she cried, running to the rail.

He landed hard on the stone of the archway, taking the shock of the landing with his legs and falling forwards. He spread his hands wide and gripped either edge of the stone path, holding himself steady. For a moment he lay there, recovering. Loren could see the pain in his face where his wound had been jostled in the fall.

"Up, boy," called one of the royal guard. "I am coming down, and have no wish to crush you." He was a burly man with a trimmed beard, somewhat advanced in years but still strong. As Chet scrambled to his feet, the guard lifted himself carefully over the railing, then held on to it as he lowered himself as far as he could. When he was at the limit of his reach, he dropped. Because he was facing backwards, he landed badly and fell onto his rear with a grunt, nearly rolling off the edge. But Chet gripped his shoulder to steady him, and he got back to his feet.

"Make haste," said Loren, for she was looking past the arch to the ground far below. The Shades had broken through the soldiers in the courtyard. Even now they were in the palace, ransacking its halls in search of the High King. "Your Majesty, are you ready?"

"Send them first," said Enalyn, gesturing to Xain and his son.

"Your Majesty, I—" Xain began.

"No time to argue," she snapped. "Your son first, and then you."

Xain took his son, Erin, and held him under the arms. "Look at me, son. I am right here. I will come right behind you. Be brave for me." Erin nodded, though his eyes were filled with tears.

Slowly, ever so slowly, Xain lowered him over the edge. Loren helped, leaning over to grip one wrist while Xain held the other, and together they hung as far over as they dared, until the boy's ankles were just a pace above the outstretched arms of Chet and the royal guardsman. Loren nodded to him, and they let go. Erin fell into Chet's arms, where he clung to his chest.

"You next, wizard," said Loren. "I can lower you down, if you like. You cannot weigh more than a sack of potatoes."

Xain glared at her a moment before climbing hastily over the rail. He landed without trouble, and then they lowered the High King. She jumped down quite nimbly, and Chet was there with her guard to steady her landing.

The door to the balcony flew open, slamming into the wall with a crash. Loren looked over her shoulder to see Shades run into the sunlight, sun gleaming from their gore-soaked blades.

"Run!" she cried, waving desperately to Chet and the others. "Get the High King to safety!"

Xain was already walking carefully along the arch with his son, and was a good distance ahead. The royal guard looked up at her with a grim nod and seized the High King, dragging her away. Enalyn fought him desperately, trying to return to the balcony.

"Eamin!" she cried in anguish. "Eamin!"

"Jump," said the Lord Prince, hefting his sword in his hand. "We will do our best to hold them off."

Three royal guard remained with them on the balcony, and one of them spoke gruffly over his shoulder. "No, Lord Prince. You must get to safety. We shall remain here."

"I am afraid they are right, Your Highness," said Loren. "Forgive me."

She nodded to Gem, and together they gripped Eamin's arms and half-threw him over the railing. He went over the edge with a shout, and they held him at the last second before he dropped. Just before he had time to recover and try to climb back up, they let him go, and he fell to the arch. Chet caught him and dragged him back, just as Loren and Gem jumped over together.

Gem had vaulted a bit farther, and landed catlike on the stone. But Loren had misjudged the width of it, and landed too close to the edge. As she fell forwards on her knees, her left hand came down on air instead of stone. She pitched to her left, and for a terrifying moment hung out over empty space, and her body froze in terror.

"No!" cried Chet. He leaped, landing in a slide on his back and gripping her tunic. Desperately he dragged her back, until she rolled over and came to land on top of him, her face less than an inch from his own.

"Keep your mind on the matter at hand, hunter's son," she mumbled, but her voice shook, as well as her hands where they gripped his shirt.

"It is not my mind that wanders, woodsman's daughter," he replied.

"If you two are quite done?" cried Gem, who was already up and running along the arch, and had turned back to see them there.

They scrambled to their feet and ran. Loren risked one glance back only, to see the royal guard holding the railing against the Shades. But there were too many, and one by one they fell. The last one took a blade to the gut, the tip of the sword thrusting out the back of his jerkin. He seized two of his foes and pitched backwards over the railing, and the Shades screamed as their bodies fell to break on the pavement below. Loren turned forwards and ran on.

Hissing filled the air as arrows whizzed by them, but by now they were too far to get a clear shot, and soon the arch dipped back down to block them from view. The slope was gentle enough to keep firm footing, and soon they had reached the top of the tower at the end. There the others waited for them, but other than that the tower was empty. Loren looked off down the walls and saw no one. The Shades had broken into the palace, and all the wall's guards had been slain already.

"They are coming," said the royal guardsman. Loren turned to see that some Shades had braved the jump, and even now came along the stone archway towards them. One more tried to jump as she watched, but he missed his landing and pitched off into empty space.

"They are foolish," said Xain. Loren could see how it pained him, but still his eyes glowed as he summoned his magic.

Flames burst forth, striking the Shade in the lead, and she screamed as she beat at the fire. Lurching back, she struck the man behind her, and together they fell screaming from the arch. But more were coming down from the rail, and from somewhere they had found a rope. Even now they were tying it about the railing, and then they would be climbing, not jumping.

"Rope!" said Loren. "We need to flee, not fight."

The tower's hatch lay gaping open, and she went down into it to search. There in the corner she found what she was looking for: a long coil of rope, thick and strong and well-woven. She threw the coil over her shoulder and climbed back out into the daylight. Chet helped her tie it around the tower's outer rampart with solid knots. Xain held the archway against the Shades as they advanced, while one by one the others climbed down the tower's outer wall.

"Your turn, wizard," said Loren.

"Go first," he said. "I will be right behind you."

"Do I need to throw you again?"

He growled and turned, climbing down the rope. Loren kept a careful eye on the archway, but the Shades were too far away. As soon as Xain was far enough down, she followed him, and soon they were all fleeing through the streets of the city.

THIRTY-SIX

THE GREATER PART OF THE FIGHTING HAD MOVED WITHIN THE PALACE, but there was still much of it in the streets. They had to move cautiously, ducking out of sight whenever a group of Shades came running by. They had climbed down the northwest tower of the palace wall, and did not have far to go to reach the western gate. But the way was slow, and they could not take the main streets, for those were well patrolled.

Loren felt as though she were suffering the fall of Northwood all over again, for all about them they saw the corpses of citizens in the streets. Only this time she was the one escorting others out of the city's destruction, rather than the one being rescued. She made a silent vow to herself: if need be, she would give her life to save the High King's, in token of payment for Mag, Sten, and Albern, who had sacrificed their lives for Loren.

They heard the tramping of boots and pressed themselves against the wall of a shop. Shades ran by, along the street and towards the palace. Loren leaned out to watch after they had gone, ensuring they were out of sight.

"How will we reach the western gate?" said Eamin. "Surely they will have it guarded, especially if they know we have escaped the palace."

"We may be able to break through," said Xain. "I have my magic, and you have your blades."

"Swords we have, but no armor, unlike our enemies. And forgive me for saying so, my friend, but you are nearly at the end of your strength."

Enalyn turned to Loren. "What say you, girl? We have made it this far by your counsel."

"I do not know, Your Majesty," said Loren. "In truth I had not thought that far ahead, for I was not certain we would escape the palace at all."

"How comforting," said Enalyn.

"We scaled one wall," said Chet. "We can scale another. Where can we go where the Shades will not be gathered in strength, where we can make our way into a tower and then down the other side?"

"To the north," said the Lord Prince. "But the problem is not the city wall. It is the docks. They will all be swarming with Shades, and we cannot escape the island without a boat."

"One bridge at a time, my lord," said Chet. "If we can make it beyond the north wall, then let us go to the north wall."

"I see you share Loren's gift for not thinking far ahead," said Enalyn.

But Loren was looking out beyond the edge of the building, her brow furrowed in concentration. Not far away, a strong wind whipped at the banners that flew from the western wall. "They have not burned the buildings," she said.

Xain looked at her sharply. "What?"

"They have not burned the buildings. In Wellmont, the Dorsean army sought to burn as much as they could. Here, the Shades are sacking the city, but they are not trying to destroy it. Why?"

"Likely they mean to occupy it," said Eamin. "If they can take the Seat for themselves, it will be a demonstration of their power."

"No," said Enalyn, eyes widening. "They cannot risk their fleet. If the flames spread from the city to the docks, their ships will be destroyed. Then they will be trapped here, unable to flee if we should attack them in strength."

"I do not see how that can help us," said Xain. "Unless we mean to burn the city down ourselves, in the hope that it spreads to their ships."

"I think that is precisely what Loren has planned," said Enalyn with a grim smile.

Loren turned to them. "The ship's crews will have remained with their vessels, as well as some soldiers to guard them. If they see the city beginning to burn, they may leave the ships to come and fight the fires. We could slip past them then, to take a ship for ourselves and flee."

Eamin stared at her as if she had gone mad. "You mean to burn our own city?"

"It is lost already," said Enalyn, who had begun to nod. "I think this plan may be a wise one. A strange sort of wisdom, certainly, and yet it may work."

"Can you muster the flames, wizard?" said the royal guard.

Xain's skin was pale, and his arm shivered as it wrapped around his son's shoulders. "I have little strength left. But I will do what I must."

"You may not have to," said Loren, struck by a thought. "Torches will suffice. Find them, and collect more as we move to the western wall. We will set flames wherever we think they may catch. Then, Xain, you can spread the fires with wind."

"That would be easier," he said.

"Let us go, then, and quickly," said Enalyn.

They set off once more, this time faster, for their steps held purpose again. Many fixtures on buildings held torches, and soon each of them had collected a great armful.

When they reached the west wall, they looked to see if any Shades were nearby to spot them. But none were about. One torch sat in a fixture on the wall above them, but rather than remove it, Loren had Xain light it. Then, one by one, she held the other torches in its flames until they caught.

She, Chet, and Gem ran out and among the buildings. Any place they found a shop with wooden shingles, or an inn with a stable full of hay, they flung their torches. Soon smoke rose from several buildings, and before long the smoke turned into flames. They reached for the sky with angry red fingers, and their heat filled the air.

"Now use your magic, Xain," said Loren.

Eyes glowing white, he put forth his power. The air howled and whistled before his hands, and a heavy gale swept in from the sky. It struck the houses and carried the flames south, throwing sparks and flaming brands across all the western side of the city. In no time it seemed that half the island was burning.

Casting her cloak about her, Loren ran to the western gate. As she neared it she slowed, searching warily for anyone who might spot her.

But no one was in sight as she sidled up to the gate. The great wooden doors lay broken upon the ground, torn from their hinges by a battering ram, or else by some powerful magic. The portcullis still hung in the air; the attackers must have raised it during their assault.

She peered around the corner of the wall towards the docks, and her heart sang. There were the Shades who had been left to guard the ships, and they were running towards the city walls. Behind them the ship crews streamed from their vessels, carrying buckets which they dipped into the waters of the bay.

Hastily she withdrew, and ran back to the others. "It worked," she said. "They are running to douse the flames. We should get closer to the gates, and be ready to run the moment we find an opening."

Step by step they followed her forwards, coughing and casting their cloaks across their mouths to stop themselves from breathing in the soot. Xain's son buried his head in his father's shoulder, crying. Loren soon realized she did not have to worry overmuch about being spotted; the smoke that poured through the streets, as well as the scorching heat of the flames, kept the Shades' attention. Sometimes they passed soldiers only a few paces away in the smoke, but attracted no notice.

Soon they emerged coughing, running as quick as they could into the open square before the western gate. But the moment the smoke left their eyes they skidded to a halt on the paving stones.

There stood Rogan, framed by the gate. His axe and shield were battered and stained, and his armor bore many rents from blows he had taken in the fighting. He stood alone, for all his soldiers were in the city to fight the fires. But Loren quaked in her boots, for she knew that he was easily a match for all of them.

"I see I was right," said Rogan. "As soon as I saw the smoke rising from the city, I knew you were making for the boats. A clever tactic."

Her throat was dry. But Chet stepped forwards to stand at her side, and Gem and Eamin with him.

"You may stand aside, if you wish," said the Lord Prince. "I swear we will let you live."

Rogan laughed at that, blood standing out shockingly red against the white of his teeth. "A precious sentiment, princeling. Here is my counter: kneel and present your necks for my axe, and I will make the killing quick."

"Remember the tattoo. You cannot defeat him," Loren said quietly. Then she turned to Xain and the royal guard who stood by the High

King. "Get yourselves out of the city, and the High King as well. We will hold him off as long as we can."

"I will not leave my son," said Enalyn.

"You will if you must, Your Majesty," said Loren firmly. "If he will not run from this fight, still you must reach the shores of Selvan in safety."

"What are you whispering there, Nightblade?" said Rogan. "I think you have used your last clever strategy. Come, let us make this quick. There is no need for you to suffer as Jordel did."

Loren turned on him. Her bow was light in her hand, and she ached to use it. "You may not speak his name."

Rogan smiled, and despite all she knew of him, it looked kind. "You truly loved the Mystic, did you not? The look in your eyes . . . it is almost worship. He should not have died. He should have been on our side. I can only imagine the sort of captain he would have made in our ranks. I am what he could have been—but better, for I will never die."

She nocked the arrow without thinking and loosed. It sped true, but Rogan lifted his shield to block it. Then he was charging forwards, and Eamin met the first blow with his sword.

"Get her away!" cried Loren.

Enalyn began to circle around, making for the gate under the escort of her guard. Xain only stood there, looking at Loren in wordless fury.

"Go," she said. "You remember what happened when you tried your magic on Trisken. You are even more useless here than I am."

He nodded and followed the High King, his son in tow.

Loren turned, another arrow nocked. Gem had edged forwards, his sword held forth, but his hands shook and he looked ready to flee at any moment. Chet was a couple of paces ahead, holding his staff, but he seemed just as lost. They knew, as Loren did, that they stood no chance against Rogan. They could only distract him.

But Eamin was doing a remarkable job of that for the moment. He matched the brute stroke for stroke, and even without a shield his guard was impenetrable. His armor had been left atop the palace, and he used that to his advantage, dodging around blows rather than trying to meet them head-on, and returning light, quick strikes that Rogan had to move quickly to avoid. He hoped to tire his opponent, who was burdened by his armor, and then move in for the final blow.

As Eamin and Rogan backed away from each other for a moment, Loren drew and fired. The arrow glanced from Rogan's pauldron, knocking it sideways. Chet swung with his staff, and Gem took another step forwards. But Rogan recovered quickly and blocked the staff with his shield, then swung wide, forcing them both back. Eamin lunged and struck again, and his blade found purchase in Rogan's hip. The brute grunted and stepped back, hiding behind his shield.

"I had heard you were a mighty warrior," said Eamin lightly. "But it looks as though your enchantment is your only strength."

"It is strength enough," said Rogan with a smile.

Loren looked past him to the gate. Enalyn and Xain had almost reached it, her guard at her back. Rogan's attention was on the Lord Prince—it was going to work.

But that hope proved false. Rogan whirled on the spot as though he had eyes in the back of his head and came at them in a rush. Eamin ran to follow as the King's guard stepped forwards to block her. But with three swift strokes, Rogan knocked the man's sword aside and planted the axe in the guard's chest. He sank to his knees with a grunt, dropping the sword to grip the axe with both hands.

That gave Eamin a moment's advantage. He plunged his sword into Rogan's back beneath the backplate. Rogan cried out in pain, arching backwards and grasping at the hilt of the sword. It was out of his reach, and Eamin held fast, pushing him away from the High King.

"Go!" cried Loren. She slung her bow on her back and ran forwards, seizing Gem's and Chet's arms and dragging them through the gate. Enalyn was beside them, and Xain, with his son. Just beyond the wall she stopped and turned to look.

Still Eamin held Rogan like a pig on a spit. But Loren could see the glow of dark magic around the Shade captain's neck, and already his flesh stitched itself together around the blade.

Like a snake he turned, ripping the hilt from Eamin's hand. His mailed fist crashed into the Lord Prince's face, then his chest. Loren had a horrifying flash of memory, of the way Jordel's chest had caved in under Trisken's mighty blows. Eamin struggled to hold his feet, but Rogan struck him hard with both fists clenched, and he went flying to land on the ground beside Loren.

"Impotent children," snarled Rogan. "Come here, that I may show you the true power of death."

He took a step forwards—and then stopped to look down. The royal guard still lived, and had wrapped an arm around one of Rogan's ankles. The head of the axe was still buried in his chest. With what remained of his strength, the guard used his free hand to pull it out with a roar. He flung it away, and it went skidding across the pavement towards Loren's feet.

"Girl!" he cried. "The chain!"

Loren's eyes widened. She ran to the axe and wrapped both hands around its haft.

Rogan, oblivious, tore his plated boot free from the guard's grip. The foot came up, and then down with a horrifying crunch. Again and again he stamped, until the sound of it grew horrible and wet.

His gaze rose to Loren, bloodlust making his eyes nearly glow. She stood facing him, at the edge of the gate, all her strength barely enough to lift the axe. Rogan bared his teeth in a grin, and then threw back his head to laugh out loud.

"What do you mean to do with an axe you can scarcely even wield, girl? You cannot kill me."

"I know," said Loren, and swung with all her might at the chain that held the portcullis.

Rogan barely had time to look up before it came crashing down, crushing him under its weight. Two of the three-foot spikes along its bottom pierced his chest, sinking into the stone below, while he screamed in agony.

Loren dropped the axe and ran, helping Lord Prince Eamin to his feet. Rejoining the others, they fled to the docks where a fleet of boats waited for them to sail away on.

THIRTY-SEVEN

THE GATES OF THE PALACE OF GARSEC, SELVAN'S CAPITAL CITY, SWUNG open before them. Limping and sore, Loren and the others made their way through. Inside stood Anwar, king of Selvan, along with a retinue to receive them. Quickly his healers ran forwards, their right robes swishing about their feet, to tend to Enalyn.

"I am well," she said, waving them off. "See to the Lord Prince and the others."

Anwar came forwards at once, taking a knee before her. "Your Majesty," he said. "I cannot express my relief at seeing you alive and well."

Enalyn reached down and took his hands, drawing him to his feet. "King Anwar. Thank you for your hospitality in our time of need."

"I could do no less," he said earnestly. "I blame myself for this. With so many of our soldiers south in Wellmont, we did not keep watch over the Great Bay, and did not see the attack upon the Seat until too late."

"You could not have known."

Loren watched as the healers saw to the Lord Prince Eamin's injuries. They were bruises only, and would heal with time. He kept trying to push them off, but with the High King's command ringing in their ears, they would not leave him alone.

They had sailed the short distance southwest across the water and to the docks of Garsec, and immediately sent word of the High King's arrival. While they waited for a carriage to be sent, they had stood upon the docks and watched the Seat across the water. The smoke grew thicker and thicker, until the orange glow of the flames could be seen all across the island. The fires they had set consumed nearly everything, until the Shades were forced to flee the island's destruction. Across the strait they sailed, to land on the coast and vanish once more into the Birchwood. Meanwhile the Dulmun fleet set sail for the east, returning to their homeland to plot their next stroke. One whole kingdom had risen in rebellion against the High King that day, and who knew which others held treason in their hearts?

"You are deep in thought, girl."

Loren blinked, and then ducked her head in a half-bow. While she had been distracted, looking out through the palace gates, Enalyn had approached from behind. "I apologize, Your Majesty."

"Do not. I, too, find my mind much occupied. Will you walk with me?"

Loren nodded, and Enalyn led her out through the gate. The palace sat upon a great hill, almost a mountain, in the middle of the city. Outside its walls was a wide open space, from which they could survey the city and all the lands beyond. Enalyn took her north, where far away they could see the green of the Birchwood. There she stopped, and stared at the forest for a while.

Just as Loren was beginning to grow uncomfortable in the silence, the High King spoke. "I owe you a great debt. Many times over, in fact."

Loren shook her head quickly. "I did only the duty that was passed down to me."

"Many do their duty. Sometimes that duty requires much of us, and carrying it out should be seen as a fine thing."

"As you say, Your Majesty."

Enalyn turned to her suddenly, meeting her gaze unflinching, and Loren felt overshadowed despite standing a head taller. "I have need of those with honest and loyal hearts. I have had many such servants, but they are all of a type. Like the lord chancellor, or even my son, they think only of the great battle, the wartime stratagem. We need something else now. The strength of the Shades is not their might of arms, but the plans they hatch when they believe we cannot see them."

"Indeed, it seems we cannot. None of us knew their plans, and thus we played the very game they set out for us."

Enalyn looked into her eyes. "That is what I mean to fix, if you will help me."

Loren balked. "Your Majesty? I do not understand."

"I would have you enter my service, Loren of the family Nelda. My personal service, answerable to me, under the direction and guidance of Chancellor Kal, to whom it seems I should have been listening for some time now."

"You . . . desire my service," said Loren. She could not wrap her mind around the idea. *I am a simple forest girl,* she told herself. *A daughter of the Birchwood.* And yet here she stood, and there was the High King. "Your Majesty . . . I do not know what to say."

"Say you will serve me, of course," said Enalyn, but she softened it with a smile.

Loren fell to her knee at once. "Of course, Your Majesty. You do me great honor. But . . . what am I, exactly?"

"I have told you your task already."

Loren shook her head. "That is not what I mean. I will be the agent of your will. But what am I? When I act in your name, what will I call myself? Your advisor? Your messenger?"

"Your title? There is a name already, I hear, in the stories people whisper about you. Let that be your title. Let them call you my Nightblade."

EPILOGUE

ROGAN'S BOOTS SHUFFLED UNCERTAINLY THROUGH THE SOIL OF THE Birchwood, and his path swayed back and forth. He tried to muster his strength. It would not do for the Shades at his back to see their commander weak and wandering. His hand went to his chest with a grimace. Still the wounds had not fully healed, where the portcullis had punched through plate, flesh, and bone all at once.

His teeth ground together. He did not fear his father's wrath, but only the thought of failing him. Rogan was the favored son. All his life it had been said to him. And now he had failed the man to whom he owed everything.

"Are you disappointed, my son?"

Rogan staggered to a halt, as did the soldiers behind him. His eyes filled with tears at the voice.

"Wait here," he said, keeping his back turned so that they could not see his face. "Do not move until I give the order."

He stalked off into the woods, towards where he had heard the voice. He did not have to search far before he stopped, the tears spilling down his cheeks.

"Father," he whimpered. He sank to his knees, leaves crunching beneath him. "My father. Forgive me."

"Forgive? You committed no sin, child. Stand. This was no fault of yours."

He bowed his head. "I took the task upon myself. Tomorrow should have been a day of rejoicing. We should have sent word to all the nine lands that the High King was dead and the Lord Prince captured."

"I gave you your task, Rogan. The blame lies with me, not with you."

Rogan shook his head fervently, almost maniacally. "No, *no*, Father. You are the greatest among us. No design of yours is at fault. I am your arm, meant to carry out your aims, and I am weak."

He felt the fingers resting on the top of his head, gently stroking his hair. His tears fell harder, and he curled in upon himself at the touch.

"When Trisken fell in the Greatrocks, I was wrathful. I held him accountable, for I thought he had underestimated the girl. But now I have made the same mistake. She was the perfect messenger, but I did not think she could save the High King."

"I should have stopped her," whimpered Rogan. "Forgive me."

"You are forgiven. Her victory will soon be hollow, like wine turned to ash in her throat. The High King has lost this war before it is begun. For I have found the trail of my great foe, and soon my children will bring her to me."

Rogan tensed, eyes glittering, and he looked up with hope. "You have found the Lifemage?"

He was answered only by a smile.

WEREMAGE

BEING BOOK TWO
OF THE SECOND VOLUME

OF THE
NIGHTBLADE EPIC

ONE

The door to their chambers opened easily under Loren's hand, and in the creaking of the hinges there were no echoes of the battle cries and bloodshed that still haunted her thoughts.

Cool air brushed her face as the room was revealed to her, and she sighed. The scents of the High King's Seat came rushing through the door, the heady salt of the Great Bay and the acrid smoke of the city's ten thousand hearths. She closed her eyes and drank them in.

"Loren?"

Chet's touch on her arm brought her back to herself. She glanced over her shoulder at him. "I am sorry. It . . . it feels a lifetime since last we were here. A span of months, not days."

"I feel the same," he said quietly. "But now that we *are* here, might we not go inside, rather than standing in the hall without purpose?"

She chuckled and took his hand to draw him in after her. Inside, they removed their cloaks and hung them on hooks beside the door. To the left were Xain's and Gem's rooms. To the right were two more rooms where Chet and Loren had once slept apart—though that had changed in the days since first they came here.

Much of the furniture in the common room was new, its wood fresh-hewn and the cushions too bright to have seen much use. The tables and chairs that had once been here must have been destroyed in the fighting. That thought further dampened what was already a solemn day—for while many in the city rejoiced at the return of the High King Enalyn, the wise knew it was no proud thing that she had been chased from her capital in the first place.

Seven days it was since the Seat had been attacked and Loren had helped Enalyn escape the fighting. Her forces had fled to the kingdom of Selvan, thinking to muster a counter-attack—but then, as swiftly as they had come, the attacking armies had fled. The fleet of Dulmun sailed east across the Great Bay, vanishing into their mighty coastal fortresses. The Shades had rowed the short distance between the Seat and Dorsea's eastern coast, and had disappeared into the Birchwood. All the scouts the High King could muster had failed to find them since, and many who were sent to do so had never been heard from again.

Since then, Enalyn had granted Loren a new position: Nightblade of the High King, her personal agent. It was a recognition of the valiant way Loren had saved the lives of Enalyn and her son, the Lord Prince Eamin. But other than a pretty name and a great honor, Loren was not quite sure what it meant. The title of Nightblade had been a childhood fancy, something she had thought up when she was a girl of the forest. The world she found herself in now was all too real, all too perilous. What good was a daydream in the face of the dangers that Loren had seen?

"Sky above. Come look at this."

Chet's voice came from their balcony. The words made her tense for a moment—but his voice held only awe, and no trace of fear. She entered their room, briefly noting the new bedclothes, before she passed through it to the balcony.

He stood leaning out into the open air, wiry arms spread as they gripped the railing. They were mayhap thirty paces high, and had an excellent view northwest across the Seat. The sun was still rising in the east, for the day was young, and the youthful warmth of its shine turned the winter air bracing rather than chilling. The city's smell struck her again, stronger than before, and she smiled without thinking.

"What?" said Loren. "What is it?"

"All of it," said Chet. "Look at it. Look at them."

He pointed. There, far below, she saw figures scurrying through the streets. A multitude of colors could be found: the red cloaks of Mystics, the russet armor of constables, the white and gold of the High King's guard, and all the liveries of soldiers and servants from across the nine kingdoms. But most wore simple clothes, and carried tools or pulled them in carts. Saws and hammers, lumber and ladders, all the accoutrements of craftsmen and artisans. They looked like a colony of ants from this high up, running frantically about in the chaos of a careless step that had crushed their hill. But their scurrying had a purpose: their home had been destroyed, and they meant to rebuild it.

"It seemed so simple when Enalyn called for them," said Loren quietly. "I know that it was not, but it seemed so. And just look how many of them have come to obey her."

"My father always said he would never take the High King's power, not for anything in the world," said Chet. "How frightening it must be, to hold such influence that your slightest whim can move an entire kingdom to action."

Loren nodded as if in agreement. But in her mind, she felt her thoughts turning in another direction. Yes, the great and mighty could do much with a simple command—the High King Enalyn, and the Lord Prince Eamin, and even Anwar, the king of Selvan. Yet who now walked in the halls of those mighty figures? Loren of the family Nelda. The High King's Nightblade. The thought should have been terrifying—and she supposed it was, to a degree—but she could not deny that it excited her. That, too, had been part of the dream of the Nightblade.

Her hand brushed her dagger, which she now wore inside the waist of her trousers, covering the hilt with her green vest. The feel of it on her skin cast a shadow over the bright and beautiful day.

The dagger was an ever-present source of danger. She could never stop thinking about it, and was always wary of letting it be seen by anyone but her friends. If it were ever revealed, the effects could be disastrous—not only to Loren, but to the Order of Mystics who might be the best defense against the rise of the Necromancer.

Yet she could not bring herself to get rid of it. It had been her first theft. And by now she had learned two of the dagger's magical qualities—the ability to find wizards, and the sight it could grant her even in pitch darkness. These had proven beyond useful, and had even saved her life on occasion. The Nightblade could not afford to throw away her most powerful tool.

"Where has your mind gone?" said Chet, looking at her with his brow furrowed. "You have been drifting away more and more often of late. Do not think I have not noticed."

"Nowhere," said Loren, shaking her head. She ran her fingertips along his arm, sending gooseflesh rippling. "I am here with you."

He smiled and put a hand on her cheek, his question forgotten. Her smile widened—but her thoughts turned sadly to how easy it was to guide his mind, just as on the day she fled their village in the Birchwood.

They heard a gentle knock behind them and turned to see Gem. The urchin boy stood in the doorway back to their bedroom, his knuckles still held close to the doorframe as though he might knock again. He was dressed in finer clothes than Loren was used to seeing him in, though somehow he had already found a way to get them dirty.

"I have been sent to summon you," said Gem, looking at Loren.

Her stomach did a somersault. Without thinking, she reached for Chet's hand. Only once he had squeezed her fingers did she glance at him, earning a smile that should have encouraged her. But she could see a lingering sorrow behind it.

"I must go," she said.

"I know. Do not be afraid. You will do well."

"You are more confident than I am, I fear."

"I have followed you for enough leagues to know it." He stepped before her and kissed her lightly. "And what is more, I call anyone who doubts you a fool."

Gem cleared his throat a bit more loudly than he needed to. "Yes, well and good," said the boy. "Yet the council requires her presence."

Loren gave Chet's hand one last squeeze before brushing past him and into their chambers. She rushed through the common room, but Chet's voice stopped her again halfway through the door.

"Stop."

She turned, steeling herself for him to ask her not to go. He did not want her to, and she knew it. But he only came forwards and reached past her to the hook on the wall. He brought down her fine black cloak from where she had hung it, and with gentle fingers clasped it at her throat.

"The Nightblade must be the Nightblade, after all," he murmured.

"Thank you," she said, kissing him again—and this time it was not gentle.

"Sky above. *The council.*"

"Oh, still your tongue, Gem," said Loren, rushing past the boy and into the hall.

Gem scowled. "Why should I, when the two of you never do the same?"

TWO

ONLY ONCE BEFORE HAD LOREN BEEN TO THE HIGH KING'S COUNCIL room, but she remembered the way. Therefore she did not let Gem guide her like some page, but quickened her pace so that he had to trot to keep up, though he maintained an air of long-suffering dignity.

"Who else will be there?" said Loren.

"I do not know," said Gem. "They did not summon me into the room, but sent someone out to tell me to fetch you. It is like when messengers ride day and night, relaying a letter from one to the next, except a bit more ridiculous, since it all takes place in one small palace."

Loren shook her head. Only Gem had a high enough opinion of himself that he could think of the High King's palace as small. "Did you see Xain at all?"

"No," said Gem. "In fact, I have not seen him since we came off the ship."

They paused outside the council room. One of the High King's guards stood there, resplendent in her armor. She looked down at Gem with vague disdain. The boy stuck out his tongue at her. Loren put a hand on his shoulder.

"Thank you, Gem. Now be off."

His eyes widened, like a dog whose master was displeased with it. "Might I not wait here, ready in case you should need me?"

"I do not think I shall," said Loren. "And you will likely grow bored to death, for this may take some time."

Gem's shoulders slumped. "Very well, then. You may find me in my chamber if you need me."

She watched him go until he turned the corner. Then, carefully avoiding the eyes of the guard, she entered the room as quietly as she could.

The High King Enalyn's council chamber was much like the woman herself: restrained, imposing, but not without warmth. There were some chairs around the walls—for retainers, Loren supposed, though she had yet to see anyone sit in them. The main focus of the room, of course, was the table in its center, but that table was nowhere near so large as might have been expected. Rather than feeling ornamental, it gave the place an air of wartime preparation—and that air was particularly appropriate now, with all of Underrealm embroiled in conflict.

At the head of the table sat Enalyn herself, with one elbow propped up on the arm of her chair, her chin resting on her fist. To her right sat the Lord Prince Eamin, scratching at his short, well-trimmed beard, and beside Eamin was Xain, much to Loren's relief. The wizard was often bitter and always sarcastic, but he was still the closest friend she had in this room.

But to Enalyn's left sat a woman Loren did not recognize—short, fat, and clearly old, for her hair was silver and her face bore many wrinkles. Something about her seemed similar to the High King, the sharp eyes and the severe twist to her mouth, though hers held something more of a smirk than Enalyn's did. On her shoulders was draped the red cloak of a Mystic.

The four of them looked up the moment Loren stepped through the door, and Xain hesitantly put his hands on the arms of his chair to stand. But Enalyn lifted a hand to stop him.

"Greetings, Loren," she said. "I have ten thousands of councils to hold in the time it would take me to hold ten proper ones, and so we must do away with decorum. You will pretend that these others have stood to greet you, and I will pretend that you have knelt to me. Please sit there." She pointed at the chair beside the grey-haired woman.

"Yes, Your Majesty," said Loren, hastening to obey. The woman scooted her chair over slightly to make it easier for Loren to sit.

"You two should know each other. Lord Chancellor, this is Loren of the family Nelda, Nightblade of the High King. Loren, this is Hollen of the family Konnel, the new lord chancellor of the Order of Mystics."

"Well met," said Loren, nodding. *This is the lord chancellor? I thought the Mystics were all warriors.*

Hollen flashed her a wide smile, as though she guessed at Loren's thoughts. "Well met indeed. Do not fret over my looks, dear. I am not such a bumbling old woman as I appear—but only half so much, thank the sky."

Loren's eyes widened, and her cheeks flooded with red. "I . . . I do not think . . ."

Hollen laughed, and Enalyn's lips pressed tight. "Forgive the lord chancellor. She has a habit of making people uncomfortable—which is often a useful skill—as well as a sense of self-deprecation that she finds most amusing. At another time, I might agree with her, but there are urgent matters to discuss."

"Of course, Your Majesty. My apologies," said Hollen.

Across the table, Xain caught Loren's eye and winked. She gave him a quick smile in return.

"Loren, we three have spoken about you already, and I have come to a decision," said Enalyn. Loren did not much like the sound of that. "I know that the politics of the nine kingdoms are not familiar to you, but I cannot take the time to explain them in detail. Suffice it to say that while we balance on the brink of open war, we have not yet fallen into it, and now we must put forth every effort to keep that from happening."

That made Loren balk. "Forgive me, Your Majesty, but how can that be? A battle has already been fought."

"One, yes," said Enalyn. "But it is my understanding that you were at Wellmont. Did that battle mean that Selvan and Dorsea were at war?"

Loren pursed her lips. "I suppose not. But Selvan would have been well justified in declaring such a war."

Enalyn frowned, but across the table, Eamin's jaw clenched. Loren wondered if he dared disagree with his mother.

The lord chancellor interjected. "War brings only destruction, girl. No one should wish for that, no matter how justified they feel their cause to be. A ruler's noblest purpose is the preservation of life whenever possible. All here agree that open war with Dulmun may be inevitable. But we must do all we can to avoid it, while any chance of doing so exists."

"Forgive me, Your Majesty, for I would never think to advise you on matters of which I know little," said Loren slowly. "But is there nothing to be said for justice? Has the kingdom of Dulmun not wronged the rest of Underrealm, and should they not pay a price for it?"

The High King leaned back in her chair, steepling her fingers beneath her chin. The room went suddenly very quiet, and Loren's throat became as dry as sand.

"I have spoken out of turn," she said quietly, ducking Enalyn's gaze. "Forgive me."

"No, this should be addressed," said Enalyn. "After all, you are now an agent of a king, and therefore you ought to know the way a king's mind works. Tell me, Loren: how many people have you killed?"

"None, Your Majesty," said Loren at once. And then she felt a pang of shame as she remembered her father. "Or, one, but it was not my intent to do so. I only tried to defend my life and the life of . . . of another." She risked a glance at Xain, who met her gaze solemnly.

"That is what I have been told," said Enalyn. "You have decided that lives are not yours to take, and that if someone must die for their crimes, then that is up to the King's law. Do I have the right of it?"

"Yes, Your Majesty."

"Yet a moment ago you seemed to wish that Selvan had gone to war with Dorsea, and now you think that we should go to war with Dulmun. Tell me, Nightblade: what happens in war?"

Loren looked up with a frown. "Your Majesty?"

"You have seen battle. What do soldiers do to each other in battle?"

"They . . . they kill each other."

Enalyn nodded. "I could say that it was the fault of my soldiers for doing so. It would be easy to blame them for cutting down my enemies upon the field. But the truth is that if I declare war, every life lost is my responsibility. I say my responsibility, and not my fault, for they are not the same. I will bear that burden if I must, but I am not eager for it. You say you will not kill, and that might be called a noble vow. But if you only wish for others to swing the sword in your place, then you do not hate death—you only want to be able to tell one and all that your hands are still clean. And that is not so noble a purpose."

Loren wished that she could vanish from sight. None of the others at the table would look at her, like children sitting awkwardly while their mother chastised a sibling, only wishing for the moment to pass. But then she steeled herself and raised her head, meeting the High King's gaze.

"Again I apologize, Your Majesty." She kept her tone measured but earnest. "I am unaccustomed to sitting at so high a table, where matters such as these are discussed. I vow to you that I will learn, and I beg for your patience as I do."

Enalyn smiled, and the room's tension evaporated at once. "That is well said, and shows a humble heart. It is a wise soul who seeks to learn instead of clinging to the belief that they are right. Now, back to the matter at hand: ending the war with Dulmun before it begins."

"The key to such a strategy is making war appear not only undesirable, but hopeless," said Eamin. "That could divide Dulmun and turn the nobility against their king."

Loren cocked her head, confused, and Xain spoke up. "It is our hope that some in Dulmun may be convinced they cannot win. If the noble families think that war is hopeless, it may prompt them to overthrow Bodil, Dulmun's king, and appoint a new ruler who will make peace."

"I understand," said Loren, though that was only half true. "How may I help?"

"In all honesty, I am not certain," said Enalyn. "Yet something tells me that you have a role to play. You have displayed two talents in great abundance, Loren: an ability to gather information, and a strong sense of duty. These are valuable skills, and I regard them highly, but they are yet untempered. Therefore I mean to place you in the service of Kal of the family Endil, who sent you to me in the first place. I have raised him to the position of grand chancellor of Feldemar—the lord chancellor's former position—and he is also my Master of Spies. Under his guidance, I have no doubt you will prove yourself most useful to the preservation of the nine kingdoms."

Loren's heart skipped a beat. Almost she blurted, *You are sending me away?* She looked to Xain.

"Kal was Jordel's master also, you will remember." He spoke quietly, and she saw pity in his eyes.

She swallowed hard. *Do not be a foolish girl,* she told herself. *You entered the High King's service. What sort of servant would you be if you disobeyed her command?*

So she stilled her hands on the table and turned to Enalyn. "Very well, Your Majesty," she said. "I serve at your pleasure."

From the corner of her eye she saw Hollen give an approving smile, while the Lord Prince nodded.

"Excellent," said Enalyn. "I ask only that you obey Kal's instructions, and learn from him what you can. Never forget, Loren: our task is of the utmost importance. We do not fight for peace only to keep me on the throne. That would be a limp and insipid reason to ask so much from so many. We fight instead for the preservation of Underrealm itself, and that is a greater purpose than any one person's simple ambition. Without the order of the nine kingdoms, all would be chaos. Can I count on your aid to preserve them?"

The Lord Prince looked solemn, and his brows drew together. Loren gazed at him for a moment, wondering what must be going on inside his mind—he, the presumptive successor to the throne, and not all that much older than she was.

"You can, Your Majesty," said Loren. "And you, Your Highness, and Lord Chancellor. I have already seen the fires of war licking at the trees of the Birchwood that I call home. I will do anything I must to douse the flames, and give my life if need be."

Eamin met her gaze then, his eyes bright and his head held high. He nodded, and though he spoke no word, she could almost hear him thank her.

"Well-spoken," said Enalyn. "Though I pray it does not come to that, and I hope you will not throw your life away needlessly. Serve Kal as best you know how, and I will consider your duty fulfilled. Arrangements will soon be made for you to go to him in the stronghold of Ammon, where he resides."

"Ammon?" said Loren quickly.

"Yes," said Enalyn. "Jordel's home."

Loren's breath caught in her throat. Jordel had meant to bring her to Ammon, her and Gem and Annis all, before he had fallen in the Greatrocks. But moreover, Annis was there, and Loren's heart leaped at the thought of seeing her friend again.

"Now we must discuss something more somber," said Enalyn. She looked to Xain. The wizard cleared his throat and sat up, folding his hands on the table before him. Loren had felt a sense of warning before, and that had faded, but it redoubled now. Whatever "decision" Enalyn had come to, this was the heart of it.

"I cannot travel with you any longer," said Xain.

The room fell to silence—except that at the edge of hearing, Loren thought she heard a high whine, like a gnat buzzing in her ear. The whine was soon replaced by her own pulse, thundering as she grew suddenly light-headed.

"I thought you were done trying to abandon me on the road," she said, trying to keep her tone light.

Xain did not so much as smirk. "I was," he said. "But now I have returned to the Seat, where I always meant to go. And I have my son. I could not come with you and bring Erin along."

She did not answer. She *could* not answer. *Of course not. And you know I would not ask it.*

"Moreover," Xain went on, "the High King has asked a duty of me, and I have agreed to it."

"No doubt you remember the dean of the Academy," said Enalyn. "Cyrus of the family Drayden. You met him briefly."

"I do remember," said Loren. She also remembered that Cyrus had not been there to defend the High King in the battle of the Seat, and rumors flew that he had abandoned his charges at the Academy as well.

"Cyrus has not been seen since the day the Seat was attacked. It may be assumed that he perished in the fighting." Enalyn kept her tone carefully neutral, but Loren saw the disdainful sneers that twisted the faces of both Xain and Eamin. She herself wanted to laugh out loud, but she kept her composure as Enalyn went on. "Now the Academy needs another dean, and I require an ally in that position. With Underrealm on the brink of war, I cannot choose a dean for political reasons, the way I did when I chose Cyrus."

"You mean that it would be foolish to appoint another Drayden," said Eamin lightly. "This is a small council, Your Majesty, and all upon it are trustworthy. You may speak freely, I think."

Enalyn gave him a cool stare, and then went on as though he had not said anything. "In any case, I require someone I can trust to remain loyal, and I have selected Xain. I asked him, and he accepted."

"Then it appears congratulations are in order, *Dean.*" Loren could not help the way her mouth twisted.

Enalyn must have sensed her mood. She put her hands flat on the table and said, "Very well. Those are the only matters I required you for. Your travel to Ammon will be seen to shortly."

The dismissal was clear. Loren stood from her chair and bowed. "Thank you, Your Majesty." But before she turned away, she saw Xain give the High King a quick glance. Enalyn nodded in response, and Xain stood to follow Loren from the room.

"I shall see you out," he said.

Loren shrugged. "If you wish."

In fact she did not want him anywhere near her, but thought it would be unseemly to recoil from him in front of the High King. Once they were in the hallway, however, she walked as far from his side as she could and stormed into the palace garden. Winter bit at her cheeks, and she drew her cloak close about her, thankful the first snows had not yet begun to fall.

"I am sorry," said Xain from behind her.

"You have done nothing that requires an apology," said Loren. "The High King commanded you."

"She did not command me. She asked, and I accepted. And I am sorry."

"Then take it back." She turned to him, blinking against the sting in her eyes. "Take it back and come with me."

"I . . . I cannot," he said, fists clenching by his sides. "Loren, my son—I cannot leave Erin again, and I cannot bring—"

"*I know!*" cried Loren, far louder than she meant to. But it felt good, and so she kept shouting. "I know you cannot take Erin into such danger. Why do you think I am angry with you? Because I cannot *be* angry with you at all. Nor could I be mad at Jordel, or Albern, when they—"

She stopped short and turned away, blinking harder. That had not been a fair thing to say, and she knew it. Why, then, did she not turn and apologize? But she could not, not when Xain meant to leave her alone the way he had often enough before.

"I thought the same thing," he said. To her shock, Loren heard the thickness of tears in his voice, and when she turned he wept openly. "The moment Enalyn asked me, I thought of how I was leaving you again, the way I had promised not to—and the way Jordel and Albern did. That thought has plagued me since. Yet I do not see another choice. Erin—I have my son, and I—"

"Be *silent,*" said Loren. She forced a smile. "Still your bleating tongue, wizard. You only repeat yourself, and we have said all we can say. And if there is one thing we have learned after all the leagues we have walked together, it is that you always wanted to be rid of me."

Before he could answer, she seized the front of his coat, drawing him in for an embrace as his tears fell upon her shoulder.

THREE

CHET DID NOT TAKE THE NEWS WELL. HE SAT SILENT WITH HIS FISTS clenched as Loren spoke of the council. Across from their couch, Gem sat almost sideways upon his chair, swinging his legs back and forth over one of the arms, his eyes wide and his mouth slightly open.

When Loren finished, he straightened and gave a bright laugh.

"Wonderful! Helping to prevent a war will make a fine addition to the tales of you that already fly across the nine kingdoms."

"I think you greatly overestimate how far such tales have spread," said Loren.

"How can I? The High King herself had already heard of the Night-blade before she brought you into her service. What better bard could you wish for, than one who brings tales of your exploits to the highest of thrones?"

But Chet sat silent in his chair, picking at one fingernail with another. Loren could feel his sullen displeasure, and it worried her. The look on his face was not unlike the look he had worn in the Birchwood when her father threatened her, or hit her, and Chet had held himself back only at Loren's urging.

Gem, however, seemed oblivious to it. He sat forwards in his chair and slapped his knees. "And we will get to see Annis again! We have not received word from her in days. I wonder if she already knows we are coming? I should write her a letter."

"It can hardly get there before you will," said Loren. "It will not be long before we leave the Seat."

"Might Loren and I speak alone, Gem?"

Chet's voice was quiet and firm, and it cut its way into the conversation like a footman's sword. Gem's smile dampened, and he glanced at Loren. She nodded.

"Very well," said Gem. "I am famished anyway, and I think one of the cooks likes me, for she hardly tries to strike me at all any more when I steal food from her. I will return shortly."

He bounced carefree on his feet as he slipped from the room, but Loren did not miss the worried look he gave them. Once the door had closed again, Chet sat up on the couch and placed his elbows on his knees, folding one hand over the other before his eyes.

"Why do we not leave?" said Chet.

"I mean to," said Loren lightly. "For Ammon."

"Do not do that," he said softly. "Do not pretend ignorance of my meaning. Why do we not leave this war behind?"

"We have come this far," said Loren. "Why not see it through? And besides, I took the role of Nightblade."

"You did, and what of it?" said Chet. "What is the Nightblade, in truth? She has given you a title without a duty. It is meaningless. There has never been a Nightblade before, and so you cannot declare with any certainty what service you are expected to perform."

"I suppose, then, that it is for me to decide. I am able to determine the course of my life, the way I never could before."

"Hardly. You have put that control in the hands of the High King. Enalyn has my allegiance as well as yours, but do you truly think she holds your safety as her highest concern?"

Loren looked at him sharply. "Do you think that is *my* highest concern?"

She thought to shock him, but he only rolled his eyes. "Have you even decided how long you mean to serve her? Will you do so for the rest of your life?"

"I had not given much thought to it. But I will not leave the nine kingdoms to their own devices while the threat of war looms over them."

Chet stood and went to a side table that held a flagon of wine. He filled a cup for himself and arched an eyebrow at her. She nodded, and he filled a second.

"And what does the High King mean for you to do?" he asked, changing tack. "Obey Kal, of course, but what does that mean? Have you wondered what they intend to do with you? For I have an idea."

He placed the cup in her hand. Loren took a sip, but a light one, for she wished to keep her mind sharp. It felt as though they were sparring, and she did not like it.

She let some of her bitterness come through in her tone. "Let us hear it, then, oh wisest of advisors, for surely I would be lost without you."

"I think they mean to send you after Rogan."

That gave her pause, as he must have known it would. Just the brute's name was enough to strike fear in her. Suddenly the High King's palace seemed no safer than a flimsy woodland shack. Loren did not often dream, but in recent days, Rogan's dark face had plagued her sleep more than once.

Her silence had stretched long, and Chet wore a self-satisfied look that irked her. She sipped her wine again and shrugged. "Mayhap that is indeed their plan. If so, it is Rogan who should be afraid. When he found us in Northwood, he had the advantage, and we were the ones pursued. Now I walk with all the power of the High King behind me. Who does he have? The Shades? They lick their wounds in some unknown hole, likely hiding in the Birchwood and hoping we will forget about them."

"Dulmun backs him."

Loren snorted. "One kingdom against the other eight. And do not forget that the Mystics are on our side."

Chet frowned into his cup. "Rogan does not seem the type of man to begin a war without some hope of victory." But he could not put much strength in the words.

"Never would I compel you to walk a road you deem dangerous. I told you in Northwood that you were under no obligation to come with us."

"So you did, and I said then that I do not follow you out of obligation," said Chet. "I came because . . . well . . ." He trailed off, and his cheeks flushed with something other than the wine.

"We are no longer children, Chet," said Loren. "Speak plainly."

"Because I love you," he said, the muscles of his jaw twitching. "I know it, and you know it, though I may feel like a moon-eyed child when I say the words. I have only ever wished to keep you safe. When that meant fighting beside you, I did so willingly. But when it meant urging you to flee the troubles of Underrealm, I did that as well. You refused, and still I followed you, and I will again—but I will not stop warning you of peril when I see it."

"Do so if you must," said Loren. "Only do not forget, for both our sakes, that I will continue to ignore you and press on regardless."

His nostrils flared. "How can I forget, when you have never done anything else?"

She bit her tongue and turned her gaze away from him. She knew well that this was futile, and Chet likely did as well. "I should like to take a walk," she said.

"No, I am sorry," he said, slumping back and shaking his head. "You do not have to leave."

"It will give us both time to cool our heads—and to think upon this," she said. "Each of us knows what the other will say. Let us, then, have the argument separately, in our own minds, so that it need not drive a wedge between us."

She gave him a wan smile. He did not look up at her, and only put his hand to his forehead, as though he wished to say more but did not dare to. But as she passed him on her way out the door, he reached suddenly forth and took her hand, squeezing it. She returned the pressure, and at last their gazes met for a moment. She left.

FOUR

SHE DID NOT RETURN TO THE ROOM UNTIL AFTER NIGHTFALL, AND Chet had gone to sleep already. She lay beside him, and he stirred without waking to wrap an arm around her. His warmth soon sent her to slumber—but then a dark dream seized her, dragging her mind into its depths and filling her with despair even in sleep.

Loren found herself standing beneath the boughs of the Birchwood. Somehow she knew it was the day she had left. But instead of the brown cloak she had worn on that day, in the dream she wore the black cloak Damaris had given her. Xain was nowhere to be seen. Dark storm clouds churned in the sky.

She panicked as a branch snapped behind her. Whirling, she saw her father. An arrow was buried in his chest, just below the collarbone, so deep that the head of it protruded from the flesh in the back. His body was covered in blood, and from the squelch he made when he moved, she knew it had run down to fill his boots.

But I did not shoot you in the chest! It was the leg!

She thought the words, but she could not say them aloud.

When she saw his face, she gasped. It was twisted in hate, and his flesh had begun to rot. Something had eaten away most of his left cheek, and his teeth showed through the hole. His eyes were sunken, for the meat around them had wasted away. A few fingernails had torn off. Dirt was caked deep beneath the ones that remained, dirt from his attempts to drag himself back to their village.

"You ungrateful wretch!" he screamed, so loud that she jumped. He spat at her feet. "You were never my daughter."

He lunged at her, and she cried out. But in midair he vanished, and the world around her dissolved to mist and shadow. Then the shadows took form, and the light turned silver. She looked up to see the moons peeking at her between the rooftops of Cabrus. The alley she was in seemed familiar. A figure in a deep green cloak stood only a few paces away. Loren stirred at the sight, and her breath quickened, for the figure's shape was familiar to her.

The green cloak rippled in the moonlight as she stepped forwards, hips swaying. Her movements were every bit as enchanting and seductive as the first time they had met, and Loren's heart fluttered just as it had then. In the waking world, of course, she knew that Auntie was a sadist, a murderer, and worse beside, but in the dream she knew none of these things.

Auntie stepped around and pressed up against her back. Delicate fingers traced along Loren's arms, and she shivered, her chest tight, her skin aching for the touch to linger. She could not force herself to move.

"It is the way you hold yourself," whispered Auntie, her breath brushing Loren's ear. A hand took Loren's hip firmly, and she released a shuddering sigh. "The way you put one foot before the other—just so."

She placed a foot before Loren's, so that now they were pressed even closer against each other. But then the foot moved quickly to the right, and Auntie pushed her hard. Loren yelped, tripping over the woman's ankle. She rolled quickly onto her back, but Auntie was atop her, her fingers grasping for Loren's throat.

"This is not vengeance," she hissed. "It is justice."

Loren fought, trying to wrestle herself away, but then the world dissolved to nothing again.

There was wood beneath her hands, and warm air blasted her face. She was on the deck of a riverboat. Upstream, a ship pursued her, but no crew manned it. The captain, Brimlad, was nowhere in sight, and neither were Gem or Annis. But Xain sat against the wall of the riverboat's cabin, his hair thin and wispy, withered arms wrapped around himself. Loren shuddered as she saw the black glow in his eyes.

The ship had seemed at least a league away, but suddenly it appeared only a few paces behind them. Looking up, Loren saw a small figure in a red cloak. Vivien's eyes glowed with magelight, and she raised her arms.

"Abomination!" she cried. Black burns rippled along her skin, turning her into a twisted, mangled thing.

Loren turned to see Xain, but the wizard had gone. Had he gone below? But then she saw her own hands. They were wasted, the skin almost transparent, just as Xain's had been when he ate the magestones. She clutched at her hair, and it came away in her hand. A scream ripped from her throat, thin and feeble and blood-curdling.

She fell to hands and knees, and the world vanished again.

Now her fingers scraped on stone. Loren feared to look up, but something compelled her to.

Damaris stood before her.

They were in a cavern—Loren knew not where, for unlike all the places she had seen thus far, this was nowhere she had been in real life. The edges of the room were dark, with not a torch to be seen, and the only light fell from a hole in the ceiling far above to pool around Damaris in a perfect circle. Loren's body had returned to health, so that she could have stood, but fear shuddered in her limbs. Damaris' eyes were filled with an icy fury, and Loren cowered before it, certain that the merchant was here to take her revenge at last.

"Get up," said Chet. "We are with you."

His hands took her shoulders, and with his help she found her feet. He stood to her right, and looking to her left she saw Gem and Annis. Gem had his sword out and held forth, as though ready to do battle, while Annis' fists were clenched at her sides, as though she might try to box her own mother.

Then Loren's gaze drifted past Damaris, to a man standing just behind her. He had the brown-skinned, dark-eyed look of a Wadeland man. His black hair was cropped short, and a scar split his chin. He wore the blue and grey clothing of a Shade. She knew she had never seen him before.

"Who is that?" she asked Annis, but when she turned, the girl was gone. Gem and Chet, too, had vanished—and then she saw that they all knelt before Damaris, facing Loren. Chet was chained, and his eyes were mad with fear. Damaris held a dagger at his throat, but it was an old, rusted, twisted blade, nothing fine like Loren would have expected the merchant to have.

"You take my daughter?" said Damaris, her voice a harsh rasp. "Foolish girl. I will take *everything.*"

The dagger hissed as it laid Chet's throat open. His lifeblood splashed across the stones, and his mouth worked silently as he tried to cry out.

Loren screamed and fell on her knees before him, putting her hand to the wound, trying helplessly to hold it closed. But she could feel his life slipping away between her fingers. Her shouts could not save him. Nothing could.

"No!" cried Loren. "Gem! Annis! Help me!"

But when she looked up, she found that they were not chained after all. They never had been. A hungry light was in their eyes as they regarded her. Gem bared his teeth with an animal's snarl, and he pounced upon her. She felt his teeth sink like needles into her neck.

Loren woke at last, screaming and thrashing in her bed.

"Stop! Stop! Loren! Someone help!"

Hands seized her in the darkness. Loren swung a fist in the dark, screaming louder.

She struck Chet right where the dagger of a Shade had wounded him. He screamed in pain, and the sound of it was like agony in her heart. At last her mind was dragged to the present.

"Chet! No, no, no. I am sorry, I—"

The door to their room crashed open. Xain and Gem ran in, stopping just on the threshold. Xain's eyes glowed white with magic, and Gem brandished his sword. At the sight of the boy, fear seized Loren, her mind returning to the dream and his bared teeth.

"What is it?" cried Xain. "What is wrong?"

"I—I . . ." Loren shook her head, forcing herself to speak. "It is nothing. Nothing. A nightmare."

Xain's brow furrowed, and the light did not fade from his eyes. He ran to the balcony door and opened it, looking outside as though for a prowler. Then he rushed to the closet at the other end of the room and peered within.

"I am fine, Xain," said Loren, growing exasperated. "There is no one there. It was a dream." When he knelt and looked under the bed, she got to her feet and lifted him back up. "Stop. It is nothing."

"Nothing?" said Chet, still rubbing his chest where she had struck him. "It did not sound like nothing."

Xain stood, and at last he doused his magic. But his frown remained. "You sounded as though skilled torturers had you under their knives."

"Mayhap they did," said Loren. "But only in my mind. Look at me. Do you see any wounds?"

Without answering, he went to the wall, where two robes hung on hooks. He pulled one down and threw it to her, and she put it on gratefully. But no sooner had she covered herself than he seized her face, and she yelped as he pried at her eyelids with his fingers.

"Your eyes are wild," he said, ignoring her attempts to escape. "Gem, fetch an apothecary, and tell them to bring dreamwine."

"No, Gem," said Loren, finally forcing Xain's hands away. "Sky above, Xain, I tell you I am *all right.*"

The wizard's frown deepened. "I am not sure of that, though I will allow that you seem to be safe. Have you been eating?"

"The same as you."

"Have you been . . . how much wine did you drink?"

Loren forced a laugh. "I am no drunkard."

"So says every drunkard." But she could hear the tension leach from his voice.

"I could fetch *more* wine, if you wish," said Gem from behind him. "I feel I could use a cup myself, for your screams still ring in my ears."

Loren's spirits dampened at once as she looked at the boy. Gem looked the same as always, and the same impudent smirk tugged at his lips. Yet the memory of her nightmare would not leave her mind.

She shook her head and tried to smile. "No, Gem. I only need sleep, and I would wager you do as well. Off with you both."

Xain did not move, not until she took his shoulder and ushered him gently out. Gem went more readily, and was already yawning by the time he reentered his room. Once they were gone, Loren closed her door and turned to the bed.

Chet sat up, his bare chest glistening in the moonlight, one hand still on the scar of his dagger wound. He studied her in the dim silver glow through the window.

"Loren, what is wrong?"

"Nothing," she said lightly. She cast her robe on the floor and gave him a moment to take her in before sliding beneath the covers. But it did not distract him.

"You can fool Gem and Xain, but I know you are lying."

She was not so sure she had fooled Xain, for the wizard's eyes had been troubled. But still she kept her smile and ran a hand up his arm.

"That is a strong accusation. How is your wound? I did not mean to hit you. I was not myself when I woke."

"It is all right," said Chet. "The pain is fading."

She bent to kiss the scar, and as her other hand squeezed his shoulder, she felt him relax. "Good. It is a mark of honor. I would hate for you to regret earning it."

Though his eyes were still grave, that forced a chuckle from him. "As though *that* is why I would regret it." His frown returned. "Are you certain you are all right? What did you dream of?"

Loren felt her smile grow strained. "I do not remember," she said. A sick feeling grew in the pit of her stomach at the lie. "Mayhap it was the battle of the Seat. That was no happy memory."

He hesitated, and for a moment she thought he would answer. But he only shook his head, and turned away to lie upon his side.

Soon he was asleep once more. But Loren lay awake all the rest of the night, until the silver of moonslight gave way to the pink blush of dawn. And she felt that eyes watched her in the darkness, the eyes of every enemy she had left behind her between the paths of the Birchwood and the palace of the High King.

FIVE

As they ate with Gem the next morning, Loren could sense Chet's concern for her. It fairly radiated from him, like heat from a flame. When she tried to reach for more food, he would offer to fetch it for her, and he kept asking her if she would like any more water to drink. She avoided his gaze all the while, and spoke lightly of small matters, but his worry remained—until a thought seemed to strike him, and he cocked his head.

"Where is Xain?" he said.

Loren glanced towards the wizard's room. "Sleeping, I imagine."

"Normally he rises earlier than any of us," said Chet.

Loren and Gem gave each other a dark look. That had not always been Xain's way, and had only begun after his battles with magestone sickness. Sometimes Loren wondered if the wizard slept at all any more. But now her thoughts were drawn to the night before, and her dream.

A chill went through her. She had recently consumed magestones—once, in Dorsea, when the Elves had forced her to do it, and then once again here upon the Seat when she sought an agent of the Shades. The fact that she had them, and had eaten them, was unknown to anyone but Chet, and even he only knew of the first time.

Could the magestones be linked to her nightmare? She could only find out by asking Xain, and that was not something she could do carelessly. If the wizard found out she possessed magestones—indeed, if anyone other than Chet learned of it—her very life might be in danger, for it was a dark crime under the King's law.

She shook off such thoughts and rose, going to Xain's room. Cautiously she tapped on the door, and when she heard no reply within, she pushed it open. Xain's bed was empty, the covers tousled, and his clothing from yesterday lay upon the floor.

"Gone," she said, shrugging. "Off on some business as the new dean, no doubt."

But she proved to be wrong, for Xain returned to them before they had finished eating. He stepped through the door wearing something that looked utterly foreign upon him: a full and beaming smile.

"What under the sky are you grinning about?" said Loren.

"I have a surprise for you," said Xain. "Or rather, the Lord Prince has arranged it, and he has allowed me to present it. Come with me."

Loren glanced at Chet, but he only shrugged. They rose, along with Gem, and followed Xain out into the hallway.

The wizard led them to a part of the palace they had rarely visited, where many of the High King's guards were stationed, as well as a great number of Mystics. Soldiers watched them pass with great interest. Loren's cheeks flushed as she realized that many of them were looking at her. She fought the urge to raise her hood and instead held her head high. As the Nightblade, she would have to grow used to this, she supposed.

Xain stopped at a heavy door, pausing before he opened it to ensure they were gathered behind him. He pushed it open to reveal a sort of barracks, with beds along the walls, each with a small chest at the foot. In the center of the room was a long wooden table, and around it sat several Mystics, their red hoods cast back from their faces. Loren stood in the doorway, wondering why Xain would bring her here. Then the Mystics looked up at her, and stood from their places at the table. A smile broke out on her face, wide enough to match Xain's, and she laughed.

"Weath! Jormund!" she cried.

The Mystics came forwards to embrace her, laughing—even large Jormund, who had hardly ever said a word to her. They had met her in

Brekkur when Loren was fleeing east across Underrealm, and Kal had sent them to the Seat to help deliver his message to the High King. Now they clapped her on the back and shook Chet's hand, and Jormund even picked up little Gem, who squealed like a pup. But as she released Weath's wrist, Loren looked past her to the other Mystics at the table. They studied her with interest, but they had not risen, and she did not recognize their faces.

"Where are Erik and Gwenyth?" said Loren.

The room fell silent. Jormund looked at her solemnly, and Weath cast her gaze to the floor. Loren's breath caught in her throat.

"In the battle?"

"On the eastern docks," said Weath quietly. "We pursued the armies of Dulmun there, and pressed the assault as they tried to board their ships and escape. Erik fought like a madman and killed three of them on his own. But an archer, darkness take them, fired from the stern of a ship as it fled, and the arrow pierced his heart. Gwenyth fell later, as we tried to clear the Shades from the palace."

Loren bowed her head, blinking hard. "I wish I had been there."

Weath put her hand on Loren's shoulder. "Do not be sorry. From what we have heard, you were more sorely needed in the palace, and the nine kingdoms are grateful for your actions."

She forced a smile. The other Mystics stood from the table—three of them, and none looked alike. One by one they came forwards to be introduced. First was a short, slim woman of middle years, whose narrow eyes were quick and unsmiling. She was called Shiun. There was a tall, broad youth named Uzo, whose shaved head was darker even than Annis'. He squeezed Loren's wrist harder than he needed to, and she fought away a grimace as she tried to do the same. He smiled at that and clapped her shoulder. Gem gaped at Uzo, his mouth hanging open, and did not seem to hear when the young man offered him a hand to clasp.

The last Mystic was called Niya. Though she was only a finger or two taller than Loren, she was far more heavily muscled, so that Loren felt minuscule in her presence. Beneath a shirt of chain she had a leather jerkin with a high collar that covered her neck, but its sleeves were short, so that her thick arms were on display. She wore a secretive smirk as she approached Loren and held forth her hand. When their wrists clasped, her skin was smooth and warm, and the hairs on the back of Loren's neck tingled.

"The Nightblade," said Niya. "I suppose this is meant to be an honor. The High King holds you in high esteem. That is impressive indeed, for such a young woman."

Loren's cheeks flushed. "Not so young," she said.

"Not *too* young, I suppose," said Niya.

"Niya has been appointed the captain of our squadron," said Weath. "She fought beside the former lord chancellor at the eastern gate, and took a wound in the battle."

"It sounds as if you are a hero," said Loren.

"Mayhap," said Niya. "It was only a small cut, and it was not the High King who raised my station for it, unlike you."

Loren realized that they had not released each other's wrists. She did so at last, though her hand seemed reluctant to obey. "There is time yet."

Chet eyed the woman as they shook hands. "I did not see you in the fighting," he remarked.

The smirk she had worn for Loren vanished, and Niya raised her eyebrows. "And did you take count of every Mystic before the gate? You have a cool head for battle, it seems. What is your position, by the by? Other than bedfellow of the Nightblade, I mean."

His jaw clenching, Chet opened his mouth to reply, but Loren barked a laugh despite herself. He turned his glare on her and held his tongue.

"Oh, come, Chet," she chided him. "Do not be so serious. It was a joke."

Niya grinned at Loren, and Chet forced a smile as well. "Well met, then," he said.

"Indeed," said Niya, and returned to her table. Gem stood there looking crestfallen, his hand still outstretched to clasp hers, but she acted as though he was not there.

The other Mystics told Loren something of themselves. Uzo was a spearman, though he was quick to explain his spear was likely not similar to the ones Loren was used to; it was short and flexible, and he used it half as a staff. Shiun was a scout, and skilled with a bow, but when she heard that Loren had been learning the Calentin style of shooting, her brows lifted, and she extracted a promise that the two of them would trade advice the next time they were in the training yard. After a time, Xain put his hand on Loren's shoulder and gave her a smile.

"I am glad to see you reunited," he said, "but that is not the end of the news I have for you. I did not bring you to see your friends only so you could have a happy reunion. Ammon is in need of reinforcements, and these five will come with you on the journey there."

Loren's eyes shot wide, and she looked at the Mystics anew. Her expression must have shown her shock, for Weath smiled, and Jormund loosed his huge, booming laugh. Shiun and Uzo gave her a polite smile—but Loren looked past them, to the table where Niya sat. The Mystic woman had not taken her eyes from Loren, and for a moment they locked gazes. Loren's stomach did a pleasant turn, and she swallowed hard before turning away.

Her gaze met Xain's, who still smiled at her in delight of his surprise. A grin stole across her face to match his—but then she realized that this was his parting gift. A replacement, though a shoddy one, for his own company upon the road. That thought seemed to throw a dark cloud over her joy, and her smile faltered.

Xain saw it, and his own smile grew sad in response. "There is time yet before that bitter parting," he said quietly. "And I mean to fill it with happiness where I can. Tonight, you must let me take you out upon the Seat. We will eat and drink our fill, and pretend for a little while longer that no darkness waits beyond an ever-nearing dawn."

SIX

Loren returned to her quarters, along with Chet and Gem, and there Xain left them for the rest of the day. But he returned at dusk, bringing them fine clothes to wear. He handed the boys their outfits, but when he came to Loren he paused.

"I did not know which you would rather wear," he said. "I have brought you trousers of dyed black leather, to wear with a blouse and a vest, if you wish it. That is the sort of clothing I have always seen you in. But I also have here a dress. I am not sure if it is quite your size, and I had the clothier choose the cut. I am no expert in these things you understand, and—"

"Oh, sky above, Xain," she said, laughing at his sudden awkwardness. "Let me look at the thing."

Xain lifted it from his arm. Loren went still at the sight of it, her breath escaping in a soft sigh. Hesitantly she reached out and took it, marveling at the feeling of the cloth between her fingertips. It was as blue as the ocean, and worked through with thin threads of sea-green in delicate patterns like tree leaves. She had never seen a fabric that shimmered just so, reflecting the torchlight when she turned it over in her hands. Its sleeves ran all the way to the wrists, where they closed with small buttons of some cream-colored stone she had never seen before.

"It is a silly thing, I know," he said at once, looking embarrassed as he pursed his lips at it. "Most likely you do not—"

"I do not often wear dresses," said Loren. "The last one I owned was made by my mother, and she intended for me to wear it to a dance, the very night you and I met." She pressed the dress to herself, smiling softly at him. "I ground dirt into that dress with my heel and spat on it, for I hated her. But this one I will keep. It is beautiful." Then she frowned. "Though I hope you do not expect me to wear it often. I could not possibly mount a horse in this thing."

He laughed and ran a hand through his hair. "Of course not. And you will find little occasion for dresses in Ammon, I assure you. But I am glad you like it, regardless."

When Chet saw her in the dress, he could not stop staring, and in the end she had to force him to continue getting dressed himself. Once they were ready, and Loren had donned her black cloak, Xain led them out of the palace and into the streets of the city, heading southwest.

Lamps burned from the corners of many buildings along the way, lending the city a cheery look despite the cut of the frigid air. The island was full of people about their business, and if there were more soldiers among the crowds than there had been a few weeks ago, still the mood was cheerful and boisterous, with much laughter, and songs that poured from nearly every tavern they passed. The rebuilding of the Seat had raised the mood of all upon it, and there was a sense in those who dwelt there that the war, if indeed it ever came, would be a short and simple affair, and no source of great trouble or worry.

Xain stopped before a tavern, and over its door Loren saw a stag painted in silver. Inside, a fire burned in the wide hearth, and the lamps along the walls strengthened its warm glow. Xain introduced them briefly to the matron, Canda, and she showed them to a table where they found well-cushioned chairs with intricate designs carved into the wood. When the food came, they found that it tasted nearly as delightful as the place looked. Seldom had Loren tasted any meat so finely spiced, even in the palace, and there were sweet roasted fruits the likes of which she had never seen before. The wine, too, was uncommonly good, and she wondered how much Xain had paid for it all. When she asked him, he shushed her with a wave of his hand.

"Tonight we are not concerned with such things," he said. "Tonight we think only of having one last happy memory together, at least until the next time we meet."

"Speaking of meetings," said Gem, who had snuck himself a cup of wine when Loren was not looking, "I have had a thought recently. How in all the skeins of time did the two of you meet each other? I have never heard the tale."

Loren blinked. She had told Chet the story, of course, but then they had spent far more time together since their reunion in Northwood. But she had never thought to tell Gem, for their journey together had consisted of one flight from danger after another.

So she settled back in her chair and told the story now, of how she had caught Xain running through the Birchwood and had begged him to take her with him. She skipped briefly over the description of her father and the reasons she wished to flee, and Gem did not press her for more details. But when she reached the part of the tale where they slept that first night on the riverbank, she scowled at Xain in mock fury and brandished her wine cup at him.

"And then this buffoon, darkness take him, *abandoned* me on the riverbank."

Xain's cheeks burned red, and he had to force a smile.

"I did. Though in my defense, I thought it would be safer for you."

"Oh, yes, very safe," said Loren, leaning over to Gem and muttering conspiratorially. "It only landed the constables hot on my heels, and then dropped me in the lap of Damaris of the family Yerrin, who, you will remember, has tried to kill me more than once."

The wizard barked a laugh. "And do you think I *planned* for that?"

They argued over that for a bit, and then Loren went on with the story, and by the time she had come to the part where Gem entered into it, the boy was so tired that he had nearly fallen asleep in his food. He perked up at the mention of his own name, but almost immediately his head began to sag again.

Loren looked towards the door, wondering what time it was. The common room was not so full as it had been when they entered, but there were more than enough patrons to keep it open for some hours more. Her heart sank at the thought of ending their night so soon, and she looked reluctantly at Xain. He gave her a sad smile.

Then Chet stood from his chair. "It grows late, and our urchin is almost asleep where he sits. I will see him safely to the palace and leave you two be."

Loren blinked at him. "You need not do that. I can come with you."

"Stay," said Chet, smiling and putting a hand on her shoulder. "You and I have all the coming journey together, and many days after that as well. But your time with Xain is nowhere near so plentiful, and should be savored. And besides, it would be a crime if you did not spend as much time in that dress as you possibly can, for I do not know when you shall get to wear it again."

Her sight grew misty, and she wondered if she had had too much wine. "Thank you," she murmured. Chet smiled and forced a grumbling Gem to his feet, and then walked the boy out into the night.

"He is worth more than his weight in gold, that one," said Xain quietly. "Do not forget it."

"I will not," said Loren. "All our lives he has cared for me, and some time ago that care grew into a love unlike any I have seen before. I only worry that it is too much, for if his feelings for me ever caused him harm, I could not bear it."

Xain cocked his head. "You speak as though you regret his feelings for you."

Loren shook her head quickly. "No, of course not. How could I, when I love him as well? Only sometimes I think he sees me as more than I am."

"Mayhap," said Xain. "Or mayhap you see yourself as less than you are."

She did not know what to say to that, and so they sat for a while in comfortable silence. Loren finished her cup of wine, and Xain refilled it with the rest of the bottle. They sipped gingerly, and Loren could sense the same hesitance in the wizard that she herself felt—a reluctance to move on, to see this night end and the next step in their journey begin.

It was Xain who broke the silence. "Loren, I must ask you something. Do you still carry your dagger?"

She tensed. "Yes."

"You mean to bring it with you?" he said, studying her.

"I do. What else would I do with it?"

His eyes grew far away, staring over her shoulder. "I do not know. Once you asked me if you should throw it into the Great Bay. Mayhap you should do that now. I fear what might happen if Kal should learn that you have it. Jordel was worried enough about it, and he was a much more forgiving man. I wish I were going with you."

Loren frowned. "Kal was Jordel's master, and Jordel was the one who told me the truth of the blade in the first place. I had hoped to tell Kal of it, and seek his council."

Xain leaned forwards and shook his head, speaking in a low voice. "I do not think that would be wise. He seemed a man more prone to pragmatism than to kindness. Jordel did not press you to rid yourself of the dagger, because he trusted you. Though we met him only briefly, I do not know that Kal trusts anyone. If indeed you keep the dagger in your possession, you should not tell him of it."

She pursed her lips. "Very well. I shall keep it a secret."

"Promise me."

Loren rolled her eyes. "I promise you."

He smiled. "You are too confident in yourself by half. But it is one of your endearing qualities. I hope you will send my regards to Annis, by the by, as well as my apologies. That girl will never have much affection for me, I fear."

"Who would?" said Loren, raising her brows and drinking deep of her wine.

"Careful now," said Xain, scowling with mock severity. "Have you not heard I am a mighty firemage? I might catch you in my flame."

Loren chuckled. "It is good to see you happy, Xain. You have not had much occasion for joy since I have known you. And when Jordel . . ." She took a moment to swallow past a lump in her throat. "When Jordel told me how you used to be—before you fled the Seat, I mean—I could scarcely believe it. Now I see that he did not tell me even half of the truth."

Xain's eyes sparked with interest. "I never knew that. What did he tell you?"

"Do you wish to hear tales of your praise?" she teased. "He said that you were mayhap too quick to anger, but you were quick to laugh as well. He said that was how you earned yourself favor among the great, especially the Lord Prince. When I met Eamin, I could not understand why he would befriend such a dour man as yourself. But I have since seen a new part of you, and I am glad. If this is how you were before you left the Seat, then I would not take you away from it for all the gold in the nine kingdoms."

The wizard's eyes shone with tears for a moment. He cleared his throat, and then slapped the table abruptly. "Come. I wish to show you something."

Loren straightened. "What? Where? It is the middle of the night."

"All the better," said Xain. "Come."

She hesitated a moment more, but Xain had already stood and was making for the bar. There he spoke briefly to Canda and, after he placed a pair of coins in her palm, she handed him two more bottles of wine. One of these he placed in Loren's hand before drawing her through the room and out into the street.

SEVEN

THE NIGHT WAS NO LONGER YOUNG, AND THE FIRST SNOW HAD BEGUN to fall earlier that day—not enough to cause drifts in the streets, but enough that Loren drew her cloak tighter and blew into the side of her hood to warm her face. Xain led her west in the moonslight, and before long they approached a huge black building surrounded by a wall ten paces high, all in black granite with silver trim. Loren stopped short.

"The Academy?" she said, a shiver running up her back. "Xain, where are we going?"

"Inside, of course," he said. "Did you not know that I am the dean?"

He threw open the front door and strode in. Loren hastened to follow, looking nervously around. The front hall was wide, with two staircases leading up from it in different directions, as well as halls leading to endless rows of doors in all directions. Moonslight poured through the windows high above, though it weakened considerably before it reached the floor, and most of the illumination came from a chandelier high above.

She jumped as the doors slammed shut behind her, and turned to see that an old woman had closed them. The woman was short and wizened and had a mad look in her eye, but she ignored Loren entirely as she returned to her post by the door.

"Come," said Xain, making for a hallway off to the left. Loren followed, not daring to trail too far behind. She knew that anyone they met would likely be a wizard. It was a curious thought, for everywhere else in the nine kingdoms, wizards were a rare thing.

She need not have worried, for they did not see anyone until Xain stopped before another thick door, this one made of thick oak. Next to the door was a chair, and in the chair was a shriveled crone who could have been the sister of the woman at the front door. This woman's back was not so hunched, and her fingers not so gnarled, but her eyes held a mean and cruel sneer.

"What do you want?" she grated. Her nose turned up as she observed the bottle of wine Loren carried.

"I believe you meant to ask, 'How may I help you, Dean Forredar?'" said Xain. "And my answer, Carog, is that you may stand aside."

"Certainly," said Carog, giving him a nasty smile.

She hobbled out of the way. Xain stepped forwards and put his hand on the latch—but it did not budge. His shoulders heaved with a sigh, and he turned.

"Open the door, Carog."

Carog's eyes shot wide with mock innocence. "Oh, dearie me, is it locked? Now, where would I have placed the key? It gets so hard to remember these things at my age." She made a great show of fumbling at the pockets of her robes.

Xain glared at her. "If you have lost the key, then I have no choice but to declare you derelict in your duties and replace you. I am certain Mellie will recommend a suitable steward in your stead."

In an instant, Carog's face turned to a bitter grimace. Angrily she thrust a hand into her robes and withdrew a key, which she hastened to turn in the lock.

"Thank you, Carog," said Xain graciously, as he led Loren within. After the door slammed shut behind them, he smirked. "She has hated me ever since I was a student. I would sneak in here often without her knowing. She only caught me twice, but she never forgave me."

"She is horrid," said Loren.

"And age has not improved her. But I am the dean, and no longer need to care about such things. Come, and let me show you one of my favorite places."

Looking up, Loren saw that they were in a great circular tower—and then she realized that it was the Academy's bell tower. A wide staircase ran along the wall, built into the stone itself, and there high above them was the bell, massive even from this far down. Xain started up the steps, and she followed behind. His pace soon slowed, and she heard him pant heavily. But Loren had lost none of her hardiness from a lifetime in the forest, and she chuckled as she outpaced him.

"You are as slow as the day we met, wizard," she said. "Now that you are a man of books and learning, do not forget to leave your desk every once in a while, or I shall find you fat and lazy when I return to the Seat."

"Some would be glad to grow fat and happy in their later years," gasped Xain. But he quickened his pace to keep up with her.

They reached the top, and Loren marveled at the sight of it. The bell was surrounded by a wide platform, and at the edge of it was a rail. Beyond that was only open air, so that in all directions she could look out and see the city laid before her like a blanket, but shining with the light of torches and hearths. The wind was stronger here than it had been on the street, but Loren hardly noticed it, so taken aback was she at the sight before her.

"Xain," she breathed. "This . . . this is . . ."

"It is, is it not?" he said, his smile widening.

He guided her to the edge, and there he sat, draping his arms over the railing. Loren did the same beside him, laying her cloak beneath her so she did not dirty her dress. From within his coat Xain pulled his bottle of wine and removed the rag that sealed it. Loren took that as a signal, and she opened her bottle as well.

"To the High King Enalyn," said Xain. "Long may she reign, and her enemies be vanquished."

"To lengthy roads traveled together," said Loren. "May our memories of them never dim."

They clinked the necks of the bottles against one another and drank deep. For a while after that, Loren was content to enjoy the sights and smells of the city far below, and track the slow progress of the moons across the sky as they blotted out one star after another. The wine was the finest they had had so far that night, and half of hers was gone before she realized it. The edges of her vision had begun to grow blurry. She held up the bottle.

"How much gold have you spent on me tonight, Xain?"

Xain held up his own wine. "On us, you mean. Do you think I would spend a small fortune just to please you?"

She snorted. "I should say not. I have given you no end of reasons to be annoyed with me during our time together."

"And I have, in turn, made your life horrible upon occasion," said Xain quietly. He drank again from his bottle.

Loren shook her head. "Even at its worst, I would not call it horrible. Frightening, yes, and sometimes painful. But horrible was the Birchwood, and my father. Whatever else you have done, you took me away from that. And that would be cause enough for thanks. But I have learned, too, just how honorable you are at your core—that is, when you are not being a colossal idiot."

Though she spoke in jest, Xain looked at her solemnly. "And you, Loren of the family Nelda. How could I know, when first we met, the greatness in your own heart? Were you royalty, I do not doubt you would one day be the High King. Were you a merchant, your family would become the richest in the nine lands. And as things stand—well, what commoner could claim to be greater than you?" He raised his bottle in another toast, and then drank deep.

"You are drunk," Loren proclaimed. "And I mean to join you." She took another swig.

"Join me? You are further along than I am."

Loren looked up at the moons, which were close to vanishing behind the roof of the bell tower. But that brought thoughts of sleep, which brought thoughts of dreams. Her good mood dampened.

"Xain," she said carefully. "When you ate magestones . . ." She felt him stiffen beside her. "I am sorry. I should not have presumed to ask."

"It is all right," he said. "Only that is a tale I would rather not spread through the Academy. But none are near us to eavesdrop now. Go on."

"Did you dream?" said Loren. "I remember, when we carried you through the Greatrocks, that you would lie there twitching and moaning at night."

He arched an eyebrow at her. "What has brought you to such a question?"

Loren shrugged. "I do not know. It worried me then. There were many things I wondered during those times that I have never had the courage to ask you until now. You seem well recovered, but how can that be when you suffered so terribly?"

Xain gave a grim chuckle. "I did. But no, I did not dream, nor would I have. Magestones have other properties beyond strengthening a wizard's power. They quell the appetite entirely, for one thing. Do you remember how Jordel almost had to force me to eat? And they purge the body of other influences. The remedies of the apothecary have little effect upon a wizard who eats magestones, and the same is true for poisons. And as I said at the first, a wizard who consumes the stone does not dream."

"That is good . . ." said Loren absentmindedly. Then she realized how that sounded and hurried to correct herself. "I mean, it is a little sad, I suppose. But I am glad you do not have the nightmares I thought you did."

"Are you worried about last night?" said Xain, his brows drawing close. "Loren, what under the stars did you dream of?"

"I told you I do not remember." She had made a mistake, and drawn his thoughts far too close to her secret. "I was only wondering if the sickness still troubled you at all. If you should fall back into darkness, I will no longer be here to box your ears and tie you up until you come to your senses." Pushing his shoulder, she flashed him a wide smile.

He returned it, and her fear left her. "You need not worry on that account. Those dark days are behind me, and will never return. I can hardly believe that you and I once conspired to sell those thrice-cursed stones. Do you remember?"

"Of course. It was not so long ago," said Loren.

Xain fixed her with a look. "Now that I think of it, that is a piece of information that may yet prove useful. If you remember, I had a contact in Dorsea who I thought might buy the stones. You may have need of such a man."

"But I no longer wish to sell magestones," said Loren, studying him carefully.

"Of course not, not any longer. But there are other goods beyond the King's law—and if you do not wish to sell them, or buy them, a spy should still know someone who deals in them."

"Oh?" said Loren. "Very well then. Where might I find him?"

"His name is Wyle, and he lives in the city of Bertram. It is in Dorsea, west of the King's road where it runs by the Greatrocks, halfway between their southern tip and the Moonslight Pass to the north."

"Very well," said Loren. "If I ever have occasion to visit him, I shall send him your regards."

"He will not take kindly to that," said Xain with a harsh laugh. "You might do better to pretend you never knew me. But now we have spoken overmuch of such things. It is a fine night. Too fine to spend it with talk of magestones and other dark matters beyond the King's law."

"I feel as though there are few matters these days which are *not* dark."

"That is true enough. This morning I gave my first speech to the Academy students. It was in the front hall, the one we passed through. They looked so young—and so frightened. And it was my duty to convince them not to be afraid, and that I would protect them."

"But you will," said Loren. "Is that not part of your duty?"

"It is, and I will not abandon it like that faithless steer, Cyrus," said Xain. "But I am one man—a wizard, and a strong one, I can say without boasting. Yet I do not know if I have it in me to keep them safe from all harm."

To her own great surprise, Loren squeezed his shoulder. *I must be more wine-addled than I thought.* "No one has that power, but few could come closer to it than you. Your only fault is that you are so stupidly serious about everything. If you can only shed the idea that you bear all the world's burdens, you will do much better."

Xain laughed. "Wise words from one so young. And I think you may be right. Besides, now that my son is returned to me, I need not worry half so much."

"I do not jest. You are a great wizard, Xain, and may even be a great man."

He lowered his gaze, looking down on the city again. "Jordel was a great man," he murmured.

For the second time that night, Loren swallowed past a tightness in her throat. "I thought you wished not to speak of dark matters."

"Even in death, Jordel is a light. That is what *you* must remember, Loren. If you think me great, know that I hold you in even higher regard. But you are young, and the nine lands hold grief enough to fill the lives of all within them. No matter how dark your road may grow, you must remember Jordel. If you live by what he would do, you will rarely go far wrong."

With another pang of guilt, she thought of the magestones. "I will remember," she said softly. "I have entered the High King's service because of him, after all."

Xain's eyes narrowed, as though that answer did not entirely satisfy him. But he gave no answer.

Another thought struck Loren. She took a deep breath. "Will we ever see each other again, you and I?"

She thought Xain might answer easily with a casual reassurance. Instead he shrugged. "Who can know? But I think we might. The answer lies more in your hands than mine. My duty will keep me on the Seat for the foreseeable future. Yet who knows what fortunes the coming war may bring?"

"I think the war will be over quickly, and easily, if it is not entirely bloodless," said Loren.

"Already it has claimed its share of blood," said Xain, quiet and solemn. "And I fear it has only begun. We are among the few who know the true enemy—not the kingdom of Dulmun, but the Shades' master. The Necromancer."

Loren shivered at the name. But she thrust out her hand to him. "A promise, then, between you and me. If we survive this war, I will return, and you and I will sit here together again, and here we will stay until all the tales of our journeys have been told."

Xain clasped her wrist in agreement. But Loren seized his and dragged him closer, until his nose was almost touching hers, and she scowled.

"And if you break your word to me *this* time, I will *drag* you to the top of this tower and throw you off of it. We will see if you can summon a storm to carry you safely to the ground."

The wizard burst out laughing, the longest, loudest, and clearest she had ever heard from him, and it was as if, in an instant, he had cast off all the cares that troubled him, all the way back to before the moment they had met in the Birchwood. She did not doubt that that laugh could be heard for a great distance in the city below.

"You have my word, Nightblade."

"I will hold you to it, Dean Forredar." Her mouth twisted. "It sounds odd upon my tongue."

"And mine," said Xain. "But now come. We have spent long enough up here already, and I grow cold. Besides, what would people think if they found the dean drunk at the top of his own bell tower?"

He stood and helped her up, and they stumbled down the stairs together. And for the first time in all their journey together, Loren thought that she could call Xain her true friend.

EIGHT

ONE DAY MORE PASSED, A DAY THAT LOREN SPENT MISERABLE AFTER THE
wine from the night before. As the sun lowered in the sky, Xain came
to sit with her in the common room between their chambers, and they
discussed the road from the Seat to Ammon. The wizard looked even
worse for wear than she did.

When night came and supper passed, they did not remain awake
for long. Loren would have relished one more night spent together,
but they would wake early the next day, and she would rather not be
exhausted for the beginning of their voyage across the Great Bay.

A palace servant roused them before dawn, and Loren and Chet
dressed together in silence. They shook Gem awake twice, and still he
did not rise from his bed. In the end Loren lost patience and threw a
pitcher of water on him. Xain awakened, too, and left with them so
that he could say a final farewell before they set sail.

In the palace courtyard were the Mystics who would accompany
them. Two carriages took them all quickly to the western docks. It
was the same place they had landed just weeks before, as fugitives and
refugees. They had risen far since then. Now the dean of the Acade-

my was there to see them off—and, to their delight, so was the Lord Prince. Eamin awaited them in the dim grey glow just before dawn, and stepped forwards with a smile as they clambered down from the carriage.

"Fare well, Chet of the family Lindel, and Gem of the family Noctis. Fare well, Nightblade. I would have a promise from you, that the next time we see each other, you will tell me the tale of that time you met the Elves, eh?"

Loren bowed deep. "I give you my word, Your Highness."

Eamin's smile widened. Then he withdrew, and Xain took his place. He and Chet clasped wrists, with Chet regarding the wizard silently.

"I was not myself when first we met," said Xain. "You have shown yourself to be nothing but an honorable man, yet in the course of our travels I have given you no great cause to love me. I wish you well on the roads ahead, and beg that you think of me better than I mayhap deserve. Promise me that you will care for Loren."

"That I will do, promise or no," said Chet. "Fare well here upon the island, Xain. I may not love you, but you have proven yourself an honorable man as well, in the end."

When Xain went to Gem, the boy put his hands on his hips and sniffed. "Farewell, wizard. I suppose you have proven not to be such a poor traveling companion—though some times were better than others."

Xain chuckled. "I wish, my boy, that you were a wizard, for it would be my pleasure to oversee your instruction personally. As it is, my days will be emptier of laughter until we meet again."

Gem seemed to enjoy the thought of being a wizard very much, for his eyes shone. All pretense of bravado fell from him, and he leaped forwards to give Xain an awkward hug around the waist before scampering bashfully away and towards the ship.

Only Loren remained, and they looked at each other in silence. They had said all they needed to at the top of the Academy's bell tower. In the end she seized him in a great bear hug, and he squeezed her back, though his arms were far weaker.

"Fare well, Loren," he said. "Remember Jordel."

"And you. Fare well."

The captain set sail almost the moment they had boarded. Thus began their journey to Ammon, and a miserable journey it was. Winter had come at last to Underrealm, well and truly, and storms wracked their vessel all the way to the southern coast of Feldemar. Loren and Chet spent most of their time in their bunk, which could hardly have been less private, for it was only one bed of eight in the same cabin. Gem was in the room with them for the larger part of the journey, curled miserably under his blanket. He had not been overly prone to seasickness in the past, but this voyage was unlike either they had taken together before.

After six days of sailing, they docked at a town on Feldemar's southern shore, and there they rested overnight. Loren noticed a curious tension in the town that she did not understand at first. But then she realized that they were perilously close to the kingdom of Dulmun, the kingdom that had risen in treason against the High King. Though Dulmun had taken no military action since their assault on the Seat, most believed it was only a matter of time before the seafaring kingdom made war again, and coastal towns like this would likely be among their first targets.

The day after they landed, Niya purchased horses for all of them with a purse of coins that had been given to her upon the Seat. They had brought no mounts with them, for moving steeds by boat was most difficult with the strength of winter's storms. Loren was glad she had sent her horse, Midnight, to Ammon before her journey to the High King's Seat. Their reunion was one more thing to look forward to when Loren reached Jordel's home at last.

Their road north through Feldemar was hardly any more cheery than the ocean voyage had been. The kingdom proved to be a wet and marshy land, where the air was muggy despite the cold of winter. It did not snow here, but that was little comfort, for it rained heavily and always. Often the roads would be flooded, or covered by mudslides, causing long delays. Thus, a journey that should have taken them four days on horseback took seven instead.

When they camped for the night, or stopped for a midday meal, there was little conversation beyond what was necessary to build camp. But Loren did snatch some tidbits of information from the Mystics they rode beside, particularly the new ones. She learned that Shiun was a woman of Dulmun, an awkward fact considering that nation's treachery. But she had left that land when she was a young girl, and had spent the last many years in the southwestern reaches of Underrealm.

Uzo hailed from Feldemar, and seemed the least uncomfortable with the heavy rains that pelted them. It was the way of winter in this land, he told them, and this was far gentler than the worst storms he had seen growing up. Jormund was a man of Calentin. That caught Loren's attention.

"Truly?" she said. "But you are a swordsman. Why do you not use the bow?"

"You know something of our archers, then," said Jormund, flashing his easy grin. "But a whole kingdom cannot stand back and fire upon their enemies from afar, for then they would be in grave trouble should those enemies ever get too close. And besides, I am too large to be an archer. When they put a bow in my hands as a boy, it snapped to kindling when I drew it." He laughed.

Gem's eyes went wide, but Loren leaned close and said, "He is joking."

She had meant to be quiet, but Jormund heard her. "I am not," he insisted. "Give me your own bow, if you do not believe me, and I will show you."

Loren declined.

Niya proved more reticent to speak of herself. When Loren asked the land from which she hailed, she said only "Wadeland." But she did not have the look of one from that kingdom, and she told them nothing of how she came to join the Mystics. Loren thought at first to press her for the tale, but soon realized that this was neither the time nor the place. She herself did not enjoy speaking of her childhood in the Birchwood, particularly when it came to her parents.

But that did not quell her curiosity about the Mystic woman—a curiosity, she admitted to herself, that was stoked to greater heights by the intense, smoldering look she often saw in Niya's eye when the woman thought she was not looking. Mayhap, Loren decided, she would be able to learn more once they reached Ammon.

Gem tried often to get Uzo to drill with him, for the boy still practiced the sword stances Jordel had taught him in the Greatrocks many months ago. He was much better at the forms now, and his arms had begun to fill out with his constant practice. But Uzo seemed to regard Gem as little more than an annoyance, and only joined in his training with great reluctance. Over and over again he trounced the boy, but Gem always sprang up off the ground beaming.

"You are a great warrior indeed," he said one evening, after Uzo had thrashed him thoroughly.

Uzo raised an eyebrow. "Greater than a boy with almost no practice? Stay your praise, for my pride cannot bear to be stoked any more."

Gem laughed as though that were a great joke.

One by one, Loren followed the landmarks that Xain had laid out for her on the route that would take them to Ammon. Sometimes they were easily found, and lay beside wide roads that were well kept. Other times they led her off into unbroken land, where there was nothing but thin goat trails to go by. But at last, after seven days, they came upon a wide plateau with a hill atop it, in the middle of a flat grassland, and upon that plateau was the stronghold of Ammon.

It was an impressive sight from the first, even when it was only a shape on the horizon that she could cover with her thumb. As they drew closer, they could see that it was built in three levels: first, a high wall that rimmed the edges of the plateau, from which there was only a single gate at the top of a ramp leading down; the middle wall, halfway up the hill, had two gates, and what looked like several structures built inside for the housing of troops; finally, the keep itself sat upon the hill's crown. It looked large enough to house half a thousand troops in comfort. As they neared, the plateau seemed to grow larger and larger, and the stronghold with it, so that Loren felt smaller the closer she drew.

Leagues away, they knew they had been spotted when they heard the clarion peal of horns signaling their approach. Soon after, they reached the bottom of the ramp, and felt eyes upon them all the way up. But when they reached the top, the gate was still closed. There, on the wall just above them, was an old man with a long white beard, wrapped in the red cloak of a Mystic. Loren recognized him, of course, for they had met only weeks before; he was Kal of the family Endil, and he looked just as severe as the first time she had laid eyes upon him.

"Who approaches the stronghold of Ammon, home of the family Adair?" said Kal.

"Loren of the family Nelda, Nightblade of the High King," said Loren. "But you know that already, and it is raining, so be quick and open the gate."

Kal scowled, but he turned to the men in the gatehouse and gave a nod. The drawbridge began to lower as they bent to the wheel, spanning the gap between the top of the ramp and the portcullis leading into the first level of the fortress.

"I would advise you be more careful with your manners," muttered Weath beside her, though Loren could see the wizard was hiding a smile. "I have known the grand chancellor for many years, and while he is not a stickler for ceremony, he sees great value in military decorum."

"I see greater value in a warm bed, especially now," said Loren. "I will not be kept huddling outside his fortress in the rain because I have not saluted to his liking."

After the drawbridge slammed into place, they walked their horses across it. Kal had descended to the courtyard and waited within, backed by a household guard of Mystic knights. Loren dismounted before him and gave a curt bow, pulling her gloves from her hands.

"Well met, Kal of the family Endil."

"And you, Nightblade. If you will follow me, there is much to—"

But a high-pitched squeal cut him off, and from between Kal's Mystics came a black and silver streak. It was Annis, in a dark dress that she had hitched up to run full tilt, and with a scream she flung herself into Loren's arms. Loren shouted in joy and hoisted her up in the air, and Gem launched himself from the saddle where he had been sitting behind Chet, tackling them both so that they all fell to the ground. He covered Annis' cheeks with kisses, and she laughed as she tried to hug him and Loren at the same time. Tears poured down the girl's cheeks, and Loren found it hard to keep her own restrained.

"Sky above!" barked Kal. "Are you servants of the High King, or children in truth? Get up, for though you may have all day to roll about in the mud like pups, I do not."

Loren rolled her eyes, but she got up and pulled the children with her. But Annis and Gem did not let go of each other.

"Very well," said Loren. "We are weary after our journey. If you will show us to our quarters, we will take our rest, and you may go about your business."

"Rest must wait," said Kal. "As I had begun to explain, you and I have much to discuss."

Stepping aside, he waved her on with a wide sweep of his arm. Loren sighed, hoping their discussion would be brief, for she was indeed weary and sick of the rain besides. But just as she stepped past Kal, she froze in her tracks.

In the group of Mystics who stood there, there was a man who looked to be from Wadeland. His hair was black and cropped close to the scalp, and a scar split his chin. He wore a red cloak now, but when last she had seen him, he had been dressed in the grey and blue of a Shade—and he had stood behind Damaris, in her dream.

"Loren?" said Chet behind her. "Is something the matter?"

The man was looking at her oddly—and did she catch a trace of fear in his eye? Loren tore her gaze away from him and looked to Chet.

"No. Nothing," she said. "Only I am tired, and my mind went far away. But I am sure the chancellor has no care for our weariness. Come, let us accompany him before he bursts with his impatience."

Kal growled something inaudible, and Chet snickered as they followed him onwards. But Loren stole a brief glance behind her. Mayhap she imagined it, but she thought she saw the man swallow with relief as she passed him by.

NINE

KAL TOOK LITTLE NOTICE OF LOREN'S HESITATION, AND PRESSED QUICKLY on until they had reached the keep atop the plateau. But Chet took her arm and drew her back a pace, and leaned in to whisper. "What was it? You looked as though you had seen an Elf."

Loren shook her head. "I . . . I am not certain. We should speak of it later."

Inwardly, she was not even certain what she would tell him. She knew nothing of the man she had seen. They had never met, so far as she could recall. All she knew was that he had been in her dream, dressed as a Shade. Should she even try to do anything about it? A part of her wanted to believe it was a coincidence, but another part knew that was foolish. It was not exactly a common thing, to see something in a dream only to see it later in the waking world.

And then she thought of the rest of that dream—Damaris, and Chet's death, and Gem's teeth on her throat.

No. No, there was some explanation for this. There must be.

Kal stopped short, and Loren was so absorbed in thought that she nearly ran into him. He threw open a door in the hall and drew her into a small council room. Two Mystics took up positions of guard, one on either side of the door. Loren was relieved to see that neither of them was the dark-haired stranger from her dream. But when the rest of Loren's party started to follow them in, Kal waved his hands at them as if they were cats.

"Off with you—all except Loren. My men will see you to your lodgings, such as they are. You knights will receive your assignment in time. The rest of you may sit on the ramparts until the rain has pierced you through, for all I care. Go."

They went, with Chet giving Loren one last worried look before the door closed between them. But it was not until Loren turned to Kal in the center of the room that she saw Annis had remained. Kal acted as though it were the most normal thing in the world—in fact he hardly seemed to notice the girl. He had eyes only for Loren, and he seized his long beard in his fingers as he narrowed his eyes at her.

"You certainly took your time to get here," he said.

Loren blinked. "I beg your pardon? I came here by the route that was given to me."

"Aye, and weeks after the attack upon the Seat," said Kal.

"When the High King ordered me."

Kal snorted. "If we all waited for orders, the nine kingdoms would already have fallen to ruination. Everyone moves too slowly, too slowly by half, and even the High King is no exception."

Unbidden, a flush of anger rose to Loren's cheeks. "You should not speak ill of your liege lord."

"Criticism should never be forbidden—least of all when it comes to kings," said Kal. "If a few more had been brave enough to speak against the Wizard Kings in their day, how many dark wars might have been avoided? But enough of this. I did not call you here to bandy words of politics and philosophy. Tell me of your journey, and what came before it upon the Seat."

"A moment," said Loren. "First, I saw someone in your courtyard. A young man, not much older than I, with dark hair and a scar that split his chin. Who is he?"

She was not displeased to see Kal frown in confusion, caught off guard by the question. Behind him, Annis' eyes narrowed with interest. "Hewal? What of him?"

"He had . . . he looks familiar."

Kal snorted. "That is hardly possible. I have known him since he

266

was a boy in Wadeland, and he has been stationed here since first he joined the Mystics. He was not with me when we met in Brekkur. If you have taken a fancy to him, that is not a matter I wish to give you any counsel upon whatsoever."

It was Loren's turn to be caught off guard, and she grew even angrier as she blushed anew. "I told you, I only thought he had an odd look." If she had thought for a moment to tell him of her dream, that impulse vanished.

"Forget my soldiers and their odd looks, and tell me of the attack upon the Seat," said Kal.

She did, at least in brief. When Loren spoke of some of the details of the battle, Annis' eyes went wide with shock and fear—especially when Loren told how she had brought the city gate crashing down to crush Rogan. Then Kal had her tell him of everything that had come after—when those who lived upon the Seat had fled to Selvan, and then returned, and finally when Enalyn had assigned her to Kal's service. She told him of the journey to Ammon as well, though he seemed to have little interest in that, and only studied the map that was laid out on his table, running his fingers through his beard in thought.

"Very well, very well," he muttered when she had finished. "It is good you have come, even if it took you an age. I find myself with more duties than I can easily assume, especially after the High King named me Master of Spies. Hah! A useless title if ever there was one. She wishes for me to work for her in secret—yet because she names my position, I am known more widely than before, and secrecy comes scarce."

Loren felt that they must be coming to the heart of the matter now. "If you cannot act in secret, then let me act in your stead. What would you have me do?"

It was Annis who answered her, and once again Loren was surprised as Kal let the girl speak without interruption. "The answer to that is not entirely certain. Just now, the nine kingdoms are in a precarious position. The way that people perceive this war is even more important than the next battle. We have been trying to devise ways to sway the minds of the people, rather than outmaneuver our enemy on the field, for we are not generals. The High King's subjects, as well as her enemies, must see that she is resolved and capable, and that the kingdoms are unified behind her. None of the other kingdoms must be tempted to join with Dulmun."

That made Loren balk. "Would any of them do so? The treason of one kingdom is hard enough to believe. I cannot imagine that others would break their oaths."

To Loren's great annoyance, Kal and Annis looked at each other and rolled their eyes in unison.

"If that is true, why have the other kingdoms been so slow to answer Enalyn's call?" said Annis. "Oh, Selvan is with her, for she hails from that land. Dorsea was quick to bend the knee—no doubt they feared her reprisal after the Battle of Wellmont. Hedgemond, too, has pledged their strength—but that is an easy oath to keep, for they could not be farther away from the war itself. But where is Feldemar? Where are Wadeland and Idris and Wavemount? In days to come, their kings will no doubt claim that the High King's messengers were delayed by winter storms, or that their own messengers had been slow to return. Yet the truth is that they hesitate. And if even one of them joins Dulmun, the hesitation of the rest will only increase—and then we will have a true war on our hands, one that cannot be quelled easily."

All of this was a bit beyond Loren. In truth, she was shocked to hear Annis speaking of it so plainly, as though it were second nature. Her gaze lingered on the younger girl. Kal saw it, and a wry smile lifted one corner of his mouth.

"She is impressive, is she not? At first, I will admit that I was dismayed to be saddled with the girl. But she has proven herself to have an uncanny mind for strategy."

Annis' dark cheeks turned darker still, and she lowered her gaze demurely. But Loren saw the grin she could not banish.

"Very well," said Loren. "I will leave such lofty matters to your hands, for the two of you seem more than capable of dealing with them. Yet my question remains: what shall I do?"

"If I have my way, you will be used to set an example," said Kal. "Those who have acted against the High King must be brought to justice—and the more powerful the enemy we can lay low, the better. Do you know of any mighty enemy who might serve such a purpose?" His eyes narrowed.

Loren felt a chill steal up her back, and her heart turned to ice. "You mean to send me after Rogan."

"Yes," said Kal, nodding slowly. "No one knows where he is, but we must find him. Tales have spread throughout Underrealm of this warrior, the man no one can kill, who leads the armies that march against the High King."

"He is not the only one of his kind," said Loren. "We defeated another in the Greatrocks, one named Trisken. I would not doubt that there are more in the service of the Necroma—"

"*Hist!*" cried Kal, slamming his hand down on the tabletop. He looked at the door, almost fearfully. "Do not speak of such things where others may hear you."

Loren arched an eyebrow. "I thought you trusted your soldiers, Kal."

Kal scowled. "I do. And I am also responsible for their safety. Some knowledge is dangerous—something I know Jordel taught you, or tried to, though it is clear you did not heed the lesson."

That hurt Loren more than she wished to show him, and so she lowered her head over the map. A thought came to her, and she pursed her lips. "It seems clear, then, what purpose you intend for me. Yet you seem to speak of dark deeds. I told the High King that I would not kill in her name, and she vowed never to command me to do so."

"Are you a fool, or have you not been listening?" said Kal. "I do not wish for you to murder Rogan. That would accomplish little. Our display of the High King's power must be as public as possible, and well within the law. We do not mean to kill him in darkness and shadow. He must be captured, and the King's justice brought down upon him in such a way that word of it will spread as fast as his exploits in battle."

That sounded far more palatable to Loren. And in fact, now that she thought of it, it sounded just like the stories of Mennet, the ancient thief of legend from whom Loren had drawn her first daydreams of becoming a thief. Mennet had never killed. But when a noble or great merchant was unjust and cruel to those who served them, Mennet would bring the King's justice down upon them without ever swinging the sword himself.

"Well and good," said Loren. "Then my oath is intact. When do I begin?"

"You are too eager by half," Kal grumbled. "And I have told you already that I do not know. If we knew where Rogan lurked, I would have acted already. I have learned what I needed from you. Go. Find your friends and settle into your lodgings. I will send for you again when I know our next step."

He bent over the map. Loren turned to make for the door—but she paused upon seeing a pained look on Annis' face. Kal noticed the room's silence after a moment, and he looked up, frowning. When he saw Annis' anxious expression, he sighed.

"Very well," he growled. "Spend this day in greetings and reunion if you wish. But I will expect you back on duty tomorrow."

"You shall have me," said Annis, barely restraining the glee in her voice. She ran towards Loren, seizing her arm and drawing her out into the hallway.

TEN

"COME!" SAID ANNIS, EYES BRIGHT AS SHE CLUTCHED LOREN'S HAND. "I want to see the others."

But Loren pulled her to a stop around the corner where no one could overhear. "In a moment. Annis, when did you become so wise in strategy that a grand chancellor of the Mystic Order would rely so strongly upon your counsel?"

Annis looked away bashfully. "Oh, that? That is no great matter."

"No great matter? He had you by his side the way the High King keeps the Lord Prince near her."

The hallway grew quiet as Annis searched for words. "Do you remember, long ago, when I told you of . . . of my mother, and what she would invite me to do?"

Loren's smile died as she nodded. Damaris of the family Yerrin, Annis' mother, was a cruel and ruthless matron. To achieve her ends, she had killed and tortured many. And when Annis was still a very little girl, Damaris had invited her to join in the violence. It was why Annis had been so desperate to escape her family when she and Loren first met.

"I remember," said Loren quietly.

"Well, she did not only draw me into her darker activities," said Annis. "I was there, too, for all the business one would expect in a merchant family—supply lines, and the movement of men from kingdom to kingdom, and things of that sort. Well, after I came here to Ammon, I was bored nearly to tears. I thought I would go mad for want of something to do. Then, mayhap a week after I arrived, Kal sent for me. He called me to his council chamber and asked me some questions of Yerrin activities in Dorsea. I answered him, and more besides, for he was asking the wrong sorts of questions."

Loren frowned. "What do you mean?"

Annis waved her hands as though she could pluck her explanation out of the air. "It would have been better if you were there. He wanted to know why our holdings in Selvan were so much stronger than in Dorsea, since Dorsea borders more of the nine kingdoms than Selvan. He did not understand that Selvan, though it may be farther from the other kingdoms as the bird flies, is yet more deeply connected because of its wealth and its relationship to the High King, with whom all curry favor, and that trade routes are therefore more easily—"

Quickly Loren waved her hands. "Never mind. I am sorry I asked. Go on with your story."

"Well, I went on that way for some time, and when I paused to take a breath, I saw a strange look in Kal's eyes. I cannot think he has had many dealings with anyone from a merchant family before, for I did not tell him any great secrets of trade or commerce, but only the simplest truths we are taught as very young children. In any case, after that, he began inviting me to many of his strategy sessions. I think you spoke in jest before, but I suppose I *am* a part of his council."

A smile came to Loren unbidden, and she clapped a firm hand on Annis' shoulder. "Well, I for one am glad. You seemed at ease, and confident. Happier, mayhap, than I have seen you since after Cabrus."

Annis giggled. "I think I am. I have always thought of such things as a game—which my tutors did not favor, I can assure you, though they could not complain much, for I did well at my lessons regardless. And it has earned me some small amount of renown among the Mystics who dwell here."

Loren's smile widened—but mention of the Mystics made her think of the dark young man from the courtyard, who Kal had said was named Hewal. Her good mood evaporated. "As for that—do you know many of the soldiers in Ammon? Have you met them, or learned anything about them?"

"Not very much," said Annis, shrugging. "Why do you ask?"

Her dream flashed before her eyes. But how could she explain that? "No, nothing. Pay me no mind."

Annis' eyes narrowed, and the girl crossed her arms over her chest. "You asked Kal something of this, did you not? What is your interest in this Hewal fellow?"

Loren grimaced. She had forgotten how sharp and observant Annis could be, and always at the most inopportune times. "It is no great matter. Or, I do not believe so. But if it should become important, I will tell you before anyone else—other than Chet, of course. Does that satisfy you?"

"I suppose," said Annis. "Though you make it all sound very mysterious, and that is rarely a good sign with you. I could speak with Hewal if you wish, and try to learn what I—"

"*No!*" said Loren, far more sharply than she had intended. She tried again, softening her tone. "No, that is all right. But thank you."

Annis' eyes shot wide, and for the first time the girl looked truly worried. "Loren, what is it?" she whispered. "Are we in any danger?"

Loren thought of Chet's ruined throat, and the feral look in Gem's eyes as he attacked her. But she forced a smile. "No. Of course not. We are in a stronghold of Mystics, the greatest warriors in Underrealm. Where could we be safer?" She could see that Annis was not entirely convinced. But she took the girl's arm and led her on down the hallway. "Come. You have hardly had a chance to speak with Gem, and though you might not care overmuch, Chet, too, wishes to see you."

"Not so much as he wishes to see you, I am sure," said Annis with a sigh. "Are the two of you . . . is it much the same as when I saw you last?"

A furious red sprang into Loren's face. When last she had seen Annis, she and Chet had been chaste, but now . . . "Er, it is not—that is, not *quite* the same."

Annis must have taken her meaning, for her mouth formed a small circle. "I . . . I did not mean to . . . that is, forgive me for prying."

Loren could not help a laugh at that. "Still the modest merchant's daughter, I see. It is not prying that worries me—only I did not wish to embarrass *you*."

"Yes, well . . ." Annis looked thoroughly miserable through her bashfulness. "Might we speak of something else?"

"Mayhap our friends can distract us," said Loren. She took Annis' hand, and led her running and laughing down the hallway. Annis pointed the way to the stronghold's great dining hall, and there was Loren's party, seated and eating a meal from the kitchens.

Gem sprang to his feet at once and flung himself into Annis' arms, screaming with delight. Annis clutched at his shoulders, and then pushed him away to look at him—and Loren saw it. There, in Annis' gaze, was a pure and true love, even stronger, mayhap, than the way Loren felt for Chet. Tears came freely to the girl's eyes as she smiled and clutched Gem to her again. But Gem only smiled and laughed, and Loren saw no trace of the same feelings within him. Her high mood dampened for a moment.

Chet gave Annis a warm enough greeting, and then came to Loren. He took her hand in his and led her to the table.

"I will fetch you some food. What did Kal wish to discuss with you?"

Loren's mind returned to the council room, and the mission Kal had given her. Just as Chet had warned on the High King's Seat, she would soon hunt for Rogan. Her mood darkened, and he saw it. But she only shook her head.

"There is time to discuss it later," she said. "Let us wait until the happiness of this reunion has passed."

He frowned, and she feared he might press her. But then Annis sat beside her, and Gem on her other side, both of them talking animatedly. And in the face of their joy, Chet closed his mouth again, and went to fetch Loren her dinner, while Loren picked up a knife and began to pick at her nails with it.

ELEVEN

AFTER THEY ATE, ANNIS TOOK LOREN AND CHET AND GEM TO THE stables, where they found Midnight waiting. Loren gave a happy cry when she saw the mare, and scratched at her nose as Midnight whinnied in delight. But then the horse turned to Annis and pushed her muzzle against the girl's shoulder. Annis giggled and gave Loren an embarrassed look.

"We have become fast friends during our time here," she confessed. "I have visited her often, and usually bring a treat from the kitchens. Though I think that duty should now pass to you. Here." From a pocket in her cloak she drew an apple, and Loren fed it to Midnight, who gave a sharp nicker of pleasure.

They remained there for some time, and Loren brushed Midnight's coat, though it was already clean and shining. Then Annis took them out into the courtyard and atop the wall, where they looked out over the surrounding lands. It had stopped raining. Night approached swiftly, and the last of the sun's pale light dimmed through the clouds. From their high perspective, Annis pointed out this or that part of the fortress, sharing tidbits she had learned from the Mystics—who were growing more and more plentiful, the way she described it.

"Ever since the attack on the Seat, they have come in ever greater numbers," said Annis. "But they do nothing. There are no plans to engage in battle, at least not yet. They are only gathering their strength, and it is hard to escape reminders of the brewing war. I was only just starting to learn the names of those within the stronghold when all the newcomers started to arrive. Now I am nearly lost again."

"Are you? I can tell you where to find yourself, if you wish," said Niya.

They all gave a little jump and turned. The Mystic woman had appeared behind them as if by magic, and the others had come as well—Uzo, Shiun, Weath, and large Jormund. They each gave Loren a nod.

"You did not hear us coming?" said Niya, giving Loren a wide smile. "You should keep a better lookout."

"I am in a stronghold full of allies," said Loren, rolling her eyes. "I thought I might let my guard down for half a moment."

Niya smiled at her, and then turned to Annis. A curious light shone in her eyes. "Well, if it is not the Yerrin girl."

Annis frowned. "I was not aware that we knew each other."

"But everyone in the stronghold knows you," said Niya, and her smile grew wider. "Those who dwell here already speak of you as though you are their little sister."

That mollified Annis considerably, and she held forth a hand. "I am Annis of the family Yerrin. Well met."

Niya clasped her wrist. "I already said I know who you are. I am Niya. These ones with me are Weath, Uzo, Shiun, and Jormund."

They greeted her one by one, and then stepped up to the ramparts beside Loren and Chet as Annis went on describing the lands that surrounded the stronghold. It seemed that Niya quickly grew bored, however, for she moved next to Loren and leaned on the ramparts just to her right. Loren saw that Chet took notice, and his mouth twisted in a frown.

"How went your council with the grand chancellor?" said Niya. She spoke quietly, so as not to interrupt Annis.

"Nothing very important came of it," said Loren lightly. She tried not to pay attention to how close Niya was, so close that she could almost feel the woman's breath on her cheek. "At least not yet. Though it seems the next leg of my mission might begin sooner than I had expected."

Niya straightened slightly, and forgot to speak quietly. "You are to ride forth? When?"

Annis' conversation halted, and the other Mystics looked to Loren. She shook her head quickly. "That has not been decided. Kal does not yet know where to send me. As soon as that changes, I am sure I shall be summoned."

The woman frowned. "But he will not send you out alone, I hope. We were charged with your safety."

"To see me here, yes," said Loren. "But after that?"

Niya's jaw twitched as she searched for words. "I would rest easier knowing you were in our hands than guarded by others in Ammon."

"Yes, and any excuse to march out the gate," muttered Uzo. "Already the air here cloys my nostrils."

They all went silent for a moment. Weath and Niya looked to Uzo, and from their expressions Loren felt that he had said something wrong, though she did not know what. But, too, she saw Annis look at Uzo, and Loren saw something in the girl's eyes—anxiousness? Mayhap even fear? But certainly a sense of warning.

Chet saw none of it, and it was his unknowing response that broke the moment's tension. "I am not eager to leave. Here we are protected, and beyond Ammon's walls I think we will find only danger."

Weath turned to him and smiled, her troubled expression vanishing. But Annis and Niya still wore dark looks, and both of them looked far away as though lost in thought.

"I would welcome some danger," said Jormund to Chet. "We have been idle since the attack on the Seat. I feel that if I do not do something soon, I may go mad."

"I have not seen as much battle as you, certainly, but I do not wish for more," said Chet.

"Mayhap you have no reason," snapped Uzo. "I was in the palace when they came. I knew a lover there, a courtesan of the High King herself, and some others as well."

"Meaning yourself?" said Niya, smirking.

Uzo's dark cheeks went darker. "In any case, I saw him during the battle. I was in formation, and we could not break through the lines of the Shades. I watched, helpless, as two of them dragged him from a side room. They cut him open there in the hall, and let his guts splash upon the marble floor. There was no reason for it. He had no weapon. It was slaughter for the sake of slaughter."

They were all silent for a moment after that. Loren saw Gem looking up at Uzo, his jaw hanging slack. The boy's eyes shone wet, and not from the light drizzle that fell from the sky.

One of Jormund's massive hands tightened into a fist. "I was stationed on the north wall, but I went running to the eastern docks as soon as the horns sounded. I saw the Dulmun fleet land, and the gate had already been drawn up against them. Some of the folk from the city had been trapped outside, but rather than flee north or south, they only pounded on the gate. We tried to get it open and let them in, but before we could, the Dulmun soldiers set upon them, piercing them with spears so that their bodies were pinned to the wall."

"We all saw dark things that day," said Weath quietly. "We all have reason to hate the Shades."

Loren thought of the part she had played in the battle of the palace, and found herself nodding in agreement. But then she thought of Xain—and that, in turn, made her think of Jordel.

"Vengeance," she said—but her voice broke. She cleared her throat and tried again, quietly. "Vengeance is a poor reason to ride into battle. Let us not make war for hatred. We should seek justice instead. A wise man—and a Mystic—taught me that."

Weath and Jormund bowed their heads. Loren knew that they had been Kal's soldiers for some time, and had known Jordel, at least in passing. But Niya gave Loren a wry look.

"Why should it matter if justice or vengeance swings the sword? A head will roll free regardless. I have fought before, and I have learned this: give yourself whatever reason you need to fight. But when you go to battle, fight to win. Then you may dream up whatever reason you wish. You cannot do that if you are dead."

Loren's ears burned. "I only mean that having a clear mind and a clear purpose may—"

Niya shook her head. "I know what you meant."

Somehow the reassurance left Loren feeling even more embarrassed. She knew that she had been naive when she left the Birchwood, and had thought that everyone she met could be held to her own rules of right and wrong. But that had ended in disaster more than once, and no more so than when Jordel had fallen in the Greatrocks. She could keep her own vow, yes, and never take a life—but she knew that if she led these Mystics upon their mission, and did not look upon the world with both eyes open, it would lead only to tragedy and death.

The Nightblade must have honor, she told herself. *But the Nightblade must also be wise—for who would call me honorable if I let others die?*

Her gaze drifted, and she looked down from the wall into the courtyard. The door to the stronghold opened, and a Mystic stepped out. The daylight was almost gone, but she recognized him from the scar that split his chin: Hewal. Her brows drew together.

"What?" whispered Chet, catching the look on her face. "What is wrong?"

Loren did not answer him, but turned to the rest of them. "I am weary from the road and desire rest," she said. "I bid all of you a good night."

"I will show you to your quarters," said Annis brightly. "Follow me."

She led them down into the courtyard. The Mystics stayed atop the wall, with Niya giving Loren a final nod, along with a secretive smile that made Loren's heart flutter. As Annis scampered down the steps, Loren lagged behind to speak with Chet.

"You remember my dream upon the Seat," she said.

"I do," said Chet, frowning.

"I saw a man in my dream—a man dressed in the clothes of a Shade. And then, when we arrived at Ammon today, I saw him again. He was in Kal's guard. He had a scar on his chin."

Chet's eyes widened. "I remember the one. You are certain? He was in your dream?"

"I am. It was not a likeness—it was the same man."

"What . . ." Chet stopped and looked about, as though he expected to find eavesdroppers. "What do you suppose it means?"

"I do not know," said Loren. "You do not think I am going mad?"

"Why should I think that?" said Chet, shrugging. "I often dream of those I have met in the waking world, and sometimes I see people in my dreams who do not exist at all. But never have I seen someone in my sleep, only for them to appear in true life. And besides, you have spoken with Elves."

The memory made Loren shudder. "That was my thought as well. They are fey, and I never had such dreams before I met them. But even if this is some work of theirs, what does it mean? What should we do?"

"Who can we trust here?" said Chet. "Annis and Gem, of course, though I do not know if they will be of much help. What about Kal? Could you not tell him what you saw?"

"I do not think he would place much stock in a dream," said Loren. Her thoughts drifted to Niya, and she remembered how the woman often looked at her. "We might tell the Mystics who came with us."

"No," said Chet at once. "We barely know that Niya woman, for we scarcely met her a week ago. And though we have known some of the others a while longer, still we have not spent much time with them. I would hardly call them friends."

"Yet they are capable warriors, and Niya seems wise besides," said Loren. "She is a captain, as Jordel was. We need someone who knows something of the Mystics."

"If you must speak to one of them, speak to Weath, or Shiun or Jormund or Uzo," said Chet. "But not Niya."

Loren gave him a look, and she thought she heard what he was unwilling to say. Almost she took him to task for it, but now hardly seemed the time. "Very well," she said. "Let us mention it first to Annis—only I do not think it would be wise to tell her everything at once."

Chet gave a sigh of relief. "I agree."

They increased their pace to catch up with the children again. Soon they reached their quarters, and Annis stopped them before a wooden door. "I am just across the hall, in a room where some Mystics stay as well," she said. "Gem is in the next room over. Loren and Chet, your room is your own."

"Thank you, Annis," said Loren. She glanced up and down the hallway. No one else was in sight. "Would you mind stepping within for a moment? Both of you? There was one more matter I wished to discuss."

Annis and Gem frowned at each other, but they followed Loren into her room. It was a meager place, with only a bed, a single chest, and a bureau against the wall. There were neither chairs nor rugs nor drapes, as they had had upon the Seat, nor even a window, and only a small hole near the ceiling so that burning a lantern did not make the room too stuffy. Loren closed the door behind the children and stood before them, fidgeting with her hands.

"What is it, Loren?" said Annis. "Clearly something troubles you greatly."

"I must ask you to trust me," Loren blurted out. "But I cannot . . . I cannot tell you exactly why."

The girl's nostrils flared. "Is this about Hewal? *What* is the matter with you—or with him? Spit it out." She put her hands to her hips, and for a moment looked just like her mother as she scowled.

"Yes, it is Hewal," said Loren. "Is there anything—anything at all—that you know about him? The smallest detail might help."

Annis threw up her hands. "I have told you I know almost nothing. I believe he is a messenger, but I am not even certain of that."

Loren and Chet shared a look. A messenger? Who better to act as a spy for the enemy?

Gem was frowning at the both of them now. "What under the sky has you so worried?" he said. "I have not seen you this anxious since . . . well, since just before the attack upon the Seat."

"There is nothing for it," she said quietly to Chet.

"I know," he said.

Loren took a deep breath and spoke in a whisper. "I think he may be a Shade."

The room went very still. Annis and Gem both froze, as though they were afraid a movement might reveal them to some unseen enemy. At last Annis licked her lips.

"Why?" she said.

"I cannot explain that," said Loren. "But for my peace of mind if nothing else, we must look into it."

"How?" said Gem. "I do not think I could walk up to him in the dining hall and ask, 'Say, do you have another change of clothes that are blue and grey? Have you lost a friend named Trisken recently?' What do you mean to do?"

"I do not know exactly," said Loren. "But we can start with his personal effects. The chances are small that we will find anything to prove what I suspect, but we have to try."

Annis shivered. "Very well. We can do it tomorrow. I will find out where his quarters are."

"Thank you," said Loren. "Now go to bed, both of you, and ready yourselves. Let us all hope that I am wrong."

TWELVE

ANNIS WORKED WITH REMARKABLE SPEED. WELL BEFORE THE NEXT midday meal, she approached Loren and Chet with Gem in tow. After bidding them to follow, she led them unerringly through Ammon's halls to the part of the keep where Kal's household guard slept. When she pointed out the door to Hewal's room, Loren led them all off down the hallway and around the first corner.

"Wait here," she told Chet. "Annis, you go down to the other end of the hall. If someone approaches, cough as loudly as you can, louder than someone struck with plague. We will slip out of the room as quickly as we can."

Gem puffed out his chest. "Mayhap I should stand guard. I may have the loudest cough in all the nine kingdoms."

"Who could doubt it?" said Loren, letting no trace of a smile touch her lips. "But you can read, where Chet and I cannot."

The boy blinked. "I had not thought of that. Very well."

As Annis ran down the hall to the next corner, Loren and Gem slipped into the room. *His bed is the first on the left,* Annis had told them. They found it at once. A small cupboard stood near the head, and at the foot, the customary chest. The chest had no lock, and at first Loren was glad. But then she realized that Hewal would not keep anything incriminating in an unlocked chest, and her heart sank.

Still, they had come this far, and it would be foolish not to look while they could. Within the chest they found some folded letters. Loren handed them to Gem, for she could not read them, but they contained nothing nefarious. Other than that, it held only several changes of clothes and a second pair of boots. Loren turned the boots upside-down and shook them, but there was nothing hidden within. The cupboard at the other end of the bed was no better, holding only a few tunics. Loren probed them with her fingers to see if something was folded inside, but they were only harmless cloth.

They left the room as quickly as they had entered, and walked away with Chet and Annis in tow. Loren scowled as they walked, slamming a fist into her palm.

"Nothing," said Loren. "Not that there was any great hope. But I thought I might find some sign—a pendant with the Shades' mark, mayhap."

"I mean you no offense," said Gem, "but if this Hewal were careless enough to keep such a thing in his possession, I think he would have been discovered long before we arrived."

"If he is even a Shade in the first place," said Annis. "And since you will not tell us why you think he might be, I cannot offer any other ideas of how we might learn whether it is true."

"Mayhap it is nothing," said Loren. "This was likely a foolish idea in the first place. Forgive me for bringing you into it."

Chet stopped short, forcing the rest of them to do the same. "You did not summon us on some lark, Loren," he said quietly. "I think you should tell them. Then they may understand why this is so important—and why we should not stop our search here."

Loren looked about. The hall was empty, but still she felt out of place, as though there might be spies eavesdropping around either corner. "Very well. But not here."

Annis raised an eyebrow. "You said only yesterday that this was a stronghold filled with allies. Are you so fearful of being overheard?"

"I said that to the Mystics, who no doubt believe it themselves," said Loren. "I myself am not entirely convinced. Come. We are not far from our rooms, and can speak more privately in my chamber."

"*Our* chamber," muttered Chet, but he smiled as he said it to soften the words. Loren led them onwards, and soon they had enclosed themselves in the room. When Loren had checked twice that the door's latch was secure, she turned to the children. But looking upon their expectant faces, she suddenly balked, and turned to pace the room instead.

"Spit it out, Loren," said Annis. "Whatever you have to say, delay helps nothing and no one."

"I do not myself understand it," said Loren. "Therefore I am leery of trying to explain, for it is a mad tale."

Gem scoffed. "And we are all of us strangers to mad tales, after all the leagues we have ridden together."

That made Loren smile, and her worry eased slightly. "I see your point. Very well. I . . . saw Hewal in a dream. While we were still on the Seat. You remember, Gem, how I awoke in terror one night." Gem nodded, frowning. "I saw many things in my dream, but among them, I saw your mother, Annis. And behind her stood Hewal—but he wore the blue and grey of a Shade, and not the red cloak of a Mystic."

"Wait, what do you mean you saw him?" said Annis. "That is, do you mean that you saw *him?*"

Gem blinked at her for a moment before he said carefully, "I think she means to ask whether you saw some man who looked *like* Hewal?"

"No," said Loren. "It was no likeness. It was Hewal. He looked into my eyes, and he smiled. He had the same scar on his chin, the same hair, and . . . it was him."

"That is . . . odd indeed," said Annis. "I have never heard of anything like it. I would say it is some sort of spell, except that I have never heard of a wizard who could do such a thing."

Chet spoke quietly from where he was leaning on the wall. "Tell them why the dream matters."

"Yes. There is more," said Loren. "One night, when we traveled across Dorsea, I woke while the moons were still high. When I rose, I saw Chet had been charmed into slumber, and a party of Elves surrounded our camp."

The room went silent, and the lamp flickered, as though a chill breeze had blown through to freeze them all solid. Gem seized Annis' sleeve in fear, and Chet's hands balled to fists at his sides. But then the moment passed, and Loren let loose a quiet sigh of relief.

"Elves?" squeaked Gem. "They came upon us? How did you make them leave?"

"She did not," said Annis, her voice shaking. "You cannot *make* an Elf do anything, no more than you can send away a winter gale by scolding it. What did they want, Loren? What did they *do?*"

"They wanted nothing, and they did little," said Loren, speaking carefully. She had no intention of telling Annis about the magestones that she held, even now, in a pocket of her cloak. Not even Chet knew that secret. "But one of them touched my skin, and when it did, I could . . . I could *see* everything, inside and out, and the threads that bound it all together. It almost drove me mad. Mayhap, for a moment, it did. But this dream . . . it came after I met the Elves. And in the dream, I felt the way I did when they stood before me."

Gem snapped his fingers and pointed at her. "When the Lord Prince met us upon the Seat, he said it. He said you were Elf-touched. That is why."

"Yes," said Loren.

"And he is right," said Annis quietly. "I did not see it so clearly before we parted, but I see it now—whether because I am searching for it, or because it has grown more pronounced in the weeks that have passed. But there is a light in your eyes that was not there before, Loren, and a . . . a sort of *sharpness* to you. Are you certain the Elves did nothing else?"

Nothing but the magestones, thought Loren. But she already knew from Xain that that had nothing to do with it, or with her dreams. "Nothing," she said. "It must have been their touch."

"But even if this is true—no, do not look me that way, you know what I meant," said Gem. "But how can we be certain of your dream's purpose? None can know the thoughts or intent of Elves. They may not have even meant to do . . . whatever it is that they did to you."

"Whether they meant to or not, Loren saw what she saw," said Chet. "I do not think that is something we can easily dismiss."

"I think you are right," said Annis. "This paints everything in a different light. Even if Hewal is not a Shade, such a vision cannot be cast aside without careful thought. Mayhap the dream was only a message, leading you down the right path to find them. Hewal could be the link that leads you to the Shades, without being one himself."

Loren had not thought of that. "It is possible. But how can we know?"

"By watching," said Chet. "It seems the only thing we know about him for certain is that he is a messenger for Kal. Thus, when next he delivers a message, we should watch him—even follow him, if we can."

"Will you know when he leaves, Annis?" said Loren.

"I can find out," said Annis. "And I will tell you at once."

"Very well," said Loren. "Let us hope I am not wrong about this, and that we do not waste our time on some useless flight of fancy."

THIRTEEN

Beginning the next day, Annis kept a careful watch on all messengers entering and leaving Ammon. But Hewal was not one of them, and days passed while they waited impatiently. The longer the waiting went on, the greater grew Loren's frustration. Before a week had passed, she had begun to fidget incessantly with her hands, and often caught herself picking at her fingernails with a knife, though they were already immaculately clean.

Chet tried to be patient with her, but after she snapped at him on the fourth day, he loosed his own irritation. "If this bothers you so, why do you not bring the matter before Kal? You are the Nightblade. Word of your suspicion should be enough for him to take at least some action—or, at the very least, he might tell you when he next plans to send Hewal out on some errand."

"And what, exactly, should I say? 'I saw your messenger, Hewal, whom you have known since he was a boy, in a dream, and he was dressed as a Shade.' Kal seems to place *such* great faith in me; he will likely clap Hewal in irons straightaway."

They did not speak the rest of that day. Loren managed to bring herself to apologize the next morning. But the situation only grew worse, and not least because Kal himself did not seem to need Loren for anything at all. When she tired of lurking around the stronghold, hoping to catch Hewal in some wrongdoing, she would often make for the chancellor's council chambers. But every time she entered after a timid knock, Kal would send her away, saying that he knew no more than the last time he had seen her, and that she must be patient. He kept Annis close, however, and so at meal times Loren would ply her for information—yet Annis knew precious little, for she and Kal still spoke only of logistics and supply lines, and these bored Loren almost to tears.

After a time she accepted her fate, and she began to spend most of her days on the stronghold's training grounds. There, wrapped in her black cloak against the persistent rain, she practiced her archery. Albern had not had enough time to teach her the finer points of Calentin archery, but she remembered his lessons clearly, and over and over again she went through the forms he had shown her. By now she had advanced to the point where she could draw an arrow and fire it in the space of a heartbeat, but her aim often suffered. If she wanted accuracy, she had to revert to the way she had learned to shoot growing up: placing the arrow on the left of the bow, and holding it steady with her forefinger.

Sometimes Chet came to join her. At first she tried to pass on what Albern had taught her, but he gave it up after only one afternoon. "I prefer shooting the way I have learned," he said. "My father taught me to shoot that way, and it was how I put game on the table for many years. Why should I need to learn another style?" Loren wondered if he would say the same thing if he had had more opportunity to see Albern shoot. The Calentin man had been able to empty a quiver in the time it took her to fire only two arrows; every shot found its mark, and could puncture chain mail besides.

Chet did not spend nearly so much time in training as she did, however, for he spent most of his days within the stronghold. He and Weath had become fast friends on their journey north to Ammon, and now she had taken it upon herself to teach him to read. He told Loren that it came to him slowly, but that he was learning the way of it.

"That is well," said Loren. "I have little time for such learning, and so you can read my letters for me." He gave her a mock scowl.

Many of the Mystics in the fortress spent their days in the training yard as well—and Niya was among them. Though Loren often bundled up against the weather, Niya took no such measures, and she still wore her high-necked leather shirts with no sleeves. Loren lost count of the number of times she found herself standing and staring at the Mystic's thick and muscular arms. They bore no scars; either Niya wore armor when she went into battle, or she was a far better fighter than any opponent she had yet faced. The Mystic often caught Loren staring at her, and Loren would blush as she hurriedly returned to her archery.

Once, Niya approached her while she was shooting. Loren paused and looked at her expectantly, one arrow halfway to the string. But Niya only shook her head and waved her hand, prompting Loren to continue. Loren nocked and fired, drew, nocked and fired. But with Niya watching, she tried too hard to make the motions look smooth and fluid, and her aim was even worse than usual. One arrow missed the target entirely, and snapped in two against the stone wall behind.

"Who tried to teach you the Calentin style?" said Niya.

"You recognize it," said Loren. "I thought you were from Wavemount."

"I am, and yet I have fought beside soldiers from all the nine kingdoms. And I have seen enough Calentin archers to know that whoever instructed you was a poor teacher—or, mayhap, they did not have as much time for your lessons as they should have."

Loren thought of Albern with a stab of heartbreak—and of guilt. "It was the latter," she said quietly. "My instructor was . . . well, he is lost now."

Niya let a silent moment pass. "He taught you the forms all right—but only from the waist up." She came over and, before Loren knew what was happening, Niya was right behind her, with one hand on her waist and the other on her left shoulder. "You lean the way you should, and you have your left shoulder lower than your right, the way you ought to. But your legs are the problem."

"What about my legs?" said Loren. It was suddenly hard to speak around the quickening of her breath.

If Niya noticed how flustered Loren had become, she did not remark upon it. She knelt and took Loren's right knee in her hands, pushing it gently so that it bent. "You learned the more ordinary type of shooting, and so you lock your knees when you fire. But your back leg should be coiled, like a serpent ready to strike, and you must use it when you loose." Her hands slid over, and then down Loren's left leg to her ankle. She pushed it forwards, almost causing Loren to lose her balance as it slid on the ground. "This should be extended forwards, so that your body can move over it when you shoot, like a hinge."

"I . . . I do not entirely understand," said Loren. One hand rose to draw her hood a bit farther around her face, to hide how red she had become.

With a chuckle, Niya rose to stand behind her once more. She put her left hand on Loren's waist, and her right on Loren's torso, just under the pit of her arm. "You use your whole body to fire, not just your arms. Act as a lever to propel the arrow forwards. Like this." She pushed her hands together, so that Loren leaned forwards. "That sort of motion, every time you shoot. It adds only a little more power to each arrow, but that little bit of power can be the difference between a killing shot and only a deep wound—and in the meanwhile, it adds a motion to your body that gives you better control over the arrow."

Loren could feel the woman's breath on her cheek. She had to force herself to speak. "You did not learn all of this only watching Calentin archers."

"I did not say I only watched them. Try it. Loose an arrow."

Her fingers fumbling, Loren drew as Albern had taught her, and loosed towards the target. But the motion of her legs was unfamiliar, and the arrow clattered off the cobblestones before skittering past the base of the target.

"Your training has gone amiss. That was my worst shot yet."

"My advice is sound, but you are too well practiced at doing it the wrong way," said Niya. "Keep at it, and mayhap one day you will shoot like a true Calentin."

She stepped back, and Loren loosed a long, low breath—but then Niya slapped her rump, and she jumped into the air, barely restraining a scream. Whirling, she readied herself to give Niya a tongue-lashing— but the Mystic was already striding away, and had soon vanished into a door leading into the stronghold.

Loren tried to still her racing pulse as she drew her cloak around her again. She surveyed the training yard to see if anyone else had been watching—and felt sick to her stomach as she saw Chet standing nearby. He was under an awning, one hand still on the door through which he had emerged, and for half a moment Loren hoped he had only just come out—but the look on his face told her that he had been there long enough, at least, to see the moment when Niya left. Loren forced a smile and waved to him, and slowly he made his way over to her.

"Who could have known that Mystic training was quite so involved?" said Loren lightly. She knew at once that it was a foolish thing to say, but she could not remain silent against the smoldering anger in his eyes. His expression was not unfamiliar to her; she had seen it often enough in the Birchwood, but then it had been directed at her father, every time he would lay his hands upon Loren.

Chet ignored her poor attempt at a joke. "I do not like that Mystic woman."

"You are being ridiculous."

His nostrils flared. "Do not do that. Do not dismiss what I say, as though it has no foundation—as though we both did not witness what just occurred."

Loren sighed. She stepped up to him, and placed a hand upon his cheek. "You should not worry over such trivial things. We have been sent here to Ammon for a purpose. Whatever game Niya plays at is nothing compared to that."

He glowered in the direction the woman had gone. "We were sent here for a purpose, yes. What was she sent here for?"

Now Loren was beginning to grow frustrated. "Are you angry at her, or at me?"

"I . . . why should I be angry with you?" He blinked twice, clearly flustered. "She is the one who behaves poorly."

"Then do not show anger when I am around and she is not. Let her act how she wishes. Why should we care? I am my own person. Do you not trust me?"

Chet looked at her for a long moment. She studied his chestnut eyes, never flinching. "Very well," he said at last, quietly. "You are right. Of course I trust you."

Loren smiled at him. But in the back of her mind, she could not quite quell her own doubts. She still felt a flutter in her chest when she thought of Niya's hand on her waist, and she could still smell the woman's breath on the edge of her cowl.

Without warning she snatched Chet's hand and dragged him towards the door that led in to the stronghold. "Come with me."

He nearly stumbled as he trotted after her. "Where are we going?"

"To our bedchamber. I mean to prove myself still further."

FOURTEEN

Trisken stood upon the stone bridge, menacing in his armor. One massive fist clutched his spiked warhammer near its head, and its butt rested upon the stones near his feet. The feathers of one of Albern's arrows protruded from his eye socket, but through the blood that streamed down his face, white teeth gleamed in a grin.

"You brought me the Yerrin girl, an abomination, and a Mystic to kill," he said. Sick laughter poured from his throat, dragging rotten fingernails of terror up Loren's back. "I could have asked for no finer gifts."

"I brought you nothing!" she screamed, for the storms had started, and she could hardly hear herself over the thunder. "We killed you!"

"How can you kill that which will not die?" he said, throwing his head back and cackling. "How can you kill that which serves death itself?"

Then she saw that he stood on a cairn. She remembered it well. They had built it over Jordel's body. She fell to her knees, weeping as she had when first they buried the Mystic—and then she fell back, shrieking in terror, as a hand covered with desiccated flesh burst from the mound of stones.

She landed hard on her rear end, wincing from the impact on the stone bridge—except that she was no longer on the stone bridge. Instead she lay upon a soft and silken bed, and fine cloth of many colors was draped upon the walls of the small room. Two torches were mounted in sconces, but to Loren they seemed far too large, and their flames licked at the drapes. Her sharp intake of breath brought the scents of fine perfume and wine, and she realized that she was in a house of lovers. Blushing furiously, she pushed herself up, intent on leaving. But she went stock still as the room's door opened.

The lover entered—a woman Loren had never seen before. She looked like an Idrisian, and her long black hair was worked into a single fine braid. Though she was clothed, the fabric was sheer enough to deepen Loren's blush considerably. The lover's gaze locked on Loren, and she swayed as she made her way towards the bed. When she reached the foot of it, she did not stop, but crawled forwards on hands and knees.

"I . . . I did not mean to come here," said Loren. How *had* she come to be here, anyway? She could not remember. "I must go. Chet awaits me."

"Not for long," said the girl. "Stay with me. You have paid, after all."

"I assure you I have not," said Loren. She tried to leave, but her body would not respond—as though it knew she did not truly wish to go. Her eyes went to the torches on the walls. Their flames rose ever higher. How had they not already caught the silks in a blaze?

The lover was close now, too close for Loren to escape without pushing her away. Her lips pressed against Loren's ear. "Would you like to meet my parents?" she whispered.

The question was so unexpected that Loren was shocked out of the moment. "I . . . what?" she said. "Who are your parents?"

"He wonders," said the lover. All of a sudden she drew back and curled her knees up to her chest, wrapping her arms around them, like a child huddling against the cold. "He wonders, and I cannot tell him."

Loren nearly asked who the lover was talking about—but then she cried out, for the torches had caught the walls on fire at last. She leaped from the bed, trying to pull the lover with her. But the lover merely lay on the bed, curling further in on herself, and began to weep. And now the door was wreathed in flames. They could not get out. The smoke burned her eyes, forcing her to shut them as she coughed and coughed and fell back to the bed—

—only she did not land upon the bed, but in a foul-smelling flow of filth and refuse. She fought to get clear of it, and her hand struck stone. It was the edge of the channel, and she knew that she was in the sewers of Cabrus. Coughing and spluttering, she emerged from the stream, falling breathless upon her back.

Snik.

Cold steel pressed against her throat. Loren froze.

"Sweet, simpering little tart," hissed a familiar voice. It was Auntie. Crouching, she held Loren's own dagger to her throat. "Why did you come back here? You should never have returned."

"I did not mean to come here," said Loren, unable to stop the tears that poured from her eyes. "Please, forgive me. I will leave, I will never come back, I will—"

"It is the way you hold yourself," said Auntie, lifting the dagger. Loren thought she was free, but then Auntie's other hand seized her throat. "The hip juts out slightly."

With a shriek, she plunged the dagger into Loren's heart.

Loren screamed.

"That might be a stance of rest, but this hand you hold a bit farther from your body than the other."

She withdrew the dagger, but only to sink it into Loren's heart again, and then pull it out, and then again, and again, and now Loren could not even scream, for only blood came bubbling up from her lungs.

"It is ready to leap to the hip and draw forth the knife, the knife, *the knife, the knife, the knife!*"

The world slowly went black, and Auntie's furious screams faded to nothing. Then, in the blackness, Loren heard the sound of rushing water. She opened her eyes—when had she closed them?—and saw that she stood in a city of gold. It was built around a waterfall, the source of the sound she had heard. The city was built in two levels—one at the bottom of the falls, and one at the top. The buildings all glistened and gleamed with gold trim, which shone all the more in the light mist that pervaded the air.

She was on a balcony not unlike the one she had had in the High King's palace, one that afforded her an excellent view of the city and the lands all around—a landscape similar to the one surrounding Ammon, with strange trees that hid dark pathways.

"Welcome to Dahab."

The voice made her jump. She turned to see Hewal standing beside her on the balcony. He did not look at her, but only leaned on the railing, looking out. Again he wore the blue and grey of the Shades. Without warning he sprang up on the railing, and then his mouth became a beak, his feet claws, and his hands wings. He had turned into a crow. With a raucous cry he took to the air, soaring higher and higher as he spiraled up into the mists coming off the waterfall. Her mind flashed a word: *Weremage.*

Loren watched the bird soar for a moment—and then she found that she was no longer upon the balcony. Now she stood on a huge pillar of stone in the midst of the river near the bottom of the waterfall. Its roar deafened her, and she could barely keep her footing upon the slippery rock.

Then she saw that Damaris stood there, just out of arm's reach. And behind Damaris was Gregor, and now the bodyguard was truly giant-size, with hands as large as Loren herself. He reached out for her, and though she wanted to flee, there was nowhere to go. His fingers wrapped around her, and she barely managed to squeeze out between them. But they wrapped around her again, and again, each time dragging her closer.

"I will take *everything,"* said Damaris.

Gregor seized her at last, and he lifted her to hold her suspended over the waterfall. Between his fingers she could only just glimpse his face, and his cheeks that were sliced open, and the bloody ruined mess of his mouth, the stab wounds all over his body that seeped blood through his clothing and chain mail.

His hands fell away from her, and she thought she would plunge into the river far below—but she landed on the pillar again. She looked up, wondering why he had released her, only to find that he now held Gem, Annis, and Chet, and that they now hung over the water in her stead. Loren rose to her knees before the giant and clasped her hands to beg.

"Please, let them go," she cried. "Let them go. You want to kill me—since the beginning, you have only wanted to kill me."

"I told her to kill you, yes." Gregor's voice was like thunder. It struck her like a fist to the chest. "She would not listen, and her love for you made a corpse of me."

"Everything," whispered Damaris in her ear.

Gregor released her friends, and they fell into the water. But at the last moment, Chet reached out and grabbed an outcrop of the pillar Loren stood on, and the children clung to his arms. He tried to lift them all, but the weight was too much. Screaming, Loren fell to her stomach and reached for him, trying to help him up. The children climbed over him and took her hands, and she got them to safety. At last she reached Chet, but she could not raise him—he was too heavy.

Chet looked into her eyes for a long moment. Then his arms slipped, and he fell into the abyss—for it was not the waterfall, but the stone bridge again, and his body fell to lie, broken, beside Jordel's forever. Even as Loren's screams redoubled, she felt hands seize her cloak. She looked up, expecting to see Gregor again. Instead, she found Gem and Annis. They had ruined mouths just like Gregor's, and they laughed as they pitched her over the edge of the bridge.

She came awake screaming again.

Chet was fighting to hold her down. This time she had just enough presence of mind not to strike him. But she could not still her panicked screams, and guards in red cloaks came bursting into the room, swords drawn.

"It is all right!" cried Chet. "She is all right. Just help me hold her!"

One of them came, taking Loren's arm and holding her in place as she slowly got her bearings. Her gaze roved all over the room, and she could not force it to stay any one place for long.

"Loren. Loren!" said Chet. He took her face in his hands and forced her to look at him. "Loren. It is me. You are here, with me, in Ammon. It is all right. There is no one there. Come back to me."

At last her hands stopped trying to find purchase on a bridge that was not there. A long, shuddering breath escaped her. "I . . . I am all right. I am all right."

"Yes, you are," he said, and pulled her close. She clutched him to her, staring over his shoulder into nothingness.

"Is she ill?" said the guard who had remained by the door. "Should I fetch an apothecary?"

"No," said Loren at once.

"Are you certain?" said Chet. "Mayhap some dreamwine . . ."

"No, Chet," she said, pushing back to look at him. "I am all right. It was only another dream."

A look of recognition crossed his face. He heard what she had not said—that once again she had seen visions. He turned to the Mystics and shrugged. "As she says. Thank you."

The guards did not look eager to leave. But Loren seemed to have grown calm again, and so they stepped out of the room.

Chet turned to her and whispered, "Did you—"

"Shush," said Loren, putting a finger to his lips. She listened hard. Finally, after the space of several heartbeats, she heard the quiet foot-steps of the Mystics slipping away. A sigh slipped from her. "They are gone."

She fell back upon her pillow. It was the eve of Yearsend, some days after Niya had given her instructions in the training yard, and they had learned nothing more in the meanwhile. Hewal still had not been sent from the fortress, and they had seen him do nothing nefarious within it. Why, then, had she had this dream now? Was it a sign of something soon to come?

"What was it?" said Chet. "Did you . . . did you *see* anything? Was Hewal there?"

"He was," said Loren. "And he was dressed as a Shade again. But this time there was more—he turned into a bird, and flew off into the sky."

"A . . . a bird?" said Chet. "Do you mean that he is a weremage?"

"I do not know that, any more than I know for certain that he is a Shade," said Loren. "But that is what I saw. And . . . and I saw a golden city built on a waterfall. It is not a place I have ever seen before, and yet . . . and yet it was so *real*. I think it must be a real place—just as I first saw Hewal in a dream, and then found him in the waking world."

Chet frowned. "But why were you screaming? None of this sounds very terrifying."

Almost she answered him. Almost she told him of Trisken, and Jordel's grave, and Auntie, and what had happened to him and Gem and Annis. But at the last moment, words failed her, and she shrugged. "I saw nothing else. Or at least, I remember nothing else. Whatever frightened me, it slipped away as I awoke."

He looked at her for a long moment. She could see in his eyes that he did not believe her. "Loren," he said at last. "I have told you that I trust you. Do you not trust me in turn?"

A pang of guilt struck her, and she pushed herself up on her elbows. "I . . . I do, of course, Chet. And yet there are things I do not wish to say. Not because I fear for you to know them—but because I fear to say them aloud, and give strength to the thought behind them."

"You cannot truly believe that."

Loren shrugged. "How can I know what to believe? I see things in my dreams only to find them in the waking world. And there . . . there are things I see that I could not bear if they ever to pass. Do not force me to say them out loud. I beg you not to."

He did not answer her. After a long moment's silence, he lay down again and turned his back to her, drawing the blanket tight around himself against the cold.

She waited until his breath had deepened with sleep. Then she went to her cloak and reached within one of the pockets for her brown cloth packet. From it she drew a magestone. For a long while she looked at it.

A wizard who consumes the stone does not dream, Xain had said.

She was not a wizard. Yet mayhap it would help.

Loren broke the stone in half and slid one piece onto her tongue. It dissolved into nothing, and she swallowed. The room did not grow brighter, for she did not have her dagger close to hand. But she felt a calm slip through her. She lay back down beside Chet, and was soon asleep—a dreamless sleep at last.

FIFTEEN

FOUR MORE DAYS PASSED IN CHEERLESS RAIN. LOREN TOLD GEM AND Annis of her dream—as much of it as she had discussed with Chet—but they had no more inkling of its meaning than she herself had. The four of them were more watchful after that, but Hewal was just as inactive as he had always been, and nothing of interest happened within Ammon's walls.

The last day of Yearsend arrived, and the stronghold held a feast to celebrate the new year. It had been more than two weeks since Loren arrived at Ammon, and her frustration had now dwindled to a pervasive apathy. She rarely went into the training yard anymore, and spent most of her time either in the stables visiting Midnight, or in her own chamber, from which she emerged only for meals. But the Yearsend feast drew her out of hiding at last, if only because Annis was very excited about it. Somehow, the girl had convinced Kal to let her arrange the whole thing, and it promised to be a merrier affair than Ammon had seen in years.

Just after dawn on the day of the feast, Loren rode with Chet to a nearby river to bathe, and she also laundered her clothes. When at last they went to the dining hall after midday, they were not disappointed. The smell of the food struck her from a good ways off, well before she walked in the door. Most of the tables had been moved to the edges of the room, except for a line of them down the center. Upon these were placed all manner of fine foods, from meats and vegetables to sweet treats baked with honey, and still other dishes made with spices that smelled wholly unfamiliar to Loren. They found not only the usual wine and ale waiting for them, but brandywines and meads and other, clear liquors that Loren had never seen before, but which smelled stronger than anything she had ever tasted.

There were minstrels as well, a small party of them clustered off to one side of the room. They did not wear the red of Mystics, and so Loren guessed they must have come from one of the towns that lay not far away from Ammon. They plucked and pounded and blew upon their instruments enthusiastically, if not particularly well, and Loren saw many of the Mystics around the room stamping their feet and pounding their fists or mugs upon the table in time with the music. But from his elevated table at the head of the hall, Kal often glared at the minstrels, and tore more savagely at his meal the longer they played.

After Loren had taken her plate down the row of tables and loaded it high with food, she found a place at a table with Chet and Annis and Gem. Gem looked to be nearly done with his first plate by the time she reached them, and he soon rose to go fill another. Annis ate more delicately, but she savored her bites, moaning gently at each morsel and dabbing at the corners of her mouth with the edge of her sleeve.

"Having planned the feast myself, I was able to instruct the kitchens in preparing all of the dishes just the way I like them," she said. "I have not enjoyed so many of my favorite treats since I left my family's home upon the Seat."

"However did you convince Kal to let you do this?" said Loren. "This is a fine celebration. One might almost call it joyous, and that is a word I would never have used to describe the grand chancellor. I am surprised he did not flay you when you presented your plans to him."

Annis giggled. "I offered my expertise in planning the feast, and Kal accepted easily enough. Then, when he saw the list of things I intended to procure, he almost boxed my ears. But then I showed him my figures, and how this feast would cost him just over half of what he normally spent, for I did my duty and secured the best prices for the wares I required. He fell silent quickly enough after that, and left me to handle the rest of it." She leaned over the table and dropped her voice to a murmur. "Though I waited until *after* that to hire the minstrels."

Chet laughed aloud, and Loren joined in. They began to eat, and she swiftly discovered that she and Annis shared similar tastes, as it was the best food she had had in some time, and even compared favorably to the meals she had been served in the High King's palace.

After some time, and more food, and more wine as well, some Mystics pushed tables against walls to clear a section of empty floor. Then the minstrels redoubled their playing, and the drummers took the lead, and the dancing began. Loren had never dreamed she would see these warriors, who were always so grim in their red cloaks, laughing and prancing upon the stone floor like the villagers from her home in the Birchwood. The comparison seemed especially apt when Chet got to his feet and drew her up after him, pulling her into a dance that she laughed all the way through.

"We have never danced together. Do you realize that?" he said, as one song finished and they waited for the chords of the next to begin.

She smiled at him—but then the smile dampened, for his words brought her parents to mind. They, after all, were the reason Chet had been forbidden to approach her at the village dances.

"I am sorry," he said quickly. "I only meant that I am happy to do so now."

"And so am I," she said. "I wish we had had years of this. We should not let that fate befall others."

She pointed back to their table, where Gem and Annis still sat. Annis had begun to fiddle with her fingers, and every so often she looked nervously over at Gem. The boy did not seem to notice her, for his gaze wandered the room, lingering on the table where their Mystic friends sat. Chet's gaze met Loren's, and he nodded as he took her meaning. As the next song began, they ran up to the table. Loren seized Gem's hands and drew him up, while Chet did the same to Annis.

"Come, master urchin," said Loren. "I know you are a scholar and an expert thief. Let us see if you are a dancer as well!"

It soon became apparent that he was. The minstrels struck up a tune as old as the mountains, to which Loren had learned the words of a song of the moons, Enalyn and Merida. But half a hundred voices in the hall broke out into nearly as many songs, for bards in all the nine kingdoms had written different poetry for the same notes. That made the dancers laugh, and Gem's feet danced lightly upon the stones in time with Loren's as they whirled around each other. Loren was almost as surprised at his practiced ease as she was at Annis' awkwardness, for the girl's feet fumbled as she did her turns with Chet. But then the middle of the song came, and Loren and Chet gave each other a look. They took the children's hands, and spun them off to each other, an effortless trade that reunited them at the same time it pitched Gem and Annis together.

Loren leaned in close. "That was well done."

"You had an equal hand in it," said Chet, and kissed her cheek. They kept on with the dance, sneaking glances at the children all the while. Gem danced as easily as he had with Loren, laughing and smiling at Annis, whose cheeks had gone darker as their hands clasped. Her steps were still staggered and halting, but Gem led her easily enough, making up for her stilted movements with his own liquid grace.

The song ended. Chet and Loren bowed to each other. Gem stepped back to do the same, but Annis was slow to release his hands, and he laughed as he pried his fingers free and bowed. Then he ran over to the table where the Mystics sat, extending his hand towards them. Shiun waved him off. Weath, too, shook her head, and he went to Uzo. The dark young man gave Gem's outstretched hands a bemused look, his eyebrows rising slowly. Then he shrugged and got to his feet, following Gem away from the table as the next song began. But Annis still stood in the middle of the floor, looking after the boy.

"May I?" came a voice. Loren turned to find that it was Niya, who had risen and approached them. She held one bare, muscular arm forth, hand extended in an invitation. Loren's cheeks burned, and she saw Chet glare.

"I have tired myself out, I am afraid," said Loren. "Mayhap Chet would accept your offer."

"Mayhap I would not," said Chet, crossing his arms.

"That is just as well," said Niya, shrugging. "I do not think his spindly frame could withstand me. Another time, then."

Chet's scowl deepened, and he took a half-step forwards. But Niya turned and left them, striding straight past her table and out of the room. Loren returned with Chet to their own table, for indeed she had grown weary with dancing, and drank deep of the cup of wine she had left there.

When they had rested, they danced again, and then they drank again, and after they had done that a few times more, they fetched themselves more food to eat. The feasting had begun soon after midday, and would continue until everyone in the hall had gone to bed or fallen senseless beneath their tables. At some point Loren lost track of Annis, and then of Gem, and then Annis reappeared, and then she stopped looking after either one of them at all. She had just taken it into her head that she might retire to her chamber with Chet—mayhap for the night, or mayhap just for half an hour—when a hand clutched at her sleeve.

She turned to find Gem standing before her, wide-eyed and breathless. At once she sensed that something was wrong.

"What is it?"

"I went to relieve myself," he said. "When I was walking back through the courtyard, I saw someone standing there. At first I paid them no mind—until I saw that it was Hewal. He looked to be readying a horse for travel."

Loren and Chet looked to each other. Travel? On the final day of Yearsend? "Kal could have sent him on some errand," said Chet, but even he did not sound as if he believed the words.

"Any message could surely wait until tomorrow." Loren looked to the head of the room. There sat Kal. Wine had not appeared to improve his mood, for he scowled ever more heavily at the minstrels and the dancing. She could go and ask him . . . but he looked to be in no mood for questions. And if something *was* wrong, the delay meant Hewal would likely vanish before she could follow. "We must go after him."

"We should be quick," said Gem. "He will leave at any moment."

Together they flew from the dining hall. Loren was thankful she had worn her cloak to the feast, but Chet and Gem had no such protection, and they huddled into themselves against the sudden, biting cold. At least there was no rain. The day had waned on, and the sun was only a finger's breadth above the horizon, but night's chill had come early.

At once they saw him there in the courtyard: Hewal, fiddling with the straps of his saddlebags. He paid no mind to them, nor to the few others who milled about the courtyard or the walls. And why should he take notice? It was well known that he was a messenger for Kal. Anyone would assume that he was on the grand chancellor's business.

"Go and fetch cloaks for travel," said Loren. "I will ready horses for us."

Chet nodded and turned to obey—but the door opened behind them, and he stopped short. Framed in the light of the doorway was

Niya, and beside her stood Weath. Weath merely looked confused, but Niya's eyes were narrowed, and her brows drawn together.

"What is it?" she said. "What is wrong?"

Loren hesitated only a moment before replying, "It is nothing. I only wanted a moment of fresh air."

"That is a lie," said Niya flatly. "I saw the three of you when you ran out of the dining hall. Something is the matter."

Loren looked uneasily at her friends. Chet was glowering at Niya, while Gem balanced on the balls of his feet, hesitant to leave now that the Mystics had arrived. But what should she say? She had known Weath for some time, and had traveled a ways with Niya—but how would they react if she told them she meant to chase down one of their own?

"Out with it," said Niya. "I shall not leave it be, and so you had better tell me now, lest I keep you from whatever mischief you are about to get up to."

"A messenger is about to leave the stronghold," Loren began.

"Loren," said Chet, a warning tone in his voice.

She pressed on, ignoring him. "We believe he may be up to something. I cannot explain why, and I may be wrong, but we mean to follow him and find out for certain."

A long moment of silence stretched. Weath looked to Niya, but Niya did not take her gaze from Loren. At last she nodded.

"Weath, fetch Shiun. We may need her to track him."

"I . . . what do you mean?" said Loren.

"We are coming with you, of course," said Niya. "Or have you forgotten that the Lord Prince himself assigned us to your service?"

Loren had pointed out before that the Lord Prince only bound the Mystics to bring her to Ammon, but she did not repeat the point now. They had wasted too much time already. Glancing over her shoulder, she saw that Hewal had already left the upper courtyard. "Very well," she said. "Get ready to ride as quickly as you may—and Chet, fetch those cloaks *now*."

He frowned for a moment, looking distrustfully at Niya, but then ran to do as she said. Loren looked at the Mystics and tossed her head towards the stairs.

"Let us get on with it, then, and hope that we are not already too late."

SIXTEEN

LOREN LED GEM AND NIYA TO THE STABLES AT A DEAD RUN, GOING straight to Midnight's stall. As she began to ready the blanket and saddle, the mare nickered and tossed her mane, sensing the excitement on the air.

"After so many days of idleness, I am relieved we have something to do at last," said Niya from across the stable.

Loren could not help smiling at her, though she quickly masked it as she noticed Gem eyeing her. "I must admit I feel the same."

They had almost readied the horses to ride by the time Chet returned, and with him came Weath and Shiun. He had already donned his own cloak, and he threw another into Gem's hands. The party brought their horses into the courtyard and mounted quickly, with Loren dragging Gem up to sit behind her in the saddle. They rode out of the gate and through Ammon's two levels to the final gate that opened upon the ramp. There they stopped, and Niya hailed one of the gate guards.

"The messenger who just left through here," she said. "Which way did he ride?"

"South," said the guard.

They did not pause to answer, but rode out at once. Loren spurred Midnight to the head of the group, but Niya slapped the reins of her horse until the two were neck and neck. At the crossroads they pulled to a stop again, looking down the south road. But they saw no sign of Hewal upon it, nor of any rider.

"Shiun, take the lead," said Niya. "If he diverts from the road, you will see it better than any of us."

"Chet should ride beside her," said Loren. "He is a hunter."

Niya raised her brows. "Of rabbits, mayhap. I doubt he has often stalked men on horseback." Loren frowned, and Niya sighed. "Very well. Shiun and Chet, ride in front."

The Mystic said nothing, but only nodded and nudged her horse. Now they made their way more slowly, for Shiun could not keep a good lookout at a gallop. The reduced pace grated on Loren's nerves, but she knew from her own limited experience at hunting that they could not press on any faster, lest they lose the way.

After a time, Shiun stopped her horse and pointed off the road. "There. Fresh tracks leading that way."

Loren gave Chet a glance. He rolled his eyes and shrugged at her, and she smirked.

Niya nudged her horse forwards beside Shiun's. "Can you follow him more quickly now?"

Shiun nodded. "Yes. He has cut through the land heedlessly. He does not think anyone is following him."

"That is his folly. Lead on."

They rode on at a light canter, with Shiun giving her horse only the slightest nudge to keep on track, until they reached the edge of a forest. The last sliver of sun just barely showed above the horizon, and the way ahead was dark beneath the trees. Shiun looked to Niya and raised her brows.

"The trail will soon be hard to see, at least until the moons rise," she said. "But if he continues to ride straight, I think we might follow him easily enough. From here, though, we should go on foot, or we might alert him to our presence sooner than we would wish."

Niya frowned. Then she looked to Loren. "Nightblade? Should we press on?"

Loren blinked. Niya had seemed forceful enough so far. Why now did she wish for Loren to give the orders? "I . . . we should. If my suspicions are correct, we cannot be too stringent in our pursuit."

With a nod, Niya turned to Shiun again. "As she says."

They dismounted, and Shiun led them between the trunks. Very soon, sunlight vanished from the sky that was just visible through the branches above, and they had to make their way more slowly, with Shiun leading them straight down the same direction they had already been traveling. Eventually the moons appeared, and then they were able to increase their pace once again.

"How does he know where he is going?" said Gem.

Loren glanced back at him. "We are following his tracks."

"I did not ask how we are following him," said the boy. "I know we can see his tracks—or at least, that woman can, because I feel blind as a bat in this forest. What I mean is—how does *he* know where he is going? There is no path here to follow. How does he pick his way so unerringly?"

Chet shrugged. "Paths are not always necessary. If one comes to a place often enough, the feet begin to remember the way, better than a sailor steering by the stars."

Weath raised her head to look at the rest of them. "Then he comes this way often. This is not his first time—nor, likely, his second or third, but one of many."

That cast a solemn silence over them all. What purpose could Kal's messenger have for coming so often to the middle of this wood?

Soon Shiun bid them all to halt with an upraised hand. Drawing Loren and Niya to her side, she pointed ahead through the trees.

"What is it?" whispered Niya. "I see nothing."

"I see it," said Loren. There, a few hundred paces ahead, was a horse tied to a tree. She could not be certain it was Hewal's from such a distance, but it was black, as his had been. "It seems his horse is there. But where is Hewal?"

"Close, no doubt," said Shiun. "We should leave our own horses nearby. Hidden. Then the three of us—or, better, only two—should go on alone."

"Three," said Niya. "He would not come out here to be on his own. He is meeting someone. If it comes to a fight, I would rather outnumber them."

Shiun nodded. Loren handed Midnight's reins to Chet. But when she turned to go, he caught her hand. "Be careful," he whispered.

"I shall," she told him. "And besides, Shiun and Niya will be with me."

Chet eyed Niya. "Forgive me if I am not greatly comforted."

Loren smiled and touched his cheek. "Take the horses and the others and get out of sight, in case Hewal should circle around and return for his steed before we can come to warn you."

She turned to follow Shiun. The Mystic led the way through the woods, bow out and an arrow half-drawn. Niya had not had time to fetch her sword, but she had a knife. Loren had only her hands—and the dagger hidden on the back of her belt, though she would not draw that unless it was a matter of life and death. They moved as silently as they could. Loren knew how to muffle her steps, and Shiun was quiet as a mouse. Niya did her best, but the woman was clearly not well practiced in woodcraft, and Loren winced at her every footfall. A light drizzle began to come down upon them. Loren put up the hood of her cloak and brushed the hair from her eyes.

Shiun stopped and held out a hand for them to do the same. She pointed ahead to where two figures huddled together against the rain. The one in the red cloak was clearly Hewal. The other, a Feldemar woman, was unfamiliar—and Loren was a little disappointed, though mayhap not surprised, to see that she did not wear blue and grey.

"Do you recognize her?" said Loren.

"I do not," said Niya. "But that means little. This whole kingdom is strange to me."

"Hist," said Shiun, and drew them back into the shadows of the forest—for Hewal had turned away from the other figure and begun to walk back towards them. After he passed them by, Loren leaned forwards and peered towards the other figure. In her hand she held a piece of paper—a message from Hewal.

"There," she whispered, pointing.

"I see it," murmured Niya. "Wait a moment longer for him to get out of earshot. Then let us take her."

"The two of you go," said Shiun. She raised her bow. "I shall watch from here, and prevent her from escape if she should slip from your grasp."

Niya rolled her shoulders, casting her red cloak off her bare, muscular arms. "That is unlikely."

Loren struck out to the left, circling around through the woods as she approached the figure. The woman, whoever she was, made her way through the trees in the opposite direction from where Hewal had gone. She moved slowly, clearly not expecting any threat in the darkness. Loren shadowed her steps several paces to the left, while Niya drew closer and closer from the rear.

When Niya was almost close enough to charge, Loren made her move. She ran forwards a few quick paces, letting her feet fall heavy and loud, and then slapped her hand on a tree trunk for good measure.

The woman came to a stop at once and froze, her eyes searching the darkness. Niya pounced from the shadows and bore the woman to the ground. She fought like a wildcat, but Niya wrestled her facedown into the loam, holding one arm twisted behind her back and jerking it upwards until the woman grunted with pain.

"Give us the message," hissed Niya through gritted teeth.

"I have no message," said the woman.

Shiun appeared from the darkness nearby, her arrow trained on the woman. Loren pulled her cloak aside and dug through its pockets. In a moment she heard the crinkling of parchment, and soon she had the letter. She pulled it out, broke the seal, and unfolded it, leaning far over so that her body shielded it from the drizzle. The words meant nothing to her, but she did not need to see them. There, at the bottom of the page, was a symbol she knew well—a twisted, spiked design, like a vine that wound in and around itself, but covered with thorns. The symbol of the Shades. She sucked a sharp breath in between her teeth.

Niya looked up. "What? What does it say?"

"Enough," said Loren. "We may return to Ammon now. Bring this one with us."

But the woman on the ground gave a great heave, and Niya lost her balance for just a moment. The woman's hand darted to her belt and drew forth a dagger. Loren cried out a warning, diving at Niya and bearing her backwards to take her out of the dagger's reach—but the woman plunged the dagger into her own heart. She collapsed, hunching over the blade, and her lifeblood splashed upon the dark mud to turn it darker still.

SEVENTEEN

"Darkness take her!" snarled Niya. She flipped the woman over, mayhap hoping to keep her alive. But it was far too late for that.

Loren seized her shoulder and drew her back. "I am sure the darkness below will indeed take her, but we have more pressing business. Hewal has gotten too far already—mayhap he will return to Ammon where we can find him, but mayhap he will not. We must catch him at once."

"Very well," said Niya. She gave the woman's corpse a final glare before turning to go. "Let us chase him down. I will take my anger out upon his hide."

As quickly as they could, they ran back the way they had come. When they reached the place where Hewal's horse had been, they found it already gone. Chet and the others emerged from the jungle, the horses in tow. Gem's eyes were wide, while Chet's brows had drawn together in concern.

"What happened?" said Chet. "Hewal came back this way, mounted, and rode off. We were just about to go and find you, for we feared something had gone wrong."

"Not for us, but for someone he met with," said Loren. "We must catch him, and quickly. Gain your saddles and ride!"

They did, spurring to a fast trot, for they could not safely go any faster between the trees. As soon as they emerged from the forest into open ground, Shiun stopped them. They all scanned the horizon, but could see nothing in the moonslight.

"Blast it," said Niya. "He could have ridden south, or he could have gone north, back to Ammon."

"We could divide ourselves," said Weath. "Let me take the boys back towards Ammon, while the rest of you ride south. If you find him that way, you will need more strength than we, if we should find him returned to Ammon and in the midst of our brothers."

"How can he have gone so far in so short a time?" said Niya, as though Weath had not spoken.

"We search by moonslight," said Shiun, shaking her head. "No doubt I could see him if the sun were still up."

Loren thought quickly. In her cloak she had her magestones, and upon her back she had her dagger . . .

She jerked in her saddle, looking back towards the forest. "A moment. I dropped the letter."

Without waiting for an answer, she turned and galloped Midnight back into the trees. Gem clung to her back at the sudden movement. Once he had righted himself, he leaned forwards to peer at her.

"Why did you lie to them? I can hear the crinkle of the letter in your cloak pocket."

"Because there is something else in my cloak pocket, and I would rather they not see it," said Loren. "Gem, you have proclaimed many times that you are my man, and loyal to me. You must prove it now—for you can never tell anyone what you are about to see. Promise me, and quickly."

"I—I promise," he said, though he looked even more confused.

She steeled herself, and then reached into her cloak to draw forth the brown cloth packet. From it she drew a shard of magestone—a remnant of a piece she had already broken in half—and quickly put it between her lips. It melted upon her tongue, utterly tasteless, and slid down her throat with ease.

Gem's eyes shot wide. "I . . . Loren—"

"Shush," she said. "You promised."

Her boots dug into Midnight's ribs, and they came riding back to the others. Niya looked at her with a scowl.

"That has wasted even more time," growled the Mystic. "I have decided that Weath's plan is best, and that we should—"

Loren let Niya's voice fade to the back of her mind. She reached within her cloak, placing a hand upon the hilt of the dagger on the back of her belt.

The night grew bright as day, for in her sight the moons glowed like suns. She saw all the landscape around them in brilliant, vivid color. Even the darkness between the trees was illuminated, as though each leaf was a small lantern casting a silver glow upon the ground. She scanned the horizon in all directions, and her eyes caught upon a movement. There he was—Hewal, riding upon the road, making his way south and away from Ammon. He rode at an easy pace, a light trot his horse could maintain for leagues at a time.

"There!" she cried, shooting up straight in her saddle and pointing. "I see him!"

Niya stopped talking abruptly and frowned. She looked in the direction of Loren's outthrust finger. "What? I see nothing."

Neither did Loren, for she had loosed the grip on her dagger. But she feigned surprise. "What? He is just there. A good distance away, and small, but it is him. I am sure of it. Come!"

She set off without waiting for an answer, sending Midnight into a headlong gallop upon the road. The others had little choice but to follow her, and so they did, and soon the lot of them were riding hard. Loren could almost sense the shock that went through the others when they, too, spotted Hewal at last.

When they had closed the distance to half a league, Hewal heard them and pulled his horse to a stop. In a few moments they had reached him, and they fanned out to create a semicircle facing him. Hewal did not seem particularly alarmed, but only bemused. After surveying the group, he focused upon Loren.

"Nightblade," he said, inclining his head. His voice sounded as it had in her dream: smooth and bright, fresh with youth but heavy with the weight of duty. "Has Kal sent you? Is there some news concerning my errand?"

"No one sent us," said Loren. "Though, I wonder what masters have sent you upon your ride this night, Hewal. I do not think it was Kal of the Mystics."

She reached into her cloak to draw out the letter, and held it up so that it fell unfolded in the moonslight. The symbol of the Shades was plain to see, even from the few paces that separated them.

Hewal stared at it for a moment as though he did not comprehend what she had said. Then, brow furrowed, he climbed down from his horse. He took a step forwards.

"Stay where you are," said Niya, drawing her knife and pointing it at him. Shiun drew an arrow and nocked it. Hewal stopped in his tracks. "You will return with us to Ammon, and if you make no trouble, you may even survive the journey."

Hewal raised his hands, and a small smile crossed his lips. "I do not think any friendly reception awaits me at Ammon. Therefore I do not think I shall come with you."

An image flashed into Loren's mind—Hewal in her dream, when his eyes had glowed white and he had transformed into a crow.

"Wait!" she cried. "He is a—"

She was too late. Hewal's eyes filled with light, and his body erupted into a mass of flesh, muscle and fur. A black bear stood where he had been a moment before, and around its feet pooled the shredded scraps that had been his clothing.

Hewal roared and lunged at them. A massive claw took Weath's horse in the side, and the beast screamed as it died. Weath flew from the saddle and rolled away from the road.

"Back away!" cried Loren, wheeling Midnight around and dancing a few paces off. "Shiun!"

The Mystic had already sprung into action, drawing and firing an arrow. The shaft pierced Hewal's side, and his bestial roar took on a note of pain. But he sprang towards her, and Shiun had to spur her horse away before she could fire another shaft.

Leaping from Midnight's saddle, Loren threw the reins into Gem's hands. He caught them on instinct and opened his mouth, but before he could speak, Loren cried, "Get to Ammon!" and slapped Midnight's flank hard. With her nostrils filled with the scent of bear, the horse brayed in fear and rode north for the fortress, with Gem desperately clinging to her back.

Loren thought of reaching for her dagger, but what good would it do her? Its short blade would not save her against a bear. It was proof against magic, yes, but did that mean it could stop a weremage's claws? She had never had a chance to test it. Now did not seem the best time to do so.

Shiun was dancing back and forth, giving Hewal no clear way to charge. Niya stood a few paces off, brandishing her knife, but it seemed as impotent as the dagger. Chet had dismounted and stood beside Loren. His face was grim.

Loren took his shoulders. "It is a bear. How do you hunt a bear?"

"Go into its cave with spears," said Chet.

"We do not have a cave, or spears," said Loren. "And we are not dealing with a savage beast. Hewal has a human's wit."

Chet shrugged helplessly. "What do you want me to say? I have never hunted a weremage before."

Loren gave a frustrated growl—but then the ground shook beneath their feet, and she heard Niya shout. She flung herself to the side, seizing Chet's cloak and dragging him after her. Hewal barreled past them in a flash of black fur, roaring his anger as his terrible claws passed through the air where they had just stood.

Niya and Shiun seized them and pulled them to their feet. Shiun had another arrow nocked, but she did not draw. Weath stumbled over to them, shaking her head dizzily.

"Shoot him!" said Niya, looking to Shiun.

"I am not a good enough shot to strike the eye, and nothing else will be a worthwhile strike," said Shiun. Loren saw that Hewal had turned back towards them, and was edging to the right, presenting only his front. "The skull is too thick, and the shoulders are useless."

"Not if we can drive a knife into them," said Weath. "But that is a dangerous job, to be sure."

"I will do it," said Niya. "Only I will need a distraction."

"If I had a spear . . ." Weath shook her head, and then reached to her belt and drew a knife. "I will do my best."

"And I," said Loren. "But I have no blade. Does anyone have a knife to spare?" She feared to reveal her dagger with all of them so close to her.

Niya knelt and took a blade from her boot. "Here."

Loren followed Weath, who approached the bear slowly at a half-crouch. Behind her, Loren heard Chet mutter, "No one offers *me* a knife."

There came a *snikt* from Shiun, and soon Chet crept up beside Loren and Weath with a blade in hand. The three of them moved slowly forwards while Shiun stepped to their right to flank Hewal.

Hewal let out a low growl. It rumbled from his chest and thrummed in Loren's boots. She breathed deep to steady herself. "I doubt he will charge again," she muttered, hoping the weremage could not hear her. "He has seen we can evade him too easily. Likely he will stand his ground and swing at us. He does not need to press forwards into our midst, for he knows he can wait for us to step within reach."

"What should we do, then?" muttered Chet, speaking from the corner of his mouth. "We need to get his attention."

"Feint at him," said Weath. "I will do it."

"You have been hurt already," said Loren. "Let me."

She did not wait for an answer, but took two quick steps forwards. She slashed at the empty air, three paces from where Hewal stood. He lurched backwards and swiped at her, growling. But quickly he turned his focus to Shiun, for she had raised her bow and begun to draw. Loren took another half-step towards him—but he lunged suddenly, forcing her to dance back.

Just then, she saw movement over his shoulder. There was Niya, creeping forwards through the grass, little more than a shadow in a red cloak. She lifted one hand, her dagger held ready to bring down in a stab. Hewal paused. He raised his muzzle into the air, sniffing.

With a wordless cry, Loren lunged and slashed at him. He jerked away, just as an arrow from Shiun flew forth and lodged in his foreleg. Chet, Loren and Weath pressed forwards, brandishing their knives. Hewal bellowed and reared up on his hind legs, and then Niya struck. Leaping forwards, she wrapped one thick arm around Hewal's neck and plunged the knife into his shoulder. He cried out anew—but this time the sound was pure fear.

Loren's elation lasted only a moment, for whether by accident or intent, the weremage toppled backwards. Niya had to throw herself clear and roll away, taking the knife with her. Hewal rounded on her, swiping at the air, but Niya rolled again, distancing herself. No sooner had she risen to her knees than she flipped the knife into her fingertips and threw it. Hewal only just raised a paw in time, and instead of driving into his throat, the dagger buried itself up to the hilt in his foreleg. A low whine issued from the bear's throat, and white light came from its eyes once again.

Slowly Hewal shrank, his thick coat of fur sinking back into his body. In the shrinking of his frame, Niya's knife slid free. It fell to land in the dirt, coated in red. At last Hewal stood before them, naked and panting in the moonlight, blood pouring from his wounds.

For a moment, all was still. Then, though nothing had been said, Hewal began to laugh.

"Oh, you are a clever one indeed, Nightblade," he said. "I do not know how you learned the truth about me, but once again you have shown your worth as a foe."

His familiar tone made her pause. "What do you mean? I have never seen you before, and you know nothing of me."

"You are the Nightblade. Everyone knows of you," said Hewal, and now his smile turned cruel. "Rogan and his undying brutes. My brothers and sisters. And sweet Damaris of the family Yerrin. She, in particular, sends her regards. And she looks forward to her reunion with you—which, now that I am exposed, will certainly be soon in coming."

"What reunion?" said Loren. "Tell us what the family Yerrin is planning, and you may yet escape with your life."

"Do you think I believe that?" he snarled. "I have played at being a Mystic for years. I have seen how they treat those they put to the question. No, such a fate is not for me."

His eyes began to glow. Beside Loren, Niya straightened with a start, and then lunged. "He is healing himself!"

Hewal jumped straight up—and in the air, he grew a beak, and black feathers sprouted from his skin. The crow's wings flapped desperately as Shiun's hastily-loosed arrow pierced the air below him. He flew off through the sky, giving a raucous, braying caw.

The sight of the beak erupting from his face, indeed his whole transformation, made Loren weak. It threw her mind back to her dream, and she saw Chet's opened throat—but then she turned to see him standing beside her, alive and whole. Her mind could not reconcile the images from her dream and the sight before her eyes. Her knees gave out, and she sank to the ground.

"Loren!" cried Chet. He knelt beside her. "Are you all right?"

"I—it is nothing," she said, shaking off the vision. "A moment's dizziness, that is all."

He frowned at her. "Did he hurt you? I did not see him land a blow . . ."

She shook her head quickly. "He did not touch me. I am all right." With his help, she fought her way back to her feet. Niya, Weath, and Shiun all stood there, looking at her. "I am fine. Except that he has escaped, and we have nothing."

"We have enough," said Chet. "You have the letter. That is proof enough of his guilt."

"And what use is guilt?" snapped Niya. "He could lead us to those who commanded him, and now we have not the faintest clue where to find them. Who cares if we know the dog misbehaved? I wish to find the masters who told him to bark."

"Well, we have not done that," said Chet. "Scowl about it if you wish."

Niya opened her mouth to reply, but Loren cut her off. "You said he healed himself? What did you mean?"

The Mystic glared. "Weremages. They transform their own bodies, and therefore many are able to close their own wounds and stop themselves from bleeding to death."

"That is a useful talent," said Loren.

She had not meant it as a joke, but Niya gave a grim smile anyway. "Mayhap—but it is almost as painful as suffering the wound again. I take some small comfort that I caused him that much pain, at least."

Loren sighed. "I find little to give me comfort just now. Come, let us mount our horses. We have a long ride back to Ammon, and we do not bear good news."

EIGHTEEN

Two horses were gone, so Loren rode with Chet and Weath with Shiun. They rode back to Ammon quickly enough, but Loren did not press them too hard. There seemed little need for haste, since it would not change what they would find at the end of their ride.

As they rode up the ramp to the front gate, Loren stole a glance at the Mystics beside her. She had not thought of it until just now, but if there were any consequences to face for their actions that night, the Mystics would likely suffer worse than she would. She was the Nightblade, and it was not entirely clear whether Kal was her master or not. But these were Kal's soldiers, and they had ridden off in Loren's company without orders. Kal did not seem the sort to take such things lightly.

"It might be best if we do not mention your involvement tonight," said Loren. Niya looked over at her. "In coming with me, I mean. I can tell the grand chancellor that it was only Chet and I, and eschew any mention of you at all."

Weath pointed up ahead. "Though I appreciate your selflessness, I doubt that that would work."

Loren looked up. There, at the top of the ramp, the drawbridge had already been lowered. Standing just inside of Ammon's gate was a party of Mystics on horseback. At their head was Kal, and beside him was Gem, who still rode Midnight. Loren felt her stomach do a turn. They reached the top of the ramp and stopped.

"Nightblade," growled Kal.

"Grand Chancellor," said Loren.

"I had meant to ride out to your rescue, for I gathered that it was necessary. It seems that is no longer the case. I imagine you have some tidings for me."

"I do, though I fear they are ill news."

"What other kind is there these days? Very well. Come."

He turned and led her—not quickly, but at a walk even slower than if they were on foot—all the way back up through Ammon's three levels. In the space of a few heartbeats it became monotonous, and then tedious, leaving Loren's mind free to wonder about the tongue-lashing he no doubt had in store for her. As she considered it, she realized that that was likely the point—this plodding pace was meant to give her as much time as possible to contemplate her impending fate.

When they reached the stronghold's keep, Kal dismounted and handed his horse off to a stableboy. Loren quietly asked Gem to see to Midnight, and then followed Kal into the fortress. As they approached his council chamber, they found Annis waiting in the hallway. The girl paced back and forth, hands twisting together anxiously in front of her, as though she awaited news of some close relative lying upon their deathbed. When she saw Loren approaching, she came running up.

"Are you whole? Gem said—"

"I am safe," said Loren. "We all are. I must speak with the grand chancellor."

"Indeed you must," said Kal. "But the girl comes, too. The rest of you, however, may leave us—I have no wish to move the entire Yearsend feast into my own chamber."

Chet looked to Loren—and to Loren's surprise, so did Niya. She steeled herself. "The rest should be present as well. Our tale is . . . unusual, you might say, and I would rather that you did not hear only my account of it."

Kal glared, but he did not argue with her, and the whole party followed Loren into the room. They all stepped back towards the room's edges, away from Kal and the council table—all except Niya, who stood just beside Loren, but a half-step back, the way a soldier stood by their commanding officer. But Loren pushed that comparison out of her mind at once, and began to tell her story. She left nothing out, save for the moment she had eaten magestones. Soon she came to the end of her tale.

The moment she finished speaking, Kal snorted. "A weremage? I told you I have known Hewal since he was a boy. I have known his father. He went through the trials. There was no trace of magic within him."

Loren looked at the others in the room. Weath and Shiun shifted on their feet, not meeting Kal's gaze. Only Chet and Niya looked straight ahead, unflinching.

"It is true, Grand Chancellor," said Chet. "We were all there."

Kal looked at Niya. She gave him a small nod. His scowl deepened.

"Hewal made mention of how long he had been a Mystic," said Loren. "He called it a charade, one he had been forced to play for a long time. Mayhap he was entered into your service for just this purpose—in which case, his father may not be so close a friend as—"

"Be silent!" said Kal, slapping his hand on the table. "If what you say is true, do you not think I can come to that guess on my own? The High King's favor has given you too high an opinion of your own wit—high enough that it spurs you to foolish courses of action, like pursuing one of my own men into the wilderness without orders."

Loren had to restrain a grim smile. Her tone had mayhap been too condescending, but in truth, it felt good to throw Kal off-balance after the way he always grumped at her. "You call that foolish? Had I gone to you, we might have missed Hewal altogether, and you would know nothing."

"I know little enough now," said Kal. "Had you done things properly, Hewal might not have escaped."

Loren's hand tightened where it held her belt. "I serve the High King," she said, quiet but firm. "I will do what I think is in her best interests."

Rather than answer, Kal turned to the rest of them. "You are all dismissed."

The Mystics began to move for the door, but Chet tried to speak up. "We have told you already why we—"

"You are here to corroborate Loren's tale," said Kal, his voice rising. "Now that that is done, you are as useful as a second nose. Get out! You are neither in the High King's service, nor mine. You are nothing more than the Nightblade's bedfellow guest."

Chet's whole body tensed. Loren saw the muscles working in his jaw. But she put a hand on his arm and turned him to face her. "It is all right," she murmured. "Go."

He did, but only after giving Kal a final dirty look. Niya held the door until he was through, and then, as she closed it behind them all, she locked gazes with Loren for a moment. She gave a small nod and a smile, and then she was gone. But Loren noted quietly that, again, Annis had remained in the room, and Kal still paid her no mind.

Loren braced herself, certain that now Kal would loose the full strength of his wrath. He looked like a pot about to boil over, his anger frothing just below the lid. But rather than shout, he held out a hand. "You said there was a letter. Give it to me."

Tension bled from her, and Loren reached into her cloak with relief. After she handed it to him, Kal whipped the letter open and looked it over. Loren wished she had had someone read it to her before she returned to Ammon, but there had been no time. Kal frowned. "Darkness damn this place. Girl, fetch me that lamp."

At first Loren thought he meant her, but he waved his hand at Annis. She started, as though she was surprised to be called upon, and then hastened to obey. Kal sat down in his chair and held the letter close to the light, his eyes skittering back and forth across it. When they reached the bottom of the letter and the symbol of the Shades there, his frown deepened.

"This is, in part, a report," said Kal. "A report of your arrival here at the stronghold, and a brief account of your actions, few though they have been. It seems you have attracted someone's interest."

"You mean Damaris," said Loren. "It must be her."

Beside Kal, Annis' expression grew solemn, and she dropped her gaze to the table. But Kal raised his brows and leaned back in his chair. "That seems quite a guess."

"Hewal mentioned her. He said we would be reunited soon."

"If . . ." Kal paused, and his mouth twisted as though he had just bitten into a piece of spoiled meat. "If Hewal is indeed an agent of the enemy, he may have spoken only to throw you off the trail. We can put no stock in any of his words."

Her recent dream flashed back into her mind. The city where she had seen Hewal, and what he had told her there. *Welcome to Dahab.* She braced herself, and then she took the leap.

"There was something else Hewal mentioned before he escaped. A place called Dahab."

The room fell utterly quiet. Annis looked up, her eyes wide with wonder, and then she and Kal traded glances. Loren had feared she might get only blank looks from them, but this was somehow worse. Was Dahab indeed the city she had seen in her dream? And if so, *how* had she seen it?

What was happening to her?

"That is quite a detail," said Kal. "Why did you not tell us that when you first mentioned the tale?"

"It has been a long night," said Loren. "It slipped my mind."

"Is there anything else that 'slipped your mind?' Surprise is not healthy for the elderly, and tonight has turned the last of my beard grey."

Loren shook her head quickly. "That is all."

Kal studied her for a moment, and then he threw the letter down. He began to pull at his beard, while Annis leaned surreptitiously over the table, trying to see the letter.

"I think that Damaris is in Dahab," said Loren. "I think that this letter was for her. I wish to go there, and capture her."

A loud snort erupted from Kal as though by accident, so loud that for a moment he dissolved into a fit of coughing. "Do not be ridiculous. You propose a perilous mission, led by little more than a far guess. Damaris is of no interest to us now. Rogan is the greater threat. You do not even know anything of Dahab."

She had gone this far, and so there seemed little sense in restraining herself. The visions in her dream had proven correct. "A city of gold. It is built around a waterfall, is it not?"

Kal rolled his eyes. "Very well. You have heard of it. But the rest of what I said holds true."

"This is the best chance we have seen," said Loren. "Damaris is there. I can . . . I can *feel* it. After our confrontation in the Greatrocks, she went to ground, and there she has remained ever since. She *must* be in Dahab. And furthermore, it makes sense to pursue her. She worked with Rogan, and with the Shades. When the attack on the Seat failed, Rogan and his soldiers would have needed somewhere to hide, and someone to help hide them. Who better than the family Yerrin, and Damaris in particular? Finding her could lead to him. It seems to me that this is but the first step in the mission you set before me."

"Pardon me if I do not trust in your *feelings*," said Kal. "I have only ever trusted information from reliable sources, and I will not change that now."

Loren shook her head and leaned over the table. "Where do you get such information? From your spies. You have them across all the nine kingdoms, do you not? Let me be one of them. It is better than sitting here idle, as I have since I arrived. Enalyn did not raise me up so that I could languish away here."

But she had gone too far at last, for Kal shot to his feet and slammed both hands on the table. "Do not bandy the High King's name about here as though you are her kin, you upstart little sow. She appointed you the Nightblade so that you could follow *my* orders, and that is what you will do."

His fury almost made her quail, and for a moment she saw not Kal, but her father, and his meaty fists clenched by his sides. She shook away the image. Her father was not here. He was dead. And she would never flinch before an angry old man again.

"Before the High King brought me into her service, I always acted on my own. It is what I did during that time that made me valuable enough that she desired my assistance in the first place."

Kal roared so loud and with such force that a fleck of his spit splashed upon her cheek. "No, what you did during that time led to the death of Jordel!"

She froze. Kal had made no move towards her, had not made to hit her, as her father had. Yet she felt as though she had been struck in the gut, and a far harder blow than she ever suffered at home in the Birchwood. She felt a stinging at the back of her eyes, and she fought it away. Kal would not get the satisfaction of seeing her weep. But he seemed to know how deeply he had hurt her. Though he did not smile, she thought she saw a grim satisfaction in his eyes as he leaned back.

"Did you ever consider that mayhap Enalyn brought you into her service so that she—or *someone*, and I suppose the duty is now mine— could keep an eye upon you? Left to your own devices, you helped Xain escape the law, and then escape Jordel. By your side he fled halfway across Underrealm. Because of you, Jordel was banished from his or- der—*my* order, I should say. And then he died for it. You do not need to be left to run free. You need someone who knows what they are doing to instruct you—and darkness take you, you must heed those in- structions. It is even in the name you have been given. You call yourself Nightblade. A blade is a tool. A knife in the hand, to be wielded—not some thrice-damned hero of legend."

Loren wanted to answer him. Nightblade was no one's tool. Mennet had never been a tool, he had been his own man. And had she not always desired to be Mennet? But words would not come—not because she could not think of them, but because they would not emerge past the tightness of her throat, and if she forced them to, they would come with tears. She would not allow that in his presence.

In the silence that had consumed the room, it was Annis who saved her by speaking up at last. "If she is a tool, then use her. That is a tool's purpose, is it not? To be used. Honed. I have walked beside Loren almost since the beginning of her travels. I know her as a girl far more capable than many give her credit for, when first they meet her. You sent her to the High King's Seat with little more than a message to deliver. In turn, she saved the Lord Prince, the High King, and all the nine kingdoms. She may surprise you again. But she will learn nothing, and serve no purpose, if she stays here in Ammon."

Kal glanced at her. "Nor will she learn anything if she gets herself gutted in some back alley in Dahab. You may have your uses, girl, but that does not mean I hold you in much higher regard than the upstart here."

"Yet you need a spy to investigate this information," said Annis. "And by sending Loren, you may solve two problems at once, for she will need a party of Mystics to accompany her."

She looked at him steadily as she said it, and when he looked to her, they shared a long moment of silence. It seemed to Loren that something passed between them, something she could not understand. Finally Kal gave a frustrated growl and turned back to Loren.

"Very well," he said. "But there will be rules. Vow to obey them, and I will send you. Refuse, and you can stay locked in your bedchamber until you rot."

Loren lifted her chin. "What rules?"

"You will do nothing foolish," said Kal. "That means you will not take any action—real, meaningful action, I mean—without consulting me first, by letter. You will go to Dahab to see if Damaris is there. If she is, you will send word—and you will *only* send word. You will take no action against her in Dahab without my express approval and guidance."

The thought of finding Damaris there, and then not capturing her, grated on Loren's very soul. But if she did not agree, she would be forced to stay here.

"Very well," said Loren. "I vow I will obey you, to the letter."

Kal snorted. "'To the letter.' Very well. We are done here, and you may take your dramatics elsewhere. It is late. Girl, I shall not need you any longer." He waved Annis off and turned to his desk in the corner. Annis came to Loren, and they left the chamber together.

NINETEEN

No one waited in the nearby hallways. Once they were out of earshot of the guards, Loren drew Annis aside.

"I am sorry," she said. "I should not have asked to pursue Damaris without speaking with you first."

Annis shook her head slowly. She looked as though she were gazing at something behind Loren, but there was nothing there to see. "There was no time. And besides, I think you are right to do this. I think my mother is a worthier target of the King's justice than Rogan would be. I have had my reservations about pursuing him for some time. Even if we should catch him, and execute him, I do not know how much it will accomplish. Yes, there are rumors of his exploits, of course, but to most of the kings and nobles he is utterly unknown. But my mother . . . yes, if my mother was brought low, that would truly give pause to the mighty across the nine kingdoms. Of course, Kal may not wish to anger my family even further than they already—"

Loren put a hand on her shoulder, and Annis stopped abruptly. Her gaze focused on Loren, as though she were just waking up.

"I am sorry. Was I babbling?"

Loren smiled sadly and gripped her shoulder a bit tighter. "No one could blame you for being hesitant to pursue her. Damaris will be treated fairly, Annis—mayhap not mercifully, but fairly."

"Yes, I . . . yes," said Annis. Tears welled in her eyes. She stepped closer to Loren, who put an arm around her shoulders and held her tighter. Annis did not return the embrace, but she put her head on Loren's shoulder. "I know. And I know that I must sound like a monster, saying these things of my own kin. Yet this—is this not why I wished to escape with you in the first place? I have known since I was a child that Mother's ways were evil, and that she must be brought to justice. But that has only recently become a possibility. I suppose I have been trying to steel myself for it to happen. I fear I have done a poor job."

"You have done marvelously," said Loren, rubbing her arm. "I am with you, and will help see you safely through this."

"I know," whispered Annis. One shaky arm came up to wrap around Loren's waist. "Thank you."

Loren pushed her back a bit. "All of that having been said, I should warn you—this will likely be perilous. It may make sense for you to remain in Ammon while we pursue her. Kal will certainly want your counsel."

Annis shook her head at once. "No. I must be there to face her when she is brought down—the same way I was there in the mountains to confront her. I did not ask to be a Yerrin, but still I am one of them, and it is my duty to see their evil put to rest."

Despite herself, Loren chuckled. "And Kal says I am one for dramatics. But very well. If you can convince Kal, I would be happy to stand by your side. Thrice we have been separated, and each time I have missed you worse. I will never by my own choosing part ways with you again. I swear it by the sky."

"And I," said Annis. Then she put her hands on her hips. "But as for convincing Kal—why should I need to? I am not in his service."

Loren gave an uneasy look back in the direction of Kal's council chamber. "I wonder if he would agree."

It turned out that Kal did not agree. When Annis came to him with her proposal to accompany Loren on her mission, he raged for almost an hour at her foolishness. From the way Annis described it to Loren afterwards, she bore it all patiently until it seemed clear that Kal was only ranting to hear himself shout. Then she stamped her foot, and when the noise shocked Kal to silence, she said, "I have never entered your service. I have never entered the High King's service. I am pledged to no one at all, in fact. And though I have taken your room and board, I think I have provided counsel enough to pay that back several times over. So unless you wish to tie me up and throw me in one of your dungeons, I will accompany Loren of my own free will."

Kal scowled and complained a bit more. But in the end, she spoke only the truth. And his anger may have been mostly for show, because he gifted her a horse from his stables for the journey.

The morning after they pursued Hewal from the stronghold, Gem came to find Loren. At first he only acted as though he was bored and looking for something to do, but he hovered around, and often she caught him studying her with worry in his eyes. Therefore she found an excuse to send Chet away, and when they were alone she fixed the boy with a look.

"What is it, Gem? You are hovering about me like a fly over rotting fruit."

"An insect, am I?" said Gem, sniffing. "I thought I had earned better than petty insults."

Loren rolled her eyes. "I am sure you will survive the slight to your honor. Tell me what troubles you."

"It is . . ." Gem glanced at the door to Loren's chamber nervously, and then leaned forwards to whisper. "It is the magestone I saw you eat."

Loren blanched. Of course. She should have known he would come to her. "I asked you not to speak of that," she said.

"Not to others, of course. But Loren . . . I have seen what they can do—"

"To wizards," she said quickly. "I do not have the gift of magic."

"And so I thought the stones would have no effect upon you at all," said Gem. "But it seems that that is not the case."

Loren sighed and cocked her head, thinking for a moment of how to explain it best, and also how to do so quickly, for Chet would soon return. "You know that Jordel and I often took counsel together, alone, yes?" she said.

"I remember," said Gem softly.

"And you know also that my dagger has been something of interest to me since before you and I met."

Gem snorted. "If by 'interest,' you mean you treasure it enough to nearly get yourself killed."

"Well, in our time together, Jordel taught me some of the secrets of the dagger. I cannot tell them all now. But then when I met the Elves, they showed me one more of the dagger's secrets. When I eat a magestone, and place my hand upon the hilt, I can see in the dark, as though it were day—mayhap even better."

The boy's eyes went wide, until she thought they might pop from his head. An eager grin stole across his face. "Really?" he whispered. "That is astounding. What a tool for a master thief!" But then his expression fell to doubt. "Yet if it means you must eat magestones . . ."

"I have eaten them ever since that night in Dorsea," said Loren. "Not very often—four times in all, and each time only half of a stone, broken and dissolved on my tongue. Have you seen me descend into madness? I am not a wizard, Gem. They do not do me any harm, the way they did to Xain."

Eagerness claimed him again. "But then this is wondrous!" he cried. "This is fantastic! What a thrilling addition to the tale of the Nightblade! A dagger that lets you—"

"No!" she said sharply, silencing him at once. "No one must ever know of my dagger. No one. Not even Kal and the Mystics, not even the ones who travel with us. That is another tale I cannot tell you now, but you must trust me in this—and you must never mention the dagger."

To her surprise, Gem narrowed his eyes and nodded conspiratorially. "Very well. Mayhap that is even better. If they do not know it is because of the blade, that is all the more impressive. A girl—a woman, I should say—who can see in the dark, and . . ." He paused, frowning. "What else did you say it could do?"

"Sky above," she muttered, shoving him by the shoulder towards the door. "That is enough for now. Off with you, and forget all that we have discussed here—except that you must not speak of the blade."

"Secrecy is my specialty, my lady," said Gem, giving her a bow at the door. He threw the latch, but paused just before he left, grinning at her. "And, it seems, it is yours as well—Nightblade, master of the shadows."

Loren reached for a boot to fling at him, but he ran off down the hall, cackling. He did not even close the door behind him.

TWENTY

To Loren's immense disappointment, it took them days more to ready for the journey. As she had done with Xain on the Seat, she spent her time studying maps and learning the routes to reach Dahab. She did her planning with Annis, rather than Kal—the grand chancellor did not see fit to provide any advice, nor compel Loren to spend any more time with him than necessary, and for that she was grateful.

Dahab was an old city in the south of Feldemar. It had once been the kingdom's capital. It was also the ancestral home of the family Yerrin, and had been as far as anyone could remember, or discover in tomes of history. Fat with wealth and power, Dahab exerted its influence over all the nine kingdoms, though ostensibly it still served the king of Feldemar, who dwelt in the city of Yota farther to the west.

At this time of year, the roads there would be hard. They would be crossing the heart of Feldemar, a dense jungle where bogs and marshes could trap the unwary. Indeed, throughout the nine kingdoms, Feldemar was thought of as a particularly wild place. Its kings through the centuries had built and maintained roads as best they could, but the land fought them at every turn. And without many wide stone roads to carry troops, supplies, and the King's law, the "kingdom" was more akin to a collection of provinces scattered across the wide and wild landscape. Sometimes lesser lords would claim rule over one part of it or another, disregarding royal decree or birthright. As long as taxes still made their way to Yota, the king rarely put forth much effort to suppress them. Thus small conflicts of territory and dominance often raged across Feldemar, fought in bitter skirmishes of only a few dozen soldiers at a time, in the wet and marshy underbrush that covered much of the landscape.

But the wealth and power in the city of Dahab kept it free from such infighting. War was only good for business when it was fought on a grand scale, and Feldemar's petty border squabbles contributed little. The family Yerrin had enough coin to maintain order by any means necessary. Their own guards were above such work, but whenever bandits grew too bold, the Yerrins would hire mercenaries to root them out of their jungle holes for the slaughter, and all in the name of commerce.

Therefore the roads Loren would take would be mostly free of bandits and highwaymen. Loren and her party would face only natural dangers on their journey, and those were none too perilous.

As for the party itself, Annis informed Loren that she would be sent out with the same Mystics who had accompanied her to Ammon in the first place. That reminded Loren that Annis had said something to Kal about solving two problems at once, and she asked what it had meant. But Annis avoided her gaze and equivocated.

"Ammon was never meant to hold so many soldiers at once," she said. "It is a constant chore to keep it supplied, and every hungry mouth removed from it makes the job easier." But Loren knew that when they left the fortress, they would take enough food with them for the journey, and so that seemed a poor explanation. Yet Annis would say nothing more.

On the morning of the second day after their confrontation with Hewal, Loren awoke early and could not return to sleep. After tossing and turning for some time, she sighed and gave it up. She was thankful at least that she had not been woken by one of her dreams. While Chet snored peacefully, she put on her clothes and made her way to the stronghold walls.

She had no particular aim in her wandering, but soon she found herself on the southwestern end of the fortress, looking out at the lands that fell away until they reached the jungle on the horizon. The sky grew lighter with every passing moment, and would already have turned from grey to pink if it were not for the thick clouds overhead that threatened rain. Loren studied the lush green before her. Soon she would ride out across those lands, in the very direction she was looking now, until she reached a city that she had seen only in her dreams.

She heard footsteps on the wall behind her, slow and easy.

"What wakes the Nightblade so early in the day?"

Niya's voice made Loren swallow and take a moment to compose herself. But even as she hesitated, the Mystic came and leaned on the wall just next to her, so close that their elbows pressed against each other. Through the thin fabric of her sleeve, Loren could feel the warmth of the other woman's bare arm.

"I do not know," said Loren. "I awoke for no reason."

"Not another dream, then?" said Niya. "I heard that a nightmare came upon you recently."

Loren shook her head. "No. No dreams today. At least none I remember."

Niya nodded. Loren glanced at her, but the woman kept her gaze trained on the landscape.

"How did you know about Hewal?" said Niya.

Loren floundered. "I . . . what? Why do you ask?"

"Because I do not know the answer," said Niya, smirking. "At first I assumed that Kal had had you watch him. But when we returned to Ammon, and the grand chancellor did not believe your tale, I realized that Hewal's betrayal was a surprise even to him. So then I wondered: how did you know, when Kal suspected nothing?"

Loren shrugged, but that made their arms rub together. She thought about shifting so that they were no longer touching, but she held her place for the moment. "Hewal had a suspicious look to him."

Niya smirked. "Do not most people look suspicious? Many would say that I have an odd look to me."

"I have not decided about you, yet. But I have seen nothing to make me suspect you. Should I?"

The Mystic's smile grew broader, and she nodded as though conceding a point. "Very well. But there is another reason I came to speak with you, after I saw you brooding here on the wall. I have been told that I, and the other Mystics who came here to Ammon with you, have been assigned to accompany you on your next mission."

"Yes," said Loren.

Niya sighed—it sounded like relief. "That is good. As I have mentioned, I feel you are safer in my hands than in others'."

A deep flush crept up Loren's neck. "You mistake the way of things. I am the one leading the expedition."

"Can you tell me where we are bound?"

"Kal did not tell you?"

The Mystic snorted. "Kal did not even tell me that I was assigned to you. That news came down through the chain of command."

She could see no harm in it. "We make for Dahab, to gather information for Kal's plans."

"I see," said Niya, nodding. "And did Kal assign me to you, or did you request my presence?"

The red had begun to seep from her cheeks, but now Loren felt it return anew. "I do not know what you mean."

Niya rolled her eyes. "Very well, if you wish me to couch my meaning behind other words: did you request *my squadron* of Mystics?"

"I requested nothing," said Loren. "In either direction. I did not request for you to come with me, or to remain here. The decision was Kal's."

"You do not care either way, then?" said Niya, smirking again.

"I . . . have not spent much thought on it."

The smirk turned into a grin. "When will you stop pretending that you do not think about me, just as you know I think about you?"

Loren flushed a deeper red, but she held the woman's gaze. "I have not pretended anything of the sort. Yet you, in turn, know that Chet loves me, and I him."

Niya did not look away. She only edged a little closer. "And what do I care about love? This is war time, and I am not looking for a wife. Only a pair of green eyes, and everything beneath them."

Neither of them moved for a long moment. Loren was not sure which way she *wished* to move. Or rather, she was torn between what she wished to do, and some sense of . . . duty? Obligation? She was not certain. But in the end, she stepped away from Niya. The spark in the air faded to nothing.

"No," she said. "What you seek is not important. What Chet and I have agreed to, is."

"Oh?" said Niya, who did not look put off in the least. She folded her arms—*Those thick, thrice-damned arms,* thought Loren—and cocked her head. "And what have you agreed to? You have discussed such things?"

"I . . . not in such detail," said Loren. "Yet I know what would hurt him, and what would not."

Niya growled in frustration and looked away. "Do you think he knows anything of hurt? I suppose I should expect such foolishness from youth. You will learn, eventually, that young love rarely ages as well as either of the parties involved."

The words came surprisingly harsh and bitter. But the vicious look on Niya's face melted away as quickly as it had come, and she summoned a sad smile—though it seemed forced.

"I speak from passion, and not wisdom," she said. "Forgive me. It is your decision, of course, if you wish to limit yourself to a boy who . . . well, he can hardly know what he is about, can he? But now I must return to my duties. Fare well, until our journey together begins."

She turned and ambled off down the ramparts towards the western tower. Loren felt confused, and more than a little restless. She looked out across the landscape again, but it no longer held such attraction as when she had first arrived. So she made her way down the stairs instead, and through the hallways back to her chamber.

Chet sat at the edge of the bed, looking as though he had just woken. His hair was mussed, and he rubbed sleep from one eye with the back of his hand. "Good morn."

"Shush."

Loren threw her cloak upon the floor and pushed him back down upon the bed, and they did not speak for some time.

Afterwards, he lay breathless beside her. "Sky above," he muttered. Loren smiled, but it quickly faded. He saw it, and propped himself up on one elbow. "What is it? What is wrong?"

What could she tell him? He had said often enough what he thought of Niya. Anything Loren could tell him that was close to the truth would only turn his distrust to anger, and just before they all set out on a journey together. It would not do to have them battling with each other the whole way to Dahab. And if their tempers got the better of them once they reached the city, that could be disastrous.

One thing, at least, was close enough to the truth. "I am worried about the road ahead," she said. "Just as with Hewal, I saw it in my dreams. It is unsettling, to say the least."

"Mayhap your dreams are trying to guide you," he said. "Though I know it comes at a price, for the terror of your visions is plain to see, this could yet be a gift."

Loren looked away. "A gift. Hardly."

"Not all of us can see what is to come in days ahead."

She looked up into his eyes. "I do not see our fate. Do you understand? Sometimes I see things from the past, only they are twisted and horrible. Other times, I see things that do *not* come to pass, and could not. This is not prophecy. No one has that power. I only see . . . clues. Hints. Things that can help guide me in what to do—and, mayhap, what to avoid doing."

The sight of his slit throat flashed through her mind, and she craned her neck as she felt the phantom pain of Gem's teeth at her neck.

Chet had gone solemn. Loren feared he might ask her again about her visions, even after she had asked him to trust her. But he only said, "And what must you avoid doing?"

She gave him a smile and leaned forwards to kiss him before pushing him onto his back once more. "Not this, certainly," she said, as she climbed atop him.

TWENTY-ONE

No trumpets blared when they set forth from Ammon, and there was no assembly of troops in the courtyard to see them off. They received even less of a parting ceremony than they had had upon the Seat. Only Kal was there to bid them farewell, his hood drawn up against the rain. He wore his cloak of red, but the Mystics who accompanied Loren had stowed their own cloaks in their saddlebags and wore plain brown. The success of their mission relied upon secrecy, and it would not do for a party of Mystics to be seen making their way across the kingdom.

As Loren gained the saddle atop Midnight, Kal gripped her ankle. She looked down at him, bracing herself for a final biting remark. But he only said, "Remember your vow to me, girl."

She softened somewhat, and nodded. "I will."

"I believe it." Then he stepped closer, and his voice dropped so that Loren had to stoop to hear it. "Forgive what I said in anger and after too much wine. Jordel's death was not your doing. He was his own man."

Loren could not reply for a moment, and she blinked hard as she drew her hood up against the rain. "He was that," she said at last.

A single guard at the gatehouse observed their passing, and before midday Ammon was lost from sight behind them. Niya and Loren led the procession. Chet followed just behind Loren and to her side, almost as if he was ready to spur his horse between her and Niya at a moment's notice. Loren saw, but she made no mention of it. The last thing she wished to do was call attention to the rapidly growing divide between him and the Mystic.

They stayed on the main road all that day and camped within sight of it that evening. But early on the second day they split off onto a less-traveled path that plunged straight into the heart of the wilderness. If they were lucky, and the weather not too harsh, the side roads would only cost them two days on the journey, and it would be that much harder for the family Yerrin to observe their approach.

But the sky did not cooperate. On the third day they were blasted by the heaviest rainstorm Loren had ever seen in her life. It forced them from the road to ride beneath the trees, and even that did little to shield them. Niya called them to a halt long before the sun had gone down.

The storm did not pass the next day, or the next. They had under-estimated the fury of Feldemar's winters, and the journey became a cheerless affair.

After the second night camping in the rain, Shiun let them build a fire against the weather. "No one will be able to see its glow through this storm, unless they have almost stumbled upon us already," she said. "And secrecy will do us no good if we freeze to death."

Loren was surprised that they even *could* build a fire in such weather. But Uzo set about with sticks and leaves, and built a little shelter against the rain. He did it effortlessly, and though it looked a flimsy thing, it did not rock in the wind, and it kept the rain from dousing the wood.

"We learn this trick as children," he said, the first time Gem praised him for it. The boy had scooted up close to the fire, practically sticking his frozen hands right into it. "These storms come every year, and there is nothing to be done about them. The world cannot stop to appease the sky's anger, and so those who travel in such weather must learn how to endure it."

One morning, when the storm was particularly fierce, Niya commanded them to remain camped there for the day. When Loren objected, Niya shook her head firmly. "We are at your command, Night-blade, but it would be foolhardy to press on through this. The winds might pick us up and carry us away. And besides, the horses will tire themselves to death against such a battering. We must hope that one day's rest will not make any great difference."

She found a place in the jungle where the trees kept off the worst of the rain, and there she commanded the Mystics to drill. Uzo and Jormund practiced against each other. Loren marveled at how Uzo, though he was by far the smaller, was able to keep up by using his speed and skill as much as his spear. Though young, he seemed a most capable warrior. She was not surprised that he had survived the battle on the Seat.

Gem followed along with the two of them for a while, off to the side, until Weath took pity and practiced his sword forms with him. Shiun stood apart from the rest, practicing her archery against a tree. Loren stayed with them for a while, but she had no interest in training. Instead she returned to her tent, which Chet had never left, and fumed to him.

"Here we sit, helpless against the weather," she said, trying without success to wring the water from her clothes. "Some agents of the High King we have proven ourselves."

"I do not know that I think this is so terrible a thing as you seem to," said Chet, grinning at her. "I can imagine many fates worse than being trapped in a tent with you for days on end."

Loren scowled and slapped his shoulder.

The sixth day was the worst yet, but at Loren's insistence, Niya commanded them to press on. They had already lost too much time, and a day of rest had filled them all with an urgency to keep moving. But the road grew worse and worse, and their horses kept slipping in the mud. They had to ride upon a riverbank for almost two hours straight, and the footing was so uncertain that they almost lost Jormund to the floodwaters. Niya called them to a halt hours before sundown, and the frustration in the camp was palpable as they all built their tents.

Soon afterwards they sat around the fire, staring into its licking flames, saying nothing. Out of all the party, Weath had seemed the least affected by the sour mood. Now she looked around the fire and gave a low chuckle. "A sorry lot we all look, and all for the sake of a little unpleasant weather."

"I would call this more than a little unpleasant," said Jormund. The big man's broad shoulders were hunched over his bread and meat to keep them dry. He tore another chunk off his loaf with his teeth.

But Gem seemed to appreciate Weath's attempt to lighten the mood, or else he was still grateful for how she had practiced swordplay with him, for he smiled at her. "I do not know about that. I grew up in a city that would become filthy in the summer, so that the smell of it pervaded the countryside all around. During those times, I would have welcomed a storm such as this to clean out the gutters and the back alleys."

"As you say," said Weath, smiling in turn. "I think the kingdom of Idris would welcome a storm to soak their lands. They have lain dry and barren for generations beyond count."

"Indeed!" said Gem, puffing out his chest. He raised his voice, shouting into the storm that still pelted them. "In fact, I am glad to be in such a storm as this, and not back in Ammon, where I could be warm and dry!"

But across the fire, Uzo snorted. "I do not love the storm, but I *am* glad to be gone from that place, darkness take it. Better these wildlands than all the old guard staring down their noses at us."

A cold snap seemed to rush through the camp. Weath and Shiun went stone still, looking at Uzo in shock. Niya sat up straight from her place by the fire and slammed her wooden plate down upon the ground. Loren tensed, though she was not entirely sure what was wrong.

"Enough of that talk, Uzo," said Niya. "We are all of us Mystics, old and new. I will not have you bring division to our ranks."

Uzo avoided her gaze. Beside him, Loren saw that Jormund was scowling, though he did not speak in Uzo's defense.

"Am I understood?" said Niya.

"Yes, Captain," said Uzo, though no one could miss the tinge of defiance in his voice.

Niya stared at him a moment longer, as if daring him to look up. Weath looked ashamed on Uzo's behalf, which was well, Loren supposed, since Uzo did not look ashamed in the slightest. Jormund's face had gone a shade darker, as though he barely restrained himself from an outburst.

At last Weath cleared her throat. "I spoke in jest before, of course. This storm can take itself back to whatever pit in the darkness it crawled out of."

Jormund let loose a long, low sigh. He looked up and forced a smile, as though determined to forget the discomfort of a moment ago. "And do you notice how it only started after our journey began, and grows stronger the farther south we travel? It is like this mission is Elf-cursed."

Weath chuckled easily. "I doubt the Elves care one way or another about a party such as ours."

But Uzo's scowl deepened, and he shook his head. "Elves. Do you all believe in such tales?"

"Uzo," said Niya in a warning tone.

Loren looked at him in confusion. "What do you mean?"

He met her gaze, unflinching. "You mean you believe in Elves as well?"

"Uzo!" barked Niya.

His eyes flashed as he met her gaze at last. "Can I not speak my mind on something so trivial, Captain? Or does your order for silence extend even to my disbelief of superstitious tales?"

Niya was about to answer, but Weath spoke first, cocking her head. "Do you mean to tell me that you do not even think Elves are real?"

Uzo turned to her, his glare softening somewhat. "Of course not. No one but the witless would think so."

Loren did not even know what to say to such a thing. She looked at Chet and Annis beside her. They both raised their brows and shrugged. But Gem looked between Uzo and Loren, his brow furrowed, as though he were suddenly unsure.

Niya spoke, a contemptuous smile playing at her lips. "Uzo is a farm boy from here in Feldemar. From the north, are you not?" Uzo stared at her and gave a slow nod. Niya shook her head at the rest of them. "He is practically an outlander. Elves rarely trouble that part of the world, and as a result, many of their elders have begun to forget."

But Uzo rolled his eyes. "They have forgotten nothing. They only stopped believing campfire stories. Do you ever notice how every time a story is told about Elves, it is always a tale of someone far away? And always, too, it happened a long time ago. Who has seen an Elf in living memory? Have you, Captain?"

Niya did not answer. Uzo looked around the camp, but no one spoke up. Loren felt a curious burning in her breast, a heat that crawled its way up the back of her neck. She realized suddenly that her hands were clenched to fists. Chet put a hand on her arm in warning, but she ignored it.

"I have," she said.

That sent the whole camp into silence. Gem and Annis looked at each other nervously, while Chet ducked his gaze. It sounded like a boast, and she had not meant it to. The Mystics all stared at her in wonder—even Uzo, who clearly had not expected to be challenged. But he recovered quickly, shaking his head.

"What do you mean?" he said. "You cannot mean that *you* have seen them. You heard from someone else—"

"I saw them," said Loren. "With my own eyes. As close as you and I are now. Closer, in fact."

His nostrils flared in anger. "Then tell the tale of it. Explain yourself, if you are so wise in the way of such things."

"I do not know that I need to follow your orders, Uzo," she said.

Uzo's anger became a smirk. "I thought not. By all the tales that are told of Elves, if you had seen them, you would be dead."

But Weath shook her head. "That is not true. There are all sorts of tales about Elves, and the only thing they agree upon is that you never can tell what they will do. Sometimes they will kill everyone in sight. Sometimes they will walk straight into the middle of a campsite—or even a city, if some tales can be believed—and kill one person. Just one. A king, or a peasant, or even a babe. Once they decide you must die, you die. Other times they leave you be. That is the great terror of the Elves: that no one can know their intentions, and that there is no escaping their wrath if they turn it upon you."

She turned to Loren then. "This explains much," she said. "I knew there was something odd about you from the moment we met, on that ship in Brekkur. It is something in your eyes. I have never seen its like before, but I have heard it can be a sign of those who are Elf-touched."

Loren frowned. "Others have said much the same thing. The Lord Prince even remarked upon it. I thought it was only their color—that seems to catch most people's attention easily enough."

Weath shook her head quickly. "It is not only that. Wizards like me can see it more easily than most, but it is clear to all, if you know what to look for. Look at her, Uzo. You can see it, can you not?"

Uzo stared at Loren for a moment, and she saw recognition dawn upon him. He turned sullenly away. "I see only a pair of green eyes," he muttered.

But Weath looked at Loren and gave her a little smile. Loren tried to return it, but she felt suddenly out of place. Everyone around the campfire returned to their meals, studiously avoiding looking at her. Only a moment ago, Loren had felt like a member of their company—if not a Mystic herself, then at least a friend to this group of them. Now, though, other than to Chet and Gem and Annis, she felt like an outsider—somehow apart from the rest of them, and someone to be avoided.

But one pair of eyes lingered. Niya still looked at her, and the Mystic's face was a curious mix of trepidation and wonder.

TWENTY-TWO

Loren rose with the dawn the next morning and left the camp to relieve herself. When she had finished, she straightened and drew her trousers up again. Just as she finished tying the drawstring, Niya stepped out from behind a tree, making Loren jump.

"Good morn, Nightblade."

"Sky above!" cried Loren. "What were you doing there? Were you *watching* me?"

Niya only rolled her eyes. "We are on campaign, at least of a sort. There is little room for modesty in a war party. Do you think the rest of us cannot your hear the grunts you and your lover let out when the moons are high?"

Loren could feel herself turning a deep shade of red. "I . . . I thought the sounds of the storm—"

But Niya cut her off with a sharp wave of her hand. "Enough. I only came to ask you if it is true, what you said last night about the Elves."

"I am no liar."

They studied each other for a long moment, Niya searching for something in her eyes. At last she gave a small nod. "Very well. I meant no offense. But it is a most unusual tale. Then again, much about you seems unusual, and mayhap this explains why. When did you see them?"

Loren shrugged, a little put off. "Some time before I came to the Seat, when I traveled east across Dorsea."

Niya's shoulders slumped, as though she had hoped for a different answer. "I see. It was after the Greatrocks, then? When Jordel fell?"

Loren cocked her head. "Yes. Did you know him?"

"No. I have only heard stories. Who does not know the exploits of the Nightblade, after all?" Her look of burning curiosity faded, to be replaced by a familiar small smirk. "In particular, they speak of the hatred between you and the merchant Damaris. Is that why you are so eager to pursue her to Dahab?"

"I do not hate Damaris. I only wish to see her brought before the King's law."

"Oh, but she is worthy of hate, is she not?" said Niya, her smirk taking on a feral quality. "Many in the Mystics have tales of the family Yerrin, of their cruel dealings and the corpses that may be laid at their feet. Yet we only mean to capture Damaris. Would it not be easier to kill her? Does she not deserve it?"

A chill went through Loren. "That is not my duty. No doubt the King's law will deliver whatever sentence is just."

Niya snorted. "Mayhap. Yet if the end result will be her death, why should we not do it ourselves?" She studied Loren's face for a moment, but found no agreement there, and so she sighed and looked away. "Oh, do not look at me so. I am half jesting, after all. Though it *would* be cleaner, certainly."

Loren peered at her, a thought slowly forming. "What did Damaris do to you?"

Niya's nostrils flared. "I do not take your meaning."

"Whence came this thought? You have known from the start that we did not set out to kill her."

"I have never seen the woman before in my life." Niya shook her head and turned away—but not angrily. Rather she looked like a woman who had just remembered something she had not meant to forget in the first place.

"The family Yerrin, then," said Loren. "What are they to you?"

Niya turned back, and it was as though she had never been angry at all. "Nothing, Nightblade. Nothing more than an obstacle in our mission. Only sometimes I think the King's law is too slow, and in the name of justice it allows injustice to live too long. But though you may wish to believe differently, the Mystics are not above assassination to achieve our ends."

Loren suppressed a shudder. She supposed it was no great surprise, but still it was not pleasant to hear. "That is hardly honorable."

"Nor are those we are sometimes forced to kill. Yet if Kal wished Damaris dead, he would not have sent us. He would no doubt employ a Drayden. Then the whole affair would be taken care of with little fuss."

The name of Drayden made Loren pause and study the Mystic more closely. "What do you mean?"

"Have you never heard of them?" said Niya, raising an eyebrow. "That is odd. They are well known throughout all the nine lands."

"I have heard of them, certainly. But I do not understand . . . why would Kal employ one of them? Theirs is a dark name."

"So is the family Yerrin's, and yet we Mystics have many dealings with them. Do you know nothing of the Drayden killers?"

Loren shook her head.

"They are assassins without peer. They work in the shadows, and they never fail to eliminate their mark. Mostly they work for the benefit of the family Drayden itself. But sometimes they can be hired, though it takes a hefty weight of gold."

"But surely Kal . . ." Loren let her words trail off. She had almost said that Kal, at least, would not employ assassins, even if the Mystics would. Yet before the thought could reach her lips, she knew it was foolish. Mayhap he would not do so lightly, but if he thought it was the only way to achieve an end, she did not think he would hesitate.

She realized that Niya was studying her face as these thoughts raced through her mind. "Poor little Nightblade," said the Mystic. Her voice had gone quiet, and held none of its usual veiled barbs. "You are surrounded by dark deeds, and darker times."

"Yet not all is darkness," said Loren, lifting her chin. "And the darkest night is still lit by the moons. I knew a Drayden—Qarad, your former lord chancellor. He proved his loyalty when he died, battling the Shades within the High King's palace."

Niya turned to the tree beside her and picked at it with her fingernail. "Yes. I never met him myself, and I had always heard he was a terror to the soldiers who served him. But he knew his duty."

They let a long silence stretch between them, a respectful moment for the dead. Then Loren cocked her head, remembering the night before.

"What did Uzo mean last night, when he mentioned the old guard?"

"Nothing," said Niya at once. "He is young, and newer to the Mystics than some. Such a combination rarely breeds temperance."

"I have never had much temperance myself," said Loren. "But what did he mean? He said something else, when we were in Ammon—something that turned your mood dour, as it did last night. I will have an answer."

"Oh you will, will you?" A spark of mischief shone in Niya's eye, the jibe returning to her voice. But then she sighed, and her expression grew more somber. "Kal is of the old guard, and he assembles Mystics to his side who share in his beliefs. For hundreds of years, the Mystics have had one purpose: to preserve the King's law, and through it, the nine kingdoms."

"Of course," said Loren. "That *is* their purpose, is it not?"

"It is. But some Mystics have grown weary of that being our sole pursuit. Our order holds much power now over the nine lands—not only because of our soldiers and the great number of wizards within our ranks, but because of our many connections to the wealthiest and most powerful families across the nine kingdoms. Only in the Order of Mystics will you find Yerrins and Draydens working side by side, as well as many members of the nobility. In our oaths, we forsake all ties to the families whence we came. But in truth, blood is not so easy to cast aside. If all the Mystics with powerful connections were to act in concert, united by some common purpose, we would be powerful indeed. Have you never heard our order called the Tenth Kingdom?"

"I have not," said Loren.

Her mind went racing back to the village of Strapa, where Mystics had pursued her and Jordel as they searched for Xain. Derrick, the leader of their pursuers, also thought of the Mystics as being of two kinds. He had even slain one of his own soldiers. *This one was a poison within our ranks,* he had said. But Jordel had been furious with him, for he believed that all were equal who wore the red cloak.

"But still I do not understand," said Loren, shaking her head. "You say that they are not happy with their duty. But what else is there?"

"Nothing," said Niya. "There is nothing else."

"Do not be coy with me," said Loren. "What do they *wish* to do? You say they have influence, and could wield it. To what end?"

"There is no end," said Niya. "They are aimless. Unhappy with their state of affairs, but with no plan to improve upon it. And do not worry, Nightblade: you will never find me being coy with you."

That made Loren's cheeks burn—but, too, she could sense that Niya still withheld something. It made her suddenly nervous to be traveling in this grim company of red-cloaked soldiers. She felt as though for some time now, she had been swimming with the flow of a river, and had only just become aware of a dangerous undercurrent that she could neither see nor predict.

Niya must have seen her anxiety, for she gave a sad smile and stepped forwards. With two fingers she reached up and brushed a lock of hair behind Loren's ear. "These are far too many worries for a woman so young. Free your mind of such troubles, Nightblade. They are for the red cloaks, not the black."

Loren stared into her eyes for a moment. Then she pushed past the Mystic, making for the camp.

Two days later, they awoke to a grey morning with rain lighter than they had seen in some time. They were nearing the journey's end, and the sight of better weather brought their spirits up.

"This is a good omen," said Shiun. "If this holds, we could reach Dahab before sundown."

"Then let us press on as quickly as we may," said Annis, rubbing at her arms through the sleeves of her shirt. "And when we have concluded our business in Dahab, let us remain there a while, or mayhap forever. I mean never to spend another night in the wilderness battered by rain, if I can help it."

After a meager breakfast they set off. And whether because of the prospect of reaching the end of their road, or the weather, their mood was now almost cheerful. There were snatches of conversation as they followed the winding paths through bogs and marshes, and once, Gem offered to sing Uzo a song, though Niya quickly told him to be silent.

"We have seen nothing to tell us that we are being watched, but still we should be cautious," she said. "And by no means should we go singing through the woods and call our foes down upon our heads."

Shortly after midday, they heard swift hoofbeats ahead of them. Niya and Loren shared a glance. They had sent Shiun ahead to scout the way, and if she was returning now, she was coming quickly. Niya waved them all off the road, and they retreated into the trees.

"Swords," muttered Niya. She and the other Mystics all drew. After a moment, Gem fumbled his own blade from its scabbard.

"If it is not Shiun, let them pass us, and only fight if we are spotted," said Loren.

But it was Shiun after all. As soon as she reached the spot on the road where the rest of them were hiding, she pulled to a stop and waved to them. Loren walked Midnight out into the open.

"If you meant to conceal yourselves, you did a poor job," said Shiun. "The marks of your passing are like signal fires."

"Enough of that," said Niya. "What is wrong?"

"There are soldiers," said Shiun. "Yerrin guards, up ahead."

Loren frowned. "Where our path meets the main road?"

"No," said Shiun. "Upon the road we travel."

That cast a grim mood over all of them. They had taken this way specifically to avoid detection, believing Yerrin would only be watching the major routes.

"So we have wasted days in our journey, and for little purpose," said Chet.

"No," said Loren. "The main road would have been little better, and there would be no way to keep their watchmen from spotting us— which is what we must try to do now."

"Why would they have guards posted, unless they knew we were coming this way?" said Niya.

"There could be any number of reasons," said Loren. "It could be a precaution, or they could be on the lookout for another foe entirely."

"Do you not think Hewal has arrived ahead of us?" said Weath. "If he has warned them that we are coming . . ."

Loren and Chet shared a look. Hewal would not have given such warning, because Loren and the Mystics should not have known he was in Dahab. They had only come because of Loren's dream, which only Chet, Gem, and Annis knew about. She could not explain it to the rest of them, not now at any rate.

"Of course Hewal could have told them we might come, but he could not have known we would take this route," said Loren. "And regardless, we cannot turn back now. If anything, we should take this as a sign that Damaris is in Dahab for certain. We must not let her slip away."

"There might be a way past the guards," said Shiun. "The path we ride now leads to a log bridge. That is where the Yerrin guards have placed themselves. But the river beneath the bridge can be crossed another way, bypassing the guards—with Weath's help."

Loren frowned, but Weath only nodded. "Say on."

"The river runs through a small divide in the land, several paces below the bridge. If we walk through that divide, there is a place close by where the water grows shallow and somewhat calm, despite the flooding from the rain. There, Weath could turn the water to stone, giving us a bridge to cross over. If we are silent, we should be able to avoid the guards' attention."

"Why not cross the river somewhere else?" said Annis. "We should do it far from the bridge, so that there is no danger of the guards seeing us." She looked more nervous than the rest of them. Loren realized that, if they were spotted, word would surely fly to Damaris that her daughter had been seen near the city of Dahab. If that happened, Loren doubted that all the Mystics in Underrealm could keep Damaris from hunting them down.

But Shiun shook her head. "There is nowhere else, at least not that I have seen. Upstream and down, the river moves too quickly. I could search for another calm section, but that would take time—mayhap days."

Loren looked to Weath. The alchemist nodded. "Shiun and I have known each other a long while. I trust her judgement in this."

"Very well," said Loren. "When only one path presents itself, the wise take their first step. Lead the way, Shiun."

But the Mystic hesitated, looking at Niya. Loren turned to find Niya studying her own hands.

"Why do we not simply take the bridge?" said Uzo. "We could dispatch the guards and be on our way in no time."

Niya looked up to meet Loren's gaze. "It would be faster."

"No," said Loren. "There is no need for fighting if subterfuge will serve."

"Yet speed is imperative to our mission," said Niya. "And we have wasted days already."

"You speak of saving less than an hour's time," said Loren.

Niya turned to Shiun. "If we *are* discovered while we try the more difficult crossing, what will be our position?"

Shiun's expression remained carefully neutral. "It will be difficult. They will have the high ground, and we would have to climb the riverbank to engage them."

"There. You see?" said Niya. "If anything should go wrong, we will all be at far greater risk."

Loren felt as though the argument were slipping away from her. "If we kill their guards, our advantage will be lost. Speed is important, but so is secrecy. Do you wish to warn all of the family Yerrin that we approach Dahab?"

"If we do our job well, no guard will escape to bring such a message."

"Yet if they do not hear from their guards at all, they will be suspicious regardless. And we will move more slowly than before if one of us is injured in the fight."

"That is unlikely," said Jormund with a grim smile. He pressed his fists together until his knuckles cracked.

"You risk all of our safety, for the sake of some guards you have never met," said Niya, brows drawing together.

"While you are willing to wantonly sacrifice the lives of strangers," said Loren. "I am in command here. We go by the river."

Niya's face turned a shade darker. But at last she jerked her horse's reins to the side, nudging it away from the rest of the group. Weath let out a low *whoosh* of breath. Shiun studied Loren for a moment, and then turned to lead them off the road.

TWENTY-THREE

THEY WERE CLOSER TO THE RIVER THAN LOREN HAD THOUGHT, AND soon reached the bank. Looking down, she saw at once what Shiun had meant about the difficulty in crossing. Its surface was a roiling mass of angry white foam.

"We will remain atop the bank for a ways," said Shiun. "There is no place to safely climb down closer to the water."

They had to ride in single file, for the trees pressed close to them on the right hand side. Loren rode just behind Shiun, with Chet behind her, and behind him, Niya and the rest of the party. Once or twice, Loren glanced behind her, excusing the motion by peering around the jungle first. She caught a glimpse of Niya's face, but the Mystic's anger seemed to have faded—or else she was suppressing it. But at least her complexion was no longer so red, and she was not glaring as she had been before.

Finally they reached a place where the ground grew a bit more solid underfoot. There was a little shelf not far below them. Shiun led them down, so that now they walked on the river's very edge. Loren guided Midnight to the right, so that the horse did not risk losing her footing in the river's soft mud. Midnight hardly needed the urging. She eyed the water nervously and nickered. Loren stroked her mane.

They reached a curve in the river. Before they turned it, Shiun stopped them and bade them to dismount. "On foot from here," she whispered. "Keep yourselves quiet, and mind the horses." Loren passed the command back down the line.

As they made their way around the curve, Loren saw the bridge at last. It was made from a single thick log, taken from a tree so massive that four people could not have wrapped their arms around its girth. The trunk had been shorn in half down the middle, so that its top formed a large platform almost three paces wide. It lay across the river, one end on each of the banks, which were now six paces above their heads.

Shiun stopped and pointed. Loren peered in the direction of her finger. After a moment she saw it: a figure in a dark green cloak, concealed in a tree on the other side of the river. One of the Yerrin guards. But the guard was looking the wrong direction—across the river and up—and was half hidden by branches besides, so she could not see the party making its way along the bank.

Raising two fingers for silence, Shiun led them onwards. They crossed beneath the bridge in dead silence. Just after she passed under it, Loren heard a loud sniff from above. She froze, standing stock still for a moment. Cautiously she glanced up. But she could not see who had made the noise, and there was no other sound. Shiun pressed on, and Loren hastened to follow.

At last they saw the place Shiun had mentioned. A tree had collapsed, smaller than the one that formed the bridge, but still sizable. It lay directly across the river as though human hands had laid it there. It turned the water upstream into a still pool, which gently flowed over the top of the log before turning into the raging floodwaters they had walked beside all this time.

There was not enough space for Weath to press forwards to the front of the group, so they all moved down until the alchemist had reached the still waters. Loren glanced back down the river the way they had come. The log bridge was a ways off, but still too close for comfort. Now would be the most dangerous part of the whole affair.

Weath took a deep breath. She knelt at the water's edge and put her hands into it. Loren could only imagine how cold the water must be, but the alchemist did not complain. From behind her closed eyelids, a gentle light spilled forth.

As they all watched in wonder, the water around Weath's hands began to change. It swirled and then solidified. For a brief moment it looked to Loren as though it had turned to ice. But then the ice went grey, and turned harder until it had become stone. The stone rippled farther and farther out into the river, at first in a perfect semicircle, but then, as Weath found her focus, it became a straight line, little more than a pace across. It edged forwards slowly, ever so slowly, and each moment seemed an eternity under the threat of the nearby bridge. At last the stone touched the bank on the other side. There it sank into the silt and mud, creeping into the earth like the roots of a tree and anchoring itself to the shore.

Weath's eyes opened, and the glow in them brightened. "All right," she gasped. "I shall have to hold it here while the rest of you cross."

"What about you?" said Loren.

"I can hold it up for myself at the end, but the rest of you must go first. One at a time—I cannot bear the weight of more."

Niya pressed forwards without answering and led her horse across the stone. She walked a bit too slowly for Loren's liking, but the stone bridge was wet from the splashing water, and Niya had to pick her way carefully. When she had reached the other side, she pressed herself and her horse up against the riverbank and waved the rest of them on. Jormund stepped forwards and placed one foot on the bridge. Weath gave a wry smile.

"You should eat less, big man."

Jormund grinned at her and pressed on. After him went Chet, closely followed by Gem, and then Shiun and Uzo. Only Weath, Annis, and Loren remained to cross. Annis looked to Loren, but Loren waved a hand at her. "You first."

Annis gave her a wan smile and stepped forwards. Loren's smile vanished the moment Annis turned her back. The girl looked terrified. As a merchant's daughter, she had never engaged in as much physical activity as the rest of them. Across the river, Loren caught Chet's eye and tossed her head at Annis. He nodded and stepped to the end of the bridge, holding forth a hand, ready to help Annis once she was close enough.

The girl moved step by step, each one more cautious than the one before, each one agonizingly slow. When she reached the halfway point, her shoe slid on the wet stone. For a panicked moment, Loren thought she would fall over. But Annis recovered, throwing both her arms out to steady herself. On she pressed, but now she moved even more slowly, frightened by her near miss. Chet leaned farther forwards, grasping for her outstretched hand.

Annis slipped again. Almost within reach of the riverbank, she teetered on one foot. Chet lunged for her, seized the back of her collar, and flung her to the riverbank. But Weath's concentration wavered, and when Chet's foot came down, it slipped right through the stone. He did not cry out as he fell into the river, but that did not matter—for Annis' horse fell, too. It struck the water with a thunderous splash and a loud whinny. After their quiet sneaking, Loren nearly jumped out of her skin at the sound.

Shouts came from downriver, and two figures in green cloaks appeared on the bridge. One of them pointed at the party.

"Darkness take us," said Loren. She flung herself onto Midnight's back. The mare plunged into the stream under Loren's heels and struck out, swimming hard for Chet, who was fighting to reach the shore. The cold river clutched at her legs, making her gasp, and she had to force herself to push Midnight on through the water.

Weath sprang up, the glow in her eyes intensifying, and led her horse forwards. Stone rose up from the bridge to meet her hand, maintaining her connection as she held it up for herself and crossed. Behind her horse's hooves, the bridge began to dissolve away, turning to water again and sweeping away downriver. Niya, Jormund, Uzo and Shiun mounted their horses, and with a battlecry they charged up the riverbank. Gem gave his own thin scream and ran after them, though he had no horse and could not keep up.

Chet's head bobbed under the surface of the water until he struck the dam. Loren thrust out a hand and seized his shoulder, and he pulled himself onto Midnight's back behind her. The horse's hooves found purchase on the bank at last, and she emerged from the river, scattering water in all directions.

"Watch after Annis!" cried Loren, as Chet jumped from Midnight's back.

"I will, but where are you—?"

His question was lost as she spurred Midnight after the Mystics.

The fight had already begun. One Yerrin guard lay on her back. Her hands clawed futilely at an arrow in her throat. Jormund had two more occupied, keeping them at bay with great sweeps of his sword. Niya and Uzo had one each. *Why are there so many?* thought Loren.

But all thought fled her as she saw a green cloak rippling. Unseen by the Mystics, another guard ran from the fighting.

A messenger. They would ride for Dahab and warn the family Yerrin.

Loren sent her heels into Midnight's side and went after the guard with a cry.

She caught up to the Yerrin soldier and tried to leap from the saddle, tackling him to the ground. But Loren was still not as practiced on horseback as the rest of the party. Her foot caught in the stirrup, and she fell atop him without any control. Her ribs struck a rock, driving the air from her lungs. Dazed and gasping, she rolled away.

There came a *hiss* as the guard drew his sword. He and Loren fought to their feet almost at the same time. Her bow was unstrung and on Midnight's saddle. She only had her dagger, but she hesitated to use it. What if the guard recognized it and escaped? Or what if one of the other Mystics came upon them and saw it?

The guard lunged forwards, thrusting his sword. Loren backstepped and almost stumbled. He swung to the left, and then down. Loren did not let him draw close enough to reach her, but it seemed he was guiding her in some particular direction. She glanced behind her and saw only trees.

He swung again, and she ducked behind a trunk. Too late, hasty footsteps told her his aim: he ran away from her, straight for Midnight. Loren went after him.

No doubt he had hoped to gain the saddle and ride off before she caught him. But he wore chainmail and heavy boots, and Loren had always been a fast runner. She tackled him in the knees just before he reached Midnight. To her relief, his sword slid away on the grass. But he surprised her with a kick, and she fell back with explosions of light dancing before her eyes.

If he had pressed his advantage, he might have choked the life from her before she could stop him. But he went for the sword instead, and that gave Loren time to regain her feet. He charged wildly, swinging without skill, hoping to catch her by surprise. Loren danced back again—but this time he gave her no room to glance behind her. One haphazard swing sent her leaping away, only to strike her head on a low branch. Loren fell to hands and knees. The guard attacked, sword raised.

A knife came flying. It sank into the Yerrin guard's side just below the arm. He cried out and dropped his sword. Niya appeared and tore the knife out. The Yerrin guard sank to his knees. She seized his hair, placing the blade to his throat.

"Is Damaris in the city?" she hissed.

The guard spat at her but missed. "Darkness take you and your kin."

Niya drove a knee into his side where she had stabbed him. He screamed. "I will not ask again. Some other of your fellows survived. Only one must live to tell me what I need to know. Tell the truth, and it could be you."

Loren rose, her shoulders heaving with deep gasps. But when she saw Niya, she paused. The Mystic's clothes and hair had become badly mussed in the fighting, and the high collar of her jerkin had come undone. There, where the leather parted, Loren could see a mass of scar tissue from some old and terrible wound.

The jungle had gone too silent, and Niya looked up at Loren with a frown. Her skin went a shade paler when she saw Loren looking at her scar. With a savage twist, she plunged her knife into the Yerrin guard's throat. As he fell to the ground, coughing his life into the soil, Niya buttoned up her collar again.

The forest went very still for a moment, except for the thrashing of the dying guard. Loren felt that she should say something. But then they heard the sound of hooves in the underbrush, and Shiun came riding into view with Chet. They both pulled to a halt. Chet was still dripping from his dunking in the river.

"Where is Annis?" said Loren.

"S-safe," said Chet, shivering. "We won the fight. W-Weath and Gem are w-with her."

"We must get you dry," said Loren. "You will catch your death of sickness." She brought Midnight to him, and as he dismounted, she fetched a dry cloak from her saddlebags to wrap around him.

"The Yerrins?" Niya's voice was thick with some emotion hastily hidden, though whether it was anger or embarrassment, Loren could not tell. The Mystic woman was still looking at her. Indeed she had not removed her gaze since Loren saw the scars at her throat.

"All dead," said Shiun. Chet's expression grew dark. "The Yerrins in Dahab will know something is amiss, but no one remains to tell them just what it is."

"Very well," said Niya. With her gaze still locked on Loren, she bared her lips in a fierce grin. "It appears we might as well have charged the bridge after all, Nightblade."

Loren flushed with anger. She tilted her head towards the corpse on the ground. "Mayhap—but then this one might have gotten away, for he would have had time to escape while you were fighting."

That gave Niya pause. At last she turned away, staring at the man on the ground. "Mayhap. We cannot change what has happened. Only now we must move with haste, and accomplish our aims in Dahab before Yerrin notices their missing patrol. The moment they do, they will send someone to search for them."

She reached up a hand, and Shiun pulled her into the saddle. They rode off back towards the others while Loren rubbed Chet's arms to warm him.

"They k-killed the Yerrins," said Chet quietly. "All of them."

Bowing her head, Loren wrapped her arms around him, trying to pass her warmth to him through the cloak. "I know. They are warriors. This is what they are trained to do."

"Y-yet you are s-supposed to be in c-command of them, and you told them you did not w-wish—"

Loren released him, climbed onto Midnight's saddle, and met his gaze. "I am not their master. They are my guards, not my servants."

Chet turned away from her to look ahead through the jungle.

"I did not wish for this," she told him quietly.

"I know."

TWENTY-FOUR

THEY HAD TO HIDE THE BODIES, SO THAT IF THE FAMILY YERRIN CAME to investigate why their patrol had not returned, it would take some time to find them.

"We might drag them off into the trees and hide them behind cut branches," said Jormund.

Loren was uncomfortably reminded of when she had first met Damaris, who had slain a squadron of constables and forced Loren to help her men bury the bodies. As she studied the grim look on Annis' face, Loren wondered if the girl was thinking the same thing.

"Too easy to find," said Shiun. "They will see the hewn trees, and then they will know what to look for."

"Throw them in the river," said Uzo. "No doubt the bodies will wash up on the bank, but it will be a ways downstream. It is fastest, and will not be any easier for searchers to discover than anything else we might do."

So it was agreed. The Mystics took care of the grisly work. Chet donned a new change of dry clothes and huddled off to the side under three cloaks, trying to dispel his chill. Loren wanted to be with him, but he was still dour after watching the Mystics slay their foes. It seemed distance was what he needed now, and so she gave it to him. The ride would warm him anyway, as well as the heat from his horse's body. As the others dragged the corpses to the log bridge and threw them off, Shiun rode back across the bridge and downriver a ways. She soon returned with Annis' horse. Its recovery seemed to be the only bit of good news from the whole affair.

All of them readied to ride on. Loren saw that Annis was staring down at the ground and went over to the girl. "What is wrong?"

"It is my fault we were discovered," said Annis. "If I had not slipped, they would not have seen us."

Loren shook her head. "No. Any one of us could have done the same. You should not blame yourself."

Annis looked around at the rest of the party and frowned. "I should not have come. It was the foolish notion of a foolish girl. I am no warrior."

"I would call you many things before I called you foolish," said Loren, putting a hand on her shoulder. "Strength of arms is not the only worthy quality in this world. A great enough wit will not only triumph over might, but make it look a fool. I value your mind far more highly than a simple swordsman."

That drew a small smile from Annis, though the girl did not look entirely convinced.

They rode hard once they set out, with Shiun scouting the way again. Gone was their high mood of that morning. No one spoke, but only watched the road as it passed beneath the horses' hooves.

They drew upon Dahab just before twilight. The clouds had mostly dissipated from the sky, and half the sun showed above the horizon to light the land. When they crested the last rise, the whole party stopped in awe.

North of them, the river they had crossed met an even greater waterway that ran south. But almost immediately, it reached a high shelf in the land and fell off into a great waterfall. "There is the Nelos," said Uzo, pointing to the river. "It flies away south until it reaches the Skytongue, which flows into the Great Bay many leagues away."

But Loren could not speak. As beautiful as it was, she had no eyes for the river, or even for the waterfall it formed. She could look only at the shelf, upon which was built the city of Dahab.

Just as she had seen in her dream, it was built in two levels. Both held palaces and mansions aplenty, and all of them with gold trim. The dying sun upon the gold made the whole place shine like a jewel in firelight, so that they could not long observe it without having to shield their eyes. Upon the higher level were built grander mansions, and ones fairer to look at. Many of them were made of white marble that gleamed nearly as bright as the gold, and Loren was reminded of the High King's palace. But even a stranger could see that the true power rested in the city's bottom layer. There the buildings were more solid, more sinister—and far older, from the look of them.

It was not only the sight of the city that struck Loren dumb, but the fact that she beheld it, in truth, for the second time. She could not be sure, but she thought she even saw the pillar of rock where Gregor had held Annis, Gem, and Chet over the abyss. Suddenly she was struck with terror at the thought of bringing her friends here. She wanted to turn back, to spur Midnight into the jungle and hide away, never to return.

Instead she nudged the horse's side. "Onwards," she said. "We should try to reach it before the moons rise."

Your dreams are not the future, she told herself. *You are not so important that the Elves would give you that gift.*

But that did nothing to quell the fear in her heart.

As they neared the city, three buildings in the lower level caught their eye. They were massive, flat on top, but with sloping sides so that they almost resembled pyramids. They were wrought all in black granite, and the style looked familiar to Loren. Then she realized that they looked very similar to the Academy of Wizards on the Seat. But while the Academy stood tall and proud, these mansions sat like spiders in the shadows. Even their bronze trim looked like crooked legs, coiled before springing forth to snatch some unwary prey.

"Those buildings are the homes of the family Yerrin," said Uzo. His jaw clenched. "If there are answers for us in this city, they will be there."

"A great many of your kin must dwell here," said Gem, looking over to Annis. "Have you not visited the city before?"

"No. Before the journey that brought me to Cabrus, I had never left the Seat." Annis straightened suddenly in her saddle and turned to Loren with a curious expression. "I have only just now realized that that was my first journey away from home, and I am still upon it. It has been eight months since I saw the place where I was raised. What a long and wandering road it has been."

That gave Loren pause as well. Had it really been so close to a year since she left the Birchwood? Her birthday had passed some time in Octis, unmarked. She had been in the Greatrocks then, and Jordel had been alive. But that had never held great importance for her, since her parents had never celebrated it.

Not far from the city, they had to rejoin the main road. It was close enough that Yerrin would have little warning, even if they were spotted, but still they did not wish to be noticed. Therefore they split up and entered the city in twos and threes. Chet and Loren rode in together, and reached the city's gates just as the last of twilight faded from the sky. The guards did not even seem to notice them riding alongside the trading carts and wagons.

Once inside the city walls, they passed a few streets and then regrouped with the rest of the party. Then Uzo led them on through the winding streets.

Despite the ominous presence of the Yerrin mansions, which were visible over the neighboring buildings, the rest of the city seemed a far less sinister place than Loren had expected. The knowledge that Dahab was the ancient home of the family Yerrin had made her think it would be some dark den of evil. But in fact, the buildings looked much the same as they did anywhere else, except that here they were often walled with a reddish-brown plaster and had roofs of red tiles made with clay. The people talked and laughed and joked as in any city Loren had visited so far, and she saw many street performers here, which had been a rarity in Cabrus and Wellmont. Even upon the High King's Seat they were not so plentiful. She saw dancers swinging wide staves that were set on fire, and two duelists performing an elegant dance with blunted swords. One woman beckoned to wide-headed snakes on the ground, and at her command they bobbed and weaved into intricate patterns like whirlpools.

As they neared the black mansions, Loren saw that not only were they built close to one another, but they were in fact in a sort of compound, with a single great wall that surrounded all three of them. Uzo led them in a wandering path around the wall, as though they were merely travelers taking in the city's sights. But they all studied the place surreptitiously, eyeing the few gates, which were closed, and the many guards that patrolled the ramparts.

When they had finished their circle, they stopped at a tavern. There was no stable, but there was a long post outside where they could tie their horses, and a servant girl there who Loren paid to watch the steeds. Inside they found a cheery room full of many patrons. The tables were low, and each was surrounded by cushions placed directly on the ground. Loren smelled wine and ale, but also a sweet, spiced scent she could not place.

"Tea," said Uzo, lifting his nose and taking a deep sniff. "Sky above, it smells wonderful."

At a table near the back of the room, they ordered ale and wine, and tea for Uzo. They waited for the drinks to be delivered before they spoke. When they had all had a few sips, Loren leaned forwards.

"What can we expect inside the Yerrin walls?" she asked Uzo in a low voice.

Uzo shrugged. "I have only visited this city twice before," he said. "And I have never been inside the Yerrin dwellings. They permit no outsiders to come within, except for important guests on official business—usually nobility."

Loren thought of how she and Jordel had infiltrated the Shade fortress in the Greatrocks. "Mayhap we could disguise ourselves as guards. That might get us inside."

But Niya shook her head. "We could never pass for Yerrins. Did you not see the guards' helmets? The fronts are open, so that their faces are plain to see."

"At least Uzo could get in," said Loren. "He comes from Feldemar, and has the look."

Niya rolled her eyes. "You must listen better. *None* but Yerrins are permitted inside the wall. Uzo's skin is not enough. They are a family. They know each other. He would be recognized—or rather, he would not be, and therein lies the problem."

Loren's face flushed with embarrassment, which she tried to pass off. "What, then?"

To everyone's surprise, Gem spoke up. "Are there other buildings inside the wall?"

They all looked to Uzo, but he shrugged. "I do not know for certain."

"But there would have to be," said Weath. "We see only their great manors, where the family's important scions live, as well as the people who serve them. Yet the Yerrins would need more than that—storage for food, granaries for horse feed, and even cleaning sheds for the groundskeepers."

Gem's face broke into a smile, and Loren guessed at his idea just before he gave voice to it. "There will be rooftops, then. There is no one better on rooftops than I. If we can climb the wall, mayhap we can travel across the smaller buildings to reach the manors, and without anyone seeing us."

Niya's nostrils flared, and she snorted. "Good on rooftops, are you? Mayhap in the city you called home. But you do not know this place."

"Loren can pick her way through any forest, even if she has never been there," said Gem. "I am the same with cities."

"He does have a sense for such things," said Loren. "With him to guide me, mayhap I can slip into the Yerrin dwellings."

"You?" said Chet. "You speak as if you mean to go alone."

"I am the spy," said Loren, shrugging. "Surely you do not think that all nine of us can sneak in together."

"Two may conceal themselves better than nine, yet three are not much more noticeable, and may be much safer if it should come to a fight," said Niya. "I will come with you, for you will need someone by your side who will do what is necessary to get back out alive."

Loren thought she heard the meaning behind that: *who will kill, if need be.* She met Niya's gaze, but the Mystic did not flinch.

"I should like to come as well," said Chet. "Surely one more will not make a difference."

But her dream flashed into her mind, and she saw Chet in Gregor's clutches. "No. You must remain here. Each person added to the mission only increases the danger."

"Then let me come instead of Niya," insisted Chet. "I can look after you as well as she can."

"That is not what I said I would do," said Niya. "I said I would get her—and *all* of us—out alive. You might look after her, but you will not drive steel into a guard's gut if they stand between you and escape."

Chet gave her a glare, and she returned it. But before either of them could speak again, Weath put her hand on the table to draw their attention. "The plan all sounds well," she said. "But what do you mean to *do* once you are inside? That is still unclear."

"We must learn if Damaris is in the city," said Loren. "Surely someone inside will know."

"You mean to interrogate them?" said Uzo. "You will hardly have the time."

"I do not require much time," said Niya. Her hand dropped to the knife at her waist.

"If a corpse is found, Damaris will know someone is after her, and may flee the city," said Weath.

"I said nothing of corpses," said Niya. "But if Damaris should learn that we are here, and if she then tries to flee, then so much the better. We can follow her while sending word back to Kal, and the Mystics will bring her to bay—removed from the proud manors of her family where her defenses will be strongest. It is harder to shoot a bird in flight than when they are roosting—but when a swallow hides within the earth, it cannot be shot at all, and one must draw it into the open."

Annis looked at Loren across the table. Loren thought she knew the girl's mind: this was somewhat beyond the orders Kal had given them. Yet Loren knew of no other way to learn whether Damaris was in the city, and they were running out of time. If Yerrin had not already discovered their missing party of guards in the jungle, they soon would.

"It is decided, then," said Loren. "The rest of you will wait here for our return. And if anything should go wrong, and the three of us do not return, you must send word back to Ammon at once."

Chet glared into his cup of wine. Loren had barely touched hers, but now she threw the rest of it back all at once. Niya smirked.

"Bolster your courage however you must, Nightblade, and then let us carry out your plan."

Loren thought to herself that in fact, the plan had been Gem's. But she said nothing, and only returned Niya's smile.

TWENTY-FIVE

LOREN, GEM, AND NIYA LEFT THE TAVERN SOON AFTERWARDS. CHET and Weath came with them, to provide as much help as they could before the three of them passed beyond the wall.

Now that the moons had risen, Dahab was like an explosion of light. Its many lanterns and torches caught on the gold trim that adorned every building, so that the whole place shone nearly as bright as during the day, but warmer, a soft orange glow that wrapped them within itself. Yet everything was edged by the blue glow of the moons, and it blended with the firelight to give the buildings an ethereal, magical look. As she marveled at the sight of it, Loren realized that every torch and lantern was placed to cast its glow on as much of the gold as possible, as if each structure had been built for just that purpose.

"Now the whole city glows like a gem," said Gem. He looked up at Loren, grinning. "I call that a good omen for us—or for me, at least."

Loren smiled back—but then her mind turned to her dream, and she saw his face turn savage, his teeth bared as they tore at her throat. Her smile became forced. "I hope so."

The streets had begun to clear with the day's end, and they found a section of the wall with almost no one nearby. Just before they climbed up, Chet took Loren aside for a moment.

"You must promise me to return," he said, looking into her eyes.

"I can make no such promise," said Loren. "But I promise to try."

"That is hardly comforting." Chet glared over her shoulder, and even without turning, Loren knew his ugly look was for Niya.

"Whatever your feelings towards Niya, do not let them blind you." Loren had to fight to keep her irritation from her voice. "She has proven herself loyal so far."

"So far," said Chet.

Loren put a hand on his cheek. "Dear, dear Chet. Look after Annis. If all goes well, we shall return soon, but if it does not, she will be in greater danger than the rest of you."

"I hardly agree," said Chet. "If they catch us, we will be killed. I do not think she faces that fate."

But Loren remembered when last she had faced Damaris in the Greatrocks, and she remembered the merchant's wrath. "Yet she faces her own sort of horror. Look after her."

He gave a slow nod. Then he laced his fingers together and knelt. Loren glanced up the street. Weath had cleared the few passersby from sight, and she gave a nod. Loren placed her foot in Chet's grasp and her hands upon the wall. They looked at each other, and he nodded three times in quick succession. After the third nod he heaved upwards, and Loren jumped. Her fingers seized the top of the wall, and she gripped it tight, bracing her feet against the surface to steady herself. Then, slowly, she pulled herself up to the edge.

Cautiously she raised one eye over the lip of the wall, and then ducked back down at once. There was a guard not three paces away, walking in Loren's direction. But the guard's gaze was turned up and outwards, over the city, and she took no notice of Loren's fingers as she passed.

Once the footsteps drew away, she pulled herself over. No other guards stood nearby, and so Loren waved down to Gem and Niya. One by one they followed her. Chet did not look happy to heave Niya up the wall, but he did it, and soon they were all up. There was a rooftop within easy jumping distance, and another beyond that. Indeed, just as Gem had predicted, there seemed to be a route that ran all the way to the bottom of the first manor far ahead.

"Better and better," whispered the boy, grinning at them in the moonslight.

"Stop prattling and jump," growled Niya.

Gem rolled his eyes. He scampered off and made the leap to the first roof, landing catlike upon the tiles. Loren feared the sound he would make when he landed, but she heard nothing at all when he came down. When she followed him, she found that the rooftop was very solidly built. They could not have made a noise upon it if they tried.

"Stay close, and stop when I do," said Gem, and ran off.

He jumped from one rooftop to the next, always lurking in the shadows of higher buildings when he could. Sometimes he would turn left or right, though Loren saw no reason for it, and then a moment later she would see that they had avoided an obstacle they would not have been able to climb over. The boy's skill was marvelous. Truly he looked at a city the way she did a forest: each one different and yet all of them sharing a common set of rules.

Suddenly Gem stopped. Ahead of them was a building with a second story, though there was another roof on their level to the left.

"Why do you halt?" said Niya. "This is no time for nerves, whelp."

Loren glared at her before speaking to Gem more patiently. "What is it, Gem?"

"I think we must climb this way," said Gem, pointing at the taller building ahead.

"That is a waste of time," said Niya. "We should go around."

"It is too heavily lit," said Gem. "This way keeps us out of the torchlight from the walls."

Niya scowled at him, but Loren spoke first. "Very well. Up it is."

"It is a waste of—" Niya began.

"We will waste more time arguing," said Loren. "If Gem says this is the way to go, I believe him."

The Mystic snorted and turned away. Loren could not understand her frustration with Gem. She had never seemed fond of the boy, but now it was worse. It seemed fear of discovery was wearing on the woman's nerves.

The two-story building was not made of the same granite as the manors, but plaster like the other smaller buildings. There were window ledges and wooden beams to take hold of, and Gem scaled them easily enough. Loren was not quite so quick, but she followed close behind, and Niya's powerful arms propelled her up easily. At the top, Gem reached up and gripped the edge of the tiles, using them to pull himself to the roof. He lowered a hand and took Loren's arm as she did the same. But Niya did not wait for Gem's help, instead grabbing one of the tiles on her own.

With a *clink,* the tile came away in Niya's hand. She lurched away from the wall. For an instant it seemed the Mystic would fall to the cobblestones far below. But Loren had just gained the rooftop, and she threw herself flat to seize Niya's hand. The Mystic slammed back into the wall with a grunt, while Loren clung desperately to the roof, trying to keep herself from sliding over. The tile that had come off spun away, shattering as it struck the cobblestones far below.

"Hurry!" gasped Loren. Niya got her hand atop the roof, and with Gem's help, Loren pulled her up. No sooner had they ducked out of sight than they heard a voice on the ground below. They all froze—but it was no shout of panic or alarm. Peeking back over the edge, Loren saw a solid-looking man in fine green clothes step out the front door of the building atop which they lay. He looked at the tile on the ground for a moment, and then turned his gaze skyward. Loren retreated just in time. There was a long moment of silence. After her pulse had resumed its normal pace, Loren risked another peek. The man had gone, and no alarm had been raised.

"A stroke of luck, that," said Gem.

Loren looked to Niya. The Mystic woman did not look chagrined at her mistake; if anything, she only seemed angrier at Gem. But when he led them to the other end of the roof and helped them climb down, Niya waited patiently, and followed his lead as he took them farther along the rooftops.

At long last they reached the closest manor. Now that they were up against it, it was even more imposing than it had been when viewed from the streets. The buildings pressed close here, up to its very walls. There was a window just in front of them, and inside was an empty room with no lights. Loren reached out to the window, but it would not budge under her hand. "Locked," she muttered.

There was another window just a few paces down, but it, too, was locked. They tried one after another, but without success. Niya muttered a curse. "The family Yerrin, it seems, are not all fools. Likely it is one duty of the manor guards to ensure all windows on this level are secure."

"The higher floors might be open," said Loren.

"That is my thought," said Niya. "Boy, climb to the next floor and try one of them."

But panic seized Loren's breast, and she shook her head. "No. I will do it."

Niya frowned at her. "He is a better climber."

Loren hesitated. In truth, she was already nervous to have brought Gem this close to the manor. Certainly she did not want him to come inside with them. She did not truly believe that her dreams showed her the future, but the thought of Gem in Gregor's hands—or, worse, the thought of the boy going mad and attacking her—would not leave her mind.

"He should remain here, on guard. If anything goes amiss, he will serve as a lookout, and can come to warn us. His purpose here was only to help us reach the manor, after all."

To her relief, Niya shrugged. "Very well. But we have tarried too long here already. If you wish to lead the way, then lead."

Loren nodded and looked up. There was a window there, and a granite ledge below it, just a pace out of reach. She stepped back and then took a running leap, feet scrabbling on the wall. Her fingers just reached the ledge. From there she was able to pull herself up enough to grip the bottom edge of the windowsill, and then it was a simple matter to stand upon the ledge. She tried lifting the window. It swung open easily, without a sound.

"It is open," she whispered down.

"Very well," said Niya. Without a glance at Gem, she jumped up and caught the ledge. Loren slipped into the room, and Niya was not a moment behind her.

Loren leaned back out the window. "Wait here for us," she said to Gem. "If you hear sounds of alarm from within, ready yourself to run. If you think for a moment that you are in danger, flee, and do not look back."

"I will not leave you here," said Gem.

She glared at him. "You will. You have pledged yourself to me, and this is the most solemn order I have ever given you. Do you understand?"

He matched her scowl with one of his own, but in the end he nodded.

"Good. We will return as quickly as we may."

Loren drew back into the room. Niya stood facing her, a curious expression on her face. The moment's silence stretched a bit too long, and Loren looked out the window. From this vantage point the city was laid out before them like a blanket of stars, mirroring those in the sky, except that its light was orange to match the silver-blue from above.

"A fine sight," said Niya in a careful tone.

"I suppose so," said Loren.

In truth the city only filled her with dread, for she could not see it without seeing her dream. Niya inclined her head, inserting herself into Loren's field of view.

"I meant to say . . . earlier, during the fight in the jungle. You saw my wound."

Loren blinked at her for a moment, uncomprehending. Then she remembered the terrible scars at Niya's throat. "Yes."

The Mystic searched her eyes. But then she shrugged with a humorless smile. "I hide it behind this collar. I think it is hideous to look at, and some others have agreed."

"Few of us go through life without wounds, and many of them scar. I am only amazed that you survived such an injury. It looks as though your throat was cut more than once."

Niya's face turned a deep, angry red, and Loren balked.

"I am sorry. I did not mean to bring forth a grievous memory."

"Grievous indeed," said Niya, though she sounded more angry than mournful. "And impossible to forget."

"You should not let it trouble you," said Loren. "You cannot help the scar, and anyone who remarks upon it is not worth worrying about."

"That is more easily said than believed."

Loren frowned and turned her gaze out the window again. She wished she were anywhere but in this city. Her fear seemed to grow with every passing moment, and as much as she longed to find Damaris lurking within this place, at the same time she dreaded the thought that she might.

"Niya, there is something dangerous here."

Loren paused. She had not meant to speak at all. The words had come out almost against her will. But as Niya looked at her, she pressed on heedlessly. "I think Damaris is here. I am almost certain of it. And worse, there is a man, her bodyguard—a man named Gregor. He is dangerous, mayhap more dangerous than anyone I have faced in my travels, and—"

Without warning, Niya seized her shoulders and kissed her. The second their lips met, Loren's worries vanished into sparks of bliss. Her own hands rose to Niya's waist, though she did not mean to move them. More than a month of desire was now finally real, and she only wanted all the city to fade away, and all the world beyond it as well—

And then she remembered Chet, waiting for her in a tavern just beyond the wall. She pulled back, pushing Niya away.

"No," she said quietly. "Clearly I have not spoken plainly enough. I love Chet."

"And I have told you I do not care for love, nor desire it," said Niya, wearing a self-satisfied smile. "And you seem far less convinced of your words than the last time you said them. I do not regret it. You deserved a kiss, and likely needed one as well."

I did, thought Loren. But she shook her head. "You could hardly have chosen a worse time."

Niya sighed and rolled her eyes, though her smile did not leave her. "Very well. Until another time, then. In the meanwhile, let us go and find a merchant."

TWENTY-SIX

THEY LISTENED AT THE ROOM'S DOOR FOR A LONG MOMENT, BUT COULD hear no sound in the hallway beyond. Loren opened it cautiously and poked her head outside. There was no one in sight. She slipped out of the room, and Niya followed. At the end of the hall they found a stairway and took it up to the next floor. Loren waved Niya back and peeked down the hallway, but it was as empty as the first, and the rooms looked all the same.

"Not here," she said. "Let us go up another floor."

"Why?" said Niya. "What are you looking for?"

Loren thought back to Damaris' room at the Wyrmwing Inn in Cabrus. It had fairly glowed in its opulence, a wide and spacious place with drapes and fine furniture. "We seek Damaris, or someone of similar stature who would know where she is. These floors are filled with small drawing rooms and apartments, doubtless for the servants, or mayhap only for storage. If I know the family Yerrin, the higher we go, the more important will be the people who dwell there."

So they ascended. At each landing, Loren inspected the hall beyond. Her guess was right—upon each level, the doors lessened in number, and soon they were worked with fine designs in gold. But they had not climbed much higher before they heard the tramp of heavy boots coming down the stairs towards them.

"Into the hall!" whispered Loren.

They ducked around the corner of the stairwell door just in time. After the steps passed, Loren and Niya poked their heads back out. They saw four Yerrin guards, who soon vanished around the next curve in the stairs.

"We should expect to see more of them from this point on, I think," said Loren.

But Niya smiled at her. "Did you not see them? Within the manor, they have closed helmets."

At first Loren did not understand. But after a moment, she matched Niya's grin with one of her own.

The next hallway up was not empty. They saw a pair of guards within it, walking together away from the stairwell. They had little time to lose before the guards would be out of sight. After nodding to each other, they ran silently up behind.

Each threw an arm around one of the guards' necks. Niya bore her opponent to the ground and squeezed until she fell unconscious. But Loren's guard almost slipped from her grasp. He struggled mightily, reaching for a dagger at his belt.

Loren caught his wrist, struggling to twist his arm behind him. Niya rose and drove a fist into the guard's stomach. He doubled over. Snatching his helmet away, Niya brought it crashing down on the back of his head. Finally he collapsed to the floor.

"Easy enough," said Loren, panting.

Niya snorted.

They found an empty room and left the guards trussed up within, tied with some drapes they tore from the windows. Loren used her hunting knife to cut two strips of the cloth into gags. They had already stripped the guards of their uniforms, and put them on over their own clothes, including the helmets. The guards had gloves, too, so that no bit of their skin was exposed.

"Your clothes are a better fit than mine," said Niya, squeezing her hands into the gloves.

"I cannot help my lithe figure," said Loren with a smirk.

Niya eyed her. "Nor should you."

That turned Loren's cheeks a deep red, and she chastised herself.

She must try to control her tongue, and not encourage Niya in her advances.

Loren folded her black cloak and shoved it underneath her chain mail and leather shirt. It gave her the appearance of a paunch. Niya abandoned her own brown cloak in favor of the guard's green one. They made their way back to the stairwell with more confidence and climbed two more floors without seeing anyone else.

On the third story up, they ran into another pair of guards escorting a merchant. At first Loren thought to walk straight past them, pretending to be about their own business. Then she saw Niya draw aside. She did the same at the last moment, and they stood at attention as the merchant passed them by. The other guards gave them a brief glance, but the merchant did not even appear to notice they were there, and soon he was out of sight around the corner.

"Remember that we are guards, and therefore servants," said Niya.

"I will not forget again. You have some skill in subterfuge."

Though she could not see it beneath the helmet, Loren heard a fierce smile in Niya's voice. "I prefer a knife, but deception will serve in a pinch. Should we pursue the ones we just passed? He was a merchant. Mayhap he would know something."

Loren considered it for a moment, but then shook her head. "We would have to fight the guards, and would be too exposed while we did so. We should look for one in the hallways, not the stairwell, and follow them to a room where they may be subdued without witnesses."

They began to inspect the halls more carefully. They walked the entirety of each floor, striding with impunity as though they were on an errand. Their surroundings began to grow more elaborate. Now even the side tables in the halls were well-carved, and the sconces for the torches were wrought with intricate designs. No one else, guard or merchant, spared them so much as a glance. Loren was reminded again of when she and Jordel had pulled this very trick in the Greatrocks. For a painful moment, she wished he was here now. Though Niya was a competent enough companion, she was no replacement.

On the next floor, they passed by someone alone—a wizened merchant in a fine green dress. As soon as she saw the woman coming, Loren started, and only just managed to keep herself from coming to an abrupt halt in the middle of the hallway. Once they were alone again, Niya stopped and turned to her.

"What is wrong? Who was that?"

"Her face . . . I remember it from somewhere." And then it came to her in a flash. "Her name is Gretchen. She kept Damaris' accounts. I saw her when I first met the merchant, and Annis as well."

"We will not find a better target than that," said Niya. "And we have spent too long in this place already. Who knows but that the guards we subdued have awoken, and are struggling free from their bonds even now."

They turned and went hastily back the way they had come, and soon they could see Gretchen just ahead of them. The woman reached the stairwell and went up to the next floor. Niya and Loren followed close behind. In the hallway, Gretchen entered the second door on her left, closing it behind her with a soft *click*. Loren and Niya stopped just outside it and looked at each other.

"There might be guards inside," said Loren.

"There might not," said Niya. "And we are out of time."

She opened the door before Loren could answer and strode confidently inside. With little other choice, Loren followed—but inside, they both froze.

They were in a sitting room. In the center was a small table surrounded by plush chairs, upon one of which Gretchen now sat. There were no guards in the room, but there was one other person—a young man with dark hair and a scar that split his chin. Hewal.

Gretchen and Hewal looked up the moment the door opened. When Loren and Niya paused, Gretchen frowned.

"What is it?" Her voice was a shrill bark, like a small dog that thought itself a mastiff. "Are you lost?"

Loren could not think of what to say. Thankfully Niya's wits were quicker. "No, my lady," she said, deepening her voice to disguise it. She pushed the door shut and took a step into the room. Loren followed. "Only we have been sent with orders. It appears the two of you may be in grave danger."

The old woman's brows flew skywards. "Us? This is the Golden Manor, you twit. What possible danger could there—"

But Loren saw Hewal's eyes go wide, and he shot to his feet. Niya was quicker, lunging forwards and tackling the man to the ground. Loren went for Gretchen, clapping a hand over her mouth and seizing her arm as she tried to rise. Niya and Hewal wrestled for a moment, but she was stronger, and held him down while she drew her knife. She held the point of it under his chin.

"Be still, weremage," she said. "If I see the slightest glow in your eyes, I will plunge this into your brain. I know you cannot heal that wound away."

Keeping one hand over Gretchen's mouth, Loren reached up to remove her helmet. When it came off, Gretchen's eyes narrowed, and then in a moment they shot wide. She screamed something, but the words were muffled under Loren's hand.

"Yes, Gretchen." Loren gave her a grim smile. "It has been a long time. We have questions for you, and you would do well to answer them."

Hewal was nearly spitting with rage. "How?" he said. "How did you find me here?"

"You can never escape the Nightblade, weremage," said Loren. "Remember that well." *He does not need to know that we did not come here looking for him,* she thought. It would have made her laugh out loud, if the situation had been less serious.

Hewal snorted. "I suppose Kal's spies are not so incompetent as I had believed."

Struck by a thought, Loren raised her brows. "Oh, do you think you deceived Kal? You are mistaken. He has known of your deception a long time, and played you for a fool all the while."

Joy coursed through her as she saw his face grow pale—but then he calmed himself and snorted. "You lie. Kal knew nothing, or he would have been more careful with his secrets. If you could hear only half the things I know about him and his precious order . . ."

Despite her best efforts to remain calm, dread seized Loren's heart at his words. But Niya pressed her dagger harder against his skin. He went quiet. Loren saw a small drop of blood appear at the tip of the dagger.

"Be silent, wizard," said Niya. "We seek Damaris. If you wish to live, you will tell us where she may be found. In fact, I offer the two of you this chance: whichever one of you tells us where Damaris is hiding may live. I will take great pleasure in bleeding the other one all over this fine rug."

Hewal glared at her, but Gretchen's eyes went wide with terror. "Do you wish to volunteer?" said Loren. She took her hand away from Gretchen's mouth, but dropped it to her throat. "Speak. But if you try to scream, I will throttle you."

"I have nothing to say to you, ungrateful wretch." Gretchen tried to spit at her, but the saliva only splashed out on her own chin. "I told Damaris she should have killed you."

"Mayhap she should have," said Loren. "But now she never shall, for I mean to bring her before the King's justice. Tell me where she is, and I will see that that justice is lenient upon you."

"She is far away from you!" hissed Gretchen.

Loren frowned. "She is not here in Dahab, then?"

Gretchen snapped her mouth shut at once, but Loren could see the fear in her eyes and knew it for the truth.

What, then, had her dream shown her? She had seen Damaris here—*here,* in this very city. If that was a lie, then why was Hewal here? Why had she been allowed to see that he was a weremage, or that he would be in this city at all?

Her thoughts were drifting, and she forced herself back to the present. She would have to worry about these things later. Now Niya put her face closer to Hewal's, sneering at him. "The old woman has been the most helpful so far," she said. "You had best contribute something to the conversation, lest I grow bored of you."

Hewal only glared. Niya shrugged and turned back to Gretchen. "Very well. He does not seem forthcoming. Say on, old woman, and my friend and I will leave you be."

Loren saw Gretchen hesitate, her throat working. "Do not scream," warned Loren.

"She is far away," said Gretchen. "Far from here."

"You have said as much already," said Niya. "Tell us more."

"A fortress. Far to the west. Too strong for you fools to break into."

Niya clutched Hewal's throat tighter and turned the dagger on Gretchen, holding it just under the woman's eye. "What is it called? Where may it be found?"

Gretchen squirmed under Loren's hands, trying to edge away from the knife. "Yewamba! It is Yewamba, it—"

A moment too late, Loren saw the flash of light in Hewal's eyes. He slapped Niya's hand away and sprang, and as he moved, great claws of bone shot from his hands. But he did not attack Niya, nor Loren. He plunged the knifelike claws into Gretchen's throat and chest. One of them sliced open the back of Loren's hand, and she recoiled in pain. Hewal did not press his attack, but jumped back and away from them both.

Niya flipped her knife around, but Hewal flung a chair at her just as she threw it, and the blade went wide. Gretchen collapsed on the couch, blood spurting from her throat to cover Loren's chain mail.

"The window!" cried Loren.

But she was not fast enough. Hewal turned and flung himself into the window, curling his body into a ball. The glass burst outwards with a great crash. The glow of Hewal's eyes grew brighter. In a heartbeat he was gone, and a crow flew away into the night, cawing madly. Loren seized Gretchen's shoulders, trying to sit her up so that she did not drown in her own blood.

"Leave her," said Niya. "She is dead already."

It was true. A spark of life remained in the woman's terror-filled eyes, but already it was fading. Loren gritted her teeth and stood back, pressing her sliced hand hard into her sleeve to stanch the flow of blood. Niya went to the window and looked down.

"Guards heard the window breaking," she said. "It is time we left."

"But we do not know where this Yewamba is," said Loren.

"We can discover that later, or so I hope."

"I am covered in blood. I cannot walk out of here like this, for they will know that something is amiss."

Niya's eyes grew narrow as she studied Loren. For a long, curious moment, Loren felt that she was being judged, as though Niya weighed one grim option against another. Then the Mystic's face relaxed.

"Well, I hope you do not expect me to leave you here. We have a mission to find Damaris, you and I, and I will not let you abandon it so easily."

That forced a laugh from Loren. "Then I hope you have an idea."

"Mayhap we can follow our quarry," said Niya, tossing her head towards the window. "Only we cannot fly, and shall have to climb."

Loren went to the window and leaned out to look down. "It is a long way."

"Not so long as the stairwell, if we must fight our way down. And I do not think you will be much use if it comes to swords, which it surely will."

"You are correct," said Loren. "Very well. These outfits will no longer help us." Quickly they shed their guard uniforms, and Loren donned her black cloak once more. From Niya's discarded cloak she cut a strip of cloth and tied it around the cut on her hand. She lifted the window to climb out.

"A moment," said Niya, seizing her cloak and drawing her back.

"You have proven to be something of a lure that summons luck. You found Hewal when we did not even seek him. We shall need more of that luck if we are to escape. I think you should give me another kiss."

For a moment Loren could not believe her own ears. "Before was not the time for such idiocy, and now is even less so."

Niya only widened her eyes in mock fear. With two hands clasped to her heart, she simpered, "Without your luck, I fear even to attempt the climb."

Loren wanted to strike her. But in her mind's eye she could almost see the guards who even now must surely be rushing up the tower towards them. She darted forwards and gave Niya a brief kiss, and then slapped her shoulder, hard. "For your stupidity."

"A small price to pay," said Niya, and climbed out the window.

TWENTY-SEVEN

THE WAY WAS SLOW, AND LOREN FELT HORRIBLY VULNERABLE ON THE outside of the building. As she climbed, she kept a careful eye out for Hewal. In bird form, it would be easy for the weremage to spot them and warn the Yerrin soldiers. But no crow wheeled in the sky. Hewal must have flown to the ground and entered the Golden Manor from there, hoping to catch them on the stairwell.

As luck had it, they came down not far from where they had left Gem. The boy jumped across two rooftops to join them before they reached the bottom. By that time, the whole compound rang with shouts of alarm and the sound of tramping boots.

Gem stared at them both in wide-eyed wonder. "By the sky above, what did the two of you do in there? You have mustered an army."

"Time enough for that later," said Loren. "Now it is time for running."

Run they did, with Gem leading the way across the rooftops once more. This time he did not suggest they climb the higher building. He took them in a dead sprint around it—and then he cut right, running straight for the wall.

Loren skidded to a halt. "Gem, this way is exposed."

"Every way is exposed now. You have kicked the anthill."

He was right. Guards ran all along the wall. They were mustering to move through the compound in rank and file, searching for the intruders. The quickest way was safest now.

The wall was close. There were two guards straight ahead. Just before the three of them reached the last rooftop, the guards spotted them. Loren slowed in her run. But Niya sped past her.

"No time," said the Mystic, and she made the leap.

One of the guards raised his sword, but she caught his wrist, wrenching him to the side and clearing a space for Loren and Gem to land beside her. With her other hand she struck the guard hard in the throat, and as he choked for breath, she pushed him back over the wall. He fell to the street beyond with a scream, which ended abruptly as he struck the cobblestones.

The other guard came for Loren, who sidestepped the woman's wild swing and shoved Gem away. They were pressed close together now, giving no time to think. Loren lunged and slammed the crown of her head into the guard's nose where it was exposed by the helmet. She felt it snap with a wet *crunch*. The guard fell upon her back, stunned. Loren shook away the spots in her eyes.

"Over!" she cried, and nearly flung Gem off the ramparts. But she caught his hands and stooped over the edge, lowering him as far as she could before she let go. He landed well and rolled away, and Loren hopped over after him.

An arrow sailed through the air above her, and she flinched, losing her grip before she meant to. She almost landed straight on her ankles, and only just managed to roll with the impact. Her tailbone came down hard, and she groaned as she regained her feet. A moment later, Niya came crashing down beside her, turning over and over as she rolled across the street.

"Get up," said Gem, pulling on her arm. "They are almost upon us."

He dragged Loren to her feet and tried to flee with her. But Loren went to Niya and hauled her up. The Mystic's ankle had twisted, and she limped when she tried to walk.

Loren threw an arm around her and half-dragged her away from the wall. They passed the body of the guard Niya had thrown over. Loren tried to ignore it. Mayhap he was still alive, but Loren thought she would feel better if she did not know for certain.

They ducked into the first alley they saw, and Gem led them around two different turns before they came upon a well-populated street.

"Which way to the others?" said Loren.

"This way," said Gem. "At least, I think so."

"You do not remember?" growled Niya.

He frowned at her. "Do you? Then follow me." And off he ran. Loren pulled Niya after him, trying to ignore the woman's grumbling.

Gem was right in his guess after all, and soon they reached the tavern. Chet and Uzo were waiting outside, and Chet's face was nearly chalk-white. But it flushed with color again when he saw Loren, and he ran forwards to help with Niya.

"What happened?" he said in a low voice. "Half of the city seems to be in an uproar."

"Why does everyone want an explanation while danger still looms?" said Loren. "Get the others out of there. We should ride as far from this place as we can. Let us find an inn on the other side of the city."

They all made ready to leave. Loren went to help Niya up on her horse. "I am not badly hurt," said Niya, scowling at her. "It was only a little turn."

"Do not act so surly when I am only trying to help you," said Loren. "It would seem I am not so lucky as you thought."

"Yet I am alive. And I have the memory of you kissing me by your own choice."

Loren's eyes went wide, and she looked over her shoulder. But Chet was a few paces away, tending to his saddle, and had not heard. She leaned in closer. "I would rather you did not speak of it."

Niya grinned at her. "Is that an order, Nightblade?"

"It is. You can mount your horse on your own." Loren went to Midnight and climbed into the saddle. She took no small pleasure in seeing Niya struggle to do the same.

They rode off, south and away from the Yerrin manors. No one gave them a second glance, yet still Loren felt as though eyes were upon her. She drew up her hood to hide her face, and kept a wary lookout for anyone wearing green. When they had almost reached the city's southern wall, they found an inn with a sizable stable, and there they pulled to a halt.

"See to the horses and meet us within," Niya told Shiun and Jormund. Then she turned to Loren. "I could use a drink, and you deserve one."

Though Loren was still irritated with the Mystic, she could not deny that a cup of wine sounded like the finest thing in the world. Once inside they ordered food and drink and had it brought to a table near the back, out of view of the front door.

The moment they found their seats, Weath leaned forwards. "Did they recognize you?" she said. "Will they follow you, or trace this back somehow?"

"Yes," said Loren. "Hewal was there. He saw me plainly, and must have guessed who Niya was under her helmet."

Uzo smirked. "I am sure you have heard this before, but your green eyes leave you ill-suited to life as a spy."

"It was not Loren's fault."

Niya and Chet said the words at the same time. They glared at each other for a long moment before turning away.

"Very well," said Weath. "What did you learn?"

Loren looked around, conscious that there could be ears listening in any corner. "The one we seek is not in the city. She resides in a fortress—a place called Yewamba, far to the west of here."

"Then we have what we came for," said Weath. "We should make ready to leave. I suggest we spend one night here, for we are all weary from the road, and the three of you need rest even more. But we should ride before first light. Uzo and Jormund can buy us supplies for the journey back to Ammon."

"Thank goodness," said Chet. "Even on this side of the city, I cannot shake my fear that we could be found at any moment."

But Loren remained silent. Then she realized that Niya, too, had yet to answer. Their gazes locked across the table.

Gem looked back and forth between the two of them with wide eyes. "Oh, darkness take us," muttered the boy.

"We are going to Yewamba," said Niya.

Chet gawked at her. "We certainly are not. We are going back to Ammon to bring our news to Kal."

"Kal will receive his news," said Loren quietly. "We will send someone with a letter. Jormund, I think."

For a moment it seemed Chet thought she was joking, for a grin played at his lips, coming and then fading again. It was the face of someone trying to understand a joke, and it pained Loren to see it. But when she did not smile in turn, he shook his head slowly.

"You cannot be serious. Loren, you are not this foolish."

"She is far from foolish," said Niya. "She is wiser than you are, at any rate. We have waited for weeks—months, in fact—for an opportunity to bring our enemies to heel. Now we have such a chance. But it will not last long, for Hewal will surely send word of what has happened here tonight, and then our target will hide herself in another dark hole. I will not waste our opportunity, and neither will the Nightblade."

Chet and Weath both began to speak, but Loren cut them off with a raised hand. "Niya is correct. We left Ammon to accomplish a purpose."

"That purpose was information," said Chet.

"Information leading to a capture," said Loren. "But if we do not act on what we know, that will never happen. If we had learned that the one we seek was in some outland kingdom, some like Hedgemond, that would be one thing. But this fortress, wherever it is, lies far to the west. If we ride the long distance back to Ammon to tell Kal what we have learned, and then devise a plan, and *then* set out after her, weeks will have passed. Even if winter ends tomorrow and not a single storm troubles us the whole while, the chance to catch Damaris will have vanished."

"So you would rather ride west without any plan at all," said Chet. "You understand, I hope, why I see little wisdom in that."

"We will devise our plan upon the road," said Niya. "That is how commanders in the field are supposed to act."

Chet seemed to sense that he was losing, for his frustration grew more plain with every word. "But you do not even know where you are going," he said, spreading his hands into the empty air. "This fortress you speak of could be anywhere."

Loren looked to Annis. The girl had remained silent through the whole argument, staring into her own lap. "Annis."

The girl jumped. "What?"

"You know where it is."

"I . . ." Annis' eyes went wide, and she looked around at them. "I do not know *precisely* where it is. Yet there is—that is, when I was with Kal, and we studied the maps and the records, there was a place. Something I took note of. It *was* to the west of here, and it was like—like a sort of hole, but for coin. No roads passed through it. There were no cities, only mountains. Yet all around it, numbers disappeared from ledgers without explanation. Garrisons marched from fortresses to reinforce some other stronghold, but that place was never named. Food and other supplies—all went missing. And I have heard the name of Yewamba before. It was spoken in the halls of my family. It is a place we called home in the past, a long-abandoned fortress of great power."

At the words *long-abandoned fortress,* Loren felt her hackles rise. She saw the image from her dream again: Damaris standing in a vast cavern, bathed in a single pool of light. Quickly she pushed the image away.

Chet was at a loss for a moment. But he recovered, planting a hand on the table and shaking his head. "No. This is madness, all of it. You made a vow to Kal. Will you break it?"

"I vowed that I would take no action against our target in Dahab," said Loren. "And I will obey that vow to the letter."

"You know that is not what he meant."

"I must agree with Chet," said Weath. "Riding out on our own seems foolhardy."

"It is," said Loren. "And I will not ask you to come with me. I am no fool. I know this goes directly against Kal's wishes. You risk his wrath if you accompany me. Neither, Chet, would I ask you to follow me into darkness and danger. I did not do so in Northwood, and I will not now. But I am going to Yewamba. Always I have done what I thought was best. Sometimes that brought great sorrow, and not just for myself. But it is also the only reason we know as much as we know. It is the reason the High King is prepared to fight this war in the first place. Before we left the Seat, she told me that the nine kingdoms were more important than any of us. I still believe that. And this is what I must do to preserve them—and to mete out justice for a friend who fell before his time. Were Jordel here, I think he would do the same."

That cast most of them into silence. But Chet glared into his lap and shook his head. "You speak of justice, but I hear revenge behind your words."

"Then go to Ammon," said Loren. "Indeed, I would feel better if you did. There is no doubt that I ride upon the more dangerous path. Turn your road from mine, and take the children with you."

"Not likely," said Gem. "I go where you go, as I have always done. Well, since we met."

"I will not turn away either," said Annis quietly. "I cannot say with honesty that this is a wise course. But I think . . . I think it is the right one, and I must follow it. For the same reason I came with you this far already. Though I do not know what help I will be."

"You have been tremendous help already," said Loren. "We would not even know where we were going, were it not for you. Do you see? Wit above might."

Annis smiled at her. And beside the girl, Chet shook his head and sighed, even as his scowl deepened.

"Of course I will not abandon you now, Loren," he murmured. "Not ever, not while I draw breath. But my fear is not for myself, nor for the others. It is for you, Loren. I do not wish to follow you only to witness your doom."

Weath looked as though she wished to say a great deal more. But when she gave Niya a searching look, the captain's expression remained unmoved.

"Very well," said Weath, lowering her gaze. "I will send the others out for supplies. We can be ready to ride by first light."

TWENTY-EIGHT

THEY SLIPPED THROUGH THE CITY'S GATE IN A GREY MORNING, PASSING through a wet chill that hung in the air but did not fall as rain. The guards at the gate seemed more attentive than they had before. Loren guessed the uproar at the Yerrin manors had something to do with that. But she traded her black cloak for a plain brown one, and they rode out in twos and threes, the way they had entered the city, and no one marked their passing.

Just out of sight of the city walls, they sent Jormund away to ride east. Loren gave him his instructions and bid him farewell, a little apart from the others.

"This holds all of the information we were able to gather," she said, placing a scroll in his hands. She had dictated the message upon it to Gem. "It also tells him that we ride west for Yewamba. He will no doubt be angry. You must make it clear to him that it was my decision, and that you had nothing to do with it."

Jormund gave her a wry smile. "Do you think I would distance myself from you so? I will tell him it was my counsel that sent you west, and that I begged to come with you."

Loren smiled at that. "I wish that you could ride with us. We shall miss your sword."

"I hope you do not need it. Fare well, Nightblade."

"Fare well."

He bade good-bye to the rest of the party and then mounted to ride away. Loren and the others watched until he was out of sight, and then they rode west.

From the first day they left Dahab behind them, they noticed a change. Winter's storms no longer battered them as they had before, and while the air was still frigid, at least it was free from rain. The roads west of Dahab were nowhere near so ill-kept as the ones to the east, so their journey was almost pleasant. The month of Martis was nearly past, and winter was just beginning to give way to spring.

When they made camp on the first day, Loren waited until Chet had gone to fetch firewood, and then she went to Niya. "You did something in the manor that I meant to ask you about."

Niya smirked at her. "I did, and I will do it again. Or more, if you but give me half a chance and half an hour."

Loren's cheeks flamed. "Not that. I meant the knife. You threw it at Hewal—just as you did the first time we faced him. You are very good with it."

"As I said, deception and knives are my two great loves. But still you have asked me no question."

"Can you teach me? To throw a knife like that, I mean."

Niya cocked her head slightly. "I thought you were against killing."

"I am. But a knife may be used for other things than death, even when thrown. Or has it escaped your notice that you yourself have not killed Hewal with it?"

That forced a bark of laughter. "It was not for lack of intent, I assure you. But very well. I can teach you to throw, if you wish to learn a fancy trick to entertain your friends. Only you must promise me something."

Loren frowned and spoke in a low murmur. "I will not . . . that is, I will not do again the thing you made me do in Dahab. I should not have done it the once."

"Made you do?" said Niya, smiling. She dropped her voice to a murmur as well, as though respecting Loren's wish for secrecy, but it only made her tone more inviting, more electric. "I have given and received enough kisses that I know when a woman is enjoying herself."

Once again, crimson rushed into Loren's face. "If you do not wish to teach me to throw, then just say so."

She turned to leave, but Niya put a hand on her arm, gently holding her in place. "Calm yourself, Nightblade. I did not say anything of the sort, and that was not the promise I meant to extract from you—though I find it interesting that your thoughts went there so quickly. Here is your vow: that you will never throw a knife at me."

That took Loren aback, and she frowned. "Of course not. Why would I?"

Niya grinned. "I am sure I will give you reason. But no, it is only something I was made to promise by the person who taught me."

Loren allowed herself a tiny smile at that. She supposed such a tradition was no evil thing. "Then I give you my word, and easily."

The Mystic led her to a nearby tree and produced a hunting knife from her belt. "You must hold the knife by whichever end is lightest. The weight on the other end will give your throw power. Here."

She placed the blade into Loren's hand, and Loren felt the weight of it. "I would hold this one by the hilt." *But my dagger, I would hold by the blade,* she thought. Her fingers wrapped around Niya's knife.

"Just so, but you must hold it differently," said Niya. She pried Loren's fingers apart—Loren did not miss the heat of the woman's skin upon her own—and adjusted the grip. "Hold it with only your thumb and the first two fingers—three, if the knife is larger. The hardest part is ensuring that the knife does not spin in the air, so that the blade strikes your target, and not the hilt. Do your best, but do not be surprised if it does not work."

Loren drew back and threw. The blade wobbled slightly, but it sped true, and the first finger's breadth of it sank into the bark of the tree. Niya drew back, eyes wide with astonishment.

"It comes to you naturally. And to think, in Ammon you doubted my skills as a teacher."

An urge gripped her, and Loren obeyed it without thinking. She looked the Mystic in the eyes and smiled. "Mayhap in Ammon I was distracted from the lesson."

Niya's smile turned feral. "And what, I wonder, distracted you?"

They paused like that for a moment. Then Loren shook her head and took a step back. "I should not have said that. I did not mean to be untoward."

"I know what you meant, girl. I have told you before, I know when a woman is enjoying herself." Niya went to the tree and removed her knife before walking off. Without looking back, she called over her shoulder, "You have talent, but you need practice to turn that into skill. Use your hunting knife."

Loren watched her go until she felt someone's gaze upon her. She turned quickly, expecting to find Chet. But it was only Gem, watching her with a curious expression.

"It seems I have some ability when it comes to throwing knives," said Loren.

"I have always wanted to learn to do it," said Gem. "Mayhap you can teach me."

Loren arched an eyebrow. "Me? Niya should instruct you. She is a master at it."

Gem looked the way the Mystic had gone. "I suppose so, but she is . . . an intimidating woman. I do not think she likes me, and would rather learn from you in any case."

"It would be my honor—only let me practice a bit myself, so that I know better how to instruct you."

She threw the knife for an hour before she went to sleep that night. When she stood her watch in the early morning hours, she practiced with her dagger instead of the hunting knife, for no one was awake to see it. Not every throw was as true as her first, but she found herself getting better and better at it. She kept practicing as the days passed, and very soon she could easily land her throw within a hand's breadth of the spot she aimed for.

It was good to have the distraction, for the road was otherwise monotonous. It gave her something to do when they stopped to eat, or to make camp for the night. Though the road was far easier than the one they had taken to Dahab, it was not well traveled, and they would sometimes go two or more days without seeing someone passing by. When they did, they avoided speaking, or giving any greeting more than a nod.

The landscape they traveled was fair enough, Loren supposed, but she preferred the drier, taller trees of the Birchwood to the jungled land they rode through now. The vegetation always seemed damp, and the trees were knotted with great vines that clutched their trunks as if to strangle them. When they did come upon clear, green lands, it felt as if the air grew lighter, and they drank it in with deep breaths. But always the road took them back into the jungle again, where they would spend days at a time beneath a canopy of leaves so thick that they never saw the sun.

They came often upon smaller side roads that led off deeper into the jungle. Many were marked on their maps, and ran in the same direction they traveled. But when Shiun suggested they use those roads, Niya shook her head.

"It is no use trying to use back ways and lesser-known paths," she said. "Now more than ever we require speed. If we can reach Yewamba fast enough, Hewal will not have enough time to warn Damaris of our coming."

"Could he not remain in bird form, and fly there in only a few days?" said Loren.

"I do not think he is strong enough for that," said Weath. "To hold a shape other than their own, a weremage must keep their concentration, and the greater their change, the harder it becomes. Changing his form so that he looked like another person would be one thing. That requires only the smallest use of power, and many weremages learn to hold such a transformation even as they sleep. But it would be a powerful weremage indeed who could maintain the form of a bird, or any beast, for days on end. And if Hewal were so strong in his magic, he would likely have turned into something far more fearsome than a bear when last we fought him."

"How do you know these things?" said Gem, eyes alight with curiosity. "I thought you were an alchemist."

"Weremagic and alchemy are mirrors of each other," said Weath. "Indeed, they can sense each other, so that I can tell when a spell of either branch is used near me, unless the wizard has learned to conceal it."

"Can they do so?" said Annis, arching an eyebrow. "I have never heard of this."

"Magic has many secrets," said Weath, shrugging. "The children of merchants rarely learn them unless they are wizards themselves, for what would be the purpose? As for your question—yes, a wizard may conceal their spells after much practice—and the smaller the spell, the easier to hide it."

"I am surprised to hear you call them alchemy and weremagic," said Loren. "Xain insisted the branches had different names. He called himself an elementalist."

"He is a noble," chuckled Weath. "I am a farmer's daughter from

Dorsea. I never cared for the frivolities that the Academy tried to force upon the students."

Loren looked at her again, raising a brow in surprise. She had met few enough Dorseans, other than the taciturn villagers they had met for one terrible night as they fled east across that kingdom. They had been reserved and easily offended, much like the people in tales Loren had heard of Dorseans all her life. But Weath was kind and generous to the point of fault, and always the one to calm tensions among the party. She was curious if Weath knew that Loren was from Selvan, and for the first time she found herself wondering if Dorseans grew up with tales of Selvan's people as well.

The days passed quickly, if quietly, for the jungle sometimes made them nervous to speak too much. It was as though the verdant growth itself was listening to them, and was none too pleased by what it heard. The wildlife was as colorful as the vegetation. They learned from Uzo that they must not touch any of the brightly-colored frogs, for some of them had poison in their skin. Most snakes, too, were venomous. In fact it seemed that so many animals in this place were venomous that Loren wondered what people ate.

But while the creatures around them bore little resemblance to the animals of her home, they were often breathtaking in their beauty. Uzo, however, hardly spared them a second glance. Loren soon realized that to him, these were as commonplace as starlings in the Birchwood. She wondered if he had ever been to one of the southern forests, and if so, whether the squirrels and rabbits were as wondrous to him as these animals were to her.

"I think we are upon the right road," said Gem, when nearly a week of travel had passed. Some of the others gave him odd looks. He grinned at them from his seat beside Loren. "The sky itself has stopped hampering our journey. Why else would it spare us its storms, except as a sign that we are going where we are meant to go?"

That drew a chuckle from most of them. Even Uzo smiled, though he often seemed annoyed by Gem's antics and never-ending optimism. "This journey has taught me that Elves are real. I suppose I can believe in your signs and portents as well."

Gem did not stop beaming at that for the rest of the day.

But though the mood of most of the party had risen considerably,

Chet's only grew worse the farther they rode. He would not acknowledge Niya at all unless absolutely necessary, and then he would say only one or two words at a time. He was curt with the rest of them as well, and would often make snide remarks. When asked to help gather firewood, or hunt, he would sometimes mutter, "We would not need to do so if we were riding in the right direction." When they made camp each night, he made a point of sleeping out of Loren's reach within their tent.

For the first several days she bore it silently, for she thought his ill mood might fade after a time. Gem kept trying to entice him into conversation, though Chet never seemed willing. Then, on the tenth day of their ride, Gem asked curiously why Chet and Loren and Shiun did not keep their bows strung while they rode.

"Because we know how bows work," snapped Chet. "And we do not want to break ours. If you wish to learn about archery, find an instructor."

Gem balked. Loren fixed Chet with a steely glare, and then looked over her shoulder at the boy. "Gem, ride with Annis for a while. I must ask Shiun a question about the road ahead. Chet, come with me."

Chet had gone sullen. He could no doubt sense her anger, and must have known this was no ride for pleasure. "She is not far ahead," he said lamely.

"Come," she said, and nudged Midnight into a canter. She heard the hoofbeats of his horse behind her a moment later.

When they were out of sight of the others, she turned from the road down a side path. It led up a hill, and Loren slowed to a walk. He followed behind her silently, for which she was grateful—if he had made some snide remark about their course, she might have struck him. The path soon took them up to a crest that looked over flatlands to the north, running to a great lake in the far distance. She stopped and turned Midnight so that they faced each other.

"You must stop undermining this mission."

"It is a fool's errand. It is not safe, Loren."

"Of course it is not safe," she said angrily. "Where is safety to be found in this time? Nowhere in Underrealm, that is for certain."

"So your intent, then, is to seek danger? How does that seem a wise course?"

"My intent is to help stop this war. Unless the High King and those who serve her stop the Necromancer—"

"Then let the High King stop them," said Chet. "You have done enough."

"Nothing is enough until the danger has passed," said Loren, shaking her head. "The threat only grows."

"And so does the threat to *you*," said Chet. "I could bear it when you entered Enalyn's service, for if you were determined to join in this battle, it seemed better to have the power of the Seat at your back. I thought you would be safer in Ammon, far from all the battles that have yet been fought. But this . . . this is not just foolish, it is foolhardy beyond reckoning."

"You thought," said Loren, rolling her eyes. "When will you learn that your thoughts are your own? They are not mine. I never planned to seek safety."

"Why did you even leave the forest, then?" said Chet, shouting now. He nudged his horse forwards so that they were within arm's reach of each other. "You *said* you left because of your parents. They are gone now, Loren. You can do anything you want to—"

"Of course I can do anything I want!" she cried. "I *always* could, without any need for your permission. And this is the life I choose."

Chet went stock still. He stared at her for a long while as she sat there, her shoulders heaving, barely restraining the urge to throw him from his saddle and pummel his foolish head. And in the silence, Loren saw the dawning realization in his eyes. It was the look of a man who had been speaking to someone in a mask, only to have the mask ripped away and the person beneath look nothing like he thought.

"It is," he said, his voice suddenly small. "It *is* what you choose."

And suddenly Loren felt that she, too, saw someone entirely new to her. In her eyes, Chet again became the young boy who had made her promise to dance with him, the boy who had followed her with doe's eyes around their village. She did not know what she had seen him as only a moment before. That image of him was wiped away so completely that it was as though it had never existed, and now he was little more than a child again.

Of course he is a child, she thought. *You both are, if you would only be honest with yourself.* But pride kept her from giving voice to the thought.

"Do you enjoy this, Loren?"

Her fury had burned a bit lower in the long silence, but she was still angry as she shrugged. "I—of course I do not *enjoy* it. I do not enjoy danger, or the deaths of those I love. Jordel died, and Albern, and Mag with Sten by her side. Yet that is why I can do nothing else. That is why I must go on—because they cannot. You have told me often of your plans, or at least your desires, to run away from all this. You say you want to hide away in some forgotten corner of Underrealm and let this great war pass us by, like hiding in a hollow tree against a raging storm. I can never do that, Chet."

"I thought you wanted to, once," said Chet. "I thought we both wanted to run away together."

"Because that was better than the life my parents deigned to give me. But now I could not live with myself. I could not abandon the nine kingdoms or the people I love. And that is *because* of my parents, Chet. That is what they would do—run away, look after themselves, never giving a thought to anyone else. I have roamed too far and seen too much, and I love too many. A merchant's child, a city urchin, a fallen wizard, and yes, even you, you great idiot. I love you all, and more besides, and all of you will suffer if darkness is allowed to win."

Chet looked at her a moment longer before turning away. "I cannot live my life for others. Not anymore. I want to live in safety, as long as I can, and I want you to be safe. That is all I want, Loren. I do not care for Underrealm, but only for you. The nine kingdoms mean nothing to me. Not next to a pair of green eyes."

"That is some bard's sentiment, Chet," said Loren. "It is not anything useful."

He did not answer, or even look at her. Slowly he turned his horse and rode back towards the others, leaving her alone on the hilltop.

TWENTY-NINE

THEY REACHED FELDEMAR'S WESTERN LANDS THREE DAYS LATER. ANNIS told them they were close. Loren had often consulted with her during the journey, huddling together over their map, and she had pointed out the place where she thought Yewamba must be located. As she had said, there was nothing marked there. The closest thing was a small town nearby, a place called Sarafu. It was little more than a village, but it was one of the areas from which much coin and many soldiers had vanished.

"If there is a road to Yewamba, we may find a sign of it in Sarafu," said Annis. "At the very least, the area around it will be our best hope to start looking."

They could not ride into the town, for it would not do for the Yerrins to learn that a party matching their description had come there. Instead they set up camp in the jungle an hour's walk away. They sent Uzo and Shiun into the place to buy supplies and ask after information. Hewal had never met either of them, other than during their brief fight south of Ammon. Loren hoped he would not recognize either of them by their description, if he heard any word about two strangers arriving to the town.

The Mystics returned with no information that would help. They had not asked after the fortress by name, of course, but no one in town seemed to have heard of any military movements, and they had spied no Yerrin activity at all. If the family Yerrin was indeed operating in Sarafu, they did so in secret.

They began their search the day after they arrived, splitting the party in two. Loren led Chet and Weath riding north along the foot of the mountains, while Niya took Uzo and Shiun south. They followed roads when there were roads to follow, and dove off into the countryside when there were not. Gem and Annis remained at the camp, looking after their possessions.

Once again, Loren found herself at the foot of the Greatrock Mountains. These were the northern reaches of the same range, after it turned northwest and cut across Dorsea. Here they formed Feldemar's western border, just as they formed Selvan's in the south. As they had ridden west, she had feared that the sight of the mountains might call to mind painful memories of Jordel. But these peaks were so different from the ones they had traveled together that she could hardly believe they were the same range. In the south, the peaks were tall but gentle, peaked with snow atop the grey and brown of rock and soil. In Feldemar, the jungle ran straight up the sides of the mountains to the very top, even now, in winter, and their silhouette was like a row of upraised knife blades against the sky.

The first long day's search revealed nothing, and they returned to camp defeated. Niya came back shortly after Loren, and from the slump of her shoulders Loren thought she could tell how successful they had been. But she rose from her place by the fire and went to them, regardless.

"Did you see anything?"

"Nothing," said Niya, shaking her head. "We will ride farther tomorrow."

"As will we."

And so they did. Loren led the others galloping north on the best road they could find, passing in a rush the landscape that they had searched in detail the day before. When they reached lands they had not yet searched, they slowed once more to renew their hunt. But that day proved just as fruitless as the first, and their heads hung still lower by the time they had returned to the camp. This time Niya came back first. She, too, had been unsuccessful.

They were a morose party that night. As they sat eating a meager meal around the fire, they rarely looked at each other. Niya spit a bit of gristle into the flames, and the sound was so loud that Annis jumped.

"We might think of moving the camp," said Niya.

"But which way?" said Loren. "If we move north, it may take us farther away from Yewamba—but the same is true if we move south."

"We know it is not here," said Uzo. "I say we flip the coin."

"It is fourteen days since we left Dahab," said Loren. "Surely word has reached Yewamba by now. We are giving Damaris too much time to prepare."

"And what do you suggest, Nightblade?" said Niya, raising her hands in exasperation. "If you know of a wiser course, then tell us, and we will follow it."

Loren frowned and looked into the fire. Of course she had no better idea, and they all knew it. But if they took the camp in the wrong direction, their whole mission here might end in disaster.

After a moment's silence, Weath spoke quietly. "Mayhap this is a matter best left to daylight. During the night, all roads may look dark, and choosing between them becomes more difficult."

"That seems wise," said Gem brightly, smiling at the rest of them. The smile was not returned.

Gregor stood before her.

As before, the man was giant-sized, larger even than he was in life. His hands looked as though he could crush her to a pulp between his fingers; his massive legs were like oak trunks. He was so large that the trees around him seemed dwarfish, though the tops of them still stretched over his head. Now his face was not wasted, as it had been before. And his eyes were not sunken, but smoldered with a dark light, as though he were a wizard who had eaten magestones.

"I told her to kill you," he said. His voice was not thunder now, but the roar of the ocean, the inexorable tide that in time tore down even mighty mountains.

Loren wanted to turn and flee, but her feet were rooted in place. She looked around in a panic. It was Feldemar, the very land she had been searching for the past two days. Gregor stood between two peaks, peaks that stretched impossibly far above them both, yet seemed small and insignificant next to the giant.

Then, Loren saw that they were not quite alone. Behind Gregor, making its way down a little path between the peaks, was a caravan. It was small, only three wagons—but she recognized them as belonging to Damaris, from the caravan she had led when Loren first met her. Awestruck, Loren watched as the wagons vanished one by one.

Her attention was drawn back to Gregor as the man reached into his cloak. He pulled something out, holding it up before her—and then Loren saw that it was not one thing, but three. Three small, black stones that shone in the moonlight. Magestones.

Gregor flung the stones at her, and she flinched. But in midair they twisted and turned, growing as they moved, lit from within, and when they had finished they had become the bodies of Chet, Annis, and Gem. Her friends fell lifeless at her feet. Now she could move, and she fell to her knees beside them, crying their names. Chet's throat was cut, the same as always. Gem would not attack her now, for his body was broken in a thousand places. Annis had dark bruises around her throat where she had been strangled.

Someone dragged her up by the hair.

"The knife," hissed Auntie's voice. But it was not Auntie who held her—it was Damaris, and the merchant held the same knife as before, an old, rusted, twisted thing, far below her station.

Loren woke just as the knife parted the skin of her throat.

The sound of her scream escaped her, but she came to herself just in time, and stopped it there, so that she only gave a little yelp. Her hands grasped in the darkness, but she did not strike out, did not hit Chet by accident. She only found his arm and gripped it, squeezing it tight, afraid to let go.

Chet shifted in his sleep and rolled onto his back. But he did not wake.

She lay there a while, letting her pulse slow, letting the panic and the fear seep from her, like water from a rag hung up to dry. It was somewhat of a relief to know that the aftereffects of these dreams were easing. Mayhap, in time, she would even wake without feeling the terror they always left behind.

When her pulse had stilled, she sat up and dressed herself before slipping from the tent. Outside, their little clearing was fairly well-lit, for both moons hung directly above them in the sky. She looked up at them and loosed a long breath, feeling the last of the tension leave her.

"Did you dream?"

The voice startled her. It seemed the shock of her nightmare had not entirely fled, for fear went coursing through her limbs again, making them shake. She looked across the camp to find Niya sitting against the base of a tree, on watch.

Of course it would be Niya on duty, she thought.

"I did."

Niya rose and took a step forwards. "And what did you see?"

Loren blanched. "See?"

"In your dream. I heard a brief cry. Did you not have a nightmare?" Niya was studying her face, her head cocked slightly, curious.

"I . . . yes. I did. But I cannot remember it."

"Hm."

She strode forwards, and Loren tensed, though she did not know why. But Niya went straight past her and towards the trees. Just before she vanished from sight she stopped and turned.

"Will you stand for me, while I relieve myself?"

"Yes, of course," said Loren. "I will take the watch, if you wish it. I do not think I will sleep again tonight."

Niya nodded and vanished.

Loren went to where the Mystic had been sitting and put her back against the same tree. The ground still held some of Niya's warmth, and Loren sighed.

Her thoughts returned to her dream. The peaks of the Greatrocks she knew well enough—they were visible even now, a darker black against the backdrop of stars in the sky. But the path she had seen, the two peaks in particular . . . those were sights she had not seen with her waking eyes.

She thought back to Hewal and how her dreams had shown him in Dahab. Could this be the same? Was Yewamba *in* the mountains themselves? If so, she was correct in her reluctance to move the camp, for they would not find the fortress in the lands surrounding the Greatrocks.

Niya soon returned and entered her tent without a word. Loren stood watch the rest of the night, and when dawn came, she waited impatiently for everyone to rise.

"I have had a thought," she said. "We should not move the camp."

"What, then?" said Niya.

"I wonder if we have been looking in the right place. We have been searching the lands near the mountains. But those lands are open to all, even casual passersby. If Yewamba had been built in such a place, surely it could not have escaped notice all these years. It would be on the maps. But it is not. What if it is *in* the mountains?" Loren looked at Annis and Gem. "We know full well how cleverly a stronghold can be concealed in such a way."

Their expressions grew solemn, and Loren knew they were thinking of the Shade stronghold where Jordel had met his end.

Niya looked to Shiun. The scout shrugged. "It is possible. We could easily have missed a path into the mountains in our searching, for we did not look for such a thing."

"It would make sense," Annis interjected. "I told you that much coin and many supplies had vanished in this area, enough for a mighty stronghold indeed. I had been wondering how so large a place could escape notice of the High King's mapmakers."

With a sigh, Niya shrugged. "Very well. It seems as good a guess as any."

They ate hastily after that. Loren could feel it in all of them—a sense of nearing the end of their journey, that this time, surely, they would find what they sought. They mounted their horses and rode off. But this time they rode together, making as far west as they could, and did not split into two groups until they had reached the feet of the mountains. Then they went in the same groups of three as they had the past two days.

This time the going was far slower, for they had to ride around and over ridges, and the land itself seemed to try to halt their progress. Soon Loren began to grow frustrated, and with her frustration came doubts. This was taking more than three times as long. What if it was all a waste of time? What if another day went by, and they were no closer to their goal? That was only another day for Damaris to prepare for their coming, or mayhap flee Yewamba before they arrived.

She looked up and froze. Her hands jerked on the reins, and Midnight came to a sudden stop. Chet and Weath wheeled around, staring at her.

"What is it?" said Chet.

But Loren could not take her eyes from the mountain peaks. There were two of them, and she recognized them. She had seen them the night before, in her dream.

"Weath, ride south," she said. "Tell Niya to come at once."

Chet and Weath looked at each other, and then they followed Loren's gaze.

"What is it?" said Chet again.

"I am not certain."

Weath hesitated, choosing her words carefully. "Then what should I tell Niya, when I find her?"

"Tell her I have found something. Bring her to the foot of those two peaks there."

She showed Weath, and then the Mystic rode away south. She and Chet pressed on ahead.

"Did you see it?" said Chet. "In a dream?"

"Yes," said Loren. "It came to me last night."

His brows rose. "I did not hear you."

"They are growing less terrible." *At least after I wake,* she thought.

They soon reached the place, and Loren saw what she had already known they would find there: a small wagon trail that vanished between the foot of the mountains. She could almost imagine the caravan wagons making their way into the Greatrocks—but then her imagination conjured Gregor before her, and she shuddered, feeling the blood drain from her face.

"Are you all right?" said Chet.

"Yes," she said quietly. "We should get out of sight and wait for the others."

They took the horses off into the trees, but before they did so, Loren turned to look at where the trail ran off in the other direction. At once she saw the reason why they had not spotted the trail in the last two days' search: it ended abruptly just before a small gap in a ridge. It was natural, but as perfect for concealment as if it had been built by human hands. On the other side of the wall, she did not doubt that the trail resumed—but if they had seen it from there, they would only have seen a trail that led to a flat wall, and would not have tried to follow it.

They dismounted and tied their horses to a tree out of sight of the path. There they sat in silence as they studied the peaks, fixing themselves a light lunch. Loren thought of taking her bow and trying to hunt, but she did not wish to be out of sight if Niya and the others should return.

Some time after midday, there came a steady *clop-clop* of horses' hooves through the trees. Loren stepped into the open and hailed them as soon as they came into sight. They gathered around her on the path, looking over the peaks and the faint trail that led between them.

"A fortunate find," said Niya. She looked at Loren and arched an eyebrow. "I find it incredible that you should have stumbled upon this by chance."

Loren kept her expression carefully neutral. "What other explanation is there?"

Niya's nostrils flared, and she looked away.

"You think this is the way to Yewamba?" said Uzo. "That seems a narrow track to supply a fortress as large as the Yerrin girl made it sound."

"We have found no better sign," said Loren. "Let us investigate it."

"Lead the way, Shiun," said Niya. "And be wary. If we are indeed upon the right trail, there will be guards before long, if they have not seen us already."

"We should proceed on foot," said Shiun. "For the noise, and so that we may pass more easily between the trees."

Niya nodded and dismounted, and the rest of them followed suit, tying the horses in a place of concealment from the road. Then Shiun went on ahead of them, running at a half-trot into the trees, where she disappeared. Loren and Chet strung their bows, and the rest of them set off after her at a slower pace.

"It is fortunate after all that we did not move the camp," said Niya, giving Loren a careful look.

"Fortunate indeed," said Loren, not returning her gaze.

Not even an hour passed before Shiun returned to them, stepping out from behind a trunk as though she had appeared from thin air. The party came to a halt, and Niya's hand went to the hilt of her sword.

"There are guards," said Shiun. "They are many, and they are Yerrins."

Loren and Niya went on ahead with her. She took them silently through the trees, and Loren made very sure to place her feet just as Shiun did—she had some gift with woodcraft and stealth, but Shiun was a master of it. They stopped, and the scout pointed to the top of a ridge on their right. Loren saw two little bumps, and as they watched for a moment, one of them moved.

"Two up there," said Shiun. "And three there."

She pointed back down the slope they were on, towards the path, which curled and curved its way through the jungle. A motion in the trees beside the path caught Loren's eye, and she saw three more figures. They wore green cloaks—not the light green of Yerrin merchants, but a deep green meant to blend into the jungle.

"Something is close by, that is certain," said Niya.

"There are none higher up the ridge we stand upon," said Shiun. "We can press on that way."

They followed the ground up until they had almost emerged from the trees and into the daylight. But Shiun stopped them, keeping them hidden, and they followed the course of the ridge as it ran farther west. Soon they had passed the guards on the opposite ridge. Below them and ahead of them, they saw that the path took a long turn around the spurs of the mountain that stretched down on either side of it.

Ahead of them, the sun had neared the peaks. Soon it would be dark, and Loren was growing somewhat impatient. But she did not say anything, for who knew if other guards might lurk in the jungle around them?

At last, just as the sun began to sink out of sight, they rounded the spur to follow the path's curve. And there, at last, they found what they were looking for.

They walked upon the foot of a mountain, but a smaller peak stood pressed up against it, and that peak ended in a flat top. Within the mountain itself was built a mighty stronghold that Loren knew at once must be Yewamba.

It stretched out towards them into a great point, like the prow of a ship or the head of an arrow, and all along the top of it ran a great wall. The land that sloped up towards the fortress was rocky and treacherous, and only a single road had been built leading up. From where they stood, they could see arrow slits in the walls of the stronghold as well as in the slopes. Yewamba had been hollowed from the rock, descending into the earth, so that the mountain was the fortress and the fortress, the mountain.

The image of a wide cavern flashed into Loren's mind, the cavern where she had seen Damaris in her dream. She suppressed a shiver.

"Yewamba," said Niya, her voice a fierce rasp.

Loren nodded. "If Damaris of the family Yerrin is anywhere in Underrealm, she is here."

THIRTY

THEY DID NOT SPEAK OF WHAT THEY HAD SEEN WHILE THEY MADE their way back out of the valley, for they did not know for certain if there were any more guards around. It was a long walk, made longer by the fact that the sun had now gone down and they had to pick their way through the darkness. Loren's mind raced all the while, wondering what they should do. When she had first heard of Yewamba, she had not imagined it would be so grand a place, so impregnable. The thought of trying to conquer the fortress with only six of them—eight, if they counted Gem and Annis—now seemed laughable. But what was their alternative? Returning to Ammon? Kal would be furious with her, and she would not even have accomplished what she came here to do, which was the only thing that might stay his wrath now.

At last they reached the place where Chet and the others waited for them. They all came forwards and gathered in a group, but Loren held up a hand to forestall their questions.

"There will be time enough to tell you what we saw, but now we must return to camp. Gem and Annis are likely worried sick, and we should not leave them alone overnight in any case."

And she would not say another word until they had all mounted their horses and begun to ride east. Shiun had them remain quiet until they were out of the valley mouth and back near the main road again, but then Chet turned to Loren.

"Did you find Yewamba?"

"Yes," said Loren. The others looked to her with interest. "It is a mighty fortress, and from what we could tell, it is well garrisoned. Even if Kal brought all the Mystics in Ammon, I doubt he could take it by force."

Niya looked at her sharply. "It is good, then, that we mean to use subterfuge instead."

"I do not see how," said Loren.

"Then you intend to give up?" said Niya. "We have come too far for that."

Loren shook her head. "Let us discuss this when we have returned, and we can think upon it properly."

"Then ride faster." Niya obeyed her own command at once, savagely nudging her horse into a canter in the moonslight.

Gem and Annis came to meet them with palpable relief when they reached the camp at last. "We were worried," said Annis. "We feared you had been discovered and taken."

"I am glad to say we were not," said Chet. "Not yet, at any rate, though I think Niya has some mad scheme to ensure that is how we meet our end."

"Do not make snide comments at me, boy," snarled Niya. "If you have counsel to give, then let us hear it."

"Enough," said Loren. "All will be heard in turn."

They sat around the fire Gem and Annis had built. Loren and Niya described Yewamba, with Shiun interjecting every so often with some description of the place and the guards placed around it. When they had finished, Chet spread his hands.

"It seems plain to me that there is little hope of entering the fortress," he said. "We should return to Ammon and let Kal deal with it."

"I do not doubt that he will already have sent a host this way," said Loren. "Jormund will have reached him by now, and Kal will have wasted no time assembling his forces. But it is as I said before: even all the Mystics at his command cannot hope to besiege the place, not without tremendous loss."

"But neither can we hope to conquer it on our own," said Chet.

"We do not need to conquer the fortress," said Niya. "We only need to capture Damaris. That is why we have come all this way. Loren and I have proven our worth already. The two of us can drag this merchant from her hole."

Loren frowned as she looked into the fire. It was possible, she supposed. But Yewamba was not the Golden Manor. It was not in the city, for one thing. Escape would not be so easy. And neither would their entry, for she had no faintest idea how to sneak into the place. There were no rooftops for Gem to lead them across.

"We cannot pass the main gate without detection," she said slowly. "That is the first obstacle."

"You speak as though this is something you are considering," said Chet, incredulous. "Do not tell me you have begun to agree with this mad course."

But Niya ignored him and nodded eagerly at Loren. "Shiun can scout the place tomorrow. She can find us a back entrance. The stronghold is built into a mountain—there must be more than one way in, even if we must tunnel through the rock."

"I could help you there with magic," said Weath. "But I cannot withhold my own concerns. Even once we gain entry, it seems to me that we have but a slim chance of success. Damaris will be well guarded, and extracting her will be no easy task."

"Who agreed to come because they thought this would be easy?" snapped Niya. "If you wish to turn back once you have gotten us inside the stronghold, I will not stop you. The Nightblade and I can manage on our own."

"You advocate for madness," said Chet. "The wisest course would be to make for Ammon. At the least we should remain here, waiting for Kal's arrival, and watch the stronghold in case Damaris should try to escape it."

That did seem wise to Loren, and for a moment her heart leaped. It was safer, certainly, and she could not deny the pit of fear that formed in her stomach at the thought of sneaking into Yewamba. But Niya shook her head scornfully.

"There must be other ways out of Yewamba, just as there are other ways in," she said. "If Damaris learns that a host from Ammon has arrived in the area, doubtless there is some tunnel in the mountains that she can use to evade it. Our only hope is taking her by surprise."

"Hope," scoffed Chet. "I do not see hope in any part of this."

"Do you not? Then let me explain it more clearly, *boy*. Underrealm stands on the brink of war. Damaris' capture and execution could quell the flames of rebellion. The High King could declare open war tomorrow. She may have done so already, and word of it has not reached us yet. But we here, now, just we six, can put an end to it."

Niya's words awoke a flame in Loren's heart. She remembered what Enalyn had told her upon the Seat: that the preservation of the nine kingdoms was the greatest purpose there was. Niya spoke the truth now; ending Damaris' string of crimes could help bring that about. Loren could do it. And if Niya guessed correctly that Damaris had a means of escape, Loren might be the only one who could.

But more than that, she could end the nightmares, or at least remove the power of them. Mayhap the cavern from her dreams awaited her in Yewamba. Mayhap Gregor was there, too. But if they succeeded, if Damaris was captured and brought before the King's law, Loren need no longer fear the visions that came in her sleep. For a moment her mind quailed at the thought of Chet's corpse, and the corpses of Annis and Gem. But she had seen them die in Dahab as well, and that had not come to pass.

You do not see the future, she told herself once again. *And you were a self-important fool if you ever believed it so.*

"We must do it," she said quietly.

They all stopped and looked at her. Chet's expression fell into despair, and she knew he could see her determination.

"If there is more than a fool's hope of success, we must try," she went on. "Niya is right. All of Underrealm is papyrus awaiting only an ember to ignite it. We can douse the flames before they erupt. That is the duty of the Mystic Order, and it is my duty as the Nightblade."

"But we cannot do it on our own," said Chet. "Kal's force—"

"Is not enough," said Loren. "And even if it were, how long would it take? If he set out from Ammon with his whole host the very day that Jormund reached him, still the march would take more than a month. It might take two. Then they would lay siege to Yewamba. Another two months. Mayhap more. The place looked as though a dozen could repel an army for a year."

"It would become a symbol for the traitors," said Weath quietly. She stared into her hands, her shoulders slumped, as though she had just realized a terrible truth. "Our mission, our true mission, would be a failure, for it would only drag the war on."

"Yet if we succeed, we few?" said Loren. "What if the tale should spread throughout Underrealm that one small band of the High King's spies captured Damaris from her impregnable home and brought her to justice? What traitor would dare to stand against the crown then?"

The camp was silent. The answer was obvious to them all.

Niya's bright teeth shone in the firelight. "Then we are agreed. Loren and I will infiltrate Yewamba and bring Damaris forth. Once we have escaped with her, the rest of you—"

"No," said Chet.

"Chet—" Loren gave him a warning look.

"Let me speak," he said sharply. "I know—or I have learned, on our journeys—that you will not be swayed once you have decided something, Loren. But in some matters, I will not change my mind either. If you are determined to do this, I am coming with you."

"And I," said Gem at once. He beamed at Uzo as though he expected the young man to chime in with agreement. Uzo raised his brows and remained silent.

Annis gave a nervous titter of laughter. "I hope it is understood by all when I do not volunteer, for I would only get in the way."

"Of course, Annis," said Loren. "And as for Gem, and Chet, I will not deny that a part of me wants to forbid you to go. Your lives are dearer to me than my own. But I cannot command you to remain behind in good conscience, when you have urged me so strongly not to go in the first place."

"Chet urged you, you mean," muttered Gem, so quiet that Loren barely heard it.

But Niya shook her head. "That is unwise, Loren. If we should be caught in the fortress, these boys will not keep us from death. We should not risk any more lives than we must."

"You speak as though I am yours to command," said Chet. "I am not. Nor am I yours, Loren. I obey only myself, and if you do not wish for me to come with you, you shall have to tie me to a tree."

"Do not tempt me, boy," growled Niya.

Loren glared at her. "Chet speaks the truth. He is no Mystic, and so he is not yours to command."

Niya drew back, agape. "You cannot tell me you wish to endanger him."

"My wish is not important," said Loren. "I know him well enough to know that he will not hamper the success of our mission, and so if he wishes to come, he can. Or am I no longer in command?"

The Mystic's nostrils flared, and her chest heaved with quick, angry breaths. When she spoke, the words came terse and angry. "Very well, Nightblade. But might I have a word alone?"

Without waiting for an answer, she stood and walked away from the campfire. Chet watched her go, still frowning.

"You do not need to go with her," he said.

"We gain nothing by being angry and divided," said Loren. "If I can soothe her temper, it will be better for us all."

So saying, she rose and went off in the direction Niya had gone. She found her a ways off, when the fire had receded to little more than a glow in the distance. Niya was pacing back and forth before a wide mahogany tree, and when she saw Loren approaching she slammed a fist into the side of it.

"You let that boy sway your mind too easily," she said. "Few appreciate a good lover more than I. But it is a girl, and not a woman, who makes decisions with her loins instead of her head."

Fury seized Loren, and she spoke without thought. "Is that so? I think you have done nothing else since we first met."

Niya stopped dead, eyes narrowing and fists clenching at her sides. For a moment, Loren was afraid to move. She half thought that Niya meant to attack her. But then a smile split Niya's scowl, and she snickered.

"Mayhap you speak fairly," she said. "I can admit to my own distraction. But when it comes to our mission, I put such thoughts aside. I worry that you have not learned to do so."

"And I grow tired of hearing that," said Loren. "You, Chet, Kal—it seems everyone thinks I am a little girl, swaying this way and that like a willow in a gale. Just because I was silent while all gave counsel does not mean I was waiting to find something to agree with. I listened, and when I came to my own decision, I gave it."

Niya studied her for a moment. Then she took a step closer, her demeanor changing entirely. Loren no longer feared the woman's temper, but grew nervous for an entirely different reason.

"I had not thought of that," said Niya softly. "And it was wrong of me. I did not give you enough credit. You *are* young, and sometimes I forget that an old soul lurks behind those eyes."

The Mystic reached up and brushed away a lock of Loren's hair. Loren fought to keep her knees from shaking. "I accept your apology," she said, keeping her tone reserved.

"For a long while now, I have sought to be entrusted with a command," said Niya. "Now that one has been given to me, even one so small, I suppose I sometimes forget you are the one in charge here. I was a fool to call you a little girl. You are a woman grown, of course—that is why I cannot stop desiring you."

"Yet you should stop, as I have told you often enough before." Loren tried to sound indignant, but she could not even speak forcefully enough to convince herself. "At least you should make up your mind about it—I feel as though one moment you scorn me, and the next you whisper honeyed words."

"That is because the distance between here and Dahab has increased both my impatience and my hunger."

"It has not increased mine."

"That is a lie."

They both knew it was true. Niya took another step forwards, so that they were almost touching. They were out of sight of the camp. Loren knew no one would come to disturb them. Almost she surrendered to her instincts; almost she reached out for the woman. She even lifted her hands to do it.

And then at the last moment she regained control. She put her hands on Niya's shoulders instead, gently pushing her away.

"I love Chet," she said. "You must stop this."

"Why?" said Niya. She cupped Loren's cheek. "Neither of us wants me to."

"Because you are trying to make me do something that I know I would regret. He has suffered enough because of me. I will not cause him more pain."

"Then say nothing of it to him," said Niya. "I will not."

But those words doused the fire in Loren at last, and she reached up to pull Niya's hand away. "No. That is not who I am. I value honor."

Niya scowled. "So says the former thief."

"Former," said Loren. "And even then, I never meant to steal anyone's affection."

"If that were true, then you would never have looked at me the way you did when we met," said Niya. She pushed past Loren and made for the camp. It was a long while before Loren's heart had stilled enough that she could follow.

THIRTY-ONE

THE NEXT DAY THEY SENT SHIUN BACK INTO THE MOUNTAINS TO SCOUT Yewamba and see if she could find another route inside. The rest did not wait idly, but moved the camp. They took themselves west, across the main road and into the jungle at the mouth of the valley. There was a sort of cleft in the mountains there, where behind a rise there was a wide clearing. There they erected their tents once more, though Niya commanded them to light no fires.

Shortly after midday, Shiun returned with good news. "There is a path," she said. "It runs up the back side of the mountain, and it is perilous. The last part cannot be climbed without Weath. But it will bring us straight to the top of the walls, and from there we can enter the stronghold with ease."

"That is our party, then," said Loren. "All but Annis and Uzo, who will stay to guard the camp."

"And happily enough," said Uzo. "If you succeed, I confess I will be jealous of the glory you will have earned yourselves. But I have never found anything onerous about guard duty, especially when the alternative is to thrust my head between the very jaws of death."

Loren smirked, but the expression quickly died. "If we do not succeed, you must return to Ammon as swiftly as you can. Take Annis with you, and keep her safe. Her information about the stronghold will be of immense help to Kal."

Uzo nodded. "Of course. And . . . I should say, in case I do not get another chance, that I am sorry if I have been coarse with you during the journey. I thought I rode with a young girl who had been raised above her station by fortune alone. I see now that I traveled beside a brave warrior instead."

She flushed and shook her head. "No warrior, but only a spy. As luck would have it, however, that is just what was required. They say that even a dull knife is better for cutting than a golden spoon."

His teeth flashed in a smile. "They do not say that in this kingdom, but it is true enough."

Their meal that night was a somber affair, made more so because they could not cook and so had to eat the salted rations from their packs, which had begun to run low.

"If we return, you and I should go hunting," Loren told Chet. "It will make our journey to Ammon much easier."

Chet looked at her oddly. "You say 'if.' Are you that doubtful we shall come back?"

She shook her head at once. "Of course not. I only meant . . . I was not thinking."

He looked away and did not answer.

Uzo volunteered to stand watch the whole night, since he would be able to sleep the next day while the rest of them could not. Loren was in the midst of readying for bed, and wondering how she would be able to sleep, when Annis approached her.

"Loren," she said quietly. "Might I speak with you?"

"Of course. What is it?"

Annis looked around the camp, her gaze lingering longest on Gem. "Alone?"

Loren frowned, but she let herself be led off away from the camp. Annis took her out through the cleft in the mountain, into the open jungle and to a small stream that ran south not far away from the main road. The sun had long passed from sight behind the mountains that loomed over them, but its light still filled the sky. Here in the foothills, they had a clear view of the land to the east, and just near the horizon, Loren could make out the edges of the mountains' shadow. The glow of sunlight there was like a soft golden blanket being drawn back and away from her, over the edge of the world and out of sight.

Together they stood and watched it slowly creeping away, until Annis cleared her throat. "Let us sit on the bank of the stream," she said, her tone too airy, too light. "I want to put my feet in the water. I can hardly believe how long it is since last I bathed."

"Very well," said Loren. She was more curious than ever about what troubled Annis, but it seemed the girl would not speak of it until she was ready. So they sat together upon the bank beside the stream and pulled off their boots. The water was not too very cold, despite the winter. Uzo had told them that it never snowed in Feldemar, and all of the south-flowing rivers carried water from the north, where it remained hot and sunny all year round.

"This is a strange land, but I find it very beautiful," said Annis, looking out into the gathering darkness between the trees.

"I prefer the Birchwood, but I am happy to have seen it," said Loren. "Together you and I have wandered forests, grasslands, great rivers and jungles, and even the ocean. All that is left now is to visit a desert together."

"Mayhap one day we could journey to Idris," said Annis, her eyes all alight. "I have heard it is an exotic place. When all of this is over, I should love to go there with you." But then her expression fell, and she looked away. "When all of this is over."

"Annis, what is it?" said Loren. "I wish to hear what troubles you, but I must rise before the dawn."

"Of course. Forgive me." Annis drew a deep breath. "I do not want Gem to go with you. I want you to command him to stay."

Loren's heart sank. "I cannot," she said. "Or rather, I will not. I have tried it before—with both of you, in fact. You each made it plain how much you hate it."

"But you are all wandering into danger, danger that could overcome even grown warriors. He and I are both still children, and though he practices his swordplay, he is no fighter. I worry that he will try to join a battle, if one should break out, and then something will—"

"We both know why you are worried, Annis," said Loren irritably. "You worry that if he does not return, then you will never have told him how you feel, and will never know if he felt the same. The solution is simple: *speak* to him. You are an eloquent girl, when you do not let your tongue run away with your mind. You know that I love you as my sister, but frankly I have grown tired of how reluctant you are to even broach the subject with him."

To her surprise, Annis' eyes brimmed with tears, and she gave a sniff. She bowed her head and turned away. Mortified, Loren sat up and placed a hand on her back.

"Annis, I am sorry. I spoke too harshly, I—"

"No, you spoke true enough," said Annis, voice trembling. "Only . . . it is not that I am afraid to tell Gem. It is just that I wish I did not have to."

Loren frowned. But as she thought upon it, she understood, and her expression softened. "He has never fawned over you the way you have over him."

Annis fixed her with a glare, but her brimming tears robbed it of any bite. "I do not fawn, but otherwise you are right. He has never looked at me . . . in that way. I keep hoping to see it in his eyes, the way I see it when Chet looks at you. He looked that way from the first moment I met him, and I was there as the two of you fell deeper and deeper into love. It was effortless."

"Of course it was, you great fool," said Loren gently. "Chet and I have known each other our entire lives. He loved me even before I left the forest, before I met you. Everyone is different. Every love is different. He never told me how he felt, for he never needed to. But he is not Gem, and you are not me. So free yourself from both our misery, and speak to him."

Annis' eyes shone, but not with tears. "You are right," she said, quiet as a prayer. "I will. I *will* tell him. And I will tell him that if he does not return from Yewamba, I will storm in there and drag him out myself."

Loren laughed. "Good. Then go."

The girl shot to her feet, but paused when Loren remained sitting. "Are you not coming?"

"I will in a moment," said Loren. "But my feet are enjoying the water too much. I wish to relax a little while longer, for I think I shall not have another chance in some time."

Annis smiled at her and set off into the trees. Loren face fell the moment the girl's back was turned, and she looked down at her feet as they dangled in the stream.

He loved me even before I left the forest.

Loren had said the words without thinking. But why had she not said *We loved each other?*

She loved Chet—she knew that she did. But she had known for some time, in the back of her mind, that it was not the same as his love for her. If it were, she could never have manipulated him so easily on the day she left her home. If it were, she would not think of Niya the way she did now—and the proof of that could be found in Weath. Weath and Chet had become fast friends, and Loren could see how attractive the woman was, with her short copper hair and lithe, supple figure. Loren could remember one or two occasions when Chet's gaze had lingered upon her a moment longer than was proper.

Yet never once had Loren suspected that Chet might harbor any intent towards Weath beyond friendship. But Chet seemed to have more than an inkling of the connection between Loren and Niya. It made him jealous, and no matter how Loren denied it, she knew it was for good reason.

Even now, Loren could not stop thinking of how easy it would be to secretly draw Niya out of the camp. They could be alone for one night. Mayhap the last night of both their lives.

What had she told Annis? *You worry that if he does not return, then you will never have told him how you feel.*

The same could be said for Loren herself. Always she had denied what she felt for Niya, no matter how the Mystic goaded her. And now she had told Annis to be bold, to act as fear had always prevented her from acting before. Yet she would not do the same, even though she might never have another chance.

She remembered her heated argument with Niya just two nights before. Again she saw Niya standing just before her, almost pressed against her. When her mind played across it, the memory of the woman's scent flooded her nostrils.

A stone lay by Loren's hand. She picked it up and flung it hard into the water, where it broke the surface with a loud *plop*.

"Darkness take the woman," she muttered. "And darkness take me as well."

She drew her feet from the water and pulled her boots on, making her way slowly back to camp.

THIRTY-TWO

SLEEP DID NOT COME TO LOREN FOR A LONG TIME. CHET HAD ROLLED over into the corner of the tent before she entered, and he did not move as she undressed and crawled beneath their blanket. She rolled back and forth, trying to get comfortable and drift off. There was a lump beneath the tent, and she kept trying to shift around it to find flat ground again. But at last she had to admit that the lump was only an excuse, for she had slept on far worse terrain during her journeys.

"Close your eyes, woman," grumbled Chet.

Loren sighed. "I am not the only one who cannot sleep, then."

He turned over, and in the pale moonslight through the tent, she saw his eyes glinting. "Of course I cannot sleep. I am terrified of what tomorrow could bring. Do you not feel the same way?"

"I suppose so," she said with a shrug. "But on the other hand, I am somewhat used to that feeling."

"If that were true, sleep would come easy. Yet I think I understand your meaning. I do not feel as though I should be frightened. I was there for the fall of Northwood, and you and I faced Rogan more than once. I was there when assassins came for the Lord

Prince, and I was in the battle on the Seat. Yet somehow this feels different."

"It is different," said Loren. "All of those times were a surprise. The danger came from nowhere, and then it ended. This might be the first time you have planned to march into mortal peril."

Chet snickered. "I suppose that is right enough."

Loren felt herself relax at his laugh. She had not heard it in some time. Cautiously she scooted closer to him, and he did the same, placing his head on her shoulder. She curled her arm around him, fingers idly stroking his arm, and he laid a hand across her stomach. The feeling of his skin loosened her taut muscles even more. It felt natural between them again. It felt right. Suddenly the doubts she had had upon the bank of the stream faded away, and they seemed silly in her memory. This was how it had been when she first came to know that she loved him—beneath the boughs of the Birchwood, and then when their trysts began upon the Seat.

Then she remembered Niya, and the light in the woman's eyes when they looked at her. Comfort fell away, and she felt like a fraud with Chet in her arms.

"Chet, you have not been wrong about Niya," she said quietly. "I know you have suspected her for some time. And I dismissed it, but I should not have. Niya would have me, if she could. She has said as much, subtly and in ways that were less so."

He was still for a while, and then he pushed himself up on his elbow. In the midst of his silhouette, his eyes searched hers. "And? What came of it?"

"Nothing," said Loren. But then she realized that that was not strictly true. "She kissed me. Twice. In Dahab."

She could feel him tense. "You . . . why would you—"

"I did not," said Loren quickly. "She did it without asking."

He pushed himself up still farther. "What? Loren, that is only a step away from taking someone against their will, from breaking the High King's harshest law."

"That is not the way of it," said Loren. "I know how it must sound, but . . . do you remember the first time we kissed, on the shores of Dorsea, just before we sailed for the Seat?"

"Of course," he said quietly. "That memory will never fade."

"I did not ask you before I kissed you," said Loren.

"Yet you knew," he said. "You knew I loved you."

"How? You had never said the words, nor had I. We had never spoken of it at all. And when we began to—that is, when we became . . ." She flushed, and wondered if the moonslight would reveal it. "Even when we did more than kiss, we did not speak of it then. You told me you loved me for the first time just before we left the Seat. We had shared a bed for weeks before then."

He thought about that for a moment. But then he shook his head. "I do not understand, Loren. You knew my desires, and I knew yours. And so the only way I can think that what Niya did was no crime, is if she also knew your desires, and she was right."

She stared up at him. Shame burned in her breast, but she did not look away.

"I see," he said quietly. He began to turn away, to roll towards his side of the tent again.

"Stop, Chet," said Loren, pulling him back. "I do not want to be with Niya."

"You just said otherwise. So what is the truth?"

"The truth is that I am here. With you."

"That is not an answer."

"Yes. Yes, I would lay with Niya if it were not for you."

It thrilled her to say it out loud. Her skin rose to gooseflesh at the words, and she grew quick of breath. But then she raised a hand to cup his cheek.

"But that is something I would merely enjoy. A momentary pleasure, like drinking a cup of wine. Between such a fancy and what I want—what I truly desire—a wide gulf stretches. Much would have to change in this world before I would attempt to leap it."

He did not answer for a moment. Loren realized she was holding her breath, and slowly she let it out. And then, when he spoke, she heard a small smile in his voice.

"So you do not fancy me, then?"

She gave a frustrated growl and slapped his arm. "Be silent, you idiot. I love you, Chet. I will not lay with anyone else, but that does not mean I can promise I will never have desires. Can you tell me, in truth, that you have never thought of another? Mayhap Weath?"

"Anyone can see that she has a fine figure," said Chet. "But there my thoughts remain. I will never lay with her."

"And I will never lay with Niya," said Loren. "It is not precisely the same, for I feel a way about her that you do not feel towards Weath. But I have chosen love over desire. I hope you know that."

419

"I do," he whispered. "I only wish that my love was enough for you. That it did not leave you wanting another, or feeling this deep need to pursue the aims of the High King."

"That is another matter entirely, and you know it."

"Of course it is, but it comes from the same place in your heart. I believe you when you say you will be true. Yet even so, I am not enough. There is your quest—your mission. Can you not give that up for me as well?"

"No," she said flatly. "And you should not ask it of me. Not if you love me in truth."

He paused to consider that. "I understand your sense of duty," he said at last. "It is a quality I admire, in others as well as yourself. It is only that I do not see anything for you beyond this war. If I were in your position, I might do the same as you have done. But always I would dream of a quiet home in the woods, where I might spend my days after the war—if indeed it becomes a war at all. Do you want that, Loren?"

"I do not know. It sounds fine enough, I suppose. But when I think of it, I do not feel the yearning for it that is plain in your voice."

"That is what I thought," he said, sighing. "Is there even a time after the war, in your mind? And what do you see there?"

She sat up, and he rose from his elbow to sit beside her. She took his hands into her own and traced a finger along the back of his hand. "I have no easy answer for you. I cannot say what I know you want me to say. How can I know what the distant future holds when I cannot even know what will happen to you and me tomorrow? But right now, I love you. And your love is dearer to me than any honor the High King could bestow. Can that be enough? At least for now?"

He turned his hand over to grasp hers, and lifted it to his mouth to kiss her fingers one by one. "It can," he murmured.

Loren kissed him, and they lay down again together, still and content. Soon she was asleep, a dreamless sleep more sound than any she had had since leaving Ammon.

THIRTY-THREE

Uzo went about the camp to wake them all before dawn. One by one they came out of their tents and stood stretching in the crisp air. Loren caught herself looking at each of her companions. Often they returned her gaze, but no one spoke a word.

They were silent, too, as they readied themselves for the journey. The Mystics buckled their swords at their waists and donned their shirts of chain. Loren left her bow—Albern's gift—for it would be of little use in the fortress, and only by terrible misfortune would she need it before then. Niya had her sword and a brace of knives at her belt. She caught Loren staring and winked. Loren smiled and shook her head.

Annis rose to see them off, though of course she would not be coming with them. Loren noticed at once that Annis and Gem would hardly look at each other, and each flinched when the other spoke. They kept a wide distance between themselves as well. Loren groaned inwardly. Whatever Annis had told Gem the night before, it did not appear to have gone well. But she could waste little thought on that now. She would have to ask what happened after their journey to Yewamba, if indeed there was an afterwards in which they could speak with each other.

She went to Midnight just before they left and stroked the mare's muzzle. "You will be safe here," she said. "If I do not return, I am sorry, but that only means you will belong to Annis. You like her."

Midnight blew a wet snort into Loren's face, making her laugh.

Shiun led them from the camp and into the jungle. They paused at the mouth of the valley while she went ahead to search it, making sure no new guards had been posted there since last they came. She soon returned to wave them on. The sky had only just begun to turn grey.

For a long while she led them on the same path they had taken the last time, but when she reached the place where they had seen the guards, she took them in another direction—right instead of left, up the face of the northern ridge rather than the south. Loren wondered at the change, but she did not speak. Shiun had been out all day scouting the path, and the woman was like an Elf in the woods, silent and sure. She would not lead them astray.

At one point they stopped dead, and Shiun gestured them into a crouch. Loren looked around for the reason, and then she saw two forms moving a little bit below them on the ridge. They wore the green cloaks of Yerrins, and they appeared to be eating. Shiun turned to Loren and leaned close, whispering into her ear.

"Do we remove them now?"

Loren blinked at her. "Remove . . .?"

Niya pressed forwards, her breath hot on Loren's cheek. "We may have to escape at great speed. Every guard we kill on the way in is one we will not have to fight on the way out."

"No," said Loren. "When are the patrols replaced? Do you know?" Shiun shook her head. "Then we could raise the alarm while we are still inside, and not even know it. The family Yerrin prides themselves on not killing needlessly—we should endeavor to do the same."

Shiun glanced over Loren's shoulder. From the corner of her eye, Loren saw Niya shrug. Shiun turned away without a word and pressed on.

The grey had lightened considerably when they reached the base of Yewamba's sudden cliffs. Dawn's approach filled them all with urgency. The route up looked to be a difficult one, but Loren knew from long experience that climbing up would be much easier than climbing down.

Their path began to wind back and forth, and Shiun would pause every few moments to check that the rocks gave her another path up.

But then they reached the top of the slope, and it turned into a sheer wall at least thirty paces high.

"Where do we go from here?" said Loren.

"Up," said Shiun, arching an eyebrow.

"That is why you brought me," Weath said, smiling. She stepped forwards and pulled off her leather gloves. Her eyes began to glow. "I may not be much of an alchemist, but I *am* an alchemist."

She put forth her hand at about the height of her knee, and her fingers sank into the rock like it was made of water. Soon she had carved a little depression there, and she placed her foot inside it. She made another for the other foot, and then she reached up to create her handholds. Hand over hand and foot over foot she began to climb, creating new handholds each time.

"Sky above," whispered Gem. "I would have given much to have known a girl like her when I was the best thief in Cabrus."

Niya snorted. "I will go next," she growled.

"I will follow," said Loren. "Then Gem, Chet, and Shiun. You can cover our rear best with the bow."

Shiun nodded. Niya was already climbing up just behind Weath, gripping each handhold almost as soon as the alchemist's foot left it. Loren came after her as soon as there was room, and soon the whole group was on the cliff face, making their way slowly up, like ants ascending the leg of a table.

The sun rose at last while they were halfway up, and eastern light poured upon them from the left. Loren paused for a moment to look back down. Yewamba's little valley was in view, but nothing beyond, for the mountains blocked the landscape from sight. It was the very reason Yewamba was so well hidden. She could not see any guards from her vantage point, and she hoped that none looked their way, for surely they could not miss the sight of five small figures crawling their way up the light grey stone of the cliff.

A wind had begun to blow. Loren shivered and reached up for the next handhold.

Just then, Niya's foot slipped from the wall. She gave a grunt as she slid down, reaching desperately for something to hold on to. With no time to think, Loren braced her feet and reached up to try and halt Niya's fall. It did little to slow her, but Niya gripped a handhold in time, stopping with a jolt. Loren realized suddenly that her hand was on Niya's rear.

The Mystic looked down at her with a savage grin. "Time for that later, Nightblade. We are working."

"Get on with it," said Loren, removing her hand. She looked down towards Chet, trying to send him a silent apology. He rolled his eyes and shook his head. She hoped that meant he was not upset.

Looking up again, she realized they had finally neared the top. Weath was already out of sight over the wall, and Niya was scrambling over as well. They all quickened their pace, Loren nearly leaping from handhold to handhold, and Gem following so fast that his fingers scraped on her boot more than once. But just before she reached the lip, Loren heard a muffled cry and the scuff of leather boots on stone.

We are discovered, she thought. A moment's panic seized her as she wondered if she should keep going. But then she realized Weath and Niya were in danger, and she lunged up—only to recoil again, as a body sailed over her head and fell into the open air. She caught a glance of it—and saw Weath's pale face, her red hair fluttering, bone jutting from her neck. In silence the Mystic fell, and in silence struck the rocks far, far below, too far away to hear the impact.

For a moment, horror froze them all. Then Loren vaulted over the top of the wall to land on the rampart just beyond. Niya was there, kneeling over the body of a Yerrin guard. The blade of her knife was still buried in the woman's throat. Niya looked up at Loren, her eyes wide with grief.

"She came—she surprised us, we—Weath, she did not see her, and—"

The words died in her throat, and Loren could only stare. Slowly she turned to the top of the wall again, her breath catching in her throat, as the others came over one by one and joined her in silence.

THIRTY-FOUR

AFTER A LONG MOMENT OF MOURNING, SHIUN BROKE THE QUIET. "The sun is up. We are far too exposed here."

"Yes," said Niya. She wiped something—sweat, or tears—from her eyes with the back of one hand, while the other wiped her knife clean on the dead guard's cloak. "Help me get her out of sight."

"We have no time to find a hiding place," said Shiun. She looked at the corpse disdainfully. "Throw her over the wall, where she may join Weath in death."

Niya nodded, and together the two of them lifted the guard to toss her into the open air. There was a bloodstain on the floor, but that could not be helped. Chet and Gem still sat where they had climbed up. Chet stared blankly in the direction Weath had fallen.

"Chet!" whispered Loren. His head jerked towards her. "Come."

The boys edged forwards slowly. There was an inner wall opposite the ramparts behind which Loren and the others had ducked, and now Shiun poked her head over it, looking about. When she crouched again, she spoke to Loren and Niya. "I cannot see very well, for the wall blocks vision, but I see only another half-dozen Yerrins atop it. That is a light guard, for I would guess that the wall is many hundreds of paces long. Below us, the courtyard is entirely empty. If we are fortunate, they will not notice this one missing for a long while."

"How can you think we are fortunate when Weath is dead?" said Chet harshly.

"Chet," said Loren, meeting his gaze. He lasted only a moment before looking away. "Go on, Shiun."

But Niya spoke first. "We should leave one lookout here, and the rest of us will enter Yewamba. We will find Damaris and bring her up, then carry her down the way we came."

"Carry her down the cliff?" said Loren. "How can we manage that?"

"I have rope," said Shiun, patting a large leather pack that hung at her hip. "We can bind her and gag her, and with one on the ground to guide her descent, the rest of us may lower her down."

"Good enough," said Niya. "Chet will remain here, while the rest of us—"

"No," said Chet. "I will go with Loren."

Niya glared, but Shiun nodded in agreement. "I will remain. The boy only came to keep her safe, and he is no warrior. He will be useless here if he is discovered."

"That is why he should not be here at all," snarled Niya. "But very well. If we are resigned to this foolishness, then let us carry it out."

With Shiun remaining behind, Niya led the rest of them down a stairway and into the empty courtyard. Not far from the bottom of the steps was a door. Niya paused there for only a moment, pressing her ear to the wood to listen. Then she pushed it open and stepped through, with Loren only a pace behind her, and Chet and Gem at her heels.

They were at the top of yet another staircase landing, except that this one descended to both the left and right. Both directions turned almost immediately, deeper into the mountain. Loren ran down to the corner of the one on the left, and saw that it turned away from the other.

"This one turns to the right."

"And this one to the left," said Chet, who had gone in the other direction. "Two paths in two directions, but which to take?"

Loren thought hard. Yewamba was a fortress built from a mountain shaped like an arrowhead. Yes, an arrowhead, or the prow of a ship. And on a ship, where did the captain reside? Always their quarters were towards the rear—or in this case, deeper into the mountain.

"This way," she said.

"How do you know?" said Chet.

"It is a guess, but I think it is a good one. We can argue about it if you like."

He grimaced, but Niya ran down the steps after Loren. "Listen to her. If she says she knows where to find Damaris, I believe her." She vanished almost at once around the corner and was lost from sight.

Chet and Gem ran up to Loren, and Chet's face was full of concern. "Did you see this in your dreams as well?"

"No," said Loren. "It is truly a guess. And my dreams do not show me the future."

"They have guided us well enough so far," said Gem. "We would not be here without them."

"They are—" She stopped short. Chet's corpse flashed in her mind, and Gem's madness. "I know nothing of this place. I only think that we will find Damaris in its deepest, darkest hole. Now let us hurry, for Niya has already left us behind."

They took the steps two at a time until they caught the Mystic. She had paused where the stairs ended, opening into a hallway that branched left and right while also running straight ahead. Torches lit the place, just as they lit the stairwell. Niya glanced over her shoulder. "Nightblade?"

"Straight ahead," said Loren, and took the lead.

The craftsmanship of the fortress was nothing so opulent as the High King's palace, and yet in its own way it seemed grander, more powerful. There were some pillars and beams that looked as though they had been brought here, but much of it was carved out of the rock of the mountain itself, and they did not appear to have taken much effort to make it beautiful. It was as though whoever built Yewamba had done so long before the decorative refinement that gave birth to the Seat. The stronghold had a sense of lurking, of ominous presence and malice, a long-forgotten and long-sleeping threat that only waited for the right time to wake and sweep all its enemies away into the darkness below the world.

That menace weighed more heavily on them the deeper they drove. The halls all turned exactly left and right, so that Loren was able to remember the way she was going easily enough, and led them always west, deeper into the heart of the Greatrocks. But all the while, they never saw another soul, nor any sign of one—save for the lit torches on the walls. But those made the air oppressively hot, and stuffy besides, so that soon they were huffing and wheezing even though they were not running.

"It is like being wrapped in a blanket on a summer day," said Chet, his forehead glistening with sweat.

"Where are they?" growled Niya. She stopped and ducked through the open doorway of some of the rooms as they passed. "There are tables in some of these, and dishes, and weapons in others. But where are the people?"

"Mayhap they heard us coming," said Gem. "Mayhap they fled. They must have heard I was with you." But even his customary bravado could not withstand the creeping silence, and his smile faltered.

"Hush," said Loren, stopping suddenly. They all froze where they stood. Loren listened harder, and then she heard it again—the clink of metal on pottery.

She turned to the rest of them. "A kitchen?"

"Food," said Gem, licking his lips.

"Be silent, Gem."

"I do not smell anything," said Niya.

"I think sound carries farther in this place than scent," said Loren. "And worse, I cannot tell where the sound came from."

"Then what do you propose to do?"

"Press on. Only be more careful, now that we know others are near."

They moved slower after that, careful to let each step fall silently. And then, at long last, they heard a sound. Shuffling footsteps, the sound of soft leather on stone, and moving towards them from the right.

Loren pointed to one of the rooms, and they lunged through the open doorway to hide themselves on either side of it. Loren risked leaning out slightly to look back into the hall. A young woman in a plain brown dress, her skin as dark as night, walked past them. She carried a broad silver tray in two hands, and upon the tray were several platters of food with gold covers.

Niya looked at Loren after the girl passed. "Did you see it?"

"I did," said Loren. "Fancy food for fancy people. Let us follow our little songbird."

They waited until the girl had turned the next corner out of sight, and then ran after her. Two more hallways they followed her, until she rounded the final corner and ducked into the first doorway in the hallway there. Peeking around the corner, Loren saw a guard at the door. She looked to Niya.

The Mystic pounced silent as a striking wolf. Her hand caught the guard by the throat, choking his cry of alarm to silence. Her dagger was in her hand, and Loren quailed—but Niya only brought the pommel crashing into his temple, and he collapsed. Loren ran past them both and into the room, where the servant stood looking at the door, her eyes wide with alarm. When she saw Loren, she tried to scream, but Loren covered her mouth with a hand and seized the tray to keep it from falling. Chet took it from her and set it on the ground while Loren pressed the girl back into the wall.

"Silence! Be silent," said Loren. "We will not hurt you."

But the girl's gaze went over Loren's shoulder, and she screamed into the hand that kept her quiet. Loren turned to see that Niya had dragged the guard into the room and, now that he was out of the hallway, was slitting his throat with her hunting knife.

"Niya!" cried Loren in a harsh rasp.

The woman glared up at her. "Every one I kill now is one I will not have to fight when I escape. I say that for myself, since it seems plain you will not fight at all."

"I will not kill," said Loren. "Darkness take you, Niya. Get into the hallway and keep watch. Warn us if you hear anyone coming."

Niya's nostrils flared, but she did as she was bid. Loren turned back to the girl and shook her by the shoulder to get her attention.

"Where are you taking this food? I am removing my hand so that you may talk. Do not scream."

Cautiously she lifted her hand, no more than a finger's breadth from the girl's lips. But the girl shook her head. "I will tell you nothing."

Loren sighed. "Tell us, girl. Do not make this difficult."

"Who are you? What do you want? Why did you kill him?"

Glancing over her shoulder at the dead guard, Loren remembered what Uzo had told them in Dahab: the Yerrins were family, and none but the family were allowed inside. Doubtless the guard was some cousin of the girl's. She cursed Niya again in her mind.

"My companion killed him because she is a madwoman," said Loren. "We are seeking someone. Help us find her, and you will not be harmed. I swear it. But if we take too long in our conversation here . . . well, my companion will grow impatient, and then she will speak with you herself."

429

Fresh terror filled the girl's eyes. "I am only a servant. I know nothing of the stronghold."

"I would wager you know enough. Where are all the soldiers stationed?"

The girl only shook her head. Loren glanced back over her shoulder. "Gem, fetch Niya."

"No!" cried the girl. "No, no, please. The soldiers are all in the eastern chambers of the stronghold, far from here."

"And who resides here?" said Loren.

She looked all around, desperate for some escape, but there was none. "The wealthier members of the family. The caravan heads and accountants, the higher scions."

"To whom do you bring this food?"

The girl's throat bobbed up and down as she swallowed. "The . . . the lady of the fortress."

"Is it Damaris?"

Though the girl did not answer, her eyes grew wider with fear, and her skin went a shade paler. It was all the answer Loren needed.

"But there is no one in this room," said Loren. "Where is she? How did you mean to bring the food to her?"

Gem ran up beside them, where there was a small door built into the wall. He turned the latch and opened it outwards into the room. "This way, I would wager."

Chet pressed in behind him, and Loren leaned over to look. There was a small wooden platform there, affixed to a rope that ran up and down in the pitch blackness beyond.

"What is it?" said Chet.

"I think . . ." Gem leaned in and pulled on one of the ropes. The wooden platform moved down slightly. "Yes, I think this is some device that brings things up and down in the fortress. If the kitchens are up on this level, this would be how they send food down to those on the lower levels."

"She is below us then," said Loren, focusing on the girl once more. "How many floors down?"

"Please, no," said the girl. "You cannot reach her. She is well guarded. And if it is known that I helped you . . ."

They heard footsteps at the door, and Niya reappeared in it. "What is taking so long?" she snarled. "Will she not speak? Give her to me."

Loren turned back to the girl and raised her brows.

"Fifteen," squeaked the girl. "Damaris is fifteen floors down."

"You have done well," said Loren. Then she shoved the girl back so that her head slammed into the wall. She fell unconscious at once, and Loren caught her before she reached the floor.

THIRTY-FIVE

"I WILL GO FIRST," SAID GEM.

"Let me," said Niya. "If there are foes on the other side, you will be of little use."

"I am smaller, and if there are foes, I will see them first," countered Gem. "I will be able to tell you, so that the situation may be resolved with stealth rather than by alerting the whole kingdom to our presence."

Loren looked up from where she and Chet were tying up the servant girl in the corner using the cloak of the slain guard. "Let Gem go first. He is craftier than any of us." With her dagger Loren cut a strip of cloth from the girl's dress and shoved it in her mouth, and then tied it in place with another.

"I do not doubt it," sneered Niya, glaring down at the boy.

Gem slipped into the dark hole in the wall and crawled over the edge of the wooden platform, clinging to the rope in the darkness. "I cannot see how far down it goes," he said. "But the rope is sturdy, and there are many rough patches on the wall where you may place your feet. It will not be too difficult a climb."

"Still, you may wish to rid yourself of the chain shirt, Niya," said Loren. "Doubtless that will only make things harder."

Niya arched an eyebrow. "I will keep it, though your concern is touching. I think it will come to fighting before we leave here, and I would not be defenseless when it does."

"Suit yourself, then."

One by one they entered the darkness behind Gem: first Loren, and then Niya, and finally Chet. The rock pressed in close, with only a few handbreadths to either side of them. Gem had said the climb was not difficult, but that was because his tiny body fit far more easily than any of theirs. The air grew stuffy and hard to breathe, and it was worse the farther down they went, so that Loren guessed the only source of fresh air must be above them.

"Sky above, it stinks here," said Chet.

"Can you imagine how terrified Annis would be if she had come with us?" said Gem. He snickered, but then went silent. "Still, I wish she had."

"Still your prattling," said Niya. "There could be foes less than a pace away from us even now."

Indeed, they passed several more doors like the one they had used to enter the shaft. There did not appear to be one on every floor, but almost, and from the edges of each came thin shafts of light. It was the only illumination they had, and barely enough for them to see by. Loren wondered what would happen if another servant came to use the dumbwaiter and pulled on the rope. Would they all go plummeting into the darkness to land in whatever hole lay below them?

"Go faster, Gem," she hissed.

She guessed that they had passed seven floors now. But then, as they kept going, the air grew sweeter. They could breathe more easily, and she felt a draft upon her arms. And far, far below them, there came the sound of rushing water.

The stream, thought Loren. It must be the same stream that ran out to skip beside the main road. It ran out of the mountain itself. Of course. What better way to dispose of the stronghold's waste? No doubt there was some station upriver where they could collect fresh water, which would let Yewamba withstand a siege for almost any length of time. By using this shaft, and others like it, they could dispose of their rubbish, their unused food, and even the contents of their chamber pots.

But Gem had stopped, and she almost stepped on him as her thoughts wandered. "Fifteen," whispered the boy. "This is where she meant to send the food." He paused there a moment, listening. "I do not hear anything on the other side."

"Then give it a push," said Loren.

He tried, but in the dim light she saw him shake his head. "It is shut."

"Climb down a bit farther," she said. "Let me try."

Gem slid farther down the rope, and she took his place at the door. From her belt she drew her dagger and slipped it into the crack between the hatch and the wall. She probed up and down, searching for the latch. At last she found it and lifted it, and the hatch jerked open. It sounded loud as a thunderclap after the long silence, and they all froze. But from the other side there came no sound.

She stuck her head through the opening. The room beyond was another servant's room, and it was empty. Carefully, silently, she slipped out. Niya followed her quickly, and then came the boy, and then Chet.

"The air is even worse here than it was in the shaft," said Chet. "I think I might choke."

"We can but hope," said Niya. Quickly she stole to the room's door and looked both ways down the hallway outside. "No one. But I hear sounds from that direction."

Loren went to the door and heard them, too—voices, far enough to be only a low murmur, but still close enough to be heard. They were to the left, which was west, and deeper into the mountain.

"It seems the right direction," she whispered. "Let us go, but be cautious."

The hallway now was more natural rock than cut stone, and every surface was rough to the touch, so that they could not brush too hard against the walls without scraping their skin. It was harder to muffle their footfalls, and so they had to move even slower than they had before. There was a channel cut into the rock below them, and an iron grate was laid over it flush with the floor. In the channel there flowed a thin stream of water, hardly enough to dip a hand in, though there was room for much more. Another strange feature of the stronghold, though Loren had not even a guess as to its purpose.

At last the hall turned and opened into a wide room beyond, with a domed ceiling carved in sweeping designs. Loren caught a glimpse of horses and men cut into the stone, but her attention quickly went to the soldiers in the room instead. She and the others dove behind the edge of the room's doorway before they could be seen.

There were not many soldiers, mayhap only two dozen, but that was far more than they had any hope of taking in a fight. There was a long row of tables against either wall, and there the soldiers sat, eating a meal. All of them wore shirts of chain and greaves of iron plate, and they all had helmets, though they had removed those to eat. Loren took a second glance and cursed—the helmets were open-faced.

Niya had spotted it, too. "No disguises this time," she whispered.

"What shall we do?" said Loren.

"Turn back?" said Chet. But even he did not sound hopeful that the idea would be accepted.

"There," said Gem. "Look."

He pointed to the floor. The same channel that had run beside them ran through the center of the mess hall and out the other side. And it was far removed from the tables where the soldiers sat.

"It will be a tight fit," whispered Chet.

"And filthy," said Niya. "Mayhap we can find a way to sneak around."

"When did you care about a little dirt?" said Loren. "It is the fastest route for certain, and already I worry that the servant may be discovered at any moment."

They could not argue with that, and so together they stole back down the hallway. Once they were far enough away from the mess hall that they did not need to fear being heard, Loren and Chet stooped together and lifted up a section of the iron grate. It lifted easily enough, though the iron scraped on the stone with a noise that made them all nervous.

"In, quickly," said Loren, placing the grate to the side. Niya took off her sword and, holding it in one hand, she crawled into the channel. Gem was just behind her. Chet motioned to Loren.

"I will go down first and lie on my back. Push the grate on top of me as quietly as you can, and I will do my best to hold it up while you crawl in. I can lower it down from below."

In a moment they had done it. From beneath the grate, Chet held up one side of it so that it slanted, and Loren slid in beside him. As they pressed up against each other for a moment, she kissed his cheek.

"For luck," she said.

He grinned and slowly lowered the grate, following her as she slithered along the channel. The water they crawled through was dirty, but it seemed an ordinary sort of dirt, from the earth and not from human waste. Loren was grateful for that—she had half-feared that the trough might be a secondary method of disposing of the chamber pots.

"At least this gives some relief from the heat," whispered Chet behind her.

Loren realized that might be the channel's purpose—to somewhat cool the air, here in the bowels of the fortress where it was so warm. But she looked back at Chet and put a finger to her lips, urging him to be silent.

They came to the turn in the channel where it entered the mess hall. Niya paused for a moment and looked back to make sure they were with her. She placed two fingers to her lips for silence, and then crawled forwards again, much more slowly this time.

Half a pace at a time, they made their way through the room. Above them and to either side of them, the chatter of the soldiers seemed like a shouting throng, and they flinched at every raised voice and sudden laugh. Loren's nerves nearly failed her every time she had to put one of her hands or her knees back down in the water, for she feared to make even the smallest splash. She looked up again, trying to guess how far they had gone. She might have been halfway through the room, or only two body lengths in. She could not be sure, and her view was blocked to the front by Niya and Gem, and to the rear by Chet.

Then a soldier crossed the room, and stepped loudly on the grate just over Niya's head. Startled, the Mystic dropped her sword in the water with a *splash*.

Loren looked up through the grate as they all went perfectly still. She counted the thudding of her heartbeats. *One. Two. Three. Four. Five.*

No one came into view. The sound of talking all around them did not pause for so much as a moment.

A long, shuddering sigh escaped Loren, though she fought to keep it silent. Niya looked back over her shoulder and grimaced.

They went a little faster, no longer worried about the small sloshing sounds that came from their progress. Soon they had crossed to the other side of the room, and then the channel took a turn down another hall. Still Niya pressed on, until they were well away from the mess hall. Then the Mystic woman flipped over and lifted the grate above herself, setting it gently on the stone to the side. She climbed from the channel and stole into the first room in the hall. Gem hopped out after her, but he waited for Loren and Chet to emerge and replace the iron grate before the three of them followed Niya into the room.

It was an office of some sort. There was a large ledger on the desk in the corner, though it was closed, and the opposite wall held shelves of scrolls. Thankfully the room was unoccupied, at least for the moment.

"This looks more like the sort of place we seek," said Niya.

"Yet Damaris is not here, either," said Loren. "Let us move on, and quickly, for now I expect the place will be well populated."

They began to steal from room to room, pausing at each one to ensure there was no one around to see them dashing by. Only when a hall was lined by doors that were all closed did they dare to run, and even then they did it at a crouching sort of shuffle to keep quiet. But they only found more offices, and rooms of accounts, and once a study, with a fine upholstered chair and many books upon its shelves.

They passed a grand staircase, with bannisters of wood embedded in the stone walls to either side, and the entire length covered by a woven stair runner. It was patterned like a fine rug, and the edges looked new, but the middle was worn and dirty. Gem stopped and stared at it for a moment, but Loren took his shoulder and pushed him on.

Finally Niya rounded a corner and stopped dead before immediately backing up into Loren again. They pressed themselves to the stone wall, and Niya met her gaze. She held up two fingers, and then pointed to the sword at her hip. *Two guards, both armed, in the next hall.* Loren nodded, and then slid around Niya to see for herself, peeking around the corner. They stood together on the left side of the hallway, hands on the grips of their weapons, staring straight ahead at the opposite wall.

From within the room where they stood guard, Loren could hear voices. Some were deep, some were shrill, but they did not speak over each other, and she could make out each of them with crystal clarity. And she heard one that she knew better than most in Underrealm: a powerful, velvety voice, almost melodic, rich with power and well used to it. The voice of Damaris of the family Yerrin. She drew back again.

"Come," she whispered, motioning towards an empty room they had passed. The door was open, but Loren had seen that it had a bolt. They entered the room and closed the door behind them, and Loren slid the bolt into place before turning to the others.

"We have found her," she said. "Damaris is in that room. Now we must figure out how to remove her from this fortress, even if we must drag her screaming the whole way."

THIRTY-SIX

"I FEEL AS THOUGH WE HAVE TRAVELED ACROSS A KINGDOM TO FIND a door, but no one told us the door would be locked and bolted and protected by magic besides," said Chet. "Tell me I am not the only one who sees this as hopeless."

"Keep your voice down," said Niya.

"And take heart," chirped Gem. "I have always seen this entire affair as hopeless."

Chet glared at him. "That is not comforting." He wiped one sleeve against his forehead. "I might not mind if it were not so hot down here."

Loren ignored them. "We must subdue the guards before we can capture Damaris. I think the two in the hall will not be much of a problem. But if I know Damaris, there will be other guards within her council room. And I heard other voices within besides, voices I do not recognize. Also, though I did not hear him, Gregor will be here." Even saying the man's name sent fear coursing through her very soul. Gem's cheerful smile vanished in an instant. He, too, had met the giant bodyguard.

But Niya sliced her hand through the air, as though banishing Loren's warnings. "Darkness take the guards. We can rush the room and take the ones at the door—I trust that you three can subdue one, while I kill the other?—and slay whoever we find inside as well."

"You do not know Gregor. He is a beast in human form," said Loren.

Niya spat, sending a thick glob of saliva to splash on the open pages of a book on the desk beside her. "Say what you wish of him, but I will gut him regardless."

Loren only shook her head. Chet spoke up. "But that is not all we must do," he said. "Once we have Damaris, how do you mean to get her out of the fortress? She will not cooperate just because you have her in hand. And we are fifteen floors below our only means of escape."

They all went quiet at that. But in a moment Gem looked up with a bright smile. "The shaft. The same one we came down in. Why do we not use the platform to bring her up, like a tray of food?"

A slow smile overcame Loren, and she nodded. "That could work. And I will admit that the idea of escorting her out of here in such an . . . *undignified* manner amuses me no end. Yet the way to that shaft is back through the mess hall."

"It cannot be the only one, not in a place this large," said Gem. "We have come through many passages on our way here. I am certain I can find another."

"Go, then, and search," said Loren. "Only be careful, and do not let yourself come to harm."

"Yes, my lady," said Gem. He gave her a quick half-bow and vanished. Niya rolled her eyes.

"That leaves us with the council room," said Loren.

"We can take the—" Niya began.

"We cannot take the guards," said Loren, shaking her head. "Not with any degree of certainty. You are a powerful warrior, Niya, I will not deny that, but I will not hinge all of our success upon your skill with a blade."

"Unless you have a better suggestion, you have little choice," said Niya, folding her arms.

The room fell to silence, for of course Loren had no answer. Chet shook his head and tugged at the collar of his tunic. "Darkness take this place," he muttered. "The air is so *thick.*"

At his words, an idea came to Loren in a flash. "Fire," she said. "We can build a fire of wood, cloth and parchment, so that it fills the hall with smoke. The smoke will drive them out of the council room and make it hard to see besides. In the confusion, we can snatch Damaris right out of the hands of her guards."

Niya frowned, but Loren could almost see the idea taking root in the Mystic's mind. "Mayhap. But they will move fast once they smell the smoke, and could slip past us before we can act. We should block their first means of escape."

"The stairwell we passed," said Loren. "The rug was new, but its fibers have already been worn down. It sees much use. That is the route they use to come and go from this floor."

"We must block the stairwell, then, and we should do the same to the hallway at its feet," said Niya. "That way the guards in the mess hall will not be able to come and help their lady."

"But if we fill it with furniture, we will be spotted before we can set the flame," said Chet.

Loren thought hard. "The floor above. If there are not so many of them up there . . ."

Niya straightened. "Why wonder? Let us go and see."

They slipped out and went back the way they had come, quickly reaching the stairwell. They stole up it and looked down the hallway in both directions. At once Loren thought she must be right in her guess, for only every other torch was lit, and they saw no one in any direction. A quick search of the rooms confirmed it: this floor was used little, if at all, though it still had furniture aplenty for their purpose.

"We will build a small mountain of chairs and tables at the top of the stairs," said Loren. "When we are ready to begin, Chet, you and Gem shall send the furniture crashing down. We will return to the room where we just were. Damaris and her guards will pass that way, but they will find the hall blocked. By the time they return in our direction, the smoke should be too thick to see. That is when Niya and I will snatch her away and take her down the hall in the other direction. We will take the first stairway up that we can find. You will meet us there. Then Gem will take us to the shaft leading up, if he can find one."

Gem burst around the corner just then, bouncing on the balls of his feet. "He can," he said. "I found it only a short distance away. I poked my head inside just to be sure—it does not have a door for the level Damaris is on, which is why they did not use it to send her food."

"Good work," said Loren. Despite the gravity of their situation, her mouth split in a grin. "We have our plan, then."

"As far as schemes go, it seems less than simple," grumbled Niya.

"Simple schemes are more easily countered," said Chet.

"Elaborate ones have more chances to fail."

Loren stifled a laugh and clapped one hand each on their shoulders. "Enough. This plan will work. I can feel it. Ready yourselves, for now we snare a merchant."

THIRTY-SEVEN

Loren and Niya ran hurriedly from room to room on the lower level. They built stacks of books and drapes beneath tables in half a dozen offices. At any moment Loren feared a guard would come wandering down the hallway, and the plan would be foiled. But soon they had their little pyres built, and Loren ran quickly to the stairwell. On the floor above, she found Chet waiting for her. Beside him was a huge pile of chairs and couches, all of them stacked atop a pair of tables at the head of the stairs.

"Are you ready?" she asked breathlessly.

"Yes," he said. Then he seized her shirt and drew her in to kiss her. "Be safe."

"And you." She kissed him back.

"Ahem," said Gem. He did not clear his throat so much as he simply said the word aloud.

"Oh, be silent, Gem."

She fled back down the stairs to Niya, who had been watching them. As they ran down the hall towards the first room to set their fires, Niya arched an eyebrow. "Do I get no such consideration?"

Loren ignored that. "Here." She took a torch from a sconce and placed it in the Mystic's hand before seizing another for herself. They split off and ran to separate rooms

In the first, Loren thrust the torch into the pile of books. The dry parchment caught at once. The smoke was even thicker than she had thought it would be, and she quickly ran to the next before it grew too heavy to breathe. Two more fires she set, and at the last one she threw the torch into the flames. She and Niya met each other in the hallway and ran back to the room where they had concocted the plan. To ease their breathing, they held the edges of their cloaks over their noses and mouths.

Scarcely had they shut the door before they heard shouts from Damaris' council room, and they quickly pressed themselves to either side of the door to wait. Many boots came tramping towards them, and Loren tensed. The party passed them by, the guards rushing their lady towards the stairs. Any moment now, Chet and Gem would throw down their barrier . . .

A crash shook the walls, ending with the sound of splintering wood, shards of it scattering upon the stone floor. A renewed cry sprang up from the guards, and the sound of running came back towards Loren.

"Now!" she cried, and she and Niya threw their shoulders into the door. It flew outwards like a battering ram, and she felt it strike bodies. Three guards were bowled to the floor, two of them unconscious and the third stunned. Loren blinked against the smoke that flooded her vision, trying to see the figures ahead of her. She spotted one in a dark green dress pressing a green handkerchief to her mouth. Loren seized an arm and dragged the figure forwards. The face came into view, and her heart skipped a beat. Damaris of the family Yerrin stood before her, in Loren's clutches at last.

"We have her!" cried Loren. "Go!"

She dragged Damaris off down the hall. The merchant's eyes were still pressed so tight against the smoke that she had not realized who had taken her arm. But Niya did not follow them at once. Behind Damaris there were several other figures—some in the fine clothes of merchants or noblemen, and others in guard uniforms.

Niya slew them all.

Loren paused for a moment, horror-struck. First Niya cut down the unarmed figures in the fine clothing. Then she attacked the guards. The smoke had begun to work on her by then, but the guards were nearly poisoned from it, and they all fell beneath her blade. She hacked them down as though she had gone mad, leaving them mangled on the floor in their own blood.

Loren could not stop it. She could not help them. So she turned and ran.

It was a long way before she found another stairwell. This one was plain stone, and it was crumbling, so that she had to take care with her steps. But as she started her ascent, Damaris began to recover from the smoke at last. She swiped desperately at her eyes with the sleeve of her dress.

Her eyes focused on Loren's face.

Damaris recoiled, trying to snatch her hand away.

"You!" she cried. "Guards! *Guards,* darkness take—"

Loren wrenched Damaris' arm around and behind her back, and with her other hand she covered Damaris' mouth, taking care that the merchant could not bite her.

"Be silent, Damaris. You know that I will not kill you, but I can make your path out of this place more painful than it has to be." She shoved the merchant up the stairs, and Damaris had to walk or fall flat on her face. Whenever she tried to break free, Loren wrenched on her arm again, until the woman cried out beneath her hand.

But all the while, Loren looked fearfully back over her shoulder as they went. Suddenly the thought of Niya coming up behind her was terrifying, for she did not know what strange war-lust had seized the Mystic. It reminded her of when Mag had fought the Shades in Northwood. She had entered some sort of battle-trance, and become something inhuman. Only that had been a cold and dead-eyed fury, and Niya's seemed born of pure rage and hatred. It frightened Loren to her core, and she only wished to get as far away from it as possible.

At the top of the stairs, she headed back towards where Gem had shown them the shaft leading up. The smoke had begun to rise to this level, but it was nowhere near as bad, and she found the place easily enough. But when she found the room, only Gem was there. Loren looked behind him, and then inside the room, but Chet was nowhere to be seen.

"Gem," she said, panic seizing her limbs. "Where is Chet?"

"Some guards spotted us just after we threw down the furniture," said Gem. The boy panted heavily, as though he had just run a great sprint. "We split up and said we would meet here. He has not returned yet."

Loren spun, dragging Damaris with her as the merchant cried out in protest. She looked both directions down the hallway, and then ran to the next intersection to look there. Chet was nowhere in sight.

She did not know what to do. She had been willing to leave Niya behind, at least while the woman was in her bloodlust. If worst came to worst, Niya could find the shaft and escape on her own. But Chet . . . how could she go on without him?

You cannot, came the answer in her mind.

Damaris took advantage of her distraction and opened her mouth to bite down on Loren's forefinger. But Loren felt the motion at the last moment and dragged her hand away. The merchant's teeth cut into her skin, but not the flesh. She seized the back of Damaris' hair and slammed the merchant's whole body into the wall, screaming with rage.

"Still yourself, you noxious witch!" she cried. With another great heave, she crushed the merchant into the stone again. "I swear by both the moons that I will end you."

Damaris only laughed. "We both know that that is a lie, *Night-blade.* Tales of you fly all across the land, of the mercy of your hand. And I know you still better than those stories."

"Gem, find rope," said Loren. "Or cord, or anything to bind her with—the more painful the better."

The boy ran off to obey her. Loren shoved Damaris into the room with the hatch and then drew her dagger. She hacked a long strip from the back of Damaris' dress, heedless of the large hole it made there. Her knife slipped for moment and drew a thin line of blood from Damaris' shoulder blade, and the woman hissed with pain.

"My apologies, *my lady,*" said Loren. "Mayhap if you struggled less, that would not have happened."

She balled up most of the cloth and shoved it into Damaris' mouth, tying it in place with the rest. Damaris grunted as Loren pulled the knot as tight as she could. Gem returned in a moment with a thin rope that looked as though it had once belonged to fine drapes, though Loren could not imagine why there would be window coverings in this place, so far from the sunlight.

"Loren!"

She whirled. Chet stood there in the doorway. His clothes were so scorched that she hardly recognized them, and he was covered in soot, but his skin was unmarked by blade or burn. Loren's eyes filled with tears in an instant.

"Chet," she said. "Thank the sky. I thought you were lost. I meant to go and find you, I—"

"That is all right. I am here." He went to her and put a hand on her arm. "You have Damaris. I can scarcely believe it."

"It worked," said Loren. "Now come, quickly, and help me get her into the shaft." Gem already had the thing open, and was hauling on the rope to lower the wooden platform so that they could put Damaris onto it.

"Of course, of course," mumbled Chet. "Only forgive me . . . the smoke . . ." His eyes wandered, taking her in, and then looking to the door of the room. He seemed dazed, half senseless.

She looked at him with concern. "Are you all right? What is wrong? Are you hurt?"

But before he could answer her, Loren heard footsteps from the hall. They all froze, even Damaris, and Loren watched the doorway with wide and fearful eyes. The footsteps stopped just out of sight. Then, with two great staggering steps, Niya appeared in the door.

Loren's first instinct was to loose a sigh of relief, but then she tensed again. The Mystic had taken a wound in the fighting. It looked to be a stab wound from a knife, but it was high on her shoulder and did not seem fatal.

That was not what gave Loren pause. It was the look in Niya's eye—still furious, still filled with a lust for blood and death. Loren felt that she must do something, but she did not know what.

"Niya," said Chet. "You are here, too. What a relief." It did not seem that he saw any sign of the woman's dangerous mood.

"You . . ." growled Niya. She staggered into the room, and Loren saw that the stab wound was not her only injury. Her left arm was badly burned near the shoulder. *"You."*

The sword fell from her hand, and relief washed through Loren. But then Niya strode into the room and seized Chet by the front of his shirt. Before anyone could react, the Mystic drew her dagger and slit Chet's throat.

446

THIRTY-EIGHT

"No!"

Loren fell to her knees beside Chet as he slumped to the ground. She seized his throat, trying hopelessly to staunch the blood as it poured out over her fingers. Her dreams played in her mind, the dreams where Chet always died, always, just as he was dying now.

Gem gave a scream and launched himself at Niya. But the Mystic struck him a heavy backhand blow, and he landed hard on the floor. Damaris struggled against her bonds, trying to fight to her feet. Niya kicked her back down, and she lay still. Then Niya seized Loren by the back of her cloak and hauled her up.

"Stop your fretting, Nightblade," she growled. "Look."

Loren struggled against her, fighting to reach for Chet again. She knew she could not save him. But darkness take her if she would not be with him as his life slipped away, if she would not give him at least that comfort.

Then she froze.

From Chet's eyes poured a glow she knew well: magelight. And as she watched, his form began to change.

His skin darkened, and his sandy brown hair turned black. When the glow faded from his eyes, he was Chet no longer, but Hewal. He raised a hand, reaching for her, but she could not know whether it was in anger or in fear, for the blood that bubbled up around his teeth was all she could see.

Life fled him at last, and his hand fell to the stone floor.

Niya let go, and Loren jerked away from her.

"You . . . how did you . . ."

"Sky above, girl." Niya's voice was a low growl, still holding some of the fury of her battle-rage. "Look at him. He wears different clothes. Chet wore boots into the stronghold, but Hewal has shoes on."

She spoke the truth. Hewal's clothes were burned and torn, but they were clearly different. In her relief at seeing Chet again, Loren had not seen the details of his appearance.

"I . . . I thought . . ."

"I know what you thought," said Niya. "But we are out of time. All of Yewamba will soon be mustered against us, and we must escape before that happens."

"But Chet—the real Chet, I mean, where is—"

"Loren!" Chet's voice rang out from the hallway. A moment later he appeared there in the doorway, gripping its edges with his hands. Loren ran to him with a cry, but she stopped a pace away, hesitant.

"Sky above, *listen*, girl," said Niya. "Look at his boots."

Loren did, and they were Chet's, and she ran forwards to embrace him. He started, surprised, but then his arms folded around her.

"What is it?" he said. "What is wrong? Gem and I became separated, and—"

He froze, and she knew that he had seen Hewal's body. Loren pushed away from him and followed his gaze.

"He took your likeness, and when I saw him I thought you . . ."

And then she recalled her dream. Chet in the depths of Yewamba, before Damaris, his throat cut. Even Auntie's appearance, over and over again, every night.

Weremage, she thought.

All at once she understood, and she began to laugh. It rang from her clear and loud, mayhap her first true laugh since that final night with Xain upon the Seat. She laughed until her knees were weak, and she had to hold Chet to remain standing.

"Loren, I do not understand what has happened," said Chet.

"You will," she said, touching his cheek. "Everything, I promise you. I will tell you all. But after we have escaped."

"That may be a problem," said Gem. He had thrust his head into the shaft with the wooden platform, and now he withdrew it. "The way is shut."

"What do you mean?" said Loren. She went to him and looked for herself. Far above, she could see a large metal grate. It had been placed to block the way up, with only a tiny gap in its middle so that the rope could run through it.

"It looks to block the top five levels, if I guess the distance correctly," said Gem. "A measure to prevent escape by the very route we had planned to take."

Loren turned to Damaris, who sat against the wall now. Though the merchant's mouth was covered, Loren could see the smile in her eyes. She knelt and pulled off the gag.

"How can we escape?" she said.

"You cannot," said Damaris. Her voice was calm, measured, and utterly in control. "You will die here, slain by my soldiers. Your only possible consolation will be taking my own life before that happens—and I call that a small price, for your end is assured."

Loren saw no doubt whatsoever in the woman's face, and it sent a chill through her. But Niya seized the front of Damaris' dress and dragged her to her feet, slamming her back into the wall.

"Do not toy with us, wretch," said Niya. "There is a way out. A way that you would use to escape, if Yewamba were besieged beyond hope of victory. Tell us where to find it."

Damaris cocked her brows. "I do not know you, woman."

"You will know me before the end," hissed Niya. "Tell us how to get out."

"Never," said Damaris. "Not in a lifetime could you understand the depths of my loathing for this girl, with her simpering eyes and stolen cloak."

"I have stolen many things, but not this," said Loren, smiling fiercely at the merchant. "The cloak you gave me freely. And, too, you drove your daughter away from you and into my company. You may blame yourself for that as well."

Damaris jerked without warning in Niya's arms, breaking free and flinging herself at Loren. But with her hands bound behind her it was a feeble lunge, and Loren caught her by the shoulders. Damaris thrashed and struggled, screaming in Loren's face.

"Never speak of her to me, you mewling sow! You will beg me for death before I am through with you. I have spent a lifetime plumbing the depths of pain. I will plunge you into them again and again until you have forgotten your own name, until you have forgotten everything but agony!"

Loren pushed her slightly away. She drew back her hand and gave Damaris a calm, measured, crushing slap across the face.

"No. You will not."

Chet put a hand on her shoulder. "We have remained here overlong," he said. "If we cannot use the shaft to escape, we should find a better place to hide."

Niya seized Damaris once again and spun her around before driving a knee into her gut. The merchant gave a thin grunt, wheezing as she tried to suck air into her lungs. "Tell us," said Niya. "Tell us before I end you."

Damaris only laughed.

The Mystic squeezed her by the throat, cutting off the laugh and pressing her windpipe until her eyes bugged out. "I give you one final chance. Speak. I have killed many here today, and I will kill more before the end. Speak, or you are next." She drew her knife and pressed the point against Damaris' jugular.

"Stop it," said Loren. She seized Niya's wrist and pulled it away. "That is not the mission."

"The mission?" snarled Niya. "The mission now becomes escape—and if we cannot capture Damaris, better to kill her."

"Our situation is not hopeless. We saw on the way in how sparsely populated this place is. We may still make our way to the top." Loren's hand tightened on Niya's wrist. "And we may need Damaris as a bargaining chip. Without her, our chances dwindle."

Rage still burned in the Mystic's eyes, plain for all to see. But a spark of cunning flashed within them, and Loren felt the tension in her arm fade away. "Very well," she said in a low voice. "Because we need her."

Loren nodded, and then turned to Damaris. "That is twice now when I could have killed you and did not. That is in repayment, for you have done so twice for me."

"And never a greater mistake," hissed Damaris. "But you have no power over me, girl. You have only ever called off the trained dogs who march by your side—the wizard who became a dean, and now this Mystic."

"You are a fine one to talk," said Loren, arching an eyebrow. "When have you ever held a blade yourself, rather than commanding the one in Gregor's hand? Gag her."

She turned away as Chet did as she asked. But then a thought struck her, spurred by her own words. Gregor.

"Hold a moment," she said, and turned to Damaris. "I did not see Gregor with you below. Is he here in Yewamba?"

The merchant froze. Above the gag, she studied Loren with narrow eyes.

"You seem fairly obsessed with this Gregor fellow," said Niya scornfully. "Is he another lover, mayhap, whose affections you scorned?"

Chet glared at that, but Loren ignored it. "He is her guard. And he is loyal to her beyond measure or reason. Her other guards obey her to the letter, for their duty is to their family. If Damaris ordered them to kill us at all costs, even if it meant her own life, they would obey." Loren smiled at Damaris. "But not Gregor. If we offered her life in exchange for our escape, Gregor would accept in a heartbeat."

Niya's hand tightened on Damaris' shoulder. "We will not surrender her."

"Of course not," said Loren, her smile broadening. "But Gregor will believe that we will. He knows I am . . . an *honorable* thief."

Damaris screamed into her gag and lunged for Loren again, but Niya dragged her back. Loren looked over to Chet and Gem, who wore hopeful smiles for the first time since they had all entered the room.

"Find us some Yerrin guards, my friends. It is time we got out of this place."

Damaris struggled all the while they dragged her down the hallways. Niya held her arm across the woman's throat, placing her in front of the party as they sought for guards to bargain with. They had to find a staircase down to the next level, for the one they were on was still abandoned.

Eventually they neared the mess hall they had snuck through earlier. Around the corner from it they stopped, and Niya looked to Loren. With a nod, Loren ushered her around the corner.

"Guards of Yerrin!" she cried.

The room went utterly silent, and everyone within froze.

The guards had mustered in groups around the tables on either side of the room. It seemed that two captains had gathered their men around to inform them of what had happened and to issue orders. Loren saw that many of the men had burns on their bodies or their clothing, and wondered how long they had been fighting the flames, trying to find their lady among the smoke and the blaze. Now they edged away from the tables and towards the center of the room, hands going to the hilts of their swords.

"That is enough of that," said Niya, tightening her grip on Damaris' neck. "Stay your hands, or see her body broken."

They froze, looking at each other uneasily. Then one of them stepped forwards, a barrel-chested fellow with a thick beard flecked with grey. "Unhand our lady, or things will not go well for you."

"We will not," said Loren. "Not until we have spoken to Gregor."

At that the man paused. He glanced at Damaris. From beneath her gag she shouted, and with her eyes wide she shook her head back and forth. But her words could not be understood, and the guard captain frowned.

"Run and fetch Gregor," he said to one of the men.

"Captain—"

He lifted three fingers. "Do as I say, and do not return without him. Am I understood?"

The guard gave Loren and the others a worried look. "Yes, Captain."

The guard ran out the room's other exit at once. The captain turned back to Loren. "What do you want?"

"Assurance of escape," said Loren. "Once we are safely on our way out of Yewamba, your lady will be freed."

"I cannot allow that," he said at once.

Loren smiled. "We will see, once Gregor arrives. Where is he?"

"Not far," said the captain.

"Good, then," said Loren. "If it is all the same to you, we will be in the hallway with your lady, to ensure that none of your men think to try their luck with an attack."

The captain took a quick step forwards. Niya jerked Damaris up until the merchant was forced to stand upon her toes. The captain froze. "Do not take her out of our sight," he said.

"Very well," said Loren. "She and my friend will stand in the doorway where you may see her."

They backed away slowly, with Loren and Chet and Gem taking up position just to the left of the door. Niya stood in sight of the guards, holding Damaris before her. The merchant continued to struggle and fight, flinging her hands back and forth where they were bound before her.

"Be still," snarled Niya. She drove a fist into Damaris' side, causing her to groan and sag.

"Niya!" said Loren. "Enough. If you harm her too badly, they will not help us at all."

"I will do more than harm her if she does not stop her squirming," said Niya.

Chet looked up and down the hallway. "What is taking the guard so long?" he said. "I thought Gregor was nearby."

"If I know him, he searches high and low for Damaris," said Loren. "He might have gone farther than the captain knew." But she understood his anxiety—she, too, felt more ill at ease the longer they remained here.

"*Still* yourself, witch!" said Niya. Her arm constricted on Damaris' throat just a bit more.

"I think you squeeze her too tight," said Gem, frowning. "She is twitching."

Loren glanced over. Though they were still bound before her, Damaris' arms were indeed spasming back and forth—or rather, her hands were, in jerky little motions. Then Loren's eyes shot wide. The merchant was not struggling against her bonds—she was signaling to the guard captain.

"Niya, run!" she cried, but too late. A door down the hall burst open, and with a great shout of battle cries soldiers in mail shirts and green cloaks stormed into view. Niya froze in shock, and Damaris jerked away from the woman's grasp, then ran stumbling into the mess hall before she could be reclaimed. Loren ran to help, but only in time to see Damaris turn beside the captain and rip the gag away from her mouth with a triumphant grin.

"*Kill them!*" cried Damaris. "Burn this place to the ground if you must! Bring me their corpses!"

With a snarl, Niya drew her sword. But Loren seized her arm and dragged her back.

"You cannot take them all!" she cried. "Run!"

They did, turning and fleeing down the hallway as an army surged after them.

THIRTY-NINE

"WE CANNOT LEAVE WITHOUT DAMARIS," SAID NIYA AS THEY RAN.

"We cannot capture her and live," replied Loren. "If you turn back and attack her guards, they will overwhelm you. Now we can only escape, and try again another day."

"You should have let me kill her."

Loren did not answer, but she wondered if the Mystic was right. Yet Kal had been clear: justice was worthless if delivered in secret. Should Damaris die here, in the bowels of this mountain, who would ever even know? Especially if Loren and the rest of them did not escape to spread the tale. And if they killed her like common assassins, that would make them no better than the traitors they fought against who had tried to murder the High King.

But she had no time for such thoughts, not if she wanted to get them all out alive. They ran up the first stairway they saw, but it only took them up one floor, and they did not know which direction to turn.

"We do not know the way out," said Chet. "We will never get out of here before they catch us."

"Oh, stop your *whining,*" said Niya.

"There is no other choice," said Loren. "We have to keep looking and hope for the best. One floor at a time."

They turned this way and that through the halls, trying to create a weaving, winding path so that they could not be followed easily. Loren, Chet, and Gem wore only cloth, and Niya was strong enough to run fast even with her chain shirt, so that they soon left the guards behind them. But they could hear the pursuit, their shouts and footsteps thundering in the halls.

At last Loren spotted another stairway. "There!" she cried, leading the way to it. But at the foot of the stairs they skidded to a halt. Above, they heard more shouts and the sound of running. Another group of guards, and this one making its way down towards them.

"We are trapped," whispered Loren.

"Then it is a fight after all," said Chet. He looked to Niya. "I suppose we should be glad we have your sword."

"Wait," said Gem. He looked up at Loren with wide eyes. "There may be a way. The shaft."

She frowned at him. "It is shut, Gem. We cannot go up that way."

"Not up," he said. "Down."

Her mind raced. Down, down, into impenetrable darkness—but where they had heard the sound of running water. It might be a river deep enough to swim. It might be only a few fingers deep. Or the rope might not be directly over the water at all, and end ten paces above a rocky cavern floor, and they would kill themselves if they tried the jump. But they did not know that, and they *did* know what would happen if they stayed and fought the guards.

"We must try it," she said. "Come."

They ran on, and now they ducked their heads into each room as they went, searching for one that had a hatch. Chet found one in a few moments. Loren threw it open and looked up, just to be sure—but there was the metal grate, blocking the way in this shaft just as it had in the other.

"Very well," she said. "Down it is."

They slipped through the hatch as quickly as they could, with Niya going last. She pulled the hatch as far shut as she could, though she could not latch it from the inside. It would have to do. Loren led them all down the rope.

Fifteen floors they had descended before they found Damaris. Loren thought they passed at least fifteen more, but it was hard to keep count, for no light came through the hatches on the lower levels. Soon they were in pitch blackness, and when they looked up they could only barely glimpse the soft glow that had lit their way before.

"How will we even know when we reach the bottom?" called Gem. The sound of rushing water had grown loud enough now that he had to raise his voice to be heard.

"I imagine the rope will end," said Loren.

"That is not comforting," said Chet.

Loren chuckled—and then she cried out, for the wall had vanished under her feet. She had reached the bottom of the shaft, and when she put out her foot to take the next step down, it met only empty air. For a terrifying moment she swung there in the darkness, swaying back and forth on the rope as she tried to tighten her grip.

"Loren!" cried Chet, for he could not see her.

"I am all right!" she said. "The shaft has ended, but the rope has not."

"Can you see the floor?" said Niya.

I cannot see anything at all, thought Loren irritably. But she only said, "No."

Hand over hand she lowered herself once more, but now the way was harder without something to brace herself on. Her hands began to chafe on the rope, and she did not know how much longer she could keep hold. *As long as you must,* she told herself, tightening her grip again. *This place must have a bottom.* They would reach it eventually.

And then the rope ended.

Loren felt it with her feet first, where they were wrapped around the line. Suddenly they encountered the curving loop at the bottom of the rope, where it turned and ran back up the shaft to the crank that must be at the top. She went a little farther down and stuck out her feet, but she already knew she would not find the ground. The rushing water was loud, thundering below them, but too far for her to reach.

"We are at the bottom," she called up.

"Thank the sky," said Gem.

"I mean the bottom of the rope," said Loren. "The floor is still far below."

"Ah," said Gem. "That is somewhat less good news."

"What do we do?" said Chet.

"A moment," said Loren. "I am thinking." At least she was able to put a knee in the loop of the rope and take some of the weight off her arms. But that only made her realize that her friends had no such support, and their grips must be as tired as her own. Her mind raced, desperate for an answer.

They could risk the jump. Though she could not be sure, it sounded as though the water was below them. They could drop from the end of the rope, and hope that they would land in the river that would carry them out into the valley. But then again, if the river indeed emerged out into the open, would they not be able to see the light of the opening from here?

See.

She cursed the darkness. If she only had a torch, or moonslight, or—

Loren almost struck herself, she was so angry. *You stupid, stupid fool,* she thought.

The magestones. She had them in her cloak, the same place she always kept them. But she had not used them since Ammon, and had nearly forgotten about them.

"I cannot hold on to this rope forever, you know," said Gem. The boy tried to fill his voice with bravado, but Loren could sense the fear quivering beneath it. "Even one so strong as I am has his limits."

"One moment!" she said, fumbling with her cloak pocket. With hasty fingers she seized a magestone and broke off a piece, which she shoved in between her lips. Then she reached for the back of her belt and drew her dagger.

The cavern erupted in light, silver and pale, like the glow of the Elves. Now Loren could see as though she stood in the sun, or better, for every detail was enhanced, from the ridges in the rocky cavern to the cobwebs that collected in the corners.

She looked down and was glad she had not risked the jump. There was a river, yes, mayhap fifteen paces below them. But it twisted and turned through a fissure in the floor, and just beneath them was only rock, pocked with spikes of stone that jutted up from the ground towards them, like hungry teeth eager to devour.

"We cannot jump!" said Loren. "There is only stone below us."

"What?" said Chet. "How do you know?"

"My eyes are adjusting," she lied. "Are you not getting used to the darkness?"

"Then what do we do?" said Niya, her irritation plain.

Loren looked about. She could see other ropes hanging down from other holes in the ceiling—other shafts leading up to other wooden platforms, and all of them too far away to reach. But then she turned the other way, and saw that they were very near to the cavern wall, and there were shelves in the rock there. But it was at least five paces away—too far to jump, and certainly too far to reach.

"We must swing!" said Loren. "Swing the rope . . . this way." She reached up and tapped Gem's leg, on the side where the rock wall was. He did the same to Chet, who did the same to Niya.

"I see nothing that way," said Niya.

"Trust me," said Loren. "Draw back your legs, and . . . now!"

They did it, back and forth, back and forth. At first they were awkward and uncoordinated, but as they all sensed the rhythm of each other, they soon moved in unison. The rope only moved a pace at first, and then two. Then they got within reach of the shelf, but Loren missed her grasp. She tightened her grip on the dagger with one hand, and her hold on the rope with the other.

"This time!" she cried, and when she swung towards the shelf, she reached it at last. She threw herself onto the stone, and a lump in the rock struck her in the ribs, making her wince. But she seized the rope and pulled it tight, and just managed to keep from sliding off the edge again by wrapping her arm around a lump in the stone. The rope hung there, her three friends upon it, dangling over the rocky floor far below.

"Quickly!" she said through gritted teeth. "Climb down."

Gem descended like a spider, and she sighed with relief once his weight was off the line. Then came Chet, and by the time only Niya was left, it was easy. The Mystic reached the shelf at last, and Loren released the rope with a sigh. But above her she saw that the other three were fumbling blindly in the dark, their hands on the wall to hold themselves steady.

"We have to climb down from here," she said. "The wall is rough. There are handholds aplenty."

"How can you see?' said Chet. "It is black as tar."

"What matters is that I *can* see," said Loren. "I will go down first. When I tell you to, guide your foot to the edge, and I will give you your first handhold."

They did as she bid, and one by one they slid over the edge and began to climb down the stone wall. Loren put the dagger in her teeth, careful not to let it touch her lips, for it was frighteningly sharp. She was gratified to see that its magical properties remained even when she held it so.

With its help she took them all the entire long, dark, frightening way to the floor of the cavern, and when they had reached it they sighed with relief.

"If anything, I can see less than before," said Gem. "If this place is so dark, is there even a way out?"

"The water must emerge somewhere," said Loren. "It forms the stream in the valley outside Yewamba. Chet, put your hand on my shoulder, and the rest of you in a chain. I will take us to the water, and we will follow it out."

So they progressed to the water's edge. Loren could see that the river was nowhere near so deep as she had thought; she doubted it came up to her chest. But it was wide, and the way beside it was not always clear, so that it took them some time to follow it through the cavern.

When they reached the end of it, Loren hoped to find a curve in the rock, some sort of passage that would take them to the open air beyond. But to her dismay, the water ended at a wall, against which it frothed and bubbled.

"The water has ended," she said.

"What do you mean, it has ended?" said Niya.

"It dives under the cave wall here. If it emerges in the open air beyond, it goes underground for a ways beforehand."

"Then there is no way out?" said Chet.

"There is," said Loren. She turned to look at him, but then realized that was pointless, for he could not see her. "The river."

Niya snorted. "Underground? We do not know how far it is. We could drown."

"Yet there is no other way."

"Loren, I cannot swim," said Gem, and now all his bravado had fled him.

She cursed inwardly, for she had forgotten. "I can take you, Gem. You can hold my shoulders."

"He had better come with me," said Niya. "You are not as strong as I am."

Loren studied the Mystic for a moment, thankful now for the darkness. "I would rather bring him myself," she said carefully. "Gem and I have done something like this together before."

That was true enough—in the city of Wellmont, they had swum

under a gate that blocked the river. But in truth, Loren was not sure that she trusted Niya with the boy's life. The Mystic had always scorned him, likely thinking him too young to be on such an important quest. If the way became blocked, and Niya faced the choice of saving the boy or saving her own skin, Loren did not think it would be a difficult decision.

Niya only shrugged. "If you insist."

"Loren, are you certain this is the best way?" said Chet.

"Of course not," she told him. "But it is the only way. Now come. Dawdling here will not make the swim easier."

She shucked off her boots and tied them to her belt. They would not help with her swimming, but once they emerged out the other side, she could not go barefoot all the way back to their camp. Quickly she helped the others do the same, for their fingers fumbled in the darkness, and soon they were ready.

"All right," said Loren. "Gem, take my shoulders. Follow the flow of the water. It comes out the other side in the end, so it knows where it is going. Good luck."

"Luck," said Chet, laughing suddenly. "How can we think ours is good, after all that has happened?"

Niya scowled in the direction of his voice, likely thinking no one could see her in the pitch-dark cavern. Then, without warning, the Mystic flung herself into the water. After letting Gem take a deep breath, Loren followed.

The water snatched her at once and dragged her into the tunnel beneath the rock. Immediately it slammed her into the wall, and she felt Gem's grip shift. Keeping one hand on her dagger hilt, she reached up with the other and clutched his arm. It was useless to try to swim, for the current was too strong here. She only twisted and turned, keeping her body between the boy and the rocks, and used her legs to brace against the impact. Chet and Niya would not be able to see a thing, and Loren only hoped they did not take too hard of a battering.

Her lungs grew weak, and then began to burn. The tunnel ahead showed no sign of ending. She took her hand from Gem's arm and tried to swim as best she could, desperate to speed their progress. If she was losing her breath, Gem must be near to drowning. Niya and Chet were nowhere to be seen. Had they become separated? Did the water run in different passages, ones she had missed as she went by?

A dim light appeared, different from the night vision of the dagger, illuminating the channel. The end of the tunnel at last. But though they could see the glow, they still could not see the exit, and spots had begun to dance in Loren's vision.

Around her neck, she felt Gem's grip slacken.

No, she thought. She seized his arm and kicked as hard as she could, striking for the light ahead. *Hold on. Hold on, you little brat.*

Sunlight erupted above them, almost blinding in its intensity. Loren shoved her dagger into its sheath and swam up, still clutching at Gem. Her head broke the surface with a great splash, and she sucked in a greedy lungful of air.

The shore was only a few paces away, and she kicked for it. Niya was there already, on hands and knees in the grass, gasping and heaving. Loren flung Gem up on the bank first and then dragged herself from the water. Her black cloak had become dead weight intent on trying to drag her into the river again, so she undid the clasp and threw it off. She fell on the shore as all her strength left her at once, and her chest heaved with her breathing.

But then she thought of Gem and rose once more. She crawled to the boy and flipped him onto his back, pounding on his chest. For one heart-stopping instant he lay still. Then at last he coughed up water. She hauled him up to sitting and bent him forwards, and he kept coughing until no more water came out.

Loren looked up towards the stream. *Chet. Where is Chet?*

Then he appeared, breaking the surface just as she had, a little upstream. He saw them and fought to swim to the shore, gasping. Loren sighed with relief. Chet had always been a good swimmer.

"Is he all right?" said Chet, once he had gained the land.

"Well enough, considering," said Loren, giving Gem's back a final pound.

"Leave off," said the boy, waving a limp arm in her direction. "I am fine."

Loren smiled down at him. But the smile died on her lips as a horn cut the air.

She had not had time to take in their surroundings, but now she looked up. They were at the foot of the stronghold, with its peaked prow jutting out into the air straight overhead. A few hundred paces away was the bottom of the long, winding ramp that led up to the main entrance. And down that ramp figures were running and shouting, their weapons drawn.

"They have spotted us," said Loren. She fought for her feet and snatched up her cloak. "Come. We must flee if we are to survive."

Quickly she removed her boots from around her waist and pulled them on. Niya struggled to don her own boots, her movements slow and sluggish.

"I would wager that now you wish we had killed the guards in the valley as we approached."

"I do not, but thank you," said Loren, frowning. "Now is not the time for gloating, but for running."

Run they did, following the stream. Soon the guards were behind them, giving chase along the opposite side of the river. But Loren and her friends were waterlogged and exhausted from the swim, so that they could not gain much ground, and soon their lungs burned anew.

"We are not gaining any ground," said Chet. "They will follow us straight back to Uzo and Annis."

"And—" Loren almost stopped in her tracks, and only resumed her flight when Chet snatched her arm and pulled her along. "Shiun. Where is Shiun?"

"She will look after herself," said Niya. "Likely she fled the fortress as soon as the alarm was raised, for who could think that we would escape?"

It was not a comforting thought that Shiun would leave them to their fate, but certainly they could not go back to see. If they somehow evaded the guards, they would return later. But she did not see how that would happen.

And then they ran over a hillock, and an arrow struck Loren in the chest.

She stumbled in her run and barely kept herself from falling on her face, sinking to her knees instead.

Dazed, she stared at the feathered shaft that protruded from her torso, on the left side and just under the collarbone. Her gaze drifted upwards.

Three guards stood there. Mayhap they were the ones Shiun had shown to Loren on the valley floor, two days ago when they had discovered Yewamba. Mayhap they were another three. But one of them had a bow, and she had loosed the shaft that now pierced Loren's body.

Was that the arrowhead she could feel, protruding from her back?

She tried to lift her left arm to see, but it did not move. She lifted her right arm instead, reaching behind her back. But a pain shot through her, and she dropped her hand.

Someone was screaming. Who was screaming? She looked up. Chet, Chet who held her shoulders, who was trying to place his body between her and the archer.

Why do that? she thought. *I have been shot already.* It struck her then that that was a foolish thought, and her mind was wandering.

Someone else was there. Shiun, her dark eyes wide and anxious as she beheld Loren's wound. And looking over Chet's shoulder, Loren could see two of the Yerrin guards had now been shot as well, and lay still on the ground. Shiun must have done it. The third guard lay on his back, hands raised feebly as Niya plunged her dagger into his chest, over, and over, and over.

Loren fell backwards and knew nothing more.

FORTY

BLINDING PAIN WAS HER ONLY COMPANION WHEN SHE AWOKE, BUT THAT was better than the memory of a nightmare.

Loren tried to sit up. She failed, gasped, and lay still. Her chest was wrapped with bandages that covered a great pad of cloth. She tried to probe at it with her left hand, but as soon as her arm moved the pain redoubled. Hissing through her teeth, she waited for it to subside before using her right hand instead, though that limb was weak and shaking.

Touching the pad of cloth was not too bad, but when she tried to lift it, dried blood peeled from her skin. She winced and left it alone, and then looked around.

Where were the others? She knew she was in her tent, but Chet was not with her, and she heard no movement outside.

"Is anyone there?" she croaked.

She heard movement on the grass, and then the tent flap flew open. Chet eagerly poked his head in, eyes shining as he beheld her. "You are awake," he said, his voice shaking.

"I am, and I am thirsty."

"Of course," he said. "One moment."

He vanished, only to return shortly with her waterskin. She could not sit up without his help, but once she did she drank deep, ignoring the way it burned in her throat. When she was done she patted his arm, and he moved the skin away.

"How long?" she said.

"It is the evening of the day after our mission."

Loren's eyes shot wide, and she tried to look out through the tent flap. "They have not found us?"

"We moved the camp," said Chet. "Shiun found this place, and we were on constant watch in case they drew near it. But then, sometime during the night, they simply gave up."

"Why?" said Loren. "Why would they?" She frowned, looking into her lap. Then a guess came to her, and she surged forwards, trying to leave the tent. But with a grimace and a cry she fell back, and Chet only just caught her in time.

"Sky above, Loren, give yourself a moment at least. You took an arrow. That is no scratch."

Once more she looked at the bandages on her chest. "Who did this?" *Niya,* she guessed in her mind.

"Uzo," said Chet. "He has some little skill as a healer, it seems, though he told us often that he is no master at it. He did say the wound could have been much worse. The arrow struck only flesh, nothing vital."

"Nowhere near as bad as your wound upon the Seat, then?" said Loren.

Though he tried to restrain it, a guffaw burst out. "Darkness take you, Loren. We are not in contest to see who can suffer the greater injury."

Loren smiled at him and put her hand on his cheek. "Did everyone get out safely?"

"They did," he said. But then his face darkened, and his voice grew quiet. "All but Weath, of course."

"I am sorry," said Loren. Then she shook her head. *Darkness take me, my thoughts are wandering.* "But we have little time. I know why the Yerrins stopped searching for us. They mean to leave—"

"They mean to leave Yewamba," said Chet. "Annis guessed the same thing. She said it was a good thing Damaris did not know she was close by, or else she would never have left the stronghold. But now the family Yerrin feels too exposed, for their location is known, and mayhap word has already reached them that Kal marches west towards them. Whatever the reason, they are preparing to leave."

"Then this is our last chance to stop Damaris," said Loren. "We must—"

"She will ride out ahead of the rest," said Chet. "Annis guessed that, too. She thinks she knows the route Damaris will take, unless there is some road west of the mountains she can escape to. But Uzo and Shiun have gone to guard the main road, and if Damaris passes that way, they will see her. If they believe they can take her guards, they will. If not, they will mark her passing so that we may follow in due time."

Loren stared at him in wonder. "Annis did all this?"

"Annis and Niya," said Chet, smiling. "Niya commanded Uzo and Shiun to go. They should return in a few days. But all of the plans came from Annis."

"That girl has more wit than even I realized," said Loren, shaking her head. But then something he had said caught her attention, and she frowned at him. "You said Niya told Uzo and Shiun to go. She did not accompany them?"

"She is here," said Chet. "She took wounds herself, you will remember."

"I do," said Loren. "Only I wish Uzo and Shiun were not alone."

"They will not endanger themselves," said Chet. He sat back, leaning on his hands. "I for one am just glad we escaped in time, and that you are still alive."

"I am, too," said Loren, smiling at him. Despite the pain from her wound, she felt as though a great weight had left her shoulders. "Indeed, my mind is easier than it has been in some time."

"Even though we lost Damaris?" said Chet, his brows rising.

She thought of her dream, and then of Hewal's corpse. "Even then," she said softly.

He shook his head. "Well, then my mind is eased as well. Only now I should go."

"Go?" said Loren. "Where?"

"To hunt," he said. "Our supplies run low, and Niya fears to visit that little town nearby, in case the Yerrins have placed agents there to watch for us. But I will send Annis in to sit with you, and help you if you should need anything."

Loren nodded. He kissed her forehead and left.

A while later she heard footsteps again and smiled as the tent flap opened. But it was not Annis. It was Niya. Her regular clothes were gone, replaced with dark brown trousers and a cream-colored tunic, the same as Loren's. It was the nondescript outfit most of them had worn on the journey to avoid attracting attention.

"Hello," said Loren softly.

"You look well enough," said Niya.

"I suppose I am," said Loren. "At least I am not dead."

"Though not for lack of trying."

Loren smiled. "How is your shoulder?"

Niya glanced at her own bandages. She wore fewer than Loren did. "It pains me less and less. I have been going for walks. They make it easier."

"I may do the same," said Loren.

It seemed as though Niya meant to say something else, or mayhap even to come inside the tent to continue speaking. But there came the snap of a twig, and she looked off to the side. She frowned at Loren. "You have another visitor. When you decide you are strong enough for walking, tell me. I shall bring you along."

She vanished from sight, only to be replaced by Annis. The girl crawled into the tent with her and took Loren's hand with a happy smile.

"It is good to see you awake."

"And it is good to see you at all," said Loren. "I heard that you have become quite the master strategist while I have been resting."

Annis' cheeks darkened. "I suppose I have been industrious in my planning."

"Thank you for seeing to things after I was injured," said Loren. "When I woke, I feared that we had lost everything. I should have known better."

"Stop it," said Annis, shaking her head. "You make it sound as though I have performed great deeds. I have only looked at maps and read a few signs."

"Kingdoms have been conquered, or more importantly, saved, by ones who sit and stare at maps," said Loren. "Our party would neither have come so far, nor come so close to achieving our aims were it not for you. I am glad you and Gem are with me."

At the boy's name, Annis' smile dampened considerably, though she tried to maintain it. But Loren saw, and frowned.

"What is it?"

"Nothing," said Annis. "Nothing you should trouble yourself over at any rate. You should be resting."

Loren raised her hands—the left one moved far more slowly than the right. "I am resting, and I cannot do anything else. Speak on. Did Gem do something wrong?"

Annis shook her head quickly. "No, not at all. Only . . . do you remember the night before you went to Yewamba, when I decided to tell him how I felt?"

"How can I forget?" said Loren, smirking. "I have rarely seen you with your blood up to that extent."

"Well, I did it," said Annis miserably. "And in return, he told me . . . that he felt affection for another."

Loren cocked her head, wondering at the girl's despair. "Another? Who . . .?" Then a horrid thought struck her. "Oh, sky above. Do not say he means me."

Annis snorted—which Loren did not think was very complimentary—and shook her head. "No. It is Uzo."

Loren only stared for a moment. Then the meaning of it assembled in her mind. She closed her eyes and heaved a deep sigh. "I see. That . . . I am sorry, Annis."

"Why should you be?" said Annis, shrugging. "It is not your fault, nor his. And is that not the most irritating thing? If he *did* pine after you, I could box his ears for being a fool, when I have shown him plainly how I felt. But now . . ."

"Yes," said Loren, thinking of Xain, and then of Jordel. "I learned the same thing myself, just before we left the Seat. Sometimes the deepest cut comes from the one who did not intend it, and who had no other choice in the first place."

FORTY-ONE

SHE RESTED THAT DAY, AND WENT TO SLEEP SHORTLY AFTER THE SUN went down. When she woke the next morning, her chest hardly hurt at all, at least not with any sharp pain. There was a gentle soreness that penetrated deep into her chest, and it swelled when she tried to move her arms. But Chet changed her bandages, which Uzo had shown him how to do, and she got a good look at her wound for the first time. It was much smaller than she had thought it would be, only a little larger than her fingernail, and the blood was already solid.

"The guards of Yerrin use narrow arrowheads," said Chet. "It lets them pierce chain, and sometimes plate, but it lessens the wound, and thank the sky for that."

With his help, she got dressed and left the tent. Outside, she found she could walk quite easily. She did not hurt anywhere but the shoulder, and as long as she did not move that too quickly, it was almost as though there was no injury at all.

"That is good," said Chet. "Uzo told us that the injury was not very serious, and that it was only the shock of it that made you fall senseless. Even so, you seem to be healing remarkably quickly."

It was true. She wondered about it, and then recalled what Xain had told her in the Academy's bell tower about the mystical properties of magestones. Was this another of them? In any case, she was glad of it.

As she sighed and stretched in the early morning light, Niya came out of her own tent. She smiled to see Loren up and about. "Good morn, Nightblade. How is your wound?"

"Better than yesterday," said Loren. "And I suppose that is all that can be expected."

"That is good to hear," said Niya. "Are you ready to try a walk? I found a path in the jungle yesterday that leads to a beautiful clearing. I think you would enjoy it."

Loren glanced at Chet, but he smiled and patted her hand. "I should go out hunting again," he said. "Go. It will be good for you."

"I will not be gone long," said Loren. Then she followed Niya, who struck out at once, heading south between the trees.

Soon Loren saw the trail that the Mystic had spoken of. It was an easy enough walk, and went up and down a series of hills that ran along the base of the mountains. Once or twice it crossed the stream, the same one that ran out of the mountain and came flowing all the way south. Loren remembered their escape from that place with a slight shiver.

Niya saw it and looked her over. "Is something wrong? Does it hurt?"

"No," said Loren. "I only remembered the cavern under Yewamba."

Niya nodded, and then fixed Loren with a crafty look. "And I remember you guiding us through it without pause. How did you see down there, anyway? Do not tell me you have good eyes—the place was pitch black."

Loren shrugged. She had not revealed her dagger to any of the Mystics, for she could not know who among them was trustworthy with its great secret. Even now she could feel it pressing against her ankle in her boot. "I cannot explain what I do not understand. I could see, and I do not know why you could not."

"Hm," said Niya, frowning at her. "Very well. Keep your secrets, Nightblade. But come along. We are near the place I wanted to show you."

The ground rose up now, up to the top of a ridge that was like a first step leading up a grand staircase, all the way to the mountains high above. There on the top of the ridge was the clearing. When they reached it, Niya waved her arm expansively out towards the lands below, as though presenting a fine feast.

It took Loren's breath away. They were not so very high, but the land before them fell down and down, so that she could see for what seemed like endless leagues. Jungle stretched without breaking, except to the southeast where she could see the village of Sarafu, smoke rising from its chimneys. But the rest was a verdant rug that went on forever, and the sun a golden coin glinting in a sky like the ocean.

"It is wonderful, Niya," said Loren. "I am glad you brought me here."

"Come, sit with me," said Niya. "Do you need help?"

Loren dropped and crossed her legs upon the ground. "No, thank you. It is as I said—the wound hardly troubles me if I do not jostle it."

"That is good," said Niya. She flashed a smile. "I will try not to jostle it, then."

Loren returned the smile, but she did not feel the same thrill course through her that she had during all the long journey across Feldemar. The memory of Niya's battle-rage, of the way she had cut down those people inside Yewamba, would not quit her mind. "You will not have an opportunity to."

"Oh, come now," said Niya. "At least be coy when you rebuff me. After what we went through in Yewamba together, I deserve at least that much."

"It is Yewamba that is the problem," said Loren. "You went half-mad in there. You did not only attack guards, but unarmed merchants. It was as though no amount of blood could sate you."

Niya frowned. "We needed to escape, and we were bringing a prisoner with us. Any pursuer could have overtaken us easily. They were a threat, and I removed them."

"I . . . I understand that," said Loren. And inside she thought, *Do I honestly? Am I that different from the girl who left the Birchwood so long ago?* But the answer was the feeling of unease in her heart. "Yet I saw you, Niya. You enjoyed it."

The Mystic's nostrils flared, and she looked away. "Mayhap I did, but not in the way you think. I have always been angry. You must have seen that yourself. Long ago I learned to control that when I fought, to harness it into a sort of madness. It makes me strong. In the moment I may be a killer." She put a hand on Loren's knee. "But that does not mean I am always a killer. I can be gentle as well."

Loren wanted to pull her knee away, but she restrained herself. "Once, I wanted that. But I have told you that I am Chet's, and he is mine. More clearly than ever now, I know why. Chet and I have been by each other's side for most of our lives. We know each other. We understand each other. He feels the same way about killing as I do. You are a fine woman, Niya, but you and I will never have what Chet has."

"How many times must I tell you that I do not want what you and Chet have?" growled Niya. She leaned forwards, trying to kiss Loren.

"Stop!" said Loren. She shot to her feet, awkward without the use of her left arm, and her right fist clenched. "I have spoken plainly, and already you have skirted dangerously close to the wrong side of the law. Leave me be."

Slowly Niya rose to her feet. She looked down at Loren with a wry smile and shook her head.

"Oh, little Loren," she said quietly. "What a foolish, foolish little girl you have been."

Loren recoiled—and then her heart stopped. From Niya's eyes, a pale white light shone forth.

Her form shifted and rippled. First she shrank, so that she was of a height with Loren. Her dark hair grew by a few fingers and then turned so blonde that it was almost white. Her brown skin darkened further. Her lips grew fuller. And as the light faded from her eyes at last, they were a light hazel, a hazel that captivated Loren just as surely as it had the first time she saw it.

Her lips curled in a devilish grin.

"Hello, Loren," said Auntie. "I can only imagine how much you have missed me."

473

FORTY-TWO

LOREN TURNED AND FLED FOR HER LIFE.

Her feet pounded down the path back towards camp, jostling her shoulder and making her wince as she plunged into the trees. She feared to look behind her, to slow even that much.

"Oh, Loren," called Auntie. "Why have you always been so coy?"

The voice sounded close, forcing Loren to turn against her will. But the weremage had vanished. Loren whirled, seeking her in the jungle, but saw nothing.

"Why—how long?" she called out. If she could get Auntie to talk, she might be able to tell the woman's location. "When did you take Niya's place?"

"You stupid, stupid girl." The voice came floating from her left, and Loren turned. Still she saw nothing. "It has always been me. From the very first time when you made your moon-eyes at me upon the Seat."

"That is a lie," said Loren at once. "You were kind. You were even . . . you acted as though you—"

"As though I *wanted* you?" Auntie laughed, long and cruel. "As I

474

said. A stupid girl. So stupid, you very nearly betrayed the love of your life for a pair of strong arms."

She was trying to circle around, to come between Loren and the path back to camp. *"Chet!"* screamed Loren, breaking into a sprint and ignoring the pain in her chest. *"Chet!"*

The jungle was silent. For a moment she wondered if Auntie was still there, stalking her, or if the weremage had decided not to chase her, and instead to go back for the camp. She must reach it first. If Auntie hurt any of the others—

Auntie pounced from the trees, right in front of Loren, who tried to skid to a halt. But the weremage's hand darted out and seized her shoulder. Loren cried out with pain and fell to her knees. Auntie sneered down at her.

"The mighty Nightblade," she said. "How long I have waited to bring you low. But I could not have imagined how sweet it would be— almost as sweet as the taste of you upon my lips."

"Why?" gasped Loren, as Auntie continued to squeeze her wound through the bandage. "Why all of this?"

"Oh, it was so very hard not to kill you until now," said Auntie. Without removing her grip, she knelt, her face only a handbreadth from Loren's. "Even the delightful charms of your eyes, darkness take them, did not still my wrath, my desire to taste your blood upon my knife. But I knew I must be patient. I knew I must wait. For I knew in the end you would bring me to Damaris."

Her free hand pulled down her collar. Then Loren saw that she still had a ruined throat, the mass of scar tissue that spoke of a grievous wound. It had not changed with the rest of Auntie's body.

"She gave me this. She gave me this because of *you.* I lay in that sewer for days as I tried to stitch my own neck together, and still it is ruined. Because of *you.*" Her voice was little more than rasping breath now, sweet and pungent in Loren's nostrils. "That is why I needed you, needed you both, you see. But while I waited, while I followed you as you bumbled your way across Feldemar in search of her, I decided that you would be mine before the end."

Loren struck all at once, hoping to surprise her. Her right fist slammed into Auntie's neck, and the weremage coughed violently just before Loren crushed the woman's nose with her forehead. She fought to gain her feet, but Auntie recovered, sweeping her legs out from under her with a vicious kick. Loren crashed down upon her back, screaming as agony lanced her shoulder.

Auntie straddled her, drawing something from her pocket. She threw it in Loren's face—a fine powder, burnt orange. Loren gasped without thinking and felt it enter her lungs. Her body seized up, arms twitching, and then they ceased to move at all. She lay utterly limp, her limbs refusing to answer the call of her mind. Auntie grinned down at her.

"A poison," said Auntie. "It may kill you in time, if I use enough of it. For I will use a very great deal, Loren, a *very* great deal. But mostly, I will use it to hold you in place. Because I do not wish for you to go anywhere, *Nightblade*—not while I carve you up, a piece at a time."

She drew a knife from her boot and held it up. Loren tried to recoil, but she could not move.

It was the knife from her dream. Old, rusted, dirty. Far below the quality one would expect of a merchant—but just right for a madwoman who lurked in the sewers of Cabrus.

Loren could not even scream. Only her eyes obeyed her, and even that was sluggish.

"I want you awake for all of it. I want you to feel every bit of it—every cut. And I want you to remember all the while, Loren." She leaned down, her lips brushing against Loren's ear. "I want you to remember that you almost chose me. That you almost gave yourself to me, in every way, instead of the boy you claimed to love."

"Loren!"

Auntie whirled. The voice was Chet's, but it came from a distance, somewhere off through the trees. He called out again. He was closer now. He was coming this way.

No, no, sky above, no, thought Loren. *Run Chet, please, darkness take me, run. Why did I call out for you?*

Atop her, Auntie gave a growl—but then she froze. She turned and looked down at Loren, an evil glint in her eye.

"You told me that Chet knows you. That he *understands* you. You are wrong. Let me show you."

Light flowed from her eyes once more, and her body began to shift. Her blonde hair turned black and grew out, and brown skin turned to cream.

The transformation ended, and panic seized Loren's breath—for she stared into her own eyes. Auntie had taken on Loren's likeness; indeed, she looked identical, for they wore the same dark brown trousers, the same white shirt, though Auntie's was somewhat too large, for it had been sewn for Niya's larger frame.

476

"Come along, girl," said Auntie, and Loren shuddered inwardly to hear her own voice from that mouth. "I mean to give you quite a show."

The weremage rose and threw her arms beneath Loren's, dragging her off to the side of the path. She rolled Loren beneath some bushes there, and ripped some branches from the trees, throwing them over her body. But then she knelt and moved the branches slightly so that Loren could look out.

"You can see me, can you not, girl?" whispered Auntie. "I would not want you to miss a thing."

Then she rose and turned, just as Loren heard Chet approach from down the path.

"Loren!" he exclaimed. "There you are. I heard you call my name, and I feared something was wrong."

Sky above, no, thought Loren. She railed at her body, screaming for her arms to move, but they would not comply.

"Wrong? What could be wrong?" said Auntie. She waited for Chet to come to her, so that she could be sure Loren would see them. Chet stepped up to her, and Auntie slid her arms up to lace her fingers behind his neck. She drew him close and gave him a long, passionate kiss. Loren wanted to close her eyes, but even that was beyond her power. "Nothing can be wrong when you are with me."

"I am flattered, though that has not proven to be the case in recent days," said Chet, giving her a wry smile.

Chet, look to the left, thought Loren. *Please, please. Look to the left. See me.*

His head jerked up, and a mad hope filled her that somehow he had heard her. But he looked the other direction. "Where is Niya?"

"After she showed me the clearing above, she went off on her own. She said she would make for the camp in a while. I am surprised you did not see her—but glad as well, for it means I have you alone." Slowly her hands slid down his chest, and then around his waist. He responded by wrapping his arms around her and leaning in for another kiss. "And while we are here, and alone . . ." Her hands slid around to his front, toying with the buckle of his belt.

Chet drew back, laughing with embarrassment. "I—Loren, what are you doing? We are in the open jungle."

"And why should that matter? No one is near to see us." Auntie smiled up at him and cocked an eyebrow. Her lips had a wry twist, and her eyes shone with promise.

That is not my smile, Chet, screamed Loren. *You know it. You know my eyes. Look at them!*

But he only glanced back over his shoulder, a silly grin stealing across his face. "What if Niya should return and look for you?"

"She will not," said Auntie. "I told you, she makes for camp." When he still seemed hesitant, she kissed him again and finished removing his belt while their lips were still locked.

They fell to the floor of the path, tearing at each other's clothes. Soon Auntie rolled Chet onto his back and sat atop him. Their low, hushed moans mingled with the sounds of the jungle, while Loren could do nothing but watch.

And then she blinked.

At first she did not notice, but then it happened again. She tried once more, consciously—and her eyelids responded.

Loren tried to move her hand. Her fingers twitched.

Could the poison be wearing off already? Auntie had made it sound as though she would be frozen for hours. Surely the weremage would not have left her here if the paralysis would wear off so soon.

Then she heard Xain's words again. *The remedies of the apothecary have little effect upon a wizard who eats magestones, and the same is true for poisons.*

The magestone she had eaten in Yewamba. It was still within her, burning the poison out of her blood.

She tried again, and this time her hand moved, jerking from her stomach and landing on the dirt beside her. She heaved again, and it edged towards the path a little more.

Chet and Auntie were growing more passionate with every moment, and the weremage sounded nearly frenzied at their tryst. She looked down at Chet, smiling fiendishly at him. "Do you love me, Chet?"

"Of course," he said, breathless.

"Do you *know* me?"

"I—what?" Distracted for a moment, he frowned up at her.

Slowly, painfully, Loren dragged her feet up towards her body, her knee bending up into the air. Her body jerked towards the path as she let the knee fall, but though the branches that covered her rustled, it was not loud enough to hear.

Without warning, Auntie slapped Chet's face. "Do you *know* me? Better than any other?"

"Loren, what in the darkness below—"

"Tell me!" cried Auntie. Neither of them had bothered to remove their tunics, and she seized the front of his now. "Tell me you know me, better than any other in all the nine kingdoms."

Chet shook his head and tried to push up on his elbows. "Enough, Loren. I do not know what you—"

Auntie slammed him back down on the ground. In an instant her old, rusted knife was in her hand. She pressed it against his throat.

No! thought Loren.

She saw Damaris holding the knife in her dream, saw it part Chet's skin, saw his blood splashing upon the ground.

"Chet," she croaked. She lifted one hand, shaking as it rose into the air, helpless. "Chet." But he could not hear her.

"Tell me," rasped Auntie.

Chet went white with fear. "Loren, what are you—"

Loren heaved herself out of the bushes, crashing down on the grass of the path. The sound drew Chet's attention at last, and he looked over at her. His face became a mask of confusion, and then terror as he looked up at Auntie.

"Chet," gasped Loren. "Run."

Auntie smiled at her, a vicious grin, and her eyes began to glow. She transformed back into herself again, keeping the knife pressed to Chet's throat. Chet recoiled with a cry, but he could not move from under her with the blade pressing against his skin.

"Well met, lover," said Auntie. "Are you not enjoying yourself? Am I not twice the bedfellow Loren is? She is little more than a girl, after all."

Chet panicked and tried to snatch her hand away, but Auntie seized his wrist and slammed it back into the ground. She did not move the blade from his neck, nor did she stop her writhing on top of him.

"Oh, but you are no longer so excited," said Auntie, pouting down at where they were joined. With a flash of magelight, she turned into Niya. "Do you prefer another? I noticed you eyeing me from time to time as we rode together. Or was that only jealousy? No, you desired someone else, did you not?"

Another flash of magelight, and now she was Weath.

"Yes, little Weath, your 'friend.' The one whose fragile little neck broke so easily, just before I pitched her from the walls of Yewamba."

"Stop," groaned Chet, turning his head as though he could sink into the ground away from her. "Please, stop it."

Loren tried to rise, tried to crawl towards them, but her legs were still sluggish. Only her arms would obey her commands.

Then she remembered her dagger. It was still in her boot. Shaking, she reached for it.

"Do not tell me you did not want her. You have had a greedy mind, little boy." Auntie's cruel smile dissolved into a grimace of hate. "And I will make you pay for your every untoward thought."

The dagger slid easily from its sheath. Loren hefted it, feeling the weight.

The handle is the heavier end, she thought, turning it to hold it by the blade. *Sky above, do not let me miss.*

She threw the dagger.

It sank into Auntie's arm. The weremage screamed in pain and reared back—and her blade came away from Chet's throat.

He rose up and snatched her wrist, and then struck her in the face before wrestling her to the ground. With his weight he pinned her, driving a knee into her chest and holding both her hands above her head. She screamed again, but it turned into a harsh laugh. He shook as he held her down, his hands grasping at her throat. Auntie turned to glare hatefully at Loren.

Auntie glared hatred at Loren. "You promised, you sniveling little liar. You promised you would not throw the knife at me."

"Be silent!" screamed Chet. "Be silent, you vile . . . you—" He shoved her hands away as she tried to fight him off, pressing her face into the dirt.

"Oh, is this all you wanted?" sneered Auntie. "To be in control? You should have said so. Have me then, if you wish."

"You—you took me, you took me without—" Chet's eyes were wild, his lips drawn back in a snarl. He seized the hilt of Loren's dagger and twisted it in Auntie's arm, drawing a fresh scream from her. "I will kill you."

"I believe you," said Auntie. "What are you waiting for?"

"Chet," groaned Loren. "Chet, wait."

His gaze turned to her. "Wait? You tell me to *wait?* You saw what she did, Loren. It is what the High King's harshest law commands."

Loren tried to rise to hands and knees, but her legs would still not obey her. "You are not a killer, Chet," she said. The words came thick and slow upon her tongue, for the poison had not entirely left her. "Remember what happened on the shores of Dorsea, how Xain—"

"How dare you?" cried Chet, his voice rising to a great shout. "That was a prisoner. He surrendered! How dare you call this the same?"

Incredibly, Auntie giggled. "The law is clear. And I have violated it so very badly."

"Be silent," growled Chet.

"Let the Mystics do it," said Loren. "They serve the King's law."

Chet looked at her for a moment. She thought she saw the fury fading from his eyes. But at last he shook his head, and she saw that the anger was not gone—it had only turned to ice, a terrible, bloodless rage.

"We are the King's law," he said. "This is not revenge, Loren. It is justice."

He was right. Of course he was right. Every child in Underrealm knew this edict. Loren would not have blinked at Auntie's sentence, not if anyone else were to carry it out. But to see Chet with the blade in his hand, death in his eyes . . .

"Very well," she said softly.

Loren turned her gaze from him to look at Auntie instead. The weremage looked back, her eyes twitching, her teeth showing in a smile, as though she had never been happier.

She was still smiling when Chet lowered the dagger and slit her throat, sending her blood gushing across the ground. A burbling laugh poured up through her lips, along with blood. Then, even as Loren watched, where he had slit it the flesh of her neck began to knit back together. But not the mass of scar tissue—that remained as it had been, even when Auntie was Niya. The fresh cut, though—it healed as she watched. It healed.

It healed until Chet plunged the dagger through her eye into her brain.

Auntie's body spasmed once, and then lay still.

And then after a moment, a final glow came from the weremage's remaining eye.

Slowly she transformed one last time. Weath's face shifted and melted away. But she did not become the seductive, loam-skinned beauty Loren had first met. Instead her skin turned lily-white, her face a little older, mayhap the age of Loren's mother. The hair that replaced Weath's copper was not white-blonde, but frizzy and black.

A woman Loren had never seen before lay there dead. Chet rolled away from her, covering his face to hide the tears that spilled forth.

FORTY-THREE

WHEN LOREN COULD RISE AT LAST, SHE WENT TO CHET'S SIDE AND TRIED to hold him. But he recoiled from her touch, pushing her away and shaking his head. So she merely sat by his side, trying not to look at the stranger who lay dead before her.

In time Chet's tears subsided, and he rose to his feet. Loren stood too, if more slowly, and together they made their way back towards the camp. They did not bury the body. Loren could scarcely bear looking at it, and asking Chet to touch it was out of the question.

Annis and Gem saw at once that something was wrong, but when they asked, Chet only shook his head and went into his tent. Loren told them nothing she did not have to—only that Niya had been Auntie all along, and that she had attacked them, and now was dead. From the moment he heard the weremage's name, Gem's face went pale, and his eyes wide.

"Dead?" he whispered. "Are you certain?"

"Yes," said Loren quietly.

His look grew distant, and he turned from her. In a moment he, too, vanished into his tent, leaving Annis and Loren standing there, staring at each other, not knowing what to do, or even where to begin.

That night, Loren ate a meager meal. Afterwards she went to the tent she shared with Chet.

Something compelled her to stop a pace away from it. She stared at the flap for a long while. And then she turned from it, and slept in the tent that had once been Niya's.

Uzo and Shiun returned the next day. Loren was hardly surprised when they told her that Damaris had ridden south with too many guards for them to engage. So little had gone well for their party this far in the mission, that this latest lack of success seemed almost expected.

In turn, she had to tell them the tale of what had happened with Auntie. They listened in shock, and when they learned that Niya had been the weremage all along, they shook their heads in disbelief. Then, looking at each other in silent agreement, they set off into the jungle towards the path that Loren had described.

When they returned from burying her, the dark look in their eyes spoke volumes of how shaken they were. They had not buried their companion and captain, a Mystic. They had seen an utter stranger, and only Loren's word told them that she had once been their sister-in-arms.

"We should ride south when we can," said Shiun, after they had eaten a silent meal together around a small fire. "I can follow Damaris easily enough now, but the trail may grow cold, and it certainly will once she reaches Dorsea."

Loren thought for a moment. "We will spend one more night here," she said at last. "One more night of rest, for the toll has been great. On all of us."

She looked across the camp. Chet still had not emerged from his tent.

The next morning dawned grey and cold, and a light rain began to fall. Loren went a little ways off from the camp and sat on a fallen tree, face turned upwards, letting the water wash away the sweat and the dirt and the horror of the last few days. She sensed that the rest of them feared to disturb her, just as she herself feared to disturb Chet. But eventually, Annis came out to her and waited, hands clasped in front of her, until Loren met her gaze.

"Shiun says we must go. The rain makes it ever more urgent that we begin the hunt, lest we lose Damaris' trail."

"Of course," said Loren quietly. "I will rouse Chet."

"He is awake, and readying himself to leave," said Annis.

Loren shot to her feet and pushed past Annis to run for the camp. She came to a halt where the horses were tied up. Chet stood there, securing his pack to the saddle. He looked at her without smiling and nodded.

"We are riding south," she said, not sure what else to tell him. "Damaris has gone—"

"Towards Dorsea. I know," he said. "Annis explained. Let us get on with it."

He turned away and resumed readying himself for the journey. Loren ducked her head, and after a moment walked past him to take down Niya's tent—*her* tent now, she supposed.

Soon they had mounted, and Shiun led them through the jungle towards the main road. Once there, they increased their pace to a steady trot, and made their plodding way south. The jungle stayed thick on both sides of them as they passed the town of Sarafu, and long after, so that for many hours they could see nothing but the trees on either side of them.

Then the trees fell away, and they came to a lip in the land, from which it spilled down a long, long way towards a great basin. The western rim was the Greatrock Mountains, and a wide river formed the eastern side. They themselves stood on the northern lip, and where it ended in the south, the jungle gave way to a sparsely wooded land of light brown dirt.

"That is the border of Dorsea," said Shiun. "Damaris rides south, no doubt hoping to evade us, as well as Kal's host, which still marches west."

"She will not succeed," said Loren quietly. "We will capture her. I swear it."

There was no longer any question of whether they should continue to pursue the merchant or return to Kal. She knew without asking that every one of them would not have turned back, not for all the gold in all the nine kingdoms.

Still they did not ride on, but only sat upon their horses, looking down at the lush land as the falling rain soaked it. The day was winding towards evening, and Loren knew they should be pressing on as quickly as they could. Damaris would not slow for anything, not until she believed herself to be safe. But still she hesitated. And after a time, she glanced at Chet.

"Go ahead," she murmured to the others. "We will be with you in a moment."

The party obeyed without comment, and soon she and Chet were alone on the road. But he did not look at her, not even when he broke his silence at last.

"I do not care if you understand why I did it or not," he said.

"Yet I do understand," she said quietly.

He snorted. "Do you? I was not so forgiving when you showed Xain leniency in Dorsea."

"It is as you said. That was different, and I was wrong to gainsay you when it came to Auntie."

Chet turned his face away from her. "You may say it, you know. You may tell me I am a hypocrite. I scorned you, though it was not even your hand that held the knife."

"It has been a long journey, but I am not ready to take that step," said Loren. "Yet I no longer look with disdain on those who do. I still think justice should come from the law, and from the King's servants who deal in it. But there is not always time. And you *did* serve the law, Chet. I know that."

She reached across the space between them and put a hand on his shoulder, but he shied away from her touch.

"I cannot," he whispered. "Please. I still see—I see her. I am sorry."

"You have nothing to apologize for," she told him, feeling tears brim in her eyes. She blinked them away. "Never. Not to me."

A moment longer she waited, until he turned his face forwards again and nodded. Then she spurred Midnight into a walk, and Chet followed just behind. The sun neared the horizon, heralding the approach of night, as she led him down the long road into the lowlands.

EPILOGUE

A LIGHT SNOW HAD ONLY JUST BEGUN TO FALL, AND IT DUSTED THE Yerrin camp. Damaris' tent was fine, more than fine enough to keep her head warm and dry. But she had eschewed that shelter to drink in the frozen air. She took deep breaths, standing to the north of the camp, only vaguely aware of the guards who stood close to hand. Her gaze lingered on the Dorsean landscape they had been traversing for the last several days.

Do you pursue me, Nightblade? she thought. *That is good. Follow me. Follow me and never stop. Let me draw you to your doom.*

A shout came from behind her, and she whirled on the spot. Her guards drew closer and unsheathed their blades.

Damaris' heart skipped a beat as a figure emerged from the camp. His form was in silhouette, rimmed by the firelight, but she knew him—not only from his size, but from the way he moved, every little quirk of motion that had accompanied her on all the long roads of her life since they were both children. The guards fell away before him.

"Gregor," she sighed.

He fell to one knee at her feet, bowing his head. "My lady," he said.

His voice was thick with emotion, and he hid his face from her, as well as the guards to either side.

Damaris glanced at them. "Leave us," she said. They obeyed at once, marching back towards the camp.

"Rise, my friend," she said, taking his shoulders and lifting him up. "Sky above, I have missed you more than I can say." She drew him into an embrace for a moment only, but it was enough that she could feel him shaking.

"I should never have left you," he said. "If anything had happened at Yewamba, I would have taken my own life the moment I had slain the vermin who had harmed you."

"Left me?" said Damaris wryly. She did not smile, but she let her eyes crinkle with amusement. "If you will recall, I ordered you to remain upon the Seat."

"And I failed you there, as well," he said. "I could not secure the support you require, and then a boy—"

She raised a hand, and he fell silent at once. "I know," she said smoothly. "I have heard all the tale of it already. And I do not blame you, Gregor. We are stretched thin, you and I, and we will not win every battle. All that matters is that we win more of them than we lose."

"We will, my lady," said Gregor, bowing his head once more. "I swear it."

"I believe you," said Damaris. "And the next confrontation swiftly approaches. Something happened at the Battle of Wellmont."

"A rumor only," said Gregor.

She fixed him with a look. "It is not a rumor."

His eyes did not widen, nor did his brows shift by so much as a hair. Yet from a pace away she could feel his whole body go rigid. "Then . . . are we to make our way east?"

"Not yet," said Damaris, sighing. "At least not while hounds nip at our heels. I am being followed."

"I have heard." Gregor's voice rumbled with fury. His fists, each almost as large as her head, coiled by his sides. "The girl."

"The Nightblade of the High King, you mean," said Damaris, letting her mockery emerge plain in her tone.

"I will take a party. We will come upon them in the night and destroy them."

"No, no, that will not do at all. Loren herself played no small role in the Battle of Wellmont, though she cannot possibly have learned what has occurred because of it. Yet we will ensure she comes to regret it."

Damaris' eyes narrowed as she remembered the storeroom in Yewamba, where Loren had dumped her like a sack of flour with her wrists bound together. And she remembered the boy, the boy Loren's age who had been there with her. Damaris had seen the look in Loren's eyes when she beheld him. It sent a lance of vicious joy through her, and her breath quickened.

"And when we are sure she is well-acquainted with the deepest pits of sorrow—then, Gregor, you may do what I should have ordered the moment we first laid eyes upon her. Then, you may kill her."

YERRIN

BEING BOOK THREE
OF THE SECOND VOLUME

OF THE
NIGHTBLADE EPIC

ONE

Winter had always had a way of being especially cruel to Loren, and so she hid now with her friends from its bitter snows. Which was not to say that they had entirely avoided the rough weather; for weeks, they had pursued the merchant Damaris back and forth across the northwestern reaches of the kingdom. Through snows and storms they followed her, from tiny villages to modest cities, through woods and over fields and across rivers. Always Damaris had remained just ahead of them, taunting them, ever out of reach.

Now they had a room at an inn in the town of Sidwan, far south of Feldemar and west of the Greatrock Mountains. They had arrived only the night before. Some might have called the dwelling modest, but Loren thought that would be far too generous. She guessed the inn's master rarely had his floors scrubbed or bedding changed, for everything reeked. Two threadbare pallets of straw lay on the floor, but Loren could almost see the fleas crawling across them. They ate rarely of the inn's food, which caused their bellies to roil and complain, but instead ate from the rations they had kept in good supply during their travels. Of all the inn's offerings, only the ale was passably good, and so of that they drank freely.

Loren's little council was even smaller than normal, for Uzo and Shiun were away at the moment. Chet sat on one of the pallets, idly rubbing his arms and staring at nothing. His oft-washed skin was red and raw, but mayhap not so bad as it had been last week. Loren hoped that was a good sign. Gem had gone to fetch himself a snack—the boy's stomach seemed to be made of iron, and he was the only one who did not turn up his nose at the common room's meager fare.

Annis, as was her custom these days, sat on the floor with a map of the nine kingdoms. With her forefinger she traced lines between towns and cities, her eyes darting back and forth, her lips slightly parted but never moving. Every so often she would wince and shake her head, then return to tracing routes that were clear only in her own mind. Loren worried about her. Annis' determination to find Damaris had neared obsession. The merchant was her mother, and that made her feel a greater burden than all the rest of them.

Other than Chet, of course.

Loren sighed, kicking her boots against the floor and toying idly with the knives at her belt. The blades were new, purchased at the first blacksmith they had found after entering the kingdom of Dorsea. They were neither so fine as the dagger on the back of her belt, nor as modest as the hunting knife in her boot. The smith had balanced them perfectly for throwing. Half of her wished to go out behind the inn and practice, but she feared to be away if Uzo and Shiun returned with news.

She thought of the one who had taught her to throw knives in the first place. Her fingers recoiled as though the blades had burned her.

It is a useful skill, she told herself. *It does not matter who taught it to you.*

She looked at Chet and wondered if she truly believed that.

He seemed to feel her gaze upon him, for he looked up at her. He tried to give her a smile, but it came out frail.

"I think I may try to sleep," said Loren.

His smile faltered. "Oh? Have you rested poorly?"

"It has been a long road, and we have ridden hard."

"Yet too much sleep can make one even wearier."

Loren spread her hands. "There is little else to do just now."

Now his smile died at last, and he stared at the floor. "Those are pretty words, but not true ones. We both know why you want to sleep. Yet that is not how the dreams work, or so you have said."

"I suppose not," said Loren. "But we know I cannot have one if I am awake."

He subsided, turning away from her. Loren's pulse had quickened, and she forced herself to take a deep breath. It was not Chet's fault that her sleep had been dreamless, but she was frustrated, and it made her irritable. A small part of her feared what the dreams might mean and where they might be leading her. But the greater part of her wanted any clue, any hint about where Damaris might be. If that knowledge came to her in a dream, she thought she could accept whatever harm her visions might bring.

She sighed and pushed herself up from the floor, going over to sit beside Chet—but not too close, not where she might accidentally brush against him.

"I want a clue that will lead us to the end of this road," said Loren. "I want to bring Damaris to justice."

Chet shook his head slowly. "I suppose I do as well. But will that truly be the end?"

Loren gritted her teeth. Damaris' capture would not entirely end the war, and they both knew it. "It will be a good first step. And the dreams will help. When they come, we will use whatever I see to find her. I swear it."

Chet drew a breath as though he was about to speak—but then the door flew open. Loren shot upright, hand going to one of her knives. But it was only Gem, stumbling in with a tray of food and ale. He kicked the door behind him, and it closed with a loud *thud*. Annis' head jerked up, but the moment she saw Gem she flushed and turned away.

Loren scowled. "Sky above, Gem. Are you trying to wake the whole inn?"

"Wake them?" said Gem, eyes wide and innocent. "It is scarcely sundown. If anyone is abed already, let them rise so that they may know how lazy I think them."

"This from the boy who has spent more time asleep than all the rest of us combined," said Chet. He chuckled and shook his head. It warmed Loren's heart to see. Whatever chill had settled between him and Loren, he had lost none of his affection or good cheer towards the children, nor even towards Uzo and Shiun.

"But that is another matter entirely," said Gem, lifting his chin. "I am unquestionably the handsomest of our party, and retaining such beauty requires more rest. That is not laziness, but only due consideration for the beautification of your lives."

"What noble sacrifice. What a selfless gift," said Loren, clutching her hands over her heart. Then she snatched the tray with one hand and shoved him gently with the other. "Now if you truly wish to make all our lives better, still your flapping lips for a little while and let us drink in peace."

Gem rubbed his chest where she had pushed him, but his smile remained. "I suppose I can do that," he said. "After all, my lips have flapped enough for one day—in the common room, where one or two of my tales were most welcome."

Loren's heart skipped. "What tales? Gem, what have you—"

He waved a hand airily. "I did not tell them who we are, or where we are bound, or why. But I heard some patrons in the common room discussing our black-cloaked friend. I gave them a few nods and winks at the right times, and told them some small stories that I had heard and they had not."

"Stories you heard?" said Loren, arching an eyebrow. "It is more accurate to say that you lived them."

Gem spread his hands. "They are different words, but they mean much the same thing."

Loren sighed. Gem had been spreading tales everywhere—not only since they entered Feldemar, but a long time before that, ever since the two of them had escaped from the city of Cabrus. She had long ago given up trying to stop him.

Gem snatched two mugs of ale from the tray and went across the room to Annis. He stopped more than a pace away, looking at her fitfully. One foot scraped at the back of his other ankle to scratch an itch. He wore thick and warm shoes, recently bought—a necessity against the snow outside, but clearly something he was unused to.

Gradually Annis became aware of the room's quiet. At last she looked up to see Gem. Her cheeks darkened, and she quickly looked back down at the map.

"I . . . er, would you like to have a drink?" said Gem, proffering one of the mugs.

"Oh, ah. No. Thank you. Or, wait, I suppose so." Annis' hand jerked back and forth a few times, as though her mind kept changing even in the act of reaching for the mug. At last she gripped the handle and pulled it towards her—but the movement was jerky, and a bit of ale spilled over to splash on a corner of the map.

"Blast!" said Gem. He knelt and tried to scrub at the stain. "I am sorry."

"No, it was my fault," said Annis.

She took a corner of her sleeve and reached to wipe away the ale. But as her hand brushed Gem's, they both yelped. Gem leaped up as though stung and scuttled away. Then he realized he had forgotten his own mug on the floor beside her, and he darted back to get it. He retreated to the farthest pallet and sank into it, studiously inspecting his drink.

Loren winced at the exchange. Things had grown more and more awkward since Annis' disastrous confession of love in Feldemar. Gem clearly felt awful for rebuffing her, and Annis seemed determined to forget the whole thing had ever happened. But it hung between them always, and what had once been a bosom friendship was now an ever-strained and painful interaction.

It did no good to dwell on such thoughts. Loren went over to Annis and sat across from her, ignoring the girl's flushed cheeks. She studied the map, but it meant very little to her. Loren could recognize the drawings—the mountains and rivers, the lakes and oceans—but she had never learned to read, and so the names of places were a mystery. But Annis looked at the map as though it were an elaborate tapestry, with every detail plain before her and no mystery hidden. Or at least, none but the greatest mystery of all—the one that kept her hovering over the map day and night, trying to unravel the secret.

"How goes your search?" said Loren. "Have you any idea why Damaris might have come here?"

"If I had, I would have said something," grumbled Annis. She sighed and rubbed her eyes with the heels of her hands. "I am sorry. I grow ever more frustrated the longer this goes on. My mo—Damaris' course through Dorsea makes no sense. First she goes in one direction, and then another. It seems clear she is trying to throw us off her trail. But even if that is the case, I feel I should be able to guess her ultimate aim. Yet the only thing I can see is that she always goes farther south, and there is no place in the south of Dorsea that makes sense as her final destination."

"What if it is a ruse, then?" said Chet. "What if her ultimate aim lies farther north, and she plans to double back?"

Annis pursed her lips. "I have considered it, of course. But there is nothing significant west of the Greatrocks, and I do not think she would go east of them. There lies Dorsea's capital, Danfon. There is no greater concentration of officers of the High King's law in the kingdom.

She would put herself at far too great a risk. That, I believe, is why she has restricted herself to smaller towns—like this one."

"I think even the word 'small' overstates the case," said Gem. "'Tiny' might be more accurate. I have seen no horses in Sidwan besides our own."

Loren sighed and shook her head. "I am less worried about where Damaris is going and more worried about what she means to do."

"Are we so sure she means to do anything?" said Chet. "I thought her goal was to take Yewamba, but we chased her from there. She may simply be trying to escape."

"Never," said Annis. "Oh, I am certain she wants to evade us. But there is something else at work here. There always is. She has not given up on . . . well, on whatever goal drove her to Yewamba in the first place."

"But what goal?" said Loren. "Something to do with the war, no doubt."

"Yes, but that is far too general," said Annis. "She will never be an ally of the High King—not after what she has done—but she may not be on the side of the Necromancer any longer, either. She seems aimless, but that is only because we do not know what larger game she is playing."

"Could she be making her way towards one of your family's holdings in Dorsea?" said Loren.

"She could—except that those are few and far between, and none are very grand." said Annis. "I think that may be why she wanted Yewamba. She could have given it to the Necromancer as a great stronghold in the war. Or she might have meant to lurk there in safety while the war raged on without her. Without knowing the machinations of all our enemies, it becomes harder to predict what any one of them is doing."

"I, for one, doubt she still stands by the Necromancer," said Chet. "The High King has declared war at last, and eight kingdoms stand behind her. Not even a great fool would join the wrong side of that fight, and your mother is not a great fool."

The room went silent, and Loren shot Chet a look. Annis dropped her gaze to the floor, and Chet's cheeks flushed. They had taken to avoiding the fact that Damaris was Annis' mother. It was not a comfortable truth for the girl to hear, and even less so now that their mission was to bring her before the King's law—a law that was always swift and always fair, but not always merciful.

"In any case," said Loren, "all our wonderment might be for nothing. If she is indeed here in Sidwan, and we can bring her to heel, then her ultimate aim becomes of far less consequence."

As if in answer to her words, they heard footsteps in the hallway outside. The footsteps stopped outside their door, which opened to reveal Uzo. The dark young spearman wore plain clothes for travel, and had changed his red Mystic cloak for one of brown. Snow dusted his shoulders, already melting into little droplets at his feet.

"It is time," he said. "Shiun has found her."

They were on their feet in an instant. Chet snatched up his quarterstaff from where it leaned by the door, and Gem began to buckle on his little sword.

Almost too little, now, thought Loren. The boy was growing by leaps and bounds. She had already noted that he needed new clothes, and now it seemed he should have a new blade as well.

Loren turned to Annis. "Wait here for us. We will return soon."

"Be sure that you do," said Annis. "Sky above, I hope we have found her this time."

"We have never been so close," said Loren. "If the worst should happen, and she evades us again, we shall catch her in the next town."

Annis dropped her gaze to the floor. "Her escape would not be the worst that could happen. At least not to my mind."

Loren gave a little smile and stepped forwards to wrap the girl in a quick hug. "We will be safe. See that you are the same."

She turned, cloak whirling about her, and followed Uzo from the inn.

TWO

SIDWAN WAS A TINY CLUSTER OF INNS AND CRAFTSHOPS THAT MIGHT NOT have existed at all, except that a bend in the nearby road met a bend in the nearby river, and the fertile land all around was perfect for farming. Farmers thus formed the largest portion of the town's populace, and of the patrons of its taverns and shops. Travelers would stop in the town for a drink or to repair a shoe or harness, and in the evenings the locals would gather around to hear news of the wider world. Loren and her friends had worked hard to dissuade such interest. The less notice any-one took of them, the better.

Near the center of the town was its largest inn: a stone building, and one of the few that had a second floor. That was where Shiun and Uzo had gone to search for Damaris. But Uzo turned away, leading them down a smaller side street towards the edge of town.

"She was not at the inn?" said Loren.

"No, though we wasted a fair amount of time searching there. It was only by chance that we saw two dark men passing through the town. They did not wear green cloaks, but they looked and moved like trained fighters. Mayhap they had been sent to fetch supplies for the next stretch of the journey. In any case, Shiun followed them to one of the finer houses on the edge of town. There we saw many more guards and some horses in the stables, and soon we spotted Damaris in one of the windows."

"It *is* her, then," said Loren. A thrill of excitement ran through her. Their long hunt that had now stretched across two kingdoms might finally be over.

But not yet. First they had to capture Damaris, and that would be no easy feat. The merchant traveled with several guards—hardly an army, but more than the paltry five of Loren's party. And there was always the threat that Gregor had rejoined her.

Gregor. The bodyguard had not been in the stronghold of Yewamba. But if he had heard what happened there, Loren knew he would cross the sky and the darkness to be by Damaris' side again. His devotion to her dwarfed even his massive size. He was a terrifying fighter, and Loren feared to face him even with all her friends at her back. If Gregor was here, Loren knew they might not all survive—if any of them did.

Uzo stopped them behind a cobbler's shop, and he and Loren peered around the corner. Before them was a home that would have been modest in any of Underrealm's great cities, but it looked like an opulent jewel here in Sidwan. Loren smirked to herself. Even when on the run, it seemed Damaris could not help her taste for finery. Two guards stood at the front door, and though they did not wear the family Yerrin's colors, they had the right look.

"We saw her upstairs."

Loren jumped. Shiun's voice had come from nowhere, and now she crept up behind them. The woman was a scout beyond peer, and Loren still marveled at her ability to move silently, to see even the smallest sign of her quarry's trail in the wilderness. Chet had grown up a hunter, and he had taught Loren the ways of tracking a beast in the woods, but Shiun's knowledge eclipsed even his.

Gem's face had paled. "You move more quietly than an Elf."

"I doubt it, though I have not seen one," said Shiun.

"Are you certain it was Damaris?" said Loren.

"No," said Shiun. "I have never seen her, either. But she was a Yerrin woman in fine garb, and the others certainly seemed to obey her commands."

"Very well," said Loren. "We should take the house, and quickly."

"One thing more," said Shiun. "There is a man I have not seen before. He is large, and he wears more armor than the other guards."

Loren shuddered. "Gregor."

Shiun's mouth twisted. "I thought it might be, from the description you gave."

"He is only a man," said Uzo. "Even a giant may be taken by surprise."

"You do not know him," said Loren. "We must be cautious. He is twice as vicious as he is large, and he will defend Damaris with his dying breath."

"Then I will make him take that breath." Uzo's hand tightened on the haft of his spear.

Loren's jaw clenched. "Kill only if you have no other choice. The more of them we capture, the more information we can gather about the High King's enemies."

Uzo rolled his eyes, but Shiun nodded and spoke for them both. "As you say, Nightblade."

There was a long pause. After a moment, Shiun and Uzo glanced at each other, their brows raised. At last Uzo cleared his throat. "It might be best to secure the bottom floor first. That way we can watch to make sure she does not slip away."

Of course. Loren was supposed to come up with the plan of attack and tell the rest of them what to do. In Feldemar, Niya had given orders when it came to fighting, and Loren was still unused to it. Her cheeks flamed, and she hoped they attributed it to the cold air.

"That seems wise," she said. "Do not climb to the second floor until the first is in our hands. And Gem—you must run into town and summon the constables."

"What?" said Gem. "But there are only two of them, and they hardly seemed to be trained fighters. They will be of little help."

She fixed him with a hard look. "They represent the King's law, and we will need them to restore order once the fighting is done." She extended a hand to Uzo. He gave her his Mystic badge, and Loren placed it in Gem's hand. "Give them this so that they know you are not some urchin boy."

He folded his arms and pouted at his feet. "I *am* an urchin boy," he muttered. But he turned and left them, slipping through the buildings back towards the town's center.

Loren motioned the others off, and they spread out to attack the building from both sides. Loren approached the left corner of the manor with Chet close behind her. She drew one of the throwing daggers from her belt.

One of the guards was only a pace away. Loren leaped from her hiding place and brought the hilt of her dagger crashing down hard on the back of the woman's head. The guard fell senseless to the ground. The other guard whirled, scrabbling for his sword. Before he could muster the wits to shout, Uzo pounced from behind. His arm wrapped around the guard's throat, and he squeezed. The man's eyes rolled back, and Uzo lowered him to the ground.

"Two taken care of, and easily," said Chet.

"Do not gloat until it is done," said Loren. "Fate despises the boastful."

"The back door," said Shiun. "Less chance of a heavy guard."

Loren nodded. "Uzo, stay here to prevent escape through the front."

The rest of them moved single file around the building. No guards were posted at the rear. Peeking in through a window, Loren saw a small sitting room with a fireplace. Two guards sat on chairs there, holding their hands out towards the flames.

She looked back at Shiun and Chet and held up two fingers. They nodded. Loren gripped the door's latch and looked at the crack of the doorjamb. There was no lock or bar. She lifted the latch and threw the door open.

Both guards shot up from their chairs with a cry. One was a spindly woman, the other a stout man. Chet struck first, his quarterstaff cracking down on the spindly one's shoulder. She grunted with the pain, but she managed to draw her sword before he swung again.

The stout man launched himself at Loren. She sidestepped his first swing, but it was no wild attack. These were disciplined soldiers. His reverse swing almost caught her arm, and she had to drop to her knee to avoid it.

Shiun leaped in to the fray, landing two quick punches at the man's throat. He fell back, gasping. Loren took advantage, shooting up to kick him hard in the groin. He wheezed and fell. She kicked him full in the face, and he rolled over, unconscious. The two of them leaped in to help Chet, whose opponent was forcing him back with wild swings. In a moment Shiun had disarmed her, and soon she went down to a punishing strike of Chet's quarterstaff.

They heard a commotion from the front of the house. Two guards burst into the back room, swords already drawn. They paused in shock for half a moment.

Shunk

The tip of a spear burst through one of the guards' chests. She looked down at the spearhead, eyes wide. The other guard only had a moment to be surprised before Shiun leaped forwards and planted her short sword in his gut. Both of them sank to the ground, their last breaths gurgling. Behind them stood Uzo, a grim smile on his lips as he gripped his spear.

Loren glared at him. "That was not necessary."

Uzo shrugged. "You said we needed to be fast."

Shiun said nothing, wiping her sword clean on one of the guards' cloaks. Loren shook her head and made for the stairs.

The staircase was short and open at the top, so she crept up carefully. There was little chance that anyone upstairs had missed the noise of all the fighting, but no one had come down. She hoped that meant there were no more warriors above. Mayhap Gregor was not here after all, but that seemed too fortunate to hope for.

She reached the top of the stairs. A large foyer stretched before her, and at the other end of it was a guard. There were no lamps lit here, and the windows cast him in a large silhouette.

Loren's steps faltered, and her throat went dry with fear. But it lasted only a moment, and then her eyes adjusted to the darkness. The man before her was large, truly, and he carried a sword and shield. But it was not Gregor. He did not have the ice-grey eyes, and a thick beard covered his face. Though he still stood taller than any of Loren's party, he was nowhere near the size of Gregor.

Relief washed through her just as suddenly as the fear had. It seemed the bodyguard had not yet found Damaris.

"Leave now," said the man, "and you may live."

Loren could not help herself. She snorted. "I have heard the same promise from foes far more dangerous. I have never taken them up on their offer, yet here I stand."

He growled and stepped forwards. But there was a *hiss,* and an arrow planted itself in his thigh. He roared and fell to one knee. Glancing back, Loren saw that Shiun had taken her bow from her back and was already drawing another arrow.

Chet stepped forth. When the man tried to swing his longsword, Chet blocked it with his staff. Another strike knocked the blade from his hand, and then he cracked the butt of his staff right between the man's eyes. His head snapped back, and he fell.

Uzo snickered. "'Leave now and you may live.' Honestly."

Loren allowed herself to share a smile with him. She motioned them all forwards. "Come. It is almost over."

The final door opened easily under her hand. Loren stepped through it into the master bedroom. And there she stopped.

A woman stood before her. But it was not Damaris. She wore clothes just as fine as the merchant, and there was something similar in the haughty tilt of her head. Mayhap she was another Yerrin. But Loren had never seen her before.

Loren growled in frustration. "A ruse. Darkness take that woman. She knew we would follow her here, and she set a false trail to lead us to this impostor." She shook her head and gestured at the woman. "Capture her. She may still have information that can help."

But the woman did not recoil in fear. Instead she smiled.

And then her eyes glowed black.

"Stop."

Everyone in the room froze. Loren frowned, her eyes flicking to her friends. They stood rooted in place as though held by some unseen force. Uzo was even in mid-stride, but there he remained.

The woman spoke again. "Kill each other, but leave the Nightblade alive."

Slowly, Chet, Uzo, and Shiun turned towards each other, raising their weapons.

Loren's blood ran cold. The woman was a wizard, and she had eaten magestones—the black glow in her eyes said that much. But this was some magic Loren had never seen before, and her mentor, Jordel, had never told her of it.

But her dagger kept her safe. This wizard could not know of the weapon—an ancient tool of the Mystic mage hunters, and proof against all spells. It had saved her life from a mad wizard before, and it kept her from enchantment now.

She drew the dagger and leaped forwards. The Yerrin woman barely had an instant to look surprised before Loren brought the hilt crashing down on her temple. Her eyes rolled back, and she folded like parchment.

Loren whirled. Shiun had eschewed her bow in such close quarters and was attacking Uzo with her sword. Uzo managed to keep her at bay while also trying to strike Chet with his spear, but Chet was defending himself well with his staff—at least for now. Their movements were slow, sluggish, as though they fought to throw off the mental commands they had been given.

"Stop!" she cried. "The woman has no power over you."

They acted as if they had not heard. The command had been planted, and they would not stop until they carried it out.

Loren leaped and took Chet in a flying tackle. She winced as his head cracked on the wall. Chet cried out, groping gingerly at the back of his head. Slowly his eyes focused on Loren.

"I . . . what happened?" he said.

"I do not know," said Loren. "But stop the others!"

She leaped up and dashed at Uzo and Shiun. With Chet out of the way, they had turned their full attention on each other. Loren thrust herself in between both of them.

They both froze, weapons held high. The wizard had commanded them to leave the Nightblade alive, and now they could not attack each other without striking her.

Chet gripped Shiun from behind in a tight hold. Her sword arm dangled, useless. But her other hand came up, scrabbling for Chet's eyes. She scratched his face, and he grimaced.

"Chet!" said Loren. She lunged, trying to pull Shiun's hand away.

Uzo took advantage of her distraction to move around her, and slowly his spear came forwards, poking for Shiun's gut. Then, from outside the room, Loren heard the pounding of footsteps making their way up the stairs.

More guards, she thought. Her heart sank. She and her friends could not fight their way out while two of them were determined to kill each other.

A voice came from outside. "Loren?"

Her pulse skipped. "Gem! In here!"

The boy burst into the bedroom. On his heels were two constables in red leather armor. Both of them huffed and wheezed mightily. It appeared they had run all the way here.

"Uzo and Shiun are enchanted!" she said. "Stop them, but do not hurt them badly!"

With the help of Gem and the constables, she and Chet managed to pry Shiun and Uzo apart. Then Loren remembered how Chet had come out of the enchantment. She went to Uzo and punched him full in the face—not as hard as she could, but hard enough. He recoiled from the blow—and then his eyes cleared. He rubbed at his jaw.

"What . . . did you *hit* me?"

Loren sighed with relief. "I did, and you will have to forgive me."

She went to Shiun, who was still trying to fight off Chet and the other constable. Balling a fist one more time, Loren struck her. Shiun blinked hard as the enchantment passed away.

"You all were gripped by some spell," said Loren. "It came from the wizard. I have never seen anything like it."

"Mindwyrd." Shiun spat on the floor. "A mentalist power, gained by eating magestones. It lets them control the will of others."

Loren shuddered. "I am glad we rid you of it in time."

Uzo gave Loren an odd look. "It did not seem to affect you."

Loren kept her face carefully neutral. Jordel had often warned her against revealing her dagger to anyone. "It must have been a weak enchantment."

"It was," said Shiun. "Else we would not have been freed from it so easily. And her magic must have been weakened further by trying to control more than one person at a time."

Uzo's curious expression lightened, much to Loren's relief, and he shook his head. "Sky save us from wizards. We should have brought a mage hunter."

Loren had nearly forgotten about the constables, but now one of them stepped forwards—a large man with a drooping mustache. As he studied the prone Yerrin woman, confusion made his lips twist and jump, and the mustache shivered like a dying squirrel's tail.

"I beg your pardon, but what exactly happened here?"

"Everyone in this house is a member of the family Yerrin," said Loren. "They are criminals under the King's law, and that one is an abomination." She pointed at the wizard.

Both constables blinked at Loren before giving each other an odd look.

"An abomination?" said Loren. "An eater of magestones?"

They jumped and took an involuntary step away from the woman.

Loren sighed. "She is harmless now. Blindfold her and bind her before she wakes. That will keep her from being able to use her magic. But do it quickly, and do not remove the blindfold for any reason. Do you have a jail here?"

"I . . . yes. Yes, my lady, and we will secure them right away." The large constable motioned to his companion. "Fetch some helping hands from the village, and be quick."

"I leave it in your capable hands," said Loren. She beckoned to her friends, leading them down the stairs.

"Capable hands?" said Gem once they were out of earshot. "I do not know that I share your assessment."

Loren frowned at him as she led them out behind the house. "We will remain here for a moment, at least until all the Yerrins are taken into custody."

Chet shuddered. "That woman . . . her magic was terrifying. It was if my body was not my own."

"Be thankful she was a weak wizard," said Shiun. "Else it would have taken more than a simple knock on the head to remove her spell."

Loren pursed her lips. "You know something of this . . . mindwyrd. Are you a mage hunter, then?"

Shiun shook her head with a wry smile. "No. But in my time in the Mystics, I have met many who are. Some of their secrets are not for others to know, but they loose some of the smaller details from time to time—if you get them drunk enough."

"I am glad to know it," said Loren. "There may be more dark wizards ahead in our future."

"There are too many in our past, if you ask me," muttered Gem.

Loren looked away from the house, over the snow-covered farmlands that ran to a forest in the south. A long breath escaped through her nose, and her hands formed fists before she managed to relax them.

Chet saw the movement, and he frowned. "Damaris was not here."

"No," said Loren. Did he think she did not know that?

"We will find her."

Loren almost snapped at him, but she restrained herself just in time. "I need a moment." She began to walk south.

Chet took a half-step forwards. "Where are you going? You should not be alone."

She glanced back at him. "I will not be long. I need to relieve myself."

He flushed, but his mouth remained a firm line. "Still, someone should go with you."

"I will do it," said Shiun. She slung her bow across her back and went to Loren's side.

They walked a road between two farms, their breath misting on the frosty air. A light fall of snowflakes danced around them, eddying in the wind of their passing. Snow lay in shallow drifts, and the people here waited for spring's warmth to welcome new plantings. That would not be long now. The season's turn was nearly upon them.

Soon they had reached the outskirts of the forest. Loren felt better the moment she stood beneath its boughs. She leaned back against a tree, folding her arms and staring into the far distance. Sidwan was reduced to the size of a candle, the lights of its homes shining in protest against the approaching evening. Loren blew another long sigh, enjoying the way it floated around her like smoke.

The impostor was troubling. How long had they been following a false trail?

Curse the visions from my dreams, she thought.

Her foresight should have come as they rode across Dorsea, giving some clue that they no longer pursued Damaris. Loren could not guess at the purpose of the visions, of course. Mayhap there was no purpose at all. But she needed every bit of help she could get, and if she must wrest that help from dreams and visions, she would. Yet she seemed to have lost even that advantage.

Shiun cleared her throat and turned away. "I will give you some privacy."

"There is no need. I do not actually have to relieve myself."

The Mystic's eyes sparkled. "That was obvious, but I thought I might help you keep up the pretense."

Loren's mood did not lighten. She only frowned harder and scuffed her boot in the snow.

"I thought we had her this time. Now she has slipped away, and who knows if we will find the trail again?"

"We could not have done anything different than we did."

Shiun's tone was less reassuring than her words. She sounded irritated. Loren glared at the ground. No doubt Shiun blamed Loren for losing the merchant. And why should she not? Loren was in charge. Yet this whole expedition seemed to have become a flight from one disaster to another. Jormund had left them some time ago—albeit at Loren's orders—and two other members of their company were dead. Worse, one of them had turned out to be an enemy in disguise. Loren should have known. Should have seen. Even without her visions.

"I will not rest until it is done. Until Damaris is in our hands and the hands of the King's law, and order is restored to the nine kingdoms."

Shiun was silent for a long moment. "That would be a great feat," she said at last.

Loren flushed. She had spoken like a silly girl. When had Underrealm ever been a place of perfect order? Border squabbles raged and bandit squadrons roamed, creating a thousand conflicts great and small, and each led to bloodshed in the end. Yet they faced a far greater threat now—a war that might lay whole kingdoms low. Loren had not started it, but she had taken a solemn vow to help finish it.

But she did not say any of this to Shiun. "I suppose we have wasted enough time for them to think I did my business," she muttered. "Let us return."

She pushed off from the tree and strode north, Shiun at her side.

THREE

THE DREAM TOOK HER.

She stood on the High King's Seat. Both moons hung full in the sky above her. The streets looked familiar, but she could not place them. Then she recognized the main road that crossed the city from east to west. She had passed this way when . . .

Again she looked up at the moons. Yes. It was the night she had followed a wizard's trail across the Seat. She had found a lock of hair and burned it on her dagger. Its magic led her east, but she had found nothing there. Dejected, she had returned to the palace—but not before visiting a tavern.

She whirled. There was the tavern. A warm glow poured from the edges of its door, which was poorly mounted in the frame.

But now a man leaned on the door. He was tall, his shoulders broad. Many knife scars crossed his arms and face, and even his nearly-shaved head. He was clad all in black leathers, making it hard to see most of his body in the darkness. But his eyes were bright even at night. The glow was akin to magelight, yet Loren had never seen anything quite like it.

Before she could ask who he was, he laughed and pointed to her left. Loren caught a flash of movement at the edge of her vision. She turned and saw a woman in a red cloak. Her brown hair was cut short in a bob, and her sleeveless shirt and vest showed her thick, muscular arms.

Niya.

Rage filled Loren, a rage more terrible than she had ever felt while awake. She launched herself after Niya, who ducked into an alley. Loren plunged into the darkness, pulling a magestone from her cloak and eating it to gain night vision.

Auntie stood there, no longer disguised as Niya. Her clothes had changed as well. Now she wore black robes in a style that looked somehow familiar. Yet it was Auntie's thin, svelte form, her smooth brown skin and dyed blonde hair. And her eyes, which Loren knew she could never forget.

"You!" cried Loren. "You live!"

Auntie frowned at her. There was no recognition in her expression, no anger—only confusion.

"Who are you?" she said.

Loren screamed in rage. If the witch thought to escape by deception, she would find that a folly.

Loren raised her dagger and leaped. Darkness take her vow not to kill. Auntie had died already, but Loren would kill her again in her dreams. She would do it a thousand times, and relish each kiss of the dagger.

Auntie cried out in fear. She raised a hand, and her eyes glowed.

Loren froze in midair, held in place by mindmagic.

But . . . but that was impossible. Auntie was a weremage, not a mindmage. A wizard could only command one branch of magic.

Just as Loren was about to scream her frustration, Auntie vanished. The magic released her, and Loren fell hard to the ground. A hand took her shoulder, and she almost recoiled—but the hand was gentle, and it raised her up.

Before her stood a young woman of surpassing beauty, mayhap a few years older than Loren. But this woman had none of the raw, animal seduction of Auntie. Hers was a softer, gentler grace, a promise of great love and great kindness. She was clad in wispy, silky blue. Loren wondered how the winter air did not freeze her to the bone.

But it is not winter, she realized suddenly. She had visited the Seat in early autumn.

Recognition crashed in upon her. She had seen the woman before. Not in true life, but in another dream. Loren had seen her in a house of lovers, and she had wept for a man Loren did not know. But now she did not weep. She only gave Loren a sad smile.

"That was not the one you fear," said the woman. "The one you fear is dead. You must remember that when you see her."

"When I—what?" said Loren.

The woman smiled and leaned forwards to kiss Loren's cheek. Her sweet and pungent scent penetrated the air, and Loren's heart went skipping.

"You shall have such a hard time after he goes," said the woman. "But you will carry on. Because you must."

"Please," said Loren. "Please, tell me what you mean. I do not understand."

"That boy Chet," said a voice behind her—a voice she knew. "He will leave, you know."

Loren whirled as she shot to her feet. Her surroundings shifted, and now she shivered in bitingly cold wind atop a mountain. Snow covered the landscape in all directions. Loren's stomach lurched as she tried to place herself.

She was in the Greatrocks. The knowledge came crashing upon her, the way it does in dreams. Her peak overlooked a mountain pass. They had taken such a pass through the mountains only a few weeks ago, chasing Damaris into Dorsea. She studied the mountains, trying to find something familiar, but she could see nothing.

And then, there was Mag.

The woman stood in the snow, wind gusting around her. She wore a shirt of chain with thick, fur-lined leather beneath it. Fresh blood covered a mighty spear in her right hand, and a battered shield hung on her left arm. A mournful expression pulled at her cheeks, the corners of her eyes. She stooped, seemingly weary beyond reckoning—nothing like the proud barmaid Loren remembered from Northwood. Where she and Albern had sacrificed themselves so that Loren might live.

Loren fell to her knees. Tears sprang to her eyes unbidden.

"Mag," she whispered. "Mag, is it really you?"

"I cannot come with you," said Mag. Her eyes, too, glistened with tears. She sank to the ground and seized Loren's shoulders, drawing her into an embrace. "Darkness take me, Loren, I cannot come with you. And I cannot tell him."

I cannot tell him. The lover in blue had once spoken the same words. Did they speak of the same man? Who was he?

"Who, Mag?" said Loren. "Please, tell me."

Mag only tossed her head, indicating something over Loren's shoulder. Loren turned to look.

There stood the man in black, the one she had just seen outside the tavern on the Seat. Now he leaned against a different building. It looked like a smithy. The sound of ringing hammers came from within, and smoke poured from its chimney. Its door was plain wood, but above it hung a blue sign with a yellow hammer.

What was a smithy doing in the mountains?

"Your boy," said the man.

"My . . . boy?" said Loren. Then she realized he might have answered her question. "Do you mean Chet? Is that who you all keep speaking of? Mag, what do you wish to tell Chet?"

She turned. Mag was gone. Only the dark man remained.

"Your boy," said the man again. He gave a leering smile. "He is leaving—but then, you have known that for some time."

Grief coursed through her. "You are lying," she said, striding towards the man in black. "You know nothing of Chet. Or of me."

"Ask him yourself." The man pointed over her shoulder. Loren did not want to turn, to find herself somewhere else again with questions still unanswered. But the dream took hold, and her body moved without her intent.

Chet stood a pace away, in the vast entry chamber of a grand palace. Its beauty nearly rivaled that of the High King's palace itself. But no one walked the halls, and no guards stood at the doors. Red plaster formed its pillars, and the roof peaked in two great curves. Just next to them stood wide doors leading outside. Beyond those doors, Loren heard voices.

She ignored them and took a step towards Chet.

"Chet," she said. "Are you all right?"

"I am leaving you," he said. "You cannot follow me anymore."

Loren balked. "What? What do you mean?"

"You cannot follow me anymore."

"Chet, I have not followed you anywhere. *You* have followed *me,* no matter what I—"

He ignored her, stepping out the palace's front door. That door had been closed a moment ago, Loren was certain.

She followed Chet, expecting to find herself in another strange place. But the world did not shift around her. Before her, a massive staircase led to a wide courtyard. The stairs were wider than some ships she had sailed on. On the other side of the courtyard stood a white wall, and beyond that, a grand city. She could see manor houses and military strongholds, as well as countless smaller homes and shops. Nearly all of them had the same sort of curving, peaked tile roof as the palace, barely visible under snow.

But at the bottom of the steps sat Damaris and Gregor.

Loren panicked, looking for Chet. She must not let Damaris find him. But Chet had vanished, and Damaris did not look the least bit interested in finding anyone. In fact, she and Gregor did not seem to have noticed Loren. They sat at fine chairs beside a fine table, furniture that seemed more at home in a merchant's study than out here in a palace courtyard. They had a bottle of wine, and Damaris took delicate sips from a pewter goblet.

"Sidwan?" she said.

Gregor shook his head. "A failure. They overcame the wizard and captured or killed the rest."

Damaris' eyes sharpened. "But we gave Unwe magestones. How did they overcome her mindwyrd?"

The bodyguard's glower deepened. "I do not know. She was never very strong with the gift."

"Yet the magestones . . ." Damaris sighed and pinched the bridge of her nose. Loren's stomach did a turn. She had seen Annis make the same gesture countless times. "I suppose we should not have expected it to be so easy."

"No. It appears they have more wit than I gave them credit for."

"Forgive me, but that is no surprise," said Damaris. "You have always hated Loren, and it blinds you to her many admirable qualities—of which her resourcefulness is among the greatest."

Gregor's jaw clenched. "Just because she is cunning—"

Damaris chuckled and leaned over to pat his hand. "Oh, do not get so angry. We knew Sidwan might not be the end of it. This is not even a setback. It was planned for."

Loren thought she had gone unseen. But now Gregor looked up the steps at her. She quailed at the hatred she saw in his eyes. Suddenly his face changed, becoming the pale, decaying corpse she had seen in dreams before. His throat gaped from a wide wound drawn by a terrible blade. Loren shuddered to think of a warrior who could best the giant in a fight and inflict such damage upon him.

His throat rasped hideously as he spoke. "And when the plan is complete, I shall have her at last."

Damaris, too, turned to look at Loren. She smiled with teeth covered by a red stain. Loren took it for wine, until she realized it was blood.

"And you shall take your time with her."

Loren tried to run, but her legs would not answer the call of her mind. The ground began to shake beneath her feet. Through the courtyard's front gate poured soldiers in strange armor. More came marching from around the edges of the palace. They converged and made their way up the steps towards her—but they parted around the table where Damaris and Gregor sat, flowing like waves around a rock. They stared at Loren from beneath horrible, twisted masks.

A hand gripped Loren's arm, making her jump. She turned and saw Niya. Loren tried to recoil, but Niya held her firm.

"There is only one way out," she said. She was not panicked, but only solemn—even a little sad.

She pulled Loren back into the palace. They went at a dead run through the halls. Niya led her this way and that, past tapestries on the walls and fine urns on side tables, until Loren was hopelessly lost.

Finally Niya skidded to a halt with Loren just behind her. Ahead of them stood wide double doors that opened to a great dining hall. The other end of the hall had another set of doors, beyond which was a courtyard, and beyond that, a gate leading out to the city. No one blocked their path to freedom.

Niya pulled Loren away, towards a small iron door in the wall. Loren drew back.

"That way is safe," she said, pointing through the dining hall.

"That way is for the others," said Niya. "It is not for you."

Loren looked around. There were no others. "What do you mean?"

"Come."

Niya pulled her through the iron door. Inside was a small serving room with trays and dishes. There was no other exit.

Loren froze. Niya had trapped her.

But then Niya went to the other end of the room and pulled down a shelf of dishes. Pottery smashed on the floor. Behind the shelf was a passageway, open but utterly dark inside.

"What is in there?" said Loren.

Niya did not answer. Instead she pulled Loren close and kissed her. Loren's knees went weak, and she shivered as she had when their lips met in Dahab. All the knowledge of what had come after, of Niya's betrayal and her crimes against Chet, seemed for a moment not to matter. She gripped Niya's shoulders, and they clung to each other for a few precious heartbeats.

Then Niya pushed Loren into the passage. Loren stumbled and fell. Before she could rise, Niya had lifted the shelf to cover the way out again. Loren tried to push it away, but the shelf did not budge.

Beyond the shelf, Loren heard the room's door crash open. There came the sound of many feet tramping in. The masked soldiers had found them—or rather, they had found Niya, for Loren was now hidden.

The Mystic's battle cry split the air, a berserker scream that Loren had heard in the halls of Yewamba. She shuddered as she remembered how Niya had hacked down every foe in reach. Now she pictured the Mystic tearing into the masked soldiers that must be pouring into the room.

A blade pierced flesh with a sharp *shunk*. The berserker cry faltered.

Niya laughed instead, a feral noise. Loren heard still more soldiers dying. But at last Niya began to cough blood, and then her voice failed.

There came the sound of many, many swords sinking into a body.

Bitter tears ran down Loren's cheeks. But she could do nothing for Niya now. She turned back to the passageway.

It was utterly dark, but a magestone still coursed through her veins. When she put her hand on her dagger, she could see as if by daylight. The passageway turned twice before ending at a ladder leading up. She climbed it and found herself in another passage like the one below. Again it turned, but she saw no branches to go in any other direction.

After a little while, she reached the end. Before her hung a tapestry, and below it came a gentle breeze. A room lay beyond, but Loren feared to enter it.

Her the only other choice was to return to the room full of soldiers—and Niya's corpse.

Loren set her jaw and pushed the tapestry aside.

She was in a chamber with two doors on either side leading to bedrooms. A third door led out to the rest of the palace. A small table rested in the middle of the room, with a plush couch and two chairs surrounding it. Three lamps lit the place, but they were not on the walls—they sat on side tables at the edges of the room, and they cast many shifting shadows. Everything was of the finest make, just as Loren had seen downstairs.

At the other end of the room was a fourth door, leading to a balcony that overlooked a courtyard. The same courtyard Loren had seen below, on the other side of the dining hall.

Standing in front of the door was Gregor.

The giant faced out into the world beyond. But now he noticed Loren, and he closed the door as he turned to her.

Loren turned and threw the tapestry aside, desperate to escape. But the passageway had vanished. Now she faced a wall of solid stone. She could not get out.

"This is the only way," said Niya.

She stood just beside Loren. Wounds covered her body, and her throat was cut—because, of course, Chet had cut it in Feldemar. But her voice did not rattle, her words did not rasp. She looked at Loren with tears in her eyes.

"It is the only way out," she said again. "Even the Elves told you."

Gregor stalked towards Loren in the darkness.

FOUR

The dream released her.

Loren woke in their room in Sidwan. For a moment she panicked, clutching at her thick blanket.

But she did not scream. She kept still and silent, squeezing the blanket, feeling the rough wood floor upon which she lay. In a moment the terror passed. A long sigh rushed out of her, and she closed her eyes.

She gained greater control of the fear each time, much to her relief. The terror of her dreams had been awful in the beginning, and she did not miss that in the slightest.

The others still slept, and she heard no noises from the inn downstairs. Slowly, quietly, she dressed herself and went to the common room. The innkeeper gave her barely a glance as she walked by him to the front door. Outside, the sky had just begun to grey. Dawn would come in an hour or two. Loren went to the innkeeper and bought breakfast—bread and water only, for she did not trust the meat they served here.

After eating, she went for a brief visit with Midnight in the stables. Modest though the inn was, the staff kept the horses well supplied with oats. Midnight nuzzled Loren's shoulder, as though offering comfort against the fear of her dreams. Loren fed her an old apple she had saved.

She returned to the room and waited for the others to wake. It did not take long. Shiun and Uzo stirred before dawn, and Chet and Annis rose from their pallets soon after. Only Gem remained asleep, curled in the back corner and snoring loudly.

"Shiun, Uzo," said Loren. "We will ride out today. Go into town and replenish our supplies. Get a new waterskin for Gem—his has nearly fallen apart."

"We shall need some more coin," said Shiun.

Loren's gut did a turn. "Of course," she said lightly.

She went to her saddlebag and pulled out her coin purse. A few forlorn weights fell into her palm. Loren handed two of them to Shiun.

They were near the end of their money, and she dreaded having to fetch more. Loren served the High King; by law, she could fetch more gold from any Mystic stronghold. But Loren had feared to turn to the Mystics thus far, and she still did. The redcloaks would have to report the transaction to Kal of the family Endil, and that might cause a reunion with the grand chancellor that Loren would rather put off.

Kal had sent them chasing after Damaris in the first place. He had once mentored Jordel, and now the High King had placed Loren under his command. But Loren had been overzealous in her pursuit of Damaris, and Kal would be furious. Strictly speaking, Loren had not disobeyed any direct order. But Kal had not granted permission for her rash course, and Loren had not even captured Damaris. Now her best hope was to find the merchant before Kal found her, and hope her belated success might earn some forgiveness.

She cast her thoughts aside as Uzo and Shiun left the room. The Mystics knew nothing of her dreams, and she meant to keep it that way. Once she was sure they were out of earshot, she went to the corner and roused Gem by shaking him hard. He came awake with a start, swatting at her with his scrawny arms.

"Wha—what?" he groused. "What is it? I am resting."

"Yes, and overlong," said Loren. "Get up, for we must all take counsel. I have had a dream."

"And so have I," said Gem. "In it were many beautiful young men and an overabundance of food. I wish you had not dragged me from it."

Loren fixed him with a look. Gem glared back for a moment, but then his eyes widened.

"Oh. You mean *that* sort of dream."

Soon he had dressed himself, and then he, Chet, and Annis gathered around Loren in a little circle on the floor. For a moment she felt a rare nostalgia—she knew they must look similar to when the old storyteller, Bracken, would gather the children in her village and tell them tales.

"What brought the dream?" said Chet. "Was it something that happened yesterday?"

"I have never known what causes the dreams," said Loren. "It is nothing I can control, nor has the waking world ever had much influence upon it. It is as though some unseen force jerks on my strings, dragging me this way and that like a puppet."

"Yet whatever this force is, it seems to want to help us," said Annis.

Chet stared at his hands. "If the dreams were meant to help, they might have warned us about Niya."

They all went silent at that. Chet drew his knees up to his chest. His right hand scrubbed at his left arm, though he was already immaculately clean.

One by one, Loren held them in her gaze. "I mean to tell you everything," she said. "Everything I saw. No more half-truths. If I had told you everything from the beginning, we might have avoided much sorrow—and then again, we might not have. But I think now that avoiding the truth helps no one."

But even as she said the words, she winced inside, for there was one thing she could not say. The magestones. Gem knew she had them, and he knew something of their power. And Loren had told Annis not long ago. But she still had not told Chet. He worried too much about her as it was, and he was still too righteous. He held a greater respect for the King's law than any of the rest of them. The urchin and the smuggler's daughter took her use of magestones in stride, but she knew in her heart of hearts that Chet would not do the same.

But the magestones had not been an important part of the dream in any case, and so it was easy to avoid mentioning them. She told them all the rest, about the mysterious lover in blue, the cruel man in black, and Mag. Gem wept a bit when Loren mentioned her. Loren told them every strange place she had visited, the ones she had seen in the waking world and the ones she had not.

Then she came to Chet's part in the dream. Loren paused. She heard his words again as though he spoke them now: *I am leaving you. You cannot follow me anymore.*

Loren repeated the words exactly. She neither avoided Chet's gaze, nor looked at him too closely. Then she paused, while Gem and Annis shifted uncomfortably where they sat.

"Of course, I have seen many things in my dreams," said Loren. "It means nothing, as we all know."

"Naturally," said Annis. Gem nodded eagerly.

But Chet met her gaze for a moment. He quickly looked away. But in that moment, she saw an aching sadness within him. As she carried on with the story, he refused to look at her.

The dream spoke true, thought Loren. *Sky save me. He is going to leave.*

It made her pause, her voice faltering to nothing. In the moment's silence, Chet glanced at her by reflex. They looked at each other quietly for a long moment.

How could Loren blame him? He had never wanted to go on this mad quest in the first place. Chet had only ever wanted to return home with Loren, there to build a quiet and happy life, letting the world's troubles pass them by. But he had followed Loren out of love, and he had suffered a fate worse than Loren could imagine. Auntie had bedded him without leave. He would bear the scar of that always. It was what made him sit in the corner staring past the walls, what made him scrub at his too-clean skin.

It was why he could no longer stand to have Loren touch him.

She forced herself to go on. When she finished the tale, Gem shook his head.

"It is an absolute mess. How are we supposed to read the tale of it? Can you not make any of it a bit more clear?"

Loren frowned at him. "And how do you think I should do that? I do not control the dreams, Gem. They come when they wish, and they show me whatever they will."

"*I* can control my dreams," said Gem, sniffing. "Most often I turn into a firemage and roast my enemies with flame. Can you imagine me as a wizard? No doubt fate kept the gift of magic from me because I had been given such a long list of exceptional qualities already."

"Who could doubt it?" said Loren evenly.

Annis had been sitting in thought after Loren finished her dream-tale. Now she tapped a finger on her chin. "The city you described . . . it sounds like one of the great cities of Dorsea. And the palace you described sounds very like the king's palace, in the capital of Danfon."

Loren frowned. "But I thought you said your mother would never go there."

"I thought not," said Annis, shrugging. "Too much power is concentrated there—and therefore too many agents of the King's law. She could be seen by any constable or Mystic, and then she would be in grave trouble. King Jun and his royal senate have been seeking a way to appease the High King. They could hardly think of a greater gift than to capture and turn over the merchant Damaris, one of the most renowned traitors in the nine kingdoms."

"Then there you have it," said Loren. "Damaris could not have gone to Danfon. It is no more true than the idea of her sitting at a fine table in a snowy courtyard."

"Yet the dream showed her in Danfon," said Annis. "Did you not say that you saw Hewal in Dahab? And that is where we found him."

"I did," said Loren. "But I saw Damaris there, too, and we know now that she never went to Dahab."

"This is still the best clue we have," said Annis. "And your example only proves the point. Even when your dreams are unclear, they bring us to Damaris in time."

Loren shook her head. "I am not sure. Fetch your map. Let us at least see where Danfon is."

Annis hurried to retrieve it. She laid it out on the floor and began to point out markings. "This is Feldemar to the north, and here is Sidwan, where we are now. To the northeast is the Moonslight Pass that leads to Danfon. If we faced no delays, we could reach the capital in less than a week."

But Loren's eye was drawn, almost against her will, to another part of the map. She saw the Greatrocks where they bent south, and little drawings of trees that marked the Birchwood. But to the west of the mountains was the name of a place. She could not read it, but she could not draw her eyes from it.

As she studied the name in silence, something appeared. A small building, almost like a model built of little sticks. At first she did not recognize it, but then she saw that it was a smithy. Its door was plain wood, but above that was a blue sign with a yellow hammer.

Loren shuddered. The building she had seen in her dream. The smithy in the mountains.

Her visions had only ever come to her in dreams, never in the waking world. Was this the same thing? Some effect of whatever magic she had? Or did her imagination play tricks on her now?

Loren put her forefinger on the map. To her eyes, her finger seemed to pass right through the little smithy. That sent another shiver of fear up her spine.

"What is this place?"

Annis frowned. "That is Bertram. A sizeable city, and very important to Dorsean trade. Why?"

Bertram.

She had heard the name before. Xain had told her of it in past days, when they had conspired to sell the stones. He had mentioned it again just before Loren left the High King's Seat. A smuggler named Wyle lived in Bertram, buying and selling goods beyond the King's law. In particular, Xain said the man trafficked in magestones.

"I think we should go there," said Loren slowly. "There is a man in Bertram named Wyle. Xain told me of him. He is a smuggler, like your family, though I am sure he is less well connected."

The others frowned at each other. Loren knew she must appear mad.

"But Loren," said Gem, "what does he have to do with Damaris?"

Loren shook her head. "I do not know. Only . . . only I . . ." She swallowed against a suddenly dry throat. "The smithy I saw in my dream. I see it again, sitting there on the map."

A long silence stretched. Gem leaned in to peer closely at the name of the town, as though he expected to see the smithy drawn there.

"That has never happened before," said Chet.

"No, it has not," said Loren. "But it is happening now. And Xain told me of Wyle. This cannot be a coincidence."

Annis shook her head. "I still do not see how it would help. Wyle may be a smuggler, but he is not the criminal we seek."

"Yet he may be a valuable man to know," said Loren. "He must have friends and contacts across Dorsea. He may know something of the family Yerrin's activities. Damaris is gone, and we do not know to where—not for certain. I do not think we will find her by relying on Shiun's skill as a tracker, considerable though that skill might be. Mayhap Wyle has information that can help."

"If what Annis says is true, your dream showed us the capital, not Bertram," said Gem.

"It *could* have been Bertram," said Annis, pursing her lips. "They are both great cities. Bertram has at least one palace that could have been the one Loren saw."

"And even if my dream showed me Danfon, the visions are not always clear," said Loren. "In Feldemar I saw you turn feral and rip out my throat with your teeth."

Gem sniffed. "I would use a dagger," he muttered. Then his eyes widened. "Not that I would ever do such a thing at all, of course."

Loren flipped one of her throwing knives from her belt and pointed it at him. "You had best not try it." But she smiled at him.

Annis tilted her head side to side, her expression thoughtful. "In any case, Bertram is a good deal closer to where we are now than the capital is. Even if our search there reveals nothing, we will not have wasted much time."

"Then it is settled," said Loren. "We go to Bertram, and then, mayhap, to the capital."

Gem gave a long sigh. "More riding for endless leagues," he groused.

But Chet sat silently, his arms folded across his knees. His left hand still idly scrubbed at the skin of his right arm, and his gaze looked at something far away.

"Chet?" said Loren. "What is it?"

He jumped. "What? Nothing."

"Your thoughts seem to be elsewhere."

"They are," he said, shaking his head. "But they are of little consequence."

"Not to me," said Loren quietly. Almost she put a hand on his arm, but she stopped herself just in time.

"I . . ." He frowned. She could see some battle taking place behind his eyes. "I do not think this is a good idea."

Annis arched an eyebrow. "What? A journey to Bertram?"

"Yes," said Chet. "I think you are wrong about it."

Annis' voice took on an undercurrent of annoyance. "I was not aware you knew much of the great cities of Underrealm. What gives you doubt?"

Chet's cheeks flushed. "I think . . . I think we should carry on the way we are going."

"But we have run out of ideas," said Loren. "We do not know what to do, if not this."

"And do you not think that odd?" Chet spoke quickly now, his words pouring as though through a widening chink in a dam. "That we have pursued Damaris this long, and you dreamless, only to finally have a vision after she has evaded us entirely?"

"But that is a gift," said Gem. "Whatever force has granted Loren these visions, they have given us another just when we needed it most."

Chet snorted. "Forgive me if I doubt the kindness of whoever has infiltrated Loren's mind. But it seems no one else is even curious why the dreams come at all."

And would you feel the same, if the visions did not reveal that you plan to abandon me?

The thought came before Loren could stop it. She hated herself for it, biting her own tongue to keep the words from escaping.

Gem opened his mouth to speak again, but Loren stopped him. "Enough," she said, quiet but just sharp enough to halt his words. "This is the only plan we have. If we think of a better one, we shall act upon it. But in the meantime, we cannot remain in Sidwan until we rot."

Chet's gaze darted to her. For a moment she thought he would argue, but then his shoulders sagged. "Very well," he muttered. "If that is your wish."

She gave him a smile, and after a moment they began to pack their things for travel. But Loren glanced at him as they worked, and her thoughts gave her no peace.

FIVE

Once Shiun and Uzo returned, Loren told them she meant to ride for Bertram. They accepted the news with silent nods and readied their packs for travel. Loren wondered what they thought about this sudden change in tack. Thus far in their travels, the party had relied on Shiun's tracking. This new course must have seemed strange, but the Mystics neither complained nor questioned her.

In truth, she had begun to question herself. The visions in her dreams were strange enough, and she drew no closer to understanding them than she had ever been. But the vision of the smithy on the map . . . that was something new, and it disturbed her even more. What else might she see in the waking world? When something from her dreamsight appeared in true life, a great unease and disorientation came over her. Sometimes it left her almost unable to act. Now she feared that, in a moment of danger, she might see something that was not there at all. The thought discomfited her. As the day wore on, she caught Chet and the children stealing glances at her from the corners of their eyes, and she wondered if they thought the same thing.

Loren decided to spend one night more in Sidwan before setting out. Damaris' trail had grown stale, and one more day would make no difference. Since entering Dorsea, they had never spent more than one night in the same place. They needed a rest, and they more than deserved one.

A short while before going to bed, Loren caught Chet's eye. "Our quarters grow stuffy. I could use a walk in the fresh air before sleep. Would you come with me?"

He smiled too quickly, the way he always did these days, and nodded. But he donned his boots slowly, and after they left the room he walked sluggishly a half-pace behind her. He likely thought she meant to discuss her dream with him.

In fact she wanted to, but she promised herself she would not. They had not spent much time together lately—especially because they had not lain together since Yewamba. Niya's crime—or Auntie's—had left a lasting mark upon him. The mind required time to heal from such a thing, but it also needed help. Few people were better suited to help Chet than Loren. And more than that, she was partially responsible for what had happened. She owed him more attention than she had given.

The town shone in the afternoon light around them. The low sun's red glow bounded from every snowy surface to fly back into their eyes, so that Loren had to squint whenever she turned towards it. Lazy smoke drifted from smokestacks all around, floating up into a clear sky. Loren hoped the weather remained this fine on their journey.

Soon they walked through farmlands. The path south went up a hill and then turned east, bending back and forth at the corners of each farm until it joined the main road that would lead them to Bertram. Here in Dorsea, farmers used small copses of trees to mark the borders of their property. Each time Loren and Chet walked beneath the branches, it felt for a moment like they walked in the Birchwood again.

"Do you remember Northwood?" said Loren. "The way you used to take me walking each day?"

Chet's head jerked towards her as she started talking. But her words calmed him, and he gave her a genuine smile this time—warm, and not too fast. Loren thrilled to see it on his face again.

"Of course I do," he said. For a moment his eyes clouded. "Those were dark days for you. As these days are for me."

"It was painful, then," said Loren softly. "But it was better to know the truth about my father. Indeed, I think it helped me. I had traveled for months, and I thought I rode a tall horse, staring down my nose at those below me who resorted to violence. Little did I know I had made my first kill before I even left home."

Chet shook his head. "That is not the whole truth, Loren. You did what—"

"I did what I had to," said Loren. "I know. And even after learning the consequence, I have not turned into a killer. Yet it *has* shaped me. I know now that others, too, do what they must."

"You are speaking of me and . . . and her," said Chet.

Loren shook her head quickly. "That was different."

For a moment she forgot herself. She reached out to him and took his arm. But Chet jerked away from her as if she had pressed a red-hot poker into his skin. Loren recoiled, drawing her hands to her chest.

"I am sorry," she said.

"No, it is I who should apologize," said Chet. "I . . . I have been getting better about it. But still, when I see you, still some part of my mind sees . . ."

"*No*, Chet," she said, trying to keep her voice kind and firm at the same time. "You must never apologize. You did nothing wrong, and you have done nothing wrong since. I am at fault. I have been ignoring you. That is why I wanted to walk with you now—to try and bring back the memory of Northwood, when the world was a better place and we were . . . well, not happy, entirely, but happier. So much darkness has come since then."

"It has," said Chet. His hand rose to his chest, to the place just above his heart where the dagger of a Shade had pierced him. It no longer gave him pain, but he would rub at it on occasion—and ever more often since Auntie. "Darkness came, but it always passed. But not this darkness. Not now."

Loren ached. She wanted to reach out to him, wanted to hold him. She felt the desire constantly, and she knew she only meant to help him. Always she had to remind herself that it would *not* help, that it would only hurt him more.

She folded her arms and turned to walk again, keeping her pace slow so that he did not feel the need to hurry. "I thought the same thing, you know. After Jordel died, I mean. I thought the grief would never leave me. In truth, I suppose it has not. But it has become bearable. Mayhap you can hope for that."

Chet was silent for a long moment. Then he stopped walking. Loren turned and, to her shock, found him weeping.

"I do not want to leave you," he whispered.

She did not answer at first. She did not trust herself to speak. Tears did not come, but she felt the ache of them in her heart, her throat. They choked her, and she fought to master them.

"I do not want you to go," she said at last. "But I want you to be happy, and I want you to be safe. I fear that neither of those may be possible if you remain with me."

A sob burst from him, and he scrubbed at his eyes with his hand. It was all Loren could do to keep from embracing him then.

"I am not faithless," he said. "I came with you to find Damaris. That is what all this has been for, and I think . . . I *feel* that we are close. Even after learning that she has evaded us, I think I can sense her just in the next town. I want to see it through."

Loren looked down at her feet. "Do you think it will help? Help *you*, I mean?"

He sucked in another cry as his head swung back and forth. An answer? A rejection? Loren did not know.

She could not hold him. She could not take his hand. So she gestured back towards Sidwan.

"Come," she said. "Let us return to the others. We have a long ride tomorrow, and we both need our rest."

Chet nodded and walked beside her. By the time they reached the town and returned to the inn, he had mastered his emotions. Likely the others thought his flushed face came from the cold. But Loren lay awake long into the night, listening for every sound of him shifting on his pallet, wondering if he hid the motion of another silent sob.

They set out for Bertram the next day. The folk of Sidwan seemed sorry to see them go. They had likely caused a greater commotion than the town had seen in years.

Before leaving, they checked in on the constables one last time. The Yerrin wizard was bound and blindfolded. Magestone sickness had not yet set in, but Loren knew it soon would. She did not envy the constables, who would have to remain here to witness it. The other Yerrins sat in a small cell, the only sort of jail for leagues in any direction, and not built to hold five prisoners.

"We shall see to them," said the fat constable with the drooping mustache. Loren had learned he called himself Ham. The name was almost too appropriate. "A letter has been sent to the city of Chosun, and some of our brethren will arrive soon to escort them to better holdings."

"Thank you," said Loren. "Do not forget to tell them of the mind-mage. She will no longer be so dangerous as she was, but no wizard should be trifled with."

Ham shuddered. "I will remember it. Thank you, Nightblade."

Loren gave him a sharp look. She had not told him that title. No doubt this was some work of Gem's. Glancing back, she saw the boy's crooked teeth flashing in a grin.

"You are welcome, constable," said Loren. "Your service will not be forgotten."

He puffed up his chest and saluted with his hand over his heart. Loren gave him a final nod and led her party out of the town.

The road to Bertram was easy enough, though somewhat slower because of the snow. The king paid local workers to clear it away from time to time, but they had not done so since the last snowfall. Sometimes Loren's party had to cut into the countryside to avoid a large drift that had piled up. They rode as long as they could while the sun was high, and each night they stopped early enough to gather firewood before dark. At first Loren had been hesitant to light fires, but Shiun had advised it.

"Bandits are more active during winter," she said. "But they are not likely to trifle with our party. At least four of us look like we can fight."

Gem glowered. "I would say five."

Shiun arched an eyebrow. "As you say. In any case, I think they will leave us alone. Our greatest foe is the cold."

One night Loren and Gem went out to fetch firewood together, taking Chet's hatchet with them. Loren cut down dead-looking branches and piled them into Gem's arms, and soon the boy had a sizeable stack. Once he might have struggled with such a burden, but now he bore it easily. Over their long journey together, he had shot up like a weed, and he had begun to grow some muscle as well.

"I have been meaning . . . er," Gem began. He cleared his throat and tried again. "I have meant to ask if I might start taking a watch at night."

Loren looked at him in surprise. "That would be most welcome," she said carefully. "But mayhap we will pair you with someone else, at least to start. I would hate to wake in the morning and find you had fallen asleep."

Gem scowled at her. "Do you think I cannot remain awake when I wish to?"

"I would never say such a thing," said Loren, keeping her face carefully neutral. "Except that I would, for you have tried standing a watch before—with me, in the Greatrocks. I had to nudge you thrice an hour. You enjoy your rest, master urchin."

His scowl deepened. "And what wise man would not?"

Loren chuckled. The boy's insouciance and seemingly bottomless cheer had been a comfort through many dark times. She wondered how she had ever thought to leave him behind, as she had long ago. A journey without Gem seemed a foreign concept after they had ridden so many leagues together. And the same went for Annis.

At that thought, Loren turned to regard Gem carefully. "I have been meaning to speak with you, as well, but of another matter. How long do you and Annis mean to keep up this strain between you?"

Gem's cheeks and ears grew bright red, and he ducked his gaze. "I . . . it is not something either us have planned, exactly, I think."

"And I notice it has not been pleasant for either of you. That goes for the rest of us as well."

He sighed. "I know it."

"You know that what happened is not your fault. Nor is it Annis'. If either of you blames the other, or yourself . . ."

Gem shook his head quickly. "Of course not. I know that. Only . . . only, is that not the worst part? When no one is to blame? If she had done something wrong, I could take her to task for it. Or if I had done something wrong—outlandish as the notion might seem—I suppose she could do the same to me, and then there might at last be an end to . . . to the discomfort. But neither of us have done anything wrong, and so what can we do to fix it?"

His words were all too familiar to Loren. She had said something very similar to Xain back on the High King's Seat. Many whom she held dear had left her, one way or another—first Jordel, then Albern and Mag, and finally Xain. Yet they had had no choice. Jordel, Albern, and Mag had been slain, all of them in defense of Loren and her friends. Xain had been reunited with his son, and had remained on the Seat to see to the boy's safety. None of them had any choice in what they had done, and Loren had had no choice but to move on. Yet that had not diminished the pain of their parting, and in some ways had only inflamed it. It had taken her a long time before she could think of them with anything but heartache.

"Mayhap it only requires a bit more work," she said. "On both your parts, I mean. Finding a way to turn your friendship warm and easy again, the way it used to be."

Gem looked down at his boots. Then he shrugged, feigning a nonchalance Loren knew he did not feel. "In any case, I suppose it was foolish of me not to predict such an outcome. I should have known long ago that Annis would confess such feelings for me."

Loren cocked her head. "Because of the way she acted? She *has* fawned on you almost from the moment you met."

"She has?" Gem's eyes went saucer-wide. "I have not seen that, nor is it what I meant. I mean only . . . well, how could any young maiden keep herself from desiring such a man?" He held the bundle of sticks in one hand while gesturing at himself with the other.

Loren kept herself from cuffing his ear, but it was a mighty struggle. Still, she felt the need to pierce the bubble of his high opinion of himself.

"I hope she did nothing wrong by it, but Annis told me something of your conversation. And she made some mention of Uzo."

It worked. Gem deflated at once, and his cheeks flushed anew. "Yes, I . . . well, he is very . . ."

"He is," said Loren, nodding. Uzo was indeed a beautiful young man, though she had never felt the same connection towards him that she had with Chet. *Or with Niya,* whispered her mind, though she quickly banished that thought. "But unless it has happened without my noticing, I do not think that you have said anything more to Uzo than Annis said to you for a long while."

"You have not missed anything," said Gem with a sigh. "I may think very highly of myself—and with good reason—but I hold no illusions about Uzo. He scarcely seems to notice me, and when he does, he seems to regard me mostly with annoyance. And besides, how old do you think he is? What would he want from one who is scarcely more than a boy?"

"You are not much younger than I am, and Uzo is not much older," said Loren. "Yet I see what you mean. He is a soldier, after all, and from what little he has told us about himself, I do not think a great romance is something he desires."

"Well, I long for such a romance enough for the both of us," said Gem. He looked up at the sky as if searching for strength. The firewood almost fell from his hands. "But I suppose that is my lot. I think every great scholar, and artist and warrior—and sometime medica—only lives a more complete and fulfilling life if they have suffered a great unrequited love in their youth."

Again Loren's hand twitched, itching to slap the back of the boy's head. "No doubt," she said instead. "It seems almost a requirement."

Her thoughts went to her dreams again, the way they so often did these days. She saw Gem's terrible snarl, the way his face twisted in a rage she had never seen there in the waking world. Her head twitched as she felt his teeth tearing at her throat.

She cut down another branch. But after she put it atop the pile, she took the firewood from his arms and set it down on the ground. Then she took Gem by the shoulders and turned him to face her. He looked up at her—though they were getting near to a height of each other now—and they remained that way for a little while, studying each other in silence.

"You know that I care for you, do you not?" said Loren. "You are one of my dearest friends. I will never stop looking after you."

Gem's brow furrowed. "What under the sky are you talking about? It is my job to look after *you,* not the other way around."

Loren shook her head. "Your wit is one of my favorite things about you. But be serious for a moment. I do not jest."

His mouth worked. Without warning he leaped forth, wrapping his arms around her in an embrace.

"I know it," he said. "And you may be my favorite person in all the world. And that is quite a statement, as I have seen so much of it."

She patted his hair gently. "Good. I never want you to forget it."

Gem drew back and looked up at her, and she saw recognition in his eyes. "This is about your dream. About how you have seen me attack you."

Loren nodded, suddenly nervous to speak.

"Then take my vow, though I have given you one before. I vow never to do you harm. I would end my own life first." He cocked his head and pursed his lips. "Though I would rather not do that either, if it is at all possible."

Loren smirked and embraced him again. "And I command you never to do so. I only wanted you to know how high of an esteem I hold you in. As long as you know it, I am satisfied."

He bounced on his feet and stooped to gather up the firewood. "Then be satisfied! Only we should be getting back, for I am sure the others will not be happy until they have had a chance to warm their frozen limbs."

She smiled and hung the hatchet at her belt, leading him back towards the camp. But a shadow remained over her heart. She had told Gem of her dreams, yes. But she had left one thing out, something she had only realized recently. Whenever she saw Gem turn vicious with rage and attack her, he had been a grown man.

It means nothing, she told herself. *Do you trust your dreams more than the boy at your side?*

Loren glanced at him and hoped she believed her own answer.

SIX

Two days into their journey, the road began to wend through the western foothills of the Greatrocks. The skeletal trees grew fewer and farther between, giving way to an open but hilly landscape that must have been brilliant green in summer, but was now a dead, dark brown where it was not covered in snow. After four days of hard riding, they emerged through a great cleft in the earth onto a highland, and there they came to Bertram at last.

The city had been built at the confluence of two rivers that came leaping down out of the Greatrocks to the east. The waters joined to form the Fanrong, which ran west to Dorsea's coast to meet the western sea. No kingdoms contested that coastline, and Dorsea drew great wealth from its fertile lands. Eventually, that wealth spread through the rest of the kingdom by way of the river.

They paused for a midday meal of rabbit that Chet had shot that morning. While they ate, they gazed down at the city. Gem leaned forwards suddenly and pointed. "Is that the King's road running through the city?"

"It is," said Shiun, nodding. "Bertram was the capital of Dorsea for hundreds of years. When the Dark Wars ended and the last Wizard King vanished, the High King took some of Feldemar's lands and gave them to the Dorsean king—or, you might say, returned them to her. They were Dorsean lands in the beginning, or else the kingdom would not have earned its name, for it would have bordered only two of the oceans."

Gem's eyes widened as he stared at her. "The last Wizard King? What do you mean they vanished?"

Shiun paused for a moment, and she looked at the boy carefully. "It is not something that is widely known, and it might have been better for me not to mention it. But the last Wizard King ruled in Feldemar, and held her kingdom long against the other eight. When the war turned against her, she vanished. The High King Andriana searched everywhere, but never found her. Underrealm lived in fear of her return for many years, but that is now centuries past. She died long ago, though we may never know where. In any case, when the northeast lands were reclaimed, the Dorsean king moved the capital to its original home in Danfon. Therefore Dorsea has had two capitals, but they are both on the King's road, in accordance with the ancient edicts."

Loren stared at the scout. She did not think she had heard the Mystic woman speak so much in all the time they had ridden together. "I thought you were a woman of Dulmun."

"I am, but I was stationed in Bertram for a number of years," said Shiun. "In that time I learned something of its history." She bowed her head and tore another hunk of rabbit from the bone, looking slightly embarrassed.

They reached the city just after nightfall. Loren feared they might find the gates closed, but they stood open. The war with Dulmun was far away, and Bertram had no reason to fear any attack. A constable at the gatehouse asked a few questions, but when Uzo and Shiun flashed their Mystic badges, the woman quickly waved them on.

"You should have a badge," Gem told Loren as they rode through the gate.

Loren frowned. "What sort of badge?"

"A mark of office," said Gem. "You are not some simple traveler. You are the Nightblade."

She gave a quick glance around in case anyone was close enough to overhear, but the street was mostly empty. "I have a writ with the High King's seal," she said in a low voice. "That is good enough."

Gem lifted his chin. "It is not as impressive, certainly."

To Loren's surprise, Uzo snickered aloud at that. Gem beamed for the rest of their ride through the city.

They found an inn with good stables for the horses. In the common room, Loren bought dinner and a few bottles of passable wine. They had not had the opportunity to eat well since leaving the city of Dahab in Feldemar, and that seemed a lifetime ago. Loren thought a decent meal might be good for the others' mood—and mayhap hers as well. It took half the coin left in her purse, but she tried not to think of that. Once they found Wyle in Bertram, she hoped she could sell some of her magestones to replenish her reserves. And if nothing else, she could find a presence of Mystics in the city. Her identification from the High King would be as good as a bank note to them, and they would fill her purse to bursting. They would send word to Kal, but Loren could leave Bertram far behind before he found her.

In the middle of their meal, she turned to Annis. "How might we go about finding Wyle?"

Annis thought hard, and then gave a quick glance at Uzo and Shiun. "The only thing we know about him for certain is that he traffics in certain goods beyond the King's law. But we cannot simply walk into a jeweler and ask for such a man."

"A jeweler? Why a jeweler?" said Gem.

Annis arched an eyebrow. "They are familiar with the transport and safekeeping of small but very valuable objects. It makes them particularly suited to smuggle similar goods."

"Can we not simply ask for Wyle by name?" said Chet. "He does not need to know what we wish to speak to him about."

Gem and Annis rolled their eyes in unison—then they each saw the other doing it, and there was a moment of uncomfortable silence.

"That is not quite how it works," said Annis, a flush in her cheeks. "Smugglers do not like strangers who ask about them. Too often, such people are the King's law in disguise."

"How does one meet a smuggler, then?" said Loren.

"By personal introduction," said Annis. "A friend who knows the smuggler brings in a new contact. If Xain were here, he might be able to help us, but he is not."

"So we must find someone with whom we can establish trust quickly enough to get such an introduction," said Loren. "That seems a tall order."

Annis sighed. "It is. These circles are carefully guarded even in the meanest of towns, and Bertram is a grand city. Still, if we promise—or at least hint—that there may be a considerable amount of gold available to our contact as a reward . . ."

"Very well," said Loren. "We will rest well tonight and start tomorrow."

They went to bed soon after their meal, and rose before dawn. In the morning, Loren faced a dilemma. She had to leave someone in the room to guard their possessions. During their travels so far, that person had been Annis, but now she needed Annis for the negotiations. Gem was streetwise beyond compare, and could be of great use in the city. Shiun knew something of Bertram already, and Loren wanted Uzo in case things came to a fight. That left Chet, and she did not think he would enjoy being left behind. But when she proposed it to him, he accepted quite easily.

"I am the best choice," he told her, giving a small smile. "Besides, how could I complain about being allowed to rest? We are all road-weary. If anything, I feel guilty that the rest of you must remain on your feet while I sleep the day away."

With the matter settled, the party moved out into the city. Loren had not been able to see much of Bertram during the night, but now its splendor was laid before her in the dawn. It was nowhere near as grand as the High King's Seat, but it rivaled Dahab for both its size and its proud history. The buildings were crafted with exquisite care, with solid white walls and glistening red tile roofs. Contrary to many cities she had seen in her travels, this one seemed to have been laid out with careful consideration. Streets did not twist and turn with the land, but had been laid out in a careful grid that made navigation easier. The roofs peaked the same as many in Dorsea, and very similar to the ones she had seen in Danfon in her dream.

Shiun led them towards the part of town where the jewelers lay. All the crafters' shops clustered near to the river, where the workers could easily dispose of the refuse and rubbish of their daily work. Annis carefully considered the jewelers one by one, and stepped into only the ones that seemed exceptionally fine.

"Would it not be better to try the poorer ones?" said Loren. "Surely the less reputable shops would be the ones to associate with someone like a smuggler."

Annis arched an eyebrow. "Do you think so? There is a great deal of coin to be made in dealings beyond the King's law, at least until you find the noose around your neck. Those who walk such dark roads know it, and they like to spend their coin while they have the chance."

Loren smirked and deferred to Annis' judgement. But though they entered many shops, and while Annis dropped many broad hints that they had "very valuable gems" to sell, they did not seem to have any luck. The shop owners did not seem to take the hint, except for one or two who vigorously denied dealing in cargo they called "too valuable." When Annis pressed the point, they asked Loren's party to leave, no matter how much coin was offered.

After their fifth such attempt, Loren was beginning to grow nervous. "Some of these jewelers almost certainly understand what we are talking about," she told Annis. "But they are nervous to speak to us for some reason. Do you not think they might send word to Wyle that we are searching for him?"

"There is little we can do about that," said Annis. "We must hope that we find someone more amenable before Wyle catches wind of us."

Loren sighed and nodded—but then she came to a sudden stop in the street. The others paused, looking at her curiously.

"Loren?" said Annis. "What is it?"

Only a few paces away was a building. It had a plain wood door and a blue sign with a yellow hammer. It was the smithy she had seen in her dream, and in miniature on the map—and now it stood before her in Bertram. Loren felt a sensation that had become too familiar, a wild churning in her stomach and a disorientation that made her dizzy.

"I think we should look here," she said, pointing to the smithy.

Annis looked at it and frowned. "This place? It is a smithy. If I read its sign right, a steelsmith, though they may deal in silver as well. But they do not traffic in gems, and that is where our interest lies."

"Yet I think we should investigate," said Loren. She gave Annis a look. "Something about the place looks familiar."

Annis' eyes widened slightly, and she glanced at Gem. He looked from her to Loren, and the three of them nodded at each other.

"If you are finished passing messages back and forth with your eyes, mayhap we should go inside?" said Uzo. His tone was carefully neutral, but Loren thought she heard an air of exasperation behind his words.

"Very well," said Loren. "Annis, lead the way."

They went in. The smithy was larger than it looked from the outside, for the room stretched far back, mayhap twice as large as most of the other buildings. On the other end of the wide workroom, Loren saw another door leading to the street on the other side. With such an impressive presence, she guessed this place had a great deal of business.

Near the room's center was the smith. She leaned over a bench in conversation with a young man—one of her apprentices, Loren assumed. But when she looked up and noticed Loren's party, she came to them at once. Her arms and chest were bare beneath a leather apron that covered her front, and every bit of her bristled with muscle. Her black hair was long but bound up in a folded ponytail—no doubt to keep it free from the heat of the forge while she worked. She spent a moment sizing the party up, considerable arms folded over her chest. Loren was reminded of Niya for an uncomfortable moment.

"Good morn," said the smith. "Or near enough to afternoon, I suppose. I am Kanja, and master of this place. Are you here with business? I hope you do not wish to apprentice with me, for I have help enough, as you can see."

"Not at all," said Loren. "We are travelers who have come far on the road. Some of our possessions require repair. Bits and bridles, and things of that sort."

Kanja nodded, her eyes roving over the group. They seemed to linger for a moment on Uzo, and her cheeks reddened. "I can be of help there. But you should know that my shop's craftsmanship is famous. My apprentices and I do good work, and my prices reflect our quality."

"We would expect no less," said Annis smoothly. "Indeed, an artisan who takes pride in their work is a treasure beyond the value of mere gold. If that is how you feel about quality, could we beg a recommendation?"

The smith dropped her gaze from Uzo to Annis. Her eyes sharpened as though she was surprised to hear such careful words from such a young girl. "I am not fond of begging. But what sort of recommendation do you seek?"

"While we are in Bertram, we have certain goods we wish to sell," said Annis. "We have been searching among jewelers all morning, but none of them seemed quite right for the sale, you might say. It is as you just said—our goods are very valuable, and we price them in equal measure to their quality."

Kanja's nostrils flared. "I may know someone who could give a fair price for such valuable jewels."

Loren leaned forwards and dropped her voice. "I have heard of a man in Bertram who is just such a friend to many people. Mayhap you know the name?"

The steelsmith looked over her shoulder to ensure none of her apprentices were close enough to hear. "What name would that be?"

"I was told it was Wyle."

Kanja gave a very slight nod. "I know him. And if you seek to trade in certain very fine goods, there is no one better. I would know." Her gaze rose to Uzo again, and she gave him a little smile. "Indeed, it is something I pride myself on. I have an eye, and a taste, for only the finest things in life."

Uzo's brows rose almost imperceptibly. Loren looked back and forth between him and Kanja, and she almost burst out laughing as she realized what the smith was saying. Just to be sure, she cocked her head as if curious. "And do you have a husband who shares in those fine tastes?"

The smith's cheeks reddened slightly, and she dropped her gaze from Uzo demurely. "Who would want such a thing as a husband? It would be only a denial of other, mayhap better opportunities that present themselves."

Loren almost guffawed out loud, but she restrained herself. Instead she met Uzo's gaze and raised her brows. He glared back at her, and she could almost see him withhold a groan. Loren tilted her head and smirked.

Uzo gave a great sigh. Then he stepped forwards, flashing Kanja his widest smile. It was so bright, it even dazzled Loren.

"I myself have never thought to deny any of life's pleasures," he said, voice almost a purr.

Loren thought the steelsmith might bounce on her toes like a child. Behind them both, Gem looked between Uzo and Kanja with a scowl on his face. A little pang of guilt struck her, but she dismissed it. Gem looked more annoyed than devastated.

"I am glad to hear it," said Kanja, grinning at Uzo. "Mayhap I could arrange an introduction, then—after a fine meal spent together? I promise you that my tastes extend to wine as well. You look like a man of Feldemar, so you may not know fine Dorsean wine. We make it with rice, and it is clear and sweet."

Uzo inclined his head. "I shall look forward to . . . a new taste, then."

Loren and Annis turned away suddenly, both hiding their mouths behind their hands to stifle a laugh. Gem only snorted.

Kanja shifted on her feet. "I cannot wait. Come and see me before the sun goes down."

"It would be my pleasure," said Uzo. Then he actually drew her hand up and bent his lips to kiss it. Kanja shivered.

They left the shop and made their way through the streets back towards their inn. All were silent for a long moment. Annis and Loren kept sneaking glances at Uzo, who stared stoically ahead. But at last he growled through his teeth.

"If you mean to say something, you may as well get it over with."

The girls burst out laughing, and even Shiun could not keep herself from a grin.

"I thought she meant to have you on the spot!" said Annis. "I wonder if she would have, if the apprentices were not in the room."

"What sort of dastardly woman is she?" grumbled Gem. "Why, she only *just* met you. Is no one else suspicious that she agreed to give up the secret so easily?"

"I, for one, am not," said Annis. "In the backroom dealings that take place between smugglers and thieves across the nine kingdoms, such transactions are neither rare nor frowned upon. Indeed, many welcome them, for there are darker deeds that can pay for goods and services."

Gem glowered in evident disagreement. Loren forced her smile away. "But of course, Uzo, you know you need not do this if you do not want to. It would be an aid to the mission, but we can find another way."

He heaved a sigh. "I do not prefer women, but neither do I loathe them. You are not asking anything I am not willing to give for the sake of our quest. But may I speak freely?"

Loren nodded at once. "Always."

Uzo stopped walking and caught her gaze. "Soldier to commander, I expect you to get me very, *very* drunk before you send me out to my doom."

Loren could not stop a single loud bark of laughter, but she forced herself back to solemnity at once. "You have my word—commander to soldier. And when the bards sing the tale of our adventures, I will see to it that none of them forget the great sacrifice of Uzo the Spearman."

Annis doubled over and screamed with laughter while Shiun chuckled. And even Uzo and Gem wore reluctant smiles as they set off towards the inn again.

SEVEN

LOREN DID HER LEVEL BEST TO FULFILL UZO'S REQUEST, DOLING OUT precious gold to fill him with fine Calentin wine during their midday meal. Uzo drank deep and often, while Annis tittered and Gem shook his head ruefully. Uzo had not often complained during their journey, but as the wine set in, he began to make long-suffering remarks about his fate.

"Am I to blame for the way I look?" he said, the words slurring slightly. "I only ever sought to be a warrior. Yet all my life, lechers have eyed me like a mountain to be climbed."

"That is, mayhap, an unfortunate metaphor," said Shiun. "But come now. I know you had lovers on the Seat. You have never wanted for fine company."

Uzo slumped over the table and shrugged. "I suppose I have had my share of good companions in my time, yes."

"There, you see?" said Shiun, smiling as she sipped her wine. "Do not look so morose. We all honor your great sacrifice in the name of the High King."

Loren and Annis chuckled. Uzo's scowl deepened, and he pushed his chair back from the table.

"I suppose I have had enough fun poked at me. I shall go and get this over with."

"Fare well," said Gem, who had not looked up from his food in some time. "Be safe."

Uzo gave the boy a small smile. He ruffled Gem's hair before walking away. "I shall. Best to put the matter from your mind, little master."

Gem's head came up, and he watched the Mystic go. Then he lowered his chin to rest on his folded arms again, looking a little less forlorn.

There was little to do until Uzo's return. They went to their room after they had finished eating, and there Loren and Annis sat discussing the map while the others rested. Annis read the names of various cities to Loren and explained some of her thoughts about them, the pieces she had been trying to put together in their search for Damaris.

"As we traveled, I sometimes wondered if she might be making for Bertram," said Annis. "But I thought that would be folly. Bertram is not the capital, but all the same, the King's law has a strong presence. She would attract notice here, no matter how stealthily she traveled. It might have made sense as a brief waystop before some other destination. But when she began to cut back and forth across the northern countryside, I thought that possibility had vanished."

"Could it still be possible?" said Loren. "We lost her trail in Sidwan. What if she evaded us long before that? What if we pursued her retinue for the last week or so while she made for Bertram and beyond?"

Annis frowned. "Anything is possible. But if that is the case, we have almost certainly lost her."

A while later, Uzo returned at last. His jaw was set in a firm line as he quietly entered their room. His clothing was mussed. When he stopped before Loren, he gave her a quick salute.

"I have returned, Nightblade."

"No need for formality," said Loren. "Do we have what we need?"

"We do," said Uzo. "Kanja waits downstairs, there to lead us to Wyle."

From the other corner of the room, Shiun looked at him with a carefully neutral expression. "And did Kanja get what *she* needed?"

Annis nearly died from trying to restrain her giggling, and Loren hid a smile. Gem looked morose. But Uzo only glared at Shiun. "Even when it points in a less desirable direction, my spear is still strong."

Loren leaped to her feet and clapped him on the shoulder. "And that is all we need to hear about that, I think. Thank you again, Uzo. Now let us go and fetch the moon-eyed smith while she is still amenable."

They left Chet in the room again and went downstairs, where they found Kanja waiting for them. A beatific smile played across the smith's face. She draped an arm across Uzo's shoulders and kissed his cheek before nodding warmly to the others.

"Greetings, all. Let us do our business. It is a fine evening for it."

"Fine indeed," said Loren. "We are ever grateful for your willingness to make an introduction."

"Oh, I am more than willing," said Kanja, stroking Uzo's hair. "And please accept my earnest wish for many more favorable dealings in the future."

Several of the common room's patrons looked at Kanja and rolled their eyes. From the way they muttered into their drinks, Loren doubted this was the first time they had seen the smith conducting such business. Uzo gave Loren a weary look. She hid a smile and gestured Kanja out the door.

The streets were lit with strange lanterns like Loren had never seen before. Their sides were made with parchment, not glass, and they were open at the top and bottom, with a small cover a finger or two above the top to keep their flames from falling prey to wind or snow. The paper gave them a warm, soft glow, less harsh than a regular lantern, and it bathed all the streets and walls of the city as they made their way along.

There were few dancers or other street performers here, the way there had been on the Seat or in Dahab. But as the sky above grew darker, some people climbed to rooftop balconies built into many of the houses and shops. There they would stand, leaning on a railing, and sing. The words were in no tongue Loren recognized, and the tune was unfamiliar, though it sounded old. Then she noticed that the words and the tunes blended together from one singer to the next, with just enough difference to tell they were somewhat different songs. It created an odd sensation as they walked, for the same song seemed to shift and meld into different forms of itself the farther they went.

Most of the party looked up at the singers as they went, mouths hanging open slightly in awe. But Kanja walked as if she did not even notice them, and Loren supposed that might be true, since she likely heard them often enough. But Shiun tilted her head back, a pleasant smile tugging at her lips. It was the look of one meeting a friend they had not seen in a long time.

"Why do they sing?" said Gem. His voice was hushed with reverence.

"It is a farewell to winter," said Shiun softly. "The calendar of Underrealm says that spring has come already, of course, but tradition dictates that they sing it on this night. That custom was built on the fading of the snows, and not the marks of some scholars upon a piece of paper."

"What luck that we should be here," said Annis. "To think that they only sing like this once a year."

Kanja and Shiun gave a quick snort of laughter together. "That is not the case," said Kanja. "Soon they will sing the song to greet spring. Then they will sing another song to mark spring's peak, and then another to say farewell to spring, and then *another* to greet summer, and so on. If you spend any length of time in the great Dorsean cities, you will likely grow sick of all the singing."

"I do not see how I could," said Loren. "I hope I get to hear it again, and often."

They reached the point where the two rivers became one and spun away westward. Each current was spanned by a great bridge. In the center of the confluence was a massive pedestal built of unyielding stone, upon which were hung many lanterns. From what Loren could see, it was crafted out of a rock that had been in the water already. Atop the pedestal was a great statue of bronze, mayhap six paces tall. She was a woman, that much was certain, clad in armor and with her long flowing hair splayed out in the wind. On her shield was a device of the sun.

"Renna Sunmane," said Annis with reverence. "She resided here in Bertram during the Kinslayer War."

"She did," said Kanja. "But that statue was built a long, long while after those times. Now they say she stands guard over the riverboats that wind along the waterways. I myself think she is a great nuisance that too many ships crash into. But who would waste the effort to remove such a large rock from the river, especially when many of the simpler folk nearly worship her?"

Annis scowled at the smith's back.

They crossed to Bertram's eastern district, built on the wedge of land between the two smaller rivers. Shortly after that, Kanja stopped in front of a large building. It looked like a simple shop, but its front door was locked and barred shut. Kanja began to lead them around to the back of the building, but Loren stopped her, turning to Uzo and Shiun.

"Wait here," she said. "I will take Annis and Gem inside. Only come after us if you hear trouble."

Shiun nodded, and she and Uzo took position to either side of the alley beside the building. Kanja gave Uzo a little wave as she left. He returned it with a sickly smile.

They followed her around the back of the building, where a small door led to an apartment built in the building's rear. She knocked, and soon they heard a voice on the other side of the door.

"Who is that?"

Kanja smiled at Loren and winked. "It is Kanja, you rascal."

"I can see that, my dear. I am asking about the others with you."

Loren looked closer at the door. She could not see a peephole. How could Wyle see them?

"I have brought some new friends who wish to meet you. For business."

"Normally, new friends are my favorite people. But recent events have soured me on company. Mayhap another time."

Kanja drew back, looking nervously over her shoulder at Loren's party. "But Wyle . . . I vouch for them."

"And I trust you implicitly, my dear. Yet I do not trust them."

The smith pulled nervously at her collar. Loren licked her lips and stepped forth. "Trust is not always necessary for business," she said. "Especially when such business may fill your pockets for many months to come."

A long silence stretched from behind the door. "That is a mighty promise. You do not know how deep my pockets are."

"Yet I know what I have brought to fill them."

Another long silence. When Wyle spoke again, Loren thought she could hear some amusement in his tone. "Never let it be said that I do not respect confidence—even when that confidence borders on arrogance. Come in, then, I suppose."

They heard a bar sliding. Kanja breathed a sigh of relief and reached out to open the door. No one stood inside. Loren saw only a steep staircase leading up to the second floor.

"Where is he?" said Loren.

"Upstairs," said Kanja. "Come."

She led them up the stairs. The second floor was entirely separate from the first, and a half-wall divided part of the back of the room from the front. The place looked as if it had once been well furnished. The chairs and cabinetry were of fine craftsmanship, fine rugs were on the floor, and Loren spotted dishes with gold and silver inlay. But the apartment looked as though a disaster had struck it. There were bits of splintered wood on the floor, as though some furniture had been destroyed in a fight and no one had yet tidied up. There were stains on some of the rugs, and while they might be wine, Loren suspected blood.

In a blue, winged armchair sat a dark man with sharp eyes. He wore a black vest over a long, cream-colored tunic, and dark blue pants that went into high leather boots. His appearance was immaculate, utterly at odds with the state of his dwelling. In his hand was a glass goblet full of wine, which he set down as he rose from the chair to greet them. Loren thought to herself that that was entirely unnecessary, since he must have been standing when they arrived, and had only sat so that he could stand up again. His eyes roved across Loren's little group, studying each one of them with interest. His gaze lingered long on Annis, and he blinked more than once at Loren's striking green eyes.

"Greetings to all, and a good evening to you," he said, bowing low. "As Kanja has no doubt told you, I am known as Wyle—or, likely, you knew that already, for I heard that you have been searching for me. But I do not think I know you, or have heard of you, and you are a bit younger than the friends I am used to meeting." His eyes flicked to Loren again as he said it.

"But . . . but Wyle!" cried Kanja. "What on earth has happened here?" She gawked at the destruction all around them.

"Nothing you should worry your muscular self about," said Wyle. "It is a small situation with which I have only recently dealt. I shall have the place in order by tomorrow."

Kanja still looked upset. But Loren cared little for whatever trouble Wyle had had, as long as it had passed. She stepped forwards to speak before Kanja could ask further questions.

"We are friends and travelers passing through, and our age does not diminish the quality of our goods. We have some items that we wish to sell to you, if you are interested. They are of the finest quality, and nothing we would want to sell where certain . . . red-clad friends might catch wind of it."

Wyle's eyes widened, and the corners of his lips turned down in thought. "Of course, of course," he said. "Naturally. Well, if we are to do business, then I should don my business garments. A moment, if you would."

He retreated to the back section of the room, where the half-wall hid him from view. Loren and Annis gave each other an odd look. Gem looked at Kanja and frowned. "Business garments?"

"Some finery of his, no doubt." Kanja gave a little smile. "I have seen him in many fine clothes, as well as none at all."

From his expression, Loren thought Gem might be sick.

Then they heard the crash of a window from the back of the room.

"Dark below," growled Loren.

She ran around the half-wall. A window in the front of the building had been broken, and Wyle was nowhere to be seen.

"Gem, down the stairs!" she cried. "I will go after him."

Loren ran to the window. Wyle was already halfway to the ground. There were tiles and bricks set in the wall. Loren had thought them a decoration, but now she saw they formed a sort of ladder leading down. An escape route, in case Wyle found himself cornered. Loren admired the precaution.

She leaped out the window and took the same route down. Wyle jumped the last two paces to the ground. He landed in a crouch and came up running.

But he had not predicted the Mystics. Uzo leaped out of the alley, hands grasping. Wyle seized the spearman's arm and flipped him around, then kicked his legs out from under him. Uzo landed hard on his back. But Shiun appeared, driving a fist into Wyle's stomach. He fell to the street, wheezing.

Loren reached the ground a moment later, and Gem appeared just after. Loren helped Uzo to his feet. He had hit the back of his head when he landed, and he rubbed it ruefully while glaring at the smuggler. Loren tossed her head towards the back of the building.

"Bring him back to his hideout," she said. "This is not a conversation for the open air."

They took him back to the door leading to the staircase, but Loren commanded Shiun and Uzo to wait again. "One of you remain here, and one at the front of the building. I will not let him try the same trick twice, but be ready just in case."

In truth, she had no wish for the Mystics to learn of her magestones. Uzo and Shiun nodded and went to do as they were bid. Loren put a hand on Wyle's shoulder. He tried to shake her off, but before he could react she pulled one hand up behind his shoulder blades and shoved him up the stairs.

"Be still. You will not escape me a second time, but I have no wish to hurt you."

"You are hurting me now," said Wyle. But to her surprise, his tone was affable. He stopped resisting and walked up the stairs without further trouble. Once they had entered the apartment again, Loren released him with a shove.

Kanja still stood where she had been, eyes wide and head swinging back and forth. "I do not understand. What is wrong?"

"A sudden change of heart has come over me," said Wyle. "I decided—rather abruptly, it is true—that I would rather not do business with these new friends."

"But why?" said Kanja, blinking.

Wyle sighed and rubbed at his temples. "Kanja, you are a lovely woman—if too trusting—and a more than passable lover. But you are a terrible judge of people. Your new friends are the King's law."

Kanja gasped and took a step back. Her eyes grew panicked, and she seemed as if she might run.

"He speaks the truth," said Loren. "But you need not fear."

"Not her, mayhap," said Wyle. He shook his head with a sigh. "But I hold no illusions for myself. What a tragedy. I am too pretty and too clever to die under the knives of Mystics. And just after ridding myself of another gaggle of troublemakers."

Gem gave a loud snort. Loren shot him a glare.

"You have no reason to fear us, Wyle, nor was that little display of yours necessary," said Loren. "We are not here to kill you, nor to put you to the question. But I think I would prefer the rest of our conversation to be conducted in private. If you do not mind?"

She tossed her head towards Kanja. Wyle stared at her for a moment, and then a slow smile crept across his lips. He went to Kanja and put his hands on her shoulders.

"Whether she tells the truth or no, neither of us gains anything by your being here, my sweet," he said. "Go, and take care of yourself. I will see you soon, if I can."

Kanja gave Loren one last uneasy look, but she nodded. Then she pulled in Wyle and kissed him deep and long. Loren and Annis studiously averted their gazes, and Gem openly made a gagging noise. But the moment passed, and then Kanja left through the apartment's back entrance.

Loren waved a hand at the staircase. "That one hardly did much to guard your presence here. Whatever made you entrust her with the secret?"

Wyle shrugged. "Kanja is a fine woman, as I said. And when someone comes to Bertram looking for those who deal beyond the King's law, they never look twice at a steelsmith. I wonder, in fact, how you found her."

"How painful it must be to wonder," said Loren.

To her amusement, Wyle very nearly pouted. "Painful indeed." The pout turned into the same curious smile she had seen earlier. "But now we have wasted enough time on . . . shall we call them pleasantries? I wish to hear the real reason you sought me. Servants of the King's law, seeking to deal with a man like me? I begin to think you may be even better friends than I first thought."

"We may be," said Loren. "It has come to my knowledge that you deal in certain goods of inestimable price. And because of that, we know that *you* know a great deal about the family Yerrin."

Wyle's amused look fell away at once. He folded his arms over his chest. "I feel my mind changing again. On second thought—or rather, third, or is it fourth?—I think I would rather not have any dealings with you after all."

"How unfortunate for you," said Loren. "We have come to the point where your preferences matter very little to me."

The smuggler's eyes narrowed. "How *did* you come to be here, anyway? You seem to know a very great deal about me, but I only know that you are the Nightblade."

That took Loren aback. "You know who I am?"

Wyle shrugged. "Rumors are one of the most—no, *the* most important tool of my trade. Many people whisper about the green-eyed girl in the black cloak." He pointed at her face, and then her body. "Green eyes. Black cloak. And servant of the King's law."

"You know more about me than you make it sound," said Loren.

"Just because I hear rumors, does not mean I rely overmuch on them," said Wyle. "Many tales about you are obvious lies, like how you escaped a constable's prison with a magic cloak. I wish to learn a truth or two instead."

Loren well remembered Xain's warning: Wyle had no love for the wizard, and would not be pleased to find out Loren was his friend. "It does not much matter how I heard of you," she said.

"Come now. I am at your mercy. Who cares if I know how it came about?" Wyle began counting on his fingers. "Was it Torbrik who told you? He has never forgiven me for that mess with the Calentin ship. Or mayhap that girl Jessa. She has caused me more than a fair share of troubles, and all because of a little misunderstanding over hemlock. Ah, I have it. It was that idiot of idiots, Robb. If I hear one more word from him about that den of lovers—"

"Stop!" said Loren. "If it will cease your prattling, I will tell you. I learned of you from Xain, of the family Forredar."

Wyle's already annoyed expression turned to dismay. *"Xain?* Sky above. A trio of misfortunes has befallen me at once. A girl made out of rumors, sent by one of the worst investments I ever made, on some business concerning the Yerrins. No. That is three reasons for me to have nothing to do with . . . with whatever this is, and any of the reasons would be good enough on its own."

Loren felt herself at somewhat of a loss. The man clearly wanted nothing to do with her, and whenever she tried to argue with him, he only talked circles around her. But in the moment's silence, Annis stepped forwards.

"You need not have any dealings with the family Yerrin at all," said Annis. "We only wish to know what they are up to. A small group of Yerrins have been crisscrossing their way across Dorsea. We need to find them. Surely you must know something."

Wyle eyed her. "How much do you know about the family Yerrin, exactly?"

Annis' cheeks darkened for a moment. "Quite enough."

"Oh?" said Wyle. "I wonder. I wonder if you know what they do to anyone who attempts to interfere with their trade. No, not even interfere, but just to skim a small bit on the side. I have had friends who attracted their attention—*have had,* I say, for none of them still live. And they were not quick in dying. The Yerrins saw to that. No, I do not imagine you know very much about the Yerrins at all, or you would not pursue them in the first place."

Annis smiled, though the expression was devoid of humor and held only a clear threat. Loren shuddered at how closely she resembled Damaris in that moment.

"You guess wrong. I myself am of the family Yerrin. You have the honor of addressing Annis, daughter of Damaris."

Wyle's mouth opened at once, as if to reply by reflex. But once he heard Annis' words, his voice died in his throat. His skin went several shades paler. At last he choked out, "I . . . I had not heard that you still traveled with the Nightblade."

"Yet you can see that I do," said Annis. "And I would *ever* so much appreciate your help. But of course, if you will not give it, I shall be forced to send a letter to my darling mother."

"You . . ." Wyle swallowed hard. "I know you would not. They say you have sundered yourself from her. There are precious few rumors about you, but they all agree on that."

"If so, they speak the truth," said Annis. "And certainly we are on no friendly terms. Yet whatever opinion she holds of me, my mother—and in fact, all my kin—would be most interested to learn the name of a man dealing in magestones, and just where in Bertram he might be found."

Wyle stared at her for a long, silent moment. Then his gaze rose to Loren, and he flashed her a wide smile.

"The Nightblade of the High King," he said, giving her a deep bow. "I am most pleased to make your acquaintance. It will, of course, be my pleasure to serve you."

EIGHT

WYLE HAD A BROAD, SOLID TABLE OF OAK, AND ACROSS IT HE UNFURLED a map, holding down the corners with large tomes bound in leather. When that was done, he had Annis lay out their journey in Dorsea thus far. They started with riding south out of Feldemar and crossing the Sunmane Pass, and then the mad crisscross through Dorsea's western towns, finally ending in Sidwan where they had lost Damaris' trail. Gem soon grew bored by the conversation and went to sit in Wyle's great armchair, where he promptly fell asleep. When they had finished telling the tale, Wyle pursed his lips and pulled at the thin scrub of beard on his chin.

"That is quite the journey, and I hear little information that may help," said Wyle. "She could have thrown you from her trail long ago, and you never realized it until Sidwan."

"We thought of that," said Annis. "But to a man so clever as yourself, surely such a setback would be merely a distraction."

Wyle arched an eyebrow. "You wound me, my dear, though doubtless you do not intend to. There are some kingdoms where the word 'clever' carries a more sinister connotation, and Dorsea is one such."

Annis' eyes went wide, and she tilted her head to the side like a bird. "Is it? I had not the slightest idea. You *must* forgive me."

The smuggler hid a smile. "I shudder to think how sharp your wits will be in adulthood."

"I will choose to take that as a compliment," said Annis, giving a perfect curtsey.

"I think you are right that Damaris would stay well away from Danfon and the other major cities," said Wyle, looking back at the map. "It would simply be too great a risk. But then again, an unexpected course is often the best way to accomplish something nefarious. And it is well known that Damaris is both crafty and devious—meaning no offense to her daughter, of course. Very well. I will send word at once to my friends in the city, and we shall see what may be seen. But there is nothing else we can do tonight. After I send my letters I will retire, and I suggest that you do the same. We must all hope that the morning will bring news."

"Well enough," said Loren. "In that case, there is only one matter more we must discuss with you." She looked at Annis and tapped her cloak where an inner pocket held her magestones.

"Ah, yes," said Annis. "We did not entirely lie to you when we came here. We *do* carry a certain valuable cargo, and we *do* mean to sell it— or at least a portion of it."

Wyle drew up, looking back and forth between them. "Truly? Agents of the King's law, dealing in magestones? Wonders never cease."

"I think these are days when all of us will see many things we have never seen before," said Loren. "What price would you give us for them?"

For a moment Wyle did not answer, only pulling at his beard again and staring at the table in thought. "Let us see . . . I could give you mayhap fifty weights per stone."

Loren's knees went weak. With fifty weights she could make a pauper's journey from one end of Underrealm to the other, and with a hundred she could do the same thing but eat like a king the whole while. She had heard often that magestones were very valuable, but she had never known just how much so. She thought back to when she had found Damaris' caravan in Selvan, its wagons containing secret compartments holding hundreds of magestones each. She did not have a great enough command of numbers to calculate how much coin that cargo would bring, but she guessed it was enough to buy half a kingdom.

And then she almost fell over as Annis immediately replied, "Eighty weights."

Wyle frowned. "Are you mad? On my best day I cannot sell them for eighty-five, and five weights of profit is nowhere near enough for the risk I take."

Annis rolled her eyes. "You can sell them for nearly double eighty-five, you brigand. We will sell them to you for eighty if you will buy at least ten of them."

The smuggler's frown deepened. "Seventy-five—but I will buy fifteen."

"Seventy-six."

Wyle threw his hands up in the air. "You are a merchant's daughter," he cried. "You should conduct yourself with dignity. It is unbecoming to haggle for scraps."

Annis spread her hands with a disarming smile. "I must preserve at least some of my dignity as my mother's daughter."

Wyle rolled his eyes just as she had—but Loren thought she saw him hiding a smile as well. "Very well. Seventy-six, you beggar. I shall collect the coins tonight and have them ready for you in the morning."

Loren did not think her tongue would work. Visions of piles and piles of gold weights danced in her mind. But she forced herself to be calm again, and she gave Wyle a little half-bow. "Though at first our meeting was fraught with tension, I am glad to have made your acquaintance regardless. We shall see you upon the morrow."

Wyle returned her bow with a deeper one. "And you, Nightblade. If I am still uneasy about our association, I grant at least that it will be an interesting one. I beg only that you do not make it interesting in the same way that Xain did—leaving me alone and forlorn upon a riverbank without a copper in my pocket."

Loren raised an eyebrow. "It seems that you and I have had at least some similar experiences with Xain, then."

"Oh?" Wyle looked surprised. "You should have told me from the beginning that you and the wizard were not friends. It might have changed my opinion of you."

"Our road together was long," said Loren. "Things changed."

Wyle sniffed. "Very well. I hope to hear the tale some time. But that will have to wait for another day."

Annis gave him an even deeper bow than he had given Loren. They roused Gem and left. Shiun waited outside the apartment's back door, and she pushed herself from the wall with a raised brow.

"Since I have not had to chase him down again, may I assume that negotiations went well?"

"Well and better," said Loren. "He will begin gathering information at once, and we will return in the morning. I think we can trust him to do as we have bid him, but just in case . . ."

Shiun nodded at once. "I will remain here to watch the building and make sure."

"Thank you," said Loren. "I shall send Uzo to replace you after the moons have begun to lower in the sky. We are all of us weary."

They fetched Uzo from the front of the building and made their way back towards their inn. Gem was nearly asleep as he walked, and Uzo had to keep a hand on the boy's shoulder to prop him up. Loren took advantage of the Mystics' distraction to step aside with Annis.

"How did you do that magic with Wyle?" she murmured.

"Hm?" said Annis, raising her eyebrows. "I did no magic."

"You sold him the magestones for thousands of gold weights!" said Loren. "When we first met, you did not even know what the stones were, much less their price."

"Oh, that," said Annis. She dropped her gaze and smiled, brushing a lock of hair behind her ear. "It is simple, really. It would have been better if I *had* known their value to start with, for I likely could have fetched a better price. But I had to let him make his proposal first. I knew he would bid far, far less than they were worth. Once he gave his first offer, I picked what seemed a good amount higher and worked from there. And not that it matters much, but he is not giving us *thousands* of gold weights—not much over one thousand, in fact."

Loren scoffed. "You speak as though that is not simply *unimaginable* wealth to almost all in Underrealm. Sometimes I forget you are a merchant's daughter in truth."

Annis' smile widened but for only a moment. "We shall have to find some way to store them safely, of course. He will likely give us the coin in lockboxes, and we can spread them between all our saddlebags. At some point we should find a banker."

Loren hesitated a moment. Annis noticed it and looked at her curiously. Loren's mouth worked for a moment before she spoke, more quietly and slowly than before.

"Let us not spread the coins among all our saddlebags," she said.

"Just yours, Gem's, and mine. It would be better if Chet did not know about it at all."

There was a long silence between them as Annis looked away uncomfortably. "This is about your dream, is it not?" she said at last. "I could understand Chet wanting to leave, after . . . after what happened. But do you really think he would rob us into the bargain?"

"I do not," said Loren. "But remember that Chet knows nothing about the magestones. How would we explain where the coin came from in the first place?"

"Ah," said Annis, nodding quickly. "Of course. That is very wise. I should have thought—"

But her words died as the night's silence shattered. Deafening as thunder, the city's bells began to toll.

The sound made them freeze in their tracks, and Loren's hand went to her dagger. In all their journeys, they had heard many bells tolling in alarm, and her first thought was that somehow she had been discovered. But she realized that was a ridiculous thought.

A second thought flashed through her mind to replace the first: *Damaris.*

"Something is happening," she said.

Gem had been startled to full wakefulness, and now he cringed every time the bells tolled anew. "Is the city under attack?"

Loren turned to Uzo. "Go to Shiun at once. Make sure that Wyle does not try to escape in the confusion. If you must, escort him to join the rest of us at the inn."

Uzo nodded and ran off while Loren turned to Annis and Gem.

"Whatever this is, I do not like it. We must reach Chet at once."

They set off at a sprint, only slightly hampered by Annis with her shorter legs and longer skirts. Soon they found the inn and ran inside. Loren had planned to dash upstairs and find Chet. But she skidded to a halt on the threshold as she saw him there in the common room.

"Chet!" she said. "Are you safe? We heard the bells—"

"As did I," he said, "and I came down to see what the fuss was all about. Then a crier come to the square outside. He . . . he told us the reason for the bells."

His words died, and one hand rose to scrub at his face. His skin had gone ashen, and his fingers were shaking.

"Chet?" She almost lifted a hand to reach for him, but she pulled it back at the last second. "What is wrong?"

"King Jun, the king of Dorsea," said Chet. "He has been murdered. The crier said he was assassinated by the High King. Dorsea has joined the war on the side of the rebels."

They stood there in silence for a moment, staring at him. Then Loren shook herself out of her thoughts. The common room buzzed, and no one seemed to pay them any attention. But that might change. She had to get them out of sight.

"Upstairs," she said. "Let us speak no further word until we are safe in our room."

Annis began pacing the room's length even before Gem closed the door behind them. "This cannot be," she said. "It *cannot* be. Dorsea pledged its support to the High King. Jun was one of only three kings to do so at once. Enalyn would never kill him when she so desperately needs the support of the other kingdoms."

"It is a ruse, then," said Loren. "It must be some work of the Necromancer. Only they stand to benefit from the tumult this will cause."

"And my mother must be behind it," said Annis.

Loren frowned. "Damaris? What makes you think so?"

Annis shook her head, looking miserable. "It is just as Wyle said. She has done the unexpected. We thought she would stay away from the capital, just as she wanted us to think. She went there and put this plan in motion, knowing we would be unlikely to follow her and discover her plot before she could carry it out. We thought she would avoid Dorsea's king, but all along she meant to kill him."

"But assassinating a king . . ." said Loren. "That is no small feat. And she has only been in Dorsea a scant few weeks."

"Oh, she must have set events in motion long before," said Annis. "I should have foreseen this. We wondered if she still served the Necromancer, and now we know. Seizing power in Dorsea was a part of the grander scheme. Now this kingdom is a strong foothold. Indeed, Dorsea's betrayal is far worse than Dulmun's. Dulmun's strength of arms may be greater, but it lies far to the northeast. Dorsea is in the center of Underrealm, and it borders more kingdoms than any other. There is some small comfort: this threat would have been even greater if Damaris had managed to capture and hold Yewamba. From that stronghold, she could have staged assaults into both Feldemar and Calentin with relative ease."

"At least we thwarted her there," said Gem. "And we will stop her here as well."

"It will not be so easy," said Annis, shaking her head. "Yewamba was a mighty stronghold, but Damaris was isolated. Now she is in Danfon itself. She will have the full support of whoever has taken the throne after Jun's death. Yet I do not know how they think to thwart the will of the senate."

"You mentioned that before," said Loren. "What is the senate?"

"A body of twelve representatives, two each from the six states of Dorsea," said Annis. "They govern most domestic matters within the kingdom, while the king has ultimate authority when it comes to war. But even in that, the senate may gainsay him if enough of them unite in common purpose."

Gem sniffed. "That sounds hideously inefficient."

"It is meant to be," said Annis. "A precaution so that no mad tyrant can lead the kingdom to ruin through warmongering."

"Yet Dorsea is the most warlike of all the kingdoms," said Loren.

Annis raised her brows. "Spoken like a true daughter of Selvan. They are often embroiled in battles, yes, but they content themselves with small border skirmishes. The senate is supposed to keep the king from doing anything too consequential."

Loren bit back her first angry answer and took a deep breath before answering in a calm voice. "The people of Wellmont would say that Dorsea's actions have been consequential enough."

Annis spread her hands. "No kingdom is perfect. Some are merely less terrible than others."

Gem looked back and forth between them with an uncomfortable expression. "Mayhap we should put aside philosophy for a moment and consider our next action. It seems clear we must stop Damaris, as well as the new Dorsean king."

Loren heaved a sigh. Gem was right. Her dislike of Dorsea mattered little in the face of their current predicament. "Who would that be? Who would turn this kingdom against the High King?"

"I do not know," said Annis. "Jun is of the family Fei, and it will be someone else in that house who takes his place. But I do not know the royal families of all the nine kingdoms very well. I know only that Jun has no siblings, and so it will be one of his cousins, or mayhap an uncle or aunt."

"So we mean to pit ourselves against a king, then?" said Chet quietly.

Loren looked at him. He sat on one of the beds, leaning against the wall beside it. His knees were up, his arms draped over them. He was not looking at any of them, but only picking at his nails.

"Only so far as we must," said Loren gently. "It seems clear we shall find Damaris in the capital, and she is our true aim."

We hunt Damaris, she thought, wishing he could hear the words. *You said you wanted to see it through, to catch her. Stay with me at least that long, before you tell me you mean to leave.*

He glanced up, meeting her gaze. His face filled with the sad smile she had seen too often lately. "Very well. It appears we ride for Danfon."

Loren nodded. "Thank you," she whispered. Then she turned to the others. "But not at once. We aimed to get a good night's rest, and I still mean to. Gem, go to Wyle's hideout. Tell Uzo and Shiun to split the watch between themselves, and that we ride from the city tomorrow. Then return here as quickly as you can, and get to sleep. We should try to be up before the sun."

Gem gave a quick nod and flew from the room. Chet readied himself for bed and fell asleep almost at once. Loren prepared to do the same, but Annis stopped her for a moment.

"We should bring Wyle with us," she said.

Loren's brows rose. "Why?"

"He is a smuggler," said Annis. "Danfon will be in great turmoil, and the guards at its gates will be vigilant. We must enter the city with all possible discretion, and I do not doubt he can sneak us in without anyone seeing."

"That seems wise," said Loren, nodding slowly. "We will bring him, then, though I doubt he will enjoy it."

Annis grinned. "I do not think he has enjoyed any part of his dealings with us yet. What is one more unpleasant duty?"

Loren smiled. "Thank you again, Annis. Our quest would be doomed without you."

The girl waved a hand. "You would muddle through somehow. You always do. I only do my best to make things a bit easier."

"And you do a marvelous job. Good night."

They went to bed, Loren on the floor and Annis on the pallet next to Chet's. But for a long while, Loren's thoughts would give her no peace. She had wondered why her dreams had led her here. Now she had a guess. They had a smuggler now, who could help them enter Dorsea's capital without being seen. That seemed a boon, but if the dreams were truly meant to help her, they would have led her to Danfon long ago, before Damaris carried out this coup.

Her hands tightened to fists. Chet's misgivings about her dreams wormed their way into her mind. Yet she could not bring herself to ignore them as he wished. How could she, when they were the only help she had?

Back and forth her mind whirled as she lay on the room's floor. When Gem and Uzo returned, she shut her eyes and pretended to sleep, but slumber came slow. At last, shortly before Uzo went to replace Shiun, Loren's eyes closed.

NINE

THE NEXT MORNING, THEY FOUND WYLE NO MORE EXCITED ABOUT their proposition than they had expected. The merchant greeted them drowsily in a fine coat of blue with golden trim, but he walked around his apartment in bare feet. He had cleaned the place up somewhat during the night, and there were now several chairs upon which to sit. When Annis explained what had happened and what they guessed about Damaris' role in the rebellion, he waved his hand in dismissal.

"I have learned of King Jun's death already, of course, and furthermore I know who has succeeded him. The man's name is Wojin, and he is Jun's uncle. Was, I should say. And I had already guessed that Damaris might have played some small part, though I am glad, of course, to hear it corroborated by such a capable mind as the Yerrin girl's. Ah, well. Our meeting has been a blessed one, and I have enjoyed every instant of it. Your departure aggrieves me, but I suppose it is fate's cruel wont to force such bitter partings."

Loren gave him a faint smile. "Then let your poetic heart rejoice, smuggler. We do not mean to part ways with you at all. I need someone to get me into Danfon, and that person must be well acquainted with secret ways and passages that the King's law would not use. Who better for such a purpose than the great and honorable businessman, Wyle?"

Wyle tried to turn his expression into a smile, but it only became something of a grimace. "I might have guessed that would be your aim. But your words are truer than you know: I am great and honorable, but I am a *businessman* above all. You mean to end a rebellion. There is little profit in such a scheme, and therefore I decline to offer my further service."

"Only the poorest of merchants can find no profit in a war," said Annis. "Surely you can find some way to draw coin from a venture like ours."

All humor left Wyle's eyes. He leaned over his thick table, planting his hands flat upon it. "I enjoy my jibes with you, girl. But never insult me that way again. I am no warhawk."

The sudden vehemence in his voice surprised Loren, and she felt ashamed without truly knowing why. Even Annis was taken aback for a moment, and Gem stared at Wyle with wide eyes.

"Our apologies," said Loren carefully. "Indeed, I would not work with one who earned coin from the deaths of others. But we do need you, and our cause is honorable. We do not aim to join the war in Dorsea, but to end the far greater war across all of Underrealm. If you help us, you will be serving the cause of the High King herself. Can you not imagine that she would be grateful for such aid? How full might your coffers be after she expressed that gratitude?"

Wyle drew back for a moment, pinching his chin between two fingers. But then he shook his head. "My coffers are plenty full, and from dealings that are far less dangerous."

"Less dangerous, but still beyond the King's law," said Loren. "I am the Nightblade. I serve the High King directly. Imagine it, Wyle. Imagine me in her council chamber, speaking to her of your bravery. Imagine her scrawling a writ upon parchment—a writ of amnesty for your past . . . shall we call them indiscretions?"

Annis stared at Loren in surprise, but only for a moment before recovering. "Think of it, Wyle," she said. "A bank account full of the High King's gold, and a paper that absolves you from past crimes. You could become an honest businessman at last, making far more coin than you do now, and never fearing a constable's noose. Even my family would avoid you if you had the High King's favor."

Twice Wyle opened his mouth to answer, pointing his finger at them as if about to present a counter-point. Twice he closed his mouth again, looking off distantly as thoughts seemed to flit behind his eyes. In the end he tilted his head at them with a wide smile.

"I will admit you present an attractive offer, though you hide insults within it. I have *always* been an honest businessman. But in this, you have changed my mind. My heart sings at the opportunity to be of further service to Her Majesty."

Loren sent Chet and the Mystics to fetch the last of the supplies they would need for the journey. When they had gone, Wyle brought out eleven lockboxes full of gold coins to pay for her magestones. Each box was made of iron and had a small latch at the bottom through which a lock could be placed. All the locks had the same key, which Loren took from Wyle and put in her coin purse. Each box held four rows of twenty-five gold weights each, and they were packed tightly with velvet so that the coins did not jingle when the boxes were moved. Annis insisted on opening all of the lockboxes to verify their count, and Wyle seemed to take that as a great insult.

"As though I am a swindler," he complained. "As though I would have lived this long in my line of work if I had acquired a reputation of shortchanging my customers."

Annis inspected the lockboxes, and then the pile of gold weights that would go directly into Loren's coin purse. She pointed at the pile. "There are thirty-eight coins here where there should be forty."

Wyle's eyes darted to the pile. He picked it up and fingered through it before looking at Annis uneasily. "An honest mistake. My apologies."

He put the pile down and pulled not two, but six extra coins from the purse at his belt.

"By way of amends," he muttered.

"Most excellent," said Annis, clapping her hands. "Let us store them for travel, then."

Loren and Gem had stood silent through the whole exchange, gawking at the money before them. More than eleven hundreds of gold weights. Before leaving the Birchwood, Loren would have laughed at the thought of a single person owning that much wealth. Since then, of course, she had learned that some people had much more. But to see such riches laid out before her and know they were her own . . . she suddenly understood the gold-lust in the tales of Bracken, the old storyteller who came to her village in her youth. They closed the lockboxes, and Loren put six of them in Midnight's saddlebags. The other five went into the bags of the horse that Gem and Annis shared.

They ate an early midday meal and rode from the city just before noon. Loren feared that with the news from last night, they might face extra scrutiny at the gate, but the guards waved them on.

"A good thing, that," said Uzo, after they had passed well beyond earshot of the gate. "I do not think it will be wise to flash our Mystic badges any longer."

"Why?" said Gem. "The Mystics have no quarrel with Dorsea," said Gem.

Uzo scoffed. "Do you think our order is free from the politics of the nine kingdoms? Every Mystic vows to serve no king but the High King—and now the Dorseans have declared the High King their enemy."

Loren glanced over her shoulder. "What about the Mystics in Bertram itself?" she said. "Are they not in danger?"

Shiun and Uzo looked at each other uneasily, but this time it was Shiun who spoke. "I do not think so. Not so far from the capital. Not yet. Our holdings in Bertram are strong, and the Dorseans would be loath to assault them without a pressing reason. As long as the Mystics do not take overt action against Dorsea, they should be safe. In Danfon itself, things may be different."

That thought remained with Loren for a long while. She knew the Mystics had a presence in almost every great city across the nine kingdoms—a castle here, a fortress there, sometimes in the heart of the population, sometimes in long-distant wilderness. But now the Mystics in Dorsea were cut off from the rest of their order—and now that she thought of it, so were the Mystics in Dulmun. For three months now, they had been isolated in a kingdom at war with the High King. If the Mystics here now faced a brittle peace, could such peace have lasted so long in the very heart of a treacherous nation?

Some referred to the Mystics as the Tenth Kingdom. Many in their ranks had held great power before donning the red cloak, and if unified that power would be no less than that of a true king. Yet Loren saw now that their power was scattered all across the nine lands. It would be near impossible to consolidate it in order to achieve any end, great or small. Sometimes she was not sure of her own feelings towards the Mystics. Some, like Jordel, served high ideals. Others, like Uzo and Shiun, were honorable enough soldiers, willing to follow orders and fight for the greater good. Loren had met others who were self-serving and hungry for power. But she did not relish the thought of small pockets of the red-cloaked warriors suddenly finding themselves isolated in rebellious kingdoms, there to wait until the king finally decided to eliminate them.

It was only a short ride from the gates of Bertram to the King's road, and from there they pushed their horses as hard as they dared. They ate their supper in the saddle, only stopping once the sun was well below the horizon and its last light faded from the sky. The hard ride brought them to the beginning of the Moonslight Pass, the southern route that would take them through the mountains to Dorsea's northeastern reaches.

The next morning they climbed into the Greatrocks themselves. As a section of the King's road, the pass was well tended. The road was laid in stone, and in many places it went straight through the mountains themselves, where large clefts had been cut as if by a giant's axe. But it was a steep climb even so, and in some places the road had no choice but to cut back and forth, following the contours of the land.

The mountains were beautiful in the last days of winter. The well-cleared road left the travelers a great deal of unused attention to study their mighty peaks and splendid valleys. It struck Loren how different this mountain range could be, at different points along its length. She had first seen the Greatrocks to the south, where they had ridden with Jordel. Those peaks were high, but they were somewhat gentle, and the summer sun had painted their grey cliffs and stones in hues of warm red. Then they had come to the Greatrocks in the north, searching for Damaris and the stronghold of Yewamba. There the mountains rose into the sky like knives, mighty and sheer, but still covered in green, for the jungle climbed even to their utmost heights. The range they rode through now was somewhere in the middle. Though the peaks had been tamed by human hands, they still stood proud and regal, and each was covered in snow like a robe of office. Indeed, when the sun bathed the slopes in amber at the beginning and ending of the day, Loren was reminded of the white and gold of the High King, and she wondered if this might be the place from which those colors had been drawn.

The day's end found them in the town of Midgar, which meant 'waystop' in the ancient tongue of Dulmun, from the days when Renna Sunmane had conquered this land in the name of the first High King. It was an entirely appropriate name, for the town had been built for the sole purpose of being a place for travelers to rest as they rode the Moonslight Pass. There was a Mystic stronghold just outside the town, a little farther up the slope of the mountains, as though it had been placed there to oversee the town. Loren stared at it as they entered Midgar. The shape of the stronghold was all too familiar. They had seen one just like it in the southern Greatrocks. Jordel had told her that all ancient Mystic strongholds were alike, so much so that he would know the placement of every stone within it. It was still disconcerting to see the truth of his words.

They stopped at one of the town's more modest inns. Midgar had several, and for a moment Loren had the wild thought of staying at the finest of them. She had a great deal of newfound coin, after all. But she doused the thought in an instant. She had riches, yes, but she would not hold them long if she spent them too freely. So she guided the party towards the meanest-looking inn, which was called the Jolly Rat, though Wyle protested mightily.

"I have visited Midgar before, and I can tell you the Jolly Rat is apt-ly named," he said. "The rats are so jolly because they are well fed, and that is because the innkeeper lets them run freely through her kitchen and the guests' rooms. Let us board at the Silver Boar instead. If they have the same cook as the last time I was here, you will never taste finer boiled carrots in all your life."

"We stay at the Jolly Rat," said Loren. "Though you may go and eat your supper at the Silver Boar if you wish, and pay for it as well."

Wyle sniffed. "I am no beggar who must accept free meals, especial-ly when they are served in such a place. I will indeed eat at the Silver Boar, and stop by the blue door afterwards into the bargain."

Loren flushed. The blue door was known across the nine lands as the sign of a house of lovers. She had not thought there would be one here so far from any city. "What you do is your own business, as long as you use your own coin. But since I would rather not leave you alone to do it, take Shiun with you. You can buy her dinner as well."

Wyle scowled. Shiun smirked at him, but then she shook her head at Loren. "If I may make a suggestion, Nightblade, send Uzo instead. He will be just as fine as a guard, and he would likely get some use out of the blue door, whereas I would not."

Indeed, Uzo looked surprisingly eager. Loren nodded at once. "Of course. I am sorry I did not think of it already, Uzo, after your service in Bertram."

Uzo ducked his head. "Do not trouble yourself, Nightblade. And thank you."

Wyle's expression had darkened still further at the prospect of paying for Uzo's lover as well as his dinner. But the smuggler took one last dark look at the Jolly Rat and turned on his heel, beckoning Uzo to follow him. Uzo threw a wink over his shoulder and went. With a little smile, Loren watched them go before leading the others into the common room of the Jolly Rat. They quickly secured a room and stables and then bought dinner. Loren thought it looked a bit meager, but nowhere near so bad as Wyle had made it sound. Indeed, they had stayed in far worse places in their travels.

Gem spoke up as they settled into their seats. "Is it wise to let Wyle go off, do you think? If he puts his mind to it, he might yet evade Uzo."

"He will not," said Annis. "The prospect of the reward at the end of this journey will keep him close. Indeed, Loren, you offered him more than I would have. A royal pardon is not something easily obtained."

Loren shrugged. "I am not wise in all the politics of the nine kingdoms. Yet it seems to me that whatever small mischief Wyle has gotten up to here in Dorsea, it pales in comparison to the threat of the Necromancer and the rebellion. If he can help us deliver Damaris, and even the kingdom of Dorsea, I do not doubt that Her Majesty will grant him a life as a honest merchant."

"And if she does, she will have removed a smuggler who traffics in illegal goods," said Shiun. "He may even begin to pay taxes on his dealings, furthering the king's and the High King's might. It is the wisest of generals who can defeat an enemy by turning them into a servant."

Loren laughed at that, as did Gem. But Annis did not join them, and now stared morosely at her meal. Loren saw it and leaned over, placing a hand on the girl's shoulder.

"Annis?" she said. "Is something wrong?"

The girl's head jerked up, and she shook her head too quickly. "Not at all," she said. "My thoughts are far away. Forgive me."

Loren frowned. She glanced briefly at the others around the table and then back to Annis. "Come. Let us take a walk together."

"No, we . . . we should eat," said Annis.

"Yet you have scarcely touched your food," said Loren, pointing into the girl's bowl. "Stand and walk before I am forced to drag you."

They rose and left Chet, Gem, and Shiun to their meal, fetching their cloaks and stepping out into the wintry night. Annis gasped at the chill and rubbed her arms.

"Step lively," said Loren. "You should get the blood flowing. It will loose whatever words you have bottled up inside yourself."

"It is no great matter, truly," said Annis. "I know I am only being foolish. Yet I still find myself shocked that Dorsea joined the rebellion. It is difficult to imagine a greater disaster for the High King, and it was orchestrated by my own mother."

"Your mother's misdeeds are not yours, and they never have been," said Loren.

"I know that. Yet we are in pursuit of her, and I have bent all my thought towards finding her. I should have seen this coming." Annis spoke faster and faster. "But then again, *should* I have been able to predict it? Why should I? My mother is much older and, it seems, infinitely more cunning. I have begun to think this is a fool's errand. The two of us chasing her across the kingdom, I mean. It seems that we run off on one mad course of action after another. Yes, it seems like the right thing to do every time. But what if we are only making things worse? I—"

Loren put a hand on Annis' shoulder and squeezed. Not hard, but just enough to get her attention. Annis' words cut off at once, and she looked up. Loren smiled gently.

"I am sorry," said Annis. "Babbling is a difficult habit to break."

"You are being too harsh with yourself, as usual," said Loren. "It is as you said: Damaris must have been planning this rebellion for some time. If we had not followed her to Yewamba, and then to Dorsea, this still would have happened. And furthermore, she would be sitting safe in a stronghold of power, one that even the High King's armies might have had trouble removing her from. Mayhap our actions have forced her hand sooner than she wished to reveal it. Her strength now—and the strength of the Dorsean rebels—is likely less than it would have been if we had not remained on her trail, nipping at her heels."

Annis ran her hands through her hair, mussing it for a moment before pulling it back into place. "You are right, of course. And these things are what I keep telling myself. But after such a long pursuit with nothing to show for it, I am becoming a bit discouraged."

At those words, she glanced back at the inn. Loren frowned, and then she thought of Gem sitting inside. She shook her head and wrapped an arm around Annis' shoulder, pulling her close.

"It would be good to have *some* sort of victory," said Loren. "I agree with you there. Let us hope that one is just around the next corner—or the next turn in the mountain pass, as it may be."

Annis looked up at her and smiled. "Thank you, Loren. But now let us go inside and finish our meal, before I either starve or freeze to death. I am not sure which would come first, and I have no wish to learn."

Loren chuckled and led her back inside the Jolly Rat.

TEN

O<small>N THE THIRD DAY OF THEIR JOURNEY, THEY RODE DOWN THE OTHER</small> side of the Moonslight Pass to find the city of Danfon laid out before them.

Dorsea's capital had been built at the very feet of the Greatrocks. There the River Marsden spilled from the foothills, winding its way north and east until it joined the Skytongue to form the border between Dorsea and Feldemar. The Marsden flowed throughout the year, for winter's chill was too weak to tame its mighty current this far north. Danfon sprawled wide across the landscape on both sides of the river, and beyond its walls, farmlands reached almost to the horizon. Loren had traveled the countryside east of here and knew it for a brown and arid place, but here the soil was rich and loamy, and it gave the capital a fine yield.

They paused as they reached the final bend in the pass out of the mountains. Now they stood on a flat place in the land that seemed built for the sole purpose of observing the city, which seemed only a stone's throw away. The streets, like Bertram's, were laid out in neat rows that crisscrossed each other in a simple pattern. Near the western walls was the king's palace. Its red tile roofs were free from snow, either because they were swept by attendants or because their height left them more open to sunlight. The tiles shone proud in the midst of the city, like a pattern of rubies set on a veil of white lace.

Loren was struck by a feeling both unsettling and all too familiar. She had seen the palace before. Her dream had not shown it from this angle, but still she knew it. And when she turned, she saw the Greatrocks looming above her just the same. The world seemed to spin around her for a moment, and she clutched tight at the horn of Midnight's saddle. The mare blew a loud snort as though she sensed Loren's disquiet.

"Welcome to Danfon," said Wyle. Despite the city's splendor, the smuggler looked at it with an upturned nose and a frown. "A city that I thought not to visit for a long time, if ever I returned here. We will ride around it to the river on the other side."

That distracted Loren from her thoughts, and she frowned at him. "The east? Why?"

Wyle arched an eyebrow at her. "Did you not hire me to sneak you into the city unnoticed? There are secret ways that only I and others like me know of, and I mean to lead you to them. But they cannot be traveled on horseback. To the east is a town called Yincang, and there I know a man who will care for our steeds while we see to our business in the capital. We should reach the town just after nightfall, and there I suggest we remain for the night."

"We should enter the city overnight," said Loren. "Doubtless we will attract less notice that way."

But Annis shook her head. "The capital will be in turmoil after the death of King Jun," said the girl. "This new king, Wojin, will have established a curfew. We will attract more notice if we are on the streets after dark."

"Just so," agreed Wyle. "And as for the secret passages, we are no less likely to be seen there after nightfall than during the day. Thieves and scoundrels—for so I am often called, very unjustly—do not keep the same hours as more honest folk."

After they came down out of the mountains, Wyle led them off the King's road to a smaller courseway that curved through the farmlands. The plots of land were all sunken into the earth, and there were no people out working them. Loren knew little of farming, but at home in the Birchwood there were many crops that could be planted even in winter. This stillness was strange to her.

"What do they grow here?" she said.

"Rice, mostly," said Wyle. "They will begin planting a bit late this year, for winter has lasted longer than it usually does. But the capital does not lack for food stores, and the king takes good care of his people when the seasons are unkind." He paused for a moment and shrugged. "Or at least, King Jun did. I know very little of Wojin's temperament, nor how he will care for his citizens."

Loren scowled, and her hands tightened on the reins. "I am surprised to learn that the Dorsean king cared so much for his own subjects. He gave little enough thought to the suffering of other kingdoms."

Wyle glanced at her. "You were no admirer of Jun, I take it."

"I did not know his name until only recently," said Loren. "Yet if he was the king of Dorsea, then no, I had no love for him."

"You refer to Wellmont, I assume," said Wyle. Loren jerked in her saddle and looked at him. Wyle nodded. "Your Selvan accent gives it away—and that is something you should try to rid yourself of, by the by. It is always better when others cannot guess everything about you simply from the way you sound."

"Why does everyone insist I have an accent?" growled Loren. "How can I rid myself of it if I cannot even hear it?"

"Surely you can recognize that your voice is different from mine, and from the Yerrin girl's," said Wyle. "Even the boy's voice is harder to place than yours. In any case, you do yourself no favors with your concern for Dorsea's border squabbles. The Battle of Wellmont was little more than an overenthusiastic war holiday for our great king. Former king, I should say."

"You say those words easily," said Gem quietly. His gaze was far away. "But we were in the city when it was attacked. It was far from a holiday."

Wyle only shrugged, increasing Loren's irritation. "Battles rarely seem so to those who experience them, which is why I make a habit of avoiding them. But all manner of mad rumors have been spun about Wellmont since that attack. Something happened there, they say, that has turned the greatest heads in all the nine lands."

Annis arched an eyebrow. "I presume you include yourself in that company?"

Wyle shook his head quickly. "Oh no, dear girl. I count myself an honest man of great wit, but I am aware of my own insignificance. I am no mighty figure in the affairs of the nine kingdoms, nor would I wish to be so. A life of good food and good wine and some little excitement is enough for me."

Loren did not wish to speak further of Wellmont, but Gem turned to the smuggler with interest. "What did you mean before?" he said. "What happened at Wellmont?"

Wyle shrugged. "Rumors and speculation fly, but the truth is not so easily found. It seems that certain powerful parties have been trying to conceal the truth of the matter, and that is most interesting. I do not suppose you noticed anything unusual while you were there?"

"Other than the battle itself?" said Gem. "That was unusual enough for me."

"Enough of this talk," said Loren. "I do not wish to hear more about Wellmont."

"As you wish," said Wyle. The party fell silent for a time.

They followed the road in its wide loop around Danfon to where it met the Marsden half a league to the east. There they found a great construct of stone and iron, with many great pipes sticking out of the riverbank to empty into the waters, pouring a steady stream of refuse. The smell of it struck them hard even in the cold air. Gem turned away and pinched his nose, shoulders heaving.

"There you have it," said Wyle. "The secret passages. Danfon's sewers are some of the best in the nine kingdoms, and one can get entirely lost inside them. Which means, of course, that it is easy to avoid being found."

"Sewers," muttered the boy. "I had hoped I had escaped sewers forever when I left Cabrus."

Wyle laughed and shook his head. "For those who skirt the King's law, sewers are like a second home. You should enter a new line of work if you seek to avoid them."

Uzo glared at the smuggler. "We *are* the King's law."

Wyle gave Loren a broad wink. "Of course you are."

He turned them away from the sewers and took them back to the road, which went east for a ways before turning south to reach the little town of Yincang. The sun had disappeared over the Greatrocks by the time they reached it, and twilight had set in. Yincang had no wall, and so they came unchallenged to its streets. Wyle took them straight to the inn. It was a small, nondescript building with only one floor, smaller than the stable at its rear.

"Many travelers like us leave their mounts here while they do business in the city," said Wyle. "This place was built to take better care of horses than humans."

The innkeeper, a spindly man with a thin beard, took their coin without comment and directed them to three rooms where they spent the night. They woke before dawn, dragging Gem from bed as usual, and set off for the capital.

It was an hour's brisk walk to the sewers. A small staircase led down from the riverbank to the opening of the pipes, but there was no platform leading directly inside. They had to take a few precarious hops from the end of the staircase along the water's edge before they could get a handhold on one of the pipe's edges. One by one they pulled themselves up and into the dark tunnel. Loren helped Annis make the climb, but Gem leaped up by himself, eschewing her help. His foot slipped, and his shoe came down in the sludge with a *splash*.

"Ugh!" he cried, lifting his foot up. "What do the people of this city eat? That smells ten times worse than the sewers of Cabrus."

Wyle flashed an easy smile. "We spice our foods well in Dorsea, and nowhere more so than in the capital. Alas, our concern has never been what some foreigner will think of the smell of our shit."

Annis blushed at the smuggler's frank words. Wyle seemed not to notice, and he led them on through the sewers without a pause. The passages twisted and turned, intersecting with each other in such a confusing manner that Loren was lost almost at once. Soon the smell of the tunnels became little more than a background sensation in her mind. She focused on keeping one hand on the wall and her feet out of the muck that ran just below the narrow walkway.

After a time, she became aware of a noise. It grew steadily the farther they walked: a low, murmuring hum that echoed gently from the stone walls around them. Soon she placed it. It was the sound of many voices, human and animal both, as well as the low rumbling of wagon wheels. They were under the city.

"Have we passed beyond the walls?" said Loren. "When will we surface?"

"Soon enough," said Wyle. "But I do not want to lead you back into the sunlight in the middle of some busy thoroughfare. It would not do to have King Wojin's soldiers catch sight of us climbing out of the sewers in the middle of the street. There are back alleys where no one will observe us."

"And the smell will be worse there, I imagine," grumbled Gem. Loren shushed him.

The smuggler was as good as his word, and soon he led them up a ladder that took them into the open air. They had been in the sewer for hours by that time, and Loren gasped at the smell of cool, fresh air again. She could almost taste it on her tongue, and it seemed sweeter than honey.

Wyle paused for a moment to get his bearings. "There is a place not far from here where we may settle in," he said. "The innkeeper always has a warm bath ready with perfumes on hand, and she knows better than to ask me very many questions."

They came to the inn shortly, and Loren paid for their rooms. Some of the patrons in the common room turned their noses up as the party walked through, and the innkeeper offered them baths without being asked. They took turns, for there were only four tubs, but Loren commanded them to hurry.

"I wish we had not spent a night in Yincang," she told them, "and I want to make up for it by getting straight to work. I would rather not rest until we have spent at least some time in the city learning what we can."

After they were refreshed, they ate a quick meal and planned their next move. Wyle had many contacts in the city, but he did not think it wise to bring a large party with him when he went to visit them.

"Take Shiun with you," said Loren.

Wyle put a hand to his breast, frowning. "Do you not trust me? I would neither run off on my own nor betray you, for I have always been—"

"—an honest businessman. Of course," said Loren, raising an eyebrow. "My assurances, smuggler, that she will only be there for your own protection."

His smile grew somewhat forced, but he bowed gracefully in his chair. "Of course. How thoughtful of you."

"The rest of us will get a feel for the city's mood," said Loren. "Chet and Uzo, visit some taverns and inns, any place that the city folk gather to have a drink. See what they think about the new king, and whether or not anyone has noticed the presence of the family Yerrin within the city walls. I will take Annis and Gem with me and visit shops. We can tell them we are gathering supplies to go on a journey. Let us try to get a few tongues wagging while we barter for prices."

ELEVEN

WITH THEIR PLAN FORMED, THEY QUICKLY FINISHED THEIR FOOD AND set off into the streets. Loren took Annis and Gem to a marketplace near the inn. They had lodged in one of the city's finer districts, which must have been a deliberate choice of Wyle's; the smuggler enjoyed a good bed and good wine. Now they passed between stores with fine luxury crafts displayed in the windows, which were often paned with glass and framed by ornamented wrought iron. Annis took the lead at once and led them towards the first shop—a tailor. Just before they reached the door, Loren paused and turned to her.

"Barter hard for everything we purchase," she said. "And if the price is too high, let us take our business elsewhere. We are only here for information, and it looks like the goods here are expensive."

Annis tilted her head. "We will have to spend some coin, Loren. We have plenty of it now, and a merchant's tongue never wags so freely as when their purse is being filled."

"We do have coin, but that was not the case a few days ago, and I did not enjoy it," said Loren. "Our gold may have to last us a long while. I do not have an endless supply of magestones to sell, after all."

Annis arched an eyebrow at her. "Do you think I would waste our funds? I am a Yerrin, Loren. I can buy information without emptying our purse. My mother taught me that much, at least."

"Oh, let her handle it, Loren," said Gem. "I should so love a new suit of clothes."

Loren frowned. "You will only get them filthy. Indeed, I think you know some spell to coat your garments with grime, for it seems to happen instantly."

Gem scowled. Annis giggled at them both. "Trust me, Loren," she said. "This is why you have brought me along, after all."

Loren sighed. "Very well. Of course I trust you—and I brought you because you are my friend, not just because you are useful."

Annis smiled and led the way into the shop. Inside, they found the tailor to be a man both portly and incredibly short, a finger shorter even than Annis. At first he looked at them with disdain; though they had just bathed, their clothes were still worn from long leagues on the road, and were modest besides. But when Annis flashed a pair of gold weights in her palm, his demeanor changed at once.

"Of course it would be my pleasure to serve you," he said, beaming a smile. "Do you want new clothes for further travel, or something a bit more elegant for functions within the city?"

Annis eyed the fine gowns displayed on mannequins along the walls. But after a moment she turned from them with a quiet sigh. "Indeed, we mean to ride from the city soon," she said, "though it pains me to refuse such dresses as yours. Such fine craftsmanship is rare to see, though I should have expected it from an establishment as well kept as this."

The merchant's smile grew still wider, and he bowed. "You learned your manners too well, for they compel you to be overly generous. Mine is a humble shop. But let me see what insufficient garb I can clad you in. My only hope is that you remember this mean little place with some fondness."

Shelves of fine cloth ran along the shop's back walls, and there were more standing shelves in the center. He led them along the rows, bouncing on the balls of his feet and pointing out this or that weave and color, inviting them to feel the textures. Loren was glad she had just bathed, or she would have feared to smudge dirt all over the bolts of fine fabric.

Annis appraised everything in the shop with an expert eye. Loren remembered how they met almost a year ago, when she had snuck into a Yerrin caravan just south of the Birchwood. The wagons had been filled with fabrics, for the Yerrin's chief trade was textiles—at least on the surface. Loren did not know much about clothing, but she guessed that the Yerrins trafficked in only the best, which must have been why Annis' interest alighted only on the shop's most precious samples.

At last Annis selected a few different materials. Once she had, the tailor took them back to the mannequins. He offered suggestions of various cuts, pointing to some riding dresses for her and a suit of clothes for Gem. The clothes were far too large for the boy, but the tailor promised he could deliver the same look on Gem's slighter frame.

"And for you?" he said, turning to Loren. "A riding dress as well, mayhap? Or a shirt and trousers?"

Loren balked. "Me? I do not require anything new," she said.

"Oh, yes you do," said Annis. She pursed her lips, tapping them with a finger. "But something quite different for her, I think. Not a dress, certainly, but not a suit like Gem's, either. Here."

She went to the back corner of the shop. There stood a mannequin in fine clothes that yet seemed entirely useful—somewhere between a peasant's garb, meant for hard work on a hot day, and a suit that a noble might wear. Loren could see at once that the tunic and pants would be easy to move in, and yet they had an elegant sort of flair. There was also a vest with many stylish pockets that buttoned shut.

The tailor turned to Loren with wide eyes, and a little smile played at his lips. "Ah, I see it at once," he said. "Yes, of course. Perfect. And the material?"

Annis took him back to the shelves. She must have anticipated this, for she immediately pointed out a few bolts of cloth that were all black or dark grey. But then she went to the next shelf over and pointed at a bolt of muted green velvet.

"Trim it in this," she said. "For the eyes."

"Of course, of course," said the merchant. To Loren's surprise, he was very nearly bouncing in anticipation. "And might I suggest this for the inside of the vest? You will see only a flash of it when she moves, of course, but that will make all the difference." He put his hand on a bolt of satin, green as well, but closer in color to the sea.

Annis gave a sharp clap, her eyes shining. "Sky above. It is perfect. Mayhap on the inside of the collar as well?"

The tailor snapped his fingers. "Just so. It is the final piece to make it perfect. You have a fine judgement for this, my lady. I am further humbled by your presence in my modest place of business."

"Modest you may be, but not deservedly so," said Annis. From the pouch at her waist she pulled four gold weights. These she placed in the tailor's hand, and then she deliberately pulled forth another and added it to the pile. "I hope we can retrieve the clothing tomorrow."

"I will delay some other orders to ensure it," said the tailor. "But your offer is far too generous." Yet Loren noticed his fingers closed over the gold at once.

"Not at all," said Annis. "For the quality I see here, I think I make a more than shrewd bargain."

The tailor bowed lower than ever before and drew them to the back of the shop to take their measurements. Annis went first, holding out her arms while he pulled out a ribbon and ran it along her limbs. She smiled as he did it, but then her brow furrowed for a moment.

"I do so hope the road is safe to the west," she said. "What a shame it would be for our new garments to be endangered by bandits."

The tailor frowned at that. "Things are uncertain these days, to be sure."

Annis nodded. "Still, I am certain that Wojin—pardon me, King Wojin—will maintain order."

That drew a snort from the tailor. But he quickly suppressed it, and Loren saw him look askance at Annis. He tried to pass it off by coughing quietly.

"It sounds so strange to say." Annis shook her head. "King Wojin. My heart breaks for King Jun. I saw him once, you know. He was a good man."

"He was that," said the tailor fervently. "It was my great pleasure to make clothing for many members of the royal family—though never King Jun himself, of course. I was invited to the palace more than once, and though I never had the honor of meeting His Grace, I saw him on occasion. He was a regal man, and so handsome. Not like . . . well, I mean to say that we will not see his like again for a long time."

"I can only imagine your sorrow at his passing," said Annis. "Yet at least his kinsman sits the throne."

"That is a blessing, I suppose," the tailor grumbled. "And Wojin has what he wants, in the end. That is all for you, dear. Young master, if you would?"

Gem stepped into Annis' place, his chest puffing out at the title of "young master." Annis drew aside, her eyes widening.

"Do you mean to say that Wojin desired the throne already?" she said. Her voice dropped almost to a whisper. It was the voice of a girl sharing some bit of scandalous gossip with a close friend.

The tailor responded in kind, looking over his shoulder at her and giving a wink. "That is the most ill-kept secret in Dorsea, and mayhap all the nine kingdoms. Wojin was the youngest brother of King Jun's mother, Min, of course."

"Of course," said Annis, nodding as though everyone knew it. Loren hid a smile.

"Well, everyone in Dorsea knows Wojin resented the throne passing to his nephew when Min passed away. Later, when King Jun's son, Senlin, was born, they say Wojin flew into a rage that lasted for days." The tailor sighed and shook his head. "Still, that was a long time ago. Long before King Jun met his end—at the hands of agents of the High King, or so they say." He snorted again, louder this time, and rolled his eyes.

Annis' eyes grew still wider. "Do you not believe it?" she said, her voice a sing-song.

The tailor's eyes narrowed, and he paused before answering. "The intrigues of palace life are far above my station," he said slowly. "Keep your head from the clouds lest it be removed, or so they say. Yet I have my doubts."

A thought struck Loren all at once. "And what of those others?" she said. "They say Wojin has the support of some foreigners, recently arrived here at the capital. I heard the family name, but it escapes me . . . Yamen? Yarvin?"

The tailor went still. "Yerrin? The family Yerrin?"

Loren snapped her fingers. "That was it. Yerrin. Did they not arrive here only just ahead of King Jun's death?"

"I had not heard that." The tailor pursed his lips. "I wonder . . . hm."

Over the tailor's shoulder, Annis gave Loren a small smile, but she also shook her head. Loren shrugged and turned to look out the shop's window. "I do not mean to suggest anything untoward, of course. I am a stranger to this city, after all. I only repeat what I have heard."

The tailor went silent after that, and Annis deftly turned the conversation to talk of lighter matters. But after they left the tailor's shop, she fixed Loren and Gem with a look.

"That was most telling," she said. "If the first shopkeeper we met

581

was willing to whisper of such rumors, that means many in the city must secretly believe them. And what a stroke of genius, Loren, to plant the idea of my family's involvement. Dorseans are not fond of foreigners meddling with their kingdom. Word will spread, and when it returns to us we may learn something of my family's plans."

"Indeed," said Gem quickly. "I had thought of doing the same thing, of course, but you beat me to it."

"Of course you did," said Loren, arching an eyebrow. "But what can we do with such information?"

Annis shook her head. "Nothing yet. But it is a start. Let us go to a few more shops and see what else we may learn."

As it turned out, there was little else. They went to a cobbler, a carpenter, a steelsmith, and some other little shops of various trinkets and oddities. Most of the owners seemed to hold a similar opinion to the tailor, but none expressed it so plainly. Loren wondered if that might be because they did not spend their coin so freely at the other shops, but she did not encourage Annis to spend more. The girl clearly knew what she was doing.

A few hours before sundown, they made their way back to their inn. Uzo and Chet sat in the common room, and both had clearly had a few cups of wine. Chet's nose and cheeks were ruddy, and when Loren asked Uzo how they had fared, the Mystic blinked three times before answering.

"We did well enough," he said slowly. He leaned closer and dropped his voice. "Certainly there is some disagreement in the city about Wojin taking the throne. No one was willing to speak very plainly, but there was much to be read in their quiet words and sidelong glances. It seems King Jun is greatly missed."

"It was much the same with us," said Loren. "That is good for our purposes, I think. If we faced a happy populace with great love for their liege lord, I think it would be harder to seek information about the Yerrins."

"I find myself ever more curious about the senate," said Annis. "If the kingdom does not support King Wojin, the senate may be persuaded to take action against him. Hopefully Wyle's contacts will know something of that. I am interested to hear what he has to say when he returns."

Loren nodded—and then she noticed Gem sitting very still, his eyes darting furtively over her shoulder. She barely stopped herself from following his gaze.

"Gem?" she said quietly. "What is it?"

He frowned. "Mayhap it is nothing. Only there is a girl over there—no, do not turn and look, any of you. She seems very interested in us. I have caught her looking at our table often."

Loren's stomach lurched. What if it was some spy of Damaris'? That seemed impossible. The merchant could not have heard about their presence in Danfon so soon. Yet Loren had learned long ago that the Yerrins could not be underestimated.

"I will fetch us some wine," she said. The others nodded.

Loren stood and made her way towards the bar. As she did, she stole a surreptitious glance at the girl. She wore the simple garb of a Dorsean peasant, loose pantaloons and a tunic that gathered at the wrists. She wore a wide-brimmed hat like many in the city, and her hair was black, as was common here. Yet her features were a bit softer than a typical Dorsean's, and her freckles were unusual in this kingdom. The girl did not look up—indeed, she studiously turned her gaze away. But Loren sensed a tension in her.

Loren bought a bottle of wine and returned to the table. "She does not look dangerous, at least," she said quietly. "If she is a spy, what then?"

"We should capture her," said Annis. "She may be able to help us find my mother—if indeed that is who sent her."

"Agreed," said Loren. She gave Uzo a quick look. "But we must be careful. We need her alive."

Uzo rolled his eyes and nodded.

"Very well," said Loren. "Everyone come with me."

She rose, leaving her cup and the wine. Quickly she went towards the inn's front door, and the rest hastened to follow. Just before stepping outside, Loren saw the girl shoot up from her table.

Loren darted to the corner of the inn and directed the others to file around the side of the building. She went last, waiting until the girl started to emerge through the front door. She timed it so that the last flap of her cloak was just visible as the girl stepped outside.

Quickly she directed the others to hide in the alley's dark corners. She herself stood behind a stack of crates. Soft footsteps sounded from the street. Loren drew a throwing knife from her belt.

The girl stepped into view. Loren threw the dagger, but aimed wide. The blade plunged into the wall near the girl's face, making her jump. Uzo pounced, snatching her arm and clapping a hand over her mouth. Loren stepped up beside him and slowly tugged her dagger free to sheathe it.

"Hello," she said amiably. "You seem most interested in our little party. Why?"

The girl only stared at them with wide, terrified eyes. Uzo withdrew his hand slowly, ready to replace it if she tried to scream. But the girl made no sound at all.

Loren sighed. "How long have you been following us?"

That made the girl glance at Uzo and Chet. "I was not following you. I was following them."

"Fair enough," said Loren. "Why?"

"I . . . I heard them asking questions about Wojin."

"And do you work for him?" said Loren. "Or do you work for the family Yerrin?"

The girl's brow furrowed. "Who?"

Loren glanced at Annis. The reaction seemed genuine. Mayhap the girl was a skilled liar, but Loren did not think so. Annis gave a barely perceptible shake of her head.

"What is your name?" said Loren.

"I . . ." The girl's voice faltered. She drew herself up straighter. She had some spirit then, and not just a pretty face. "I am Keridwen, of the family Ogun. Why are you in Danfon?"

Loren cocked her head, unable to keep herself from a small smile. "That is a proud question to ask ones who hold you captive."

Keridwen blushed, but she did not relent. "Are you here to help the king?"

"We do not know Wojin."

Keridwen shook her head quickly. "Wojin is not the true king."

Annis stepped forwards. "Yet he sits upon the throne, for King Jun is dead."

The girl's eyes widened and darted around nervously.

Sky above, thought Loren.

She gently pushed Uzo aside. He moved, if somewhat reluctantly, and Loren stepped within a pace of Keridwen. From her cloak pocket, she pulled her writ from the High King.

"Can you read?"

Keridwen stared for a moment before nodding slowly. Loren handed her the writ. Keridwen opened it and read it. Loren saw the color drain from her face and then come rushing back in a flush.

"You serve the High King," she said. "I hoped, but I could scarcely believe . . ."

"And now I ask again," said Loren. "Why did you follow my friends?"

Keridwen seemed to steel herself, and she drew up even straighter than before.

"King Jun was not killed," she said. "He is still alive. And if you truly serve the High King, I will take you to him."

TWELVE

After they had recovered from their shock, Loren sent Gem to check the inn. But he returned to report that Wyle and Shiun had not yet returned. At first Loren wanted to wait for them, but Annis counseled against that.

"The city has a curfew now," she said. "Nightfall is close at hand, and we will have a harder time of it if we do not go at once."

"And I do not think you should go at all," said Chet. "If this is a trap, you will be in grave danger. Send one of us as an intermediary instead."

"It is not a trap," said Keridwen, frowning.

"And besides, I *am* the intermediary," said Loren. "Though I think you are right in one respect. Not all of us should go. I will take Annis. The rest of you remain here in case something goes wrong."

"I am coming as well, of course," said Gem. "But you knew that already."

Loren sighed and turned to Chet and Uzo. "Wait here for Wyle and Shiun to return, and tell them what has happened. We will send for you as soon as we know it is safe."

"Yes, Nightblade," said Uzo.

Chet's eyes were troubled. "I do not like this."

Loren gave him a smile. "This could be the best news we have had in some time. If Jun remains alive, he can doubtless help us get to Damaris. I must at least try."

He turned away. "I see that. But please, return as quickly as you may."

Loren nodded. She had to stop herself from reaching out to take his hand. In the back of her mind, a voice whispered. *He did not insist on coming with you. Is this when he plans to leave?*

She forced the thought away and turned to Keridwen. "After you."

Keridwen nodded and raised her hood before leading them into the street. Loren and the children did the same as they passed through the crowds. They made their way south and west, and soon they had come very close to the place where the river entered the city. Not far away was the palace itself, but Keridwen turned from it and took them due west. Here the homes were all grand and towering, with multiple floors and little courtyards walled off from the rest of the city. This must be where the mightiest families lived. It had been the same on the High King's Seat and the other great cities Loren had visited: power gathered to power, and wealth to wealth.

Soon they came to a manor with a hipped roof and two great wings stretching forth from either side of the front door. Surrounding it was no stone wall, but only a wrought iron gate. Guards watched them as they went around the side. Two more guards stood at the smaller rear entrance. When Keridwen threw back her hood, they nodded in greeting.

"Welcome back," said one of the guards. "But who are these with you?"

"Friends," said Keridwen. "They are here to help the mistress's special guest."

The guard looked at her companion. He shrugged, and she turned back. "We shall have to send word."

Keridwen nodded. "Of course."

The second guard left to deliver the message. Keridwen stood back, folding her arms to keep warm. Loren appraised the manor.

"Whose home is this?"

Keridwen glanced at her and then at the home. "She is a merchant. Her name is Yushan of the family Ying. She remains loyal to—" She paused to look around, but the street was empty save for the guard. "To King Jun. She has helped us conceal him since Wojin's betrayal."

"Is she trustworthy?" said Annis. "Wojin knows the King is alive, of course, and I imagine he has offered a considerable sum for his capture."

"I imagine he has, but we have heard no word of it," said Keridwen. "It is not exactly something he can publicly declare, since his right to the throne depends on His Grace being dead already."

Soon the second guard returned, and he gave the first a curt nod. She opened the gate and motioned them all inside, and Keridwen took them in through the manor's service entrance.

Just inside, they met the merchant Yushan. She was tiny and fat, her round head balanced on her round body like a snowman's. As Loren and the others shook the snow from their clothing, she took them in with sharp eyes.

"Well met. I am Yushan, of the family Ying. I was told you are here to help?"

"And to receive help in return," said Loren. "We serve the High King Enalyn."

Yushan's eyes flashed. "I trust those who are here in my employ, but even my trust only goes so far. I would ask you not to speak so plainly—not of whom you serve, nor of anything you might see while you are here. Absolute discretion is the only thing that has kept my special guest alive so far. Do you bear any proof that you are who you say you are?"

Loren produced her writ, and Yushan scanned it quickly. But her hard look softened not a whit. "It looks to be in order," she said. "Yet I still find myself suspicious. We only sent for aid a few days ago. How did you respond so quickly?"

"That is easily answered," said Annis. "We did not respond at all, but were traveling on other business when we heard of the turmoil in the capital. We came to Danfon with no idea that your special guest was alive, for we pursued another goal entirely."

Yushan sniffed. "That has the ring of truth to it. Very well. Follow me—but be warned. I have guards aplenty, and not only the ones you can see. You will not come too close to my special guest, or they will cut you down. The fact that two of you are children will not stay their hands."

"Children?" said Gem, lifting his chin. "I would wager I have seen more battles and traveled more miles than you have."

Loren slapped his shoulder hard. But to her surprise, Yushan's face finally cracked into a smile.

"I like you, boy," said the merchant. "Come, then."

She snatched Gem's hand and drew his arm into her own as she led them into the manor. Gem looked back at Loren in a small panic as she forced him along, but Loren only smiled at him and shrugged.

Keridwen walked beside Loren and Annis as Yushan took them through the rear entry hall into the kitchen, and then opened the door to a staircase leading down. At the bottom of the staircase was a pantry with shelves along the walls. But no one waited within. Loren's hackles rose, fearing a trap.

Yushan turned to them. "Keridwen, if you would? My bones are old."

Keridwen nodded and went forwards to one of the shelves. She knocked on the side of it, thrice and then twice. After a long moment's pause, four knocks sounded from the other side. Keridwen squatted and took one end of the shelf, heaving it from its place.

"Let me help," said Loren. She seized the shelf, and Keridwen gave her a grateful smile that made her freckles dance. They swung the shelf out together.

Behind the shelf was a small doorway that Loren had to stoop to get through. A chamber lay beyond, with rugs on the floor and chairs and a table in the center. But the room was empty. Loren wondered briefly who had knocked on the back of the shelf, but then Yushan led them through this chamber to another door. This one she opened without knocking, and inside they found their prize.

The chamber into which the door opened was far larger and grander than the first. Leading off from it were four more doors, but Loren had eyes only for the people in the room. Two guards stood before the party, clad in armor of leather and chain. They had their hands on the thin swords at their belts, but they had not yet drawn them. Behind them was a larger man with a short beard whose hair was cut close to his scalp, revealing a long scar that ran back from his forehead. But behind them all was a man who Loren knew at once must be King Jun.

The king was not as tall as she might have guessed, certainly not as tall as any of his guards. But he had an imperious air that commanded attention. It was not only in the immaculate cut of his hair, nor in the fine robes that he wore, though Loren guessed they were worth more than all the cloth in the whole tailor's shop she had visited that day. Nor was it in his eyes, though they were piercing and wise in equal measure. It was the way he held himself, the subtle pose of his body that somehow elevated him above the others in the room. Loren had seen such presence before; the High King Enalyn was much the same. She almost felt compelled to take a knee.

But then she thought of Wellmont, and her thoughts soured. She inclined her head instead. "Your Grace."

King Jun did not answer her. Instead, the man with the long scar stepped forth. "And who are you?"

"I am Loren of the family Nelda, Nightblade of the High King." Loren pulled the writ from her cloak. "This letter bears her seal, and will show I speak the truth."

One of the foremost guards took the writ and handed it to his commander. He did not even glance at it before handing it back to King Jun. Loren guessed that he could not read any better than she could.

Jun took the writ and unfolded it. Each movement of his fingers was graceful, and he did not lose his poise even when he held the writ close to read it in the dim light of the room's candles. After a moment his brows rose, just a hair. He handed the writ back to his guard, and it was passed forwards to Loren.

"Greetings, Nightblade," said King Jun. His voice was like silk, and though he was quieter than his guard had been, it only served to make them listen more closely. "You have my gratitude for coming to my city."

Loren bowed her head again on instinct, but she looked up at once to match his gaze. "Of course, Your Grace. But as we have told the lady Ying, I did not know you were alive when I came to Danfon. It was only by fortune—and by the wits of Keridwen here—that we discovered you at all."

"I see," said Jun. "Why, then, did you come?"

"We seek the merchant Damaris, of the family Yerrin," said Loren. "We believe it was she who backed Wojin in his bid for your throne."

Jun frowned. "The family Yerrin. That makes some sense, I suppose. Wojin is too much of a craven to plot rebellion without powerful aid."

"Though it should be noted that Damaris does not speak for all the Yerrins," said Annis. "She has been cut off from the family. Though she is dangerous enough on her own, we do not contend with all the might her clan could bring."

The large guard with the scar glared at her. "You speak of 'we.' But who are you, girl?"

Annis gulped and lifted her chin. "I am Annis, of the family Yerrin. And I am Damaris' daughter."

All three guards tensed, but Jun lifted a hand at once. "Stay yourselves. I have heard of this girl. She sundered herself from her mother, just as the rest of the family did. We have nothing to fear from her."

Annis bowed her head. She had gone a shade paler, and her voice quivered. "Thank you, Your Grace."

Jun inclined his head. "But that makes only two introductions. The Nightblade has a second companion."

For a moment, all was still, and then Gem jerked upright as he realized Jun was talking about him. "Oh, I—yes. I am Gem, of the family Noctis." He smiled weakly, and then after a moment he added, "Your Grace."

Jun pursed his lips. "Well met. And what purpose have you here?"

Loren was about to answer, but Gem stood forth and threw out his chest. He actually had the audacity to stare down his nose at the king.

"I? I am the Nightblade's bodyguard."

The room was dead silent for a moment. King Jun's guards stared at Gem, the corners of their lips twitching, while the large one with the scar frowned. But Jun showed no trace of a smile when he nodded. "Then you are most welcome. Loyal servants are worthy of the highest honor."

Then he flapped out his robes and took a seat on the chair behind him. "Very well. Whatever your reasons for coming to Danfon, Nightblade, I am glad you are here. I know that I can rely on your help to retake my throne—not only for my sake, but for the sake of my son."

He waved an arm at Keridwen. She bowed and went to one of the room's doors, ducking within for a moment. When she emerged, she had a young boy in tow. His resemblance to Jun was obvious at once. But where King Jun had an imperious and commanding air, the prince's eyes shone with curiosity as he looked at Loren and her friends. He went to his father's side and then gave them all a deep bow.

"My son, Prince Senlin of the family Fei," said Jun.

"It is an honor to make your acquaintance," said Prince Senlin.

Annis bowed in response. Gem stood stricken for a moment, his mouth hanging slightly open, before he did the same. But Loren only inclined her head again.

"Well met," she said. "But Your Grace, I must correct you on one point. I was sent here on a mission from the High King. That mission has not changed. I am sure we all hope Damaris's capture will help you regain your rightful place as king—but her capture is my only purpose in the city."

Jun frowned—barely a small turn of the lips, but it chilled the air in the room. Annis tensed and put a hand on Loren's arm, but Jun spoke before she could. "As an envoy of the High King, and a servant of her laws, you have a duty to help me restore order."

"I know my duty," said Loren. "Her Majesty herself was the one who gave it to me, Your Grace."

The room was silent for a long moment, silent enough for Loren to hear her own pulse in her ears. Her hands had formed fists without her realizing it. Jun studied her for a moment. Then his eyes widened, and he cocked his head.

"Ah. I believe I understand. You are a girl of Selvan, are you not? I can hear it in your voice. No doubt you resent my kingdom's role in the Battle of Wellmont."

Loren frowned. "Who would not? I was in the city when your forces attacked. I watched its buildings burn and its citizens roast alive in flames—not only the warriors, but the simple folk as well. And it is not the first time you have attacked Selvan without provocation."

To her mounting irritation, Jun nodded. "Of course I understand. And who could blame you? Yet I am a king. It is part of my duty to bring prosperity to my people, and to keep them happy."

"You . . . you do not even deny it."

Jun spread his hands. "What would you have me deny? I have made war with the blessing of the senate, and my people have prospered as a result."

Annis held up a hand. "Mayhap we could turn our discussion to the matter of—"

"Your people have prospered, have they?" said Loren. "Yet some of them—many of them—died for it. And so have my people. If your son were on the battlements, I doubt you would think so lightly of war."

"I have fought in war myself," said Jun. "When he is of age, Senlin will do the same. If his fate is to die, that is as it shall be. The nine lands make widows and orphans of us all in the end."

Loren snorted and gave him a savage grin. "I have heard that wisdom before. It came from Damaris of the family Yerrin, who took your throne from you."

Jun frowned. For the first time, Loren thought she saw a flash of anger in his eyes. But Annis stepped forth and spoke loud enough to quell the conversation.

"If I may," she said. "Much has happened to us this day, Your Grace, and we are only recently come from the road. I must take a moment to speak with my compatriot. May we retire to the outer chamber, for a moment only?"

Jun blew a small sigh through his nose. He looked away and waved a hand in dismissal. Loren almost refused—but Annis took her arm and gripped it tight. Relenting, Loren followed her into the sitting room outside, and Gem came at her heels. Thankfully, none of the bodyguards followed, nor did the merchant Yushan. Behind them, someone closed the door with a soft *click*.

Annis fixed Loren with a stern glare. "You must control yourself."

Loren's nostrils flared, and her jaw worked. She wanted to argue against Annis—in fact, she wanted to shout at her. But she restrained herself to terse words through gritted teeth. "He speaks of death and killing the way a sane man speaks of cutting his fingernails."

"I know," said Annis. "You know I agree with you. I, too, was at the Battle of Wellmont. Yet you must realize that Jun is not entirely in control of his own position. He must do as the people expect, and he cannot thwart the will of the senate, for they would make things very difficult for him. Power comes with laws that Jun must obey—and one of the most important laws is that might always requires sacrifice. He does what his position forces him to do."

"Do you think that makes him blameless?" said Loren. "Your mother taught you to be cruel, and a killer. Yet you rose above it."

"And many others have not," said Annis. "It does not earn them forgiveness—yet it can give us some sort of understanding. Whatever Dorsea's faults, one of Jun's chief loyalties aligns with ours. He is a servant to the High King. Wojin serves only himself—and he is allied with my mother."

Loren held her gaze. "What will happen if we put Jun back on the throne?"

Annis' mouth opened with a quick reply—but then she paused and sighed. "In truth? One day, he will likely make war on Selvan again. Yet Wojin will certainly do the same. And restoring Jun's kingship will stave off the greater war—the one between the High King and the Necromancer. Jun and the senate may be dealt with later, when Underrealm itself is no longer in danger. Indeed, if we survive this mess, I will help you fight him."

Loren turned away with a frown. Then she pushed past Annis and made for the door to Jun's chamber.

"Loren—!" Annis reached for her arm, but Loren threw off her hand and opened the door.

The bodyguards looked up. The one with the scar had gone to Jun's side and was leaning over him, muttering. He straightened, and Jun turned to Loren. She stopped at the front of the room, feet apart, hands at her sides.

"I will return you to your throne, Your Grace," she said. Behind her, she felt Annis freeze in place. "But once I have, I will expect you to remember that it was the Nightblade—a woman of Selvan—who put you there."

"And her friends!" said Gem brightly. Loren did not turn, but she heard Annis cuff the boy's arm.

Jun met her gaze, unflinching. Then, after a long moment, he inclined his head. "If you manage it, I will not forget—and I will see to it that the senate does not forget, either."

Loren nodded. "Very well. I suppose we had better get to planning."

"Actually," said Annis, holding up a finger, "while I appreciate our eagerness, we are all of us weary, as I said. And doubtless His Grace must spend time considering how our arrival may work into whatever plans he had already begun to concoct. I recommend that we retire to our other friends and resume this work on the morrow."

"A sensible proposal," said Jun. "I accept."

But the bodyguard with the long scar scowled. "You cannot take lodgings in the city," he said. "It poses far too great a risk to you, and now, therefore, to His Grace. I will have one of my men fetch your companions, but you will bed here."

Loren glanced at Annis. The girl tossed her head slightly and nodded. "Very well," said Loren. Then she turned to the merchant, Yushan. "And I thank you for your generous hospitality."

Yushan bowed low, and her sharp look softened with a smile. "It is my honor. I am only ashamed that His Grace must bed here in my basement while I continue to move about my house in freedom."

"You have nothing to be ashamed of," said Jun. "It is only by your loyalty that we have survived this far. When I am restored to the throne, you and I may discuss how best to fill Wojin's position in the senate. He will have difficulty holding his seat when he is a corpse."

Yushan bowed still lower. Then she beckoned Loren and her friends out of the room and led them up into her manor. One of the bodyguards came with them and then ducked out the manor's rear entrance to fetch their friends.

Loren pulled Annis aside to murmur to her. "Why did you call an end to the meeting?" she said.

Annis blinked at her as if it were obvious. "Because of the exact reasons I said. Mayhap *you* are not ready to fall over from exhaustion, but I am. At the moment, I could hardly plan an escape from this manor, much less the overthrow of a king."

Gem snickered—but ahead of them, the merchant Yushan turned on them sharply. "You shall not need to plot any escape from me, but if you do I hope you will not damage my tapestries. They are expensive. And remember that we who are old have not necessarily taken leave of our senses. My ears, in particular, are still sharp."

Loren barely hid a smile. Annis flushed and bowed low. "I will remember it, my lady."

"Hmf." Yushan turned and led them on down the hall.

THIRTEEN

While they waited for Chet and the others to arrive, Loren looked around the rooms they had been assigned. Yushan had put them in one of the manor's front wings, where four rooms had wide windows that overlooked the surrounding streets. Yushan had a servant draw drapes across these. "I doubt many in the city would recognize you, but it is best to take precautions," she said.

"Thank you," said Loren.

"Think nothing of it," said Yushan. "I will have my servants fetch you something to eat. Do you take wine?"

"As much of it as we can," said Gem. Loren glared at him, and he flushed. "And, of course, we thank you for your generosity."

Yushan chuckled. "Oh, I *do* like you, child. Someone will be along shortly."

The food arrived just before their friends. Chet looked around cautiously when he was shown into the apartments. Uzo and Shiun went straight to their room once Loren pointed it out. But Wyle stood in the common room of the wing, looking about with pursed lips.

"Passable, I suppose," he said. "At least we are not paying for it."

"Oh, be silent," said Annis. "You will be glad to learn you have a room to yourself—not out of courtesy, but because no one wishes to share it with you."

"I am glad indeed," said Wyle. He went to the meal that had been laid out for them, ate a few bites and drank a cup of wine, and then made for the room Annis had indicated. "And with that, I bid you all good night."

"Wait!" said Loren. "You went out seeking information today. What did you learn?"

"Nothing," said Wyle, shrugging. "I merely sent out word and asked for information to be gathered. These things take time, my dear."

Loren suppressed a growl as he went into his room and closed the door. She sat with the others and picked at the food, but her appetite had suffered after her angry words with Jun. She had not been sitting long, however, before a knock sounded at the door. Loren glanced at Annis, but the girl only shrugged.

"Come in," said Loren.

The door opened to reveal Prince Senlin. Just behind him were Keridwen and the large bodyguard with the scar, who pushed into the room first, looking all around. When he was done, he ushered Senlin inside. Gem shot to his feet at once, bowing to the prince, and Annis and Loren did the same a moment later.

"Your Excellency," said Annis.

"Lady Yerrin," said Senlin. "I wonder, Nightblade—might I have a private word with you and your companions?"

Loren's brows rose. "Of course, Your Excellency. Although there are more people than I think would fit comfortably—Uzo and Shiun, would you remain here?"

Shiun nodded at once. "Of course, Nightblade," she said.

Loren motioned towards her room. Senlin made for the door, and Loren followed, with Annis, Chet, and Gem behind her. But at the threshold, Senlin stopped and looked up at the bodyguard behind him.

"I wish to speak with them alone, Jo."

The bodyguard frowned down at him. "My duty is to see to your safety, Your Excellency."

Senlin gave the man a frigid look—an odd expression on his soft, youthful face. "There is only one way into the room. They are no threat, and no one else can harm me if you guard the door. You will remain here."

Jo's face darkened, but he bowed his head and took a step back. Keridwen, however, remained by Senlin's side, and he did not order her away. They stepped into Loren's room—Gem scampering in even though Loren had not asked him to—and closed the door behind them. Inside were two fine armchairs. Senlin took one. But when Keridwen went to stand at his side, Loren shook her head and waved towards the other.

"I will sit on the bed. You may have the chair."

Keridwen blinked in surprise. "I thank you, Nightblade." Quickly she went and sat next to the prince, looking somewhat uncomfortable.

Loren and Annis sat beside each other on the bed while Gem sat on the floor by their feet. For a moment Loren merely looked at the prince, and Senlin studied her in turn. The prince was little more than a boy—Gem's age, or mayhap a year or two older. He had a thin build. Everything about him looked scholarly and thoughtful, rather than noble and dashing. But Loren could see a keen wit and a deep mind behind his eyes. She suspected they rarely missed a detail. Indeed, Senlin seemed somewhat akin to Annis, though he carried himself with greater confidence—likely the result of a lifetime where every need was attended to without question, to a degree that even Annis had never experienced.

Senlin spoke first. "I have heard tales of the Nightblade for some months now. I thought you would be a bit older."

Loren tilted her head. "I mean you no offense, Your Excellency, but you yourself are hardly a grown man."

Senlin smiled. "Pardon me—that must have sounded like an insult. Indeed, I am heartened to find you so close to my age. And that goes double for your worthy companions." He gave Annis and Gem each a nod in turn, and they returned it—Gem somewhat more eagerly. "I often feel that my age limits the influence I can have. It is heartening to meet people like you, who have managed to do so much good in so short a time."

It might have been only flattery, but Loren blushed all the same. "Thank you, Your Excellency," she said. "You are not lacking in kindness or grace."

Senlin sighed and leaned back in his chair. "Yet mayhap I lack in effectiveness. I came here to tell you that I do not disagree with what you said to my father."

That piqued Loren's interest. "Oh? I fear my words may have been overly frank. Even harsh."

"They were, yet they were not unearned," said Senlin. "I am no fan of warfare, nor of fighting in general. And I do not think Dorsea's wars serve the greater good."

Loren gave Annis a look, recalling their conversation in the basement. Senlin must have been brought up learning the same laws of power as his father—yet he rose above them, or tried to. That, at least, was heartening.

"I thank you for your agreement," said Loren. "Yet I do not entirely understand how it helps. Will your father listen to your counsel, if that counsel is to cease his wars?"

Senlin sighed. "He will not. Though I disagree with him, he does as he believes he must—and as the senate pressures him to do. Victory in battle pleases them, and for the most part it pleases the people they serve. Without the senate's support, my father's rule would be toothless. Because it is not, he is able to do great things for our people."

"So he does great good, but pays for it by doing great harm?" said Loren. "That is a weak justification in my mind. I will take a benevolent king, like King Anwar of Selvan, who can help his people without having to kill strangers."

"I have heard that Anwar is a good king," said Senlin. "But what of his daughter? She will take the throne from him one day. What if she is mad? Or cruel? There will be no senate to stay her hand from evil."

Loren folded her arms. "Your senate has done nothing to stay Wojin's hand."

"Give them time," said Senlin. "We will depose Wojin with their help, or not at all."

"And then your father will resume his border wars, in order to please his *people* and his *senate,*" said Loren, growing ever more irritated. "And even Dorseans who are brave enough to object will have to shrug their shoulders at the same time, because that is how Dorsea works."

"It is," said Senlin. For the first time he ducked his gaze as though ashamed. "When I myself hold the throne, I hope to do things better— though I also hope it will be a long time before that happens, for I wish a long life for my father."

Rather than soothe her, Senlin's words only made Loren more angry. "I am not you, Your Excellency, and I cannot know what your life is like. But I like to imagine, at least, that I would not be content to sit and watch as my father waged endless war."

"I am not content with it," he said. "And I advise when I can. But I cannot stop him. I mean that in the strictest sense of the word—I *cannot* stop him. Therefore I do not choose to spend my time complaining about how things ought to be. I do what I can from my station." He must have seen Loren tense, for he went on quickly. "Please do not misunderstand me—I know it is not enough. That is why I find your story so heartening. No doubt you were raised in other circumstances, ones where you could act more directly."

Loren felt her wrath deflate at once. Senlin's words were far from accurate. She had been raised by cruel parents, and until her sixteenth year she had taken no action to change things. True, her parents' evil was directed only at her, not at any others. But she remembered the way they had treated her, the way they had quashed even the slightest sign of rebellion. What if they *had* harmed others? Could she really have stood up to them? It would have been hard, though she hated them and knew they hated her in turn. What if they had raised her with kindness and love, as Jun clearly had done for Senlin?

Chet spoke, his words clipped. "Forgive me, Your Excellency. But I think you underestimate just how sky-blessed your life has been. You say you cannot change things in your kingdom. But mayhap you would not feel the same way if you yourself were threatened with the consequences of your father's wars."

"That is enough, Chet," said Loren quietly.

The room fell silent for an overlong moment. Senlin bowed his head and folded his hands over each other. "I fear I have cast a shadow over our meeting. I apologize, for that was not my intent. I look forward to seeing you again upon the morrow, and I hope that we may all find a way to achieve our ends together. That is all I wished to say."

He stood, and the others did the same. But before he could go, Loren stepped forth and put out a hand. "I thank you, Your Excellency. And forgive us if we spoke too harshly—now, or before. I often forget that the world is nowhere near so simple as I would like it to be."

Senlin's thin brows rose. Then he reached forth and took her wrist. They shook once, firmly. "Thank you, Nightblade. I think we both have a great deal to learn from each other, you and I."

He turned to go. But Keridwen stepped forwards quickly and spoke. "Your Excellency. Might I remain for a moment?"

The prince looked at her in surprise. "Of course," he said. "You are no servant, Keridwen, though my father and I greatly appreciate your aid in these dark days."

Keridwen nodded, and Senlin finally left them. Loren caught one glimpse of Jo, the bodyguard, outside the door. He appeared to have been engaged in a staring contest with Uzo and Shiun in the common room. When Senlin emerged, he quickly moved to escort the prince out of the room. The door shut behind them, and Keridwen turned back to Loren.

"I have heard many stories about you. Are they true?"

Gem's eyes lit up like the moons. Loren tried to ignore him. "I do not know what stories you have heard. Likely some are truer than others."

"Is it true that you saved the High King and the Lord Prince?"

Loren's cheeks flamed. "I found a way out of the palace when it was attacked. But many others helped in the escape. Some gave their lives. Before that, Chet took a dagger in the chest as he defended the Lord Prince."

"It was nothing," said Chet at once. But he lifted a hand, tracing his fingers over the place where the dagger had nearly pierced his heart.

Keridwen slumped. She moved to the armchair that Senlin had been in and sank into it. "I wish I could have done something like that. When Wojin attacked the palace, I mean, and we were forced to flee."

That gave Loren pause. She had spoken to few enough people about her actions upon the Seat. Mostly it had been Kal, who seemed to think she might have done a better job of her rescue. "Yet King Jun and Prince Senlin survived, in the end."

"No thanks to me," said Keridwen. "It was Jo—the king's right-hand man, and the one who came here with Senlin and me—who rescued all of us. I only followed along, protected by others but protecting no one."

Loren gave Annis a pointed look. Annis had often spoken similar words—bemoaning her own role by Loren's side and her uselessness in a fight. Annis' mouth twisted, and she shook her head. Loren smiled and went to sit in the armchair beside Keridwen.

"And who are you, exactly?" said Loren. "Are you some kin of the royal family?"

Keridwen shook her head and held up her arms. "In these clothes?"

"I have often worn disguises when I did not wish to be recognized, and you have been walking the city's streets."

"That is true enough," said Keridwen. "But no. I am only an apothecary, and from my parents I have learned some skill in healing."

"But there you have it," said Loren. "You have no reason for shame. If you have been practicing for any time at all, you have probably rescued more people than I have. I can only save lives by fighting. The world would be a worse place if everyone were like me, but a better one if all were like you."

Keridwen laughed. "I agree with you there. Yet still I wish I could do more—or that I could have done more than I did." She paused for a moment, fixing Loren with an appraising look. Loren met her gaze, feeling a twisting in her stomach. "I agree with you, you know. I know that His Grace's actions are wrong."

Loren frowned. "So does Prince Senlin. Yet that does nothing to stop King Jun."

"I do not agree with His Excellency either," said Keridwen, shaking her head. "War has never come to Danfon in my lifetime, yet we feel its effects even this far north. Often our warriors return from battle gravely wounded or even without limbs. Sometimes they have a sickness of the mind instead, a memory of death and pain that they can never banish. Dorseans honor our soldiers above all others. They risk their lives for the good of the kingdom—or at least that is how they see it, no matter how misguided our wars. Yet those wars often leave them a wreck, in mind as well as in body. I am put face to face with such maladies. The prince is not. I think it makes him more complacent than he might be. He contents himself with his principles, though they accomplish no tangible change."

"And what do you do?" said Annis quietly. "When you see these soldiers, I mean. What is your answer to King Jun's wars?"

"In one respect, Prince Senlin is right," said Keridwen. "I can do nothing to stop His Grace from waging battle. And I know he faces pressure from the senate. Yet neither am I content to wait, as His Excellency is. Instead I tell myself that I will grow. I will learn more, I will gain more influence. And I will do better next time. I hope that one day it comes true, if we survive all of this."

Loren nodded slowly. "I think I prefer your way of thinking to the prince's."

Keridwen smiled and cast her eyes down. Then she stood abruptly from the chair. "I had better leave and let you get your rest. But I thank you for the opportunity to speak."

"Of course," said Loren, rising to see her out. "I am glad you found us, Keridwen. And I hope you will come speak with us again, any time you wish."

"I would enjoy that. Only please, you must call me Kerri. Only His Grace and His Excellency call me Keridwen, and as a consequence it seems frightfully formal."

Loren smiled. "Very well, Kerri."

She held the door as Kerri left and then closed it softly. Turning to Annis and Gem, she raised her brows.

"Today has been a day," she said.

"It has been that," said Annis. "These people are somewhat strange to me. Yet I think I like Keridwen—Kerri, I suppose—the best."

"And I," said Loren. Then she noticed that Gem wore a grin that split his face from ear to ear. "What are you giggling about?"

"She had heard of you," said Gem triumphantly. "She had heard tales of the Nightblade."

Loren shook her head, trying to ignore the flush that crept up her neck. "Be silent, Gem."

FOURTEEN

In the common room, they ate a small meal before retiring to their beds. Loren had put Chet and Gem in one room, with Annis and herself in another. Almost at once, Annis went to bed and fell asleep. Loren soon joined her.

They rose before dawn—all but Gem—and broke their fast on eggs and rice. Soon a messenger arrived, requesting their presence in the king's chambers.

Loren turned to the party. "It is cramped down below. I will take Annis, Wyle, and Chet with me, but the rest of you should remain here."

Wyle pulled at his collar. "Must I come?" he said. "The king has never seen my face, and I see little benefit in changing that now."

"You are here to help secure his rescue," said Loren. "If he never meets you, how will he know who to pardon when this is all over?"

Wyle held up a finger. "You promised me a pardon from the High King, not Jun. I will not forget it. And besides, I expect an open pardon—one that absolves the crimes of anyone who holds it." Wyle paused and pulled at his thin beard. "Sky above. I wonder what such a document would be worth to the right buyer."

Annis rolled her eyes.

"But you must bring me as well!" said Gem. "There is no more cunning mind in our little party."

Before Loren could argue, Chet smiled and shook his head. "Take him," he said. "I will remain behind. It is as it was in Bertram—I shall prove no more useful than a third shoe."

"The same might be said for Gem," said Loren, scowling at the boy with mock severity. But he only grinned as he accompanied her to the manor's basement.

Jun sat in the same place he had yesterday; it seemed he had adopted the chair as his temporary throne. A guard stood to either side, and the larger bodyguard, Jo, sat just in front and to the side of his king. Prince Senlin was there as well, partially hidden behind one of the bodyguards.

"A good morn, Nightblade," said Jun. "Let us now take counsel and determine our best course of action."

"Of course, Your Grace," said Loren. "I have brought Annis with me. She has a brilliant mind for strategy and politics both. I think you will find her advice far more useful than mine."

"Then I welcome her," said Jun. He gave Annis a grave nod, which she returned.

Loren motioned for Wyle to step forwards, and he hesitated only a moment before complying. "This man is called Wyle. He is a business associate, hailing from Bertram. It was he who helped us enter the city without being seen. He knows many secret ways and has friends in the capital."

From the way Jun looked at Wyle, Loren thought he must know exactly what sort of "associate" the smuggler was. But he said only, "Welcome. If you can indeed be of help, you will have my gratitude."

"I am counting on it," said Wyle, giving the king an easy grin.

A table had been put before Jun's chair, and a map was laid upon it. Chairs were brought for Loren and Annis, and they sat opposite the king. The map depicted the city—not all of its streets and alleys, of course, but its layout around the river, as well as the locations of some important buildings. Wyle bent over the map, his hands folded before his chin. But it was Annis who spoke first.

"As has been mentioned, Wyle escorted us into the city on a route that few know about. He should be able to lead us out the same way."

"Yes, of course," said Wyle. "We will be a larger party now, but we can still avoid detection if we dress you up as beggars."

Jun tilted his head. "Lead us out? Why would I leave the city?"

The room went still. Loren and Annis looked at each other. Wyle studied King Jun for a moment, and then he sighed quietly.

Annis cleared her throat. "Your Grace, you are in grave danger while you remain here."

"That will not change if I depart—not unless I leave my kingdom entirely. Wojin will not stop hunting me just because I pass beyond Danfon's walls."

"But he will have a harder time of it," said Loren. "I said I would help you take back your throne, but I cannot also keep you safe if you remain here."

"Nor would I ask you to," said Jun. "I have my guards. But I mean to take back my throne, not merely survive. If I leave, I will look far too weak in the eyes of the senate."

Loren looked to Jo. The large bodyguard's face had darkened, making the white of his long scar stand out in stark relief. "If it is not too presumptuous, I would ask Jo's opinion on this matter. Your safety is his responsibility, after all."

"I serve at the pleasure of His Grace," said Jo.

But King Jun shook his head. "Jo does not wish to gainsay me in front of others. But I will tell you what he has said in our private meetings: he agrees with you. He wants to get me out of the city, where he believes he will be able to protect me more easily. But I have told him what I tell you now. I will not leave Danfon while I still have claim to its throne. On this matter, my mind is resolved."

Loren looked to Annis. The girl shrugged.

"Very well, Your Grace," said Loren. "If that is the case, tell us where you would like us to begin."

"We must unite the people behind me," said Jun. "Wojin is not well loved, neither by my citizens nor by most of the senators—only a few of them were in his pocket before the revolt. If we can inspire a popular uprising, the senators will rally behind us, and Dorsea itself can overthrow the usurper."

Loren had to fight hard to keep from rolling her eyes. But to her surprise, she saw Annis and Jo both nodding at the king's words. "Do you think such a plan is wise?" Loren asked Annis. "We speak of ordinary citizens, not trained soldiers. Would they risk their own lives in a battle?"

"I think they might," said Annis. "Even as far away as the High

King's Seat, I heard how His Grace is beloved by the Dorseans. Nowhere is that more true than here in the capital. Yet Loren strikes upon a truth—by and large, the citizens of Danfon are *not* trained soldiers. If you reveal yourself, there is a strong possibility that Wojin will manage to kill you before you can rally enough support. A determined force of soldiers could cut their way through even a great mass of loyal citizens in short order."

"Yet the states have their own standing armies, and the senators can control them," said Jo. "And while senators can be conniving, they generally bow to the will of their people. Several senators are in the capital now, as it happens. If we can gain their support, we will have more than enough trained soldiers to resist Wojin."

"That could work," said Annis, tapping her teeth. "But still, at least for now, His Grace must not reveal himself. It would be far too dangerous."

"Then we must fight from the shadows," said Jo. He lifted a hand to scratch at his scar where it met his temple. "The people must know their true king is alive, but his location can never be known."

"That seems a tall order," said Loren. "If they cannot see you, how can you unite them?"

"We will have to proceed slowly," said Annis. "Plant the seeds of rebellion one at a time, the way a farmer turns crops—first doubt, then distrust, and finally anger. When the whole city has come to believe in Wojin's treachery, *then* His Grace may reveal himself. You will have a popular revolt already in progress, and a trained army awaiting your orders."

Prince Senlin leaned forwards suddenly. "Yet even that plan requires some level of exposure," he said. "People spread rumors all the time. But no one places much faith in such rumors unless they come from a strong source."

"You could reveal yourself," said Loren, pointing at Senlin. "If the people saw you, even briefly, *that* rumor would fly far and fast."

"No," said Jun, Annis, and Jo all at once. Jun shook his head furiously and went on. "No. I will not risk my son."

"If anything were to go wrong, it would be disastrous," said Annis. "This is not yet a battle of swords, but one of hearts and minds. If Prince Senlin revealed himself, that might stoke the flames of hope in some citizens. But if Wojin managed to capture or kill Senlin, that would quench such hope beyond chance of rekindling."

Gem smiled. "It should be the Nightblade."

They all paused. Loren turned to him with a frown. "Gem, still your tongue if you have nothing useful to say."

"But that *is* useful," he insisted. "Loren, it should be you. The people will have heard tales of you. It was not only His Grace who knew of your exploits. Keridwen knew of you, and I am sure many others in the city do as well. You can be the one they rally behind. And if Wojin should try to track you down, he will have a hard time of it. There is no one better than you at escaping danger—except for me, of course."

Loren opened her mouth to argue again, but Annis spoke first. "I think he may be right," she said. "If the Nightblade tells them that King Jun is still alive, that would be worth more than whispers from a gossiping neighbor. You could tell them Wojin is an impostor and a liar. You would be a messenger of the king himself."

"I like it," said Wyle. Loren shot him a dirty look, but he only beamed back at her. "I myself would never do something so ostentatious, but I appreciate that it has a certain . . . grandiose style. What did I tell you, Nightblade? I place a high value on courage."

Jun nodded and held up a hand. On it was a ring in the shape of a dragon, twisted around a great ruby. "I will give you this. It is one of the emblems of my office. I would wager the fact that Wojin does not have it rankles him. It will lend credence to your words."

But Loren shook her head. "You cannot be serious. I am a spy, not a general."

"You are more than a spy," said Gem. "You are a legend."

Annis silenced him with a sharp look and put her hand over Loren's. "Gem speaks with words that are more flowery than useful, but he is not wrong. He is too eager to overestimate your worth, but you are too eager to dismiss it. Let my voice be the middle ground—you cannot singlehandedly save the nine kingdoms, but you can do this."

Loren frowned. "I do not share your confidence."

Annis' eyes sharpened. "Sky above, Loren. You claim to keep me by your side because you value my advice. I am giving it now. Will you not heed it?"

Loren sighed and looked towards the ceiling. "Very well."

"Very good," said Jun. "And I believe I know what your first task must be. Wojin means to address the public tomorrow. It shall be a large event, carried out in a great square. We can expect many hundreds of people to gather. No doubt he means to lament my untimely death and decry the High King. He has not properly done so since he took my throne. We could hardly design a better place for you to reveal yourself."

"That should work well," said Annis. "If you interrupt his address, you should have just enough time to tell the people that Jun is alive and Wojin is a traitor."

Loren's throat had gone dry. "And then? I will be a poor figurehead if soldiers fill me with arrows."

"You shall have to be fast, and you shall have to escape quickly," said Wyle. "I can help you with that. My knowledge of secrets is not limited to ways in and out of this city. I know its streets as well."

"We should go there today," said Annis. "Scouting the place first will give us a greater chance of success—as well as a greater chance of getting out alive."

Jun turned to the back of the room and beckoned to Kerri, who came forth at once. "Take Keridwen with you," he said. "I do not doubt the craftiness of this man Wyle, but if I understand right, he has not been in the capital for some time. Keridwen lives here, and will no doubt have useful insight."

Kerri inclined her head towards him. "It will be my pleasure, Your Grace."

Loren nodded and stood. "If we mean to do this, we should not delay. I shall return before nightfall, Your Grace."

Jun nodded and stood. The others were quick to follow, and Loren led them from the room.

"This is glorious," said Gem. "I knew that tales of you would one day turn to legend, but this is something beyond what I had hoped."

"Stop treating this like a lark," said Loren. "It seems to me that your whispered rumors have only led me—and all of us—into greater danger. Some bodyguard you are."

Gem ducked his head, but Annis smiled at him. "That may be true—but only because his tales have added to your power. You wish to do great things in Underrealm, Loren. But great actions always carry at least some danger. You cannot have the one without the other. We all play by the same rules in the end."

Loren's scowl deepened, and she waved her hand sharply. "Let us get on with this, then."

FIFTEEN

Loren sent Gem to fetch Chet and the Mystics before they left. Once the party reached the streets, Kerri took them southeast on a path that briefly drew near the palace. Loren eyed the place with distrust. It was familiar from her dream, and this close the resemblance was even more clear. The mountains loomed above, just as she had seen them in slumber. She thought she could even see the street down which the faceless, masked army had marched, flowing into the front courtyard and breaking around Damaris and Gregor.

They passed the palace, and soon Kerri led them to a town square. In the center was a statue of a man Loren did not recognize, a man with a full beard and long, flowing robes. He had one hand raised to the sky. But before Loren could ask about him, Kerri pointed. A large manor dominated one entire side of the square, far more impressive than Yushan's home where they had spent the night. The manor looked to be of the same sort of construction as the palace itself. Two of the square's other sides were composed of shops, while directly across the way were four more manors, though they were far smaller and less impressive than the first.

"Wojin will speak from there," said Kerri, still pointing at the largest manor. Set in its side was a wide marble balcony that stretched a few paces out into the air, overhanging the cobblestones below.

Even as Loren studied it, her attention was pulled away by the people milling about. Passersby gave the manor an uneasy look. The merchants hawking their wares seemed to studiously avoid looking at the place, as though they wanted their customers to forget it was there. Loren saw two children running along, and one of them stopped to spit on the building's wall. A nearby guard gave a cry and came after the girl, but she laughed and scampered off.

"I am no great judge of people," said Wyle, making it clear in his tone that he did not think that was true. "But I would wager that these citizens do not enjoy that building."

"That is Wojin's home," said Kerri. "Or at least, it was before he moved into the palace."

"Then why would he not give his speech from the palace?" said Chet.

Kerri glanced about to make sure no one was close enough to overhear them. "King Jun used to do so," she said. "But it required opening the palace gates so that the people could fill the courtyards inside. They loved Jun, and so he did not fear to do so. I doubt Wojin feels the same. It would surely make him anxious to have so many thousands of citizens inside his very walls."

"This is heartening," said Wyle, grinning. "These people seem to be half revolting already."

Annis frowned at him. "That was a poor joke. And we should not grow overconfident. Let us craft our plan."

"The crowd could hear me from the statue," said Loren. "It stands on a pedestal in the center of the square."

"Yet you would be surrounded," said Wyle. "The crowd would hamper the guards from coming to attack you, but it would not stop them completely. And the people would be a hindrance to your escape as well. Also, there is no cover to stop an arrow."

Loren grimaced. "Of course. My first thought was that Wojin would not have his soldiers shoot at me if I stood there, for a miss might strike the crowd. Yet from what I hear of him, he might not be deterred."

Kerri's expression grew dark. "No, Wojin would care little for that."

Gem bounced on his feet. "The rooftops!"

He pointed to the manors across from Wojin's. Their roofs were the same red tile as most in Danfon, and each a gentle slope meeting in a peak. And Loren saw now that while they were far shorter than the manor across the square, they were almost of a height with the balcony from which Wojin would deliver his speech.

"That would do," Loren mused. "But I should like to get a better look."

"I will find us a way up," said Gem, and scampered off to do just that. It was only a few moments before he returned. "Follow me."

Just beside the middle building was a huge pile of fresh-cut lumber. It was stacked neatly and formed a sort of staircase leading to the roof's edge.

Loren nodded. "This is perfect. It will let us get up and down from the roof, and I can address the crowd from there."

"Yet it still proves a poor means of escape," said Wyle. "If the space is indeed packed with the citizenry, you will not be able to get through them after climbing down."

"There is likely another way off the roof," said Gem. "Let us climb up and see."

He leaped up the piles of timber like a satyr, and Chet started up behind him. But Wyle took a quick step back and raised his hands. "I shall leave such exertions to you. I have a physique built for cleverness and charm, but not for climbing."

"That goes for me as well," said Annis. "Besides, someone should keep an eye on the smuggler."

Wyle held up a finger. "Ah, ah. I work for the king now. That means I am an honest businessman."

Loren arched an eyebrow. "Indeed. But all the same, I think Annis is right—Uzo and Shiun will remain here with the honest business-man."

"Certainly," said Shiun. She took a step closer to Wyle, as though she were ready to catch him if he tried to sneak away. Uzo stepped up on the smuggler's other side.

Wyle shook his head with an air of long-suffering dignity. "Always so distrustful," he said. "But I forgive you. Who could blame such an upstanding servant of the King's law?"

Loren smiled and turned to climb the pile of timbers. But to her surprise, she saw Kerri starting the climb as well.

"It might be better to remain here," said Loren. "There is no need to risk yourself."

Kerri raised an eyebrow, but she did not stop making her way up. "You think this is a risk? I think the danger will come during Wojin's speech. If you fear I cannot keep up, do not worry. I am as much a city child as you are."

Loren laughed at that, and so did Gem. The boy had reached the rooftop already, and had lowered a hand to help Chet make the last few steps. "She is no daughter of a city," said Gem. "Loren came from the forests."

Kerri seemed surprised—so much so that her foot slipped. Loren quickly caught her hand and steadied her. "Thank you," mumbled Kerri. "And forgive me for assuming. You are more refined than I would expect from a backwater bumpkin."

Loren's cheeks flushed. "I am only pleased you have not made fun of my accent, the way most people do. As for refinement, I would not say that I possess much, though I have had many experiences since leaving my home."

"She has indeed," said Gem. "You should have seen her when we first met in Cabrus. She stared in wide-eyed wonder at all the buildings, and her accent was even worse than it is now."

Kerri laughed. "I think it is lovely." Loren's cheeks flamed still further.

Chet helped Kerri make the last few paces of the climb. The girl was not quite as agile as she had boasted, though she was no bumbler, either. They took a few cautious steps on the roof. Loren was pleased to find the red tiles were firm under her feet—they would not slip and make her lose her footing, and she doubted if they made any noise that could be heard in the manor below. Gem bounced close to the front edge of the roof, making Loren's heart skip nervously. She always had to remind herself of Gem's familiarity with heights, for he took risks and balanced on perches that she herself would not have dared. Chet stopped a pace behind the boy, looking at the square below.

"It is a bit more exposed than I would like," said Chet. "They might still be able to shoot at you."

"The lip of the roof will give me some cover from the street," said Loren.

"I do not mean down below," said Chet. "If he has any archers on the balcony with him, or in the building, they will have a clear shot."

Loren looked at Wojin's manor. There were, indeed, many windows with a good view of her, and the balcony was more than wide enough to allow for archers. "I had not thought of that. I suppose I shall have to keep my words brief, then."

"But at least there are many routes of escape," said Gem. "And not just to the sides, but behind."

He pointed, and Loren could see that there were indeed many rooftops leading directly away from the square. There were not many gaps, and all were an easy leap.

"That shall be my route of escape," she said. "But we should find a place to climb down. I would rather know just where to go, rather than have to discover a ladder in the thick of things."

Gem led the way, jumping from one roof to another, and they all hurried to follow him. But it was almost no time at all before he stopped and pointed again. There was a drainpipe against a solid shop wall, anchored to the building with thick iron bands that would form perfect handholds.

"There," he said. "And we are far enough from the square that I doubt they will be able to reach you here."

"It is perfect," said Loren. "Though just to be safe, let us all climb it, to make sure it will hold."

It did, and when they had reached the cobblestones, Kerri led them back towards the square. When they came around the corner of the manor, Annis and the others turned to them in surprise.

"Back so soon?" said Wyle.

"Will it work?" said Annis.

"It will," said Loren. "It is as good a place as any to address the crowd, and there is an easy way to escape once I have done so."

"Most excellent," said Wyle. "Though while you have been scampering about having an adventure, I have turned my considerable mind to our plan. I think there is a way to make your appearance do more for our cause."

Loren folded her arms. "Oh?"

Wyle flashed his easy grin. "You are an impressive woman, Nightblade, and your black cloak will do you many favors in capturing the people's minds. I think King Jun is right, and his people have no great love for the usurper. Yet while the masses love to believe in a figurehead, they are reluctant to follow them unless they see their fellows already doing so."

"Speak plainly, smuggler," said Loren. "I do not enjoy parsing the meaning from your words."

"He means that a crowd will follow a crowd," said Annis. She turned to Wyle. "That wisdom is known to many. But how do you mean to use it?"

"In the simplest way possible," said Wyle. "When the Nightblade addresses the people, no doubt some of them will listen to her. But if some of them give voice to their support, and loudly, that will sway even more hearts."

Annis' eyes lit up, and she nodded eagerly. "Agents. Plants in the crowd to raise a cry."

"I do not understand," said Loren.

"Wyle will hire some few people—beggars, mayhap—to cry their support for you as you speak," said Annis. "That will encourage others to do the same. It is one thing to whisper gossip in your own shop. It is quite another thing to shout down a king—even a false one—when his guards are close at hand, and armed."

"But even the meek will rise up if they think they have the support of their fellows," said Wyle. "If we are agreed, then, I will see to the specific arrangements."

"More of your friends within the city?" said Chet.

Wyle cocked his head with a smile. "But of course. The meaner sort—not quite beggars, as the Yerrin girl said, but close enough. They will require payment—but I do not doubt that King Jun will be willing to accommodate that. As well as a fee for business honestly conducted, of course."

Loren fumed. Wyle confused her sometimes, when he seemed so eager to help them—but only until she discovered how he meant to profit from it.

"Very well," she said. "I will speak to King Jun and secure your payment—once he has the city. In the meantime, send your messages and have your friends ready to act."

"My pleasure," said Wyle, bowing low. "I imagine one of the Mystics will accompany me, to ensure there is no wrongdoing? Which one shall you send—the handsome one, or the quiet one?"

Loren looked at Shiun. The woman barely restrained a sigh as she went off with Wyle. Loren turned to Annis and the others. "Let us return to the manor and tell the king our plan."

"Later," said Annis. "Before we do, we have some goods to retrieve. Did you forget the tailor?"

Loren's eyes widened as she stared at her friend. "You cannot mean to fetch a dress now, Annis. There are more important things to be done."

"My dress is unimportant, but your new clothes are not." Annis' tone brooked no argument, and she stepped forwards to take Loren's arm. "One cannot take too much care with one's appearance when one is about to become a legend."

"She is already a legend," said Gem brightly. Annis ignored him and led Loren northeast into the city.

SIXTEEN

THE DREAM TOOK HER.

Loren was in the sewers, and the man was there. The one whose hair was cropped close, who dressed in black leather, who had scars along his arms. His eyes still glowed with that strange light, akin to magelight and yet somehow different.

He leaned against the passage wall and put a finger to his lips, though Loren had spoken no word. She spun, looking around. They were in Danfon's sewers, but she could not place their exact location. Then she thought she heard a noise—a great deal of running water. The river. They must be near the place where Wyle had first led them into the sewers.

She turned back to the man with the scars. He still held a finger to his lips, but now he lowered it and stepped around the corner. Though she had not willed her body to move, Loren found herself following him. She stepped around the corner and almost bumped into his back. The man motioned her to silence and then stepped aside for her to see.

There were Damaris and Gregor, just a little way down the tunnel. But there, too, was a woman Loren did not recognize. She had the look of a Dorsean woman, and she sat in a chair facing Loren. Damaris and Gregor faced her, away from Loren. Then Loren realized that the woman was bound and unable to move.

For the moment, Damaris and Gregor seemed content to ignore their prisoner. Gregor strode up and down the sewer, studying its walls, its ceiling. "This is how Loren entered the city," he said. "I know that she and her party came this way, but my agents could not discover her whereabouts above ground."

"That is no matter," said Damaris. "Maintain a guard so that they cannot escape the same way. But I do not think she will try to flee. I think she came here seeking us. If that is true, then it is only a matter of time before she reveals herself, and that is when we may strike."

Loren's knees shook. Damaris knew she was in the city. Of course she would know eventually—Loren meant to reveal herself to the whole populace the next day. But how had she found out in advance? Or was this a vision of the future?

Her terror increased tenfold as Damaris turned to look into her eyes.

"Hello, Loren," she said softly.

"I . . . this is a dream," said Loren.

How did she know that? She had never realized it before—not while she was in the dream, at least. Or had she? Her mind was muddled.

Damaris did not acknowledge Loren's statement. She only came forwards, walking up until she stood less than a pace in front of Loren. Gregor did not follow, though Loren could almost feel the bodyguard grow tense.

"Thank you," said Damaris, "for bringing Annis to Danfon."

Loren wanted to flee, but she could not move. "She is not here. You have been misled."

The merchant smiled. It was a sad, lonely expression, but her eyes were warm. She stepped forwards. Loren tried to jerk away, but she still could not move.

Damaris embraced her, arms wrapping around her back to rest on her shoulder blades. She laid her head on Loren's shoulder, face turned away, and squeezed her tight—not to harm, but only to give comfort. Loren had almost forgotten that the merchant was nearly a hand shorter than her.

"You have taken such good care of her," said Damaris softly. "I know now that if she had joined me in the Greatrocks, I would have regretted it. Everything had happened so fast. My hasty decision would have been my ruin. The Necromancer would have taken her from me. They have leverage over me already, but they always want more. Thank you for seeing to her safety."

Despite herself, Loren relaxed in the merchant's embrace. Why did she feel so safe? She knew Damaris' evil—knew her love of others' pain, her desire for control.

Yet after a moment, Loren recognized the truth. This was not the embrace of a friend. It was the comfort of a parent. It was something Loren had no memory of. Jordel had given her only a pale shadow of it, more akin to a battlefield commander than to a father. Loren was always expected to look after Annis, after Gem, to console them when the world was cruel, to see to their safety. Now, for just a moment, a part of her mind could pretend that Damaris' embrace promised the same. Reassurance. Security. Protection.

"Do not forget what happened at Wellmont," whispered Damaris.

Then she pulled away, and Loren's wits returned. It was the dream. It made her see things—think things—that would never happen in the waking world. This was another lie. Another trick.

Damaris stepped back until she stood by the woman in the chair. The woman's head had hung, but now she lifted it. Loren studied her. Sharp and severe features, thin eyebrows and regal lips. But she had been beaten terribly, and one eye was almost swollen shut. Far worse than that, her clothes were soaked in blood. Loren knew it came from a thousand torturous cuts, the sort that Damaris liked to give her victims as she pried information from them.

The woman tried to speak, but a bubbling cough came out instead. She hacked for a moment and tried again, her voice like steel.

"Never again will Jun sit the Dorsean throne."

Damaris drew a dagger and cut the woman's throat. The dagger was—had been—Auntie's.

Loren took a step back, horrified. Then she heard a noise behind her and turned. The man in black had gone, but someone else stood there.

Kal.

The grand chancellor was resplendent in his red cloak, which was free from any of the sewer's grime. Behind him were many Mystics, all of them armed and armored.

Loren almost melted in relief. "Damaris is here!" she said. "We can capture her!"

Kal did not answer. He raised his sword and leaped to attack her.

She barely scrambled out of the way in time. At the last moment she fell and struck the wall—but then she fell through it. Loren looked up in shock. What had seemed a small alcove was actually a side tunnel entrance. It led off into utter darkness—but in the main tunnel were Kal and his bloodthirsty Mystics.

Loren ran as fast as she could. Away from Damaris. Away from Kal and his Mystics who howled for her blood. But more red-cloaked warriors appeared in the sewers ahead. Again Loren had to turn down a side tunnel. She was hopelessly lost. Where was the city? Where was escape? She had no idea. She could only keep running.

A figure leaped out of the darkness ahead, and Loren recoiled. But it was no Mystic—or at least, not a real one. It was Niya.

Loren turned to flee again, but Niya snatched her arm.

"Quickly! We must escape!" she cried.

The Mystics were now close behind. Loren hesitated just a moment too long, and Niya's grip was strong. Soon they flew side by side. They came to a junction.

"Bent grate!" cried Niya, pointing. Loren saw it—twisted and bent, as though it had been struck by something heavy.

"Left," said Niya, and turned to follow her own direction.

The cries of the Mystics were still close, but now at least they were out of sight. Loren almost stopped following Niya, but then the woman spoke again.

"Bronze plate. Right." She pointed again, and Loren saw a bronze plate set in the ceiling. It had drainage holes, but beyond that she could not guess at its purpose. Niya turned right, and soon they had reached a heavy iron door.

"Help me get it open," she said. She seized the door and grunted as she heaved at it. Once again Loren lost control of her own body, and she moved to help. Together they heaved the iron door open. Its hinges groaned.

Sweet, fresh air rushed in to greet them. They darted through the doorway, and Loren found herself on a low wooden dock built on the river's edge. Looking up, she could see they were in the city again. They had made it back to Danfon. But Loren had wanted to escape the city.

"This is the wrong way," she said.

"It is the only way," said Niya. "Come, or they will catch you."

Loren glanced back the way they had come. Many Mystics rounded the corner. Battle cries poured from their lips as they chased her. With no other choice, Loren turned to follow Niya. The woman climbed the riverbank and ran towards a small, nondescript shop nearby. She flung open the door and ran inside, with Loren only a pace behind her.

She was in the king's palace. Confusion struck her like a hammer blow, and for a moment she froze in her tracks. The halls and mighty pillars were familiar from the last dream. Turning, she saw the shop door behind her. It was set in the wall, and beyond it was the river. It was like a portal to another world, and her mind could not reconcile the difference.

"They nearly killed us," said Chet.

Loren whirled. When had Chet appeared there? He was within arm's reach. His limbs shook, and his eyes darted everywhere, mad with fear.

"They . . . they were so close," said Chet. Even his words quivered. "If any of us had made a misstep . . . if I had fallen . . ."

"We are safe," said Loren. "They did not catch us."

"How long?" said Chet. "How long can we keep running? How long before I stumble in the chase?"

Loren opened her mouth, but no words came out. She only shook her head.

"You cannot follow me anymore," whispered Chet.

"But you have followed *me*," cried Loren in frustration. "And I know you cannot do it anymore. It is killing you, Chet. I can see it, and I know you can as well. I only wish you did not feel the need to try."

Unthinking, she stepped forwards and tried to embrace him. But he screamed and pushed her away. Loren recoiled, cursing herself as Chet fled weeping. Loren went after him, crying for him to wait, that she was sorry. But he kept running until he had led her to the passageway—the one she knew well, the one where her dreams always led her. Ahead was the dining hall. Chet fled through it. The way beyond was clear, and an open gate led to the city. Almost Loren followed him.

Then she heard cries behind her and turned. The Mystics were there. They had found her again, and their swords hungered for her blood.

She had to lead them away. Had to keep them from Chet's trail. If she followed him, he would die.

But if she went into the secret passageway, *she* would die. Gregor would see to that.

Loren threw open the small iron door and ducked inside the serving room. She seized the cupboard and heaved—it fell to the ground with a crash, scattering broken dishes everywhere. Beyond was the dark passageway, and she ate a magestone so that she could see. There was the ladder, and at the top was the second hall. Soon she came to the tapestry and moved it aside.

It was the apartment. The same as last time. She had half hoped the dream would play a trick on her again, that she would find herself somewhere else entirely. But it was the same. In the far wall was the door leading to the balcony, and before it stood Gregor. His eyes fixed on her, and she could not move as terror filled her body.

"The Elves told you." Niya's voice floated from nowhere. Loren was alone as Gregor stepped forwards, drawing his sword.

The dream released her.

Loren started awake in her bed and sat up. For half a moment she forgot where she was, and fear coursed through her as she imagined herself in the Danfon palace. But her wits soon returned. She was in the manor of the merchant Yushan, and Gregor was far away. Annis lay within arm's reach, but the girl did not stir. Slowly Loren's breathing returned to normal. She hung her head, resting it in her hands.

The dreams were more vivid, more detailed, and yet they still brought less terror each time. That was good. Whether or not the dreams were meant to help her, she could do without the dread they always left behind. Mayhap soon they would leave none at all.

But though the fear soon passed, it left her anxious and jumpy. She needed to move, to work out the sudden tension in her limbs. So she rose and dressed herself, wearing her regular, simple garments, and not the new clothes from the tailor. She did not bother to pull on her boots. The door opened silently, and she slipped out into the common room.

To her surprise, she found Shiun there. The Mystic sat in a chair by the door that led to the rest of the manor. Loren paused for a moment, and the two of them stared at each other. After a moment, Shiun raised an eyebrow.

"Can you not sleep?"

"I . . . did, but something woke me," said Loren. "What are you doing?"

"Sitting watch," said Shiun. "Uzo and I have done so since we came here."

Loren cocked her head as she went to one of the room's armchairs and sank into it. "Do you suspect Yushan might betray us?"

"I do not. But one can never be too careful. Call it an old habit—technically we are still on campaign, after all."

Loren sighed. "You are right, and I thank you for it. It is only one more detail I should have thought of."

Shiun sighed and looked away, picking at her trouser leg with her fingernails. Loren felt shame rise in her breast, and she, too, turned away. Shiun deserved better than her. The whole party did. Too often, Loren forgot that she was only a girl. The next day—or, she supposed, later this day, for it was the small hours of the morning—Loren would play at being a legend, a master thief of great renown. Yet she could not even remember to do simple things like setting a watch.

"I am sorry you were assigned to me, Shiun," she said softly. "I know you would rather not have been. I am sure you and Uzo must be frustrated by me. I should have caught Damaris long ago. A smarter woman would have. I should never have followed her to Yewamba. Sometimes—that is, I do my best, but sometimes I feel as though I am just stumbling from one mess to another, and making each one worse as I do."

Shiun's lips pressed tight. She turned back to Loren, studying her in the dim light of the room's lamp. Then it seemed to Loren like she came to a decision, resolving something in her own thoughts.

"May I speak to you openly, Nightblade?"

"Of course," said Loren. "I am your commander in name only."

"You are *not*," said Shiun sharply—so sharply that Loren jumped a bit. "You are who I was assigned to follow, and the same is true for Uzo. Yet all the long while we have ridden together, you have . . . well, you have whined and complained and moaned to us. You speak too openly and listen too eagerly."

Loren straightened somewhat in her armchair. "I . . . you do not want me to listen to you?"

"I understand your situation, at least somewhat," said Shiun. "You are young. Few are given a command at your age, even in the Mystics, where we recruit some fine soldiers of your years. You are nervous that you will make a mistake. And before you rode with Mystics, you rode alone—or with a small group of friends. And you treat them as friends. You speak to them openly, sharing everything."

"Of course," said Loren, feeling a little defensive now. "They *are* my friends."

"But I am not," said Shiun flatly. "Do not misunderstand me. I think you are a fine woman, and honorable. I do not tell you all this only for my own sake and Uzo's, but for *everyone* you may lead in the future. Sky above, act like a commander for once. Let those who serve you *serve* you. We do not need to hear the smallest details of every thought that crosses your mind. Some information can be helpful, but too much debate gets tiresome. Uzo and I are not your friends. We are here with one purpose: to carry out your orders. That is the lot of a soldier, and that is why we joined the Mystics."

"I did not join the Mystics," said Loren. "I am—"

"Stop," said Shiun. "You did not join the Mystics, but you accepted your assignment from the High King. That grants you privileges, but it also comes with responsibilities. I swear on the darkness below that I will pull my hair out if you seek reassurance from me one more time. That is not my duty. It is *your* duty to reassure us—or rather, to reassure Uzo, if he should need it. I require little for myself."

Loren found herself on her feet, fists shaking by her sides. "How do you think I can promise him that all will be well? I have little faith in myself, much less our mission."

Shiun, too, stood, matching Loren's glare with one of equal fury. "Never say that again," she hissed. "Not to any soldier who follows by your side—and, if you *do* want my advice, which you should not, then never say it to the children, either. If you believe in some Elf-tale where you are all friends on a grand adventure, I assure you that they do not. They see you as their leader, even if you do not act like one."

Loren almost argued. She wanted to. But her mind flashed back to her dream. She saw Damaris standing before her. She felt the merchant's embrace and the peace it had brought her. Reassurance. Safety. Comfort. Things she had not felt for so long, not since Jordel had died.

Shiun was studying her, and now the woman tilted her head with satisfaction. "Yes, Nightblade." Her voice was no longer angry, but quiet—and mayhap even a little sad. "That is your place. I take no more pleasure in it than you do, I am sure. But that is the way of it all the same."

Almost, Loren apologized. But then she thought better of it and nodded instead. "You . . . you are right."

Because of course Shiun was right. Loren rarely stopped to consider her own actions. That was partly because there was little time. But, too, she did not always like what she saw. She had left the Birchwood with

624

dreams of becoming a great thief, a woman who could bring fear to kings and succour to the oppressed. Yet sometimes she still acted like a young girl, one who longed for the kindness and love of a mother and father who had never shown her either.

"You are right," she said again, slowly. "I will do better. And I thank you and Uzo for your patience with me. I could hardly have asked for better soldiers to serve in my first command—all of you but Niya, of course."

Some of the tension seemed to flow out of Shiun, and she nodded slowly. "Now *that* is the sort of thing a commander might say. And as for Niya, I hope that sow has felt all the torments of the darkness below."

Loren nodded, passing a hand over her eyes. "I . . . I should return to sleep. Do not stay up all night. Make sure you wake Uzo to replace you."

Shiun resumed her seat. "I will. Sleep well, Nightblade."

Loren returned to her room and lay down. But she could not find sleep. Shiun's words echoed in her mind. She dreaded the thought of becoming a hard-bitten commander like Kal. But then, he did seem the sort of leader whom soldiers would follow into battle. Loren pictured herself in the role and wanted to laugh.

Annis still slept, her mouth open slightly. Loren studied her. Did the girl see Loren as a commander, the way Shiun said? It seemed ridiculous. Yet the children had followed her into dangers more deadly than most soldiers faced on a battlefield. But then again, they had done so while Loren acted like herself, and not the war commander Shiun seemed to want.

She sighed, pinching her chin. Her thoughts spun around each other and seemed determined not to sort themselves out. One more worry. One more crushing weight atop all the others, threatening to snap her in two.

She could not sleep, at least not yet. So she sat up in the bed and thought about what she would say the next day. Words came slowly, and she fumbled over them. Eventually she rose and began to pace. The motion helped her, and she began to form some semblance of a proper speech. She only hoped that the plan would go smoothly, and she would in fact be able to deliver it.

Moonslight peeked through a gap in the curtains. Loren went to the window and leaned against it, pulling the cloth aside to look out.

The red roofs of Danfon were silver in the night, accented in red by torches set in the walls of the buildings.

Ever since she could remember, she had dreamed of becoming a thief of legend. Something from campfire stories. Tomorrow might be the most significant single step she had yet taken on that road. It frightened her, as she knew it should. But far more than that, it excited her, if she was being honest. She often cuffed or chastised Gem when he made too much of the stories that surrounded her. The tales were embellished, made to sound like extravagant adventures when in truth she had struggled just to survive. But now she meant to pit herself against a false king before the eyes of an entire city—indeed, an entire kingdom.

"What under the sky has my life become?" she whispered.

And who was the Nightblade? A thief in the night, gallivanting across Underrealm with her band of merry companions? Or an agent of the High King and a commander of Mystics?

She blinked, and her lids were slow to rise. Weariness had come at last. She lay down in the bed once more and drew the covers over herself. At last her head settled comfortably into her pillow, and sleep claimed her quickly.

SEVENTEEN

THE MORNING DAWNED BRIGHT AND FAIR, THE AIR AS WARM AS ONE could expect in winter. Loren woke the moment Annis began to stir. When dressing, she almost reached for her normal clothes, the white shirt, green vest, and brown trousers she had worn ever since she left the Birchwood. But her hand paused on the garments. Today was not a day for simple clothes. Today she would don the new clothes Annis had bought for her.

Carefully she untied the string that held the brown cloth package together. New boots were wrapped around the rest of the clothes—not made by the tailor, but procured by him from a nearby cordwainer to go with the outfit. Loren did not think they were all that different from her old boots, though certainly they were less worn and had a few more buttons running up the calf.

The new trousers were a bit tighter than she was used to, but they still let her move about with ease. The shirt buttoned twice, inside and out, and had more buttons at the wrist. The sleeves hung somewhat loose, and they fluttered when she moved her arms. Over the shirt was a long waistcoat with many pockets on both the inside and outside.

Loren thought it looked somewhat ridiculous, but the green velvet trim did catch the eye.

When she had finished dressing, she turned to find Annis staring at her. Loren had no idea how long the girl had been watching, but now she smiled with satisfaction.

"And the cloak," she said. "Put that on."

"Why?" said Loren. "It is warm in here."

Annis rolled her eyes. "Oh, come now, Loren. Let me *see* it. I picked these clothes, after all."

Loren sighed and went to the wall, fetching her cloak and putting it on. When she turned back to Annis, the girl squealed and clapped her hands.

"It is perfect. Every stitch of it. That merchant is worth twice what he charges. If we survive all of this, I shall have to send him a mighty gift of gold."

Loren looked down at herself. "Annis, I think I look ridiculous."

"Of course *you* think so," said Annis, sniffing. "You have never had good taste when it comes to the finer things in life. Do not worry how you *think* you look, for I assure you that you are wrong. Are the clothes comfortable?"

She had not thought about it. Loren crouched, then gave a jump, then twisted all around. "Actually, yes. Very comfortable indeed. Is this silk?"

Annis rolled her eyes again. "Honestly," she whispered, before speaking in a normal tone of voice. "No, it is not. Do not trouble yourself over the fabrics. We have more important things to worry about today."

Once Annis had donned her own new garments, she and Loren stepped out into the common room. The moment they stepped into view, everyone in the room froze. Loren stopped as well, pausing on the threshold. Chet and the Mystics were looking at her, their eyes wide. Kerri was there, too, and she had her head cocked, as if Loren were a stranger she did not recognize. Even Wyle paused in eating his breakfast, his eyes traveling up and down her new garments. Gem's mouth hung open.

"Sky above," breathed the boy. "You look like the Nightblade now, and no mistake."

Loren ducked her gaze, fidgeting with one of the cuffs of her shirt. "I think you are an idiot," she muttered. "Besides, I am not the only one in new clothing."

Gem looked down at his own little suit. Somehow he had rumpled it already, but its fine cut was still eye-catching. "I like it," he said simply. "But it is nowhere near as impressive as yours."

Chet stepped up before her, smiling. But Loren could see the sadness and doubt in his gaze. For a moment she thought of her dream, but she forced that thought away.

"It suits you."

"Thank you," said Loren. "But we should be off."

They all left the manor, making for the square where Wojin would deliver his speech. It was somewhat late in the morning, and the streets were busy. Wojin's address was scheduled for midday. They had intended to give themselves some time to prepare, but Loren suddenly worried that the crowds might make them late.

She touched Kerri's arm briefly, drawing the girl's attention. "Is there a faster route?"

Kerri glanced at her. "I can take us down some side streets if you wish."

"Please," said Loren. "I would rather not be late."

Kerri smiled, and her gaze darted down to Loren's outfit. As they ducked off the main thoroughfare down an alley, she looked at Loren again. "Your outfit truly does look wonderful."

Loren tried to suppress the burning in her cheeks. "Not you, too."

The girl only chuckled, a light sound that played musically on the morning air. "Do not look so flustered. I told you when I met you that you were not quite what I expected, from the stories I had heard. But now you look much closer to the mark."

Loren chose not to answer that, and instead only urged them on to greater speed. Soon they reached the place where Loren would climb down from the rooftops. There they left Kerri, who would guide them in their escape. Loren and the others pressed on, crossing the last few streets that took them to the square.

A large crowd had already gathered. Some were there to trade, and made their way among the merchant stalls that lined two sides of the square. But most had clearly come for Wojin's speech, for they stood expectantly, looking up at the manor from which he would address them. Loren saw more than a few of them frowning and muttering to each other. She wondered if they were agents Wyle had placed in the crowd, or merely dissatisfied residents of the city. She hoped it was the latter.

"Up we go," said Gem.

He bounded up the pile of timbers, which was unchanged from the day before. Loren followed quickly, as did Chet. Shiun and Uzo remained on the ground, there to support Loren if she should need it. If all went well, and Loren escaped on the rooftops, they would vanish into the crowd and rejoin the party at Yushan's manor. Annis and Wyle had remained there, for they would be little help today.

Atop the roof, Gem bounced on the balls of his feet. When Loren and Chet reached the top, he turned to them with a grin. "I am glad to be here," he said. "Today is the day the Nightblade turns from a campfire story into a true legend."

"Be silent, Gem," said Loren. "And get down." She followed her own directions, lying on the rooftop so that she was nearly out of sight of the square below. For a moment she worried that she might be getting her knees and elbows dirty, but she quickly shook the thought away. Darkness take her if she would become someone who always worried about her appearance.

"I am worried," said Chet. He frowned down at the crowd. "There are many guards down there. The moment they see you, they will try to find a way up. It will not take them long."

"Then I will be quick," said Loren. "By the time they reach the building, we will no longer be here."

"Of course," he said, forcing a quick smile. Loren returned it, hoping hers looked more genuine.

Suddenly the crowd below them quieted. It left the air feeling empty, yet also charged with power. Loren turned. Across the square, the balcony door opened. For a moment she was uncomfortably reminded of her dream, of the balcony where she always found Gregor.

But then figures stepped through the doorway, and she shook off the thought. First came four guards. They wore armor and carried swords, but Loren noted that they did not have bows.

Then Wojin stepped into view. His robes were red trimmed with yellow, the colors of Dorsea. Upon his head was a thin circlet of gold set with many rubies. He was thinner than she had thought he would be, and his chin came down in a severe point. The point was not lessened by his thin beard, which was combed into an even sharper angle. He wore no weapon as the High King often had, not even an ornamental one. Apparently his guards were enough of a show of force for him.

Just behind Wojin came a younger man. Loren guessed that he was

Prince Shun, Wojin's son. He wore robes like his father's, but a little less ornate. His head was bowed, and he kept his eyes averted from the crowd, almost as if he was ashamed to be there. Loren wondered at that for a moment, but then all her attention was taken by the next figure stepping through the door.

Damaris of the family Yerrin emerged into the sunlight. Gone were the kindness and concern Loren had seen in her dream. Damaris strode with purpose, her head held high and haughty. She was imperious, commanding. Loren did not doubt that many in the crowd ignored Wojin to study her. Some had to wonder who she was, and what had earned her the right to stand at their king's side.

A plan began to form in Loren's mind. She watched the balcony door a moment longer, but Gregor did not appear there. She smiled to herself.

Wojin paid no attention to Damaris. He stepped to the balcony's railing and raised his hands. The crowd, which had begun to buzz below them, quickly fell silent. Wojin looked solemnly down at them all, no trace of a smile touching his features as he gradually lowered his hands.

"My people," Wojin proclaimed. His voice was powerful, Loren had to give him that. She thought she could almost feel it in the tiles beneath her hands. The words hung on the air for a moment, and the last mutterings of the crowd faded to silence. "My people," he said again. "I give you my blessings, just as the sky has given us this beautiful day. But my heart is no less heavy. Day and night, I mourn the loss of my dear nephew. No parent should have to bury their child, and though Jun was not my son, I feel his loss no less keenly."

Gem snickered aloud. Loren shot him a glance, and he shrugged. "Oh, come, Loren. The man is a pompous fool."

"Silence," she whispered.

Wojin leaned forwards, his hands gripping the balcony's railing, and his brows drew together in a frown. "But with that sense of loss comes a sense of duty. My nephew's death must not go unavenged. For the so-called High King Enalyn, there can be no forgiveness. No amends or reparations can return what we have lost. The debt can only be repaid with blood!"

He paused for a moment, as if he expected the crowd to roar in approval. They did not, and Loren thought she saw Wojin swallow.

"That is why I have joined Dulmun," he went on. His voice rose, as though he was shouting to be heard, but no one else had made a sound. "Enalyn's tyranny has had its day. For the last time, she has interfered with our sovereignty and that of the other kingdoms. No longer will we let her meddle in our affairs, keeping us from reclaiming our birthright. Dorsea should command all the southern lands that Selvan now calls their own. We did once, and we will again. Are any of us surprised that Enalyn would intervene on behalf of the kingdom she once hailed from? Underrealm is a strong nation of proud laws—but Enalyn has corrupted those laws. She calls us rebels, as she calls the kingdom of Dulmun. But I say that we 'rebels' uphold the true ideals of Underrealm!"

The time had come. Loren could feel it. She leaped to her feet and threw back her hood.

"And do those ideals include kinslaying?"

The air fell deadly quiet. Wojin gaped at her, stunned to inaction. Every head in the square turned to look. But Loren kept her gaze on Damaris. The merchant was as surprised as Wojin—but where the king stood staring at her in wonder, Damaris wore a look of open hatred. If her eyes had been longbows, Loren would have been pierced a dozen times in the space of a heartbeat.

Loren smiled briefly at Damaris, hoping the merchant could see it from such a great distance. But then she dropped her gaze to the crowd below. For a moment, she froze. They were all staring at her, many of them as dumbfounded as their king, but all of them clearly expecting her to say something. Panic struck, and her mouth worked without producing any sound.

Say something, she shouted in her own mind.

"Wojin is a usurper," she cried. They were not the first words she had planned the night before, but they seemed to do the trick. She could see a ripple move through the crowd. It was as though her words were traveling through the people like a wave. Some of them cast dark looks at Wojin where he stood on the balcony.

"A usurper, a murderer, and a would-be kinslayer," said Loren. Now that she had managed to speak, the words began to come more easily, and she remembered her speech. "Yes, I say would-be, for Wojin was not even powerful enough to bring his plans to fruition. He may have overthrown King Jun by force, and he sits in the palace now. But he is no king. King Jun is alive, and he will soon return!"

The crowd gasped. Some of them began to mill about. Glancing around, Loren could see some figures fighting to push their way through the press—guards of Wojin's, no doubt, trying to reach the base of the building upon which Loren stood. For a moment she had almost forgotten that she would need to escape.

"Liar!" cried Wojin, capturing the attention of the crowd again. "This girl tells you falsehoods!"

"Oh?" said Loren. She reached into one of the many pockets of her new vest and drew forth Jun's ring of office. Its ruby glinted in the sun as she held it up. "Then where did I get this?"

The crowd's murmur swelled as they beheld the ring. Wojin's mouth opened, but no sound came out. Loren smiled. Then a woman jumped up on the base of the statue in the square's center. She threw a fist in the air and cried out.

"Long live King Jun! Down with the usurper!"

"Down with the usurper!" yelled someone else. Loren could not see who it was, but soon a few others took up the call.

Wyle's agents, she thought. *Bless that smuggler.*

Wojin rallied himself at last. "My people!" he cried. "Do not listen to this woman. Who is she? A foreigner, and a liar! Jun is dead, murdered by assassins of the false High King! For all we know, this girl is the one who killed him! That is how she got the ring!"

Damaris' face went a shade paler, and Loren laughed out loud in what felt like a moment of madness. The laugh seemed to shock Wojin, for he fell silent again. Loren, murder Jun? She had never willingly taken a life. Wojin could not know that, but Damaris would.

Loren's laughter died, and she shook her head. "I am no murderer, Wojin. Not like you. I am a simple woman of Selvan." The crowd muttered, and she lowered her gaze to address them once more. "Yes. My kingdom has no great love for yours. But the petty differences of kings are as nothing now. Before I am a woman of Selvan, I am first a citizen of Underrealm. A servant of the High King. I did not kill Jun—I spoke with him only last night. And I will not rest until the High King's justice finds this false king—him, and the woman by his side who holds his strings. He calls me a foreign meddler? What of her? Ask yourselves, people of Danfon: why would a merchant of the family Yerrin support a man who killed his own nephew in a mad quest for power?"

Wojin was muttering to his guards and making sharp gestures towards Loren, but they had no bows with which to shoot her. Loren looked at Damaris again. The merchant's face had gone dark, and there was an evil glint in her eyes. She looked right back at Loren, her expression holding a grim promise.

I will find you, Nightblade. And I will end you.

The crowd was chanting now. "Long live King Jun! Down with the usurper! All hail the Nightblade!" That caught Loren's attention. She had not proclaimed herself to be the Nightblade at all. Wyle must have taken liberties when he gave orders to his agents.

She almost opened her mouth to speak again, but she felt a sharp tug on her pant leg and glanced down. Gem was lying flat so that the crowd could not see him, but every so often he had poked his head over the roof's edge to peer at the throng.

"The guards are close," said Gem. "It is time we left."

Loren looked and saw he was right. The guards had neared the bottom of the building where they stood. They would soon find a way up, and she did not want Uzo and Shiun to be drawn into a fight as they tried to protect her.

One last time, she turned to the crowd. "Ready yourselves for King Jun's return!" she cried. "It will be soon, and he will be wroth. For Underrealm and the High King!"

She threw a fist into the air, and many in the square cried out as they did the same. Then Loren turned with a whirl of her cloak and scampered away across the rooftop. Gem and Chet slithered away from the roof's edge, then rose to follow her.

"That was the single most glorious thing I have ever seen," said Gem with excitement. "And considering the leagues we have ridden together, that is saying a great deal."

"Oh, be *silent,* Gem," said Loren sharply. But she could not wipe the grin from her own face—even when she saw that Chet kept his gaze low, his eyes troubled. She ignored him. Mayhap she did indeed trip from one disaster into the next. But now, for the first time in a long time, it felt like she had finally gotten one thing right.

EIGHTEEN

THEY DARED NOT RETURN TO YUSHAN'S MANOR STRAIGHT AWAY, IN CASE someone spotted them. Therefore they spent some time wandering in back alleys and deserted streets, constantly searching to make sure no one had followed them. By the time they finally reached the manor, the sun was low in the sky.

In the basement, they reported the day's events to King Jun. Their news was met with celebration. Senlin's eyes shone as Gem told them of Loren's speech—Loren had not thought it necessary to give them details, but Gem insisted—and Jun wore a fierce smile. Yushan herself actually clapped her hands when they were done, and immediately she beckoned for servants to bring them food, as well as some of her finest wines.

"A good day's work," said Jo. The bodyguard pulled at his close-trimmed beard, and though his face was characteristically dour, there was an uncommon energy in the movement.

"How many would you say spoke in support?" said Prince Senlin.

"Very many," said Gem quickly, before Loren could answer. He bounded up to the prince and bowed low. "I half thought the crowd would rise up on the spot and storm Wojin's manor. Mayhap they did, after we left."

"They did not," said Uzo. "It took us a while to withdraw from the press. Wojin departed almost immediately, and the crowd dispersed soon after."

Gem looked crestfallen, but Senlin smiled and put a hand on his shoulder. "That is no matter," said the prince. "The important thing is that they know we are alive. You have performed a great service—not only to us, but also to the High King herself."

This time Gem not only beamed, but blushed as well. "I suppose it is not the first time we have done so. But I thank you nonetheless, Your Excellency."

The servant arrived with a tray holding three bottles of wine. Yushan quickly unstopped one and poured a glass, which Loren accepted gratefully. But she paused as she caught King Jun's eye. He studied her with pursed lips and a furrowed brow.

"Today was a good start," he said slowly. "Yes. A good start. But *only* the start. We will not retake the kingdom on the strength of one victory."

The room went quiet. Loren's mood dampened at once as she recognized the truth in his words. But after he had let the gravity of it settle for a moment, Jun took another glass from Yushan and filled it himself. He raised it slightly in toast to Loren.

"Then again, mayhap even a small victory deserves some acknowledgement."

Jo grunted a laugh at that, and Loren's smile returned. She touched her glass to Jun's, and the two of them drank deep.

Jun turned to speak with Senlin in a low voice, and Loren studied them for a moment. She still had little love for the Dorsean king and the wars he had brought to Selvan. But she had to admit—if only to herself—that he was not so simple a man as she had imagined him to be, back when she had been younger and had seen so little of the world.

What would I have thought a year ago in the Birchwood, to see myself drinking with a king? she thought. *Indeed, he is not even the first king I have shared wine with.*

They all made merry in Yushan's basement for a short time, but Loren soon ordered her party to return to their quarters. Jun had been right on one count: they still had much to do, and the sooner they began, the better. They spent the day resting, and retired early. Loren spent a dreamless night in sleep and woke before the sun, rising to break her fast in the common room with the others. But before she had finished eating, an urgent knock came at the door, and a messenger summoned her to Jun's side.

Annis had risen, and together the two of them made their way to the basement. There they found Jun ready to receive them—indeed, he and Senlin scarcely seemed to have moved from where they had been the night before. If they had not been wearing different clothing, Loren might have thought they had slept in their chairs. For a moment she was struck by the ludicrousness of the king and his son and their little court in this basement. Beside them, Yushan looked like a court scribe ready to take notes of the king's proclamations. But such thoughts fled her mind as Jun looked up at her gravely.

"We have received a message, relayed through many ears," he said. "Someone in the city wishes to meet with me."

Loren balked and shot a quick glance at Jo. The bodyguard's face was grave. Beside Loren, Annis spoke carefully. "That does not seem wise, Your Grace."

"Of course His Grace will not take the risk," said Jo.

Senlin glanced at the bodyguard. "Yet neither can we allow this opportunity to pass us by."

Loren held up a hand. "Pardon me, Your Grace. But *who* wishes to meet with you?"

Jun shifted in his seat. "Her name is Duris, of the family Fei. She is a senator, and she is my kin, though somewhat distant."

Annis arched an eyebrow. "And Wojin has allowed her to remain free? Why would he do that, unless she is loyal to him?"

"I have thought much the same thing," said Jun. "Yet Wojin could hardly have had time to thoroughly test the loyalty of every senator. Most likely, he hopes that they will accept his new position because it would be too difficult to resist him. The senate's purpose is to provide a check on the power of the king in domestic matters, but that power has not been strongly tested in many years. And Dorsea has not seen anything like Wojin's treachery in centuries. If he is willing to assassinate me to take the throne, would he hesitate to kill a senator? He hopes they will obey him out of fear of being replaced, or worse."

"Yet that fear may bind them to our side instead," said Jo. "They have their own states' armies, but they would not risk using them against Wojin—unless, mayhap, they think they can win. It is not the most honorable course, but it is prudent."

"And this woman Duris?" said Loren. "Is she the sort of woman who would act with such . . . prudence?"

"We do not know for certain," said Jun. "She does not normally reside in the capital, and we have had few reasons to meet each other. She only happened to be here on state business when Wojin took control. Normally she serves in the southeastern reaches alongside that state's other senator—Shen, my cousin, and a good man. But he fell in the Battle of Wellmont."

Jun abruptly stopped talking, and his eyes flashed as he looked at Loren. He must have wondered whether it was wise to mention that battle in her presence. But Loren's thoughts went elsewhere—to something in her dream she had scarcely remembered until Jun's words brought it to the fore.

Do not forget what happened at Wellmont.

Did Damaris' words refer to the death of this senator? But how could they? How could Loren forget Shen's death, when she had never heard of it before this moment?

Her thoughts had begun to wander, and she reined them in. "It seems clear what we must do," she said. "A meeting must be arranged with Duris, though His Grace cannot attend it."

"I will go," said Senlin. "I know enough, I think, to act on my father's behalf."

"Absolutely not," said Jun. "I fear for your life more than mine. If anything were to happen to me, you would be the last of our line—except Wojin himself, and that does not bear thinking about."

"It should be me, of course," said Loren. She spread her hands. "Is that not why you have summoned me here?"

Jun lifted his chin for a moment, studying her. Loren had the feeling that he had not expected her bluntness. "It is," he said at last. "I would consider it a great service."

"I have already pledged myself to helping you reclaim the throne," said Loren. "This seems but one small step on that road."

Annis pursed her lips. "It could be dangerous, Loren. If it is a trap, this Duris may well spring it on you instead. She will think she can pry the king's location from you through torture."

"Then I will not let her catch me," said Loren. "If there is one skill I possess, it is the ability to escape the traps my enemies set for me."

She meant it as a jest, but Annis' frown only deepened. "That is what the tales say about you. Take care that you do not believe too strongly in your own myth."

Loren nodded gravely. "I will not. It was a poor jest, for I know only too well how dangerous our enemies are." She turned back to Jun. "What should I seek to gain from this meeting, Your Grace?"

"That depends very much on what Duris plans to offer," said Jun. "For now, meet with her and hear what she has to say. As I have mentioned, I know little of her directly. I hope she means to pledge her loyalty and offer help. But we must be cautious. She may seek to turn me over to Wojin, thereby earning his favor."

Annis perked up. "I should go with you," she said. "If Duris wishes to negotiate—or to plan—you will need me."

Loren's mouth twisted. "I would prefer to have you by my side, certainly. Yet it seems too dangerous. If Duris is working with Wojin, she is also working with your mother. If Duris should bring word of your presence back to her, that would be disastrous."

And she fought back a thought: *unless Damaris already knows you are here, as she said in my dream.*

No. You do not see the future. Auntie was proof enough of that.

Annis shook her head at Loren's words. "I need to be there. Forgive me, Loren, but you are simply not qualified. When it comes to a fight or to gathering information, of course you are the right choice. But not when it comes to negotiation."

"That seems to make you an even more valuable asset," said Prince Senlin, frowning. "Mayhap the Nightblade is right, and you should remain here."

Frowning, Annis thought for a moment. Then she brightened. "We will take extra precautions. We will arrange the meeting at the safest location we can manage. At the beginning, someone will meet with Duris alone while others of our party scour the surrounding area, searching for any sign of an ambush. If they find nothing, they will alert Loren, and Loren will fetch me to handle the details."

They all paused. Even Loren thought that idea had some merit. "Very well," said Jun. He turned to Yushan. "Have you any idea where such a meeting might be arranged?"

Yushan thought for a moment. "I may know a place," she said at last. "It is a warehouse owned by the family Jinso. Their trade has fallen in recent months, and the warehouse has seen little use. There will be no one around to snoop about and expose us."

"We should tell her to meet us somewhere else," said Annis quickly. "Mayhap a tavern—not too close to the warehouse, but not across the city, either. We will send an agent to meet her there and then lead her to the warehouse. That way Duris will have no chance to set a trap, if that is indeed her intention."

Jun paused for a moment, looking at Jo. The bodyguard nodded slowly before turning to his liege. "It seems wise to me, Your Grace."

"Very well," said Jun. He clapped his hands to settle the matter, and Yushan scuttled off to send the message wending its way back to Duris. When the merchant had gone, Jun turned back to Loren. "Now let us determine what your goals in the meeting should be."

"I thought I was to hear Duris out," said Loren.

"That, certainly," said Jun. "The best we can hope for is that Duris wishes to help me reclaim the throne. If that is the case, the most important thing we need is the support of as many senators as we can muster."

"Agreed," said Annis.

"And I will need their full-fledged support once I have taken the palace," said Jun. "It will do me no good to reclaim the throne if I do not have the senate ready to act on my behalf."

"Forgive me, Your Grace," said Loren. "But that seems a weak method of persuasion. Right now, Wojin holds all the power. Would the nobility not be wiser to pledge their strength to him?"

Jun smiled. It was a grim expression, fell and cold, and Loren had to hide a shiver. "Not necessarily," he said, his voice tight. "Anyone who takes a throne by force must first rally support—just as we are doing now. How do they gain that support? By promising rewards. And where do they get the rewards?"

Loren frowned. After a moment's silence, Annis answered. "They eliminate possible opponents," the girl said quietly. "Then they divide the spoils of conquest up between those who supported them in their rebellion."

"Just so," said Jun. "Until Wojin is removed from power, every senator who did not directly aid him is at risk. Duris will likely know this, Nightblade. But if she does not, you must remind her."

"I will, Your Grace," said Loren.

"Then go. Sky keep you safe."

Loren bowed, and then she and Annis returned to their quarters upstairs. The others were just rising—all but Gem, who had to be roused from bed as usual. But as the rest of them woke and broke their fast, Loren sat in her own armchair in the corner and stared into the low fire burning on the hearth, her thoughts far away.

NINETEEN

THE MEETING WAS ARRANGED FOR THE NEXT DAY—AT MIDDAY, THE time when their enemies would have the most trouble pursuing Loren through crowded streets, if it should come to flight. This time Loren's whole party came, and once again Kerri guided them. She was curiously quiet as she took them through the streets, following the directions Yushan had relayed to her. At last she glanced over at Loren.

"Do you think this will work?" she said, too quietly for the others to hear.

Loren looked at her in surprise. "You were not there when we made our plans. How do you know what we mean to do?"

"Prince Senlin told me," said Kerri. "He trusts me, and he confides in me when he has some doubt about his father's course of action."

"And does he doubt this one?"

Kerri shrugged. "He is not sure. But I did not ask about the prince. I asked about you."

Loren replied with a shrug of her own. "I do not know if it will work, but it is what we must try."

That only deepened Kerri's frown. She glanced all about, as though she expected to find Wojin's agents lurking nearby. "I am less optimistic. In all the time I have spent in Jun's household, I have learned one thing about senators: they all seek to increase their own power, no matter how much they have already. It is that exact attitude that led Wojin to rebel against his rightful king. I am leery of those who offer help for no reason."

"Yet Duris may have a very good reason," said Annis suddenly. Kerri and Loren both jumped and turned to the girl. Annis arched an eyebrow. "Yes, I heard you. By all accounts, and according to everything I have learned growing up, King Jun's rule has caused much coin to flow into the purses of his senators. Nowhere was that more true than in the kingdom's southeastern reaches, which have often borne the brunt of Jun's wars, but also benefited the most from his pillaging. With uncertainty in Danfon, and indeed across all of Dorsea's northern reaches, the south is now exposed, and it faces the wrath of neighbors who have no love for the kingdom. Furthermore, those kingdoms will now have the High King's blessing to pursue war, since Dorsea has joined the rebellion. Wojin would care little for any of this—he only wishes to strengthen his grip on the throne. Duris' homeland is threatened. Jun offers an end to that threat."

Kerri looked at Annis, studying her for a long moment as though appraising her. "That is a somewhat . . . cynical way of looking at things."

Annis shrugged. "Yet it is how our enemies view the situation," she said. "We cannot ignore that fact and expect to win in this little game."

Loren frowned. "How close are we, Kerri?"

"Not far now."

Indeed, they came to the warehouse soon after. The street was deserted, just as Yushan had thought it would be. Together the group filed around to the back of the building. There was a large iron lock on the door, but it broke after a few sharp blows from the butt of Uzo's spear. Loren went inside and inspected the place. It was nearly empty, with only a few crates scattered around. She returned to the others.

"It will do nicely," she said. "Kerri, go and fetch our friend."

Kerri nodded and left. Annis went with Gem to hide in a nearby alley, while Shiun and Uzo took up position near the warehouse, where they would watch from hiding places. Chet entered the warehouse with Loren.

While they waited, Loren found a small box and sat upon it, resting her back against a much larger crate. She indicated the other half of the box and raised an eyebrow at Chet. "You might as well sit," she said. "I think we have a little while to wait."

"I would rather stand," he said quietly. He began to pace back and forth, his steps quick. "I feel restless."

Loren eyed him carefully. "No one could blame you. Our situation is hardly free from peril."

He paused and smiled at her. "Yet you seem to be facing it easily enough."

Loren waved a hand expansively. "Long exposure has let me grow used to it."

"You said much the same thing before Yewamba." Chet's voice had gone quiet, and he stared at his boots. "I was terrified, then, too, but it is different now. I am not just afraid, I am . . . weary. And it is a weariness that does not leave me, no matter how long I sleep."

His words struck Loren's heart. She had noticed it, of course—the long hours he spent in bed, the ever-growing bags beneath his eyes. She could see it in the slow way he blinked, the way he jumped at sudden sounds. The way he recoiled from her touch.

"Chet," she said softly. "We have all seen much darkness. You more than most. I do not know how to make it any easier. But I do know that you need not feel guilty about it."

He looked up at her, his eyes glistening. But he smiled through it and shook his head with a sudden sniff. "Thank you. But even though you say that, I cannot rid myself of such a feeling."

She opened her mouth to answer, but a sudden knock came at the warehouse's back door. Loren shot to her feet and glanced at Chet. "You should hide yourself."

"No." He shook his head. "Let us get it over with. If they mean us harm, it will do me no good to hide in the shadows. They will find me regardless."

Loren nodded. Then she turned to the back door. "Come."

The door opened, and Loren's dreamsight struck her like a hammer blow.

Through the door stepped a woman she had seen before. Features sharp and severe, thin eyebrows and regal lips. Loren had seen her in the sewers below Danfon, and she had been a prisoner of Damaris and Gregor. Damaris had cut her throat.

But Loren had seen something like that before. Damaris had cut Chet's throat, too, in her dreams.

Was this woman—she must be Duris—was she a weremage? As Auntie had been? No, as *Niya* had been. It was Niya all along, not Auntie. No. Niya had *been* Auntie. Was Damaris a weremage as well? Who would cut Duris' throat, if not she?

"Loren!"

She was on her knees. Her shoulders heaved, and her breath came in ragged gasps. At the door of the warehouse, Duris stood in shock, looking down at Loren. Kerri dashed forwards from beside the noble-woman. She knelt at Loren's side and took her shoulder, putting a hand to her forehead.

"What is it?" she said. "Tell me what is happening."

Loren glanced up. Chet stood two paces away, hands raised as if he wished to go to her. But he held back, his fear keeping him from touching her.

"I . . ." said Loren. The words ended in a gasp. But then she forced her breathing to calm, and she got to her feet with Kerri's help. "I am fine. A . . . a spell. Nothing more."

"A spell of what?" said Kerri. Her voice was uncharacteristically sharp, and her eyes were hard as steel. "I cannot help you if you do not tell me what is wrong."

"I said I am fine," said Loren. She pushed Kerri away—but gently. Then she turned to Duris and forced a smile. "My apologies, Lady Fei. The road here has been long, and the city has not lacked in excitement since my arrival."

Duris studied her for a moment, one eyebrow raised. "Yes," she said slowly. "I have heard of your . . . performance in the city square. I cannot say that that was a wise course of action, but it has certainly had some effect on the people."

Loren was still light-headed, and her hands felt clammy. But she forced her smile to widen as she bowed. "I have never had much trouble attracting attention. Indeed, sometimes I attract more than I would wish."

Duris sighed. "I find that easy to believe." She stepped into the warehouse and closed the door softly behind her. As she came forwards, she glanced around. "Are there any guards nearby I should be worried about?"

"Why should you worry about them?" said Loren. "I thought you were here to offer your aid to King Jun."

"I am," said Duris. "And my aid will be hard to lend if someone shoots me with an arrow because I made some sudden movement towards you."

Loren cocked her head. "Then mayhap you should not make any sudden movements."

Duris gave an exasperated sigh. "I . . . I am loyal to King Jun, but I am not one for intrigue. I beg you not to bandy words, but to speak plainly. Is my aid welcome or not? I am nervous enough just being here."

That took Loren aback. She spread her hands disarmingly. "Let us speak plainly, then. I have guards nearby, yes, but you will not see them. They will not act to harm you unless they have a very good reason. They can tell when I am in danger, and they know that *you* are no great danger to me on your own."

But she remembered the words that Duris had spoken in her dream: *Never again will Jun sit the Dorsean throne.*

A long breath came rushing from Duris' mouth. "Very well. I am relieved to hear it, and I suggest we do our business quickly so that I may leave. You are, I presume, the Nightblade of the High King?"

"I am."

Duris took an eager step forwards. "And you swear your words are true? You have seen Jun? He is alive?"

"He is," said Loren. "And he is eager to learn how you may be of service."

Duris sagged. It looked as though relief had made her limbs suddenly weak. "Thank the sky. I understand, of course, that you cannot tell me where he is. I am no friend of Wojin's, but you have no way of knowing that. He must remain secret to remain safe."

"As you say," said Loren. "But as you and I have both said by now: let us get to the point. Why did you ask for this meeting, Lady Fei?"

Before she could answer, there came a knock at the warehouse door. Duris jumped and turned in a panic. But Loren held up a hand to calm her.

"Do not worry. That will be one of my agents. Kerri?"

Kerri hastened to the door and opened it. Gem poked his head inside and caught Loren's eye. He nodded.

"Excellent," said Loren. "Show her in."

Gem opened the door wider, and Annis stepped inside. Duris gave a start at that. Annis ignored her, striding across the warehouse to stand beside Loren. Gem followed close on her heels. Duris stared at the lot of them, her head tilted in confusion.

645

"Who is this?"

Annis bowed low. "I am Annis, of the family Yerrin," she said. "My mother is Damaris. You may know her as the merchant who has taken residence in the palace and pledged her service to Wojin."

Duris' skin very nearly went as pale as Loren's. "I . . . but you . . . I swear that I—"

Loren raised a hand to silence her. "Be calm. She does not serve her mother. I am an agent of the High King, remember? Annis is the same. We came to this city to capture her mother, not to help her."

But Duris hardly seemed reassured. She put a hand to her forehead and stumbled. Loren leaped forwards to take her arm and helped her to a sitting position on the same box where she herself had rested a moment before. Duris fanned herself with a hand.

"I . . . I apologize," she said. "I . . . the shock. I fear I am ill-suited for this sort of thing. And Damaris is . . ."

She trailed off, looking uncertainly up at Loren. Annis took a step forwards.

"Damaris is what?" said Annis.

"She has her claws in Wojin," said Duris. "He rules in name only. I and the other few senators here in the capital can see it, but we can do nothing. She disregards us entirely. I had thought—hoped—that Wojin might have some respect for the senate. He was one of us before he took the throne. But he ignores us at Damaris' urging. And she is ever wary of betrayal."

"She does not like being double-crossed," said Annis, raising her brow. "I can tell you that much."

Duris studied her. "I believe it. If . . . if she were to learn that I am here . . ." She covered her eyes with a hand. "Forgive me. As I said, I think I am ill-suited to this sort of thing."

"I was about to say the same thing," said Gem brightly. "What on earth prompted you to pursue this meeting, anyway, if you are so afraid of her?"

"Gem." Loren shoot him a look, and the boy subsided. But his words made Duris look up at them, and a fire burned in her gaze.

"She is a foreigner," said Duris, all weakness gone from her voice. "Dorsea is a proud kingdom. We do not serve at the will of outsiders."

Loren crouched before Duris, resting her arms across her knees. Her new clothes accommodated the motion easily. She hated to admit it, but she was growing quite fond of how smooth they felt on her skin.

"We have had enough shock and excitement for one day—or for many days, I think. Let us get on with this quickly, Lady Fei. What do you have to offer?"

"I . . ." Duris swallowed hard. "Well, I and many of the other senators like me, that is—we wish to help Jun retake his throne."

"His Grace hoped that that might be the case," said Annis. "Yet he was also somewhat reserved in his excitement. By his account, the two of you have never been especially close. In fact, you are just as closely related to Wojin."

Duris' breathing had returned to normal. Now she gave Loren a careful look. "From what I have heard about your speech in the square, you are a woman of Selvan. Is that right?"

Loren nodded slowly. "It is. Why?"

"You know, then, how the other kingdoms perceive Dorsea. Many of them see us as warmongers—and they are not wrong. Jun enjoys battle, and many in the senate are of the same mind. Yet that is primarily because of Wojin himself."

That gave them pause. Loren looked at Annis in surprise, but the girl only shrugged. "I had heard nothing of that."

Duris waved a hand. "Oh, Jun would be reluctant to admit it. Every king wishes to be seen as a strong leader, one who chooses their own path. And particularly here in Dorsea, our king wishes to be seen as the ultimate authority when it comes to war. Yet Wojin is far more warlike than Jun has ever been, and he coaxes the other senators to put pressure on Jun. When Jun commanded us to war—us in the southern states, I mean—he would never overextend his own forces. And he would never force the issue beyond wisdom, lest other kingdoms strike back. Even so, his wars cost many lives. That is why I came here in the first place—to urge him to pursue peace after the war on Dulmun."

"It is as I suspected," said Annis. "Now that Wojin is on the throne, you fear that things will be worse, not better."

Duris nodded. "It is not only a fear. I am certain of it. Wojin is concerned with northern politics now, of course. But after he has gathered his power, he will order the south to war again. But not just border skirmishes—a true war, a war of conquest against the other kingdoms. It is a war we have no hope of winning."

Loren wondered if that was true. Damaris served the Necromancer, and Dorsea now did the same. That dark wizard had clearly been plotting this rebellion for a long time, and their Shades were part of it. She doubted they would have started the war with no hope of victory. Now Loren wondered what other schemes were in place, what next would befall the nine kingdoms.

But she could say nothing of this to Duris, of course. She needed to secure the woman's support, not make her think that Wojin would soon have even more allies on his side. "King Jun thought much the same thing," she said. "But that leaves us with the same question, which you have not answered with any great exactitude. What, exactly, do you propose to do to help your rightful king?"

"We have very little in the way of exact plans yet," said Duris. "Indeed, until the day before yesterday, we did not know that Jun was still alive. But I—and those other nobles who feel the same as I do—what we do know, is that our plans must begin with the army. Wojin controls the capital's forces, but only a small portion of the soldiers are truly loyal to him. Another small portion will be loyal to Jun, once he reveals himself. They must hide their hearts now, but they wait for the right moment to reveal themselves. My daughter is one such."

Loren drew back, surprised. "Your daughter?"

Duris lifted her chin, fierce pride shining in her eyes. "Yes. She is Morana, of the family Fei. She is a captain within the palace. Right now she serves Wojin, for she believes that is her duty. But if it was confirmed that Wojin is a liar and a murderer, and that King Jun is alive . . ."

But Annis frowned. "I am sure she is an honorable woman," she said carefully. "Yet I think Jun and Wojin must command an equal number of soldiers who are loyal to them. If anything, Wojin likely has the advantage, for his warriors must have killed many of Jun's when he took the throne."

"Yes," said Duris. "But both of their factions together are only a small part of the army. The rest of the soldiers serve the same master they have always served, the same master *most* soldiers serve—simple coin. Even if Jun were to reveal himself now, most of the army will be confused at best. They may even be swayed to Wojin's side in the end, since he is in command of the treasury."

"Then we seem to face an obstacle," said Loren. "What plans have you devised to overcome it?"

Duris shook her head. "None. But if you can solve the problem of Wojin's coin, I will continue to raise support among the other senators. They will be ready to act in Jun's favor when he reveals himself, and together we can cast Wojin from the throne."

Loren glanced at Annis, and the girl nodded. "Very well," said Loren. "I will return to His Grace with this news."

Duris stood. "Thank you, Nightblade. Forgive me for my moment of fright. I am glad to have met you, and I wish us both well."

"As do I," said Loren. She made no mention of her own moment of weakness. Hopefully Duris would forget all about it. She extended a hand, and Duris clasped her wrist. Then the noblewoman let herself out through the warehouse's rear door.

Loren turned to the rest of them. Annis gave a little smile and shrugged. "An army to persuade, and a treasury to pilfer. What could be simpler?"

"A great many things, I think," said Gem. "But who wants simple deeds? That is not what builds a legend like that of the Nightblade."

"Oh, be *silent,* Gem," said Loren, and she led them all from the warehouse.

TWENTY

THEY RETURNED TO JUN AND MADE THEIR REPORT. THE KING SEEMED heartened by the news, and he nodded thoughtfully when he heard what Duris had proposed. But Loren could not help a strong feeling of doubt. She could not fully rid herself of the memory of her dream, nor what Duris had said in it.

Never again will Jun sit the Dorsean throne.

Did Duris mean to betray them? Was she serving Damaris in truth? But no, in her dream, Damaris had killed the senator. Yet those who died in Loren's dreams did not always do so in life.

Jun seemed to sense her mood. "You seem troubled," he said. "More troubled than I would expect, for I think this meeting went very well indeed. What is it?"

"I . . ." Loren considered her words carefully. What could she tell him, in truth? "I am not entirely certain we can trust her."

Jun glanced between Jo and Senlin, but they only looked bemused. "I do not understand," said Jun.

"It seems suspect," said Loren. "Mayhap her offer is too good to be true. Call it a hunch if you like, but something feels wrong."

Jun's frown deepened. "Did she do something suspicious? Could you hear some hidden meaning in her words?"

Loren flushed. From the corner of her eye she could see Annis looking at her strangely. "It is nothing so precise, Your Grace. But I have a . . . a sense for people. I only ask that we proceed with caution."

"We will do that, of course," said Jun. "But for now, this is the only path we have. We must take it, or waste away here with inaction."

Loren bowed her head. "Of course, Your Grace."

How could she explain herself more clearly? There was no way to do so without telling Jun of her dreams, and she knew that would be a mistake. She realized suddenly that she had not told Annis, Gem, or Chet of the most recent vision. That would have to be remedied, as quickly as possible. Mayhap Annis could help her devise a way to convince Jun of the need for caution.

"It seems that our next task is clear, then," said Wyle from his armchair in the corner. "We need to empty your treasury, Your Grace."

"We had already thought that might be necessary," said Senlin. "My father knows as well as anyone that many of his soldiers serve him for pay."

Gem piped up. "But how to do it? I have stolen coins before, but I do not think all the kingdom's wealth is contained in a single purse." The boy had seated himself upon the floor about a pace away from Prince Senlin's chair. Loren had noted it with some surprise; Jo and the other guards made no mention of it, though they were hesitant to let Loren get near the king and prince.

"Indeed not," said Senlin. "Our treasury is sizeable—a building near as large as a warehouse, and filled with many treasures besides mere coin. Even if we could somehow remove all the coins—which would be a considerable enough feat—Wojin would yet possess a great deal of wealth. Many of the treasures are bulky, all are difficult to remove, and they could easily be sold in order to continue paying the army."

Jun said nothing, but sat pensively in his chair with his chin in one hand. Senlin watched him for a moment, seeming to expect him to speak. But the king said nothing.

"It seems that our problems are access and time," said Loren slowly. "Might I ask, Your Grace—do you have any alchemists who are loyal to you?"

Jun frowned at the question. "One served me, but he perished during Wojin's attack."

Loren looked to Gem. "Fetch Shiun. We may have to reach out to the Mystics here and see if they have an alchemist to help us."

The boy leaped up at once to obey, but Jo stopped him with a raised hand and leaned forwards. "I do not understand. Why do you want an alchemist? If you are thinking of storming the palace, you would do better to have a firemage or mindmage at your side. But I doubt even a wizard could help us here, unless they were uncommonly powerful."

Loren could not help a little smile. "My strength is not as a warrior, but as a thief," she said. "An alchemist might help us where a firemage cannot. If Wyle could lead us to the sewers beneath the treasury, an alchemist could tunnel up through the stone into the treasury itself. From there, with enough help, we could remove the treasure without anyone being the wiser. It would still take time, of course."

"That would not work," said Senlin flatly. "Forgive me, Nightblade, but you are hardly the first to think of such a scheme. The walls, ceiling, and floor of the treasury are all enchanted against such magic. Indeed, we even have guards posted in the sewers below the treasury to ensure no one can even make an attempt, and Wojin will have maintained those guards."

Blood flooded Loren's cheeks, and she ducked her head. "My pardon. I am less educated in ways of magic than I should be, it seems." She motioned Gem to sit again, and he sank to the floor with a dejected sigh.

"There are two things you can do to remove a man's wealth," said Wyle suddenly. His voice was filled with sudden eagerness, and Loren glanced at him. He leaned forwards in his chair now, hands on its arms, no longer slouching. "Did that man Xain ever tell you how we met, Nightblade?"

Loren arched an eyebrow. "He did not, though you hinted at it before. I gathered you did not part as friends."

Wyle snorted. "That we did not. I hired him and a riverboat captain to assist me with—" He paused suddenly, eying King Jun. "Well, with a certain business transaction. Yet when Xain discovered my aim, he misunderstood entirely, and he and the captain destroyed the goods I had intended to sell."

Annis' eyes flashed. Loren raised an eyebrow at her, but the girl held her peace for the moment. "I do not entirely understand," said Loren. "What are you saying?"

"If we cannot steal Wojin's gold—or, more properly, King Jun's gold, of course—we can destroy it."

That gave everyone in the room pause. Prince Senlin frowned in thought. "I do not see exactly how," he said slowly. "Even if we were to . . . to melt it somehow . . . Wojin could simply re-melt it and cast it into new coins."

Gem spoke quickly in Senlin's support. "And I do not see that it removes our earlier problem—namely, that there is a great *deal* of treasure. How could we hope to melt it all without alerting the guards?"

"We could burn it," said Annis. "We could burn it with magestones."

At the word *magestones*, the king and prince gasped. Wyle very suddenly looked as though he would rather be somewhere else.

"Do you mean to say that you are carrying those cursed stones?" growled Jo. His hand fell to the hilt of the blade at his hip.

"Of course not," said Annis smoothly. "Yet my mother may have some on hand."

Jun's eyes narrowed. "There have long been rumors that the family Yerrin traffics in magestones, but they have always denied them. Do you mean to say that it has been true all along?"

"I would never suggest such a thing," said Annis. "What wise family would condone it? Yet we all know that my mother has been sundered from the family, and I from her. Did you not know that was the reason?"

That gave them pause. "A different reason was given," said Senlin. "It was said that she aided the Shades in their assault on the Seat."

"Sometimes the High King cannot be entirely plain in her proclamations," said Annis. "Sometimes she must give a reason for her actions that is—not a falsehood, of course, but not the entire truth."

Loren's heart thundered in her breast. Annis walked on the edge of a knife. Revealing Damaris' involvement with magestones brought a dangerous amount of attention to all of them. If Jun learned that they had trafficked in the stones, or worse, learned that they still bore some, all their lives would be forfeit. Yet Annis seemed utterly calm.

The coin was cast. If they were to remain safe and avoid suspicion, Loren had to help. She nodded slowly, as though she had been considering Annis' words and had now come to a conclusion. "I think this is the best course, Your Grace. If we can steal Damaris' magestones and use them to destroy the treasury, we will accomplish two ends: we will remove Wojin's ability to pay your soldiers, and we will remove a great store of dangerous and illegal goods forbidden by the King's law."

The room went silent. Jo studied Loren and her friends with a stony expression, while Senlin looked to his father, gauging his reaction. But King Jun looked straight at Loren. She felt as if he was trying to read the truth in her face, and she was grateful that her upbringing had taught her to lie so well. Even Damaris had praised Loren's skill at telling falsehoods.

At last Jun nodded. "If you believe she has a store of those accursed stones, then I think there may be some merit to this plan."

Gem wore a wide grin. "Do I understand our plan aright? First steal magestones from Damaris, then use them to destroy the treasury?"

Loren matched his smile. "You must admit it is audacious."

"Audacious?" said Gem. "It is brilliant!"

"We would not even require very many," said Annis. "When magestones burn, they burn with darkfire. It will not only melt the gold, it will destroy it—and the fires will last until they have consumed everything they have touched. We will have to set the flames carefully to see that they do not spread too far, but once we start them, Wojin will have no way to put them out."

But Jun held up a hand, his brow furrowing. "Yet one detail still remains to be resolved. Namely, once I have reclaimed my throne, how can I expect to pay my soldiers any better than Wojin could?"

"We would be in just as precarious a position as Wojin is," said Senlin. "Damaris—or any other foe—could overthrow us just as easily as we now plan to overthrow him."

"When my friends and I enter the treasury, we shall bring packs with us," said Loren. "We will fill them with as much gold as we are able to carry. That can be your soldiers' pay, at least for a little while."

Jo's mouth twisted in a grimace. "You overestimate yourselves—or you underestimate the size of our army. Even if you took as much as you could carry—which would be so heavy that you could not escape afterwards—that would not last us a week."

But Annis only smiled as she turned to Wyle once more. "You have wealthy friends within the city."

"I do," said Wyle cautiously. "Many of them."

"Surely they have gold on hand. And I would wager they have a considerable amount of it."

Wyle's eyes grew shifty, and he did not reply.

Annis sighed and adopted a more careful tone. "*If* your friends happen to have gold on hand, and *if* they were to use it to supplement the king's ability to pay his soldiers for a time, I am *certain* His Grace would extend his forgiveness to your business associates."

Wyle raised an eyebrow. "Mayhap he would. Why do you speak to *me* of this, when it seems only to help my friends?"

Annis snorted. "Very well. And I am certain he would repay the gift as soon as he was able—with, mayhap, a bonus of two percent for the honest businessman who made it possible? As a reward for your exemplary assistance to the kingdom?"

The smuggler's eyes narrowed. "Five percent."

"You remember what happened the last time we bartered," said Annis. "Do not toy with me."

Wyle spread his hands with an easy smile. "What was it you said to me then? I accused you of haggling for scraps, and you told me you were only trying to maintain your reputation as a merchant's daughter. I am trying to maintain my standing as an honest businessman."

"You will wind up an honest corpse if you do not aid us," snarled Jo.

Wyle eyed him uneasily. "Three percent," he muttered.

"Done and done," said Annis. She relaxed into her chair and drummed her fingers on its arm, smiling.

"You seem to have bartered on my behalf without consulting me," said Jun, though his tone was not very severe. "You speak of repayment—yet how am I to repay Wyle? I will still have no coin in my treasury, and I cannot raise such a heavy tax so quickly. There is enough instability in the kingdom as it is."

To Loren's surprise, Prince Senlin leaned forwards to speak. "Yet you will have the throne, Father. That is the only thing that truly matters. You, unlike Wojin, are loyal to the High King. Once you have reclaimed your seat and rallied Dorsea to her side, I am sure she will compensate us for our loss. Especially if the Nightblade should speak on our behalf. It is a small price to pay for having the might of Dorsea on her side again."

King Jun sat silently for a long moment. He drummed his fingers on his chin, deep in thought, but he did not look at any of them. His gaze was far away, seeing something Loren could not. Mayhap he imagined the future, thinking through the advantages and disadvantages of such an arrangement. Frankly, Loren's head spun at even the limited discussion they had had here in this room. She did not think that hers was a mind for the politicking of the nine kingdoms, and once again she felt an enormous wave of gratitude for the presence of Annis by her side.

"Very well," said Jun at last. "We shall follow the plan of the daughter of Yerrin." He inclined his head towards her.

"Thank you, Your Grace," said Annis, standing to bow in response. Loren thought that was a bit of a joke—she was helping him, and not the other way around. Annis should have been the one to receive gratitude.

Jun excused himself from the room, taking Senlin with him. With a forlorn expression, Gem watched them go. Jo stood as well. But rather than leave, he fetched a map from a cabinet across the room and spread it on the floor between them. Loren studied it for a moment, but could make little sense of it without being able to read the words.

"This is the palace," said Jo. "This building here is the treasury." He pointed to a building drawn on the palace's northern side. "There is no entrance but the front door. There are windows, but they are very high. I do not know if you could sneak in that way."

"We will see when we get there," said Loren. "I am quite good at getting into places when people do not want me to."

"And how often have you had to sneak into a well-guarded palace?" said Jo.

Loren fixed him with a look. "I once strode into the middle of a mercenary army and stole a horse I liked, then set the rest of their mounts to stampede. This seems a small feat by comparison."

Jo grunted. "Very well. But we have not been in the palace for some time. If the Yerrins are not keeping their supplies of magestones in the treasury, we have no way of knowing where they would be."

"They will be close at hand," said Annis. "My mother would not risk letting the stones out of her sight."

Loren thought back to Cabrus. There, just before she had fled the city, she had infiltrated the apartment Damaris kept at one of the inns. There she had found the woman's magestones, all kept together in a great wooden chest with a lock. It had been one of her first thefts—though she had not stolen the stones at all, but had destroyed most of them and scattered the rest for others to find, bringing the King's law down on Damaris' head. That move had been meant to remove Damaris' threat forever, though of course things had not worked out that way.

"She will have them wherever she is staying," said Loren. "I am sure of it."

"Her apartments will likely be here." Jo tapped the map with a thick fingertip. "Those are the chambers where guests of state reside."

"Then that is where we will go first," said Loren. "Sneak into Damaris' apartments and steal as many magestones as we can, and then bring them to the treasury."

"It seems a bold plan indeed," said Jo. "Audacious, as you said."

"But you have never seen us work before," said Gem, grinning. "Or rather, you have never seen the Nightblade in action."

"Oh, leave *off*, Gem," said Loren.

But despite herself, she felt a growing excitement. When she had spoken against Wojin, she had seen Damaris' face. The merchant had been furious, yes. But she had also been surprised, and that surprise had been delicious to see. After weeks spent dodging Loren, predicting her every move, the merchant had finally been caught unawares. Loren's plan was too unpredictable, too unbelievable, for the merchant to have considered. This felt very much the same. Rather than try to draw Damaris out, Loren meant to go in. Why should Damaris expect them to come after her magestones? She knew Loren had no wizard by her side. And though she might know the treasury was one of their targets, she could not possibly guess that they would destroy its wealth rather than take it for themselves.

For the first time in a long time, Loren felt hope swell in her heart. This was going to work.

She was even able to ignore the voice in her mind. Duris' voice. *Never again will Jun sit the Dorsean throne.*

TWENTY-ONE

DAMARIS PACED HER APARTMENT. TWO PEWTER GOBLETS OF WINE SAT on a table against the wall, untouched. Gregor sat in a massive chair—it had been brought in especially for him, since all of the room's normal furnishings were far too small.

The bodyguard studied his mistress with worry. Damaris' steps were calm and measured. She was not breathing heavily, and there was no flush in her cheeks. But anyone who knew her would know that she was seething, and no one knew Damaris better than Gregor did.

"This means nothing," he said softly. "The girl's theatrics only make her an easier target. Someone must have seen where she went. My agents will find her."

"Will they?" snapped Damaris. "You have said that for days now. Yet we have discovered nothing."

"These things take time," said Gregor.

Damaris stopped short. She sucked in a deep breath and let it out slowly, then lifted a hand to her forehead. "I know they do. I know it, Gregor. Yet we have no time. That was never true before. All these long years together, we have been able to take as long as we wanted. Or at least I thought we could. But now with the war, and with the Necro-mancer—"

The candle on the table guttered. Gregor looked at the room's door. A gust of wind? Most likely. But a thin sheen of sweat beaded on his forehead.

"They understand," he said. "They have told us they understand. After all, the brutes were no more help against Loren than we have been. The Nec—the *Necromancer* is more tolerant than we once feared they would be."

Damaris smiled at him, as though she could sense his heart skip as he said the word. "You have never named them before."

Gregor's jaw worked. "Forgive me. It is a foolish superstition."

"You are many things, my friend, but you have never been foolish. Indeed, in fearing them, you show your wisdom." Damaris sighed and leaned on the back of the chair opposite Gregor. "It will be all right. We *will* find Loren, and King Jun as well."

She looked up, across the room and right into Loren's eyes. "Duris will tell us everything."

Loren jerked, suddenly aware of her own presence.

When had the dream taken her? She had watched the conversation without even realizing she was there. Now she whirled about, looking around the room. Where was she? She had not seen this place before.

But the door was right beside her, and Damaris and Gregor were across the room. She threw the door open and ran through it, pound-ing down the hallway outside.

Behind her, Gregor's voice rang out. "You cannot run from me, girl."

Dark below take you if I cannot, she thought, and kept going.

A hand seized the back of her collar and hauled her around.

Loren screamed, drawing her dagger in an instant. She slashed. But the man who had grabbed her stepped back, easily dodging the blow.

It was not Gregor. It was the man in black. He gave her a sardonic smile from beneath oddly glowing eyes.

"Sky above girl, control yourself. I am not here to kill you, so do not give me a reason to. Come."

He took her arm and hurried her along. Now she recognized where they were: the palace of Danfon. Loren knew these halls well enough by now. But he did not take her where she feared to go: the hallway, and the dining room, and the secret passage leading back to Gregor.

Instead he led her to the broad front hall, and then through the wide main doors to the courtyard outside.

The sun was high in the sky, and for a moment its light blinded Loren. When she could see again, she realized the man in black was leading her north. Soon she saw a small building ahead, and the man made right for it.

The treasury, she thought. *This is where the map showed it would be. But where are the guards?*

There were none at the front door, which opened easily under the man's hand. He led her inside. The torchlight struck her eyes, reflecting off gold, and for a moment it was as blinding as the sun had been. Senlin had not lied about the size of their hoard; before her, Loren saw more wealth than she had imagined could exist in all the world.

It struck her dumb for a moment, and she barely noticed as the man in black headed to the back of the room. But at last she followed him there. A large tapestry hung on the wall. Loren did not recognize the scene it depicted, but a man stood with hands raised to the sky. Storm clouds seemed to flow from his fingers, and they rained lightning and thunder down upon the foes who stood before him. With a start, she realized that it was the same man as the statue in the square, where she had spoken against Wojin before the crowd. His pose in the tapestry was almost the same as the statue's.

The man in black pulled the tapestry aside. Behind it was a blank stone wall.

Loren froze. "What . . .?" she said.

The man grinned at her. "My job is to know the secret ways no one else knows about."

He knelt and stuck a finger *into* the wall. For a moment Loren thought he must be an alchemist. But then she saw that there was a little nook there, cleverly hidden unless one looked for it carefully. The man's fingers disappeared inside, and then he pulled something. Loren heard a *click,* and two stones in the wall swung open. It revealed a passageway large enough to crawl through.

"In, girl," said the man. "They are coming."

"Who?" said Loren. But a sound answered her. She heard the door to the treasury burst open. Turning, she saw Kal rush in, Mystics at his heels. They saw her and screamed a battle cry as they charged.

Loren fell to hands and knees and crawled into the hole. But the man with the scars did not follow her. Instead, he swung the door shut behind her. Loren crawled on, listening. She expected to hear screams as the man died, the way Niya had inside the palace. But there was nothing—only the sound of men pounding uselessly on the stone outside.

The passageway went on for what seemed like forever. First it went down, and then it twisted left and right, and eventually it climbed again. Loren felt the walls as she went, but there was no way to turn left or right. And after a time, the passage ended.

She felt the wall with her hands. There was no knob, no lever. No way to get out. She began to panic. Loren did not fear tight spaces the way Annis did, but she was still trapped in the walls of the palace, and she had no idea how to get out.

Slowly, she drew three deep breaths. Then she remembered how the man had opened the passageway in the first place. Loren fumbled, trying and failing to keep her fingers steady.

At the top right corner of the wall before her, she found a chink in the stone. Her fingers sank inside, and she felt a lever. She pulled.

The wall swung open. Loren crawled through, and she was back in the palace again.

Quickly she rose to her feet and ran on. A moment before, she had known the layout of the palace, but now she was lost again, as though she had never been there before. So she kept running, guessing which way to turn every time she came to an intersection. Loren had grown up running through the forest, and her endurance had not lessened during all the long leagues she had traveled across Underrealm. But even still, eventually her legs and lungs began to burn. She was trapped here. She would never leave the palace. She—

Loren turned the corner and found herself before the dining hall. There it was, empty and clear. Beside her was the small iron door that led to the secret passageway.

"You know where you have to go, girl."

The voice made her spin. There was the man in black again. He leaned on the wall, his arms folded, his lips twisted in a smirk. But there, too, was Niya. She stood with hands at her sides, and her eyes were sad as they beheld Loren.

"It is the only way," said Niya, her voice soft.

"Darkness take you both," said Loren. "I am here for Damaris. Gregor is nothing, and he can stay in that room and rot for all I care."

Loren leaped into the dining hall. Niya cried out and reached for her. Even the man in black tried to seize her. But she slapped their hands away and ran. No one else moved to stop her. She reached the other end and flew through the open door. There, just a span away, was the open gate that led into the city. She was almost there. She was almost free.

An arrow pierced her chest.

Loren stumbled and fell. Her mind whirled back to Yewamba. She had been shot there, too. She remembered the shaft protruding from her chest, the fletching soft under her fingers.

No, not the fletching. Now the arrowhead was in front. It had slid straight through her ribs. A drop of her blood fell from its tip as she watched. She had been shot from behind.

Loren managed to roll on her back as she sank to the ground. She looked up. There was the balcony. The one where Gregor always wait-ed. In his hands was a massive longbow of yew, at least as long as Loren was tall. He wore an evil smile as he looked down at her.

All ways lead to Gregor.

She understood now. She understood. She could not escape Gre-gor. No matter what she did.

The dream released her.

Loren woke in the night, shivering and shaking. The terror of her dreams had begun to lessen, but this was different. This time the dream had not ended with Gregor moving towards her, looming in the dark-ness. This time he had killed her. She thought she had been clever to avoid him, but it all ended the same. She could not escape her fate.

Except that it was only a dream.

Annis lay peacefully on the other side of the bed. Loren shook her, and the girl's eyes snapped open. She sat up at once, drawing up the blanket. It was unnecessary—she and Loren both slept mostly clothed, for the girl was terribly modest.

"Loren?" she whispered. "What is it?"

"I have had a dream," she said. "Two, in fact, and I forgot to tell you of the other one. Let us fetch the others."

They went to the room that Chet and Gem shared. Uzo was on watch when they emerged, but if he thought it strange to see them awake, he made no remark. He only nodded as they passed, and then leaned back in his chair by the door of the common room. Together,

Annis and Loren woke Chet and Gem, and they gave the boys a moment to collect themselves. Then the girls sat at the foot of the bed while the boys sat up against the headboard, and Loren told them all that she had seen.

When they had finished, Gem sat frowning. "I . . . I do not understand," he said lamely.

"Nor do I," said Loren. "It seems my visions are not *meant* to be understood."

"Except when they are," said Chet quietly. "Why, then, do we bother ourselves with them?"

Loren looked at him sharply. "Would you rather I did not tell you? If I had warned you of the dreams I had in Ammon, we might not have gone to Yewamba."

Chet shook his head. "I would rather we ignored them entirely—and that means you as well. You *cannot* still think there is nothing odd about this, Loren. Whatever brought these visions on—whether it is the Elves, as we first guessed, or something else entirely—it is using you, not helping you. For weeks you saw nothing, and now you have had three visions in only a few days."

"Even if I am a tool in the hand of some greater power, I am being used to achieve the ends I wish to accomplish," said Loren. "Whatever brought the dreams *is* helping me, whether or not that is the intention."

"Oh?" said Chet. "What exactly has it helped you accomplish?"

Loren spread her hands. "We seek Damaris. The dreams have helped us find her."

"You seek to capture Damaris, not pursue her. And the dreams only show you just enough to keep you always nipping at her heels."

"That is better than losing her entirely."

"You can say that now, because you do not know the end of this road."

"Nor do you," said Loren. "Nor does anyone. It is just as likely as anything else that the dreams are leading us to the end we seek."

Chet dropped his gaze. "I think you are being drawn along on that hope. For our road has led us to several ends already, and we sought none of them."

Loren fell silent, for of course she had no answer to that. Gem and Annis looked uncomfortably at each other.

"Yet . . . yet it all must mean *something*," said Loren. "To ignore the dreams would be to give up. There must be a meaning within them. Or why would I continue to see the same thing, over and over again?"

"Mayhap the answer is not in what is the same, but what is different," said Gem slowly. "Things change from dream to dream. Might we look for clues there?"

"That still seems too plain," said Annis. "Never since we came to Danfon has Loren seen the mountains, as she did in Sidwan. Yet the mountains are not a very good clue."

"And I see Niya almost every time, no matter what I do," said Loren. "Yet she is dead. Or rather, Auntie is."

Chet's expression grew dark, and he turned away.

"One thing might be helpful, at least," said Annis. "You saw a secret entrance to the treasury. If it is there, that would help our plans immeasurably."

"If it is," said Loren. "But if it is not? We might be trapped, thinking there is a means of escape when none exists."

Annis sighed. "I suppose you are right. We cannot know what will help us until we are there, and then it may already be too late."

"I fear Duris will betray us," said Chet quietly. "What if she does? What if Damaris learns—or has already learned—about her meeting with us? What if Damaris knows about our way into and out of the city, as your dream suggests?"

"Then all our plans are for nothing," said Loren. She tugged at her hair. "But if that is the case, we should leave Danfon at once and never return. Our cause is hopeless."

Chet looked up eagerly, his eyes shining in the light of the room's lamp. "Would you do that?" he said.

Loren wondered the same thing. She had pledged herself to the High King. She had sworn to fulfill the duty assigned to her, and she had vowed to capture Damaris. Yet if their plans were doomed . . . if *she* was doomed . . . could she knowingly walk into death? She could not help the High King as a corpse. Mayhap it was wiser to retreat now, to return to Kal with her tail between her legs and seek his instruction.

Her grip tightened on her dagger. If she did that, Kal might punish her. But then? He would use her again, just as he had aimed to from the beginning. He would devise a plan, and he would issue orders. What would Loren do, then, if her dreams showed her that *those* orders would lead to her death as well? Would she run from them? Was that to be the rest of her life, fleeing one dark premonition after another?

Before she could give voice to the thought, Gem spoke up. "I . . . I would not leave," he said. "Not if it were my choice. I will follow you to whatever end, Loren. But I do not want to live the rest of my life in fear. We know your dreams have shown you lies. I think we should use your dreams when we can—but I think we must ignore them when they tell us to do the wrong thing. And fleeing this city—leaving Damaris to work her evil in Dorsea—I think that that would be the wrong thing."

Loren nodded slowly. "I think you are right. I do not know why these visions have come to me, and I do not even understand them more than half the time. But I cannot—I *will* not let them turn my life to one of fear. I am a servant of the High King. I am not one of her soldiers, but I am like one. I follow her orders and carry out her will. Every soldier marches to battle knowing that they may die. We could die now, tonight, betrayed by one of Yushan's servants. That is not enough to make me flee from Danfon. Neither are my visions. I will stay."

"And I," said Gem.

"And I," said Annis.

"I will stay with you, then," said Chet softly. She met his gaze. Until he said the words, she had not realized how much she feared it—that *this* would be the moment. *This* would be when he chose to leave her. And in fact, she could see the sadness in his eyes, see his own fear. He had been hopeful, for a moment. He had let himself believe that Loren might actually abandon her duty, might leave Dorsea to its fate. She could see it in him now. He was disappointed, even crestfallen.

Yet he would stay.

Her dreams were no visions of the future. She did not know what they were, but they were not that.

"Very well," whispered Loren. "Thank you. And now we must all go back to sleep, for tomorrow we rob a king."

TWENTY-TWO

THEY ROSE EARLY THE NEXT MORNING, AND THEY LEFT YUSHAN'S MANor before the sun had come up. Loren brought all her party along, save for Annis. Kerri came with them as before, a guide through the streets. Loren had come to feel grateful for the girl's presence. Danfon was still a strange city to her, and it felt reassuring to have someone along to whom the place was so familiar. And though the words they had had together were relatively few, Loren had come to greatly value Kerri's counsel. She almost wished the girl were coming with them into the palace, but that was far beyond her area of expertise.

Soon the walls loomed above them. One six paces in height bordered the outer courtyards. It was a magnificent structure, and could likely hold well against even a determined attack by enemy forces. But the wall was built of rough white stone, and Loren knew she and her friends could scale it easily.

The problem was that the streets around them were too crowded. No guards were on patrol, but five warriors scaling the palace wall would surely draw attention from passersby. Loren already felt a bit conspicuous out in public. She wore her black cloak to hide her new, distinctive clothing, but the cloak itself was beautifully made, and she thought she caught one or two sidelong glances from people walking past.

Once they had walked the perimeter, they ducked into a nearby alley. "We should wait a bit," said Kerri. "Soon most people will have arrived at their destinations—the marketplaces and other shops. There will be fewer curious eyes around then, and we should be able to find a moment when no one is around to see us."

"I agree," said Loren. "Chet, would you fetch us some water and bread? We may be waiting here a while."

Chet took some silver pennies and headed for the nearest inn. The rest of them settled down to wait. Gem sat on the ground against the wall, silent with his own thoughts. Shiun and Uzo took up position at either end of the alley, watching for any signs of danger. Two barrels sat side by side. Loren hopped up on one, and Kerri took the other.

For a moment, Kerri looked down the alley in the direction Chet had gone. "I have been meaning to ask—where did you all come from?"

Loren blinked at her. "I am from Selvan," she said. "Most of us are. Annis is . . . well, I suppose she is from the High King's Seat, though her family's home is in Feldemar."

Kerri shook her head at once. "No, I mean . . . how did you meet, is closer to the question. I know little enough about you all, but you are a forester, and Annis is a merchant child. Chet is . . . did I hear he was a hunter? And I do not know what to make of Gem. How did such a varied party come to join you?"

Loren chuckled. "That is a tale indeed. More than one, actually, and we do not have the time to tell them all now. Chet and I have known each other all our lives. I met Annis shortly after I left the woods where I was raised, and I met Gem a little while after that, in the city of Cabrus."

"Why did you and Chet leave the forest?"

"I . . ." Loren smiled and shook her head. "He did not leave with me. I left, and he left some months later. He went looking for me, in fact, and happened upon me in the city of Northwood." Her expression fell as she remembered it, and she went silent.

"Tales reached us of what happened at Northwood," said Kerri softly. "But I had not heard you played any part in that."

"Only by accident," said Loren. "The Shades—the ones who destroyed it—they were looking for me. And I lingered there too long, for I . . . I had lost someone, and I had also learned something . . . unpleasant. I spent too many days wandering the Birchwood, with Chet trying to lure me out of my sadness."

"You say he went there to look for you?" said Kerri. "Why?"

A small smile dusted Loren's lips. "Because he loved me. In truth, he had loved me for a long while before that. And after I left the forest, he was drawn out to find me again."

Kerri's eyes widened. "Oh, I . . . oh. I am sorry. I did not realize."

Loren's smile vanished. "You would have had little reason to. Things have not been well between us since . . . well, since before we came to Dorsea. Many things have happened to us in our travels together, and some were worse than others."

To Loren's surprise, Kerri looked down at her hands in a quiet fury. "That seems to be a common thread that wends its way through all of Underrealm in these days. It is why I grow frustrated that I cannot help."

Loren put a hand on her shoulder. "Yet you yourself said that we must accept the things we cannot change, the things we are blameless for. We can vow to ourselves that we will do better in the future, but that does not mean we must stew in the darkness now."

"How do you do that?" said Kerri. "How do you keep the sorrow away?"

Loren paused to think. She had wondered much the same thing, back in Northwood. She had sought comfort in Chet's company, but that had been little help. Only leaving the town had begun to lift her mood, even though that had been a dark enough day on its own. It seemed to her that taking action had been the best thing she could have done. That, and . . .

"Look at him," said Loren. She pointed at Gem. The boy was fiddling with a small knife from his boot. He flipped it back and forth across his fingers. It might have looked impressive that he did so without cutting himself, but Loren happened to know the blade was incredibly dull.

"Gem and Annis have been my solace through many dark times. Gem is always cheerfully arrogant—excessively so—and Annis always seeks to throw herself into whatever bit of work is before her, not to mention the fact that she has a brilliant mind. When I am unsure of what to do, or when I feel a dark mood coming over me, I only have to be around them, and they bring me out of it. And when they are frightened in turn, or mournful, I do my best to return the favor. Sometimes they want reassurance of safety or some plan of action. But most of the time it is enough simply to be with them, to tell a story and share a laugh. Alone, any one of us would likely have fallen into sorrow. But we all look after each other."

"Friends," said Kerri. "I had few enough of those, even before the city was in turmoil."

Loren smiled at her. "Well, you have some now."

Kerri returned her smile, and Loren had to look away to keep herself from blushing.

Chet soon returned, and they ate the bread and drank the water. Then they waited, huddled in their cloaks against the cold, while the street beyond their alley gradually cleared. Before the sun had long cleared the tops of the mountains, Loren poked her head out. There was hardly anyone about, and the few stragglers would soon be out of sight. She looked up at the wall. There were no guards patrolling, but only some standing guard in the towers. If they climbed the wall right beside a tower, they should be able to avoid detection.

She turned to the party. "It is time. Ready yourselves."

They stood, shaking off the snow that had dusted them while they sat. Once the street was clear, Loren led them across it. She climbed first. The wall was as easy to scale as she had thought it would be, and soon she scrabbled over the top. She fell to her knees on the other side of the ramparts.

The courtyard beyond was empty. She could hear the soldiers above her moving about the tower, but their gazes were turned up and outward. Loren did not doubt that the army was on alert since her appearance a few days ago, but clearly no one expected her to infiltrate the palace directly, for the guard seemed to be lax.

Loren leaned back over the ramparts and motioned to the others. One by one they came up after her—all but Kerri. She would remain behind, for she would be of little help once they were in the palace.

Using Jo's map, they had very carefully chosen the place to climb up. Here, a smaller wall joined the palace to the main outer wall, forming a barrier between the front and back halves of the courtyard. This little blockade was less than a pace wide, and not designed to be walked on, but if they were careful they could use it to reach the palace itself. Loren glanced up one last time to ensure the guards were looking outwards, not towards the palace, and then she led her party across it. She had to control her speed—it would not do to slip on the snow and fall into the courtyard. But they reached the palace without incident. Just above them was a balcony. Loren leaped up and seized the handrail, pulling herself atop it before helping the others make the climb. Once they were all up, Loren tried the door. It was unlocked.

"Wojin is arrogant," said Shiun once they had slipped inside. "This was almost easy."

"It is to be expected," said Loren. "He only lets his most trusted guards watch the palace, and those are very few."

"They could at least check the locks," said Uzo.

"What if it is a trap?" said Chet. "What if Damaris guessed this is our aim?"

That gave Loren pause. It seemed unlikely that Damaris could anticipate such a plan as quickly as they had come up with it. Yet their entry did seem almost too easy.

She shook herself. "We will be cautious," she said. "If we see the jaws of a trap closing around us, we run. But we will carry out our mission. Let us go."

They had entered the palace very close to the apartments where they guessed Damaris would be. The hallway outside their room was empty, and Loren turned right, creeping down it. She feared that at any moment, she might recognize a location from her dreams. That could be disastrous, if the dreamsight struck her as it had when she met Duris. But nothing happened, and soon they had reached the last corner before the apartments. Loren peeked around it. There were two guards there, dark of skin and wearing green clothing. Yerrins.

Loren ducked back out of sight. "We have the right place," she murmured. "I see two guards."

"Easy enough," said Shiun.

"Gem, go back to the last turn in the hall and keep watch. I do not think we can take them silently. If more soldiers come, we will need your warning."

Gem looked up in shock. He had already begun to draw his sword. "I thought I was supposed to fight!" he whispered.

Loren gave him a hard look.

He gave an exasperated sigh. "Very well." Quickly he ran back the way they had come.

At Loren's signal, they charged around the corner. She, Uzo, and Chet ran wide, hugging the left wall to give Shiun a clear shot. Her arrow sank into the thigh of one guard, who grunted as she went down.

Before the nearer guard could draw his sword, Uzo was there. The butt of his spear cracked the man in his forehead. Finally, Chet pounced on the second guard. He struck her senseless with his staff—but not before a defiant yell burst from her lips.

"Well, someone will have heard that," said Uzo evenly.

"Then let us be quick," said Shiun, running up behind them.

Loren opened the door and leaped inside, one of her knives held before her. For a heart-stopping moment, she feared to find herself in the room from her dreams. But it was not the same room, and Gregor was nowhere to be seen. For just a moment, relief washed through her.

Then she saw the figure in the chair. It faced the window, and the sunlight cast it in silhouette. But Loren could see that its hands were bound behind the chair. It did not move.

Loren straightened, her throat going dry. Behind her, Chet and the Mystics hesitated.

She knew what she would find when she turned the chair around. She had seen it in her dream already. Loren shook her head, forcing her thoughts back to the present.

"Uzo and Shiun . . . search for a chest. A lockbox. Search the cupboards if you must. Find the magestones."

They went to do as she had bid. Slowly, Loren approached the chair. Chet went with her but remained a half-step behind.

"Loren?"

She waved him off. Step by step, she came around the chair, finding exactly what she knew she would.

It was Duris. She had been tortured to death. In the end, her throat had been cut, just as Loren had seen in her dream. But it was obvious that she had been dying for a long, long time before that. Bruises covered her face, and one of her severe-looking eyes was almost swollen shut. There were other wounds that looked far more painful, cuts all over her body that left blood running down her dress to soak into the carpet. Loren shuddered as she realized it must have been done overnight—they had met with the senator only yesterday.

"Nightblade," said Shiun. She had approached while Loren was distracted. "The room is empty. There are no magestones here."

Nothing but the corpse, thought Loren. *Duris, dead, just as I saw in my dream. What else among my visions is fated to pass?*

"Loren—" said Chet.

"Damaris outwitted us," said Loren. "She learned somehow that Duris had met with us, and she plied her for information. That means . . ." She looked up, working it out. "That means she could have traced us back to our hiding place. Somehow."

Uzo's eyes widened. "This was not a trap for us. The guard here is light because the soldiers are out scouring the city to find us."

"Or they have found the others already," said Shiun.

Loren met Chet's gaze and saw the same fright in his eyes that must be in her own. "She could not have learned from Duris about Yushan's manor," he said. "Duris did not know. We took precautions."

"She knew about Duris before our meeting, and she followed us back from there," said Loren. "It is the only possible explanation—it is the only reason Damaris and Gregor would not be here. We need to leave, *now.*"

Footsteps pounded in the hallway outside. Uzo turned, hefting his spear, and Shiun drew an arrow. But they put up their weapons as Gem appeared in the doorway.

"Guards are coming," he said breathlessly.

"Time to go," said Loren. "Out of the palace, and then back to Yushan's home. We have to save the king."

They ran down the hall, back the way they had come. Loren heard the cries and bootsteps of soldiers in all directions. Just before they reached the room by which they had entered, they came upon four palace guards.

Loren's party launched themselves into the fray. She herself downed one guard with a punishing blow from the hilt of her dagger. The rest fell before they could recover from their surprise. Gem got his chance to fight, fending one off with desperate swings until Uzo could pierce the man with his spear. Loren winced as she saw the spearhead sink into the man's chest.

The hallway was clear again, and their door was only a few paces away.

"Quickly!" said Loren.

They leaped from the balcony to the barricade and ran along it. Guards in the tower were looking inward now, but there were only two. Shiun paused, shooting one in the throat. His companion fell to the ground, taking cover. That gave them the time they needed to reach the wall, and they heaved themselves over it. As soon as they reached the ground, Kerri waved them over to the alleyway. On her face was a look of stark terror.

"I heard the alarm and feared the worst," she said. "Were you successful?"

"No," said Loren tersely. "And King Jun is in danger. Take us back to Yushan's manor, and do not stop for anything."

TWENTY-THREE

By the time they arrived, the manor had already been attacked.

They paused a street away, surveying the place. Soldiers wearing palace uniforms swarmed in and out. But they did not move with any great hurry. Whatever fight they had found within Yushan's home, it was already over.

"We could try to sneak in," said Shiun. "Mayhap the walls can be climbed."

"If we attack quickly, we could fight our way through," said Uzo.

"No," said Loren. "Until they abandon Yushan's home, we cannot safely approach. We . . . we must find another place to hide. An inn, or . . ."

A boot scuffed on a cobblestone behind them. As one they turned, weapons out. But Loren froze when she saw Jo.

"Come with me," said the bodyguard. He had a bandage around his forehead, and blood stained the left side of it—a new scar to go with the larger one across his scalp. "His Grace is alive. We got him out in time."

Without a word he turned and headed off down the street. Loren motioned the others forwards to follow him and quickly stepped up beside Jo. "What of the others? Annis? Is Annis all right?"

"The Yerrin girl is with us, and His Excellency escaped," said Jo gruffly. "But Yushan . . . she fell." He bowed his head for a moment.

Loren's steps faltered, and she had to force herself to resume Jo's rushing pace. Yushan had taken them all in at great risk to herself, but she had gone further: she had shown them kindness and hospitality like few people Loren had met in her travels. It was only by her bravery that Jun had survived this long.

Then Loren realized that the area they were in looked familiar. She peered around, trying to place it. At last it came to her: they were near the warehouse where they had met with Duris.

"The warehouse . . ." said Loren. "Jo, it is not safe here. That is how Damaris found us in the first place."

"We guessed that," said Jo. "There was a guard nearby, watching the place to warn her master if we returned." His scowl deepened. "But I found her. And now she will deliver no warning."

Soon they found the warehouse, and Jo led them around to the back door. He knocked, and a guard opened it. Loren entered to find them all there: King Jun, sitting on a crate like it was his new throne, and Senlin at his side like always. But there, too, was Annis. She leaped up from where she had been sitting on the floor against a barrel.

"Loren!" she cried.

Loren leaped forwards, wrapping her arms around the girl. She said nothing, only holding her close for a long moment.

"I was afraid . . . I was afraid you would not return." Annis' voice was thick with tears.

"I always will," said Loren. "Are you all right? Were you hurt?"

Annis pulled away, shaking her head and swiping at her eyes. "No. We were able to get out in time. Some of Yushan's guards held them off while we made our escape." She turned to Gem. He stood back for a moment, unsure. Annis waved her hands impatiently. "Oh come *here*, you idiot." She dragged him into a hug.

"I am alive as well, though it pains me that you did not care enough to ask." Wyle's voice surprised Loren, and she looked up to see him waving from one of the room's corners. He gave her a wide smile—but Loren thought it looked somewhat forced.

Loren went to him. He stood, and she extended a hand to grip his wrist. "I am glad to see you whole."

"I am glad to be so," said Wyle. "And I suppose it is good as well that you made it back safely. Good business partners are hard enough to find."

She smiled and then left him to go to Jun. The king inclined his head gravely at her approach.

"Nightblade," he said. "Were you successful?"

"No, Your Grace," said Loren. "Damaris predicted our plan. We could not find the magestones, and when we realized you were in danger, we left."

Jun frowned. "You should have remained and carried out your mission. My soldiers saw me to safety, but now we will have to make another attempt on the treasury. It will be harder next time."

Loren shook her head. "This warehouse is not safe, Your Grace. It is a half-measure, and we must get you out of the city at once."

The king's face grew stern. "I have told you I will not leave my capital."

But Jo stepped forwards to stand beside Loren. "You must, Your Grace. My duty is to keep you safe, and I can no longer do so in Danfon. Finding Yushan was a stroke of luck. But she is gone now, and we have nowhere else to hide. The Nightblade is right—though I slew one guard, it is only a matter of time before more come."

"Then let me reveal myself," said Jun, standing suddenly. Jo and the other bodyguards dropped to one knee, though Loren remained standing. "The people will join me."

"They will not, Your Grace." Loren spoke flatly, keeping all anger from her voice, no matter how great a fool she thought the king was acting. "Not before Wojin musters his army—which he is paying, not you—to have you cut down. Some loyal soldiers may rally to your side, but they will die."

Jun opened his mouth as if to reply. But before he could, Senlin shot to his feet. "Listen to her, Father. You have made your play, and it was brave. It might even have worked. But Wojin knows you. He knows you will—forgive me—but you will use more bravery than wits when you fight him. He is counting on it. You must survive, or there is no hope for the kingdom."

The king stopped short, turning to look at his son. Loren saw his expression soften, and his eyes looked almost mournful. After a long moment he turned back to them. "Take my son," he said. "You can remove him to safety, even if I fail."

"You *will* fail," said Loren. "Forgive me for speaking so plainly, Your Grace, but I serve the High King, not you. It is vital to her war effort that you are alive and on her side. You have no army, and now that Duris has been caught and murdered, none of the senators will join you."

Jun turned to look at Senlin once more—and Loren saw the fight leave him all at once. He sat back down, seeming to sag on top of the box. But the moment of weakness passed. He straightened his back, lifting his head to regard her. Slowly, Jo and the other guards got back to their feet.

"Very well, Nightblade," he said. "I will yield to your counsel. The High King is my liege lord, and I will do what is best for her. And I will see my son to safety as well."

Loren sighed with relief, though she tried to hide it. "I am glad to hear it, Your Grace." She turned and beckoned Wyle forwards. "We need to get out of the city at once. Can you lead us?"

"Sky above, yes," said Wyle. "I only wish you had asked me sooner."

Loren nodded and turned to Jo. "Ready yourselves to leave. We will be out of the city before the day's end."

TWENTY-FOUR

It was a sorrowful and bedraggled party that followed Wyle into the sewers. There were only two royal guards left, aside from Jo, and that put their number at thirteen. Loren had traveled many lands with only her friends beside her, and so it should have felt like a large group. But they walked beneath a city surrounded by enemies, one of whom had an entire army at his command. Against so many, thirteen felt useless.

At least thirteen is a number of fortune, thought Loren. *Mayhap that is a good omen.* But she could not quite make herself believe it.

Soon Loren was as lost in the sewers as she had been on their way in. Every tunnel and intersection looked the same. Occasionally there was a short slope taking them up or down, but that was the only difference in the midst of their long, trudging walk. But Wyle clearly knew where he was going. The smuggler never paused, turning at once every time they came to a branching in the tunnels.

Kerri dropped back to walk beside Loren. "How can he know where we are?" she whispered. "Everything looks the same to me."

Loren shrugged. "He knows the place well, the same way you know the streets of the city."

"Yet the city is made up of buildings. They look different. Down here, it is just the same dreary stone walls over and over again."

"You may see it that way," said Loren. "But Wyle sees it differently. I come from a forest. If you were to visit it, you would likely think that every tree looks the same. But I knew every tree in the woods surrounding my home. And even when I passed beyond the places I knew by heart, I knew the signs to look for. Where moss grew on trees, and the way certain plants leaned to catch the light. But when I came to a city for the first time, I was hopelessly lost, because every building looked like every other."

Kerri nodded slowly. "I suppose I can see the truth of that."

Wyle spoke suddenly from ahead of them. "We are almost at the end. And forgive me for saying so, Your Grace, but not a moment too soon. I should like a very long rest after this is all over."

Jun did not deign to answer, but Loren smiled to herself. She could faintly hear a sound ahead of them. A murmuring, lapping noise. Running water. They were near the river.

Her dreamsight struck her, and her steps stumbled.

She had been near the river in her dream. When she had seen Damaris and Gregor, and Duris tied to the chair, dying. When she had heard Duris whisper the words: *Never again will Jun sit the Dorsean throne.*

Loren reached out, grasping, though she did not know what she was looking for. Her hand came down on Annis' arm, and she gripped it tight. The girl stopped and looked up at her in concern.

"What is it, Loren?"

"We are in danger," whispered Loren. "I . . . I think it is a trap."

Annis froze, looking down the tunnel. The others were a few paces ahead, and the gap was widening. Only Uzo was behind them, serving as a rearguard. He stopped short just behind Loren, brow furrowing.

"Nightblade?" he murmured. "Is everything all right?"

Loren looked back down the way they had come. "Have you . . . have you seen anything?"

Uzo's frown deepened. "Of course not. No one is behind us."

"I . . ."

Loren broke into a run, heading for the front of the group. Wyle was in the lead, with Jo beside him. The king and prince were just behind. They all stopped at the sound of her footsteps, turning in alarm.

"Nightblade?" said King Jun. "What is it?"

Before she could answer, Wojin's soldiers attacked.

Warriors in palace uniforms came charging from a side tunnel up ahead. They screamed a battle cry, and the sound echoed from the walls until it was deafening. It struck all the party into inaction, and they stood for a moment, dumbfounded as their foes approached.

All but Jo and Shiun. They leaped to the fore, weapons ready. Shiun caught Wyle by the collar and threw him backwards towards the others before she drew an arrow and fired. The shaft sped true, plunging into the chest of one of the soldiers. It pierced the chain, and the woman went down with a scream. Jo lifted his sword and met their enemies with a roar.

That broke the spell. Jun's other bodyguards mustered themselves and joined their commander with a shout. Thankfully the tunnel was narrow enough that the three of them could hold off the enemy fairly well, and even better once Uzo came forwards to aid them. The Mystic's spear was shorter than most, but it was longer than the swords of their enemies, and he used it to deadly effect, thrusting and withdrawing over and over again as his foes struggled to reach him.

But past the fighting, Loren could see a figure that towered over the palace guards. There was a light farther down the tunnel, and it put him in silhouette. There was no mistaking the breadth of his shoulders, the power in his arms.

The way he always loomed over me from the doorway in his chambers, thought Loren.

And even shrouded in darkness, she could see the hateful glint in his eyes.

Gregor was here.

Loren's limbs shook. The dreamsight left her nearly unable to move. But somehow she stumbled forwards, seizing King Jun's arm. He jumped at her touch.

"Your Grace." She could barely force the words out. "We must get you away."

"The way out is through them," he said. For the first time, she heard true fear in his voice. Now he was in the midst of a battle, not planning one from afar. But Loren could not take pleasure in his sudden terror, not now. Not while her friends' lives were in danger.

"We cannot get out that way," said Loren. "We must go back to the city."

Without waiting for him to answer, she dragged him away from the fighting. Jo and the others were being forced back slowly. Loren had a feeling that would happen much more quickly once Gregor finally reached the fray. For now, the giant seemed content to press forwards at a measured pace, taking his time.

Why is he not attacking? thought Loren. *He must see that I am escaping with the king.*

More cries sounded out. Not towards the fighting, but from behind them. Loren froze. From the tunnels leading back towards the city, Loren saw more palace soldiers come charging at her.

No.

They were surrounded. There would be no escape. Her dreams had been wrong all along—or she had misunderstood them. She would not fight Gregor within the palace. He was here for her now. All her decisions had led to him in the end.

The soldiers were coming. They were only a few paces away. Shiun had fallen back, placing herself between Loren and the approaching Yerrins. Gem was by her side, his sword held forth, terror in his eyes. Annis clung to Loren's arm.

And yet . . .

Her dreams had shown her more than just Gregor.

She looked around, seeking . . . something. Did she know this place? Had she seen it?

The man in black had taken her here. And once he had her here . . .

Yes. There was a small opening. It did not even look like another tunnel, just an alcove. But she had seen it before.

"To me!" she cried, putting every bit of her strength into it. For a moment it seemed that the fighting paused, and her friends glanced back at her. "To me!" she cried again, and dived into the alcove.

It opened up into a small side tunnel, just as Loren had known it would. She followed it, dragging Jun behind her, and he pulling Senlin. Behind, the others followed one by one. Loren glanced back, squinting to see in the dim light. Jo and one guard were the last to enter the tunnel. The other guard shoved his commander on and turned, holding the alcove against pursuit.

Loren pressed on. Soon the side tunnel opened into a wider one. It was clear, but Loren could still hear soldiers shouting. They would wrap around soon and find Loren again.

"We have to keep moving," she cried. Taking her own advice, she pulled Jun further down the tunnel. She thought she remembered it now . . . she only had to keep going this way until—

Bent grate. Left. She saw it, sticking out of the wall just as it had in her dream. She turned left and pressed down the tunnel.

"How do you know where we are?" said Jun.

"It is enough that I do," said Loren. "Do not stop."

Suddenly, footsteps. Too close. Loren turned—but not fast enough.

Gregor came charging from a side tunnel. Loren did not see any other Yerrin soldiers with him, but he did not need them.

One ham-sized fist crashed into Prince Senlin. The boy flew across the sewer, striking the wall opposite. He slumped to the ground.

Most of them cried out, but King Jun was loudest. Before Loren could react, he ripped his arm from her grip and attacked. He had no weapon, but then, Gregor had not drawn his own yet. Mayhap Jun thought he did not need one.

Gregor seized the king by the throat. His fingers wrapped all the way around the back of Jun's neck, and he squeezed.

Gem had fallen on his knees by Senlin's side, weeping. He lifted the boy up into his arms, trying to pull him out of the muck. But then Senlin coughed. Loren stared in amazement. The boy lived.

Jo cried out and attacked Gregor, who still held the king. Jo's sword came flashing down. But Gregor moved fast, faster than a blink, and drew his own weapon. It licked forth, parrying Jo's strike, and then Gregor's foot lashed out. It struck Jo in the chest, and Loren heard ribs crack. The bodyguard grunted as he fell on his back.

Shiun had moved to get a clear shot, and now she fired. The arrow pierced Gregor's arm through, but the giant did not even react.

"Stop!" cried Annis. "Gregor, stop! I command you!"

It was a desperate ploy, and it did not work. And now Gregor's sword was free.

He slammed Jun into the wall and plunged his blade into the king's chest. Such was the force of the blow that the sword pierced the stone wall behind him.

Jun jerked, and then his whole body went limp at once. Kerri screamed, the piercing echo of it rebounding from the stone walls in a chorus.

Loren found herself by Gem's side, though she had not remembered moving there. She was helping him up, helping Prince Senlin as well. She was pulling them back, away from the giant.

"Come, come, we must flee," she said. "We must flee."

Where was Chet? She saw him now—standing in support of Uzo,

but a step back, his limbs shaking. It seemed he might drop his staff at any moment. Uzo's spear was steady, however, as he advanced on Gregor. Shiun was behind him, nocking another arrow. She loosed it, but this time Gregor saw it coming. He dodged, and the shot went wide.

Gregor attacked again. Uzo expected him to use his sword to deflect the spear. Gregor caught the spear in one fist instead. His sword came from the other side, and it almost caught Uzo in the neck. But the spearman released his weapon and tumbled backwards. Shiun loosed another arrow. It hit Gregor's chest, but his armor repelled it.

Gregor flipped the spear around and threw it at her. Shiun dodged, but too slow. The spear struck her in the side. It did not run her through, but the sudden weight of it made her pitch forwards to the ground.

Sky above, no, thought Loren.

Her hand tightened on the handle of her dagger. Something coursed through her—not courage, not fear. Fury. She readied herself. Gregor was still distracted by Uzo and Chet. She could—

More battle cries sounded. The fury guttered in Loren's heart as she turned. More guards? Loren's could not even defeat Gregor on his own. If his soldiers had arrived to help him . . .

Dreamsight froze her in place as red cloaks flooded down the tunnel towards them.

Mystics.

Loren could hardly move. Her anger was gone, replaced by the terror of dreamsight. There was Kal, just as she had seen him, charging at the head of his soldiers. A rage was in their voices as well as their eyes, and they had drawn their swords.

But they were not charging at Loren, as they had in her dream. They scarcely seemed to notice her. They ran straight past her and attacked Gregor.

The giant was forced back step by step. In moments he had retreated down the same side tunnel from which he had appeared. Senlin was on his feet now, and Loren looked at him. She tried to ignore her own shaking hand.

"Your Excellency," she said. "Are you all right?"

"Yes," he said, shaking his head. "I was only stunned for a moment. I—"

His words choked off as he stared. Loren followed his gaze. There was his father, still slumped against the other side of the tunnel.

Loren stepped in front of him. "Your Excellency . . ."

"No," he whispered. "No. Father."

Loren tried to think what she could say, what words would convince him to move. But before she could, a rough hand seized her shoulder and hauled her around. She found herself face to face with Kal.

The grand chancellor's expression was a mask of carefully contained rage. Loren could sense it in the way his eyes flashed, the way his fingers squeezed down on her shoulder. His red cloak was wet in places, and Loren realized his fight had begun long before he found her little party here in the sewers.

"Girl," growled Kal. "Get your misfits out of here. Follow Jormund."

Jormund? thought Loren. And then the big man was there—tall and wide, though nowhere near so large as Gregor, the Mystic appeared from behind Kal as if by a spell. He gave her a brief smile, though there was a grimness to it that looked strange on his jovial face.

"Out of the sewers," said Kal. "Now." Then he turned and joined his Mystics in the fight. More screams told Loren that the rest of the palace guards had found them, and the sewers were now home to a pitched battle.

Senlin pressed forwards, trying to reach his father. But Loren and Gem held his arms, drawing him away. He fought them, but then Kerri swept in, and she took Senlin into her arms.

"Your Excellency," murmured Kerri. "He is dead. I am sorry, but you must go on. We must get you out of here."

Uzo and Chet joined them—and they had Shiun slung over their shoulders. At first Loren thought someone had pulled Uzo's spear from her, but then she saw wood protruding from the wound. It must have broken when she fell. Chet's face was Elf-white, and his eyes were skittish.

"Jo?" said Loren.

Uzo glanced back. "I did not see him."

"Go to him," grunted Shiun. Her gaze drifted, going here and there. Loren thought she must be in shock. "I am useless anyway. Leave me here. One of the others can haul me out."

"Stop talking," said Loren, more sharply than she had intended. "We are not leaving you here. Jormund, go find the king's bodyguard. If he is alive, we need to bring him."

Jormund seemed a bit taken aback, but after a moment he went to do what she said. Shiun laughed, though her eyes still wandered. "Good. Good commander."

"Save your breath," said Loren.

Jormund soon reappeared. Jo was breathing, but unconscious, and Jormund had lifted the bodyguard over one shoulder. Now, he and a squadron of eight more Mystics escorted Loren and her friends through the sewers. They pressed on the way Loren had been leading them before the attack. Soon enough, she saw a bronze plate set in the ceiling.

Bronze plate. Right.

"Turn right," she said.

Wyle frowned. "That way does not lead to—"

"I said right," Loren said. She pressed on, ignoring the smuggler. The rest of them followed her after only a moment, with Gem and Annis giving her odd looks.

But Chet was not looking at anything at all. Loren was growing worried. He seemed on the verge of collapse.

"Let me take her," she said. She lifted Shiun's arm from Chet's shoulders and draped it across her own. Chet did not even try to argue, but only followed along, mute.

Soon they reached the door that Loren knew she would find. Jormund set Jo down and rammed his powerful shoulder against the door, but it did not budge.

"You will need my help," Loren said quietly. After all, the man in black had needed it, in her dream. "Gem."

The boy had been walking with Prince Senlin, consoling him. But he came to take Shiun's arm as Loren helped Jormund with the door. It opened, and Loren was struck by the smell of sweet, fresh air.

"It is a good thing you learned the sewers while you were here," grunted Jormund. "We would have had another fight if we had gone the way I planned."

"A good thing indeed," said Loren. She did not meet his eyes as she led the party back into Danfon.

TWENTY-FIVE

LOREN'S PARTY HURRIED THROUGH THE CITY, FOLLOWING JORMUND'S directions. Now that they were out of immediate danger, Loren found herself wondering at the man's presence. She had no idea how Kal had found them there beneath the city, but she was even more confused that he would bring Jormund with him. The large Mystic had been in Loren's party when she searched for Damaris in the kingdom of Feldemar, and she had sent him back to Kal with, in essence, a message that she was disobeying orders. She had half expected Kal to station Jormund in some remote outpost in an outland kingdom, certainly not to bring him along on a rescue mission.

But there was no time for a reunion now, and Loren doubted their meeting would have held much cheer in any case. King Jun was dead. They had managed to rescue Senlin, but this was still a disastrous blow. The renewed purpose she had found in Danfon seemed to have fled. What were they doing here? What *could* they do? The city seemed lost, and now they could not escape it. The terror of their situation wrapped around her like a shroud, threatening to choke her.

The others seemed to feel the same, but Chet was taking it harder than any of them. As they walked, he kept looking wildly in every direction. At any sudden sound, he jumped. The rest of them were trying to maintain at least some semblance of discretion—though that was hard with their wounds and the filth from the sewer that still covered them. But Chet was like a signal fire to any observer that something was wrong.

"Chet," said Loren quietly. "You must calm yourself. You will draw too much attention."

He did not answer. She was not certain he had heard her.

After what felt like an eternity, Jormund stopped outside a tavern. There was a door in the side, and he opened it to reveal a short staircase leading down to the cellar. Loren and Uzo hauled Shiun down the steps behind him. There were many more Mystics below, and several of them came forwards to help, pulling Shiun away from Loren and Uzo to help her.

"Chet!"

The panic in Annis' voice made Loren's heart skip, and she whirled as she heard a body hit the floorboards. Chet sat against the wall, hands balled to fists in front of his face. Loren fell to her knees beside him.

"Chet? What is it?" she said, her words fast with fear. "Were you wounded?"

She tried to pry his arms away so she could see if he was bleeding anywhere. But Chet shrieked and drew away.

"Do not touch me!"

Loren fell back on her rear, hands raised. Her eyes smarted as tears sprang into them. "I am sorry!" she said quickly. "I am sorry. I—are you hurt?"

It was as if he could not hear her. He took deep, heaving breaths, his chest rising and falling like ocean waves. Suddenly he turned and vomited on the floor.

"Here," said Gem. The boy knelt by Chet, pounding him on the back. Chet groaned and heaved again, but nothing came out. "Here, you are all right." Gem spoke softly, gently. It reminded Loren of the sewers of Cabrus, where he had used soothing words with Annis, trying to coax her out of her fear. He stroked Chet's back gently.

"Get up, girl."

Kal's growl drew Loren back to herself, and she shot to her feet. The grand chancellor stood before her, though she had not heard him enter. She was a few fingers taller than he, but she did not feel it now.

His eyes blazed with fury, and their long flight since the sewers had not quenched his rage in the least. His nostrils flared in and out with each breath. She half expected him to spit in her eye.

"I have had it far past the bounds of patience with you," he said. "Darkness take the first day you came to Ammon. If I had known what a fool—what an incomprehensible *idiot* the High King had sent me, I would have sent you back to the Seat on the first available ship. You spurned my orders to hunt Rogan, you pursued Damaris—and then *lost* her—and now an entire kingdom has joined the rebellion because of you."

Shame had flooded Loren from the moment she saw Kal. She had been living with it since even before they came to Dorsea, when she chased Damaris across the kingdom of Feldemar. And during all their pursuit, she had shoved that shame away, thinking that she could assuage it if she could only complete her mission before Kal found her, as he must surely mean to do. But she had failed, and now he was here. Yet even in the depths of her embarrassment, anger rose in her breast at his words now.

"That was not my doing," she found herself saying, almost before she could think to form the words. "Damaris clearly set this in motion a long time—"

"Be! Silent!" he roared, loud enough to shake the walls.

And Loren obeyed. His was the voice of a battlefield commander, and it held incredible power when he was this close. Her legs grew so weak that she was surprised she could still stand.

"Do you think me a fool? I know the Dorsean rebellion was not undertaken overnight. Indeed, I heard rumors months ago that such an action might be afoot. Do you want to know why Damaris thought she could pull it off?"

Loren did not answer. She did not trust herself to.

"Because the Mystics left Danfon. The moment I learned you had come into Dorsea in pursuit of Damaris, I sent word to the grand chancellor of the Mystics in this kingdom. She pulled her soldiers out of the capital to find you and Damaris both. But that was just the opening the merchant needed." Now he *did* spit, a fat glob of phlegm that splashed on the floor next to her boot. "The High King made a mistake the day she let you enter her service, but no greater than mine in ever believing you were worthy of the honor."

Tears had already been in Loren's eyes. Now she could no longer restrain them. But she kept her face calm. Her lip did not tremble, and she did not sob. Thin drops merely leaked from the corners of her eyes, one at a time, racing to lay little tracks down her cheeks.

She still could not bring herself to speak, and so it was with great relief that she heard Annis answer instead. "I do not know that that is the case, Grand Chancellor," she said slowly. "I know the Mystic force that was once in this city. They would not have been significant enough to deter—"

"*You* may shut your mouth as well," said Kal. He stepped past Loren, dismissing her as he went to Annis. Now he *did* loom, for he was taller than the girl, but Annis kept her back straight and did not cower. "I knew from the moment I met her that Loren was a naive thing, but I thought you had at least some glimmer of intelligence. Indeed, when I allowed you to go with her, I thought you might have some positive influence upon her. I suppose I should have known that it would be the other way around."

The room grew deadly quiet. Annis' eyes sharpened. Not for the first time in recent days, Loren thought she looked strikingly like her mother. "I told you this in Ammon," she said in an icy voice. "But you have never *let* me do anything, Kal. I have merely, on occasion, deigned to assist you in your efforts—but then, I thought you were an honorable man. I am less convinced of that, now."

"For all the good your help has done us," said Kal. "If we gained any advantage by your advice, it is lost. We managed one step forwards, but now we have taken two steps back."

"Some very pretty dances begin that way," said Gem.

The boy's mouth shut with a *click* of his teeth, his face going pale and his eyes widening. Quick as a landslide, Kal whirled on Gem and snatched him up by the tunic. Loren stepped forwards to pull him away.

"That is enough!" cried Prince Senlin.

Kal paused. The prince came from where he had stood in the corner. He wore a look of fury to match Kal's own, though his stance was a bit more composed.

"Unhand him at once, Grand Chancellor. You have made your point and more. But if it were not for the Nightblade, I would surely be dead, and Wojin's grip on Dorsea tighter than it is already. Whatever the Nightblade did before she and hers came to the capital is none of my business. But you are all in my kingdom now, and I am its rightful ruler. They serve me well—as they served my father—and they have my favor. If you care about restoring order and righting what wrongs have been done, you would do well to focus on that and stop this pointless ranting. You may think it does some good, but I am more inclined to believe it is only for your own pleasure."

Gem stared at the prince with wide and worshipful eyes. Everyone else in the room had gone still. Loren noticed Uzo looking at her, and the spearman arched an eyebrow. Loren wondered if Kal would dare to turn his ire upon the prince—the king now, she supposed.

After a long, scowling silence, Kal finally turned away. "Very well, Your Grace," he muttered. But his turn only made him face Loren again. She stiffened. Kal thrust a finger at her, and though his voice returned to some semblance of normalcy, she could hear the barely-contained fury lurking beneath it. "You are to take no action—not even the most insignificant—without telling me first. Anything more consequential than voiding your bowels requires my explicit approval. If you test me, I will pack you in a crate with straw and *ship* you back to the Seat to answer to the High King herself. You will do nothing but what I tell you, and you will do *that* the moment the order passes my lips."

Loren felt a twisting, evil feeling inside her. She recognized the tone of Kal's voice: one full of threats both explicit and implicit, promising greater harm than he would willingly speak of in front of so many witnesses. It was the same tone her father had taken with her for most of her life, and she felt a part of herself closing off, just as she had with him.

But Loren was not the same girl who had left the Birchwood nearly a year ago. She felt a sense of rebellion in her heart that she had never been able to muster with her father. So while her expression grew neutral and her hands went entirely still, her heartbeat thudded louder in her ears, and she felt a burning desire to get away from this man, to disobey him. To defy him.

She said only, "It will be my pleasure to do as you command, Grand Chancellor."

Kal studied her eyes for a moment. What he saw there must have satisfied him, if it did not entirely please him, for he nodded with a grunt. "Very well," he said. "Tell me everything you know—all that has taken place since you came to Dorsea, and especially what you have done here in the capital."

Loren glanced at Annis. The girl understood at once and stood beside her to help deliver the report. Together they gave a full account of all that had happened on their long road since Dahab.

For his part, Kal listened and did not interrupt, for which Loren was grateful. It made it easier to maintain the veneer of courtesy that had settled over her. She did not trust the anger in her heart. In one way she welcomed it, for it was a more powerful feeling than the weakness she had always felt in the presence of her parents. But she feared that if she unleashed it, it would come out in a storm that might irrevocably damage her already-tenuous relations with the Mystic and the precarious position of power she held.

When they caught him up to the present moment, Kal stood for a time, pulling his long beard in thought. Loren and Annis glanced briefly at each other.

"Our objective seems clear," said Kal at last. "We must restore Prince Senlin to the throne, and as quickly as possible."

"Very well," said Loren. They had intended to flee the city, but Kal's objective seemed far more reasonable now that they had the Mystics' strength of arms. "How shall we do it?"

Kal's scowl returned. "I shall determine that. And I shall call upon you if—*if*—I decide I require your help. In the meantime, you and your friends have quarters here. Go to them, and do not leave for any reason. And someone clean up her lover's sick before it stinks the whole place up beyond hope of cleansing."

Loren very nearly struck him. But she forced herself to remain civil, for a moment longer at least. "As you wish, Grand Chancellor."

She motioned to Gem, who helped Chet rise, and together with Annis, Kerri, and Wyle, they left the basement.

TWENTY-SIX

THEY HAD BEEN GIVEN TWO ROOMS, WITH NOT QUITE ENOUGH BEDS between them. Loren led them all into one, but Wyle excused himself to the other, claiming he needed a moment to recover from their flight and their battle.

Chet took little note of Wyle's departure and collapsed on one of the beds. He rolled away from the others to face the wall, his arms wrapped around himself and his legs curled up. The rest of them sat, morose, in a circle in the room's opposite corner. None of them looked at each other, but only stared at the floor. Kerri was the least downcast among them, but even she seemed subdued, a far cry from her usual self. At last she seemed to muster some bit of humor, for she looked up with a little smirk.

"That Kal certainly seems a pleasant fellow."

Loren barely managed a snort. Gem picked at the threads of his trousers with a fingernail.

"Yes, mayhap that was an ill-timed quip," mumbled Kerri.

"I am stifled in this room," said Loren. "I need to get some air." She got to her feet.

Annis looked up at once. "I am not certain that that is a good idea," she said carefully.

"Because of Kal?" said Loren. "I could not care less what he thinks."

But she could not stop herself from thoughts of her father. Always she had been quiet and compliant when he was nearby, when he was within striking distance. Rebellious thoughts had only come when he left her alone. Her current mood was far too similar, and it left a bitter taste of self-loathing in the back of her throat.

I am not the same girl who left the Birchwood, she told herself. *Kal will discover that, and soon.*

"You . . . at least you should not go alone," said Annis.

Loren expected Gem to volunteer. But to her surprise, Kerri spoke up before the boy could. "I will accompany her," she said. "I could use a moment's fresh air as well, especially after those sewers."

She rose to her feet. Loren gave her a grateful nod, which Kerri answered with a smile before following her out of the room.

They were on the ground floor of the inn. The hallway to their left led to the stairway down to the basement, and beyond that it bent around to reach the common room. But to the right, it ran to the inn's back door. Apparently the innkeeper, whom Loren had not yet met, was some contact of the Mystics. She turned left and led Kerri to the back door, and was pleasantly surprised to find Uzo there.

"Uzo?" said Loren. "I am surprised to find you on guard duty."

"Certainly you did not expect me to be resting," said Uzo, giving her a little smile.

"I half thought you might be imprisoned," said Loren. "Kal may not know exactly how to deal with me, but you are one of his soldiers. He can punish you how he sees fit."

"Yet I was only following orders," said Uzo. "Or at least, that is how the grand chancellor sees it. It does not do for a commander to punish his men for following the order of their officers."

"I suppose not," said Loren. She dropped her voice. "How is Shi-un?"

"She is as well as can be expected," said Uzo. "Healers are tending to her, and she will survive."

"Good," said Loren, relief flooding through her. She could not have borne it if she had gotten the woman killed. "Now, if you please, let us out."

Uzo paused for a long moment, his mouth twisting. "Are you performing some errand for the grand chancellor? Because he told me that no one was to leave the tavern this way—particularly not you."

Loren's hands went to her hips. "I wonder: did Kal explicitly remove you from my command?"

"I—" Uzo froze, and then his lips split in a broad grin. "I suppose he never did, at that."

"Then you had better let me through. In fact, I *order* you to do so. After all, a commander wants his soldiers to follow the orders of their officers, does he not?"

Uzo looked towards the ceiling, hiding a smile. "So I have heard it said." He opened the door and stepped aside. Loren gave him a grateful nod and left, closely followed by Kerri.

Beyond the door was the inn's back alley. It held a large rack of barrels on their sides, several rows high. They likely contained ale, and there was a lowering mechanism to remove them when the innkeeper needed them. Loren began to climb the rack towards the roof. Kerri paused for a moment, looking up at her with arms folded.

"You are overly fond of rooftops, I feel," she groused.

"They are a wonderful place to get fresh air," said Loren. "And that is what we came for, is it not? Come on."

Kerri grumbled, but she followed Loren up. Soon they sat on the edge of the inn's red tile roof, their feet hanging off into the empty air. It was nearly sundown, and the sky was a brilliant orange above them. Night's chill had not yet come, and the air was quite pleasant for winter. Loren tilted her head back, breathing deep of the crisp, fresh breeze. A part of her realized that the rooftop was exposed, but the far greater part of her did not care. She would not remain cooped up in an inn where, even when he was not present, Kal loomed over her shoulder.

Silence hung between the two of them as they watched the sun lower itself towards the mountains. In the end, Kerri broke the quiet, speaking carefully.

"I would guess that you do not feel particularly proud of yourself right now."

Loren snorted. She thought of Kal's accusations—that Damaris had escaped because of her, and that her actions had inadvertently led to Dorsea's capitulation. She was not entirely sure she believed it, but then again, she had long ago accepted that such politics were far beyond her scope.

"Not exactly," she said at last.

"You should," said Kerri. "Kal is wrong."

Slowly Loren shook her head. "I do not think so. He may have . . . overreacted. That has always been his way. But my actions were far from perfect."

Kerri turned to her, and she did not move until Loren at last turned to meet her gaze. "And do you think *he* is perfect? That he has never made an error, that he does not still make them even today? Everyone makes mistakes. Even if he *is* right—which I do not think he is—then he is at least complicit in your actions. If perfection is the goal, everyone is a failure."

Loren held Kerri's gaze for a moment, studying her dark brown eyes. It was Loren who turned away first. "Some failures are greater than others."

Kerri let those words hang for a moment. When she spoke, it was not to argue. "My parents were healers. When I was growing up, I saw them tend to others. They would not refuse care to anyone, and countless souls came to us for poultices, to have wounds sewn shut or bones set. I told you already that I was sick of the way Jun began so many wars. Part of the reason was that I would have to see my parents face his casualties. True, we were always far from the battlefront. But some soldiers returned with lingering wounds, and other injuries were related to the war effort—those who made weapons or constructs of war.

"After a time, I began to feel that my parents were somehow to blame, at least in part. They never did anything to prevent the wars, though I suppose it was mad to think that they could. But even in doing their duty, they would heal people who would only go back out to join the war again. But in the end I realized they had learned a lesson a long time ago, a lesson that I myself would not learn until later. It is the most important lesson of a healer, and it is something I have tried to keep in mind as I practice the art of the apothecary."

Kerri fell silent. The air was growing colder, and she rubbed her hands together to warm them. Loren knew it for a cheap talespinner's trick, but she could not help a smirk and a snort.

"Oh, go on," she said. "What is the lesson?"

Kerri smiled at her, but it was tinged with sadness. "Everyone makes mistakes, and sometimes grave ones. But the people who do the most good in life are the ones who keep trying—not in penance for what they have done wrong, but because they wanted to do the right thing in the first place. Penance is no worthy goal, not truly. Misdeeds are inevitable, but if we only try to correct them, we forget all the good we can do in life. I have only known you a short while, and I do not know what you did before you came to Danfon. But from what I have seen, you always do your best, and you fail less often than you succeed. Kal may try to pretend that he is better than you, but if he does, he is a liar."

She fell silent, and this time Loren did not prod her to continue. Kerri's words echoed in her mind, a gentle counterargument to the thoughts she had been plagued with ever since Yewamba.

She did not know if she agreed with the girl. After all, though Kerri might be the same age as Loren, she had not seen the things Loren had. It was hard to feel that she was doing the right thing when the nine kingdoms only seemed to slip further and further into chaos with every action.

Loren looked up at the mountains again, taking a deep breath and releasing it slowly. Then she pushed herself up from the roof.

"Come," she said. "We had better leave. Kal might come to fetch us from our room, and if he finds me gone, he may have a conniption."

Kerri snickered. "I know a medicine for that." But she followed Loren down to the ground.

TWENTY-SEVEN

THEY SLEPT FITFULLY THAT NIGHT. THE DAY'S BATTLE HAD PASSED, BUT it had left its mark on all of them. Though she did not dream, Loren shot awake more than once, thinking she heard the clash of steel in a sewer tunnel. Other times she woke at the sound of others stirring, coming suddenly awake with sharp cries. She heard the same thing through the wall in the next room, where Chet, Gem, and Wyle slept.

When morning finally came, Mystics brought them food to break their fast. Loren ate sparingly, not only because the food was much poorer than it had been in Yushan's manor, but also because her appetite had waned. She tried not to wonder if Kal would call upon her that day. If she had her way, she would have wasted no thought on the grand chancellor at all.

After choking down all the food she could, she got up and went to the next room. The others were all awake—even Gem, to her surprise. He and Wyle sat on the floor, eating their own meal, though they looked little more interested in it than Loren had been. But Chet was still on his bed, and Loren did not think he had touched his plate. He sat leaning against the wall, hands clasped between his knees. He looked up at Loren as she entered, his eyes like those of a corpse.

"Wyle, Gem," she said quietly. "Might you leave us alone for a moment?"

Gem glanced up at her, confused. But Wyle, bless him, did not hesitate. He rose, beckoning for Gem to follow. As they left, Wyle gave her a reassuring nod. But she scarcely saw it, for she never took her eyes from Chet's.

The door closed behind her. She stood in perfect stillness for a moment. Then she crossed the room to sit on the bed with Chet, carefully placing herself near the foot of the bed to give him plenty of room. Yesterday, in a moment of forgetfulness, she had seized his arms. Now she would give herself no chance to repeat the mistake.

Chet gave her a sad smile. "You know what I am thinking."

Loren shook her head slowly. "I do not take anything for granted. My dreams do not show me the future."

Chet dropped his gaze to his hands. "This time they are right. I have to go."

A long silence followed. Loren did not speak, could not answer. She had expected it for days now, ever since her dream in Sidwan. She had *known*. Yet the reality of Chet's words, the finality of them, left her breathless. The pain was not as sharp as when she had lost Jordel, but it was somehow deeper. After all, Jordel's parting had not been his choice.

"I do not want to go," Chet began. "Only I cannot—"

"Stop," said Loren. "I understand. I told you in Feldemar: you never have to explain yourself. Not to me. I have always understood you, Chet. How could I not?"

"Yet I must explain," said Chet, shaking his head. "I am breaking a vow. I made it to you, and I made it to myself, and it demands that at least some excuse be made."

"What excuse?" said Loren. "You have suffered more than—"

"Darkness take you, Loren, stop talking and let me speak!"

The words were neither harsh nor angry. They were desperate and pained, dragged from him as though each one agonized his throat. Loren's voice choked off, and her jaw worked to restrain a sob.

"I thought I was brave enough," said Chet. "Or, not brave. Resilient. If I could not fully give myself to your mission, I thought I could at least endure it. Last long enough, at least, for this quest to be over. I have known for some time that I would have to abandon the war. But I thought I could help you catch Damaris, and then I could leave with my conscience . . . not clear, but somewhat assuaged. Or I hoped you might tire of the chase in time, and then we could both go. But you seem tireless, and I can no longer keep the pace. Each day when I wake, I am breathless with the fear of death. Every night I fall asleep dreading that I shall never rise again. The terror creeps through me until I think it will stop my heart, and then until I wish it would. But this has been my plight since Dahab, and I kept on—but no longer. I see it now. I see that I endanger you all. I am weak. My courage will fail you at the worst time, and then your enemies . . . do you see? I am not only leaving for my sake, but for yours. I cannot follow you anymore."

I knew the dreams lied, Loren thought. *They always have. In them, he said the opposite. But I was right all along.*

"I will get you a horse," she said. "For supplies. You have a mount outside the city, of course, but you should have a pack animal as well."

"One horse is enough," said Chet. "Indeed, I never thought to own a horse in all my life. I do not know what I would do with two."

"Take the second one," said Loren. "It will make the journey easier. The Birchwood lies not far to the south. There may still be Shades in its western reaches. The High King has not yet driven them out. You should ride east for a while, but then you should be able to ride south and find home."

Chet shook his head. "Even now, you trouble yourself over me. I do not want to be any more burden than I have already—"

"Now it is your turn to be silent, Chet," said Loren. "You are not a burden, and you never will be. You have gone farther, done more, than anyone else in my life. I may have ridden longer beside Annis and Gem, but they did not leave home to find me. They did not travel for many leagues, all alone, only to seek me out. They did not . . ." She paused, forcing away the tightness in her throat. "They did not help me survive the Birchwood long enough to leave it in the first place. I pictured it often. Stealing my parents' dagger, but instead of making off with it, plunging it into my own heart. Sometimes the longing was so strong that I had to dig my nails into my own skin to prevent it. Only your friendship and, in time, your love, turned me from the path."

He was silent for a long moment before he whispered, "You never told me that."

"There was much I never told you. And I still keep some secrets. But this I will say plainly to you, and to anyone else: you speak of me as if I am some great hero, and you only a weight that I bear. I do not argue your right to leave, but I *will not* let you speak ill of yourself. I will not even let you *think* ill of yourself. Sky above, Chet, you saved the life of the Lord Prince. You are a hero of the highest renown, and Underrealm does not deserve you."

Loren forgot herself again for a moment. Her hand crept for him—just for his foot, just to feel his skin again. But Chet drew the foot back as if she were a striking snake, and Loren immediately withdrew.

"I am sorry," she whispered.

"No, it is not you," he said. "I still cannot . . . I still see . . . forgive me."

His tears broke at last, though Loren's would not come. She shook her head. "There is nothing to forgive."

Chet sat weeping for a short while, his face buried in his hands. At last he raised his head, but when he spoke, his words were still broken by sobs. "I wish that . . . I hope that after everything—if there is an anything after all of this—I hope you will come and find me."

"I promise that I will," she said. "I swear it."

"I do not know if we can . . . if it can ever be like it was before," said Chet. "But I want to know the answer."

"We will," said Loren. "But you must promise me something as well. Promise that you will try, at least, to find happiness. I was never able to give it to you, but now I charge you with that as your only mission: find happiness wherever it lies, and cling to it. Fight for it, and enjoy it as much as ever you are able. For my sake as well as your own."

"For your sake as well as my own," whispered Chet. "I cannot imagine it. But I will try."

Slowly he pushed himself up and off the bed. With cautious, tentative steps, he walked towards the door. Loren almost leaped up to embrace him—not because she had forgotten herself, but because who knew if she would ever have another chance?

Indeed, some dark voice at the back of her mind seemed to promise that she would not.

"Wait," she said.

His footsteps stopped.

Digging into the purse at her belt, she withdrew twenty gold weights. "For the horse, and for the rest of the journey home."

She held the coins in an outstretched hand, still gazing at her folded legs. She did not look up, for then she knew she would not be able to restrain herself from trying to hold him, from begging him to stay.

A long moment's silence stretched. He did not take the coins from her hand.

"Of course," she whispered. "I forgot."

She put the coins down on the edge of the bed and withdrew. From the corner of her eye, she saw his hands collect them up. Then came the sounds of him slipping on his boots, leaving, and closing the door behind him.

And then nothing.

TWENTY-EIGHT

LATER THAT DAY, KAL SUMMONED LOREN AND ANNIS TO HIS CHAMBER. In the small room, he had put an even smaller desk. Unlike the one in his council room in Ammon, this desk had no map atop it. There was only a single goblet of wine. Loren had no idea why he would have taken up so much of the room's limited space with the desk, except mayhap that it was a more impressive place for him to sit, subtly enhancing the impression he gave off as Loren and Annis stood before him.

Also in the room were Prince Senlin—*King* Senlin, Loren reminded herself—and Jo, who was now the boy's bodyguard. Jo wore no armor now, and bandages were wrapped thick around his torso. Loren vividly remembered the sound of the man's ribs cracking when Gregor had kicked him, but Jo seemed determined not to let such injuries deter him from his duties.

"I am glad to see you well," Loren told him as Annis closed the door.

"And you, Nightblade," said Jo.

"Enough of that," said Kal. He fixed Loren with a look. "I notice your lover left this morning."

Loren straightened, glaring down at him. She did not answer.

"Is it safe to have him running around out there?" said Kal. "Can we trust him?"

Loren kept any rancor from her tone, but it was a near thing. "I trust him a far sight better than I trust you."

Kal scowled at that, but when he answered, it was to change the subject. "I have been collecting information. Wojin did more than attack you in the sewer yesterday. At the same time, his soldiers rounded up those in the royal army who are loyal to Jun."

Annis gave a little gasp. Loren thought of Duris, the noblewoman who had offered to help them, and Morana, her daughter in the palace guard. "Were they executed?"

"No," said Kal. "There were too many of them, and even if Wojin is a treacherous snake, he is no fool. So many murders would only stoke the flames of anger that still burn in the people of this city. The loyalists have been imprisoned. We will free them when we can, but it shall have to wait. I have a plan. We know, of course, that we cannot let Dorsea remain part of a rebellion. It is a grave danger to all the nine kingdoms. Not only because of Dorsea's military might, which is considerable, but because it could sway the minds of other kings who have yet to join the war. Dorsea had already allied itself with the High King, and then it changed sides. Moreover, Dorsea borders five of the nine kingdoms. I know you never studied numbers, but that is more than half. Dulmun could not have chosen a stronger ally."

"Forgive me, Grand Chancellor, but we know this, and it has no effect on what we must do," said Annis. She had not lost all of her snippy tone from yesterday, being still angry at Kal for the way he had treated them. "You said you had a plan."

Kal's jaw worked. "We must depose Wojin and restore King Senlin to the throne. You lot had concocted a plan to raise the army against him. It was complex, and therefore doomed to fail. Much of that blame may be laid at your feet, I am sure, but I know, too, that King Jun was more honorable than he was practical. Meaning no disrespect to the dead, of course."

He inclined his head at Senlin. The boy's mouth had set in a grim line, but he nodded.

"In any case," said Kal, "I mean to remove Wojin the old-fashioned way: attack the palace with a small, determined group of soldiers, and kill him."

Loren balked, but she kept her mouth shut. Annis, however, did not restrain herself. "That seems a difficult task, to be sure."

"Difficult?" said Kal. "Yes. But we should be able to pull it off. The capital is in turmoil after the Nightblade's very foolish, very public display—the only good thing to come from your stupidity."

Loren's stomach did a turn. Not at Kal's words, but at his intentions. He meant to assassinate a king—a false king, but one sitting a throne nevertheless. She did not think cold-blooded assassination fit within the Mystics' purview. Yet she knew it would be little use arguing with Kal about it now. The grand chancellor's mind was set, and he would no doubt relish the opportunity to dress Loren down again. Off to the side, she could see that Senlin also looked deeply troubled. He had the same sense of honor as his father, and Loren imagined he did not look favorably upon assassination. But he held his peace. Why should he not? Kal's plan would put him upon the throne.

Kal noted Loren's hesitation. "Enalyn vowed that she would not force you to kill," he growled. "I am required to respect that vow. But if you think I will follow your foolish rules, you are very much mistaken. Though I will not order you to deliver the killing blow, you *will* aid my soldiers in this. You have ruined enough already, and a kingdom is in chaos because of it."

Loren lifted her chin. "Very well. I will help."

That made Kal subside, at least for the moment. "Good. And I have decided to grant you a boon as well. Once my men are inside the palace and have set about their work, you are to look for Damaris. You have chased her across two kingdoms. I doubt you will ever have a better chance to catch her. See if you can capture her. We will end Wojin tomorrow, certainly, but it would be better to kill two birds with one stone." He managed a grim smile. "Or rather, since you cannot be bothered to dirty your hands, to kill one bird and cage the other."

But Loren barely heard his jibe. She could think only of Gregor—and of her dreams, in which she saw him over and over again.

In the palace of Danfon.

"I will do my best," said Loren.

Kal fixed her with a hard look. "I expect you to do more than that. You will give every fiber of yourself to ensure this mission's success, as some small token of payment for your buffoonery so far. If you interfere in any way with my soldiers' mission to kill Wojin, I myself will ensure that the full weight of the King's law falls upon your head. Is that clear?"

Loren kept her face as still as a mask of stone. "It is clear."

Kal grunted. "Good. Now get out of my sight, and ready yourself. Tomorrow we topple a king. A false one, it is true, but nonetheless it will be no mean feat."

He waved them off, and together Loren and Annis left the room.

TWENTY-NINE

LOREN RETURNED TO THEIR CHAMBERS AND INFORMED GEM AND KERRI of the plan. Gem sat silently in the corner of the room, not looking at her. He had taken Chet's departure hard, and had refused to even say good-bye. When Loren saw the look in his eyes, she could not help but be reminded of how he had been when Jordel died.

But she forced herself to ignore it. If she spent too much time thinking of Chet's departure, she was not sure she would be able to go on.

When she had finished outlining the plan, Gem finally spoke in a small voice. "I am ready to go whenever you are."

"And I will guide you, of course," said Kerri.

Annis smiled ruefully. "And I suppose I will remain here—again."

"Annis," said Loren, frowning. "You know that—"

The girl's smile only broadened, and she waved a dismissive hand. "Yes, I *do* know. I speak in jest, though I do so poorly. There is plenty to keep me occupied. I think I will meet with the new king. Likely he knows something of how to rebuild his court when he is in power, but I think I may be able to help him with some specifics."

Gem looked at her with sudden interest sparking in his eyes. "That is unfair! Why should you get to stay behind and have all the fun?"

Annis winked at him. "I doubt you would call the planning of finances and court appointments 'fun'—and if you did, I think you would only do so because of the company. You will do far better by Loren's side, but I can put in a good word for you with the new king, if you like."

Blushing furiously, Gem began to pick at his fingernails. "I do not know what you mean," he muttered darkly.

Loren smirked to see them jibing with each other again. It almost helped to remove the dark cloud of Chet's absence. But she noticed that Kerri did not join in the room's cheer. She sat completely still, and her gaze was far away.

"Kerri?" said Loren. "What is it?"

"Nothing," said Kerri quickly, looking up. "Nothing, I only . . ." She sighed and shook her head. "Oh, very well. I am worried. We had one good moment in the beginning, taking Wojin completely by surprise. But ever since then, he has outsmarted us at every turn. Even when we tried to escape. It has nearly gotten us all killed, and it *did* get King Jun killed."

Loren nodded slowly. "That is true. And sometimes I feel the same sense of foreboding. But this is a new situation. It was not Wojin who predicted our plans, but Damaris, who got her information by putting Duris to the question. But she has no one to turn to for information now. And Kal—whatever else he may be—is a cunning man. If he thinks this scheme will work, I am willing to try it."

Annis and Gem frowned but did not speak. And privately, Loren wrestled with her own doubts. Did she truly think Kal was capable of outwitting Damaris? She would rather have relied on Annis than the grand chancellor. The girl knew her mother better than anyone else. Loren had a suspicion—even a fear—that she was only submitting to Kal's will because she no longer wanted to be the one in charge. Her choices had led to many deaths already. For the moment, at least, she was content to let someone else make those decisions.

In the end, mayhap, she would find out at last whether or not all the killing could have been avoided—whether she was indeed the foolish girl Kal believed her to be, or if their foe was truly as devious as she feared.

Kal spent the rest of that night and all the next day in hurried counsel. Jo and Senlin gave him much advice on the layout of the palace and the probable distribution of guard patrols. Kal even summoned Kerri at one point. She went, despite some reservations, and came back a short while later. Kal had wanted to know details about the servants' quarters and passages, which Senlin and Jo had been unfamiliar with.

"That may be a good thing," said Annis. "I feared Kal might try a frontal assault. If he wants to know about the servants' passages, he may be trying for stealth—for as long as he can, at least."

"Mayhap," said Kerri, looking troubled. "Yet this all seems to be going so fast. He means to attack tonight. He has had scarcely more than a day to plan."

"He hopes to surprise Wojin—and Damaris," said Loren. "The more time we take to plan, the more time they have to guess our aim."

In the afternoon, Loren slipped away from the group to visit Shiun. The scout had been put up in a room of her own, and two healers tended to her wound—one a Mystic, the other not. Shiun was awake when Loren came, and she tried to push up on her elbows at once.

"Still yourself," said Loren, even as one of the healers leaped forwards to hold Shiun down. "I only wanted to see how you were doing."

"There is a hole in my gut," said Shiun. She tried to smirk but only managed a grimace. "Other than that, I could not be better." Her voice was tight with pain, and every other word came through gritted teeth.

Loren sat by her side, putting a hand over Shiun's. She glanced up at the healers. "Might we have a moment?"

They looked at each other apprehensively. The Mystic healer, a stout woman with dark skin and many bags of medicine on her belt, wagged a finger. "She is not to move for any reason."

"Of course," said Loren.

They nodded and withdrew. Shiun regarded Loren carefully for a moment. A thin veil of sweat covered her face, and Loren guessed that her wound pained her much more than she wished to show.

"Some rumors have reached me," said Shiun. "About words the grand chancellor had with you."

"Let us not speak of that," said Loren. "It is nothing you should worry yourself over. And I will not apologize for the events that led to your injury, for I know you would not want to hear it."

"Certainly not," said Shiun with a snort. "But then why have you come here?"

"I said I wanted to see if you were well," said Loren. Then she blew a long sigh out through her nose. "And I wanted to tell you that Chet left. We all rode many leagues together. I thought you ought to know."

Shiun's brows rose almost imperceptibly. "I am sorry to hear that. Though I suppose he was bound by no oath of duty. None of your friends are soldiers, not truly."

"No, they are not," said Loren. "I myself am not a soldier."

"Yet you are also not faithless."

Loren frowned and shook her head. "Chet was not faithless. He did more than almost anyone else I have met in my travels. In time—if our road had been somewhat less dark—I think he would have become a great man, and a great servant of the High King. A man somewhat like Jordel."

"You cannot be serious," said Shiun. "Do you think Jordel never walked any dark roads in all his journeys? That is what made him a great man—he never turned his course from the right one, no matter the pain it might bring him."

"Yet some pains are too deep," said Loren. "You know what happened at Yewamba."

"Actually, I do not *know*," said Shiun. "You never told us. But I guessed. From the way things changed between you."

Loren gave her a hard look. "If you guessed right, then you know better than to call Chet faithless."

Shiun met her stare for a moment, but at last she turned her eyes away. "You are right. Forgive me. I suppose, in my own way, I am sad to see the lad go. And . . . may I speak frankly for a moment?"

"You may," said Loren, smirking. "Have you need to chastise me? Have I spoken too honestly with you, my underling, again?"

"Not that," said Shiun. "Sometimes honesty is necessary, as it is now. I worry for what Chet's departure might mean for your own peace of mind. He was good for you. I know he needed to look after himself, but now I worry about who will look after you."

"Why, you will, of course," said Loren. "The moment you are healed and back up on your feet, I expect you to return to duty."

Shiun gave a loud snort, then winced in pain. "I am hardly interested in providing the sort of comfort that Chet did, if you take my meaning."

Loren smiled and put her hand over Shiun's. "I am only joking. Do not worry about me, Shiun. Worry only about getting well."

A knock came at the door, and Loren turned just as it opened. Gem poked his head in the door. "It is time. Kal has ordered the attack to begin," he said. His gaze slid past her to Shiun. "How are you?"

"You have both asked me that, now," growled Shiun. "I have a hole in my stomach, master urchin. I am hardly well, though I will not die."

Gem grinned. "I am glad to hear it."

Loren gave Shiun's hand a final squeeze and then followed Gem from the room. In the main chamber in the basement, she found her party of Mystics ready to go. At their head, to her surprise, was Jormund. Loren drew up short before him, looking around, but Kal was nowhere to be seen.

"Are you to come with us for the attack?" said Loren.

"I am to lead it," said Jormund, giving her a grim nod. "I wish I had been with you in Yewamba. But I can make up for it now—at least in part."

Loren gave him a smile, but she knew it looked weak. What if he *had* been there in Yewamba? He might have died, as Weath had.

She heard footsteps coming down the stairs and turned to see Kal enter the room. Close behind him were Kerri and Annis. Kal stopped short and scowled at Loren.

"I have put Jormund in charge," he said. "He is not unfamiliar with this sort of mission. You are to obey his every command, just as you would my own. Understood?"

Loren nodded. "I will. You have my word."

Kal snorted. "The last time I thought I had your word, I—" He bit the words off. "But never mind that. I would rather not be at odds with you, girl. Do your job now, and I will consider that a good first step."

The hard wall Loren had built up around herself softened, at least somewhat. She gave him another nod, and this time it was more genuine. "Then I will endeavor not to let you down."

It was time to leave. Annis sprang forwards and gave Loren a hug, and then Gem. It was the first time in a long time that Loren had seen them share an open embrace without any awkwardness.

"Take care of yourself, you great fool," said Annis quietly.

"And you," said Gem.

Annis released him and motioned to Kerri, who started in surprise. "Come here," said Annis. "It is for good luck, I suppose."

Over Annis' head, Kerri looked at Loren with a little smile as the girl embraced her. Loren returned it. The muscles in Kal's jaw kept spasming, as though he longed to order an end to all this silliness, but he restrained himself.

Then, at last, it was time to go. They followed Jormund and his squadron of Mystics up the stairs leading to the street. A fine mist had come with the evening. Loren took that as a good portent: a dark and misty night for dark deeds. She followed the red cloaks into the greyness.

THIRTY

LOREN SIDLED UP BESIDE JORMUND AS THEY WALKED. "WHAT IS YOUR first order, O my captain?" She tried to put an indifference in her tone that she did not feel.

Jormund chuckled. "I am no captain—though who knows? If tonight goes well, the grand chancellor might promote me. But my first instruction is that, once we are inside the palace, you should avoid the fighting at all cost."

"That is an order I can follow easily," said Loren. "How do you mean to sneak into the palace? We climbed the wall, last time."

"And that is still the best way in, but they will surely have redoubled the guard," said Jormund. "Therefore we mean to make a feint at the front gate. When they are distracted there, the larger part of our group will enter the same way you did last time. Once we are inside, Keridwen will lead us through the servants' passages to the king's quarters."

Loren frowned. "The main gate will be guarded. The mists will help, but surely they will still see us when we try to make the climb. We will be exposed."

"But we will not be climbing for very long," said Jormund, smiling. "Yond here is a mindmage."

He pointed to a man by his side. Yond did not look quite like Loren thought a wizard should—he was too short and wide for that. But he smiled at her and lifted a hand, and his eyes began to glow. A dagger flipped up out of Loren's belt to spin in midair.

"I shall get you on top of that wall quickly, girl." He had a voice like two stones grinding together. "I hope you can do your job after that."

Loren smiled at him before plucking her dagger out of the air and sheathing it once more.

Soon they reached the palace. A wide main road ran in front of the walls, and they stood in the shadows on the other side. Mayhap ten paces separated them from their target—ten paces they would have to cross in the open air. Guards stood in the windows of the gatehouse and the towers, but there were also two guards on the street in front of the gate. The mists would help cover their approach, but they would be seen before they could sneak in. A thrill coursed through Loren. It was the same feeling she had had just before they infiltrated and attacked Yewamba. She only hoped that the results would be somewhat better this time.

"Time to begin," said Jormund.

They attacked.

Ten of the Mystics stormed forwards, drawing their swords, with Loren and Gem close behind. They sounded no battle cries, and so the guards did not notice them until they were almost to the wall. Then a cry went up. Four guards from above loosed a volley of arrows, but Yond's eyes flashed. The arrows scattered in midair, clattering to the cobblestones. Then the redcloaks reached the soldiers on the street. With the benefit of surprise, the Mystics slew their foes quickly. Each fell pierced by many swords. Jormund turned to Loren and clasped his hands.

"Boot," he grunted.

Loren placed her foot in his hands and leaped when he heaved. That sent her almost halfway up the wall—and then she felt an unseen force seize her under the arms.

Yond's mindmagic, she realized.

The spell threw her the rest of the way, so that she did not even need to grip the top of the wall, but flew neatly over it to land on the other side of the ramparts.

One guard was on the wall just outside the tower, and she barely had time to look surprised before Loren attacked. The woman bore only a bow, and she could do nothing to block Loren's punch. Three times Loren struck, and the woman collapsed to the ground.

Jormund landed just behind her. At once he slammed his shoulder into the door of the gatehouse. It flew open, leading into the upper floor.

Five guards waited inside. One raised a sword, but Loren threw a dagger into his arm and then grappled with another. Jormund's sword flashed, felling two of them.

Loren's opponent tried to overpower her, but she threw a foot behind the woman's and pushed her back. The guard's head struck the wall, and she fell senseless to the floor. But her companion attacked, forcing Loren back with his sword.

Jormund came to help after the first few wild swipes. His sword battered the other man's away, knocking it from his grip. Jormund plunged the blade through the man's chest, and he dropped. The gatehouse was clear.

They ran to the wheels at either end. Jormund's meaty fists wrapped around the spokes, and he had the rear gate raised in only a few heartbeats. Loren was slower, but he ran over to help her finish it. Soon the gates were up, and they heard shouting as the guards inside the courtyard realized the palace was exposed. By that time, four more Mystics had made the climb, and they filed into the gatehouse.

"Hold this place as long as you can," said Jormund. "But once you are sure it will fall, get out alive." The warriors moved to obey. Two took up positions at the doors, while two others stood at arrow slits at the rear. They would be able to fire into the courtyard as the Danfon soldiers came to attack.

"Our job here is done," said Jormund. "Now comes the greater task."

He and Loren took the stairs down and into the courtyard, immediately ducking through the gate and back out to the street. With a quick gesture, he motioned the rest of the Mystics after him. There were fifteen of them now, in addition to Loren and her friends, and they made their way around to the same place where Loren had infiltrated the palace last time.

With the help of the mindmage, they made the climb far more quickly than they had before. No guards challenged them on the walls, for all had been summoned to fight at the front gate. They made their quick run across the side wall, and Loren led them in their climb up to the balcony that would let them in. But this time the door was locked.

"They have learned that much, at least," said Loren.

"Pah," said Jormund, grinning. "What good is a lock?"

He rammed his massive shoulder into the door twice, and the jamb splintered as it flew open. They stormed into the palace—but now they turned the opposite direction from last time, for they were making for the servant passages.

"Here," said Kerri. The girl's eyes were wide with fright, and her hands shook as she pointed out the right door, but her voice did not quiver. Loren was impressed. Kerri had said she was fearful when Wojin attacked the palace, but she seemed to be handling this battle fairly well.

Jormund threw open the door Kerri had pointed to. Inside was a servant, but before he could cry out, Jormund's meaty fist struck him senseless. Kerri directed them through the passageway, turning left and right as they made their way towards the kings' chambers.

The plan of attack was brilliant, Loren realized, for it would be almost impossible to find them here. They were in the walls of the palace itself, and all attention would be diverted to the front gate. If Wojin feared any attack, he would expect it to come from the palace's front hall. The servant's passages would put them only a few rooms away from the king's chambers, and while they would no doubt be guarded, they would have bypassed the greater strength of Wojin's forces. Indeed, even the servants' chambers were surprisingly empty. She supposed most of them must have gone to bed already, and the rest were likely hiding after hearing of the battle in the courtyard.

At last, Kerri held up a hand. They all came to a stop in front of a simple wooden door, and Kerri turned to them.

"This leads to the entrance to the keep," she said. "There is a small chamber, and then a door. Then stairs leading up into the keep itself, where the king's chambers will be found."

"Good," said Jormund. "And the Yerrins?"

"Once we climb the stairs, there is a passage leading away to the Yerrin apartments," said Kerri.

"We will break off from the rest of you once we make the climb," said Loren.

"Very well," said Jormund. "If you have not returned by the time our deed is done, we will seek you out in case you need our aid."

"I would appreciate that," said Loren, thinking of Gregor. She hoped that he would have been pulled away from Damaris' side by the fighting, but that seemed too fortunate to be true.

Jormund nodded and threw open the door. They rushed out of the hallway into a small chamber with doors on either side. Two guards stood before them, but they could barely draw their swords before the Mystics fell upon them.

In a moment the guards were slain, and Jormund opened the door to the stairwell. The stairs turned back and forth twice before emerging onto a landing before the king's chamber. Loren saw the door leading to the side hallway, and Damaris' chambers.

They all paused for half a moment, and Jormund turned to look at her.

"Good fortune, Nightblade," he said. "I will see you again soon."

"Good fortune," said Loren. She ran for the hallway door, Kerri and Gem on her heels, and threw it open.

An arrow flew at her from the hallway beyond. Loren dodged too late by reflex, but the arrow missed her anyway. She caught a glimpse of soldiers in Dorsean livery, and then she fell to the floor on her back. Desperately she kicked the door shut again.

"Jormund!" she cried. "Wait!"

She was too late. She heard the door to the king's chamber burst open, and the Mystics gave great cries as they stormed in.

"After them," said Loren, pulling Kerri and Gem with her. They reached the door to the king's chamber not a moment too soon. Behind them, the hallway door burst open, and Dorsean soldiers charged in, screaming. The opposite door flew open as well, and more soldiers came running from the other side. Loren leaped into the king's chambers, Gem and Kerri close behind her, and threw the doors shut.

The chambers were empty. There was a wide bed against the opposite wall, with great windows on either side of it, and many chairs and couches for the king to receive guests. But Wojin was not here, nor were any of his household guards. Jormund stood spinning in the center of the room, his sword drawn but impotent.

"It is empty," he said slowly.

"Jormund!" said Loren. "Guards outside!"

Jormund ran to her, and several Mystics followed. They put their shoulders against the door, leaning into the force of the soldiers beyond, who had begun to batter it.

"The bar!" said Jormund. His outthrust finger pointed at a bar for the door. Two of the Mystics heaved it up and placed it in its iron fittings, and then the rest of them fell back. The pounding and shouting from outside redoubled.

Yond eyed the door, his face grim. "That will not hold long," he said.

"When it falls, we fight," said Jormund. Loren could scarcely believe it, but a smile split his lips. "I do not think they will expect a mindmage."

"Jormund, there are far too many of them," said Loren. "And where is Wojin?"

"They knew," said Gem quietly. "They guessed."

"Yes," said Jormund. His smile did not falter as he looked down at Loren. "Yes, we have been thoroughly outwitted. Even if we could guess where Wojin has been moved to, we could never reach him, and certainly we could not surprise him."

Loren frowned up at him. "Then we must escape."

A huge blow crashed against the door. It rocked on its hinges. Jormund shook his head. "A few more strikes like that, and they will be inside. We will never have enough time to get out. But you will. Take your friends and go."

"This is *not* the time for some foolish last stand," said Loren. "Your death will not help the war with Dorsea. There are windows, we could—"

Jormund only laughed. "I told you, there is not enough time. You made your vow, Nightblade. You promised Kal you would obey me. Take Gem and Keridwen and get out." He looked down at her suddenly, and his smile went from fierce to wistful. "I may not have been in Yewamba, but this is not such a bad trade. I hope you will make sure they talk about me and my soldiers here, in whatever stories they might tell about all this."

Another blow crashed against the door. A large crack appeared in the bar holding it shut. Loren bit her cheek until she could taste blood, fighting the stinging in her eyes. "Darkness take you, Jormund. Of course I will."

"Then get out, you little twit. See to your friends."

Stooping, he lifted a chair that must have weighed at least as much as Loren, but which he hefted like a toy. He threw it through one of the chamber's wide windows. The explosion of splintering glass would have been deafening, if Loren had been able to focus on anything but the pounding at the door.

Jormund reached out and ruffled Gem's hair, and then he took Loren's shoulder and gave her a gentle push towards the window. She ran to them, pulling Kerri along behind her.

"They . . . they will die," said Kerri, sounding half-senseless.

"Many have," said Loren. "Many more will."

The Elves told you, came a whisper in her mind. A memory of her dream. *They told you. They called you Nightblade. The one who walks with death.*

Pieces. Pieces of the puzzle, and always assembling themselves too late.

There was no balcony outside the window, but there was a rooftop just a pace or two down. Loren kicked out some of the glass at the bottom so that they would not cut themselves, and then she looked at Gem and Kerri. Each of them nodded in turn.

She took one last look back. Jormund and his Mystics had their shoulders against the door now, and Yond looked to be bracing them with mindmagic. Jormund looked back at Loren, still wearing his mad grin.

A berserker's grin, she thought. *Like Niya. Is that why I saw her here in my dreams?*

Loren turned and leaped.

She came down hard on the tiles, Gem landing beside her a moment later. They both turned as Kerri made the leap, and Loren did her best to catch the girl and soften her landing. Kerri was crying, but she did not hesitate as Loren turned and led her running off down the rooftop.

Behind them, they heard a great crash of splintering timber, and then a chorus of battle cries rang out. Almost at once, Loren heard the sound of steel piercing flesh, like a butcher's cleaver sinking into a side of beef. Above it all she heard Jormund's mighty shout, laughing as he cut down his foes. But the laughter faltered. One last cry he gave, and then fell silent a final time.

They darted around the corner of the keep, and Loren stuck her head back around it. No one had followed them out.

She ducked out of sight again and looked about. The roof of the palace had many peaks and slopes that they could use to hide from sight. They stood in a sort of valley between two of the peaks, and a third was between them and the walls, blocking them from view. But they could not remain here forever. Their first goal had to be finding a way out. There must be other walls, barricades like the one they had used to enter the palace in the first place, but Loren could not see any from where they stood.

"Kerri, do you have any idea where to go from here?" said Loren.

The girl stood against the wall, her gaze distant. When she did not answer, Loren put a hand on her shoulder. Kerri shook herself, then seemed to think for a moment, as though she was listening again to Loren's words in her mind.

"No," she said at last. "I . . . I know the palace, but not the rooftops."

"Gem?" Loren turned to the boy.

"I will search about," said Gem.

He crouched and crept forwards, making for the slope closest to the outer wall. Loren sat with Kerri, watching, heart in her throat. Gem poked his head up only far enough to peek with one eye, paused for a moment, and then slid back down towards them.

"Nothing easy that way," he said. "And more bad news: the walls are now well guarded. I see many soldiers with bows."

Loren shook her head. There had been few guards when they infiltrated the palace. Wojin—or Damaris—must have commanded the guards to hide themselves until the Mystics were inside. Then they would emerge, leaving Loren and her friends trapped.

"Damaris outwitted us again," she said.

"No one is that clever," said Kerri, voice trembling.

"You do not know her very well," said Loren. "But then, you do not know me very well, either. We will escape this place alive. I swear it."

Kerri nodded, and despite her fear, Loren could see that the girl wanted to believe her. She vowed to herself that she would not let her down—or Gem, either. Even if it cost her everything.

Everything.

Loren froze where she sat. Realization came crashing down on her like a wave, robbing her of breath. For a moment it sapped her will, and she felt as if rising to her feet would be an impossible task. But she shook her head, clearing the feeling away.

She knew what she must do.

"Kerri," she said, her voice wooden. "Where is the treasury from where we are?"

Kerri opened her mouth to answer, but Gem spoke first. "I think I saw it just over that slope. It lies between us and the outer wall. We can reach its rooftop, but that ends a good ten paces before the outer wall. We cannot use it to escape."

"Not the roof," said Loren. "Follow me."

She crept up the slope and saw what Gem had described. From the peak, the roof ran down a short ways before ending. There was a small gap, easy to leap, and then the roof of the treasury. High in the treasury wall were windows—somewhat small, but large enough to slip through. A pale light shone from within. Lanterns or torches were lit inside, but not many. Mayhap even just one. That meant that if there were any guards below, they would be few.

"Follow me," said Loren. "Do not stop for anything."

Loren slid down the rooftop towards its lip. She kept a wary eye on the wall far beyond, but the guards there had no hope of seeing them in the darkness. They carried torches, yes, but the light could never reach this far, and would only keep the guards blind to the shadows.

At the rooftop's edge, she did not stop herself. Instead she jumped as hard as she could, curling and striking the window with her shoulder. The glass shattered easily under her weight, and she thrust out an arm to catch herself. It caught on the lip. She felt glass bite into her skin, but not deep. Most of it fell tinkling to the floor below.

She hung there, breath hissing through her teeth against the pain in her hand. There below them was the treasury: seemingly endless piles of gold and silver, both coin and otherwise. The riches stretched from one wall to the other. But there were no guards to watch them.

Only one figure waited for them down below.

Even in the grip of the dreamsight, Loren's heart quailed. The figure was tied to a chair, its head hanging down. Like Duris had been.

But it was not Duris.

She forced her thoughts back to the present and reached up, using the hilt of a dagger to knock away the rest of the glass from the bottom of the windowsill. Gem and Kerri would follow at any moment, and she did not want them to injure themselves. Then she fell, aiming for a shelf just below her. It rocked under her weight, but it did not fall. From there she clambered down. Above her, Gem reached the window, and then Kerri. Each of them began to climb down the same way Loren had.

Loren ignored them. She walked slowly across the floor to the figure in the chair. Blood soaked his clothing, running down the chair to pool on the floor. But his throat was not cut. He still lived—and at the sound of her approaching footsteps, he turned his face up to her.

Chet.

THIRTY-ONE

CHET GASPED AT THE SIGHT OF HER. LOREN FELL ON HER KNEES BESIDE his chair, slashing at his bonds with her dagger. His arms came free, but he could not support his own weight. He slumped forwards, falling hard out of the chair to hit the stone floor.

He had been cut. Tortured. Loren had seen a great deal of cruelty since leaving the Birchwood, but this was among the worst of it.

In her mind's eye, she saw Damaris here, a sharp knife in her hand. No dreamsight, but only a product of her own imagination—her knowledge. Damaris with Chet, kneeling beside him, behind him. Damaris, plying his skin, slicing the flesh beneath. Damaris, avoiding the veins so that he did not bleed to death too soon. Damaris, taking her time, making it last.

Damaris, smiling all the while.

"Chet," said Loren. She rolled him over. "Chet, Chet." She threw off her cloak, balling it up and putting it beneath his head. Suddenly she realized she was touching him, her hands on his shoulder, his neck, his head. But he was almost senseless, and he could hardly withdraw from her even if he wanted to.

"No," gasped Gem. Loren looked up. The boy stood a pace away, looking down at Chet, his face a mask of horror.

But Kerri pushed past him, kneeling at Chet's side across from Loren. Without hesitation she tore Chet's shirt open to inspect his wounds. Where before the girl had been shaking with fear at their plight, now her hands were steady as she probed the cuts. Chet groaned at each touch of her fingers. But she only inspected him for a short moment before she looked up at Loren.

She shook her head.

Loren's mouth worked, looking for words. She found none, and looked back down at him.

"Loren," he gasped. His eyes opened, and they were clear. Loren withdrew her hands from him at once.

"I am here," she said. "I am here, Chet. I came."

"How did you . . ." He coughed. Blood bubbled from between his lips. His face was bruised. She thought his nose must be broken. His red-matted hair stuck out in all directions. "How did you know where I was?"

"I did not," said Loren. "We were . . . we were running . . . I knew I had to come here."

It seemed as if he tried to nod, but the movement only made him grimace in pain. "The dreams."

"Yes," she whispered.

Chet began to weep. Hot tears slid down his cheeks, mingling with the blood, and silent sobs made his chest jerk. "It . . . it hurts . . . yet at the same time it is like I cannot feel it. Once . . . once she started, she would not stop. No matter what I said."

Loren did not have to ask who he meant. Damaris. "How did she find you?"

"I did not make it beyond sight of the city," said Chet. "They caught me. Gregor. Some others. The moment they appeared . . . I froze. Limp. Like a fawn when a wolf seizes its throat. And I . . . it was like I knew that it would happen. That it was inevitable. The Elves. They told you. I thought about it all the way back to the city . . . trussed up on Gregor's saddle."

Kerri looked at Loren in shock. Loren ignored her.

The Elves' words rang in her mind. *The one who walks with death.*

A wave of pain struck him, and he cried out. His hand gripped his shirt. Loren squeezed her fingers together until she thought they would break, keeping herself from taking his hand, holding him, touching his face. Not now. She would leave him alone for now, at least. Until . . . until after. She forced herself to be calm, forced away the despair that clawed at her mind, her soul. She must be strong. For him, not for herself.

"It hurts," he whispered again.

Loren's hand went to the hilt of her dagger. Not one of her throwing daggers. The dagger on the back of her belt. Finely crafted, with black designs made of magestone. The dagger Chet had used to kill Auntie.

"I could help," she whispered. "I can . . . I can end it. The pain would stop."

And deep within her heart, she knew she would. If he asked her to, she would. It would be the first life she had ever taken on purpose. But she would do it, to keep him from more pain.

"No," he gasped. "It is . . . I can feel that it is almost over. If . . . if I only have a few moments left . . . I would rather spend them with you."

Fresh tears sprang from his eyes. But they were different. His face contorted in grief, not pain.

"Do not worry," said Loren. "I will not leave."

"No, I . . ." He gasped against a fresh wave of pain before he could go on. "I told her. Damaris. I told her . . . I told her everything. Your dreams. The Elves. Your dagger . . . what it means to the Mystics."

Loren quailed. She had thought that nothing could overwhelm her grief, but now terror came flooding in to replace it. It was the secret she had held ever since Wellmont, when Jordel had first told her all the secrets of the dagger. That knowledge in the hands of Damaris . . .

But she forced such thoughts away. There would be time to deal with that. There would be no more time to spend with Chet. "It is all right," she said, determined not to let him see her fear. "You could have done nothing more."

"I did not tell her where Kal was," he whispered. "It was the only thing I could hold on to. And I had told her so much already . . . when I lied at last, she believed me."

"That was brave," she said. "That was brave, Chet. You saved many lives." She forced away thoughts of Jormund, of all the Mystics who had died in the palace just moments ago. Chet knew nothing of them. He did not need to.

"I am glad they will live," he whispered. "Glad I could do that much, at least."

"You have done so much more," said Loren.

A ragged gasp wracked his body. Suddenly his hand shot out to clutch hers. Loren looked down at her hand in shock. His fingers laced through hers. His blood still ran from wounds on his fingers, and it mixed with the blood of her sliced palm. She held him back, squeezing, giving him an anchor.

"It . . . it hurts . . ." he gasped. "I . . . you deserve better, but . . . please . . ."

"What, Chet?" she said. "I have water, I—"

"No," he whispered. "Please. Hold me?"

She lifted him up at once, lifted him to sitting, ignoring the grunt of pain. Kerri opened her mouth as if to speak, but she held herself back. Doubtless this would worsen the wound. But what did it matter? It would be over soon anyway.

It would all be over.

Chet's arms snaked around her back, but slowly, and she stroked his hair. He buried his face in her shoulder, and she squeezed, letting him feel her, letting him feel her arms around him. He turned his head, and she pulled back, thinking she was smothering him. But he kissed her, softly, briefly. She returned it. No passion, no lust. No time for that now. But she poured all of her love into it, into that brief moment of the meeting of her lips. And then they held each other again.

Chet shuddered. And then she felt it. Like a felled animal in the woods. The woods where Chet had taught her to hunt in the first place. She felt the life slip from him.

He was gone. Gone, to where she could not follow him anymore.

THIRTY-TWO

THE TREASURY FELL TO SILENCE. THE ONLY SOUNDS WERE THE MUTED voices of guards in the courtyard and on the walls outside, still no doubt searching for Loren and her friends, and the quiet, wracking sobs of Gem. But after a short while had passed, Kerri reached over and put her hand on Loren's shoulder.

"I am sorry," she said. "But we are still in danger."

"I know," said Loren. "I know."

Gently she laid Chet down, then took her cloak and stood to don it. She refused to look at him. They had to leave him here. Loren hated it, but she knew she must. She went to Gem's side and put an arm around his shoulders. He turned to her and threw his arms around her, weeping, his tears soaking into her fine new shirt.

"The front door will be guarded," said Kerri quietly. "But . . . we might fight our way out. It is the only thing I can think of."

"There is no need," said Loren. She gingerly unwrapped Gem's arms from around her waist, and then she went to the corner of the room.

A tapestry hung there. Loren remembered it. The man in black had shown it to her. She pushed it aside, and there was only a blank stone wall. Kneeling, Loren felt for the chink in the stone. After a moment she found it, and her fingers pulled on the lever. Two stones swung open, revealing the passageway.

Kerri gawked at her. "How did—"

"I am the Nightblade," said Loren. Then she remembered what the man in black had said in her dream. "It is my job to know the secret ways no one else knows."

She led the way, crawling into the passage. Gem came behind her, still sniffling, and Kerri brought up the rear. Soon the passageway was completely black. Loren reached into her cloak and pulled out a magestone, breaking off a piece and eating it. Then she reached to the back of her belt and drew her dagger, holding it in one hand as she proceeded. With the magestone in her blood, and her hand on the dagger, the passageway was suddenly bright as day.

"I cannot see," said Kerri.

"You do not need to," said Loren. "There is only one way out."

Only one way out.

She crawled forwards, following the passageway as it turned left and right, warning her friends each time. Soon it sloped up, and she knew they were near the end. At last it came. She reached up, finding the chink in the stone and pulling the lever. The wall swung out soundlessly. Loren crawled into the open.

They were in the palace. The hallway was wide and tall, and there were many doors in it. To their left, Loren thought she saw the hallway reach the main front hall, while to the right it ended in a door. But in the middle there was a side hallway leading deeper into the palace.

"I know where we are. The front doors are that way." Kerri pointed to the left. "If the Mystics still hold the front gate—"

"They do not," said Loren. "They will have left, or they are already dead. This way." She started off for the side hallway.

"How do you know?" said Kerri. But she followed along, Gem by her side.

"It is enough that I do." How could she begin to explain?

Loren led them on the course she had been shown. They walked down hallways that felt familiar to Loren by now, though she had never seen them in the waking world. The dreamsight still had its hold on her, but it was not like before. Now, seeing the places from her dreams did not disorient her or send her mind spinning. Now it was like she was following a route marked on a map.

She turned the final corner, and there it was, as she had known it would be. Ahead, an open door leading to a dining hall, and beyond that, freedom. To the left, a small wooden door led to a serving room. Loren came to a halt.

"There!" said Kerri. "That gate is open! We can escape!"

"Take Gem with you," said Loren. "I must go another way."

They both stopped short. Kerri looked over her shoulder, towards the hallway that ran to the front of the palace. Voices drifted from that direction, far away but coming closer. "What do you mean?" she said. "What other way?"

"Loren—" Gem began.

"Shush," said Loren. "You and Kerri must go into the dining hall. Wait at the other end for a short while. Then run for the city. You will be able to escape. I swear it."

Gem set his jaw. "I will not leave. Not without you. Not after Chet." *That way is for others, but not for you.*

"You are not leaving me," said Loren. "But there is one thing I must do first before I follow you."

He paused. "What thing?"

Loren gave him a sad smile and gently pushed his shoulder. "Never you worry, master urchin. But I swear this now: I will find you back at Kal's hideout. I would not leave you and Annis to fend for yourselves."

Gem looked up into her eyes, studying them. *Poor Gem,* thought Loren. *You cannot recognize a lie in my eyes. In Damaris and Auntie, I met two of the most cunning minds in the nine kingdoms, and they could not tell if I spoke the truth. What hope do you have?*

"Very well," said Gem slowly. "I believe you."

"Of course you do," she said. "Now go. Look after Kerri."

His chest puffed up a bit at that. Over his head, Loren caught Kerri's eye and winked. The girl gave a smile—little more than a small twist of the lips. Kerri had one advantage over Gem: she had not known Loren long enough to *think* she knew when Loren was telling the truth. Gem led the way into the dining hall, but Kerri paused for just a moment.

"You had better not have lied to that boy," she said quietly. "I *will* expect you back at the hideout."

Loren nodded solemnly. Then she turned and ducked into the serving room, pausing for just a moment to ensure that Kerri went to follow Gem.

Inside, she found the room laid out just as she had known it would be. Against the back wall was the shelf of dishes. Loren threw it away from the wall, not caring about the clatter it made. She was past that now. The passageway beyond led to the ladder, and that led to the passageway above. That ended in the tapestry, and Loren pulled it aside.

She stepped into Gregor's room.

He stood at the other end, framed by the open doorway. In his hands was a massive longbow of yew, longer than Loren was tall. He faced away from her, scanning the courtyard below. The room was modest by Damaris' standards, but still held finery beyond anything Loren had ever seen growing up. The tapestry through which she had emerged was matched by one on the other side of the room, and all the furniture was carved of solid oak, inlaid with finely wrought gold. There were many lanterns around the room, but only three were lit, leaving the whole place dim. They were the only illumination, for outside the night was still misty and clouded. The moons and stars cast no glow upon the room, nor even upon Gregor himself.

Loren turned and closed the door to the passageway, making no effort to mask the sound.

Gregor's head snapped up, and he turned to her. For a long moment he stood there, studying her. Then, inexorable as a rockslide, he stepped into the room. One hand drifted behind him, closing the glass balcony door. He pulled a sash holding back a curtain, and it fell across the door, sealing the room against the last rays of torchlight from beyond.

This is the only way, thought Loren. *All roads lead to Gregor.*

"Hello, Nightblade," said Gregor. His voice rolled through the room like thunder. "Damaris promised me this. That together, we would make you suffer. And then, at last, I would get to kill you."

THIRTY-THREE

"I thought I might find you here," said Loren lightly.

Gregor snorted. "Did you?" But he paused, and his eyes hardened to steel. "Ah. The boy told us things. Your dreams. Did they lead you here to die? Hardly a useful tool."

Loren shrugged, letting her gaze drift around the room. Across the room was the only other door. It led to the rest of the palace. To escape.

She turned away from it.

"They have proven more useful than you might realize. After all, they have told me where to find your mistress."

The bodyguard froze. Loren widened her eyes.

"Oh, did you not imagine I would know that? That I had not planned all this? While you waste your time here with me, Mystics are even now descending on Damaris' location and—"

Gregor charged.

Loren had expected it, but the giant's speed never failed to surprise her. She leaped away from the tapestry, making for the room's door. But Gregor anticipated the move, and his hand swiped out. Loren dropped and rolled—but her foot overextended, kicking a side table. One of the lamps fell to the floor, shattering its glass. The light went out, and the room grew dimmer still.

Quickly Loren scrambled for her feet. But Gregor was almost upon her, and she had to roll away from the door. He paused there, shoulders hunched, arms to his side. Loren thanked the sky that he did not have his sword on him.

"You did not plan this night," he growled. "If you had, you would never have left Chet for us to kill."

"You have no right to speak his name," hissed Loren. But she thought, *Even now, Gem and Kerri will be making their way across the courtyard. Almost there. Almost free.*

She circled, keeping her eyes fixed on Gregor. It almost made her forget his longbow, which he had dropped. Her foot hit it, and she nearly tripped. Gregor tensed, but when she righted herself, he subsided. In one fluid motion, Loren crouched and picked up the bow. It felt like a spear in her hands. If only she were Uzo.

"Do you think that will save you, girl?" said Gregor. "That little stick?"

"Cruel words," said Loren. "After all, it is *your* little stick."

Gregor growled and charged again. Loren leaped to the side, swinging the longbow at him. He raised an arm to block it, and it cracked over his forearm. Grunting in pain, he swung his other fist at her. Loren could not quite dodge it. It smashed into her shoulder, flinging her across the room. She rolled with the landing, fighting to her feet at once. In one hand she still held half of the longbow. The broken end was jagged and splintered. She thrust it at Gregor, forcing him back.

"I think I am at a disadvantage," she said. "If only I had learned to fight. I tried to get you to teach me, once. Do you remember? I begged you for swordplay lessons. But then, as now, you could not quite catch me. Will you not give me a sword again? It is the only way this fight will be fair."

"Who wants a fair fight?" said Gregor. "I have only one goal here tonight: to end your life, and to take as long as I can in doing so."

They had spun around each other again, and now the balcony door was behind Loren. She reversed her grip on the longbow, throwing it at him like a spear. He batted it aside, but she had not truly meant to hit him. Loren turned, dashing for the balcony. She threw aside the curtain, her hand coming down on the latch—

It did not turn. Locked.

A fist bigger than her head closed on the hood of her cloak.

This is it.

Gregor flung her away from the door. She flew all the way across the room, crushing another lamp. Loren felt a sharp pain—broken glass, or a cracking rib?—and gasped.

Then she smiled.

Rolling over, she saw Gregor stalking towards her. He wanted to get his hands on her, pin her down, but he was moving slowly. He did not want to give her another chance to escape.

Loren's hand fell to her belt, closing around a knife. She drew it and threw.

Gregor halted, raising one mailed arm to stop the blade. But it flew straight past him—to strike the third and final lamp, sending it crashing to the floor.

The room went utterly black.

Loren drew the dagger from the back of her belt. In her vision, the room grew bright as daylight.

But Gregor was blind. And he would not know she could see.

Chet would not have told him, for Loren had never told Chet. She had not wanted him to know about the magestones.

Gregor took a cautious step back. His leg struck a footstool, and he stumbled, barely keeping his feet. Experimenting, Loren scuffed a foot on the floor. Gregor's head jerked towards the sound, but too far, so that he was looking to her left.

Loren's smile widened.

"You misunderstand the dreams," said Loren. He jerked again, following her voice. She let him hear where she was. "They tell me some things, but not everything. They did not tell me I would find Damaris alone in Yewamba. That you had abandoned her. And no, they did not tell me you would take Chet tonight. But if you think they did not tell me about you, here, now, you are wrong."

Gregor made his cautious way forwards, reaching for where he could hear her voice.

"I came here, Gregor, because I wanted to."

Softening her footfalls, she began to stalk around him. On the soft rugs of the room, she made less noise than the wind. Gregor swiped his arms through where she had been standing a moment before.

"This is pointless," he growled. "Do you think the darkness is your friend? It will not help when I get my hands on you."

From behind, Loren leaped. She plunged the dagger into his calf. The blade parted cloth and flesh with equal ease. It felt . . .

Loren shuddered.

It felt so *good.* So *right.*

Had she really never used the dagger on another living person before? She knew, now. That had always been the dagger's purpose. It was never meant for anything else.

She leaped back, even as Gregor groaned and stumbled to one knee. He reached behind himself, but she was already gone.

Loren darted in again. Her blade impaled his groping forearm.

Gregor gave a brief shout, quickly cut off. He tried to rise, but he had to favor his injured leg. It was useless, unable to support his weight. He swung a wild, angry blow that Loren ducked with ease. She struck again, plunging the dagger into the pit of his good arm. It fell useless to his side.

He placed her at last, and his fingers closed on the front of her shirt. But she had already stabbed that arm through. Now she sliced it again. She did not know where to cut, exactly, but the dagger seemed to. It parted muscle and tendon, and his grip slackened. His balance wavered, and he crashed to the floor on his back. Desperately he tried to push away from her with his one good leg.

Loren took one of the throwing daggers from her belt and flung it into his ankle. It flew hard enough to pin the limb to the floor beneath.

"And here I thought—" Gregor's words cut off in a groan of pain. "Here I thought you had no spine."

The words were defiant, his tone more so. But Loren could see it plain as day on his face, clear as if a lantern were right in his eyes. Fear.

Gregor feared her.

His chest heaved with every breath, and sweat ran from him in rivulets. She wondered how long it had been since the giant had been beaten in a fight—beaten so soundly that even his limbs were useless. If it had ever happened at all.

"You thought me weak for refusing to kill," said Loren. "You still do not recognize the truth. Murder is the coward's way out."

He grunted a laugh. "What do you call this, then?"

A fierce smile crossed Loren's lips. "I suppose I do not feel particularly brave at the moment."

That forced a laugh from him. "Then I go to my death with one consolation. This pain is nothing compared to the boy's. To *Chet's.*" He gave an evil grin into what was, to him, empty darkness. "I made sure he suffered. I relished every twist of pain on his face as I cut him up, one piece at a time. If I must go to the darkness below, I do so happy, knowing that nothing will ever bring back the boy you loved. The boy I took from you."

Loren crossed to kneel by his head. She leaned in close.

"I know you are lying."

He started at the sound of her voice so close. Only one arm could still move, and he swung it at her, even though it could not grip.

She caught his hand on the blade of her knife

Gregor cried out—a scream of pain that she was ashamed of herself for enjoying.

"I know you are lying," she said again, easily, as though nothing had happened. "I saw Chet. He died slowly, yes. But not by your hand. When Annis and I first met, she told me. She told me how Damaris would torture information from her prisoners, taking her time with the pain, enjoying every cut. It was Damaris who killed him. And I promise you this. I will hunt her down. I will never stop until I find her. And when I do, I will not bring her before the King's justice. I *am* the King's justice. I will find Damaris and end her, just as I have ended you here, tonight."

It dawned on Gregor. Recognition. Loren watched it spread across his face like a tide creeping up a shore. He knew she spoke the truth, that she meant what she said. It was only a matter of time before Damaris was dead.

And just as that realization came upon him, Loren drew the dagger across his throat.

He sagged back to the floor, his lifeblood bubbling up. He coughed, choking, trying desperately to breathe. Blood spurted across his face and ran down the sides of his neck to pool, soaking into the carpet below, staining it. Like Duris.

Like Chet.

THIRTY-FOUR

LOREN SANK BACK ON HER HEELS, STARING. THE MAGESTONES AND HER dagger let her see every detail of Gregor's corpse. It sat there, silent, still. Confronting her. A sick, twisting feeling ripped through her gut.

She ignored it. Kal had given her a mission, and she was still in the palace.

First she went to the balcony and opened the door. The courtyard beyond was still empty, but guards stood on the wall beyond it. They did not notice her.

But they soon would.

Loren ducked back into the room and went to Gregor. She lifted his arm and pulled, but she could not move him. Clenching her jaw, she heaved. His body barely moved.

She went to the rug upon which he lay and seized the edge of it. Again she pulled. This time it worked. The rug slid on the wooden floor. It still seemed to her that he should be too heavy, but something—the thrill of the fight, some gift of the dagger—let her move him.

On the balcony, she lifted his head up until it hung over the railing.

Then, straining and groaning, she managed to fling him over the balcony to land in the courtyard far below.

The body struck the smooth white stones with a sick *thud*.

That drew the attention of the guards on the wall. They cried out, and soon other guards came running from all directions. Soon there was a small crowd of them in the courtyard below, staring at Gregor's corpse. As one, they joined the guards on the wall in looking up at her.

Loren threw her shoulders back. Her black cloak and her new clothes were all stained in blood. She hoped they could see it.

"Gregor is dead!" she proclaimed. "Damaris of the family Yerrin is soon to follow. And the usurper, Wojin, will never escape the King's justice. Abandon him, or you, too, will face me before the end."

Then she vanished back inside the apartment.

She left by the front entrance, not the secret one. Soon there was a staircase leading down, and she emerged into another hallway full of rooms. One of them had an open door, and she stole through it to the balcony beyond. This led her to the rooftops she had traveled with Gem and Kerri not long ago. She stalked around the palace's perimeter, stopping to look and listen at every window. Then, at last, she found the one she was looking for.

A balcony just above her head led to a wide glass door. Pulling herself up slightly, Loren saw Wojin. The false king was in urgent conference with an advisor, and Loren saw two guards inside the room as well. A single lamp lit the room. But none of them were looking at her, and in any case, the lamp inside the room would keep them from seeing outside.

She clambered up onto the balcony, sidling up to the doorway to listen. Wojin raised his head to speak to the guards.

"What of the attackers?"

"At least one still remains, Your Grace. You must stay here until we have confirmed the palace is secure."

Wojin gave an exasperated sigh. "This gambit was foolish. I told that Yerrin woman often enough. And she is not even here to face the same danger as the rest of us!"

Damaris, thought Loren. *She has left, then. Mayhap it is time for me to go, as well.*

Her gaze came to rest on Wojin.

Or mayhap not.

Loren burst through the door into the room. Wojin shot to his feet, and the guards went to draw their swords. But Loren struck before they could, kicking over the lamp. It was not complete darkness, for the window let some torch light in, but it was enough for her purposes.

One guard fell to a punishing blow from her dagger's hilt. The other only managed two swings before Loren brought him down. The advisor screamed and ran for the door, but Loren tackled him, then slammed his head into the floor to knock him senseless.

But no killing, she thought. *There has been enough of that tonight.*

Loren rose to her feet. "Wojin," she said. "What a pleasure to meet you face to face."

"Assassin," gasped Wojin.

"No," said Loren, shaking her head. "But I have killed Gregor tonight, and you are utterly at my mercy. Yet I was told, a long time ago, that not needlessly does the family Yerrin kill. And the Nightblade has at least that much honor."

Wojin swallowed hard. She watched the bulb in his throat bounce up and down. "What . . . what do you mean to do with me, then?"

"Silence you, for one thing."

She cut a gag out of the drapes and tied it around his mouth. Then she bound his hands before leading him out to the balcony. Once he was up against the railing, she shoved him in the shoulder blades. Wojin screamed into his gag as he fell, but she caught him by the ankles. Loren lowered him as far as she could, then dropped him to the rooftop below so that he fell on his shoulder. He grunted in pain. Loren jumped down beside him, then forced him up and back towards the palace. She bundled him in through a lower window.

"We are going to your dungeons," she said. "If you try to signal for help, I will make you regret it."

Wojin nodded in fear—but she saw a crafty shine in his eye. The dungeons would be guarded, and they would not be easy to escape from. That was the point, after all. No doubt he hoped he could trick her into trapping herself there.

Good. It would keep him thinking he had a way out of this.

The maps of the palace were still somewhat clear in her mind. She knew she was on the southwest end of the palace, and the dungeons were close by. She only needed to find a way leading down . . .

There. She shoved Wojin into a stairwell, barely catching him before he fell to the landing below. When they were near the bottom, she stopped and knelt, tying Wojin's feet as she had tied his hands.

"Do not move," she said. "I will return for you in a moment."

She ducked around the final turn in the stairs. Behind her, she heard Wojin start to struggle immediately. That was fine. He would not free himself before she was done.

There was a guard room before the door that led to the dungeons themselves. In the room sat a man in palace livery. He shot to his feet when Loren entered, giving a cry of alarm. Loren threw a dagger into the hand that reached for his sword, then subdued him with two quick strikes to the face. He slumped to the floor, groaning.

His belt held a ring of keys. She removed them and went back for Wojin. His bonds were not even loosened yet. He moaned in fear as she hauled him up and shoved him into the guard room. She unlocked the first door and walked him down the line of cells, peering inside.

There. A cell of healthy prisoners, clearly not here for very long. Their hair was cut short, and they were well-muscled and healthy.

"You there," said Loren. "Are you palace guards?"

One of the prisoners peered up at her, blinking. "What?"

"Palace guards. Did you serve in the palace?"

"I . . . did," said the man. "Who are you?" Then he noticed Wojin, bound and with Loren's arm around his neck. His eyes shot wide.

"Yes, it is him," said Loren. "I am looking for someone. Morana, of the family Fei. Where is she?"

"I am Morana," said a voice.

Loren turned. The cell across the hall held still more prisoners. One of them, a woman with her hair cut almost to her scalp, stood before the bars. She studied Loren with keen, severe eyes. Eyes Loren had seen before, in the face of Duris Fei.

Loren reached up and ripped out Wojin's gag. "Tell them what you did."

"I do not know what you speak of," said Wojin desperately.

Loren's dagger slid free, and she pressed the tip to his throat. "Not needlessly will I kill. But neither will I be gentle. Tell them what you did to King Jun."

Wojin gasped, trying to struggle away from the dagger. "I killed him," he whispered.

"Louder!"

"I killed him!" cried Wojin. "I took the palace by force, but he and his son escaped. But I found them after, and my soldiers killed Jun."

Loren pressed harder. The dagger pricked the skin of his throat, and Wojin squeaked. "And tell her what happened to Duris."

"We learned—Damaris learned that she was conspiring with King Jun," said Wojin, nearly weeping now. "We . . . we killed her."

Loren pressed just a bit harder. "Tell them everything. Tell her how Duris died."

"Damaris put her to the question!" cried Wojin. "She tortured her for information before cutting her throat."

Morana had gone very still, her fingers wrapped around the iron bars of her cell. She met Loren's gaze.

"Do you know who else in this dungeon is loyal to Jun?" said Loren.

"I do," said Morana, her tone clipped.

Loren removed her dagger and threw Wojin to the floor, where he crumpled in a heap. She opened Morana's cell and handed her the ring of keys. "Get them all out. Take care of this thing." She spat at Wojin's form on the floor. "I will send help as soon as I can. Senlin still lives. He will return to give you orders. Can you hold out until then?"

"We can," said Morana. But as Loren turned to go, she reached out and seized her wrist. "You did all this?"

Loren met her gaze for a moment. "Not on my own," she said softly. "Many people died to return the true king to the throne. See that their sacrifice was not in vain."

Morana nodded slowly. Loren turned and ran up the stairs, back into the palace.

THIRTY-FIVE

HER KIDNAP OF WOJIN HAD THROWN THE GUARDS INTO DISARRAY. IT was easy enough to find another rooftop to sneak away on, and when she found a side wall leading out, no guards were there to block her path. She climbed down the wall and made her way into the streets of the city.

Without Kerri to guide her, it took a great deal longer to find Kal's inn than it might have otherwise. But in the end, she found it all the same. When she approached the side door leading to the basement, the Mystic on guard moved to stop her at first. But when he caught sight of Loren's face, he gasped and stepped back. Loren ignored him, throwing open the door and descending into the room.

"Loren!"

Gem screamed as he flung himself into her arms. Annis was only a half-step behind him, and then came Kerri. They huddled around her, holding her close, the children crying.

None of them paid the least bit of attention to the blood soaking Loren's clothes. But in the end, Loren pulled back. It would be a while, she guessed, before she felt that these clothes were truly clean again, and she did not wish to sully her friends with them.

Someone had summoned Kal, and he came huffing into the room. He stopped dead when he saw Loren, staring at her for a moment in shock. Loren fixed him with a grim smile.

"Hello, Grand Chancellor. You seem surprised to see me."

"I . . ." he swallowed and forced the awe from his expression. "The boy and the girl returned, but from what they said . . . I did not know if you would."

"Yet here I am."

"Were they right?" said Kal. "Jormund?"

"Dead, with all his soldiers," said Loren. "But I captured Wojin. He is in the hands of Jun's loyalists in the prison. You must get all the warriors under your command and help them take the palace, as quickly as you can."

No doubt it grated Kal to hear her give such orders, but he had the good sense to hide it for the moment. She could see the amazement in his expression. He had likely never expected her to succeed. Loren did not think he had sent her to her death, not intentionally. But she had only been a tool to get his assassins within reach of their target. No doubt he was surprised at her success when all his Mystics had perished.

"Yes, well . . ." he said. "Good. Worse than I had hoped, but better than I feared. I shall . . . I shall act at once. Excuse me."

"Of course. I shall be waiting to give you a more complete report, when you are ready." Loren allowed herself the small pleasure of waving him away. He scowled at that, but he went, going back to his room to give the orders.

Loren had lied, of course. She would not be waiting for him.

She ushered Gem and Annis towards one of the rooms they shared. Inside, they found Wyle. He sprang to his feet the moment the door opened, his face going ashen when he saw Loren.

"Nightblade," he said. "You survived."

"I did," said Loren. "Though others did not. Close the door, Gem."

The boy hurried to do as she asked, and Loren went to sit on the bed. She was likely getting blood on the blanket, but she did not care. Annis and Gem stood before her, their eyes wide. But Kerri looked at Loren's face, studying her. Loren thought she saw something in the girl's eyes . . . recognition? Understanding?

"I killed Gregor," whispered Loren. "I killed him."

The room went still. Kerri's expression grew dour, and Wyle only blinked. But Annis and Gem looked at each other in fear. Only they could know what this moment truly meant.

"And I am leaving," continued Loren. "I must go off on my own again. Because I need to kill Damaris."

Annis sagged. She sank down on the bed, sitting on its edge. Her hands were shaking. Gem took them quickly, holding them between his own. "Loren—" said Annis.

"She killed Chet, Annis," said Loren. "And not quickly."

"No, I know," said Annis. "I . . . I understand. And I will come with you."

Loren shook her head slowly. "You should not. This is not like our journeys before. I am no longer running. I am looking to right a wrong."

"But none of our journeys have been like another," said Annis. "Yet we have always been together. I . . . I know what you must do. Gem and Kerri told me about Chet. I want to go with you."

Loren found it hard to speak past a sudden tightness in her throat, and her voice broke. "Then I welcome your company. It would be an emptier road if I did not ride it with you."

"I suppose it need not be said that I am coming as well," said Gem.

Somehow, Loren found the strength to smile. "Of course not. I was going to ask you to do so."

He smirked, but it died quickly. Loren looked past him to Wyle. At once the smuggler spread his hands, shaking his head.

"No. I have enjoyed your company, Nightblade, but I have ridden quite a bit farther than I had ever planned to. I believe I will remain here, reaping the gratitude of the new king."

"You can collect that gratitude easily enough by letter," said Loren. "I am certain Senlin will accommodate you. But we need to travel by secret ways that no one else knows. And we would pay you handsomely. Why not also earn yourself the gratitude of Underrealm's greatest . . . greatest thief?"

Her stomach turned. She had almost said *assassin*.

Wyle eyed the door to their room and pursed his lips. "I suppose it is true that I would rather not be in Danfon just now," he muttered. "I trust Senlin, but that Kal fellow . . ." He sighed and held up a finger. "Very well. But you will pay me full rates. I never give a discount, even to friends. It only cheapens the friendship."

"Fair enough," said Loren. "And thank you."

Wyle stood and bowed to her. "You are welcome, Nightblade. I am at your disposal—for a while, at least."

"Then let us not delay," said Loren, pushing herself up off the bed. "The road is long, and we should begin."

"Now?" said Gem, eyes widening in surprise.

"There is no better time," said Loren. "Damaris already has a head start."

"I think you are right," said Annis.

Loren nodded, then turned to Kerri. "Farewell, Keridwen. I am glad to have known you, even for a little while. Look after Senlin for us. He will need friends in the days to come."

Kerri's eyes flashed. Her hands balled into fists at her sides, and she tilted up her chin.

"No."

That gave Loren pause. She frowned at Kerri. "No?"

"No. I will not stay here to look after a boy. I mean, he may be king, but . . ." She took a deep breath and released it in a rush. "I want to come with you."

Loren's frown deepened, furrowing her brow. "With us? Why?"

"You know why. I want to do more. More than I can do here, even if I were to help Senlin."

Slowly Loren shook her head. "No, Kerri. You are a healer, a chemist. On the road we travel, I must . . . I must be a killer."

Kerri cocked her head. "I have never believed that killing was always wrong."

Loren opened her mouth to argue again—and then she closed it. "Very well," she said, shrugging. "You may come if you wish. But it must be now."

Kerri did not answer, but only fell in behind the children as they followed Loren out the door. Loren led them down the hallway, towards the back entrance to the inn. But as they passed one of the last doors, Gem came to a stop.

"A moment," he said, and opened the door.

"Gem—" said Loren. But then she froze. It was Prince Senlin's room. Jo had leaped to his feet as the door opened, but when he saw Gem, the bodyguard dropped his hand from his sword. Prince Senlin stood to greet Gem, dumbfounded.

"Master Noctis," he said. "Can I . . . can I help you?"

"I . . . I only wanted to say," said Gem. A flush crept up his cheeks, and he took another step into the room. "I cannot explain everything now, but I think—after tonight, I mean. I think you will be a very good king."

A small smile crossed Senlin's lips. "Thank you. That is reassuring to—"

His words died as Gem leaped forwards and kissed him. Senlin's eyes widened, and next to them both, Jo froze in shock. Then Senlin closed his eyes and gripped Gem's shoulders. For a moment, all of time seemed frozen, and Loren thought even her heart must have stopped beating.

Then at last, Gem drew away. Senlin took a small, sharp breath.

"That is all I wanted to say," said Gem. Then he fled from the room as fast as his feet would carry him. He seized Loren's arm and drew her along after him. "Sky above, hurry, before he has a chance to say something."

Loren only caught one brief glance of Senlin, standing there with his fingers on his lips, before she passed from view of him.

They reached the back door. By some stroke of fortune, Uzo was on guard duty again. But then, Loren did not much believe in fortune any longer. No doubt this was some design of fate as well—the same fate that had brought her visions, curse and blessing that they were.

But time enough for those thoughts later.

Uzo glanced down at Loren in surprise as she approached, and then he eyed her companions. A grim look came into his eyes. Loren thought for a moment that he would try to stop them. Instead he merely reached over and opened the door for her.

"Thank you," said Loren quietly. "Fare well. Say good-bye to Shiun for us. She should understand."

"She will," said Uzo. "Fare well, Nightblade. It has been the greatest honor of my life—so far, anyway. Whatever you must do, make them pay."

"I will," said Loren. And she took her first step into the darkness—a darkness that she had fully embraced for the first time.

EPILOGUE

DAMARIS SAT AT HER WRITING DESK, PENNING A LETTER BOUND FOR the Seat. Her room at the inn felt . . . empty somehow. It was strange. She had spent many years of her life without Gregor at her side. Why did this time feel different? Why did she feel his absence so keenly?

She shook off such thoughts. It would not be long before he came to join her. Indeed, it was only his paranoia that had made him send her out of the city in the first place. The dear man wanted to take every precaution, now that they knew this disturbing business about Loren's dreams.

Her quill paused on the parchment. Dreams of the future. It was a terrifying prospect—but also it seemed to her to be an incredible opportunity. What might she do if she could see what was to come? But the boy had told her the dreams came after Loren met with Elves, and Damaris was not so great a fool as to trifle with them in hopes they would give her the same gift.

A tremor of fear ran through her as she thought of Gregor back in Danfon. Alone.

She shook her head. Fear was ridiculous. Knowledge of the future could not help Loren. Eventually Gregor would figure out a way to draw her within reach. What good would foresight be then? At best it would show her just how Gregor would dismantle her piece by piece. Indeed, it seemed Loren had dreamed of it already, if the boy was to be believed.

And Damaris had used all her skill with a knife to ensure that, indeed, he *could* be believed.

Sighing, Damaris stood from the desk and crossed the room to refill her wine. Foresight was a power indeed. Loren was certainly misusing it. But it explained how she had always remained on Damaris' trail, always just one step behind her. What a myopic, uninspired use for such a gift.

Damaris rolled a knot from her neck as she sipped her wine. Some things, sadly, could never be changed. That was a fact of the world that she had had to accept long ago. Loren's great weakness was that she refused to accept it. Why, if Damaris acted the same way, her life would be spent in constant terror of the Necromancer and their—

The thought pained her. She shied away. Never mind the Necromancer. That thought must be stowed until she had devised a solution for it.

A knock came at her door.

Damaris paused. It was no attack, that much was certain. She had been fleeing across Dorsea fast enough that, even knowing where she was bound, Loren would never be able to catch her. Gregor? But no, the knock was not heavy enough for that.

"Enter."

The door opened. A messenger came into the room, stopping for a deep bow.

"Good eve, my lady."

"Good eve," said Damaris. "What is it?"

"I . . ." The messenger stopped. Her lips twitched, fighting for words.

A tremor passed through Damaris' breast. Her fingers tightened on the stem of her goblet.

"What have you come to say? Spit it out."

"It is Gregor, my lady. He . . . he is dead."

The goblet fell from Damaris' fingers and crashed to the floor, sending its wine to soak into the fine rug at her feet.

"My lady," said the messenger, leaping forwards to pick it up. "I will fetch a—"

"Silence," said Damaris. The messenger froze. "Was it the girl?"

The woman's skin went a shade paler. She nodded.

"Thank you," said Damaris. "That will be all."

The messenger opened her mouth as if to say something else. But she thought better of it, turned, and left the room.

Only then did Damaris let herself collapse into the chair by the writing desk.

Gregor. Her oldest friend. Her closest companion. Theirs was the greatest love she had ever seen or heard tale about—not the love of those who share a bed, but of those who share their lives together, their every innermost thought. Indeed, he was worth more than every man she had taken to bed all put together. He had saved her life, had been there as she raised Annis.

And now he was gone.

She did not weep openly, but she could not stop the tears from slowly leaking. Her grip tightened on the back of the chair until her knuckles had gone very nearly white.

And for the first time since she could remember, a feeling wrapped its deathly fingers around her heart. An emotion she was not at all familiar with. A pure, cold, unrelenting fear.

The dream took him.

The girl in the cloak knelt over Gregor. She leaned down to whisper something in the giant's ear, but she spoke too softly to hear. The man in black could only watch as the girl leaned farther over, drawing her dagger across Gregor's throat. The giant's blood splashed across the carpet. It gave the man in black a sense of grim satisfaction. The girl in the cloak had succeeded where he had failed.

The girl slowly stood and turned to him. Her eyes had that glow—akin to magelight, and yet different. He had never seen anything like it before—and that was not something he could say for most things under the sky.

The girl drew closer. The man tensed. He had not felt fear for a very long time, but he felt . . . awareness. Caution. His every sense strained, ready to react if she should attack him.

"I killed him," said the girl in the black cloak. "But I will need to kill many more."

"Then do it," he said. "No one can stop you."

"I am not ready," said the girl in the black cloak. "Not yet. Help me."

He chuckled and shook his head. "I am no nursemaid. Get someone else to draw the knife for you."

Her green eyes pierced him, holding him in place. She lifted the dagger and pressed its point against his heart.

The man did not like threats. The man liked to end threats. But he could not lift his hands to pull her away. The dream would not let him.

"Help me," she rasped.

The dream released him.

The man in black started awake in his bed.

The dreamsight passed almost at once. He took two deep breaths to calm himself, and it was gone. Gently he massaged his temples and then rolled his shoulders to relax them.

Moonslight through the window. Still night. That was odd. The dreams did not often wake him before morning. Not any longer.

He rose, drawing on his trousers and shirt and boots. He went to the door and opened it, stepping out onto the balcony beyond.

Talib was there, standing guard in the shadows. He glanced at her and frowned. "You should have gone. I do not need a caretaker."

She arched an eyebrow at him. "I did leave. I could not sleep. I came back."

He snorted a brief laugh at that. How very like her. She was his best soldier, and he would hate to lose her—though he already knew he must. "Has there been any news about what happened in Wellmont?"

"None," she said, shaking her head. "But then, you asked very general questions."

"They will mean the right things to the right people," he said. "Just keep your ear out. We must learn what happened there, before—"

He pinched the bridge of his nose. *Before what?* It was getting harder and harder to tell. Something was changing. Accelerating. Increasing the presence of the dreamsight in the waking world, leaving him more and more confused about what he had seen in true life and what in a dream. And it all had something to do with what had happened at Wellmont.

But he still did not know what that was.

Talib still watched him, waiting for him to finish speaking. She was one of the two whom he let see him this way. The boy had to see him as all-knowing, sardonic, and certain. But with Talib—and one other—he felt he could let down his guard.

748

In fact, he knew he must. Or he would never get what he truly wanted.

"There is something else," he said. "Someone else entering the equation."

"Oh?" said Talib. "Who?"

"You have heard of the Nightblade?"

Talib snorted. "A few whispered stories."

"Then that is an advantage, because she knows little enough of us. But she will. She is coming."

Talib shot up straight in her chair. "Here? To the Seat?"

"I . . . I do not know." He frowned as he realized it was true. He had never seen her in a location that he knew. Only in Dorsea. But he could not be certain that was where he would see her. "I only know she is looking for me."

"And what do we care?" said Talib. "She is little more than a camp-fire tale. She cannot have done half the things they have said about her."

"She has not. But she has done other things that no one speaks of at all. Not yet, at any rate."

Finally Talib stood, coming to stand before him. "Mako, I do not understand. What does she have to do with anything?"

Mako grinned, his teeth glinting in the moonslight. "In truth, I do not know. But I very much look forward to finding out."

ADDENDUM A

HISTORICAL ESSAYS FROM
THE WORLD OF UNDERREALM

OF THE ELVES

"If you see them, run." — *Dorren*

Across the nine kingdoms, no creatures are more feared than the Elves, and rightly so.

Elves could be found in Underrealm before Roth, the first High King, ever landed his ships upon Southbreak. Indeed, they have appeared in tales as far back as may be traced by even the most diligent loremasters. They have been in the world far longer than humans, and they have always inspired the same terror.

Few humans have ever seen an Elf, but all accounts agree as to their general appearance. They are uniformly tall, taller than all but the largest humans. Their skin is as varied as ours, but their hair is always magestone-black, and they are always clad in white robes. Their eyes do not glow, precisely—any more than the rest of their bodies do, for Elves do appear to be bestowed with some strange glamor—but they are without pupil or iris that any human can see. Their robes float and flutter about them as though underwater, rippling in the wake of their movements, which are both quick and graceful.

No one knows where the Elves live, if indeed they have any permanent dwellings. They are only ever seen on the move, marching across the land alone or in small parties. They seem to prefer forests and woods and other places with green things growing. But they have been seen in the arid deserts of Idris, the high, snowy peaks of the Greatrocks, and even upon the three seas, where by some magic they walk upon the surface of the water as if it were a well-paved road.

Elves speak no tongue that humans have ever learned. On the incredibly rare occasions they communicate with humans, they do so by transmitting their thoughts directly into the mind. But some humans have heard the Elves sing, and they never forget the experience. The words are beautiful and melodic, imparting some of the Elves' ethereal grace upon the listener and overwhelming them with rapturous worship. It is said that the echo lives on forever in the mind of those who experience it, always just beyond the edge of hearing.

But as has been said, when humans encounter Elves, it is far less often an experience of transportive joy than one of horror. Almost always, Elves bring only death beyond understanding or hope of rescue.

Human weapons are no proof against Elves. Their skin shatters blades and snaps arrows in two. They move with exceptional speed and can easily outpace a horse. It is impossible to say whether their minds, as alien to a human as a human is to an ant, feel wrath or vengeance. But when they descend into violence, they cannot be stopped by any mortal means.

Most often they strike at travelers encountered upon the road, though it is not known whether they happen upon such travelers by chance, or whether they plan their journeys to intercept their prey. Sometimes Elves will walk straight through a caravan, ignoring those who scream or flee in terror, and kill a single human before withdrawing into the mists that often accompany them. Other times they will slaughter an entire party, leaving their bodies to rot in the open air.

When they kill only some humans, or one of them, there is no obvious reason behind their selection. It is more likely to be an unremarkable foot soldier or weary traveler than a merchant leading a caravan or a Mystic knight at the head of an expedition. On occasion they have killed only a single child, and even babes in their mothers' arms are not safe. It was once noted by a somewhat obscure Calentin scholar that there was no record of Elves killing horses or other animals, but this information was generally dismissed by other loremasters as unimportant, and thus it never reached broad knowledge.

On the rare occasions when Elves reach human settlements, their attacks can be even more terrifying. They will stride unconcerned through a city's gates. If the gates are closed, the Elves can strike them to the ground with a single sharp blow, or with a power akin to mindmagic that Elves wield often and with ease. They will stride through the streets of the city or town in pursuit of their target, ignoring the panic caused by their arrival. Indeed, when Elves attack a human city, there is usually a far greater death toll caused by the panic than by the Elves themselves. Crowds trample those who stumble and fall while attempting to flee, and some particularly opportunistic thieves will loot vacant shops and homes, clashing with any constable or Mystic brave enough to remain behind.

Elves will stride into any home or palace to find the human they seek. Once they have killed their prey, they leave just as suddenly and inexplicably as they arrived, marching out before the terrified eyes of the city's other inhabitants. It was during one such attack, centuries before the time of the Nightblade, that a particularly level-headed observer noticed something: the blood of their victims never stained the Elves' pristine white robes.

This, then, is the great terror of the Elves: that their attacks are entirely unpredictable and seem to have no reason. Yet once they have decided to kill, no human can hope to stop them. The only hope seems to be to try and avoid being noticed in the first place, though this seems pointless considering that the Elves appear and vanish with no discernible pattern.

Those who encounter the Elves and live—such as Loren of the family Nelda, who met them one night in Dorsea's northeastern wildlands—are among a tiny and incredibly fortunate minority. They are rarely believed by anyone else. But even if they were, what good would it do? They do not know why they survived, any more than others know why their loved ones were slain. The Elves are as unpredictable as an earthquake, and as deadly as a lightning strike. But while humans can erect buildings that withstand the ground's trembling, and hide indoors to avoid the lightning, they can build no shelter to stave off the Elves' wrath.

The worst attack of Elves ever recorded occurred in the Year of Underrealm 725, on the ninth day of Yulis. The nine kingdoms were then ruled by High King Aldus, who had inherited the throne from his mother, Alden. Before his ascension, Aldus had ruled the kingdom of Hedgemond which, too, came down to him from his mother.

In those times, the capital of Underrealm had not yet been moved to the island in the Great Bay that would be called the High King's Seat. The High King still ruled from Southbreak, on the throne in Rothton, which city had been built by Roth himself, the first High King. But it would not be long before a new High King would abandon Rothton, at least in part because of this very attack.

During his time, Aldus was a wise and benevolent High King, and well loved by his subjects. He was even popular among a majority of the nine kings who served him, which is a rarity in that highest office. These were still the days of the Wizard Kings and the Dark Wars, when magestones flowed freely across Underrealm and none sat a throne but those who had the gift of magic. Aldus himself was a weremage, and though he had rarely seen battle, his hellskin form was a terrible beast, more than four paces tall and capable of great slaughter. It was somewhat ironic, then, that he was known to all who dealt with him as a kind and quiet-spoken man, slow to punish or to chastise, and forgiving almost to a fault.

Under his guiding hand, many diplomatic ties were made between kingdoms that had until that time made great war upon each other. The feud between Dulmun and Dorsea was mended, and Selvan and Wadeland became closer than they ever had been before—a bond of friendship that would still exist during the time of the Nightblade. Though the Dark Wars were not over, they looked to be on their way to ending, and all the people of Underrealm seemed to hold their breath with that hope.

Then came the Elves.

They were first seen by the people of Feldemar, for they came marching out of the eastern reaches of that kingdom's jungles. They crossed the leagues of open ground between the jungle and the coast of the Eldest Deep, crossing Dulmun's western lands at a pace faster than flight, though they did not look as if they were hurrying. Never had such a gathering of Elves been seen in memory or history, nor has such a number of them been seen together since. At least a hundred there were, though no one dared draw close enough to get a better count.

Not one of them slowed when they reached the coast. They strode east across the waves, which stilled at once and lay quiet before them, calm and shining like glass. Some brave sailors of Dulmun had taken to boats, desperate to deliver warning to their High King. But the wind died, and their oars could not outpace the Elves. They caught the would-be messengers and slaughtered them, leaving their vessels to drift away on the water.

At last the guards on Southbreak's western shores saw them coming. They spread their alarm inland, and all of Rothton's bells tolled with warning. What soldiers the island had were mustered, but many refused the call, knowing the Elves could not be resisted.

The Elves reached Rothton, cast down the western gates, and strode into the city, walking upon its main road towards the palace. They came with a wrath that could not be sated or appeased. No one who came within sight of the Elves was permitted to flee or to live. Whereas many times before, Elves had let bystanders go free, ignoring them in favor of whoever they had come to kill, now they pursued the citizens of Rothton, crushing their necks until they snapped or tearing them limb from limb. It was said that blood ran in the gutters and the bodies piled so high in places that they blocked the lanes and avenues.

As soon as he heard the bells and horns of his city, High King Aldus went to the western wall of his palace. There, for a time, he watched the slaughter with his closest advisors at his side. "It is for me," they heard him say quietly, as if speaking to himself. "It is all for me, though I do not know why."

Shortly after saying these words, he descended from the wall and strode out through the palace gates. His advisors and guards begged him not to go. Indeed, his personal bodyguard and lover, Kris of the family Konnel, tried to restrain Aldus with his own body. Aldus smiled, but with a spell he turned nearly giant-sized, and with tree-like limbs pushed Kris aside, where the man fell to his knees, weeping.

Aldus forced his way through the crowds towards the Elves, though that was difficult, for his people were nearly mad with fear, and he had to push through them like a man stumbling through a blizzard. None of his guards would come with him after Kris gave up, and so he had to make his way alone. But at last he came to stand before the white-clad beings. He reached for the sword at his belt—but only to unbuckle it and throw it upon the street.

"I know you have come for me, though I do not know how I know it," he said. "Take me, then, and let my people go."

An Elf that had stood paces away suddenly appeared just in front of Aldus. It reached out and snapped his neck, letting his body fall limp to the cobblestones.

But they did not honor his second request, if indeed they understood it at all. They moved on to the palace, killing everyone they saw on their way, and then they killed everyone within. Kris was one of the first to die, attacking the Elves with his sword in a frenzy of grief. No one at the palace escaped the slaughter, from the Lord Prince herself to the meanest scullery man.

In the end, nearly a third of those who dwelled in Rothton were slain that day. Only those who fled first, who never caught sight of the Elves, survived. All of Aldus' kin on Southbreak were killed, and his line, which had run unbroken since Roth himself, was ended.

But the end of Aldus' line was not the end of Roth's. For Aldus had a younger sister, Andara, who was a student at the Academy in those days, and in her final year. The Academy, of course, was far away from Southbreak, and so she escaped the wrath of the Elves. Some few years later she inherited the throne of Hedgemond from her older brother, Aldor, who had never produced an heir after inheriting the kingdom from Aldus.

It was her position as the king of Hedgemond that enabled Andara to make a play for the High Throne, which she did some five years after the Elven attack. Teldin, the king of Wavemount, had been chosen for the throne after Aldus, but he was never popular. A sickness took him only four years later, and he soon died.

After Teldin's incompetent rule, Andara set about winning the hearts of the other eight kings. She promised them a return of Aldus' days, a time of great peace and prosperity. She did not have such a fine mind for diplomacy as her brother had had, but she knew her only hope of gaining power lay in doing her best to emulate him. Therefore she was chosen by the council of kings, though she won by only a single vote, and became the new High King.

Andara had many notable accomplishments, but two events in her life stand out among historians who study such matters.

The first is that it was Andara who moved her throne from Rothton, where it had been since the nation's founding, to an island in the Great Bay and named it the High King's Seat.

The second is that, three years after Aldus' death, Andara gave birth to her first child: a daughter, Andriana, who would one day be called The Fearless.

OF ROTH'S WARS

As has been told elsewhere, Roth, the first High King, landed upon the island of Southbreak after sailing to Underrealm from a distant land. He led a fleet of ships, which most historians agree numbered sixteen. These were vast and mighty vessels, wrought with all the skill of whatever great kingdom whence Roth came, the name of which is lost. Each was like its own sizeable town, carrying hundreds of occupants—not only sailors, soldiers, and officers, but commonfolk as well, with artisans, farmers, and crafters of every kind.

All told, they numbered at least ten thousands. It was therefore fortunate that they found Southbreak nearly devoid of intelligent life, with plenty of room for them to build their new home. A few imps in the trees saw Roth's forces land, but they quickly scuttled to their hiding places beneath the boughs and in the island's plentiful caves, and Roth's people never saw them.

But Southbreak teemed with wildlife to hunt, and it was covered with thick and hearty trees that had stood for centuries. These provided good lumber for building, which Roth's people began to do with great vigor. Soon they had established three settlements. The first, and the greatest, was Kingsmouth, central on Southbreak's northeastern shore. The second was Starview, built on the very northern tip of the island, the home of Roth's eldest and most beloved sister, Renna, who most called Sunmane. And near the island's south end, where the Wilmwater spilled into the sea, they built the city of Denharrow. In later years, Denharrow's location would make it the greatest trading port of the whole island, and larger even than the capital, though that would not be so for more than a century.

Roth soon sought out and found a new location for his capital, and upon one of Southbreak's great mountains he built the city of Rothton. But that was an endeavor that took years, and before it was complete, he had already begun to explore for more lands to conquer. The lore of Roth's origins has been lost, but it seems clear he was some great royal son of whatever family produced him. He clearly saw it as his right to rule this new land he had found, and he was most industrious in doing so.

First his captains mapped the Great Bay, charting its edges and discovering the large island near its southwestern end, which would become the High King's Seat centuries later. Then, expeditions of soldiers explored the lands that seemed most fruitful. In just over a year, Roth knew much of the lay of the country, and he took council with his generals and admirals to devise a plan to rule them.

His first three campaigns quickly took the lands that would become Dulmun, Feldemar, Selvan, and northeastern Dorsea. But Roth would soon learn that a great force of arms was not always necessary to rule, and sometimes it was worse than no help.

THE CONQUEST OF DULMUN

Dulmun is a kingdom that spans three great land masses. The first is Southbreak, the island where Roth made landfall. The second is west of the island, and the third is to the south.

The mainland to the west of Southbreak was a wild jungle country, and those dark, rain-soaked trees stretched west as far as his scouts dared to go. The scattered humans who lived there swore a somewhat vague fealty to Kijina, the king of Feldemar. But Kijina himself did not trouble with these people, and only claimed the lands as far east as the Blumkia river. In lieu of Kijina's direct influence, the jungle tribes served lesser lords who claimed to act in Kijina's name (and with his authority). But such settlements were scattered and meager, and few numbered more than two hundreds.

The mainland to the south went from dry and arid in the east, almost as inhospitable as the southern deserts, to rich and lush in the west, with rich, fertile silt carried down from vast mountain ranges. Nomads lived in the eastern deserts, small tribes who brought goods and treasures from one oasis to the next. They did not swear fealty to the Tomb-Kings who lived farther south, but lived "free," as they put it, kneeling to no lord. But the lush lands to the west were filled with centaurs. Half human, half horse, these creatures formed many packs spread all through the rich valleys that had formed between the two great mountain ranges that would one day form the borders of Wadeland.

Roth knew he could conquer the desert without much trouble. Though some humans lived there, they were scattered and disparate, and were likely to simply surrender without a fight. The jungles in the west, too, would fall easily. But these lands were also of little value. The jungles made for poor farmland, and the strange illnesses would be hard on any of Roth's people who settled there. The deserts were worse—no wealth came from those lands except what was brought from the great civilizations in the deep south. Therefore it was the southwestern mainland that Roth desired most.

He sent token forces to the other areas and, as he guessed, their people surrendered to him after only a few small skirmishes. In the jungles, he advanced all the way to the Blumkia river. At key points along that river he stationed strong garrisons of troops, but he commanded them not to go any farther west. Their presence would make the king of Feldemar nervous, and Roth was not yet ready for a war there. In the desert, he marked his southern border on the mountain range that blocked the path of his army's advance, and at every break in the range he stationed troops, who began to extract a tax from any caravan coming north from Idris.

But to the west, the centaurs were the first to resist him in strength. Centaurs are a wise and gentle people for the most part, but when stoked, their wrath is terrible. Had Roth reached out to them with envoys for peace, he might have achieved his aims more quickly. Indeed, that was the counsel of Sunmane. She did not believe that Underrealm should be taken with conquest and war, but with diplomacy and mediation. Roth's people were mighty, but each of their lives was precious to Sunmane. They had followed their king far from home, and she saw no purpose in throwing away their lives to conquer lands that, in time, they would surely come to rule anyway. She thought their troops would be better deployed to conquer Feldemar, where the king was cruel to his subjects and unlikely to treat with them.

Roth, however, was thirsty for battle. He was a warlike king, and saw it as his right to take what he viewed as his. Therefore he sent his daughter south to conquer the centaurs' lands. He had named her Renna after his sister, but she was as unlike her aunt as it was possible to be, sharing Roth's thirst for battle and for conquest. It was her hope (and her father's) that the centaurs, who roamed the land in packs, could be defeated piecemeal.

That would not prove to be the case in the end, but at first the campaign seemed to go well. As Renna's forces pushed south from the shore of the Great Bay, the centaurs fell upon them with spears and arrows. Roth had no great strength of horse, for most of the beasts had not survived the long voyage across the Eldest Deep. The centaurs fell upon him like heavy cavalry, for they forged armor like that of humans, if not of the same quality. Though Renna's first few battles were victories, because she faced only a pack at a time, they still took a heavy toll, as many human lives were paid for each centaur's corpse.

Renna's forces pushed the centaurs back until she reached the mouth of the great valley, a broad swathe of land between the northern tips of two great mountain ranges. But there her advance stopped. For the centaurs had spread word throughout the land, and all the scattered packs had gathered into one great force to resist her.

On the banks of the Zanbibi River, they made their stand. Renna commanded more than a thousand soldiers, greatly outnumbering her foe, but only a few hundreds were trained and battle-hardy. Most of Roth's soldiers had been pressed into service, enticed with promises of plunder and grants of land. But those promises alone would not pierce the centaurs' armor, nor divide their ranks, and Renna's militia fled from the creatures' fury. But neither could the centaurs cast off the invaders, for on her side of the river, Renna had built great barricades with sharp spears thrusting forth, as against a force of cavalry, and the centaurs could not pierce them.

For a month the armies tore at each other. After the fiercest battles, the waters of the Zanbibi would run red for hours. And in the end, Renna's father ordered her to halt her advance.

Roth had finally heeded the counsel of his sister. Sunmane came to take control of the army, and she began at once to treat with the centaurs. Her job was made all the more difficult now that their ire had been stoked, but after a time she managed it. Dulmun's borders were drawn at last. Roth's domain now extended to the Zanbibi river. The centaurs kept their valley, but they gave Roth leave to mine its hills and mountains for the plentiful gold and jewels that lay there, which they held as worthless. In exchange, Roth's smiths were put to work crafting fine weapons and suits of armor for the centaurs, giving them much better arms than they had ever had before.

Once his southern border was firmly established, Roth named his new kingdom Dulmun and took it as his own seat of power. To mark its borders on the shores of the Great Bay, he ordered the building of two great war-lights. These odd buildings, half lighthouse and half fortress, were a convention first brought to Underrealm by Roth, and are still much favored by the lords of Dulmun. The northern war-light he named Arod, and the southern, Hasufel. But even as his masons busied themselves with the task, Roth set his sights on the lands of Underrealm that lay farther west, and he gave Sunmane the task of seizing them. His daughter, Renna, was no longer in command, but Roth named her as Sunmane's chief lieutenant. That was a high position, certainly, but it rankled her, and led to much strife in the end, as has been told elsewhere.

THE TREATY OF FELDEMAR

Feldemar is a place of jungles, bogs, and marshes, and has always been a divided land. Kings have difficulty establishing their rule across it, for there are many pockets of civilization that are difficult and dangerous to reach.

When Roth arrived, Feldemar was ruled by King Kijina. Kijina was a cruel lord, preferring to govern with fear and threat of punishment instead of a kind and coaxing hand. If Kijina suspected a lord of disloyalty, that lord would be killed at once, and often their family as well.

Sunmane learned all this from the first messengers she sent to the lords of Feldemar, but she still thought it best to try a peaceful treaty before launching an attack on Kijina's forces. Therefore she herself led an expedition that traveled close to the city of Dahab, Feldemar's capital, and from beyond its walls she sent envoys to Kijina himself. They brought him great gifts of gold and messages from Sunmane. The messages were diplomatic but clear: Roth meant to claim Feldemar as his own, and if Kijina served him as a loyal lord, he would reap great benefits.

Kijina's response came through sign language, for of course the people of Feldemar did not speak the tongue of Roth's people in those days. Yet even through the gesticulations, Kijina's scorn and arrogance were as clear as his rejection of her offer. Sunmane was glad, at least, that he had not killed her messengers.

So Sunmane began her campaign, but it was not the wild war-making that her niece, Renna, had brought to the centaurs. She studied the land carefully, choosing cities and towns of high importance. When she moved to attack, she would first offer an opportunity to accept Roth's rule in peace. Any lord who did so was given gold, as well as weapons and armor to outfit their troops. But Sunmane, ever shrewd, also gave each of them a personal guard of soldiers loyal to Roth. The message, though never plainly stated, was nevertheless clear: if the lord thought to turn their newly-armed troops upon Roth's armies, one of their bodyguards would slay them where they stood. But because Sunmane was as fair as she was clever, she did not face much dissent from her new vassals.

Most Feldemarian lords, however, did not accept Sunmane's terms. Any ruler will inevitably foster underlings like himself, and most who served Kijina were as cruel and intemperate as the king. After decades of his spiteful rule, they often feared Kijina's wrath more than this new, foreign interloper. Therefore Sunmane had to take many towns and cities by force of arms. Always she would command her troops to do no more harm than was necessary, and she forbade them from pillaging or looting. In this way she hoped to spread word through the kingdom that Roth's armies were at least somewhat benevolent, so that some lords of Feldemar would be more inclined to surrender their holdings without a fight.

But Sunmane could not be everywhere at once, and often her lieutenants led armies in her stead. Renna was chief among these and, though she was often the most effective, she was also the most ruthless. Sunmane sent Renna north, where she cut a bloody path through the jungle towards the Nelos River. By seizing it, Sunmane hoped to strengthen her position against Dahab, which in those days was the capital of Feldemar.

Like her aunt, Renna led from the front, but where Sunmane fought with honor as well as skill, Renna was bloodthirsty. Often she would strike down her foes even after they cast their weapons down and begged for clemency, and she ordered her soldiers to do the same. Soon she had amassed a cadre of her favorite troops, many of whom had fought with her in Dulmun and had developed a taste for blood. Chief among these was a brawny and cruel woman named Leif, who was Renna's lover as well as her captain, and who strove always to match her mistress in killing and in conquest. Wherever they went, the people of Feldemar cowered in fear, though that did not stay their blades.

Things came to a head at the town of Kunde. Resting in the foothills of a small but deadly mountain range called the Sky's Knives, Kunde was an important point of strength for the Feldemar campaign. In a letter, Sunmane had confided in Renna that she thought the town would be most difficult to take, for Kijina would no doubt guess their plans and reinforce it.

But when Renna approached Kunde on a cold grey morning, she found the town's gates open. Its lord stood waiting for them in the open. She had only a small party of retainers by her side, and their weapons were not drawn. Though Renna suspected a trap, she nevertheless rode forwards to parley, bringing a dozen heavily armed riders led by Leif. They brought an interpreter as well, for some months ago they had captured a man of Feldemar from the court of a lesser lord. They had taught him their language in order to treat more easily with their foes.

As soon as they reached the lord of Kunde, she knelt to them and bent her head. Her retainers did likewise at once. Renna dismounted, sharing a look of amusement with Leif.

"Greetings, honored people of Roth," said the lord of Kunde. She spoke to them in their own language, which amazed them, though the sound of her own tongue was heavy upon her words. "I am Wumere, and I am lord of this city."

"How do you know our words?" said Leif at once.

"You have taken some of our people and taught it to them," said Wumere, risking a glance at the interpreter they had brought. "Some of them have managed to escape after a time. I thought it would be best if I spoke to you directly."

"Why?" said Renna. "What do you mean to say to us?"

"You have come to conquer Kunde. There is no need. I offer it to you in peace."

"You offer it?" said Renna. "Are you so cowardly?"

Wumere looked up at her, still kneeling. "Is it cowardly, or is it wise? I see the strength of arms you have brought, and I know how many soldiers I have. We cannot hope to defeat you. And surely you know by now that no lord of Feldemar serves Kijina out of love, nor does he rule us with grace. Yet we have heard of the mercy and the wisdom of the Sunmane. I would pledge my people to her service over the one who presses a blade to my throat and forces me to name him king."

For a long moment, Renna hesitated. The soldiers at her side looked at her, uncertain. They had come expecting a battle, even thirsting for one. The Sunmane's expectation that Kunde would offer staunch resistance had spread throughout the troops, and this capitulation came as a complete surprise.

But at last, Renna smiled. No doubt Wumere took that as a good sign, for she smiled in return. Yet Leif knew her lieutenant's mood better than anyone, and she matched the grin with a fierce one of her own, hand tightening on her sword. Wumere's praise of Sunmane was like bitter salt on Renna's wounded pride.

"I do not accept your terms," said Renna.

Wumere's smile died. "I do not ask for any terms. Kunde is yours."

"Yes, it is," said Renna. "Leif. Kill them."

Her soldiers fell upon the party with fierce cries and cut them down. Renna's army, watching from a distance, surged forwards to join their lieutenant, and the army fell upon Kunde, pouring in through its open gate.

One member of Renna's party, who had heard everything that was said, was sickened by the slaughter. His name was Radala, and he had long been discomfited by Renna's warmongering ways. He had held his peace until now, thinking that Renna must be acting on Sunmane's orders. But he knew Sunmane would never condone the slaughter of a town that had surrendered.

The night that Kunde was sacked, Radala slipped away from the army in the dead of night, evading the sentries and striking out across the countryside. He made a dangerous journey south and east, where he met Sunmane's army as it pushed its way through the jungle towards Dahab.

Once he found Sunmane, he begged an audience and told her all that had transpired at Kunde. Sunmane's wrath was great, and she sent messengers at once to summon Renna to answer for her actions. But before Renna came, an envoy arrived from the family Yerrin. Their matriarch, Manya, desired to meet with Sunmane.

This they did, as has been described elsewhere. Sunmane had the treaty she wanted—not with Feldemar's king, but with the Yerrins. Thus Dahab fell, and most of the Feldemarians were spared further slaughter.

When Sunmane took the capital and slew Kijina with her own sword, she did not put one of Roth's people in his place. She found Kijina's daughter, Frema, more than willing to bend the knee to Roth, and so installed her as the new king. In this way, Sunmane likely staved off a much longer and bloodier conflict, for the lords of Feldemar were far more willing to acknowledge one of their own as king than some foreigner.

With the campaign at a close, Sunmane treated Renna more leniently than she might have otherwise. Instead of sending Renna home to Roth in shame, she was permitted to remain as a lieutenant, though she never led troops in battle again, for Sunmane no longer trusted her.

And thus the seed of Renna's discontent continued to grow.

THE OCCUPATION OF SELVAN AND DORSEA

With Feldemar conquered, Roth could now set his sights on what were the chief jewels in his eyes: the lands that would one day become Selvan and northern Dorsea. Selvan, in particular, was a lush and verdant country that could bring his kingdom great wealth. But he had not been willing to take it while Feldemar could threaten him from the north.

He summoned Sunmane back to Southbreak and held council with her at his home in Rothton—a temporary dwelling only while his new palace there was being built. But Sunmane ordered Renna to remain with Roth's armies in eastern Feldemar. She commanded Renna, on pain of exile, not to take any action without Sunmane's explicit approval. Renna agreed, if begrudgingly, and stewed in Feldemar for months while her aunt and her father made their plans on Southbreak without her.

In their councils, Roth again urged conquest, desiring to take these new, fertile lands with fire and sword. But Sunmane spoke strongly against such a course. The lands were practically wide open to them already, with few humans to be found anywhere. It would not be wise, she said, to fall upon their few new subjects with war, nor should they stoke the wrath of the other creatures who lived there. If they proceeded cautiously and with wisdom, they would surely have an easier time of it when they eventually pushed south beyond the mountains and into the lands of the Tomb-Kings—the only other great civilization they knew of, and one which could give them much trouble if they were not cautious.

Back and forth they argued for weeks, with both of them growing ever more irritated. Slowly that irritation stoked to anger. And on one dark day, that anger spilled forth until they were shouting at each other in Roth's newly-completed throne room, alone with each other, for their advisors and retainers had quickly fled before the fury of their lords. And at the height of their argument, Roth called his sister weak and a coward.

They both stopped short, staring at each other in the silence. Roth blanched, though he hardly knew why. Perhaps he saw in his sister's face some of the fury that had been there when she had slain Kijina, or one of the other countless times she had faced her foes on the battlefield and cut them down without hesitation.

When Sunmane finally spoke, Roth flinched. But she did not shout, nor even speak in anger. To Roth's surprise, and not insignificant guilt, she sounded deeply hurt.

"Was it my cowardice that saved the lives of hundreds of our soldiers, Your Majesty?" she said. "Was it my weakness that slew Kijina and gave you Feldemar?"

At her questions, Roth hung his head in shame. He had no servant more loyal than his sister, nor more loving, and he knew it. "Forgive me, my dearest," he said. "You are one of the moons of my heart, as my daughter, who I named for you, is the other. I spoke in anger, and I regret it."

"We have tried war, Your Majesty," said Sunmane. "And you know I will not flinch from it when it is the right course. Yet you are too quick to make it, and Renna is the same. It is long since you have seen her, my lord, and you have never witnessed her in the field. I fear that she has learned too much of battle-thirst from you, and not enough of patience."

But Roth waved his hand in dismissal. "She is only eager to prove herself. You and I were not so different, when we were young. She longs for your praise more than mine, even if you cannot see it."

Sunmane frowned, for she knew that was not the truth. Yet she could see from Roth's countenance that she could not convince him otherwise, and it would not help sway his mind towards the right course. Instead, she crossed the room to stand before him, while Roth tilted his head at her, a question in his eyes.

"Give me your hand," said Sunmane. He hesitated, and she smiled, tears suddenly brimming in her eyes. Seeing that, Roth at last placed his hand in hers, and she turned it to place it on her belly. "Feel the life that grows inside me now."

Wonder came upon Roth, and his tears swelled to match hers. "A child?"

"Yes. Fathered by a lord of Feldemar who joined us shortly before we took Dahab. That was four months ago."

Roth knelt before her, wrapping his arms around her waist and pressing his cheek to her body. "A child," he whispered. "I thought . . ."

"As did I," said Sunmane. "As did the healers. It mattered little to me either way, but now . . . do you not see it, Your Majesty? Do you—"

"Not now," said Roth. "My majesty, if I have any, is eclipsed by this moment. Now I am only a brother who is overjoyed for his sister."

Sunmane smiled at that. "Very well, brother. Then hear me when I say: *this* is the gift of Underrealm. Life, not death. It is what this new land has given to us, and we must give it back. These places and these people are not ours to conquer. They are ours to cherish, to foster and to grow. To lead. Let me lead, brother, and build a legacy of growth and care rather than of war."

Roth stood again, his bearing once again regal. Sunmane's heart quailed, for she feared he would refuse her. But Roth spoke this proclamation:

"Let it so be. If it is the sky's will that I rule this new land we have found for our people, then I will. But I will do so with justice and with peace, not war. I give to you, Renna, who is the Sunmane, my authority in this. Conquer that which I have taken for my own, but do it with grace. I command only that you bend the knee to me."

With the matter at last settled, they did not take long to put their plans into motion. Sunmane soon set forth from Southbreak, and she led Roth's people in their new settlement. They spread across the lands slowly, exploring the lush forest of the Birchwood, building new towns and villages farther and farther west and south. Before long they found the Greatrocks and mapped them, as well as the Dragon's Tail River. People of Feldemar came south to join them, their blood mingling with that of Roth's people. The lands north of the Birchwood were not as fertile as those farther south, but still Sunmane took them, and she built the city of Danfon at the foot of the Greatrocks, where she installed one of her sisters as vassal. But for herself she built the city of Garsec, at the mouth of the Melnar river just south of the Birchwood, and from there she directed all her citizens and soldiery in their development of the new kingdom.

Sunmane did not take this new domain entirely without bloodshed, of course. Though few humans mustered in strength to resist them, other creatures were plentiful in those days. But Renna treated with them when she could, and tried to avoid them when she could not, only bringing the fires of war when her people were attacked first.

It was a process of years, rather than the months it would surely have taken if they had made war. Through it all, Roth's daughter Renna served her aunt, growing ever more frustrated and impatient as her blade rested in its scabbard, unused. Often she would look for an excuse to lead troops into battle once again. But Sunmane kept a watchful eye on her, and restrained her whenever her bloodthirst grew too great.

In the end, Selvan was occupied, and Sunmane gave it its name, after her daughter, Silvin, who had been born shortly after she arrived to the new kingdom. Then Roth gave his blessing to the new kingdom and took it under his rule, and named Sunmane as its king, with Silvin as her prince.

This came as a great shock to Sunmane, who had expected Roth to send her to conquer more new lands in his name and give the kingdom to Renna. Indeed, she had long planned for this, and had tried to structure her new kingdom so that it would not suffer too greatly under Renna's more violent hand. But she accepted the honor with grace and dignity, as well as with gratitude. It left her feeling lenient, so that when Renna begged to be allowed to return to Southbreak to see her father, Sunmane relented. To her mind, it was better to have Renna gone for a time, rather than continuing to serve with resentment in her heart.

She could not know, of course, how dark was the hatred already filling that heart. Had she suspected what Renna meant to do at Southbreak, Sunmane would never have allowed her to go. But Sunmane had no gift of foresight, and so Renna left, soon to set in motion the first great civil war of Underrealm.

But while some parts of that story have been told already, we must wait a while longer before the rest of it can be told in full.

ADDENDUM B

CALENDAR OF UNDERREALM
AND A TIMELINE OF EVENTS

THE CALENDAR OF UNDERREALM

There are 363.5 days in an Underrealm year. In their calendar, these are divided into 12 months of 30 days each. To reconcile the extra days, at the end of each year there is a three-day holiday called, appropriately enough, Yearsend. It takes place in the middle of winter when the world is coldest, and after which the world "comes to life" again. Yearsend is often a time of celebration, when people of all the nine kingdoms take to feasting and revelry, bidding farewell to the year that has ended and readying themselves to greet the year that approaches.

Even-numbered years have leap days, placed in the middle of Yearsend, so that it is four days long in those years.

For the sake of ease, the twelve months of the Underrealm calendar have been given their Latin names from the Gregorian calendar. However, they are arranged in the original *order* of the Gregorian calendar, with Martis being the first month of the year, as follows:

Martis — WINTER
Arilis — SPRING
Maius — SPRING
Yunis — SPRING
Yulis — SUMMER
Augis — SUMMER
Septis — SUMMER
Octis — AUTUMN
Novis — AUTUMN
Dektis — AUTUMN
Yanis — WINTER
Febris — WINTER
Yearsend* — WINTER

Martis comes just after Yearsend. As with any calendar, the "assignment" of seasons is arbitrary, and the people of Underrealm saw no reason to make them fit the calendar symmetrically. Therefore winter stretches from Yanis to Martis. Spring is Arilis to Yunis. Summer lasts from Yulis to Septis, and autumn is from Octis to Dektis.

In the strictest sense, then, the seasons do not truly fall where they are delineated on the Underrealm calendar. However, this assignment was seen as a neater solution than having the seasons begin and end in the middle of months, which would of course be chaotic and confusing to everyone involved.

* Yearsend is included for the purpose of showing its order in the calendar, though of course it is a three- or four-day period and not truly a month on its own.

THE COUNT OF YEARS

"The Year of Underrealm 1" is held to be the year Roth, the first High King of Underrealm, ruling from the city of Rothton on the island capital of Dulmun, declared the nine lands to be under his dominion. Though some scholars enjoy debating the exact count, it is generally accepted to have occurred 1,311 years before Loren of the family Nelda left her forest home. (This is, however, an inaccurate counting, since Roth laid claim to Underrealm some eighty years before his granddaughter would mark the start of the Underrealm calendar. But this truth has long been lost to history.)

Years are notated as *The Year of Underrealm 1312*.

WEEKS

The twelve months of Underrealm are further divided into three weeks of ten days.

As we have done, the days were named for planets that the denizens of Underrealm could observe. But this presented a problem: only six planets were visible in the sky. These were named Taya, Yuna, Kina, Marama, Dal, and Kasay in the time before time, and gave Underrealm the day-names of Tasday, Yunsday, Kinsday, Marsday, Dalsday, and Kasday. Two more days were named for Underrealm's twin moons of Enalyn and Merida, giving them Lynday and Meriday. The Sun led to Sunday, as it did for us, and that was also the Underrealm day of rest.

It is said that before humans came to Underrealm, the tenth day (which always preceded Sunday) had various names among different peoples. And so, when the first High King of Underrealm, Roth, founded the nine lands, he named the tenth day after himself, calling it Rothsday.

Thus the days are, in order:

LYNDAY
MERIDAY
TASDAY
YUNSDAY
KINSDAY
MARSDAY
DALSDAY
KASDAY
ROTHSDAY
SUNDAY

THE YEAR OF UNDERREALM 1312

NOVIS

19 Novis: Loren and her friends are still in Northwood. Chet tells Loren more of how her father died. Xain reveals to Loren what Jordel told him of the Necromancer.

20 Novis: They learn that Rogan has reached Northwood and is searching for Loren. They try to flee, but the Shades attack the city in strength. Mag and Albern are lost defending Loren's escape. The rest of Loren's party escapes into the Birchwood.

21 Novis: Loren tells Xain of her dagger's powers. They decide to ride east through the Birchwood until they reach the Great Bay, and then set sail for Feldemar and Jordel's stronghold of Ammon.

22 Novis: Loren first spies the Shades pursuing her in the woods. That night they hide the horses and set watch over a false camp. The Shades find the false camp and then lose their trail.

25 Novis: Shades find Loren and attack. Loren barely stops herself from killing one of them.

26 Novis: Loren finds a village destroyed by the Shades. A mutilated boy tells her Rogan was there, searching for her.

29 Novis: Annis' birthday. She realizes it, but does not mention it to the others, who are still in a grim mood after finding the massacred village.

DEKTIS

1 Dektis: Loren passes from the Birchwood into Dorsea. That night, camped upon the Dorsean plains, Elves awaken Loren from her sleep. They reveal to Loren the power of her dagger when used with magestones.

2 Dektis: Loren tells Chet of her encounter, but none of the others. Xain sees a curious light in her eyes, but he does not recognize it.

6 Dektis: Loren reaches the village where Crastus' inn lies and buy a room for the night. But before they can rest, Rogan arrives at the head of a party of Shades. They slaughter the villagers, capturing the children. Loren barely escapes.

10 Dektis: Loren reaches the Great Bay. They discover a Shade separated from his party. Xain kills him despite Chet's objections. They ride north and see the port town of Brekkur before nightfall, but Loren decides to camp rather than reach it in the middle of the night. Chet speaks with her while she is on watch, and they share their first kiss.

11 Dektis: Loren enters Brekkur. Xain finds a good ship to gain passage, and they meet its captain, Torik. He brings them aboard to show them their lodgings—only to bring them into a room full of Mystics. Kal, Jordel's old master, leads them. After learning of Jordel's death, he tells them they must bring their information to the High King's Seat. Xain agrees.

12 Dektis: Loren takes a day aboard the ship to rest. Annis decides not to accompany Loren, but to sail north with Kal and wait for Loren in Ammon.

13 Dektis: Loren sails from Brekkur to the High King's Seat. She leaves her dagger with Xain's friend Aurel. Then she and Xain allow themselves to be captured by the High King. They deliver the news of Jordel's death and the warning of the Necromancer. Enalyn places them under house arrest.

14 Dektis: The Lord Prince Eamin visits Xain in their quarters. He meets Loren and recognizes her as Elf-touched. He promises their time in confinement will be brief.

26 Dektis: Assassins try to kill the Lord Prince in Loren's quarters. The assassins are defeated, but Chet is gravely wounded by a dagger.

30 Dektis: Chet opens his eyes but is still terribly weak.

YANIS

4 Yanis: The healers pronounce that Chet's danger has passed.

5 Yanis: High King Enalyn visits Chet to thank him, and then she speaks with Loren. They determine that the war in Wellmont has been brought on by the Shades. Enalyn determines to march her army, as well as the Mystics, to put a stop to it.

15 Yanis: Chet's bandages are removed. High King Enalyn promises him a lordship if he should wish it, but Chet refuses with profuse thanks. Loren shares Chet's bed for the first time.

16 Yanis: Enalyn's armies march forth from the High King's Seat. Loren, Chet, and Xain watch them go, along with the Lord Prince Eamin. At the same time, Enalyn sends orders for King Anwar of Selvan to dispatch an army to assault the Shade stronghold in the Greatrocks as quickly as he can.

20 Yanis: A Shade is caught masquerading as a guard in the High King's palace and killed. Loren hears the sound during the night.

21 Yanis: Lord Prince Eamin tells Loren of the Shade who was captured. Loren sneaks out upon the Seat and retrieves her dagger, then finds the inn where the Shade was staying. She finds a lock of blonde hair within the room and mistakenly takes it for the Shade's. She burns the hair on her dagger and tracks the wizard as far as the eastern docks. She thinks the Shade must have fled across the Great Bay. On her way back to the palace, she stops at a tavern. There she shares a brief conversation with a boy her age attending the Academy for wizards, and another mysterious murder takes place. But though Loren at first thinks it is the Shades, the trail goes cold again.

24 Yanis: Dulmun attacks the High King's Seat from the east. Shades attack from the west. High King Enalyn and her guard try to defend the palace, but they are overwhelmed. With Loren's help, the High King and the Lord Prince escape the palace. Together they battle Rogan at the western gate. Rogan is defeated, and Loren escapes the island.

25 Yanis: Loren reaches Selvan's capital of Garsec. High King

Enalyn recruits Loren into her service and enshrines the name of Nightblade as a royal title.

In the Birchwood, Rogan speaks with his "Father," who brings news of glad tidings. Rogan asks if they have found the Lifemage, and Father smiles.

FEBRIS

3 Febris: High King Enalyn returns to the High King's Seat and takes residence again within her palace. Loren and her friends come along. Enalyn assigns Loren to the command of Kal Endil in the fortress of Ammon and commands her to proceed to the fortress quickly. Loren learns that Xain will part her company and remain on the Seat. That night, Loren has her first terrible dream. She sees Damaris and Gregor, and she witnesses Chet's death. She also sees a man in Shade's clothing, whom she does not recognize. A scar splits his chin.

4 Febris: Xain introduces Loren to the Mystics who will accompany her to Ammon. Weath, Shiun, and Jormund are among them, as well as two Mystics she has never met, Uzo and Niya. That night, Xain takes Loren, Chet, and Gem to a fine dinner on the Seat, and he and Loren end the night conversing at the top of the Academy's bell tower. From him, Loren learns that magestones wipe dreams from a wizard's mind, but that they have no effect whatsoever on those without magic. She also learns of the smuggler Wyle, who lives in the town of Bertram in the kingdom of Dorsea.

6 Febris: Loren and her party of Mystics, along with Gem and Chet, sail from the High King's Seat, bound for Feldemar and Ammon.

11 Febris: Loren's party lands on Feldemar's southern shore. There they rest for the night.

12 Febris: Loren's party sets out for Ammon.

18 Febris: Loren and her party of Mystics arrive at Ammon and are reunited with Annis. There she sees the man in Shade's clothing from her dream. She learns his name is Hewal. Kal tells Loren he wants her to find Rogan and bring him to the King's justice. Loren and her friends decide to investigate any connection Hewal may have to the Shades.

19 Febris: Annis leads Loren and the others to Hewal's room, but they find nothing suspicious. Loren finally tells Gem and Annis about the mysterious dream that led her to suspect Hewal in the first place.

25 Febris: Niya gives Loren some advice on Calentin bowcraft, flirting with her all the while. Chet tells Loren that he does not trust the Mystic woman, but Loren soothes his fears.

30 Febris: Loren has another nightmare. She sees the city of Dahab and watches Hewal turn into a bird. She sees but does not recognize the lover Adara, and then sees Gregor kill Chet, Gem, and Annis. Remembering that Xain said magestones banish dreams, she eats another one in an attempt to quell the nightmares.

YEARSEND

1 Yearsend: After an incident at the Academy for wizards, Damaris suspects she may no longer be safe upon the Seat. She sends word to Yewamba to prepare for her arrival, and to Dahab to send reinforcements to Yewamba in preparation for her coming.

3 Yearsend: Damaris sets forth from the High King's Seat and sails to Dorsea's eastern coast. From there she begins her journey to Yewamba.

4 Yearsend: At the Yearsend feast at Ammon, Loren sees the Mystic Hewal slipping away from the festivities. With her friends and some Mystics, she follows him and observes him giving messages to a Shade spy. When Loren and Niya catch the Shade, she kills herself. With the help of a magestone, Loren tracks down Hewal, but after he battles her and the Mystics, he escapes in bird form. Kal is enraged that Loren acted without his leave, but he agrees to let her lead an expedition of Mystics to Dahab in search of Hewal.

THE YEAR OF UNDERREALM 1313

MARTIS

1 Martis: Gem speaks with Loren about the magestone she ate, and she confides in him the secret of her dagger, much to his delight.

2 Martis: Loren awakens early and speaks with Niya on the ramparts of Ammon. Niya speaks plainly for the first time about her desire for Loren, but Loren rejects her out of loyalty to Chet.

3 Martis: Loren and her party of Mystics set forth from Ammon, making for Dahab.

4 Martis: Loren and her party leave the main road and take smaller paths through the jungle to avoid detection.

5 Martis: Loren and her party are blasted by a heavy rainstorm that slows their progress.

8 Martis: Niya commands Loren's party to remain camped for a day. Loren tries to argue, but Niya overrules her, fearing the horses will wear themselves to death against the weather.

9 Martis: At Loren's insistence, the party presses on again, though the weather has grown even worse. Jormund is nearly lost to floodwaters. That night Uzo makes insubordinate statements about the "old guard" that Loren does not understand. Loren tells the party of her encounter with the Elves in Dorsea.

10 Martis: Niya confronts Loren about her tale of the Elves. In turn, Loren learns from Niya about the Drayden order of assassins, who are called the Tabarzin, and a growing schism among the Mystics.

12 Martis: The weather in Feldemar begins to lighten. Loren's party come to a bridge guarded by the family Yerrin. Despite Loren's attempts at stealth, they are forced into a fight. All the Yerrin guards are killed. They reach the city of Dahab and, after briefly scouting it, Loren and Niya sneak into the Golden Manor of the family Yerrin. Niya kisses Loren for the first time. Inside the manor they find Hewal and Damaris' accountant, Gretchen. Gretchen reveals that Damaris is in Yewamba just before Hewal kills her. Loren decides to pursue Damaris to Yewamba against Kal's orders.

13 Martis: Loren sends Jormund east with a report for Kal. She and the rest of the party begin to travel west, searching for the fortress of Yewamba. That night, Loren asks Niya to teach her to throw a knife and begins to practice each day.

20 Martis: Jormund reaches Ammon late in the evening and delivers his message to Kal. Kal is wrathful and begins to rouse a small host to travel to Yewamba and rescue Loren. He immediately sends a messenger to Yewamba to find Loren and deliver a message for her to return at once.

21 Martis: Damaris reaches the stronghold of Yewamba.

22 Martis: Kal sets forth from Ammon with a small host of Mystics, his destination Yewamba.

23 Martis: Loren confronts Chet about his insubordination and snide remarks about their mission. He urges her to abandon their quest for her own safety, but she refuses.

26 Martis: Loren and her party reach the area where they are certain Yewamba must be. They send Uzo and Shiun into a small town called Sarafu, but the Mystics learn nothing useful.

27 Martis: Loren and her party begin searching for Yewamba in the lands surrounding Sarafu, but they find nothing.

28 Martis: Loren and her party spend another fruitless day searching the foothills of the Greatrock Mountains. That night she has another dream, and this time she sees Gregor between two distinctive mountain peaks with a wagon leading down a trail.

29 Martis: Loren searches deeper in the foothills of the Greatrocks. There she finds the two mountain peaks and the wagon trail. Following the trail with Niya and Shiun, she discovers the fortress of Yewamba deep within the mountains.

30 Martis: Shiun scouts Yewamba to see if she can find a way in. Loren's party prepare themselves for the next day's mission. Annis begs Loren to forbid Gem from going, but Loren refuses. She urges Annis to confess her feelings for Gem. That night she tells Chet she loves him and chooses him over Niya.

ARILIS

1 Arilis: Loren, Chet, Gem, Niya, Shiun, and Weath sneak into Yewamba. Niya murders Weath out of sight of the rest of the party. Loren's party locates Damaris and captures her. Hewal appears, disguised as Chet, but Niya sees through his ruse and kills him. Loren and Niya try to bargain with the Yerrins, but the ruse fails and Damaris escapes. With the help of magestones, Loren leads the others in an escape from the fortress, but she is shot with an arrow in the process.

Kal's messenger arrives in the town of Sarafu.

2 Arilis: Damaris flees Yewamba. Loren wakes from rest. Uzo and Shiun have left to track Damaris, leaving Chet, Gem, and Annis with Loren. Niya has remained as well, to recover from her own wounds.

Kal's messenger, noticing a disturbance in Sarafu, traces it to Yewamba, and witnesses Damaris fleeing the fortress, heading south into Dorsea. She does not find Loren, and so resolves to return to Kal with what news she has.

3 Arilis: More guards join Damaris, and Uzo and Shiun realize their pursuit is fruitless. Niya takes Loren for a walk. Far away from the camp, Niya reveals herself to be Auntie and paralyzes Loren with a poison. She takes on Loren's appearance and seduces Chet. The paralyzing poison wears off, and together Loren and Chet overcome Auntie. Chet kills her with Loren's dagger.

Kal's messenger begins her return journey towards Ammon, intending to meet Kal on the road.

4 Arilis: Uzo and Shiun return to the camp and are dismayed to hear what happened between Loren and Auntie. They bury the weremage's body and deliver their news of Damaris.

5 Arilis: Loren and her party set off from their camp, heading south in pursuit of Damaris.

7 Arilis: Kal's messenger meets him on the road around noon. She informs him that Damaris has fled Yewamba for Dorsea. Kal guesses (correctly) that Loren has pursued the merchant. He takes a small party of riders, including Jormund, to pursue her south while sending the rest of the army to clear Yewamba of any remaining Yerrins.

9 Arilis: High King Enalyn declares war on Dulmun and sends her armies to march upon it.

15 Arilis: Kal reaches Feldemar's capital of Yota. There he spends a day gathering any information that he can about where Loren might have gone.

16 Arilis: Annis guesses that Damaris may be feinting a westward course, intending to double back for Chosun. Loren's party takes a side road, and at the end of the day they find signs of Damaris' camp from only two days before.

Gregor of the family Yerrin leaves the High King's Seat to rejoin his mistress, Damaris.

17 Arilis: Gregor lands in Brekkur, steals a horse and sets off west to find Damaris.

Kal guesses (incorrectly) that Damaris has fled into Dorsea's far western reaches and that Loren has followed her there. He rides from Yota, making for the Sunmane Pass to search western Dorsea.

24 Arilis: After days of crisscrossing Dorsea, trying to shake Loren from her trail, Damaris' party meets Gregor near the southern end of the Moonslight Pass. Gregor takes Damaris with him and rids into the pass, but he sends the rest of her party towards Sidwan with instructions to delay Loren in her pursuit.

27 Arilis: Early in the day, Damaris and Gregor ride into Danfon and begin to set into motion their plan to take the kingdom.

28 Arilis: Damaris' diversionary party reaches the town of Sidwan in Dorsea. There they wait, laying a trap for Loren and her friends, with a Yerrin mindmage pretending to be Damaris herself.

30 Arilis: Loren's party arrives in the town of Sidwan and begin to search it for Damaris, while keeping watch to ensure she does not escape the town without their notice.

1 Maius: Loren's party discover the mindmage decoy and defeat her. They realize Damaris has evaded them, and Loren decides to stay in Sidwan while she considers her next move. That night, she has a dream showing Damaris in the city of Danfon, but also a clue leading her to Bertram. She sees some of the routes and passages through Danfon's palace, and a fight with Gregor. Also in the dream, Chet tells her he is going to leave.

2 Maius: After conferring with Chet, Annis, and Gem, Loren decides to go to Bertram to find the smuggler Wyle. She decides to remain in Sidwan for one more day, and they spend their time collecting supplies for the journey.

3 Maius: Loren's party sets out from Sidwan, riding for Bertram.

After riding down Dorsea's west coast for many days, Kal guesses that Loren has followed Damaris to the city of Chosun. He diverts from the King's Road and cuts east across the countryside to reach Chosun more quickly.

5 Maius: In collusion with Damaris, Wojin Fei stages a coup to steal the throne from his nephew, Dorsea's King Jun. Jun survives and flees with his son Senlin to hide in the capital city. Accompanying them is a palace apothecary named Keridwen Ogun.

6 Maius: Loren's party arrives in Bertram and takes a room at an inn.

7 Maius: Loren's party locates the steelsmith Kanja, who leads them to Wyle. Wyle attempts to escape at first, but when he fails, he agrees to help Loren. Loren's party learns that King Jun has been assassinated and the kingdom is now in rebellion against the High King.

8 Maius: After convincing Wyle to sneak them into the capital, Loren rides from Bertram with her party, including the smuggler. They make for the Moonslight Pass, there to ride on to Danfon.

Word of King Jun's death reaches Kal in the city of Chosun. He guesses that Loren is somehow involved in the catastrophe and sets off for Danfon at once.

10 Maius: Loren rides past Danfon to the town of Yincang, where her party boards their horses in preparation for their journey into the capital the next day.

11 Maius: Loren enters Danfon and begins her search for Damaris. Gem notices a girl watching them. Loren captures her and discovers she is Keridwen, servant of King Jun. Keridwen brings them to Jun. Jun convinces Loren to help him retake his throne, and Loren's party lodges in the home of the merchant Yushan where Jun has been hiding.

12 Maius: Loren and King Jun decide to rally the populace against Wojin. They decide to strike the next day when Wojin addresses the people directly. Loren scouts the location and forms a plan for how best to reveal herself. In a dream that night, she learns that Damaris and Gregor know she is in the city. Again Chet tells her he is going to leave. For a second time, she finds herself face-to-face with Gregor.

13 Maius: Loren interrupts Wojin's public address and tells the citizenry that King Jun is alive and Wojin is a traitor. The unrest in the city continues to grow.

14 Maius: Word reaches Loren's party that Duris Fei, one of the Dorsean senators, wishes to meet with King Jun. They plan the meeting for the next day, along with precautions to make sure Duris will not be able to learn Jun's location.

15 Maius: Loren meets with Duris Fei. Duris promises to rally the senators if Loren can eliminate the treasury. Annis realizes they can destroy the treasury by burning it with magestones stolen from her mother. They resolve to try it the next day. In another dream, Loren learns another secret passage. This time she tries to avoid facing Gregor, but he shoots her with an arrow, and she realizes she cannot flee from him.

Early in the day, Kal and his force of Mystics arrive to Danfon and take up residence at an inn, from which Kal begins to organize a search for Loren.

16 Maius: Loren's party sneaks into the Danfon palace. There are no magestones, and they find the tortured corpse of Duris Fei. Loren realizes they must have discovered King Jun's hiding place, and they flee the palace immediately to try and rescue him. King Jun's guards save his life and Prince Senlin's. They all try to flee the capital through the sewers, but they are ambushed by Yerrin and Dorsean soldiers. Gregor kills King Jun. Kal and a small force of Mystics arrive and help them escape. Kal blames Loren for Wojin's rebellion.

17 Maius: Chet tells Loren he has to leave. She gives him her blessing to go, as well as some coin to buy another horse for travel. Kal tells her that he means to assault the palace the next day and kill Wojin.

Chet rides from Danfon just after noon. Before nightfall, Gregor and a party of Yerrin soldiers intercept him on the road. They capture him and haul him back into the capital. Damaris tortures him for information.

18 Maius: Chet tells Damaris of Loren's dreams, her dagger, and everything else he knows about their journeys—except where Kal and his Mystics are hiding.

After nightfall, Kal sends his forces on the attack, along with Loren and her friends. They are ambushed in the palace. Jormund and all his Mystics are killed. Loren, Gem and Keridwen escape and find Chet dying in the palace treasury. After telling Loren what he told Damaris, Chet dies. Loren gets Gem and Keridwen out of the palace and kills Gregor. She then captures Wojin and turns him over to loyalist soldiers in the dungeons. After informing Kal what has happened, Loren leaves in the night with her friends by her side.

ADDENDUM C

HISTORIES OF MAJOR CITIES IN UNDERREALM

DAHAB

Dahab is the oldest and greatest city in the kingdom of Feldemar. There is a great spur in the land there called the Dahabajo, over which the Nelos spills in a mighty waterfall, the Habajo, that casts mist and haze through the air all around. At the bottom, the falls form a sizeable lake that enriches the land all around, as well as drawing much wildlife.

In this place, in the time before time, the first king of Feldemar built their city. Their name is lost to history, and even the wisest scholars debate it, pointing at half-smudged clues left across a range of ancient tomes. While most of the buildings of Dahab were built on the land at the foot of the waterfall, the king built their palace atop the shelf in the land, there to survey their subjects living below them, in truth as well as in station. They called their city Dahab, from the word *dahan* in the ancient Feldemarian tongue, which means "gold."

And indeed, Dahab's coffers have flowed with gold ever since. Though Feldemar is a hard land for trade routes and roads, and though its lords are sometimes reluctant with their gifts and tributes to their king, still they always send them. For all the long centuries before Roth's people came to Underrealm, Feldemar was a kingdom of ever-growing inequality. The rich and powerful had more wealth than they could spend in their lifetimes, and the poor struggled to survive.

It was in this circumstance that the family Yerrin first rose to power. They had for a long time been simple traders, and even before their star began to rise, they had learned that it was not wise to interfere with the politics of kings and lords. Instead, they quietly gathered as much gold as they could, wherever they could, the better to weather the storms of war.

One day, some scion of the family discovered magestones. How this came to be is the family's most closely guarded secret, and none but the most powerful of them know it. Outsiders only know that the stones exist, and that the Yerrins alone can find them—or perhaps manufacture them.

Wizards, of course, tended to do exceedingly well in a kingdom where rule was established by might and power rather than justice or law. It was rare to see anyone but a wizard sit the throne of Feldemar, and most of the lesser lords were wizards as well. Therefore the Yerrins gained a great wealth of coin, as well as extensive political connections. But as their fortune grew, so did their danger. Wizards addicted to magestones grew desperate for the secret of their origin. And as the Yerrins knew their power came from the stones, they were more determined than ever to conceal that secret. Their own customers were also their greatest threat.

Over generations, they developed and implemented all manner of magical defenses, the likes of which had never been seen in Underrealm before. A mindmage who tried to use mindwyrd on a powerful Yerrin would find they had only a decoy, and would then be cut off from magestones until they wasted away in madness. A firemage who tried to storm Yerrin holdings would be beset by other wizards far more powerful and crafty, who had studied for years to defeat their own kind.

It was the Yerrins who greatly developed and advanced the art of enchantment. And after a time—no one is quite sure when, or how— the Yerrins learned the crafting of protective weapons and charms that protected the bearer from all magical effects. These charmed objects were a secret guarded almost as closely as the magestones themselves.

After a time, the Yerrins built their great manors. They were pyramids, and the Yerrins built them of black granite, just as the Academy would be built centuries later. There was as much magic in their construction as there was the skill of masons. Curiously, the Yerrins built them in the lower level of Dahab, not atop the Dahabajo where the king's palace stood. Mayhap the Yerrins did not want to test the king by comparing their might to his; or mayhap they thought the lower city, where the common folk lived, was the true seat of power. Regardless, they now had an impregnable stronghold that not even the most determined army could break, and only the Yerrins were allowed inside the walls.

That restriction was put to the test several times. As wizards in Feldemar became more powerful, the bloody conflicts for that kingdom's throne increased. Time and again the palace was sacked and its inhabitants slaughtered. On more than one occasion the buildings were razed, to be rebuilt later by whichever new lord had claimed the crown. Through it all, the Yerrin pyramids sat on Dahab's lower level, and the powerful merchants within looked up at the slaughter, preparing new trade deals for whoever next sat the throne.

Thus, when Loren of the family Nelda came to Dahab, she observed that the Yerrin pyramids were far older than the palace and other buildings on the Dahabajo. She was right in her guess, for though Feldemarian kings had ruled from the Dahabajo since long before the Yerrin's rise, that throne had changed hands countless times through the centuries, while the Yerrins had never lost their control.

Before the Nightblade, only one person had ever breached the Yerrins' defenses and lived to speak about it afterwards. Her name was Nayala, and she was the last Wizard King, but her tale is told elsewhere.

After the Dark Wars, the High King commanded that the capital of Feldemar be moved. The new Feldemarian king took up residence in the city of Yota. In this way the High King hoped to remove at least some of the influence the Yerrins had over the king of Feldemar—though that would not prove to be entirely successful. Dahab remained, however, the richest and most powerful city in the kingdom, its splendor and history far outshining the new capital.

The Yerrins take great pride in how long they have held to their power, as well they might. They claim it is because they have never sought a throne, nor the politicking and war that inevitably follows such ascension. But there is another reason as well: their incomparable ability to keep secrets. Only the Patron, the head of the family, knows all the family's doings, and none have ever come close to capturing or threatening them through all the long centuries. That is partially because the Patron rarely visits Dahab, and is more likely to be found in one of the Yerrins' other strongholds throughout the nine kingdoms. And for a very long time, that stronghold was Yewamba.

YEWAMBA

Yewamba is an ancient stronghold of the family Yerrin, resting in the Greatrock Mountains that form the western border of Feldemar.

One of the Yerrin family's most closely guarded secrets, no one knows exactly when it was built, but it was certainly centuries before Roth's people landed on Southbreak. It is a fortress no attacker could hope to conquer without wasting countless lives, and if well manned, one few could hope to infiltrate. When Loren of the family Nelda managed it, it was only because Yewamba held the tiniest fraction of the armies it once had, and the few dozen Yerrins posted there could not watch every avenue of approach at once.

That was long centuries after the Yerrins had last been there in great strength. At the height of its use, Yewamba was as heavily guarded as any king's palace. The fortress was built to hold more than two thousands.

The necessity of Yewamba became clear to the Yerrin patron soon after their fortunes began to rise with their sale of magestones. In the very early days of that dark trade, wizards tried to discover where the stones came from. On some occasions, they even closed in on the Patron himself. The Patron who presided over the family in those early days was a man named Babo, and he realized that as long as his location was known, the Yerrins' position was precarious.

Therefore, with the first reserves of gold that the Yerrins began to accumulate with the stones, Babo sent out his most trusted kin to find a new seat of power. They scoured the kingdom in all directions, and at first all their searching was in vain. Babo's cousin Yumbi suggested a home in the Sky's Knives, but the nearby town of Kunde was too well-populated by the kin of the Feldemarian king. The Bloodtale Marsh seemed a likely hiding place, for few would dare to venture into such a dangerous area. But that same danger made it a poor location to send the most valuable members of the family, and besides, its boggy, sinking terrain was a poor place to build a castle.

Babo's kin ranged farther and farther, eventually traveling as far east as the Eldest Deep and as far south as the Birchwood, but without success. And then, one day, Babo's sister Toba returned to him with news.

Toba had gone west, searching as far as the Greatrocks themselves. She told him that from the moment she had crested a rise and seen the mountains in the distance, she had wondered if they might be a suitable place. They stood proud against the sky, reminding her of soldiers with spears, and that seemed to her a good omen. She had taken her party into their foothills and rode along them for days, seeking a location that was both secure and secret.

Then, one day, a storm had struck. Its fury had crashed upon them like nothing Toba had ever seen. The rain had drenched them even through their thick cloaks, and lightning struck the nearby ground more than once. They had been riding along a waterway, and it suddenly flooded, carrying some of the party off in a rush. Toba had been one of them. She only barely managed to struggle to the surface, where she clung to a log that swept along in the current.

At last the log struck the shore, but on the western side of the river, separating her from her party. Toba dried herself as best she could and sought shelter. After wandering for a short while, she found a cleft in the land that seemed promising. But when she drew closer, she found a passage through the rock that had been invisible from a distance. Curious, she made her way through the passage and out the other side.

She found herself in a small valley that plunged into the Greatrocks themselves, though it, too, was invisible from the outside. Something compelled Toba to press on and into the valley, and she wove her way through the densely-packed trees. At last she came around a bend in the land and stopped suddenly, struck speechless by the sight before her.

"I saw a mountain like the prow of a ship," she told Babo. "Or like a great arrowhead. It thrust out from between the mountains on either side, its sheer cliffs rising into the air. It felt as if a vessel were sailing straight for me, bearing a message of great victory. It is what we have sought, Babo. No one can reach us there."

Babo was somewhat skeptical. After so many months of searching, he doubted that Toba's finding could be as ideal as she described. But he nevertheless arranged an expedition, leading it himself in a long journey west. Toba came with him, guiding him through the cleft in the land and the valley beyond. And when he beheld the mountain, Babo knew his search was over.

For her efforts, Babo placed Toba at his right hand in all the family's dealings. And he gave her a task at once: to find the best stonemasons and crafters from all across Feldemar, and hire them to turn the mountain into the stronghold he had long desired. This she did as quickly as she could, though of course it was still a job of many years.

Babo took his seat in the heart of the mountain only three years before the end of his life, naming it Yewamba, which means "Sky Home" in the ancient tongue of Feldemar. And when he died, Toba took his place as the family's new Patron. From this new position of strength and secrecy, the Patrons of Yerrin grew their trade of magestones (and their reserves of gold) until their wealth and power was unmatched. The family grew in number commensurate to their status, and soon their soldiers in Yewamba were near enough to a standing army, though they were loath to engage in warfare.

After the Dark Wars, when magestones were banned and the Yerrins had to conduct their trade in secret, Yewamba grew less and less necessary. The Yerrins were playing at politics now, and though they had not yet made overtures towards a throne, that desire seemed to be growing in their Patrons. With their increased presence in the courts of the nine kingdoms, Yewamba's remote and inaccessible location—once its most valuable asset—was now a detriment.

So it was that between the eleventh and twelfth centuries of Underrealm, Yewamba was slowly emptied. The Patron retreated there less and less, and fewer and fewer Yerrins lived there. Now they were spread throughout all the nine kingdoms, and their holdings in Dahab were held to be the most important—that, and the holdings they had always kept on the High King's Seat since it was built.

By the time Loren of the family Nelda came to clash with the family Yerrin, and eventually followed Damaris to Yewamba, the fortress had been abandoned for more than a century. Only the Patron and some of the family's highest scions, such as Damaris, even knew of its existence. Damaris was forced to populate it in haste after Loren thwarted her in Selvan, and it was not properly guarded or supplied when Loren and her party of Mystics infiltrated it in the Year of Underrealm 1313. But what role it would play in the rest of the war between the Necromancer and the Lifemage, not even Damaris could have guessed.

DANFON

The city of Danfon is the oldest in the kingdom of Dorsea and its current capital—but that has not always been the case.

Renna the Sunmane ordered the building of the city during the years that she guided the settling of Dorsea and Selvan. Some people of Feldemar, which was newly under Roth's rule, joined the settling process, but it was mostly Roth's people who came to live there. Feldemarians tended to travel farther south to Selvan, where the land was more bountiful, and there were forests that reminded them of home—more so than the arid lands of northern Dorsea, at any rate.

Thus the first people to settle Dorsea were, in the main, Roth's people. This is one reason that Dorseans and the Dulmish, as people of Dulmun are sometimes called, bear such a resemblance to each other, while looking quite different from the people of Feldemar, who are darker of skin, or the people of Selvan, who took on a great deal of Hedgemond blood and so are quite pale.

But the culture of Dorsea became sundered from that of Dulmun, and this came about far more quickly than one would have expected from their common origin. This split was brought about by Underrealm's first civil war—which, depending on who told the tale, was referred to as the Sunmane Rebellion or the Scourging of the Blackheart, and was by scholars referred to more neutrally as the War of Roth's Kin.

When Renna slew her father Roth on the docks of Kingsmouth and earned the name Blackheart, Sunmane declared war upon her at once. But even shadowed by grief and rage, Sunmane's wisdom and strategy were without peer. Therefore she removed herself from the city of Garsec in Selvan, which was far too vulnerable to attack via the Great Bay, and relocated to the city of Danfon. There was a palace there already, in anticipation of Roth's naming a new king to rule the kingdom, and now Sunmane made her home there.

Thus, even as she prepared for war against her niece, she governed the city's layout and growth, so that it was a more well-ordered and thoughtfully laid out than it otherwise might have been. Too, she gave charge of the city's construction to the best crafters she could find. Many of these were Feldemarians, and from them Sunmane's people learned the making of tile roofs and plaster walls, which better resisted the wildly changing temperature and sometimes-torrential rains of the area. But these were refined by Dulmish aesthetics, so that the tiles were often colored a brilliant red, and the walls a pure white, a strikingly beautiful combination that became a Dorsean trademark. The roofs were often pointed at the corners and curved up slightly, allowing them to be adorned with all manner of beautiful decoration—as well as, centuries later, providing a better foothold for those like Loren of the family Nelda, who spent a great deal of time on rooftops.

As the war raged on, the Sunmane was hard put to keep her holdings in Selvan and Dorsea—which, at that time, was a kingdom with no name, for more pressing matters concerned her. Garsec, as Sunmane had guessed, often fell prey to Blackheart's attacks, and while Sunmane always cast her back, the city suffered much in those years. But Sunmane did not cease in the mission Roth had given her, and she sent parties of explorers to range ever further west. Before the war was won, they had already found the Western Sea, and learned that the Greatrocks trailed to their end far south, giving birth to the Dragon's Tail River. These lands were settled methodically, if slowly, and they brought wealth to Sunmane's armies that would help to turn the tide of the great conflict. And as they had in Feldemar, the family Yerrin would play a large part in the resolution of that war—but so, too, would the family Drayden, who had not before that time entered very far into the politics of Underrealm. But more about this will be said elsewhere.

Much has been recorded about the War of Roth's Kin, about how the Sunmane at last defeated the Blackheart and claimed her place as Underrealm's High King. As one of her first actions after taking the throne, she at last gave the new kingdom a name: Dorsea, for it now bordered all three oceans of Underrealm. Selvan's rule was given to her daughter, Silvin, while Dorsea was given to Silvin's father, Bahati, once a lord of Feldemar, who had become one of Sunmane's most esteemed generals during the war. Bahati ruled in Danfon for the rest of his days, though it was often said that he missed his homeland to the north, and only remained out of his sense of duty and love towards Sunmane. After his passing, his body was taken back to Feldemar and buried in the village where he was born.

Centuries later, a Dorsean Wizard King attempted the murder of the High King in order to take his place. But the murder was foiled, and in the ensuing war, the High King brought all the other kingdoms against Dorsea. Indeed, this is why the nine kingdoms were established the way they were. If any king thought to betray the High King, the other lands could be rallied to subdue the rebels. The king of Feldemar was instrumental in the High King's victory, and she herself led the charge over the walls of Danfon that eventually took the city.

For the Feldemarian king's service, the High King granted her all the northeastern lands of Dorsea, and they were part of Feldemar for hundreds of years. But the Feldemarian kings never took up residence in Danfon, preferring to rule from their capital in Dahab.

Then, near the end of the Dark Wars, this situation played out in reverse. King Nayala of Feldemar resisted the Fearless Decree and spurned Andriana the Fearless. In the end her forces were defeated, though Nayala herself was never captured or killed, and her name became one of terror across Underrealm for many years—a campfire story to frighten children. But this time it was Dorsea who provided a great service in overthrowing the rebels in Feldemar, and Danfon was recaptured by Dorseans. When the Dark Wars finally ceased, Danfon and all the northeastern lands were made part of Dorsea again. There has the Dorsean king ruled ever since.

ADDENDUM D

THE FALL OF JORDEL OF THE FAMILY ADAIR

What sorrow chills the heart of we
Who mourning raise our weary hands
To tragic farewell bid to he
Who watchful guarded nine the lands

O stranger here, will not you weep
Know not you he who fell from high
His bed a cairn and there to sleep
And ages now to pass him by

Know not you Jordel of Adair
Who restless walked the miles long
His arm of might, his silver hair
His blade that shone, his armor strong

For none could know a heart so bold
Or kindness in such measure great
But weep to see him lying cold
Forever master of his fate

For though he saw along his trail
And well knew he the fate that loomed
With head held high, in shining mail
Jordel rode on to meet his doom

And so your weeping bring to close
Let courage firm your tears allay
Jordel his bier in shadow chose
To bring us all through night to day

This song was heard by Loren's party just south of the Birchwood, as they pursued Damaris after their time in Danfon.

A woman sang it in a tavern where Loren had stopped for the night.

As soon as they heard Jordel's name, they all stopped to stare at the singer, transfixed. Gem's eyes shone with wonder.

"That is Albern's song," he said.

Loren frowned at him. "Do not be stupid, Gem. Of course it is not Albern's song."

"It is," insisted Gem. "I heard him sing. I heard him talk. Those are his words."

Annis cocked her head as she regarded him. "It does sound like something Albern might have sung—stirring, if a bit plain-spoken. But Gem . . . in Northwood . . ."

"I know what happened in Northwood," said Gem, his nostrils flaring. "I was there. But still I say that is Albern's song."

"Gem, it cannot be," said Loren. "He . . . he fell."

"Then he wrote it before Northwood was attacked," said Gem, his hands balling to fists. Tears filled his eyes, threatening to spill. "I am telling you that Albern wrote that song, and I will not be called a—"

His words cut off as Loren pulled him into an embrace. Now that no one could see his face, Gem let himself weep, clutching Loren's shirt.

"You are right," said Loren quietly. "It is Albern's song. It is."

After some time, Gem went to the woman in the corner and learned the words from her, and Loren would often hear him humming the tune upon the road. He always insisted Albern wrote it. Gem was both right and wrong in his guess, but none of them would learn that for a long time yet.

LETTERS CONCERNING THE BATTLE OF WELLMONT

Year of Underrealm 1312

28 Septis

Captain Trisken,

I saw something today here in Wellmont that I cannot explain. I do not know if it is important or not, but you said to inform you of any development, no matter how small it may seem.

It happened during another attack by the Dorseans. They stormed the southern wall as they have done before. But this time the city had a sortie ready, and they met the Dorseans on the plains south of the city.

I was stationed on the walls (you will remember that I am placed in Wellmont's city guard). I saw the Dorseans fall upon the Selvan soldiers and divide them up.

One group of Selvans seemed pinned against a ridge in the land by a small party of Dorsean horsemen. I thought them doomed and turned my attention away. But a few moments later, there was a flash of light—blinding even from where I stood on the wall. I turned back.

The Selvans had somehow repelled the Dorseans, all of whom lay dead or stunned. But only two Selvan soldiers had survived. I saw them stumbling back towards the walls, one supporting the other, who seemed injured.

I did not know the two figures, but they were clearly mercenaries. What is strange is that I did not think the mercenaries in Wellmont had any wizards among their ranks. Yet the flash I saw was akin to magelight, though I have never seen it shine so bright.

I have been unable to learn the names of these two mercenaries, but I will continue to search unless I receive word from you to abandon this matter. Forgive me if this is any trouble—I know you and my brethren have enough to do in the Greatrocks.

Your faithful servant,
Rorik of the family Heln

* * *

Chancellor Endil,

Captain Jordel rode from the city today, taking with him a half dozen of our brothers, including Vivien. The Captain did not tell us where he was going, though he said he would be back. He rode off with an urchin boy behind him on the saddle, oddly enough.

Our order's position at Wellmont remains secure. The Dorseans show no indication of interest in us beyond our location in the city, and I will of course inform you if that situation should change in any regard.

A small aside, if you will forgive me. Something odd happened during today's battle. It seems a wizard has been hiding in the ranks of the mercenaries hired by the mayor. They were among the sortie that fought the Dorseans outside the walls, and a party of them became separated and surrounded. There was a flash of what I am sure was magelight—more powerful than any I have ever seen—and the Dorseans were struck down. It must have been mentalism, for I could see no burns or other signs of elementalism.

Only two of the mercenaries escaped, and so I think one of them must be the wizard. I do not know why they would have concealed their gift, for of course wizards fetch a much higher price than simple soldiers.

In any case, I am sure you wonder why I would write you about this, for while unusual, it hardly seems noteworthy. But when the mercenaries returned to the city, I spotted that one of them had the mark of the family Drayden upon his forearm. He was injured, though it did not seem life-threatening. I could not tell, of course, whether it was he or his companion who was the wizard—though if I had to guess, I would say it was the Drayden, for he is slimmer of build and more bookish looking, if you take me. His companion is a brawny woman who I am quite sure would be able to lift me above her head. She carries a sword that seems much too fine for a common footsoldier in a mercenary army.

An unknown Drayden wizard was just odd enough, I thought, to warrant mentioning.

I hope Feldemar is treating you well, though I do not envy your presence there during the heat of this summer.

Only in watchfulness lies safety.
Vella of the family Persin
Knight of the Mystic Order

* * *

Chancellor Endil,

I am sorry to send another letter so quickly, but something has hap-
pened. Vivien returned to Wellmont badly injured, burned by darkfire.
She reported that the wizard Xain is an eater of magestones. All the Mys-
tics in her company were slain trying to bring Xain down—all but Jordel,
who she says joined Xain and now rides at his side. This is hard for me
to believe, but Vivien has no reason to lie, and has always been a fiercely
loyal servant of our order.

I fear the chancellor here means to throw Jordel out of our order.
Doubtless word of this would have reached you in time, but I wanted to
send a letter as quickly as I could.

Only in watchfulness lies safety.
Vella of the family Persin
Knight of the Mystic Order

* * *

30 Septis

Chancellor Endil,

I must apologize again most profusely for the frequency of my messages to you. I hope you will understand that I would not bother you so unless I thought it was important.

I mentioned two mercenaries in my letter of two days ago. They left Wellmont just this morning. From what I have been able to gather, they purchased supplies (at an exorbitant price, for all goods are more expensive due to the invaders) and also hired two lovers from a guild here in the city. They then set out from Wellmont, though I am unable to find out how they did so, since the gates are barred. It is possible they snuck out through the west rivergate, which is not yet fully repaired after that wizard Xain blasted it open. Or mayhap they escaped over the wall. We know that one of them is a wizard, and mayhap they have some clever spell beyond my knowledge. But they headed southeast, and were spotted by city guards shortly before they were out of sight. I cannot say why, but this has troubled me ever since I learned of it.

In any case, I hope my letters have been no trouble and that the information is useful.

Only in watchfulness lies safety.
Vella of the family Persin
Knight of the Mystic Order

* * *

Dearest Matron Mangas,

I hope this letter reaches you before you require it. With the battle here in Wellmont, the roads are fraught.

Two of my lovers were hired for a journey. Their names are Cara of the family Eldun and Ombi of the family Unde. Cara is dark and well muscled, and her hair juts a few fingers from her head. Ombi is fair of skin with dark brown hair and blue eyes.

The customers were named Oris and Filip, though the second one goes by Flip. They are mercenaries who fought here in Wellmont—or I should say they were, since they have left the city. Oris is tall and broad. The sun has browned her skin and lightened her hair, which she often wears in a little tail. She wore a blue vest and carried an exquisite sword. Filip wears fine clothing—a purple jacket when last I saw him—and has hair to his shoulders. Though he tried very hard to hide it, he is a Drayden.

I have no reason to suspect either of them of wrongdoing. They have been frequent customers here for the last two weeks, and they never treated any lover with even the slightest ill manners. Both seem more than capable warriors, and I think the Drayden may be a wizard. They will not fall victim to some stray bandit in the wild.

Yet I am concerned for Cara and Ombi, for the roads are dangerous now. Ombi in particular has been with me for many years, and I hate to think of him in danger. But they were most eager to be off. They claimed they wanted to be away from the city during the fighting, but I call that a lie. Business has been excellent, as you can guess, and of course the Dorseans would never think to harm anyone within my blue door. I think they were both hungry for an adventure, as they saw it. I only hope neither of them comes to regret it.

Keep an eye out for them, will you? And please write me the moment you hear anything. The mercenaries said they were heading for Kanlena, and I told them to see you the moment they had arrived so that they could account for the safety of our lovers. They understand the severity of their contract.

I wait eagerly to hear from you.

With my love,
Kenlin, Matron of the Blue Door

* * *

Rorik,

Find those mercenaries at once. Keep an eye on them. Do not lose sight of them for an instant.

I am dispatching to Wellmont all three of my brethren who reside here. I hope this impresses upon you the gravity of your situation. They will seek you out as soon as they arrive, and they will expect you to point them to the mercenaries. Expect them before the ides of Novis.

Captain Trisken

* * *

Brother Rogan,

I have told Father of the news from Wellmont, and I know he will have spoken to you already. He asked me to arrange details with you by letter, for it tires him so to speak to us across such a distance.

My soldiers are yours to command. Tell me how many to send, and they will reach the Birchwood within a fortnight. If you think it urgent enough, I will send them by the open road instead of the secret one, and then they can be yours in only a few days. We need few swords here to guard the place, for the satyrs and the harpies watch all roads south.

I ask only this: if it is possible, find a place for me in the hunt. If this is what Father thinks it could be, I do not wish to sit here in the Greatrocks and wait for others to earn glory.

Please, brother.

Until life ends,
Trisken

* * *

My dearest Trisken,

Send half the soldiers under your command. But send them by the secret way. There is no guarantee of what happened in Wellmont yet, and we must not show our hand too soon.

Brother, you are a warmth in my heart, as Father often says we are in his. You must be patient. The glory will be no greater for the hunters than for those who guard the home with ready spear. The day will not be long in coming when we gather with all our brothers and sisters and stand on the open field of battle, all together. Until then, we must each play our part.

Our greatest duty now is to draw Enalyn's eye away from Wellmont at all costs. If it is what we hope, she cannot know what we have learned. Father and I have a plan for this, and all have their role to play. That includes you and your servants in the Greatrocks, where you must remain for now.

I love you for your loyalty and for your eagerness both—but let the latter give way to the former until Father calls upon you.

Until life ends,
Rogan

* * *

Kin Vella,

I wonder at your understanding of what other people think you mean when you offer a "small aside." I would be more likely to forgive it, as you requested, if it were not longer than all the rest of your letter. And as might be expected, you took what was most important in your message and couched it in offhanded language.

Two things you must do at once:

The first is to find and keep an eye on those mercenaries. Do not lose track of them for any reason. I am sending one of my agents to you. She is a knight of our order named Silvin. Provide her whatever assistance she requires.

The second thing you must do is tell Jordel what you have told me, if he does not already know.

I have rarely given you a command more urgent. Do not fail me.

Only in watchfulness lies safety.
Kal of the family Endil
Chancellor of the Mystic Order

* * *

Sister Silvin,

Proceed to Wellmont at once. Jordel should be there, and I hope he will remain so until you arrive. If so, I place you under his command. Do whatever he requires of you.

If Jordel has gone, speak with one of our knights there named Vella about two mercenaries they saw during the Battle of Wellmont. You know what we have been seeking—I believe they may have seen the first sign of it.

Only in watchfulness lies safety.
Kal of the family Endil
Chancellor of the Mystic Order

* * *

Kin Vella,

You would do well to find some way of communicating your blunders without driving the reader into fits of exasperated anger, especially when the delay of your letter's journey makes it impossible for me to correct your foolery in any reasonable amount of time.

You must find Jordel. Find him at once, and spare no expense or effort in the search. Disobey your captain if you must, and I will take responsibility for any consequences you face. You must tell Jordel everything you know about the mercenaries.

Only in watchfulness lies safety.
Kal of the family Endil
Chancellor of the Mystic Order

* * *

Kin Vella,

I hope you have shown at least a spark of wit and initiative and either found Jordel already or had some of your people go after the mercenaries. If not, on your head be whatever darkness is to come.

I am leaving Ammon to search for Jordel. If you do not locate him first, I hope to meet him on his road to Ammon, for I am sure that is where he is bound. If I find him in time, and if you aid Silvin when she reaches you, we may yet have a chance to bring the nine lands back from the brink of darkness.

If not, I will at least ensure we all die in the attempt.

Only in watchfulness lies safety—or at least the hope of it.
Kal of the family Endil
Chancellor of the Mystic Order

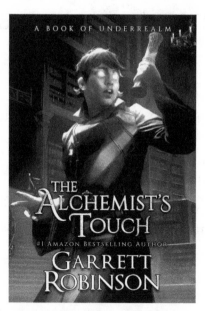

KEEP READING

More books in The Nightblade Epic are coming. But this is not the only tale of Underrealm. The Academy Journals series tells the story of the Academy for wizards upon the High King's Seat.

Either story is complete on its own—but together, they form a greater part of the tapestry of Underrealm.

Contained within the Academy Journals are answers to many of the mysteries laced throughout The Nightblade Epic. What happened to Vivien after the Battle of Wellmont? Who is the man in black? What happened to Xain after he left Loren's company?

Find out in The Alchemist's Touch, the first book in this thrilling series. Get it here:

Underrealm.net/AJ1

CONNECT ONLINE

FACEBOOK

Want to hang out with other fans of the Underrealm books? There's a Facebook group where you can do just that. Join the Nine Lands group on Facebook and share your favorite moments and fan theories from the books. I also post regular behind-the-scenes content, including information about the world you can't find anywhere else. Visit the link to be taken to the Facebook group:

Underrealm.net/nine-lands

YOUTUBE

Catch up with me daily (when I'm not directing a film or having a baby). You can watch my daily YouTube channel where I talk about art, science, life, my books, and the world.
But not cats.
Never cats.

GarrettBRobinson.com/yt

THE BOOKS OF UNDERREALM
BY GARRETT ROBINSON

To see all novels in the world of Underrealm, visit:
Underrealm.net/books

THE NIGHTBLADE EPIC
NIGHTBLADE
MYSTIC
DARKFIRE
SHADEBORN
WEREMAGE
YERRIN

THE ACADEMY JOURNALS
THE ALCHEMIST'S TOUCH
THE MINDMAGE'S WRATH
THE FIREMAGE'S VENGEANCE

TALES OF THE WANDERER (COMING SOON)
BLOOD LUST
STONE SKIN
HELL SKIN

CHRONOLOGICAL ORDER
NIGHTBLADE
MYSTIC
DARKFIRE
SHADEBORN
BLOOD LUST
THE ALCHEMIST'S TOUCH
THE MINDMAGE'S WRATH
STONE SKIN
WEREMAGE
THE FIREMAGE'S VENGEANCE
HELL SKIN
YERRIN

ABOUT THE AUTHOR

Garrett Robinson was born and raised in Los Angeles. The son of an author/painter father and a violinist/singer mother, no one was surprised when he grew up to be an artist.

After blooding himself in the independent film industry, he self-published his first book in 2012 and swiftly followed it with a stream of others, publishing more than two million words by 2014. Within months he topped numerous Amazon bestseller lists. Now he spends his time writing books and directing films.

A passionate fantasy author, his most popular books are the novels of Underrealm, including the series The Nightblade Epic and The Academy Journals.

However, he has delved into many other genres. Some works are for adult audiences only, such as *Non Zombie* and *Hit Girls*, but he has also published popular books for younger readers, including The Realm Keepers series and *The Ninjabread Man*, co-authored with Z.C. Bolger.

He now runs a publishing company, Legacy Books, dedicated to uplifting the voices of those authors traditional fantasy publishing has often ignored.

Garrett lives in Oregon with his wife Meghan, his children Dawn, Luke, and Desmond, and his dog Chewbacca.

Garrett can be found on:

BLOG: garrettbrobinson.com/blog
EMAIL: garrett@garrettbrobinson.com
TWITTER: twitter.com/garrettauthor
FACEBOOK: facebook.com/garrettbrobinson